Feline Felonies

43 Cat Crime Stories from the World's Best Mystery Writers

Edited by
Abigail Browning

GALAHAD BOOKS
NEW YORK

First Galahad Books edition published in 2001.

Galahad Books
A division of BBS Publishing Corporation
386 Park Avenue South
New York, NY 10016

Galahad Books is a registered trademark of BBS Publishing Corporation.

Published by arrangement with Dell Magazines, a division of Crosstown Publications.

Library of Congress Control Number: 00-136105

ISBN: 1-57866-114-5

Printed in the United States of America.

CONTENTS

CONTENTS

CONTENTS

ACKNOWLEDGMENTS

"The Abominable House Guest" by Theodore Sturgeon (originally titled "Fluffy"), copyright © 1963 by Theodore Sturgeon, reprinted by permission of Ralph Vicinanza Ltd.; "The Alexandrian Cat" by Steven Saylor, copyright © 1994 by Steven Saylor, reprinted by permission of the author; "Animals" by Clark Howard, copyright © 1985 by Davis Publications, Inc., reprinted by permission of the author; "Between a Cat and a Hard Place" by Jimmy Vines, copyright © 1993 by Bantam Doubleday Dell Magazines, reprinted by permission of the author; "A Case of Catnapping" by A.H.Z. Carr, copyright © 1954 by Mercury Publications, Inc., reprinted by permission of Anne Kingsbury Carr; "The Cat and Fiddle Murders" by Edward D. Hoch, copyright © 1982 by Davis Publications, Inc., reprinted by permission of the author; "Cat of Dreams" by Frances & Richard Lockridge, copyright © 1960 by Frances & Richard Lockridge, reprinted by permission of Curtis Brown, Ltd.; "Cat's-paw" by Mary Reed, copyright © 1988 by Davis Publications, Inc., reprinted by permission of the author; "Catspaw" by Sandra Woodruff (originally appeared in *From Cold Blood: Murder in Canada*, edited by Peter Sellers), copyright © 1987 by Sandra Woodruff, reprinted by permission of the author; "Chocolate" by Leslie Meier, copyright © 1992 by Bantam Doubleday Dell Magazines, reprinted by permission of the author; "Death at the Excelsior" by P. G. Wodehouse, copyright © 1976 by the estate of P. G. Wodehouse, reprinted by permission of the Scott Meredith Literary Agency, Inc.; "The Empty Birdhouse" by Patricia Highsmith, copyright © 1968 by Patricia Highsmith, reprinted by permission of the Gotham Art & Literary Agency; "The Faithful Cat" by Patricia Moyes, copyright © 1983 by Patricia Moyes, reprinted by permission of Curtis Brown, Ltd.; "A Feline Felony" by Lael J. Littke, copyright © 1967 by Davis Publications, Inc., reprinted by permission of the author; "The Highwayman's Hostage" by Lillian de la Torre, copyright © 1990 by Lillian de la Torre, reprinted by permission of Harold Ober Associates, Inc.; "Long Live the Queen" by Ruth Rendell, copyright © 1991 by Kingsmarkham Enterprises, Ltd., reprinted by permission of Sterling Lord Literistic, Inc.; "Miss Paisley's Cat" by Roy Vickers, copyright © 1953 by Roy Vickers, reprinted by permission of Curtis Brown, Ltd.; "Miss Phipps and the Siamese Cat" by Phyllis Bentley, copyright © 1973 by Davis Publications, Inc., reprinted by permission of Harold Matson Company, Inc.; "Mrrrar!" by Edgar Pangborn, copyright © 1953 by Mercury Publications, Inc., © renewed 1980 by Davis Publications, Inc., reprinted by permission of Richard Curtis Associates, Inc.; "The Nile Cat" by Edward D. Hoch, copyright © 1969 by Davis Publications, Inc., reprinted by permission of the author; "The Old Gray Cat" by Joyce Harrington, copyright © 1977 by Davis Publications, Inc., reprinted by permission of the Scott Meredith Literary Agency; "Phut Phat Concentrates" by

Lilian Jackson Braun, copyright © 1963 by Davis Publications, Inc., reprinted by permission of Blanche C. Gregory, Inc.; "The Searching Cats" by Frances & Richard Lockridge, copyright © 1956 by Frances & Richard Lockridge, reprinted by permission of Curtis Brown, Ltd.; "The Sin of Madame Phloi" by Lilian Jackson Braun, copyright © 1962 by Davis Publications, Inc., reprinted by permission of Blanche C. Gregory, Inc.; "SuSu and the 8:30 Ghost" by Lilian Jackson Braun, copyright © 1964 by Davis Publications, Inc., reprinted by permission of Blanche C. Gregory, Inc.; "The Theft of the Mafia Cat" by Edward D. Hoch, copyright © 1972 by Edward D. Hoch, reprinted by permission of the author; "The Trinity Cat" by Ellis Peters, copyright © 1976 by Ellis Peters (originally appeared in *Winter's Crimes 8*, published by Macmillan), reprinted by permission of the Deborah Owen Literary Agency; "Who Killed Wee Winky?" by Barbara Owens, copyright © 1993 by Bantam Doubleday Dell Magazines, reprinted by permission of the author; all stories have previously appeared in *Ellery Queen's Mystery Magazine*, published by Dell Magazines.

"Arnold" by Fred Hamlin, copyright © 1986 by Davis Publications, Inc., reprinted by permission of the author; "The Black Cat" by Lee Somerville, copyright © 1990 by Davis Publications, Inc., reprinted by permission of the author; "Call to Witness" by Nancy Schachterle, copyright © 1972 by H.S.D. Publications, Inc., reprinted by permission of Janet Schumer; "The Caller" by Hugh B. Cave, copyright © 1993 by Bantam Doubleday Dell Magazines, reprinted by permission of the author; "Cat Burglar" by Gene DeWeese, copyright © 1991 by Davis Publications, Inc., reprinted by permission of the Larry Sternig Literary Agency; "The Lady Wore Black" by Hugh B. Cave, copyright © 1984 by Davis Publications, Inc., reprinted by permission of the author; "Little Miracles" by Kristine Kathryn Rusch, copyright © 1992 by Davis Publications, Inc., reprinted by permission of the author; "Professor Kreller's Secret" by Ingram Meyer, copyright © 1983 by Ingram Meyer, reprinted by permission of the author; "Spectre in Blue Doubleknit" by Bruce Bethke, copyright © 1988 by Davis Publications, Inc., reprinted by permission of the author; "A Visitor to Mombasa" by James Holding, copyright © 1974 by H.S.D. Publications, Inc., reprinted by permission of James Holding; all stories have previously appeared in *Alfred Hitchcock's Mystery Magazine*, published by Dell Magazines.

"The Cat in the Bag" by Charles Peterson reprinted from *Mike Shayne's Mystery Magazine*, February 1983, copyright © 1983 by Renown Publications, Inc., reprinted by permission of the Larry Sternig Literary Agency; "Helix the Cat" by Theodore Sturgeon, copyright © 1973 by The Theodore Sturgeon Literary Trust, used by permission of Noel Sturgeon, Trustee; "Ming's Biggest Prey" by Patricia Highsmith from *The Animal Lover's Book of Beastly Murders*, copyright © 1975 by Patricia Highsmith, reprinted by permission of Mysterious Press and Marianne Fritsch-Liggenstorfer, the author's Agent; "The Witch's Cat" by Manly Wade Wellman, reprinted from *Weird Tales*, October 1939 as by Gans T. Field, copyright © 1939 by *Weird Tales*, reprinted by permission of Karl Edward Wagner, Literary Executor.

INTRODUCTION

Mystery readers love a good cat yarn, and so do mystery writers.

From the pages of *Alfred Hitchcock's Mystery Magazine* and *Ellery Queen's Mystery Magazine*, this series of 43 outstanding cat tales features stories by the top writers of short mystery fiction. Here, the time-honored relationship between mystery and cat lovers is celebrated, with cats most often playing the role of bodyguard, rescuer, or avenger.

Of course, no collection would be complete without the work of Lilian Jackson Braun, and so included are three stories by the Queen of Cats. Her feline friends SuSu, Madame Phloi, and Phut Phat all exhibit more intelligence than their human companions, which is something many of us have (uncomfortably) suspected may be true of the cats in our own lives!

In tales such as Patricia Moyes' "The Faithful Cat," the mere presence of a feline is enough to shake a criminal's resolve, and, occasionally, the animal is merely a tool in the criminal's arsenal, as is "The Nile Cat," by Edward D. Hoch. Aiding the law, both "The Searching Cats," by Frances and Richard Lockridge, and "The Trinity Cat," by Ellis Peters, direct investigators toward murderers.

Joyce Harrington's tale of murder revolving around "The Old Gray Cat," two females, and the hated woman who rules their depressing, isolated existence is deeper than it first appears. And when she asks "Who Killed Wee Winky?" Barbara Owens draws the reader into the life of an isolated old woman who takes advice from an unlikely source.

From the amusing antics of "Arnold" told by Fred Hamlin, to the "Little Miracles" Kristine Kathryn Rusch relates, to the "Death at the Excelsior" P. G. Wodehouse describes, this broad collection of cat mysteries will please every cat lover and mystery fan.

Abigail Browning
January 2001

Sandra Woodruff

CATSPAW

D ied: Croft, Jane Gilberta. At her home, after a decline bravely borne. Survived by her great-nephew Alexander de Vries and her boys: Slyboots, Courtall, Crossbite, Ranger, Fainall, Vainlove, and Furpants. She will be missed. Orchids only, by request.

Wisteria Cottage
March 28
Dear Boy,
        You will think me a morbid old woman, preoccupied with death. Do not. The thought is unworthy of you. I am alert and cheerful, as always. I write because Dr. McKillop informs me that after 83 years my heart is at last showing its age. "Tell me the worst, Doctor," I demanded. "I can take it." The man has no sense of cliché; he replied earnestly that I am failing. I deduce from his wafflings that I may linger and dwindle for a few more months or I may suddenly "pop off," as the saying goes. Accordingly, I am setting my affairs in order. My obituary is enclosed. Insert it in the quality papers, *The Globe and Mail* and *The Times*, I think, exactly as it stands. I have omitted my age because I have no wish to satisfy the appetite of the curious and because an unexpected feeling I can only describe as superstitious awe prevents me from anticipating the time of my own death.
        I have also made my will. Since you are my only living relative, it is a simple one. As you know, I have a strong sense of family obligation and an aversion to dividing property unnecessarily. I have appointed you and my solicitor, Mr. Swaine, as my executors. His firm handled your trust fund from me and your inheritance from your parents. At Mr. Swaine's excellent suggestion I have added a codicil to my will giving full legal force to any letters describing specific bequests which are found in my possession at the time of my death. These I can alter as I choose without consulting anyone. When the time comes, you will find them in the top left-hand drawer of my desk.
        Believe me, it is important to attend to these matters. However distasteful they

1

seem to you young people, be reassured that they do not unduly distress

Your affectionate aunt,

Gilberta Croft

Aunt Gilberta's letter knocked me for a loop. Don't get me wrong. I'm used to getting letters from her. Though she lives only fifteen miles from me, she refuses to use the telephone. She claims it makes communication too ephemeral. I thought nothing she did could surprise me anymore, but finding her obituary in my mail Monday morning was something else.

Aunt Gilberta took me over when my parents were killed in a car accident fourteen years ago. I was twelve. She had just been widowed, and there was no one else to have me, really. "I owe it to your poor dead mother," she said at the time. My parents always made a big thing of accepting people as they are. They had a poster that said *Dare To Be Different* over the kitchen stove. So Aunt Gilberta seemed ordinary by my standards, but my friends all thought she was a hoot.

Take the cats, for example. Every stray tomcat that wandered by got fed, neutered, and adopted as one of her boys, just like that. I'm not even sure they were all homeless to begin with. We named them together, one by one. I remember Aunt G. taking it very seriously.

"I've been doing research on the theory of cat naming," she announced. "Many people, it seems, name their cats after the nobility out of a misplaced wish for social status. Not I. My cat names must call well. The sound of the call is all important, never forget, dear boy." She had a point. "Here, Furpants" echoing on the night air is memorable. I ought to know—I had to do the calling.

In the evenings she read "the great comedies" aloud, to make me civilized— though she always regretted that she got me too late to do the job properly. We worked our way through Congreve, Sheridan, Feydeau, and her favorite Mr. Wilde and Mr. Coward. One Feydeau night she slammed the book shut in the middle of Act One and said, out of the blue, "Your Uncle Henry was always unfaithful to me. I can never forgive him for showing me that infidelity is not funny. It has quite spoiled my enjoyment of bedroom farce."

She really talks like that. Dear boy, she always calls me. I protested at that once. "But, dear boy," she answered, "I don't like your name. My niece called you Alexander against my wishes, to please my sister, so you shall be 'dear boy' or possibly 'dear' to me. You *are* a dear boy," she smiled, patting my hand.

She wanted me to be a lawyer, but took it pretty well when I dropped out of law school and went into the property-development business. I buy houses, fix them up, and sell them at a profit. Actually, Aunt G. gave me the money to buy the first houses I restored. "Seed money, dear boy," she breezed, "but from now on you must make your own way." The old girl has been good to me by her lights.

After her epistolary bombshell, I decided a visit would be a good idea.

Aunt Gilberta lives in chintz-lined seclusion at the edge of Oakes' Corners, a village about eighty miles east of Toronto. Her house is an ordinary Ontario Victorian brick cottage, but you'd never know it. The little white gate, the hedges, the lane with the church at the bottom of the hill all look like Olde England. Aunt G. has preserved herself from the least taint of Canadianism since her family came out from England sixty years ago She still carries on the lifestyle of her Edwardian country girlhood. Actually, I think she makes up her girlhood as she goes along.

I have to say that the visit was like all our visits. Aunt Gilberta was very much herself. As usual, I knocked and let myself in. She called from the living room, with Furpants (fat and striped) on her lap and Crossbite (lean and black) on the back of her wing chair.

"Hello, dear boy," she greeted me. "Does the house smell of cat?" This is Aunt Gilberta's usual greeting.

"No, Aunt G., it smells of lavender and hyacinths," I answered truthfully as she presented her cheek to be kissed. We have played this scene many times before.

"Good," she replied, right on cue. "In my childhood, of course, the best houses smelled of dogs and damp. It was a mark of social distinction. Cat is merely common."

I quickly changed the subject. "Where is Mrs. Nelles today?" Mrs. Nelles, apart from the fact that her stout dignity prevents any such term, is a dogsbody. She cooks, cleans, and copes with the daily round. She also keeps her distance.

"She is out, dear boy." Aunt Gilberta sounded huffy. "She now requires two afternoons off a week instead of one whole day. It is most inconvenient, but she claims that I shouldn't be left alone for too long anymore. In case," she added darkly in a faithful imitation of Mrs. Nelles' gloom. She brightened again. "We can talk after tea."

By talk, of course, she meant a discussion of her decline. We canvassed the subject thoroughly. Aunt G. was obviously hedging her bets. She was determined to prove her doctor wrong while at the same time obeying his instructions for babying her heart. Trips upstairs were rationed but walks to the post office permitted. As further justification for these daily trips, she trotted out one of her maxims: "Never put temptation in an inferior's way." I could imagine temptations, but not in Aunt G.'s mail.

She absolutely insisted on what she calls arranging her affairs herself.

"You will be glad I have planned carefully when the time comes" was all she would say. She had never shown the least interest in things financial before. I've certainly tried to talk about my business with her often enough. Whenever I've mentioned money she has cut me off with an Aunt Gilbertaism: "I am too well off to understand finances myself, I'm thankful to say. Concern for money becomes a man, I agree. On a woman, it is loud, like tartan trousers." There is no way to answer a thing like that.

I tried to rouse her a bit as I was leaving, partly because she had me worried, partly because it dawned on me that if Aunt G. got really sick she might become my full-time responsibility. I didn't know if I could handle it.

"You know, Aunt," I said, "you should try to meet more people. Otherwise, you'll begin to brood. Find yourself a nice young man to take your mind off your troubles." If she were the rib-elbowing kind I would have elbowed her in the ribs.

I was flabbergasted to receive another letter a week later.

> Wisteria Cottage
> April 3
> Dear Boy,
>
> You will be glad to know that I have taken your advice and have made a new friend, a young man named Alvin Ferrars. He is one of the Dundas Ferrars, I knew his grandfather. While I was arranging my affairs, it occurred to me that I might offer the art gallery one or two of those Sickerts that your Uncle Henry collected so devotedly. They are dreary things, but enjoying a vogue again, I believe. I wish to donate them now but not have them delivered until after my death. Mr. Ferrars sees to acquisitions for the gallery. He was thrilled to the marrow at my generous offer, he said. In many ways, Mr. Ferrars reminds me of your uncle when he was young. He so loves beautiful things, though he cannot see them without wanting to save them, hoard them, I might almost say. He was quite distressed at finding my small Turkoman rug by the front door in the path of dirty feet, and he actually became flustered about Courtall's blue dish. It seems that it is the best kind of carnival glass and very collectible. This seems extraordinary. Carnival glass is not what I would call good, collectible or not. As you know, I have always been one for enjoying my things, not pussyfooting around them. Courtall is particularly fond of his dish. I am sure he wouldn't drink his tea out of anything else. It was a pleasure to talk to such a cultured and considerate young man. Vainlove quite took to him, too, and you know how particular he is. The time flew. Fortunately, he will need to come again to complete the arrangements—evaluations, gift forms, and so forth. I hope you will visit soon, dear boy. I don't see enough of you.
>
> > Your affectionate aunt,
> > Gilberta Croft

She may not see enough of me, but when I did stop by for a few minutes later in the week to say that I would be away for a while, she hardly spared me a thought. It was Mr. Ferrars said this and Mr. Ferrars did that and Mr. Ferrars made such a hit with all the cats, not only with Vainlove the particular but with Ranger, who never sits on laps but sat on Mr. Ferrars' lap, who didn't even mind when he shed white hairs all over his trousers. By the time I left, I was fairly fed up with Mr. Ferrars.

The next month was incredibly hectic. I was away on business more or less continuously. Actually, the business had hit a bad patch. In my line, cash flow is everything. You have to buy at a good time and sell at the right time or you're in trouble. A sale that I had been counting on fell through and I needed to raise money right away. A loan from Aunt Gilberta would tide me over, but I didn't have any real hope of one. The few times I've wanted to borrow money from her before, she has resisted pretty firmly—refused outright, to be frank.

"You cannot expect me to pay for what I cannot approve" or a version there-of is her standard response. She's getting her own back at me for quitting law school, I guess. It's maddening, actually. Anyway, I was tired and strung out when I got home. I put down my suitcase and stooped to pick up a month's worth of mail from the hall carpet (industrial-quality grey tweed, made to withstand dirty feet). Right on top of the pile was a letter from Aunt Gilberta on her usual thick creamy paper.

Wisteria Cottage
May 4
Dear Alexander,

I hope you have concluded your business satisfactorily. In my experience, most men, even your Uncle Henry I regret to say, choose to put their work before their families and friends. It is almost a mark of masculinity. My dear Alvin is such a refreshing change; he puts the proper value on home life, friendship, and pleasant surroundings. The dear boy has been kind enough to say that my house feels like home to him. I have come to rely on him so much during your absence, particularly as I have had one or two worrying turns.

Mrs. Nelles continues to insist on her two free afternoons each week. She is quite obdurate on the subject. I must confess to feeling a shade nervous that she might leave me altogether if I were to forbid her outings. When he can, Alvin arranges his afternoons off to coincide with hers and spends them with me. He works queer hours at the gallery and is often free during the day. He is such a comfort to me. I have made him some small gifts to show my gratitude—just a silver salt cellar, Georgian your uncle always claimed, and a small porcelain dish, Meissen I believe. He was so delighted and so modest. "Don't think of giving me anything," he protested. "Leave me some small memento if you like, but nothing more." "Don't worry, dear boy," I told him, "you will be remembered in my will." Of course, I have made some alteration in my will now that

I know him. The letter with instructions is in my desk with the others. Come to see me if you can spare the time.

Your aunt,
Gilberta Croft

On top of everything else, this letter made me really angry. That putting-work-before-family crack was cheap. It was obvious that young Alvin Ferrars of the Dundas Ferrars—damn Aunt Gilberta's mania about good families—didn't put anything before himself. Don't think of giving me anything, my eye. He couldn't wait to get his hands on Aunt G.'s money—my money, as a matter of fact. I couldn't for the life of me think of what, but I knew I'd have to do something about him.

I didn't have to, however. Young Alvin overplayed his hand, the dear boy. I spent a restless few days after my trip clearing up the backlog of paperwork and trying to persuade the bank manager to give me a bridging loan. He wouldn't hear of it. He not only refused, he refused in the managerial way. "Your business is already overextended and your prospects, quite frankly, are very insecure," he said. "It wouldn't be prudent for us to lend you further monies at this time. Don't hesitate to approach us again if you can demonstrate some really solid prospects."

With one thing and another, I hadn't had a chance to visit Aunt Gilberta and I didn't much feel like it, either. I knew that I would have to go soon and at least ask her to lend me the money. I wasn't looking forward to it. Just as I finally psyched myself up to do it, I got another letter from her, in very shaky handwriting. I hardly recognized it.

Wisteria Cottage
May 9
Dear Boy,

Please come to see me very soon. That fool Dr. McKillop wanted to ring you when I was very low, but I refused. The idea of a quasi-deathbed scene offends me. However, I have important matters to discuss with you. I am afraid that I have been badly mistaken in Alvin Ferrars. He is not the innocent lover of beauty that I supposed. He is regrettably acquisitive, and I fear that mention of some small bequest—you know that I remembered him in my will—has made him greedy. Indeed, he looked at me quite fiercely the other day when he came to call. His eyes fairly glittered. I fear that he has designs on my life. I blame myself in part. I have broken my own rule and put temptation in his way. I have asked him not to come again. Do not desert

Your affectionate aunt,
Gilberta Croft

Things were obviously getting serious. Either that creep Ferrars was dangerous or Aunt G. had really flipped out this time. It was Thursday, one of Mrs. Nelles' afternoons off, so I went over right after lunch to have it out with her privately. I was fuming. Spring was in its golden phase, the time of year I usually like best, so to calm down I drove over the back way, through open country, and down her lane from the top of the hill.

About halfway there, it hit me like a ton of bricks that the simplest solution to all my problems (hers, too, for that matter) was to kill Aunt Gilberta myself. At first the thought made me so queasy I had to stop the car. I couldn't believe I could even consider such a thing. I mean, she had raised me, after a fashion, though she didn't hesitate to abandon me for Ferrars when it suited her. Finally, I got hold of myself well enough to drive on, but I still felt unreal when I arrived.

I went in at the side door. She must have heard the car because she was standing on the upstairs landing clutching a shabby housecoat around her. She looked really feeble.

We got off on the wrong footing right away. For one thing, she kept us standing in the upstairs hall. She looked ready to keel over, but she wouldn't lie down and she wouldn't sit. There were no greetings, no social niceties. All she wanted to talk about was the ingratitude of Alvin. That was fine—I didn't have a good word to say for him, either.

Warming to her theme, she went on to my own ingratitude: a) for not warning her of the evil in Alvin's heart; b) for not paying enough attention to her myself; and c) combining her grievances—for going away and leaving her in Alvin's clutches. She was completely unreasonable. I should have just left and come back later. I knew it was no time to ask for a loan, but I was desperate. I had only until Friday evening to raise the money and she was my only chance. Besides, other times I'd waited for the best moment and it didn't make any difference. I just wanted to get it over with.

She didn't take it well. I would almost have welcomed one of her chilly little pronouncements. What I got was pure fishwife at top volume. I didn't know she had it in her. The gist was that she wouldn't lend me money, now or ever. We were all the same, Uncle Henry, Alvin, and I. We had all betrayed her and used her.

At first, I tried to soothe her down, though I was pretty upset myself. She was practically hysterical. I even tried to joke with her that a lady always controls her temper. That was a mistake. She called me shallow and utterly lacking in sensitivity. Finally I lost my temper, too. I started to shout.

"You can't stand anyone getting the better of you, can you, Aunt? You've always laid down the law and doled out favors to other people. You don't know anything about being dependent on another person's whims. How do you think I feel asking for money I need badly and being treated like something subhuman? Do you think I enjoy it? Look at me! You've only given me what you thought I should have, not what I wanted. I'm not a person to you, I'm a puppet. You're not interested in me for myself. Actually, you're not interested in anyone—you just want to control people. You're selfish and tyrannical and bogus. Without your eternal posing you're nothing!" By this time I was beginning to feel better. I had done a lot of holding in over the years.

I was just starting to calm down when she smiled. She actually smiled. She was laughing at me. I felt a surge of pure rage. I reached out and shook her. I could have gone on and on doing it, just to see the pretense ooze out of her, but she wrenched away from me. She fell backward down the stairs and lay in a little heap at the bottom. One hand was reaching out to save herself, the other was still clutching her old housecoat, as if I might try to take it from her.

The first thing I thought when I saw her lying there was that she never was a good listener. The second was that she was dead and I had killed her.

I checked for a heartbeat just in case, but of course there wasn't any. My knees started to shake so much I had to sit on a step. The shouting must have disturbed Ranger, the big white cat, because he came out of the living room and, ignoring Aunt Gilberta, sat on my lap. I don't know what Aunt G. was on about— he'll sit on any lap going.

Suddenly I became cool and clearheaded, sitting there with a cat on my lap and Aunt Gilberta heaped below us in her housecoat. I looked at my watch. I had been in the house fifteen minutes.

I was about to call the doctor to say that I had found Aunt Gilberta dead, but I decided that would be asking for trouble. He would know right away that she had just died. There was no way I could explain to him what really happened— he wouldn't understand. So I decided to wait until Mrs. Nelles found Aunt G. that evening. Even if somebody saw me come to the house, by then she would have been dead long enough that a few minutes wouldn't matter one way or another. The obvious thing was to leave quickly. But I had to get rid of the letter to Alvin Ferrars first.

The letters were, as Aunt Gilberta had directed, in the top left-hand drawer of her desk. The Alvin letter was right at the back. It was short: "To Alvin, in gratitude for your attentions to an old woman, I leave you Courtall's blue dish, the one you have admired so often. I ask only that you substitute an ordinary blue glass dish for it. Courtall is fond of blue."

I could have laughed out loud—a dish, a piece of junk. Poor sod, all that effort wasted. For a moment I didn't even begrudge him the Georgian silver. In a burst of good will I put the letter back.

I left quietly a minute later. No one saw me. When Mrs. Nelles phoned to tell me the news, I managed to summon convincing surprise and grief. I made the funeral arrangements with my usual efficiency and placed the obituary in the quality papers, as instructed. Aunt Gilberta was to be buried on Monday.

The waiting time was terrible. It felt just like when my parents died. I've heard Aunt G. say a million times, "You are my only living relative, dear boy," and she was my only living relative, too. But I never really thought about what it meant. Now I know. It means that I am completely alone. I have friends, sure, but nobody who goes back all that far or who really cares about me. I told myself it was all for the best. Aunt G. couldn't have lasted much longer, the way she was looking. Even if she had really declined for any length of time (obituary or no obituary), she would have hated it.

I can't deny that I was relieved that my future was looking better. I took the risk of phoning the bank manager on Friday morning and arranging the bridging loan. I was a bit hasty, I know, but I had to be. Word had evidently gotten out, because he spread his oily charm all over me. Overnight, I had become a valued client. He had the gall to offer his condolences on the loss of my aunt and to congratulate me on my now secure prospects in the same breath.

After the funeral, at which there was no sign of Alvin Ferrars, I returned to Mr. Swaine's office with him to discuss the will. Mr. Swaine was tall, thin, and solemn. Whether he was always mournful or whether I was seeing his funeral manner I couldn't decide. He wasted no time in chat.

"Your aunt gave me to understand that you were familiar with the general tenor of her will," he began. "As you know, we are her executors. We shall discuss arrangements in due course, but for now Mrs. Croft left a letter for you, with instructions that you be left alone to read it." With that, he handed me a bulky cream envelope and beat a stately retreat.

I was surprised, but not worried. A letter from beyond the grave was a very Aunt Gilberta touch. It did give me a shock to see her handwriting firm again, though, as if she had been revitalized. The letter was dated six weeks earlier. It read:

Dear Boy,

By the time you read this, you will have killed me. You are surprised that I know when you may not even have formulated a plan for my removal. Indeed, I am not so callous as to expect malice aforethought from you, but in the end it will come to the same thing. Eliminating an ailing, possibly burdensome relative will begin to seem the expedient course, and you have always been fond of expediency.

I must confess prematurely, since I am unlikely to have a deathbed for confession, that I, too, have taken the line of least resistance. My death was not murder, but suicide at arm's length. I have been dreading the prospect of lingering death. I do not precisely relish the prospect of death at all, but given the choice I prefer quick to slow. Accordingly, I have been issuing little challenges to my heart, to no avail. An extra trip or two upstairs each day, the walk uphill from the post office, a laughable attempt to skip, even. I have survived all these.

I have, therefore, been obliged to enlist your help. You are my only living relative, and this is a familiar matter. I have decided to arrange an argument with you. You are slow to anger, but when it does erupt your temper is violent. I shall await a suitable occasion, then provoke you until you retaliate. With angry words? With an actual blow? A push downstairs? It is best that I do not know. I shall put temptation in your way and rely on you and my faint heart to do the rest. If my resolution does not falter, this scheme may even add some interest to days increasingly barren of it.

I have one other confession. To further my plan, I have practiced a small deception. I have implied strongly (though I did not lie outright—I never lie) that you would be my heir. This is not really the case. I am leaving you no money. Under the circumstances, it would not be good for your character to profit from my death. Moreover, I am a woman of strong family feeling. It has been my principle that my dear ones should be well looked after in my lifetime and not be obliged to wait until my death for financial benefit. The provisions I have already made for you and the inheritance you have from your parents should, with care, keep you comfortably. Your wildcat schemes are your own concern. You are so clever with money, dear boy. I have had the pleasure of seeing you established in life and of having discharged my responsibility to you as your only relative. I am leaving you my pink lustre teaset to remember our afternoon teas together. Do not neglect afternoon tea. It is a meal for children and the upper classes.

As my executor, you are entitled to a small fee. This fee is a convention merely; my will is an undemanding one. You know where my letters are. All of my property— the house and contents and my capital—I leave for the care of the cats. Ms. Nelles will stay on in the house at her present salary, with increments at your discretion. Should she leave, you must find a suitable replacement at once. Spare no trouble or expense. The cats must stay in their own home until the last one dies. They are so very attached to the house. Fainall would pine anywhere else and Slyboots is not as robust as he might be.

Ultimately, the house and contents should be sold and the proceeds donated to the British Anti-Vivisection Society, a group I have long supported. They have an office in Harley Street. Look after my boys as I would, and as they grow old see that they have the best veterinary care. Under no circumstances are they to be put down. Their deaths will not benefit you and in general I am against killing. I sign myself this last time,

Your affectionate aunt,

Gilberta Croft

Lilian Jackson Braun

SUSU AND THE 8:30 GHOST

When my sister and I returned from our vacation and learned that our eccentric neighbor in the wheel chair had been removed to a mental hospital, we were sorry but hardly surprised. He was a strange man, not easy to like, and no one in our apartment building seemed to be concerned about his departure—except our Siamese cat. The friendship between SuSu and Mr. Van was so close it was alarming.

If it had not been for SuSu, we would never have made the man's acquaintance, for we were not too friendly with our neighbors. Our apartment house was very large and full of odd characters who, we thought, were best ignored. On the other hand, the old building had advantages: large rooms, moderate rents, a thrilling view of the river, and a small waterfront park at the foot of the street. It was there that we first noticed Mr. Van.

One Sunday afternoon my sister Gertrude and I were walking SuSu in the park, which was barely more than a strip of grass alongside an old wharf. Barges and tugs sometimes docked there, and SuSu—wary of these monsters—preferred to stay away from the water's edge. It was one of the last nice days in November. Soon the river would freeze over, icy winds would blow, and the park would be deserted for the winter.

SuSu loved to chew grass, and she was chewing industriously when something diverted her attention and drew her toward the river. Tugging at her leash, she insisted on moving across the grass to the boardwalk, where a middle-aged man sat in a most unusual wheel chair.

It was made almost entirely of cast iron, like the base of an old-fashioned sewing machine, and it was upholstered in worn plush. With its high back and elaborate ironwork, it looked like a mobile throne, and the man who occupied this regal wheel chair presided with the imperious air of a monarch. It conflicted absurdly with his shabby clothing.

To our surprise this was the attraction that lured SuSu. She chirped at the

11

man, and the man leaned over and stroked her fur.

"She recognizes me," he explained to us, speaking with a haughty accent that sounded vaguely Teutonic. "I was-s-s a cat myself in a former existence."

I rolled my eyes at Gertrude, but she accepted the man's statement without blinking.

He was far from attractive, having a sharply pointed chin, ears set too high on his head, and eyes that were merely slits, and when he smiled he was even less appealing. Nevertheless, SuSu found him irresistible. She rubbed his ankles, and he scratched her in the right places. They made a most unlikely pair—SuSu with her luxurious blonde fur, looking fastidious and expensive, and the man in the wheel chair with his rusty coat and moth-eaten laprobe.

In the course of a fragmentary conversation with Mr. Van we learned that he and the companion who manipulated his wheel chair had just moved into a large apartment on our floor, and I wondered why the two of them needed so many rooms. As for the companion, it was hard to decide whether he was a mute or just unsociable. He was a short thick man with a round knob of a head screwed tight to his shoulders and a flicker of something unpleasant in his eyes, and he stood behind the wheel chair in sullen silence.

On the way back to the apartment Gertrude said, "How do you like our new neighbor?"

"I prefer cats before they're reincarnated as people," I said.

"But he's rather interesting," said my sister in the gentle way she had.

A few evenings later we were having coffee after dinner, and SuSu—having finished her own meal—was washing up in the down-glow of a lamp. As we watched her graceful movements, we saw her hesitate with one paw in mid-air. She held it there and listened. Then a new and different sound came from her throat, like a melodic gurgling. A minute later she was trotting to the front door with intense purpose. There she sat, watching and waiting and listening, although we ourselves could hear nothing.

It was a full two minutes before our doorbell rang. I went to open the door and was somewhat unhappy to see Mr. Van sitting there in his lordly wheel chair.

SuSu leaped into his lap—an unprecedented overture for her to make—and after he had kneaded her ears and scratched her chin, he smiled a thin-lipped, slit-eyed smile at me and said, "*Goeden avond*. I was-s-s unpacking some crates, and I found something I would like to give to you."

With a courtly flourish he handed me a small framed picture, whereupon I was more or less obliged to invite him in. He wheeled his ponderous chair into the apartment with some difficulty, the rubber tires making deep gouges in the pile of the carpet.

"How do you manage that heavy chair alone?" I asked. "It must weigh a ton."

"But it is-s-s a work of art," said Mr. Van, rubbing appreciative hands over the plush upholstery and the lacy ironwork of the wheels.

Gertrude had jumped up and poured him a cup of coffee, and he said, "I wish you would teach that man of mine to make coffee. He makes the worst *zoot-je* I have ever tasted. In Holland we like our coffee *sterk* with a little chicory. But that fellow, he is-s-s a *smeerlap*. I would not put up with him for two minutes if I could get around by myself."

SuSu was rubbing her head on the Dutchman's vest buttons, and he smiled with pleasure, showing small square teeth.

"Do you have this magnetic attraction for cats?" I asked with a slight edge to my voice. SuSu was now in raptures because he was twisting the scruff of her neck.

"It is-s-s only natural," he said. "I can read their thoughts, and they read mine of course. Do you know that cats are mind readers? You walk to the icebox to get a beer, and the cat she will not budge, but walk to the icebox to get out her dinner, and she will come bouncing into the kitchen from any place she happens to be. Your thought waves have reached her, even though she seems to be asleep."

Gertrude agreed it was probably true.

"Of course it is-s-s true," said Mr. Van, sitting tall. "Everything I say is-s-s true. Cats know more than you suspect. They can not only read your mind, they can plant ideas in your head. And they can sense something that is-s-s about to happen."

My sister said, "You must be right. SuSu knew you were coming here tonight, long before you rang the bell."

"Of course I am right. I am always right," said Mr. Van. "My grandmother in Vlissingen had a tomcat called Zwartje that she was-s-s very fond of, and after she died my grandmother came back every night to pet the cat. Every night Zwartje stood in front of *Grootmoeder's* chair and stretched and purred, although there was-s-s no one there. Every night at half-past eight."

After that visit with Mr. Van, I referred to him as Grandmother's Ghost, for he too made a habit of appearing at 8:30 several times a week. He would say, "I was-s-s feeling lonesome for my little sweetheart," and SuSu would make an extravagant fuss over the man. I was pleased that he never stayed long, although Gertrude usually encouraged him to linger.

The little framed picture he had given us was not exactly to my taste. It was a silhouette of three figures—a man in top hat and frock coat, a woman in hoop skirt and sunbonnet, and a cat carrying his tail like a lance. To satisfy my sister, however, I hung it over the kitchen sink.

One evening Gertrude, who is a librarian, came home from work in great excitement. "There's a signature on that silhouette," she said, "and I looked it up at the library. Auguste Edouart was a famous artist, and our silhouette is over a hundred years old. It might be valuable."

"I doubt it," I said. "We used to cut silhouettes like that in the third grade."

Eventually, at my sister's urging, I took the object to an antique shop, and the dealer said it was a good one, probably worth $150.

When Gertrude heard this, she said, "If the dealer quoted $150, it's worth $250. I think we should give it back to Mr. Van. The poor man doesn't know what he's giving away."

"Yes," I agreed, "maybe he could sell it and buy himself a decent wheel chair."

At 8:30 that evening SuSu began to gurgle and prance.

"Here comes Grandmother's Ghost," I said, and shortly afterward the doorbell rang.

"Mr. Van," I said, as soon as Gertrude had poured his coffee, "remember that silhouette you gave us? We've found out it's very valuable, and you must take it back."

"Of course it is-s-s valuable," he said. "Would I give it to you if it was-s-s nothing but *rommel?*"

"Do you know something about antiques?"

"My dear *Mevrouw*, I have a million dollars' worth of antiques in my apartment. Tomorrow evening you ladies must come and see my treasures. I will get rid of that *smeerlap*, and the three of us will enjoy a cup of coffee."

"By the way, what is a *smeerlap?*" I asked. "It is not very nice," said Mr. Van. "If somebody called me a *smeerlap*, I would punch him in the nose . . . Bring my little sweetheart when you come, ladies. She will find some fascinating objects to explore."

Our cat seemed to know what he was saying.

"SuSu will enjoy it," said Gertrude. "She's locked up in this apartment all winter."

"Knit her a sweater and take her to the park in cold weather," the Dutchman said in the commanding tone that always irritated me. "I often bundle up in a blanket and go to the park in the evening. It is-s-s good for insomnia."

"SuSu is not troubled with insomnia," I informed him. "She sleeps twenty hours a day."

Mr. Van looked at me with scorn. "You are wrong. Cats never sleep. You think they are sleeping, but cats are the most wakeful creatures on earth. That is-s-s one of their secrets."

After he had gone, I said to Gertrude, "He must be off his rocker."

"He's just a little eccentric," she said.

"If he has a million dollars' worth of antiques, which I doubt, why is he living in this run-down building? And why doesn't he buy a wheel chair that's easier to operate?"

"Because he's a Dutchman, I suppose."

"And how about all those ridiculous things he says about cats?"

"I'm beginning to think they're true," said Gertrude.

"And who is this fellow that lives with him? Is he a servant, or a nurse, or a keeper, or what? I see him coming and going on the elevator, but he never speaks—not one word. He doesn't even seem to have a name, and Mr. Van treats him like a slave. I'm not sure we should go tomorrow night. The whole situation is too strange."

Nevertheless, we went. The Dutchman's apartment, we found, was jammed with furniture and bric-a-brac, and Mr. Van shouted at his companion, "Move that *rommel* so the ladies can sit down."

Sullenly the fellow removed some paintings and tapestries from the seat of a carved sofa.

"Now get out of here," Mr. Van shouted at him. "Get yourself a beer," and he threw the man a crumpled dollar bill with less grace than one would throw a bone to a dog.

We sat on the sofa to drink our coffee, while SuSu explored the premises, and then Mr. Van showed us his treasures, propelling his wheel chair through a maze of furniture. He pointed out Chippendale-this and Affleck-that and Newport-something-else. Perhaps they were treasures to him, but to me they were musty relics of a dead past.

"I am in the antique business," Mr. Van explained. "Before I was-s-s chained to this stupid wheel chair, I had a shop and exhibited at all the major shows. Then . . . I was-s-s in a bad auto accident, and now I sell from the apartment. By appointment only."

"Can you do that successfully?" Gertrude asked.

"And why not? The museum people know me, and collectors come here from all over the country. I buy. I sell. And my man Frank does the legwork. He is-s-s the perfect assistant for an antique dealer—strong in the back, weak in the head."

"Where did you find him?"

"On a junk heap. I have taught him enough to be useful to me, but not enough to be useful to himself. A smart arrangement, eh?" Mr. Van winked. "He is-s-s a *smeerlap*, but I am helpless without him . . . Hoo! Look at my little sweetheart! She has-s-s made a discovery."

SuSu was sniffing at a silver bowl with two handles.

Mr. Van nodded approvingly. "It is-s-s a caudle cup made by Jeremiah Dummer of Boston in the late 17th century—for a certain lady in Salem. They said she was-s-s a witch. Look at my little sweetheart! She knows!"

I coughed and said, "Yes, indeed, you're lucky to have Frank."

"You think I do not know it?" said Mr. Van. "That is-s-s why I keep him poor. If I gave him wages, he would get ideas."

"How long ago was your accident?"

"Five years, and it was-s-s that idiot's fault! He did it! He did this to me!" The Dutchman's voice rose to a shout, and his face turned red as he pounded the arms of his wheel chair with his fists. Then SuSu rubbed against his ankles, and he stroked her and began to calm down. "Yes, five years ago," he said. "Five years in this miserable chair. We were driving to an antique show in the station wagon. That *smeerlap* went through a red light—fifty miles an hour—and hit a truck. A gravel truck!"

"How terrible!" Gertrude said, putting both hands to her face.

"I still remember packing the wagon for that trip. I was-s-s complaining all the time about sore arches. Hah! What I would give for some sore arches today yet!"

"Wasn't Frank hurt?"

Mr. Van made an impatient gesture. "His-s-s head only. They picked Waterford crystal out of his-s-s cranium for six hours. He has-s-s been *gek* ever since." The Dutchman tapped his temple.

"Where did you find your unusual wheel chair?" I asked.

"My dear *Mevrouw*, never ask a dealer where he found something," said Mr. Van. "This chair is-s-s unique. It was-s-s made for a railroad millionaire in 1872. It has-s-s the original plush. If you must spend your life in a wheel chair, have one that gives some pleasure. And now we come to the purpose of tonight's visit. Ladies, I want you to do something for me."

He wheeled himself to a desk, and Gertrude and I exchanged anxious glances.

"Here in this desk is-s-s a new will I have written, and I need witnesses. I am leaving a few choice items to museums, then everything else is-s-s to be sold and the proceeds used to establish a Foundation."

"What about Frank?" asked Gertrude, who is always genuinely concerned about others.

"Bah! Nothing for that *smeerlap*! . . . But before you ladies sign the paper, there is-s-s one thing I must write down. What is-s-s my little sweetheart's full name?"

Gertrude and I both hesitated, and I finally said, "SuSu's registered name is Superior Suda of Siam."

"Good! I will call it the Superior Suda Foundation. That gives me pleasure. Making a will is-s-s a dismal business, like a wheel chair, so give yourself some pleasure."

"What—ah—will be the purpose of the Foundation?" I asked.

Mr. Van blessed us with a benevolent smile. "It will sponsor research," he said. "I want the universities to study the highly developed mental perception of the domestic feline and apply this knowledge to the improvement of the human mind. Ladies, there is-s-s nothing better I could do with my fortune. Man is-s-s eons behind the smallest fireside grimalkin." He gave us a canny look, and his pupils seemed to narrow. "I am in a position to know," he added.

We signed the papers. What else could we do? A few days later we left on our vacation and never saw Mr. Van again.

Gertrude and I always went south for three weeks in winter, taking SuSu with us, and when we returned, the sorry news about our eccentric neighbor was thrown at us without ceremony.

We met Frank on the elevator, and for the first time he spoke! That in itself was a shock.

He said, "They took him away."

"What's that? What did you say?" We both clamored at once.

"They took him away." It was surprising to find that the voice of this chunky man was high-pitched and rasping.

"What happened to Mr. Van?" my sister demanded.

"He cracked up. His folks come from Pennsylvania and took him back home to a nut hospital."

I saw Gertrude wince, and she said, "Is it serious?"

Frank shrugged.

"What will happen to all his antiques?"

"His folks told me to dump the junk."

"But they're valuable things, aren't they?"

"Nah. Junk. He give everybody that guff about museums and all." Frank shrugged again and tapped his head. "He was *gek*!"

Wonderingly my sister and I returned to our apartment, and I could hardly wait to say it: "I told you the Dutchman was unbalanced."

"It's such a pity," she said.

"What do you think of the sudden change in Frank? He acts like a free man. It must have been terrible living with that old Scrooge."

"I'll miss Mr. Van," Gertrude said. "He was very interesting. SuSu will miss him, too."

But SuSu, we observed later that evening, was not willing to relinquish her friend in the wheel chair as easily as we had done.

We were unpacking the vacation luggage after dinner when SuSu staged her demonstration. She started to gurgle and prance, exactly as she had done all winter whenever Mr. Van was approaching our door. Gertrude and I stood there watch-

17

ing her, waiting for the bell to ring. When SuSu trotted expectantly to the front door, we followed. She was behaving in an extraordinary manner. She craned her neck, made weaving motions with her head, rolled over on her back and stretched luxuriously, all the while purring her heart out; but the doorbell never rang.

Looking at my watch, I said, "It's eight thirty. SuSu remembers."

"It's quite touching, isn't it?" said Gertrude.

That was not the end of SuSu's demonstrations. Almost every night at half-past eight she performed the same ritual.

"Cats hate to give up a habit," I remarked, recalling how SuSu had continued to sleep in the guest room long after we had moved her bed to another place. "But she'll forget after a while."

SuSu did not forget. A few weeks passed. Then we had a foretaste of spring and a sudden thaw. People went without coats prematurely, convertibles cruised with their tops down, and a few hopeful fishermen appeared down on the wharf at the foot of our street, although the river was still patched with ice.

On one of these warm evenings we walked SuSu down to the park for her first spring outing, expecting her to go after last year's dried weeds with snapping jaws. But the weeds did not tempt her. Instead, she tugged at her leash, pulling toward the boardwalk. Out of curiosity we let her go, and there on the edge of the wharf she staged her weird performance once more—gurgling, arching her back, craning her neck with joy.

"She's doing it again," I said. "I wonder what the reason could be."

Gertrude said softly, "Remember what Mr. Van said about cats and ghosts?"

"Look at that animal! You'd swear she was rubbing someone's ankles. I wish she'd stop."

"I wonder," said my sister very slowly, "if Mr. Van is really in a mental hospital."

"What do you mean?"

"Or is he—down there?" Gertrude pointed uncertainly over the edge of the wharf. "I think Mr. Van is dead, and SuSu knows."

"That's too fantastic," I said. "How could that happen?"

"I think Frank pushed the poor man off the wharf, wheel chair and all—perhaps one dark night when Mr. Van couldn't sleep and insisted on being wheeled to the park."

"Really, Gertrude—"

"Can't you see it? . . . A cold night. The riverfront deserted. Mr. Van trussed in his wheel chair with a blanket. Why, that chair would sink like lead! What a terrible thing! That icy water. That poor helpless man."

"I just can't—"

"Now Frank is free, and he has all those antiques, and nobody cares enough to ask questions. He can sell them and be set up for life. Do you know what a Newport blockfront chest is worth? I've been looking it up in the library. A chest like the one we saw in Mr. Van's apartment was sold for $40,000 at some auction in the east."

"But what about the relatives in Pennsylvania?"

"I'm sure Mr. Van had no relatives—in Pennsylvania or anywhere else."

"Well, what do you propose we should do?" I said in exasperation. "Report it to the manager of the building? Notify the police? Tell them we think the man has been murdered because our cat sees his ghost every night at eight thirty? We'd look like a couple of middle-aged ladies who are getting a little *gek*."

As a matter of fact, I was beginning to worry about Gertrude—that is, until the morning paper arrived.

I skimmed through it at the breakfast table, and there—at the bottom of page seven—one small item leaped off the paper at me. Could I believe my eyes?

"Listen to this!" I said to Gertrude. "The body of an unidentified man has been washed up on a down-river island. Police say the body apparently has been held underwater for several weeks by the ice . . . About fifty-five years old and crippled . . . No one fitting that description has been reported to the Missing Persons Bureau."

For a moment my sister sat staring at the coffee pot. Then she rose from her chair and went to the telephone.

"Now all the police have to do," she said with a slight quiver in her voice, "is to look for an antique wheel chair in the river at the foot of the street. Cast iron. With the original plush." She blinked at the phone. "Will you dial?" she asked me. "The numbers are blurred."

Hugh B. Cave

THE CALLER

Sarah Pritchard is my name. At any rate, it's the one I'm going to use in telling you what happened. That's because I want it told *my* way, not by a crowd of prying TV people and whoever writes the crazy stuff in those supermarket tabloids.

It began one summer day in the year of Our Lord '92. I was in the kitchen fixing us a supper of vegetable stew—we neither of us eat meat, I want you to know—when all at once I heard this peculiar scratching noise at the back door. Jabed heard it, too. He was sitting there at the kitchen table reading our smalltown weekly newspaper—July the eighth, it was, a Wednesday—and he looked up with a frown.

The scratching sound came again, like a raccoon or something was out there trying to claw the door open. Jabed got up and shuffled over to turn the knob. And there on the stoop outside, staring in at us, was a cat, a little old black cat with yellow eyes and one white front paw. It walked right in as if it owned the place.

Well, now, we don't dislike cats. In the sixty-two years we've been together as man and wife we must have had a dozen or more. So I put some water in a dish for this one—you shouldn't give a stray cat milk, you know; some of them can get sick on it—and I opened a can of tuna and put that down as well. Then we just stood there, Jabed and me, watching our caller till she finished filling herself.

And then—I know you're not going to believe this right off, but bear with me, please, and you'll learn to—then that little black cat looked up at us and said, plain as day, "Thank you, Sarah and Jabed. That was real neighborly of you."

And I knew that voice. Both of us did.

Where we live, I have to tell you, is out in the country, and our nearest neighbors are the folks buried in the town cemetery, just down the road a piece. I'm not going to name the town or even the state it's in, for the same reason I didn't tell you our real names. All you need to know is that the town is small enough for us to have personally known a good many of the people *in* that cemetery. And the voice coming out of the cat that day belonged unmistakably to our friend Edna Clifton, whose funeral we'd attended two years and five months before, when she passed away at age seventy-seven after a heart attack.

"How are you, anyway?" Edna or the cat said then.

We stammered some kind of reply, or at least I did—Jabed just stood there looking like he'd been turned into a pillar of salt. Then that yellow-eyed little animal asked, as natural as you please, "Have you see my Andrew lately?"

"Why, yes," I managed to answer. "He was in church last Sunday."

"Did he look well?"

"About the same," I stammered. "Though he still walks with a limp." Just before she died her husband Andrew had broke his hip, falling on an icy sidewalk when he stepped out of the town barbershop.

"Did he mention me?" asked little old Blackie with the white paw, gazing up at me as if asking questions in a human voice is a thing cats do all the time.

"Well, now, Edna, as a matter of fact he did," I heard myself saying back. "Yes, he certainly did. Jabed here asked him how he was, and he distinctly said—I remember his exact words—he distinctly said, 'Not so good as when my Edna was alive.' " Then I thought of something and hastened to add, "Why don't you go and talk to him? Unless it's too far, and you'd like us to drive you there."

"I don't have time," Edna said.

"What?"

"My little cat friend here is new at this sort of thing. She wouldn't be able to help me that long. In fact, I'm surprised she—"

Then suddenly a strange thing happened. That little black cat stopped talking right in the middle of a sentence and meowed instead. I mean, all at once she was only a cat, with only a cat's natural voice. And for the next hour or so, until she went to the door and meowed to be let out, all she did was snoop around the house, upstairs and down, the way you'd expect any normal stray cat to do.

We let her out then—or, to be exact, Jabed did before I had sense enough to stop him—and that was the last we saw of Blackie for twenty-four days. We talked about her during that time, of course. I expect you would have, too, unless you're accustomed to being called on by cats that speak like people. But we talked about her only to each other. Not for all the tea in China would we have told anyone else about her. Not at that time, anyway.

"What I think," Jabed said, "is that she may have been hanging around the cemetery, and the spirit of Edna Clifton somehow got into her. Ghosts or spirits are able to possess *people*, aren't they? So why couldn't one take possession of a cat for a time?"

"Maybe she was just sort of hanging around Edna's grave," I said. "Or sleeping there by her tombstone."

Whatever, twenty-four days after her first visit—on the first day of August, that is—Miss Blackie came scratching at our door a second time, and again we let her in. And this time after she'd been fed, she thanked us in a *different* voice.

It was a man's voice this time. It belonged to Odell Osgood, who had died more than four years before at age eighty-six, of pneumonia which he got when caught in a spell of terrible weather while out deer hunting.

Odell was buried in the town cemetery, too, of course. His wife Clara was there with him. They had a married daughter who lived in the next county with her husband and two children.

We fed Blackie same as before, this time giving her some leftover canned salmon we happened to have. After she'd eaten every last morsel, she took time to clean her mouth with that pretty white front paw of hers before turning around to look at us. By which time Jabed and I had both got over the shock of seeing her again and seated ourselves at the kitchen table.

"You two are looking real fit," said Blackie in the rusty baritone voice of old Odell. "You must be doin' somethin' right." And he—or Blackie—laughed at his own joke like he'd always used to when he was alive. In fact, if it had really been him instead of a cat there in front of us, he most likely would have slapped his big right thigh along with the hooting. Odell weighed well over two hundred fifty pounds before the pneumonia wasted him away and always made me think of a Santa Claus in overalls.

"We try to eat right and take care of ourselves," I told him.

"Good for you, both of you," he said. "Keep at it long as you can, because layin' there in the graveyard under a blanket of earth ain't much fun, I can tell you." The voice laughed again—sort of like a bullfrog croaking. And then he said, "You seen any of my kin lately, by any chance?"

We told him—Jabed did—that we'd seen Beulah and her husband Derwin *and* the two children only a week or so before, at the county fair. "All of them looked just fine," Jabed said.

"Derwin still on the wagon, would you say?"

"Yep, he was cold sober. Whyn't you—er—trot over there and pay them a visit?"

"Can't," said Odell. "I wouldn't have time."

"Like it was with Edna Clifton?" I said. "This—whatever it is—only lasts a short while?"

"What you mean, Edna Clifton?"

"Well, the last time you called on us—I mean the last time Blackie here called on us—she was Edna. You didn't know about that, hey?"

"Nope. All I know is—" And like before, though maybe not so soon, Blackie's people voice sort of faded away to a meow, and our caller was again just a little old black cat with yellow eyes, sitting there with a sad look on her face. And after going to her dish and meowing for some more of the canned salmon and being given some and taking her own good time eating it, she wandered off to explore the house again, just like any ordinary cat might have done.

I said to Jabed, after she left that time, that we should have put her on a leash of some sort and gone with her to see if she actually did go to the cemetery like we suspected. And if she did, to find out what happened when she got there.

Well, it went on and on. In September, Blackie came a third time and was yet another person in the cemetery, this time Thelma Goodis, who died of cancer at age sixty-three in the year of Our Lord '88. We talked with Thelma for quite a while, mostly about her husband and children. Then in October Blackie returned as Avery Chatwin, the town undertaker, who, if you can believe it, actually died *in* the cemetery of a stroke while burying his own mother. He'd left a wife and three children, and we talked with him even longer. Blackie was learning to hold on better each time she came, it seemed.

Meanwhile, of course—what else would you expect?—my Jabed and I had gone to the cemetery to investigate. Twice, in fact. The first time was a nice bright day and we walked, thinking we needed the exercise. It tired us out pretty much, though, so the next time we went, we drove there in our old Buick.

On each occasion we strolled about among the grave markers for an hour or more, reading off names to each other and looking for signs that Blackie had been there.

And she had.

We didn't actually see her, I have to admit, but we found more than a few places where the grass was matted down the way outdoor cats do when they make themselves a bed, and each one of those depressions had some black fur in it. One such was by Edna Clifton's grave. Others were on or close to the graves of Odell Osgood, Thelma Goodis, and Avery Chatwin.

There were three other such bedding-down spots, too. But, as I've remarked, we didn't actually see Blackie herself. Evidently she slept there in the cemetery but spent her days hunting food to keep from starving.

"Food such as field mice," Jabed suggested with a grimace. Like I said, we neither of us eat meat anymore.

But then, soon after Blackie called on us as Avery Chatwin, we had a visit of a more ordinary kind. Nothing mysterious this time. No yellow-eyed black cat speaking with the voices of dead people. This caller was only Jabed's nephew, Arnold Pritchard, who drove into our yard one day without a word of warning and asked could he stay with us awhile to do a little hunting.

Arnold was thirty-two years old at this time and still single, though handsome enough if you like your men real pretty. He lived sixty-odd miles away in the state capital, where he worked at selling used cars. We'd never liked him much.

Jabed and I grudgingly said all right, we'd put him up, but he had to promise to behave himself.

"What do you mean by that?" Arnold challenged with a grin.

"The last time you came here to hunt, you played fast and loose with that nice Mary Wharton at the drugstore," Jabed reminded him. "The townsfolk talked about it for weeks and for some reason blamed *us*. So this time, if it's hunting you want, we'll thank you to hunt things that have four legs."

Both of us knew, I suspect, that talking to the grandfather clock in the hall would have been more productive. Handsome Arnold couldn't even look at a girl without making a pass at her. And before he'd been with us a week, he'd forgot all about wanting to take home a deer.

She worked as a waitress at a restaurant in town, this girl. Her name was Nina Petrillo and her father had run off years ago and she lived with her mother in a cottage on Swamp Hollow Road. She was twenty-six, Arnold told us the first time he brought her to our house.

Later the town paper said she was only twenty.

Anyhow, she was real nice looking, with glossy black hair and a quick, bright smile and sparkly dark eyes. And with Arnold being about as handsome as a man can be, as I've said already, they made a fine-looking pair.

He saw her most every day, and the whole town was soon aware of it because he took her just about everywhere a man could take a woman in our little neck of the woods. He took her to the moving picture theater, and dancing at the Red Barn out on the highway, and even to a church supper one time. One evening when he came in late and we were still up watching television, but really waiting to lock up because we could never be sure Arnold would remember to, Jabed asked him, "Now where did you and Nina go this evening, Arnold?"

"Oh, nowhere in particular," said he with a grin.

"Just riding around, you mean?"

"That's it. Just ridin' around."

"What about the deer hunting? You give that up, have you?"

"No, no. I still want a deer to take home when I go."

"When you go," said Jabed, shaking his head. "And when will that be, do you suppose?"

"Oh, pretty soon," says Arnold, grinning again. "Why? Are you that anxious to be rid of me?"

So it went, until one morning Arnold got up from the breakfast table after eating hardly any breakfast and announced he *was* going hunting again. And took his rifle when he left the house.

About ten o'clock that morning our telephone rang and it was Claudia

Petrillo, Nina's mother, calling to ask if her daughter was at our house. I was the one answered the call, and I said, "At our house, Mrs. Petrillo? What do you mean?"

"I mean she was out with your Arnold again last night and hasn't come home," said Claudia in a truly distraught voice. "Did Arnold come home?"

"Well, of course," I said.

"Then let me talk to him."

"Mrs. Petrillo," I said, "you can't talk to him now. He went hunting right after breakfast."

"Well, when will he be home?"

"I can't answer that. I just don't know."

She hung up, but called again about twelve thirty and said the restaurant where Nina worked had called to ask where the girl was, because Nina hadn't showed up for work at eleven as she was supposed to. And so it went all through that day, with our phone ringing every hour or so and the poor woman becoming more and more distraught.

About five thirty, when it was getting dark outside, Arnold finally turned up—without any deer, I might add—and we asked him where Nina was.

He was dog-tired and dirty from being in the woods all day, and sort of just stared at us for a few seconds. Then, "What do you mean, where's Nina?" he said.

"Just that," said Jabed. "Her mother's been calling all day. Says the girl didn't come home last night and didn't show up for work today, and no one knows where she is."

Arnold gave his head a shake and stared at us some more. "I don't understand," he said. "I drove her home last night same as always."

"You drove her home," I said. "Does that mean you walked her to her door?"

"Well, no," he admitted. "I guess I just—well, I waved goodnight and drove off after she reached the porch steps."

"And what time was that?"

"What time was it? I don't know. Eleven thirty. Maybe a little later."

"And you haven't seen or heard from her since?"

"Uh-uh." He wagged his head. "I been in the woods all day."

"Then you better call her mother right now," Jabed said, "and tell her everything you know. Because the girl's disappeared, and you're the one she's been going out with for the past ten days."

That began it. Arnold called the girl's mother and she called the police, and pretty soon the whole town was talking about Nina Petrillo's mysterious vanishment. And not only talking about it but searching high and low for the girl. Nothing like that had ever happened before in our little town.

And the girl stayed missing.

Well. Arnold didn't go back to the city like he'd planned to. He stayed on and took part in the search along with every other able-bodied man in town. Even some of the younger women joined in. For days and days, teams of searchers scoured the woods for miles around. Our little town had never seen such goings-on before.

The police questioned practically everyone, even asking for help over the TV and radio and flashing appeals on the screen at the moving picture theater. But Nina Petrillo stayed missing.

Our little Blackie came around only once during those terrible days. We'd just finished a late supper one evening, and Arnold had gone up to his room to rest after being out searching all day, when there came that familiar scratching sound at the back door. "I wonder if *she's* seen Nina by any chance," Jabed said as he went to open it.

Little old yellow-eyes came trotting in and said hello as usual, and this time the voice belonged to someone younger than we'd come to expect. This time it was the voice of Charley Stimson, who had died only two years before when one of those big trailer trucks tipped over his car at Dead Man's Curve, and him only eighteen at the time.

Speaking with his voice, Blackie asked if we'd seen his mom and dad late-ly, and I fibbed and told him they were fine, which I didn't know was true because they'd moved away soon after he died, saying they couldn't bear living so near to where it happened. Then Jabed said, "Did you know Nina Petrillo is missing, Charley?" Being near the same age, Charley and Nina had known each other, of course. In fact, they'd been sweet on each other.

"Missing?" said Blackie, peering up at us. "No, I hadn't heard. You mean she ran away for some reason?"

"Well, we don't know. That's a possibility, of course."

"Tell me about it," Blackie said, twitching her whiskers.

It took quite a while for us to tell her the whole story, and she continued to be Charley the whole time, but she couldn't help us any. When her Charley voice finally changed to a meow, we gave her some canned catfood we'd bought for her and she did her usual tour of the house and departed.

A minute or so later Arnold came downstairs with a scowl on his face.

"Heard you talking to someone," he said. "Someone I know, was it?"

"Nope," said Jabed. We hadn't told his nephew about the visits from our lit-tle four-legged friend. In fact, we hadn't told anyone, being afraid they might think we were coming down with that Alazaheim disease or whatever it's called.

"Talking about Nina, were you?" Arnold persisted.

"Well, yes, we were talking about Nina. What else does anyone talk about these days? But she didn't have anything new to tell us."

"She?" said Arnold, really scowling now. "It was a man's voice I heard."

"Probably sounds like one," said Jabed with a warning glance at me. "It was old Mrs. Black—you've never met her—and she has a voice deeper'n mine."

With that, Arnold turned to go back upstairs, seemingly satisfied, but at the foot of the staircase he stopped. "I been thinking things over," he said. "This is Friday and I'll stay through the weekend, but then I really have to get back to work or I could lose my job. I'm truly sorry, but if Nina has just up and left town—and that's what it looks like, you have to admit—there isn't much anyone can do about it, is there?" He stood there shaking his head at us. "You know," he said, "I was fond of that girl. I truly was. If she hadn't run away, I might even have asked her to marry me."

He went trudging up the stairs then, and we heard the door of his room shut behind him. And Jabed looked at me the way he had when we talked about Blackie eating field mice.

"Marry him?" Jabed snorted. "That girl marry Arnold? I'll bet."

Which brings me—at last, you'll probably say—to the end of what I'm trying to tell you.

The weather was bad that weekend—cold and rainy the whole time—but the search for Nina Petrillo went on all the same. Still there was no trace of the missing girl, and on Sunday evening at supper Arnold informed us he'd be leaving in the morning. "I've done all I can," he said. "Even though I was the last person to see her, I don't have any inside track on where to look for her. Like I've told you and everyone else, I left her safe at home that night."

I couldn't think what to say to that, and neither could Jabed apparently. We just looked at him.

"I suppose it'll seem suspicious, me leaving before she's found," he said, "but I have to. Me losing my job over this won't help anyone."

"What time will you want breakfast?" I asked.

"About seven, maybe?"

"All right," I said.

He said goodnight and went up to bed about nine thirty, I remember. That was kind of early for him, but the three of us had been sitting in the living room, still talking about Nina and what could have happened to her, and it seemed to upset him more than usual. No doubt he was truly weary by this time, too. He'd searched for the missing girl as hard as anyone.

We heard him shut his door. Then Jabed picked up a book he was reading—one about cats that I'd borrowed from Abigail Watson, who had at least a dozen of them. Cats, I mean, not books. And feeling like I wanted a cup of tea to settle my nerves, I went into the kitchen to put the kettle on.

And while I was at the sink, filling the kettle, I heard that familiar scratching sound at the back door again.

"Jabed!" I called.

Jabed came running. He knows by my tone of voice when I'm real serious about something. I pointed to the door and said, "It's Blackie!" and he went straight to the door and opened it.

A gust of wind-driven rain came in along with Blackie. Jabed had to lean against the door to shut it, the wind was blowing so hard.

And Blackie—well, I felt so sorry for that poor little cat, I got down on my knees and took her up in my arms. She was soaked through and through and didn't stop shivering till I'd held her up against me for a good two minutes. Then when I let her go and stood up, she did something she'd never, ever, done before. She jumped onto a chair and from that onto the kitchen table, and made beckoning motions with that one white paw as if to say, "Come closer! I've something important to tell you!"

I felt it so strong that I reached for Jabed's hand and both of us stepped right up to the table like we were kids in school and the teacher had said, "Come here!"

"You mustn't let him go!" Blackie said then, in a voice we knew only too well. "He has to be punished!"

I looked at my husband. "Jabed!" I whispered. "It's Nina!"

Jabed just stood there returning the stare of those yellow eyes.

"We were in his car on Cemetery Road and he wanted to—to make love to me," Blackie went on, sort of sobbing the words out in Nina Petrillo's voice. "Then he tried to force me to do what he wanted, and when I fought him he got angry and—and choked me to death. And when he discovered I was dead, he buried my body where he knew no one would ever think to look for it."

I finally found my voice and said, "Where was that?"

"We were on Cemetery Road, like I said," replied Blackie in the sobbing voice of the missing girl. "He just drove to the cemetery and went from one grave marker to another looking at the dates on them. When he found one so old it wasn't likely to be visited anymore, he dug down and buried me above the coffin already in it."

I was so frightened I couldn't get a word out. But not Jabed. I'm real proud of my husband for what he did then.

Pulling up a chair, he sat down and rested his arms on the table, then leaned forward with his face up close to Blackie's and said, "What'd he dig with, Nina?"

"A license plate off his car. To break up the ground, he used a tire-changing tool."

"And which grave are you talking about?"

"It says on the headstone, 'Martha Anne Dolliver, Beloved Wife of Jonathan Dolliver, 1837–1904.' Like I said, he chose a grave so old that no one would be likely to visit it and discover he'd disturbed it."

"Now tell me," Jabed said, "how is it you can talk to us through this little cat here? You and all those others, I mean."

"What others? I don't know about any others."

"Well, there've been some, believe me. Just tell me how *you're* able to do it."

"Cats are spiritual creatures," said Nina. "Some are, anyway. Tonight this one just happened to come and bed down next to the grave Arnold put me in." The voice stopped for a few seconds, then went on with a note of determination in it, like Nina herself was actually standing there in front of us with her fists clenched. "You won't let Arnold get away with it, will you?" she said. "I'll never be able to rest right if he does."

"We'll make sure he's punished," Jabed promised.

"Thank you. Oh, thank you both!" Blackie cried, then jumped down from the table and trotted off to do her tour of the house as usual. She hadn't meowed first, I noticed—she was staying human a lot longer by this time—so she was still Nina at that point but no doubt too upset to talk anymore.

"Jabed," I said then, "what are we to do?"

"Call the police of course," said my husband.

"And tell them a *cat*—"

"What else? If they want to think we've lost our minds, that's up to them. But even if they do, they'll go out there to the cemetery and look. You can bank on it." He reached for my hand. "Come on, Sarah. Let's call them."

Have I told you our telephone is on a table in the hall, at the foot of the stairs? Well, it is. We went to it and Jabed took it up and dialed the number. We don't have that fancy 911 thing in our small town; you dial the police station. The number was on a list right there before the phone.

I heard the phone at the station ringing. Then from the staircase behind me I heard the voice of Arnold Pritchard, telling Jabed to put the phone down. "Or," Arnold snarled, "I'll drop you where you stand."

We both turned, Jabed still holding the telephone to his ear, and there was Arnold, in his pajamas, halfway down the stairs with his hunting rifle. He aimed the gun at us. "Put it down," he snarled again. "Right now! This minute!"

It seemed to take forever for Jabed to lower the phone from his ear.

"She was here, wasn't she?" Arnold screamed in a voice like—well, like he was a child again, on the verge of having hysterics. "I didn't kill her, did I? She got out of there and came here to tell you. I heard her!" His hands were shaking so hard I thought the gun would go off by itself and probably kill one of us, and my heart all but stopped beating. "Where is she?" Arnold shouted. "Where'd she go?"

He was crazy, that's what he was. Plain crazy, from hearing the voice of that girl he'd murdered and gone to such pains to bury in a place where she would never be found.

But it wasn't Jabed or me who answered him.

It was the same voice again—Nina's—from the darkness on the landing above him.

"I'm right here, Arnold," it said. And something even darker than the darkness—except for one little patch of white—launched itself from the upstairs hall and landed in a scratching, clawing heap on Arnold's head.

The rifle flew out of Arnold's hands and got to the bottom of the stairs long before Arnold himself finished falling down them. Jabed had plenty of time to snatch it up. So when Arnold finally reached the bottom and managed to scramble back onto his feet, there was Jabed pointing the weapon straight at him and saying to me, "Call the police, Sarah. Tell them we have Nina's killer right here and they should come and get him." And to Arnold he added, "You make one move, mister, and there'll be another grave in that cemetery, I promise you."

So there you are. The police came and took Jabed's no-good nephew away, and then, in spite of all that rain and wind, they went on out to the cemetery. Jabed went with them. Sure enough, someone had dug up the sod over that old grave and replaced it, and when they took it up again, using a searchlight on the police car to light up what they were doing, they found Nina Petrillo buried there, and she'd been choked to death like she said.

The man who killed her is in prison now for the rest of his life, where he belongs. As for Blackie, when we looked for her that night after Jabed got back from the cemetery, we couldn't find her. With so many people coming and going, she must have slipped out sometime when the door was opened. But she came calling again a few days later and talked to us in yet another voice from the cemetery, and she still visits us every so often.

She's getting pretty old now, though. It can't go on much longer.

We'll miss that little black cat when she dies. If we know about it when it happens, and can find her, we hope to get permission to bury her right there in the cemetery among her many friends.

Steven Saylor

THE ALEXANDRIAN CAT

We were sitting in the sunshine in the atrium of Lucius Claudius's house, discussing the latest gossip from the Forum, when a terrible yowling pierced the air.

Lucius gave a start at the noise and opened his eyes wide. The caterwauling terminated in a feline shriek, followed by a scraping, scrambling noise and then the appearance of a gigantic yellow cat racing across the roof above us. The red tiles offered little traction to the creature's claws and it skittered so close to the edge that for a moment I thought it might fall right into Lucius's lap. Lucius seemed to think so as well. He scrambled up from his chair, knocking it over as he frantically retreated to the far side of the fish pond.

The big cat was quickly followed by a smaller one, which was solid black. The little creature must have had a particularly aggressive disposition to have given chase to a rival so much larger than itself, but its careless ferocity proved to be its downfall—literally, for while its opponent managed to traverse the roof without a misstep, the black cat careered so recklessly across the tiles that at a critical turning it lost its balance. After an ear-rending cacophony of feral screeching and claws scraping madly against tiles, the black cat came plummeting feet-first into the atrium.

Lucius screamed like a child, then cursed like a man. The young slave who had been filling our wine cups came running as fast as he could.

"Accursed creature!" cried Lucius. "Get it away from me! Get it out of here!"

The slave was joined at once by others, who surrounded the beast. There was a standoff as the black cat flattened its ears and growled while the slaves held back, wary of its fangs and claws.

Regaining his dignity, Lucius caught his breath and straightened his tunic. He snapped his fingers and pointed at the overturned chair. One of the slaves righted it, whereupon Lucius stepped onto it. No doubt he thought to put as much distance between himself and the cat as possible, but instead he made a terrible error, for by raising himself so high he became the tallest object in the atrium.

Without warning, the cat gave a sudden leap. It broke through the cordon of slaves, bounded onto the seat of Lucius's chair, ran vertically up the length of his body, scrambled over his face onto the top of his head, then pounced onto the roof and disappeared. For a long moment Lucius stood gaping.

At last, assisted by his slaves (many of whom seemed about to burst out laughing), Lucius managed to step shakily from the chair. As he sat, a fresh cup of wine was put in his hand and he raised it to his lips with an unsteady hand. He drained the cup and handed it back to the slave. "Well!" he said. "Go on now, all of you. The excitement's over." As the slaves departed from the atrium, I saw that Lucius was blushing, no doubt from the embarrassment of having so thoroughly lost his composure, not to mention having been got the better of by a wild beast in his own home, and in front of his slaves. The look on his chubby, florid face was so comic that I had to bite my lips to keep from smiling.

"Cats!" he said at last. "Accursed creatures! When I was a boy, you hardly saw them at all in Rome. Now they've taken over the city! Thousands of them everywhere, wandering about at will, squabbling and mating as they please, and no one able to stop them. At least one still doesn't see them much in the country-side; farmers run them off because they frighten the other animals so badly. Weird, fierce little monsters! I think they come from Hades."

"Actually, I believe they came to Rome by way of Alexandria," I said quietly.

"Oh?"

"Yes. Sailors first brought them over from Egypt, or so I've heard. Seafarers like cats because they eat the vermin on their ships."

"What a choice—rats and mice, or one of those fearsome beasts with its claws and fangs! And you, Gordianus—all this time you've sat there as if nothing were happening! Oh, but I forget, you're used to cats. You and your Egyptian concubine have a cat which you keep as a kind of pet, don't you? As if the creature were a dog!" He made a face. "What do you call the thing?"

"Bethesda has always given her cats the name of Bast. It's what the Egyptians call their cat-god."

"What a peculiar people, to worship animals as if they were gods. No wonder we've practically taken over their government. A people who worship cats can hardly be fit to rule themselves."

I kept silent at this bit of conventional wisdom. My friend Lucius Claudius has a sweet nature and a kind heart, but he is a Roman patrician after all, and he often subscribes to the values of his class without question. I might have pointed out that the cat-worshipers he so offhandedly disdained had managed to create a culture of exquisite subtlety and monumental achievements while Romulus and

Remus were still suckling a she-wolf, but the day was too hot to engage in historical debate.

"If the creature comes back, I shall have it killed," Lucius muttered under his breath, nervously eyeing the roof.

"In Egypt," I said, "such an act would be considered murder, punishable by death."

Lucius looked at me askance. "Surely you exaggerate! I realize that the Egyptians worship all sorts of birds and beasts, but it doesn't prevent them from stealing their eggs or eating their flesh. Is the slaughter of a cow considered murder?"

"Perhaps not, but the slaying of a cat most certainly is. In fact, when I was a young man in Alexandria, one of my earliest investigations involved the murder of a cat."

"Oh, Gordianus, you must be joking! You're not saying that you were actually hired to track down the killer of a cat, are you?"

"It was a bit more complicated than that."

Lucius smiled for the first time since we had been interrupted by the squabbling cats. "Come, Gordianus, don't tease me," he said, clapping his hands for the slave to bring more wine. "You must tell me the story."

I was glad to see him regain his good spirits. "Very well," I said. "I shall tell you the tale of the Alexandrian cat."

The precinct called Rhakotis is generally acknowledged to be the most ancient part of Alexandria, the place where the city took root and about which it grew into a great metropolis. The principal landmark of Rhakotis is the Temple of Serapis, a magnificent marble edifice constructed on a huge scale and decorated with fabulous conceits of alabaster, gold, and ivory. Romans who have seen the temple begrudgingly admit that for sheer splendor it might (mind you, *might*) rival our own austere Temple of Jupiter—a telling comment on Roman provincialism rather than on the respective architectural merits of the two temples. If I were a god, I know in which house I would choose to live.

The temple is an oasis of light and splendor surrounded by a mazelike wilderness of winding streets. The houses in Rhakotis, made of hardened earth, are built high and jammed close together. The streets are narrow and strung with ropes upon which the inhabitants hang laundry and fish and plucked fowl to dry. The air is generally still and hot, but occasionally a sea breeze will manage to cross the Island of Pharos and the great harbor and the high city wall to stir the tall palm trees which grow in the little squares and gardens of Rhakotis.

In Rhakotis, one can almost imagine that the Greek conquest never occurred. The city may be named for Alexander and ruled by a Ptolemy, but the people of the ancient district are distinctly Egyptian, darkly complected with dark eyes and the type of features one sees on the old statues of the Pharaohs. These people are different from us, and so are their gods, which are not the Greek and Roman gods of perfect human form but strange hybrids of animals and men, frightful to look at.

One sees many cats in Rhakotis. They wander about as they wish, undisturbed, sunning themselves in patches of light, chasing grasshoppers, dozing on ledges and rooftops, staring at the inaccessible fish and fowl hung, with the laundry, beyond their reach. But the cats of Rhakotis do not go hungry; far from it. People set bowls of food out on the street for them, muttering incantations as they do so, and not even a starving beggar would consider taking such consecrated food for himself—for the cats of Rhakotis, like all cats throughout Egypt, are considered to be gods. Men bow as they pass them in the street, and woe unto the crass tourist from Rome or Athens who dares to snigger at such a sight, for the Egyptians are as vengeful as they are pious.

I found myself residing in Rhakotis for a number of reasons. For one thing, a young Roman of little wealth could find lodgings there to suit his means. But Rhakotis offered far more than cheap dwellings. To feed my mind, I could listen to the philosophers who lectured to their students and debated one another on the steps of the library attached to the Temple of Serapis. To feed my stomach, vendors at crowded street corners hawked exotic delicacies unheard of in Rome. As for the other appetites common to young men, those were easily satisfied as well; the Alexandrians consider themselves to be the most worldly of people, and any Roman who disputes the point only demonstrates his own unworldliness.

One morning I happened to be walking through one of the district's less crowded streets when I heard a noise behind me. It was a vague, indistinct noise, like the sound of a roaring crowd some distance away. The government of Egypt is notoriously unstable, and riots are fairly common, but it seemed too early in the day for people to be raging through the streets. Nevertheless, as I paused to listen, the noise became louder and the echoey din resolved into the sound of angry human voices.

A moment later, a man in a blue tunic appeared from around a bend in the street, running headlong toward me, his head turned to look behind him. I hurriedly stepped out of the way, but he blindly changed his course and ran straight into me. We tumbled to the ground in a confusion of arms and legs.

"Numa's balls!" I shouted, for the fool had caused me to scrape my hands and knees on the rough paving stones.

The stranger suddenly stopped his mad scramble to get to his feet and stared at me. He was a man of middle age, well groomed and obviously well fed. There was absolute panic in his eyes, but also a glimmer of hope.

"You curse in Latin!" he said hoarsely. "You're a Roman, then, like me?"

"Yes."

"Countryman—save me!" By this time we were both on our feet again, but the stranger moved in such a spastic manner and clutched at me so desperately that I thought he might pull us to the ground again.

The noise of angry voices grew nearer. The man looked back to the way he had come. Fear danced across his face like a flame. He clutched me with both hands and kept his eyes on the bend.

"I swear, I never touched the beast!" he whispered hoarsely. "The little girl said I killed it, but it was already dead when I came upon it."

"What are you saying?"

"The cat! I didn't kill the cat! It was already dead, lying in the street. But they'll tear me limb from limb, these mad Egyptians! If I can only reach my house—"

At that moment, a number of people appeared at the bend in the street, men and women dressed in the tattered clothing of the poorer classes. More people appeared, and more, shouting and twisting their faces into expressions of pure hatred. They came rushing toward us, some of them brandishing sticks and knives, others shaking their bare fists in the air.

"Help me!" the man shrieked, his voice breaking like a boy's. "Save me! I'll reward you!" The mob was almost upon us. I struggled to escape his grip. At last he broke away and resumed his headlong flight. As the angry mob drew nearer, for a moment it seemed that I had become the object of their quest. Indeed, a few of them headed straight for me, and I saw no possibility of escape. "Death comes as the end," goes the Egyptian poem, and I felt it drawing very near.

But a man near the front of the crowd, notable for his great long beard curled in the Babylonian fashion, saw the mistake and shouted in a booming voice, "Not that one! The man in blue is the one we want! Up there, at the end of the street! Quick, or he'll escape us again!"

The men and women who had been ready to strike me veered away at the last moment and ran on. I drew into a doorway, out of sight, and marveled at the size of the mob as it passed by. Half the residents of Rhakotis were after the Roman in blue!

Once the mob had passed, I stepped back into the street. Following the mob were a number of stragglers unable to keep up the pace. Among them I recognized a man who sold pastries from a shop on the Street of the Breadmakers. He was breathing hard but walked at a deliberate pace. In his hand he clutched a wooden rod for rolling dough. I knew him as a fat, cheerful baker whose chief joy was filling other people's stomachs, but on this morning he wore the grim countenance of a determined avenger.

"Menapis, what is happening?" I said, falling into step beside him.

He gave me such a withering look that I thought he did not recognize me, but when he spoke it was all too clear that he did. "You Romans come here with your pompous ways and your ill-gotten wealth, and we do our best to put up with you. You foist yourself upon us, and we endure it. But when you turn to desecration, you go too far! There are some things even a Roman can't get away with!"

"Menapis, tell me what's happened."

"He killed a cat! The fool killed a cat just a stone's throw from my shop!"

"Did you see it happen?"

"A little girl saw him do it. She screamed in terror, naturally enough, and a crowd came running. They thought the little girl was in danger, but it turned out to be something far worse. The Roman fool had killed a cat! We'd have stoned him to death right on the spot, but he managed to slip away and start running. The longer the chase went on, the more people came out to join it. He'll never escape us now. Look up ahead—the Roman rat must be trapped!"

The chase seemed to have ended, for the mob had come to a stop in a wide square. If they had overtaken him, the man in blue must already have been trampled to a pulp, I thought, with a feeling of nausea. But as I drew nearer, the crowd began to chant: "Come out! Come out! Killer of the cat!" Beside me, Menapis took up the chant with the others, slapping his rolling pin against his palm and stamping his feet.

It seemed that the fugitive had taken refuge in a prosperous-looking house. From the faces that stared in horror from the upper-story windows before they were thrown shut, the place appeared to be full of Romans—the man's private dwelling, it seemed. That he was a man of no small means I had already presumed from the quality of his blue tunic, but the size of his house confirmed it. A rich merchant, I thought—but neither silver nor a silvery tongue was likely to save him from the wrath of the mob. They continued to chant and began to beat upon the door with clubs.

Menapis shouted, "Clubs will never break such a door! We'll have to make a battering ram." I looked at the normally genial baker beside me and a shiver ran up my spine. All of this—for a cat!

I withdrew to a quieter corner of the square, where a few of the local residents had ventured out of their houses to watch the commotion. An elderly Egyptian woman, impeccably dressed in a white linen gown, gazed at the mob disparagingly. "What a rabble!" she remarked to no one in particular. "What are they thinking of, attacking the house of a man like Marcus Lepidus?"

"Your neighbor?" I said.

"For many years, as was his father before him. An honest Roman trader, and a greater credit to Alexandria than any of this rabble will ever be. Are you a Roman, too, young man?"

"Yes."

"I thought so, from your accent. Well, I have no quarrel with Romans. Dealing with men like Marcus Lepidus and his father made my late husband a wealthy man. Whatever has Marcus done to bring such a mob to his door?"

"They accuse him of killing a cat."

She gasped. A look of horror contorted her wrinkled face. "That would be unforgivable!"

"He claims to be innocent. Tell me, who else lives in that house?"

"Marcus Lepidus lives with his two cousins. They help him run his affairs, I believe."

"And their wives?"

"The cousins are married, but their wives and children remain in Rome. Marcus is a widower. He has no children. Look there! What madness is this?"

Moving through the mob like a crocodile through lily pads was a great uprooted palm tree. At the head of those who carried it I saw the man with the Babylonian beard. As they aligned the tree perpendicular to the door of Marcus Lepidus's house, its purpose became unmistakable: it was a battering ram.

"I didn't kill the cat!" Marcus Lepidus had said. And, *"Help me! Save me!"* And—no less significantly, to my ears—*"I'll reward you!"* It seemed to me, as a fellow Roman and as a man of honor who had been called on for help, that my course was clear: if the man in blue was innocent of the crime, it was my duty to help him however I could. If duty alone did not suffice, the fact that my stomach was growling and my purse was nearly empty tipped the scales conclusively.

I would need to act swiftly.

The way to the Street of the Breadmakers, usually thronged with people, was almost deserted; the shoppers and the hawkers had all run off to kill the Roman, it seemed. The shop of Menapis was empty—peering within, I saw that piles of dough lay unshapen on the table and the fire in his oven had gone out. The cat had been killed, he said, only a stone's throw from his shop, and it was at about that distance, around the corner on a little side street, that I came upon a group of shaven-headed priests who stood in a circle with bowed heads.

Peering between the orange robes of the priests, I saw the corpse of the cat sprawled on the paving stones. It had been a beautiful creature, with sleek limbs and a coat of midnight black. That it had been deliberately killed could not be doubted, for its throat had been cut.

The priests knelt down and lifted the dead cat onto a small funeral bier, which they hoisted onto their shoulders. Chanting and lamenting, they began a slow procession toward the Temple of Bast.

I looked around, not quite sure how to proceed. A movement at a window above caught my eye, but when I looked up there was nothing to see. I kept looking until a tiny face appeared, then quickly disappeared again.

"Little girl," I called softly. "Little girl."

After a moment she reappeared. Her black hair was pulled back from her face, which was perfectly round. Her eyes were shaped like almonds and her lips formed a pout. "You talk funny," she said.

"Do I?"

"Like the other man."

"What other man?"

She appeared to ponder this for a moment, but did not answer. "Would you like to hear me scream?" she said. Not waiting for a reply, she did so.

The high-pitched wail stabbed at my ears and echoed weirdly in the empty street. I gritted my teeth until she stopped. "That," I said, "is quite a scream. Tell me, are you the little girl who screamed earlier today?"

"Perhaps."

"When the cat was killed, I mean."

She wrinkled her brow thoughtfully. "Not exactly."

"Are you not the little girl who screamed when the cat was killed?"

She considered this. "Did the man with the funny beard send you?" she finally said.

I thought for a moment and recalled the man with the Babylonian beard, whose shout had saved me from the mob in the street—*"The man in blue is the one we want!"*—and whom I had seen at the head of the battering ram. "A Babylonian beard, you mean, curled with an iron?"

"Yes," she said, "all curly, like sunrays shooting out from his chin."

"He saved my life," I said. It was the truth.

"Oh, then I suppose it's all right to talk to you," she said. "Do you have a present for me, too?"

"A present?"

"Like the one he gave me." She held up a doll made of papyrus reeds and bits of rag.

"Very pretty," I said, beginning to understand. "Did he give you the doll for screaming?"

She laughed. "Isn't it silly? Would you like to hear me scream again?"

I shuddered. "Later, perhaps. You didn't really see who killed the cat, did you?"

"Silly! Nobody killed the cat, not really. The cat was just playacting, like I was. Ask the man with the funny beard." She shook her head at my credulity.

"Of course," I said. "I knew that; I just forgot. So you think I talk funny?"

"Yes, I do," she said, mocking my accent rather cruelly, I thought. Alexandrian children acquire a sharp sense of sarcasm very early in life. "You do

talk funny."

"Like the other man, you said."

"Yes."

"You mean the man in the blue tunic, the one they ran after for killing the cat?"

Her round face lengthened a bit. "No, I never heard him talk, except when the baker and his friends came after him, and then he screamed. But I can scream louder."

She seemed ready to demonstrate, so I nodded quickly. "Who then? Who talks like I do? Ah, yes, the man with the funny beard," I said, but I knew I must be wrong even as I spoke, for the man had looked quite Egyptian to me, and certainly not Roman.

"No, not him, silly. The other man."

"What other man?"

"The man who was here yesterday, the one with the runny nose. I heard them talking together, over there on the corner, the funny beard and the one who sounds like you. They were talking and pointing and looking serious, the one with the beard pulling on his beard and the one with the runny nose blowing his nose, but finally they thought of something funny and they both laughed. 'And to think, your cousin is such a lover of cats!' said the funny beard. I could tell they were planning a joke on somebody. I forgot all about it until this morning, when I saw the funny beard again and he asked me to scream when I saw the cat."

"I see. He gave you the doll, then he showed you the cat—"

"Yes, looking so dead it fooled everybody. Even the priests!"

"You screamed, people came running—then what happened?"

"The funny beard pointed at a man who was walking up the street and he shouted, 'The Roman did it! The man in blue! He killed the cat!'" She recited the lines with great conviction, holding up her doll as if it were an actor.

"The man with the runny nose, who talked like me," I said. "You're sure there was mention of his *cousin?*"

"Oh yes. I have a cousin, too. I play tricks on him all the time."

"What did this man with the Roman accent look like?"

She shrugged. "A man."

"Yes, but tall or short, young or old?"

She thought for a moment, then shrugged again. "Just a man, like you. Like the man in the blue tunic. All Romans look the same to me."

Then she screamed again, just to show me how well she could do it.

By the time I got back to the square a band of soldiers had arrived from the palace and were attempting, with limited success, to push back the mob. The soldiers were vastly outnumbered, and the mob would only be pushed back so far. Rocks and bricks were hurled against the building from time to time, some of them striking the already cracked shutters. It appeared that a serious attempt had been made to batter down the door, but the door had lost only a few splinters.

A factotum from the royal palace, a eunuch to judge by his high voice, appeared at the highest place in the square, on a rooftop next to the besieged house. He tried to quiet the mob, assuring them that justice would be done by King Ptolemy and his servants. It was in Ptolemy's interest, of course, to quell what might become an international incident; the murder of a wealthy Roman merchant by the people of Alexandria could cause him great political damage.

The eunuch warbled on, but the mob was unimpressed. To them, the issue was simple and clear: a Roman had ruthlessly murdered a cat, and they would not be satisfied until the Roman was dead. They took up their chant again, drowning out the eunuch: "Come out! Come out! Killer of the cat!"

I had decided to get inside the house of Marcus Lepidus. Caution told me that such a course was mad—for how could I ever get out alive once I was in?—and, at any rate, apparently impossible, for if there were a simple way to get into the house the mob would already have found it. Then it occurred to me that someone standing on the rooftop where Ptolemy's eunuch had stood could conceivably jump or be lowered onto the roof of the besieged house.

It all seemed like a great deal of effort, until I heard the plaintive echo of the stranger's voice inside my head: *"Help me! Save me!"*

The building from which the eunuch spoke had been commandeered by soldiers, as had the other buildings adjacent to the besieged house, as a precaution to keep the mob from gaining entry through an adjoining wall or setting fire to the whole block. It took some doing to convince the guards to let me in, but the fact that I was a Roman and claimed to know Marcus Lepidus eventually gained me an audience with the king's eunuch.

Royal servants come and go in Alexandria; those who fail to satisfy their masters become food for crocodiles and are quickly replaced. This royal servant was clearly feeling the pressure of serving a monarch who might snuff out his life with the mere arching of an eyebrow. He had been sent to quell an angry mob and to save the life of a Roman citizen, and at the moment his chances of succeeding looked distinctly uncertain. He could call for more troops, perhaps, and slaughter the mob, but such a bloodbath could lead to an even graver situation, given the instability of the Egyptian state. Complicating matters even more was the presence of a high priest of Bast, who dogged (if I may use that expression) the eunuch's every step, yowling and waving his orange robes and demanding that justice be done at once in the name of the murdered cat.

The eunuch was receptive to any ideas that I might offer. "You're a friend of this man the mob is after?" he asked.

"This *murderer*," the high priest corrected.

"An acquaintance, yes," I said—and truthfully, if having exchanged a few desperate words after colliding in the street could be called an acquaintance. "In fact, I'm his agent. He's hired me to get him out of this mess." This was also true, after a fashion. "And I think I know who really killed the cat!" This was not quite true, but might become so if the eunuch would cooperate with me. "You must get me into Marcus Lepidus's house. I was thinking that your soldiers might lower me onto his roof by a rope."

The eunuch became thoughtful. "By the same route, we might rescue Marcus Lepidus himself by having him climb a rope up onto this building, where my men can better protect him."

"Rescue a cat-killer? Give him armed protection?" The priest was outraged. The eunuch bit his lip.

At last it was agreed that the king's men would supply a rope by which I could make my way onto the roof of the besieged house. "But you cannot return to this building by the same route," the eunuch insisted.

"Why not?" I had a sudden vision of the house being set aflame with myself inside it, or of an angry mob breaking through the door and setting upon all the inhabitants with knives and clubs.

"Because the rope will be visible from the square," snapped the eunuch. "If the mob sees someone leaving the house, they'll assume it's the man they're after. Then they'll break into this building! No, I'll allow you passage to your country-man's house, but after that you'll be on your own."

I thought for a moment and then agreed. Behind the eunuch, the high priest of Bast smiled like a cat, no doubt anticipating my imminent demise and purring at the idea of yet another impious Roman departing from the shores of the living.

As I was lowered onto the merchant's roof, the household slaves realized what was happening and set up an alarm. They surrounded me at once and seemed determined to throw me into the square below, but I held up my hands to show them that I was unarmed and I cried out that I was a friend of Marcus Lepidus. My accent seemed to sway them. At last they took me down a flight of steps to meet their master.

The man in blue had withdrawn to a small chamber which I took to be his office, for it was cluttered with scrolls and scraps of papyrus. He recognized my face at once.

"But why have you come here, stranger?" he said, looking at me as if I were either a lemur sent to haunt him or a demigod to save him.

"Because you asked for my help, Marcus Lepidus. And because you offered me a reward," I said bluntly. "My name is Gordianus."

Beyond the shuttered window, which faced the square, the crowd began to chant again. A heavy object—a piece of stone or a clay bottle—struck the shutters with a crash. Marcus gave a start and bit his knuckles.

"These are my cousins, Rufus and Appius," he said, introducing two younger men who had just entered the room. Like their older cousin, they were well groomed and well dressed, and like him they appeared to be on the verge of panic.

"The guards outside are beginning to weaken," said Rufus shrilly. "What are we going to do, Marcus?"

"If they break into the house they'll slaughter us all!" said Appius, equally agitated.

"You're obviously a man of wealth, Marcus Lepidus," I said. "A trader, I understand."

"Why, yes," he said. All three cousins looked at me blankly, confused at my apparent disregard for the crisis immediately at hand. "I own a fleet of ships. We carry grain and slaves and other goods from Alexandria to Rome and elsewhere." Talking about his work calmed him noticeably, as reciting a familiar chant calms a worshiper in a temple.

"Do you own the business jointly with your cousins?" I asked.

"The business is mine," said Marcus proudly. "Inherited from my father."

"Yours alone? You have no brothers?"

"None."

"And your cousins are merely employees, not partners?"

"If you put it that way."

I looked at Rufus, the taller of the cousins. Was it fear of the mob I read on his face, or the bitterness of old resentments? His cousin Appius began to pace the room, biting his fingernails and casting what I took to be hostile glances at me.

"I understand you have no sons, Marcus Lepidus," I said.

"No. My first wife gave me only daughters; they all died of fever. My second wife was barren. I have no wife at present, but I soon will, when the girl arrives from Rome. Her parents are sending her by ship, and they promise me that she will be fertile, like her sisters. This time next year, I could be a proud father at last!" He managed a weak smile, then bit his knuckles. "But what's the use of contemplating my future when I have none? Curse all the gods of Egypt, to have put that dead cat in my path!"

"I think it was not a god who did so," I said. "Tell me, Marcus Lepidus, though Jupiter forbid such a tragedy, if you should die without a son, who would inherit your property?"

"My cousins would inherit in equal portions," said Marcus.

Rufus and Appius both looked at me gravely. Another stone struck the shutters and we all gave a start. It was impossible to read their faces for any subtle signs of guilt.

"I see. Tell me, Marcus Lepidus, who could have known, yesterday, that you would be walking up that side street in Rhakotis this morning?"

He shrugged. "I make no secret of my pleasures. There is a certain house on that street where I spend certain nights in the company of a certain catamite. Having no wife at present . . ."

"Then either of your cousins might have known that you would be coming home by that route this morning?"

"I suppose," he said, shrugging. If he was too agitated to see the point, his cousins were not. Rufus and Appius both stared at me darkly and glanced dubiously at one another.

At that moment a gray cat came sauntering into the room, its tail flicking, its head held high, apparently oblivious to the chaos outside the house or the despair of those within. "The irony of it all!" wailed Marcus Lepidus, suddenly breaking into tears. "The bitter irony! I, of all men, would never kill a cat! The creatures adore me, and I adore them. I give them a place of honor in my home, I feed them delicacies from my own plate. Come, precious one." He stooped down and made a cradle for the cat, who obligingly pounced into his arms. The cat squirmed onto its back and purred loudly. Marcus Lepidus held the animal close to him. Caressing it seemed to soothe his own distress. Rufus appeared to share his older cousin's fondness for cats, for he smiled weakly and joined him in stroking the beast's belly.

I had reached an impasse. It seemed to me quite certain that at least one of the cousins had been in league with the bearded Egyptian in deliberately plotting the destruction of Marcus Lepidus, but which? If only the little girl had been able to give me a better description. "All Romans look the same" indeed!

"You and your cursed cats!" said Appius suddenly, wrinkling his nose and retreating to the far corner of the room. "It's the cats that do this to me. They cast some sort of hateful spell! Alexandria is full of them, making my life a misery. I never sneezed once in my life before I came here!" And with that he sneezed and sneezed and began to blow his runny nose.

What followed was not pretty, though it may have been just.

I accused Appius of plotting his cousin's death. I told Marcus Lepidus all I had learned from the little girl. I summoned him to the window and opened the shutters enough to point out the bearded Egyptian, who was now overseeing the construction of a bonfire in the square below. Marcus had seen the man before in the company of his cousin.

What outcome did I expect? I had meant to help a fellow Roman far from home, to save an innocent man from the wrath of an unreasoning mob, and to gain a few coins for my purse in the process—all honorable pursuits. Did I not realize that inevitably a man would die? I was younger then, and did not always think a thing through to its logical result.

The unleashed fury of Marcus Lepidus took me by surprise. Perhaps it should not have, considering the terrible shock he had suffered that day; considering also that he was a successful businessman, and therefore to some degree ruthless; considering finally that treachery within a family often drives men to acts of extreme revenge.

Quailing before Marcus Lepidus, Appius confessed his guilt. Rufus, whom he declared to be innocent of the plot, begged for mercy on his cousin's behalf, but his pleadings were ineffectual. Though we might be hundreds of miles from Rome, the rule of the Roman family held sway in that house in Alexandria, and all power resided in the head of the household. When Marcus Lepidus stripped off his blue tunic and ordered that his cousin Appius should be dressed in it, the slaves of the household obeyed; Appius resisted, but was overwhelmed. When Marcus ordered that Appius should then be thrown from the window into the mob, it was done.

Rufus, pale and trembling, withdrew into another room. Marcus made his face as hard as stone and turned away. The gray cat twined itself about his feet, but the solace it offered was ignored.

The bearded Egyptian, not realizing the substitution, screamed to the others in the mob to take their vengeance on the man in blue. It was only much later, when the mob had largely dispersed and the Egyptian was able to get a closer look at the trampled, bloody corpse, that he realized the mistake. I shall never forget the look on his face, which changed from a leer of triumph to a mask of horror as he approached the body, studied its face, and then looked up at the window where I stood. He had overseen the killing of his own confederate.

Perhaps it was fitting that Appius received the fate which he had intended for his cousin. No doubt he thought that while he waited, safe and sound in the family house, the bearded Egyptian would proceed with the plot as they had planned and his older cousin would be torn to pieces on the Street of the Breadmakers. He did not foresee that Marcus Lepidus would be able to elude the crowd and flee all the way to his house, where all three cousins became trapped. Nor did he foresee the intervention of Gordianus the Finder—or for that matter, the intervention of the gray cat, which caused him to betray himself with a sneeze.

Thus ended the episode of the Alexandrian cat, whose death was terribly avenged.

Some days after telling this tale to Lucius Claudius, I chanced to visit him again at his house on the Palatine. I was surprised to see that a new mosaic had been installed on his doorstep. The colorful little tiles pictured a snarling Molossian mastiff, together with the stern caption, CAVE CANEM, "Beware the Dog."

A slave admitted me and escorted me to the garden at the center of the house. As I approached I heard a yapping noise, accompanied by deep-throated laughter. I came upon Lucius Claudius, who sat with what appeared to be a gigantic white rat on his lap.

"What on earth is that?" I exclaimed.

"This is my darling, my sweet, my adorable little Momo."

"Your doorstep shows a Molossian mastiff, which that animal most certainly is not."

"Momo is a Melitaean terrier—tiny, true, but very fierce," said Lucius defensively. As if to prove her master's point, the little lapdog began to yap again. Then she nervously began lapping at Lucius's chin, which he appeared to enjoy immensely.

"The doorstep advises visitors to beware this beast," I said sceptically.

"As indeed they should—especially unwelcomed visitors of the four-footed variety."

"You expect this dog to keep cats away?"

"I do! Never again shall my peace be violated by those accursed creatures, not with little Momo here to protect me. Is that not right, Momo? Are you not the fiercest cat-chaser who ever lived? Brave, bold little Momo—"

I rolled my eyes upward at this display of enthusiasm, and caught a glimpse of something black and sleek on the roof. It was almost certainly the cat who had terrified Lucius before.

An instant later the terrier was out of her master's lap, performing a frantic circular dance on the floor, yapping madly and baring her teeth. Up on the roof, the black cat arched its back, hissed, and disappeared.

"There, you see, Gordianus! Beware this dog, all you cats of Rome!" Lucius scooped the dog up in his arms and kissed her nose. "There, there, Momo, and disbelieving Gordianus doubted you . . ."

I thought of a truism I had learned from Bethesda: there are those who love cats, and those who love dogs, and never shall the two agree. But we could at least share a cup of wine, Lucius Claudius and I, and exchange the latest gossip from the Forum.

Roy Vickers

MISS PAISLEY'S CAT

There are those who have a special affection for cats, and there are those who hold them in physical and even moral abhorrence. The belief lingers that cats have been known to influence a human being—generally an old maid, and generally for evil. It is true that Miss Paisley's cat was the immediate cause of that emotionally emaciated old maid reaching a level of perverted greatness—or stark infamy, according to one's point of view. But this can be explained without resort to mysticism. The cat's behavior was catlike throughout.

Miss Paisley's cat leaped into her life when she was 54 and the cat itself was probably about two. Miss Paisley was physically healthy and active—an inoffensive, neatly dressed, self-contained spinster. The daughter of a prosperous businessman—her mother had died while the child was a toddler—she had passed her early years in the golden age of the middle classes, when every detached suburban villa had many of the attributes of a baronial hall: if there was no tenantry there was always a handful of traditionally obsequious tradesmen—to say nothing of a resident domestic staff.

She was eighteen, at a "finishing school" in Paris, when her father contracted pneumonia and died while in the course of reorganizing his business. Miss Paisley inherited the furniture of the house, a couple of hundred in cash, and an annuity of £120.

Her relations, in different parts of the country, rose to the occasion. Without expert advice they pronounced her unfit for further education or training and decided that, among them, they must marry her off—which ought not to be difficult. Miss Paisley was never the belle of a ball of any size, but she was a good-looking girl, with the usual graces and accomplishments.

In the first round of visits she accepted the warm assurances of welcome at their face value—yet she was not an unduly conceited girl. It was her father who had given her the belief that her company was a boon in itself. The technique of the finishing school, too, had been based on a similar assumption.

During the second round of visits—in units of some six months—she made the discovery that her company was tolerated rather than desired—a harsh truth from which she sought immediate escape.

There followed an era of nursery governessing and the companioning of old ladies. The children were hard work and the old ladies were very disappointing.

Penuriousness and old ladies were turning her into a humble creature, thankful for the crumbs of life. In her early twenties she obtained permanent employment as a "female clerk" in a government office. She made her home in Rumbold Chambers, Marpleton, about fifteen miles out of London, and about a mile from the house that had once been her father's. The Chambers—in this sense a genteel, Edwardian word meaning flatlets—had already seen better days, and were to see worse.

The rent would absorb nearly half her annuity; but the Chambers, she believed, had tone. The available flatlet looked over the old cemetery to the Seventeenth-Century bridge across the river. She signed a life lease. Thus, she was in that flatlet when the cat came, 32 years later.

She had taken out of the warehouse as much furniture as would go into the flatlet. The walls were adorned with six enlarged photographs, somewhat pompously framed, of the house and garden that had been her father's.

The radio came into general use; the talkies appeared and civil aviation was getting into its stride—events which touched her life not at all. Light industry invaded Marpleton and district. Every three months or so she would walk past her old home, until it was demolished to make room for a factory.

If she made no enemies, she certainly made no friends. The finishing school had effectively crippled her natural sociability. At the end of her working day she would step back 30-odd years into her past.

When the cat appeared, Miss Paisley was talking vivaciously to herself, as is the habit of the solitary.

"I sometimes think father made a mistake in keeping it as a croquet lawn. Croquet is so old-fashioned . . . *Oh!* How on earth did you get here!"

The cat had apparently strolled onto the windowsill—a whole story plus some four feet above ground level. "Animals aren't allowed in the Chambers, so you must go . . . Go, please. *Whooosh!*"

The cat blinked and descended, somewhat awkwardly, into the room.

"What an ugly cat! I shall never forget Aunt Lisa's Persian. It looked beautiful, and everybody made an absurd fuss of it. I don't suppose anybody ever wants to stroke *you*. People tolerate you, rather wishing you didn't exist, poor thing!" The cat was sitting on its haunches, staring at Miss Paisley. "Oh, well, I suppose you can stay to tea. I've no fish, but there's some bloater paste I forgot to throw away—

and some milk left over from yesterday."

Miss Paisley set about preparing tea for herself. It was Saturday afternoon. Chocolate biscuits and two cream eclairs for today, and chocolate biscuits and two meringues for Sunday. When the kettle had boiled and she had made the tea, she scraped out a nearly empty tin of bloater paste, spreading it on a thin slice of dry bread. She laid a newspaper on the floor—the carpet had been cut out of the drawing-room carpet of 34 years ago. The cat, watching these preparations, purred its approval.

"Poor thing! It's pathetically grateful," said Miss Paisley, placing the bloater paste and a saucer of yesterday's milk on the newspaper.

The cat lowered its head, sniffed the bloater paste, but did not touch it. It tried the milk, lapped once, then again sat back on its haunches and stared at Miss Paisley.

The stare of Miss Paisley's cat was not pleasing to humanity. It was, of course, a normal cat's stare from eyes that were also normal, though they appeared not to be, owing to a streak of white fur that ran from one eyelid to the opposite ear, then splashed over the spine. A wound from an airgun made one cheek slightly shorter than the other, revealing a glimpse of teeth and giving the face the suggestion of a human sneer. Add that it had a stiff left foreleg, which made its walk ungainly, and you have a very ugly cat—a standing challenge to juvenile marksmanship.

"You're a stupid cat, too," said Miss Paisley. "You don't seem to make the most of your opportunities."

Miss Paisley sat down to tea. The cat leaped onto the table, seized one of the eclairs, descended cautiously, and devoured the eclair on the carpet, several inches from the newspaper.

This time it was Miss Paisley who stared at the cat.

"That is most extraordinary behavior!" she exclaimed. "You thrust yourself upon me when I don't want you. I treat you with every kindness—"

The cat had finished the eclair. Miss Paisley continued to stare. Then her gaze shifted to her own hand which seemed to her to be moving independently of her will. She watched herself pick up the second eclair and lower it to the cat, who tugged it from her fingers.

She removed the saucer under her still empty tea cup, poured today's milk into it, and placed the saucer on the floor. She listened, fascinated, while the cat lapped it all. Her pulse was thudding with the excitement of a profound discovery.

Then, for the first time in 30-odd years, Miss Paisley burst into tears.

"Go away!" she sobbed. "I don't want you. It's too late—*I'm 54!*"

By the time her breath was coming easily again, the cat had curled up on the Chesterfield that was really Miss Paisley's bed.

It was a month or more before Miss Paisley knew for certain that she hoped the cat would make its home with her. Her attitude was free from the kind of sentimentality which one associates with an old maid and a cat. She respected its cathood, attributed to it no human qualities. The relationship was too subtle to have need of pretense. Admittedly, she talked to it a great deal. But she talked as if to a roommate, who might or might not be attending. In this respect, the cat's role could be compared with that of a paid companion.

"Excuse me, madam!" Jenkins, the watchdog and rent-collector, who had replaced the porter of palmier days, had stopped her in the narrow hall. "Would that cat with the black-and-white muzzle be yours by any chance?"

A month ago, Miss Paisley would have dithered with apology for breaking the rules and would have promised instant compliance.

"It is my cat, Jenkins. And I would be very glad to pay you half a crown a week for any trouble it may be to you."

"That's very kind of you, madam, and thank you. What I was goin' to say was that I saw it jump out o' Mr. Rinditch's window with a bit o' fish in its mouth what Mr. Rinditch had left from his breakfast." He glanced down the passage to make sure that Mr. Rinditch's door was shut. "You know what Mr. Rinditch is!"

Miss Paisley knew that he was a street bookmaker, with a number of runners who took the actual bets, and that Jenkins stood in awe of him as the only tenant of any financial substance. Mr. Rinditch was a stocky, thickset man with a large sullen face and a very large neck. Miss Paisley thought he looked vulgar, which was a matter of character, whereas the other tenants only looked common, which they couldn't help.

"I'll give it proper cat's-meat, then it won't steal."

"Thank you, madam."

The "madam" cost Miss Paisley about £4 a year. None of the other women were "madam," and none of the men were "sir" —not even Mr. Rinditch. Two pounds at Christmas and odd half crowns for small, mainly superfluous services. For Miss Paisley it was a sound investment. In her dream life she was an emigrée awaiting recall to a style of living which, did she but know it, had virtually ceased to exist in England. It was as if the 30-odd years of unskilled clerical labor were a merely temporary expedient. Through the cat she was acquiring a new philosophy, but the dream was untouched.

"I have to cut your meat," she explained that evening, "and I'm rather dreading it. You see, I've never actually handled raw meat before. It was *not* considered a necessary item in my education. Though I remember once—we were on a river picnic—two of the servants with the hamper were being driven over . . ."

She had to ask Jenkins's advice. He lent her a knife—a formidable object with a black handle and a blade tapering to a point. A French knife, he told her, and she could buy one like it at any ironmonger's—which she did on the following day. There remained the shuddery business of handling the meat. She sacrificed a memento—a pair of leather driving gloves, which she had worn for horse-riding during her holidays from school.

On the third day of the fourth month the cat failed appear at its meal-time. Miss Paisley was disturbed. She went to bed an hour later than usual, to lie awake until dawn, struggling against the now inescapable fact that the cat had become necessary to her, though she was unable to guess why this should be true. She tried to prove it was not true. She knew how some old maids doted upon a particular cat, perpetually fondling it and talking baby-talk to it. For her cat she felt nothing at all of that kind of emotion. She knew that her cat was rather dirty, and she never really liked touching it. Indeed, she did not like cats, as such. But there was something about this particular cat . . .

The cat came through the open window shortly after dawn. Miss Paisley got out of bed and uncovered the meat. The cat yawned, stretched, and ignored it, then jumped onto the foot of her bed, circled, and settled down, asleep before Miss Paisley's own head returned to her pillow. Miss Paisley was now cat-wise enough to know that it must have fed elsewhere, from which she drew the alarming inference that a cat which had strayed once might stray again.

The next day she bought a collar, had it engraved with her name and address and, in brackets, *£1 Reward for Return*. She could contemplate expenditure of this kind without unease because, in the 30-odd years, she had saved more than £500.

That evening she fastened the collar in position. The cat pulled it off. Miss Paisley unfastened the special safety buckle and tried again—tried five times before postponing further effort.

"Actually, you yourself have taught me how to handle this situation," she said the following evening. "You refused the bloater paste and the not very fresh milk. You were right! Now, it will be a great pity if we have to quarrel and see no more of each other, but—no collar—no meat!"

After small initial misunderstandings the cat accepted the collar for the duration of the meal. On the third evening the cat forgot to scratch it off after the meal. In a week, painstaking observation revealed that the cat had become unconscious of the collar. Even when it scratched the collar in the course of scratching itself, it made no effort to remove the collar. It wore the collar for the rest of its life.

After the collar incident, their relationship was established on a firmer footing. She bought herself new clothing—including a hat that was too young for her and a lumber jacket in suede as green as a cat's eyes. There followed a month of tranquillity, shadowed only by a warning from Jenkins that the cat had failed to shake off its habit of visiting Mr. Rinditch's room. She noticed something smarmy in the way Jenkins told her about it—as if he enjoyed telling her. For the first time, there came to her the suspicion that the "madam" was ironic and a source of amusement to Jenkins.

On the following Saturday came evidence that, in this matter at least, Jenkins had spoken truly. She would reach home shortly after 1 on Saturdays. While she was on her way across the hall to the staircase, the door of Mr. Rinditch's room opened. Mr. Rinditch's foot was visible, as was Miss Paisley's cat. The cat was projected some four feet across the corridor. As it struck the paneling of the staircase, Miss Paisley felt a violent pain in her own ribs. She rushed forward, tried to pick up her cat. The cat spat at her and hobbled away. For a moment she stared after it, surprised and hurt by its behavior. Then, suddenly, she brightened.

"You won't accept pity!" she murmured. She tossed her head, and her eyes sparkled with a kind of happiness that was new to her. She knocked on Mr. Rinditch's door. When the large, sullen face appeared, she met it with a catlike stare.

"You kicked my cat!"

"Your cat, is it! Then I'll thank you to keep it out o' my room."

"I regret the trespass—"

"So do I. If I catch 'im in 'ere again, he'll swing for it, and it's me tellin' yer." Mr. Rinditch slammed his door.

Miss Paisley, who affected an ignorance of cockney idiom, asked herself what the words meant. As they would bear an interpretation which she would not allow her imagination to accept, she assured herself they meant nothing. She began to wonder at her own audacity in bearding a coarse, tough man like Mr. Rinditch, who might well have started a brawl.

In the meantime, the cat had gone up the stairs and was waiting for her at the door of her apartment. It still did not wish to be touched. But when Miss Paisley rested in her easy chair before preparing her lunch, the cat, for the first time, jumped onto her lap. It growled and changed its position, steadying itself with its claws, which penetrated Miss Paisley's dress and pricked her. Then it settled down, purred a little, and went to sleep. The one-time dining-room clock chimed 2 o'clock: Miss Paisley discovered that she was not hungry.

On Sunday the cat resumed its routine, and seemed none the worse. It tackled its meat ration with avidity, and wound up with Miss Paisley's other meringue. But that did not excuse the gross brutality of Mr. Rinditch. On Monday morning Miss Paisley stopped Jenkins on the first-floor landing and asked for Mr. Rinditch's full name, explaining that she intended to apply for a summons for cruelty to animals.

"If you'll excuse me putting in a word, madam, you won't get your own back on *him* by getting' him fined ten bob. Why, he pays something like £50 a month in fines for 'is runners—thinks no more of it than you think o' your train fare."

Miss Paisley was somewhat dashed. Jenkins enlarged.

"You'd be surprised, madam, at the cash that comes his way. The night before a big race, he'll be home at 6 with more'n a couple o' hundred pound in that bag o' his; then he'll go out at a quarter to 8, do his round of the pubs, and be back at 10:30 with as much cash again."

The amount of the fine, Miss Paisley told herself, was irrelevant. This was a matter of principle. The lawyer, whom she consulted during her lunch hour, failed to perceive the principle. He told her that she could not prove her statements: that, as the cat admittedly bore no sign of the attack, the case would be "laughed out of court."

She had never heard that phrase before, and she resented it, the resentment being tinged with fear.

When she reached home, she found the cat crouching on the far side of the escritoire. It took no notice her, but she could wait no longer to unburden herself.

"We should be laughed out of court," she said. "In other words, Mr. Rinditch can kick us, and the Law will laugh at us for being kicked. I expect we look very funny when we are in pain!"

In the whole of Miss Paisley's life that was the unluckiest moment for that particular remark. If her eyes had not been turned inward, she could have interpreted the behavior of the cat, could not have failed to recognize that its position by the escritoire was strategic. She was still talking about her interview with the lawyer when the cat pounced, then turned in her direction, a live mouse kicking in its jaws.

"Oh, dear!" She accepted the situation with a sigh. She was without the physiological fear of mice—thought them pretty little things and would have encouraged them but for their unsanitary habits.

Now, Miss Paisley knew—certainly from the cliché, if not from experience—the way of a cat with a mouse. Yet it took her by surprise, creating an unmanageable conflict.

"Don't—oh, *don't*! Stop! Can't you see? . . . We're no better than Mr. Rinditch! Oh, God, please make him stop! I can't endure it. I *mustn't* endure it! Isn't it any use praying? Are You laughing, too?"

Physical movement was not at Miss Paisley's command, just then. The feeling of cold in her spine turned to heat, and spread outwards over her body, tingling as it spread. In her ears was the sound of crackling, like the burning of dried weeds.

Her breathing ceased to be painful. The immemorial ritual claimed first her attention, then her interest.

After some minutes, Miss Paisley tittered. Then she giggled. The cat, which can create in humanity so many illusions about itself, seemed to be playing its mouse to a gallery, and playing hard for a laugh.

Miss Paisley laughed.

There were periods of normality, of uneventful months in which one day was indistinguishable from another, and Miss Paisley thought of herself as an elderly lady who happened to keep a cat.

She deduced that the cat wandered a good deal, and sometimes begged or stole food from unknown persons. She had almost persuaded herself that it had abandoned its perilous habit of visiting Mr. Rinditch's flatlet. One evening in early summer, about a fortnight before the end came, this hope was dashed.

At about half-past 8 the cat had gone out, after its evening meal. Miss Paisley was looking out of her window, idly awaiting its return. Presently she saw it on top of the wall that divided the yard from the old burial ground. She waved to it; it stared at her, then proceeded to wash itself, making a ten-minute job of it. Then it slithered down via the tool shed, but instead of making straight for the drainpipe that led past Miss Paisley's windowsill, it changed direction. By leaning out of the window, she could obtain an oblique view of Mr. Rinditch's rear window.

She hurried downstairs along the corridor, past Mr. Rinditch's door to the door that gave onto the yard, skirted a group of six ashcans, and came to Mr. Rinditch's window, which was open about eighteen inches at the bottom. She could see the cat on Mr. Rinditch's bed. She knew she could not tempt it with food so soon after its main meal. She called coaxingly, then desperately.

"We are in great danger," she whispered. "Don't you care?"

The cat stared at her, then closed its eyes. Miss Paisley took stock of the room. It was sparsely but not inexpensively furnished. The paneling was disfigured with calendars and metal coat-hooks.

The sill was more than four feet from the ground. She put her shoulders in the gap, and insinuated herself. She grasped the cat by its scruff, with one finger under its collar, and retained her hold while she scrambled to the safety of the yard, neglecting to lower the window to its usual position. They both reached her apartment without meeting anyone.

During that last fortnight which remained to them, Miss Paisley received—as she would have expressed it—a final lesson from the cat. She was returning from work on a warm evening. When some 50 yards from the Chambers, she saw the cat sunning itself on the pavement. From the opposite direction came a man with a Labrador dog on a leash. Suddenly the dog bounded, snatching the leash from the man's hand.

"*Danger*! Run a-way!" screamed Miss Paisley.

The cat saw its enemy a second too late. Moreover, its stiff leg put flight out of the question. While Miss Paisley ran forward, feeling the dog's hot breath on the back of her neck, she nerved herself for the breaking of her bones. And then, as it seemed to her, the incredible happened. The dog sprang away from the cat, ran round in a circle, yelping with pain, while the cat clambered to the top of a nearby gatepost.

The man had recovered the leash and was soothing the dog. Again Miss Paisley extemporized a prayer, this time of thankfulness. Then the habit of years asserted itself over the teaching she believed she had received from the cat.

"I am afraid, sir, my cat has injured your dog. I am very sorry. If there is anything I can do—"

"That's all right, miss," a genial cockney voice answered. "He asked for it, an' he got it." The dog was bleeding under the throat, and there were two long weals on its chest. "That's the way cats ought to fight—get in under and strike *UP*, I say!"

"I have some iodine in my flat—"

"Cor, he don't want none o' that! Maybe your cat has saved 'im from losing an eye to the next one. Don't you give it another thought, miss!"

Miss Paisley bowed, sadly confused in her social values, which were also her moral values. The man's cockney accent was as inescapable as the excellence of his manners. Miss Paisley's world was changing too fast for her.

She enjoyed another six days and nights of the cat's company, which included four and a half days at the office. But these can be counted in, because the attention she gave to her work had become automatic and did not disturb her inner awareness of the relationship. She never defined that relationship, had not even observed the oddity that she had given the cat no name . . .

It was a Tuesday evening. The cat was not at home when she arrived.

"You've started being late for meals again," she grumbled. "Tonight, as it so happens, you can have ten minutes' grace." Her subscription to an illustrated social weekly was overdue. She filled up the renewal form, went out to buy a money order.

In the hall, Mr. Rinditch's voice reached her through the closed door of his apartment—apparently swearing to himself. There followed a muffled, whistling sound, as of cord being drawn sharply over metal. Then she heard a queer kind of growling cough and a scratching on woodwork—the kind of scratching that could be made by a cat's claws on a wooden panel, if the cat's body were suspended above the floor.

She stood, holding her breath, paralyzed by a sense of urgency which her imagination refused to define. She seemed to be imprisoned within herself, unable to desire escape. The sound of scratching grew thinner until it was so thin that she could doubt whether she heard it at all.

"You are imagining things!" she said to herself.

She smiled and went on her way to the post office. The smile became fixed. One must, she told herself, be circumspect in all things. If she were to start brawling with her neighbors every time she fancied—well, this-that-and-the-other—and without a shred of evidence—people would soon be saying she was an eccentric old maid. She wished she could stop smiling.

She bought the money order, posted it, and returned to her apartment, assuring herself that nothing at all had happened. That being agreed, everything could proceed as usual.

"Not home yet! Very well, I sha'n't wait for you. I shall cut up your meat now, and if it gets dry you've only yourself to blame." She put on the gloves with which she had held reins 37 years ago. "Just over a year! I must have used them to cut up your meat more than 300 times, and they're none the worse for wear. You couldn't buy gloves like this nowadays. I don't fancy tinned salmon. I think I'll make myself an omelette. I remember Cook was always a little uncertain with her omelettes."

She made the omelette carefully, but ate it quickly. When she had finished her coffee, she went to the bookcase above the escritoire. She had not opened the glass doors for more than ten years. She took out *Ivanhoe*, which her father had given to her mother before they were married.

At a quarter past ten, she closed the book.

"You know I've never waited up for you! And I'm not going to begin now."

The routine was to leave the curtains parted a little—about the width of a cat. Tonight she closed them. When she got into bed, she could soon see moonlight through the chinks by the rings . . . and then the daylight.

In the morning, she took some trouble to avoid meeting Jenkins. As if he had lain in wait for her, he popped out from the service cupboard under the staircase.

"Good morning, madam. I haven't seen your pussy cat this morning."

Pussy cat! What a nauseating way to speak of her cat!

"I'm not worrying, Jenkins. He often goes off on his own for a couple of days. I'm a little late this morning."

She was not late—she caught her usual train to London with the usual margin. At the office, her colleagues seemed more animated than usual. A fragment of their chatter penetrated. "If *Lone Lass* doesn't win tomorrow, I shall be going to London for my summer holiday." A racehorse, of course. One of the so-called classic races tomorrow, but she could not remember which. It reminded her of Mr. Rinditch. A very low, coarse man! Her thought shifted to that very nice man who owned the dog. One of nature's gentlemen! *"Get in under and strike UP!"*

She did not go out at lunch hour, so did not buy any cat's-meat.

That evening, at a few minutes to 8, she heard Jenkins's footstep on the landing. He knocked at her door.

"Good evening, madam. I hope I'm not disturbing you. There's something I'd like to show you, if you can spare a couple o' minutes."

On the way downstairs there broke upon Miss Paisley the full truth about herself and Jenkins. Madam! She could hear now the contempt in his voice, could even hear the innumerable guffaws that had greeted anecdotes of the female clerk who gave herself the airs of a lady in temporarily distressed circumstances. But her dignity had now passed into her own keeping.

He led her along the corridor, through the door giving onto the yard, to the six ashcans. He lifted a lid. On top of the garbage was the carcass of her cat. Attached to the neck was a length of green blind cord.

"Well, Jenkins?" Her fixed smile was unnerving him.

"He was in Mr. Rinditch's room again, soon after you came 'ome last night. You can't really complain, knowin' what he said he'd do. And hangin' an animal isn't torture if it's done properly, like this was. I don't suppose your poor little pussy cat felt any pain. Just pulled the string over the top of the coat-hook, and it was all over."

"That is immaterial." She knew that her cold indifference was robbing this jackal of the sadistic treat he had promised himself. "How do we know that Mr. Rinditch is responsible? It might have been anybody in the building, Jenkins."

"I tell you, it was him! Last night, when my missus went in with his evenin' meal, same as usual, she saw a length o' that blind cord stickin' out from under his bed. And there was a bit o' green fluff on the coat-hook, where the cord had frayed. The missus did a bit more nosing while she was clearing away, an' she spotted the cat's collar in the wastepaper basket. You couldn't hang a cat properly with that collar on, 'cause o' the metal. She said the strap part had been cut—like as it might be with a razor."

Miss Paisley gazed a second time into the ashcan. The collar had certainly been removed. Jenkins, watching her, thought she was still unwilling to believe him. Like most habitual liars, he was always excessively anxious to prove his word when he happened to be telling the truth.

"Come to think of it, the collar will still be in that basket," he said, mainly to himself. "Listen! He keeps it near enough to the front window. Come round to the front and maybe you'll be able to see it for yourself."

The basket was of plaited wicker. Through the interstices Miss Paisley could see enough of the collar to banish all doubt.

She could listen to herself talking to Jenkins, just as she had been able to see herself standing at the ashcan, knowing what was under the lid before Jenkins removed it. How easy it was to be calm when you had made up your mind!

When she returned to her room it was only five minutes past 8. Never mind. The calm would last as long as she needed it. In two hours and twenty-five minutes, Mr. Rinditch would come home. She was shivering. She put on the green suede lumber jacket, then she sat in her armchair, erect, her outstretched fingers in the folds of the upholstery.

"Before Mr. Rinditch comes back, I want you to know that I heard you scratching on his wall. You were alive then. We have already faced the fact that if I had hammered on the door and—brawled—you would be alive now. We won't argue about it. There's a lot to be said on both sides, so we will not indulge in recriminations."

Miss Paisley was silent until twenty-five minutes past 10, when she got up and put on the riding gloves, as if she were about to cut meat for her cat. The knife on the shelf in its usual place. Her hand snatched at the handle, as if someone were trying to take it away from her.

" *'Get in under and strike UP!'* " she whispered—and then Miss Paisley's physical movements again became unmanageable. She was gripping the handle of the knife, but she could not raise it from the shelf. She had the illusion of exerting her muscles, of pulling with all the strength of her arm against an impossibly heavy weight. Dimly she could hear Mr. Rinditch come home and slam his door.

"I've let myself become excited! I must get back my calm."

Still wearing the gloves and the lumber jacket, she went back to her chair.

"At my age I can't alter the habits of a lifetime—and when I try, I am pulled two ways at once. I told you in the first place that you had come too late. You oughtn't to have gone into Mr. Rinditch's room. He killed you in malice, and I betrayed you—oh, yes, I did!—and now I can't even pray."

Miss Paisley's thoughts propounded riddles and postulated nightmares with which her genteel education was unable to cope. When she came to full consciousness of her surroundings it was a quarter to 3 in the morning. The electric light was burning and she was wearing neither the gloves nor the green suede jacket.

"I don't remember turning on the light—I'm too tired to remember anything." She would sleep on in the morning, take a day off. She undressed and got into bed. For the first time for more than a year, she fell asleep without thought of the cat.

She was awakened shortly after 7 by a number of unusual sounds—of a clatter in the hall and voices raised, of a coming and going on the stairs. She sat up and listened. On the ground floor Mrs. Jenkins was shouting while she cried—a working-class habit which Miss Paisley deplored. A voice she recognized as that of the boilermaker who lived on the top floor shouted up the stairs to his wife.

"Oh, Emma! They've taken 'im away. Hangcuffs an' all! Cor!"

Miss Paisley put on her long winter coat, pulled the collar up to her chin, and opened her door.

"What is all the noise about?" she asked the boilermaker.

"That bookie on the ground floor, miss. Someone cut 'is throat for 'im in the night. The pleece've pinched Jenkins." He added: "Hangcuffs an' all!"

"Oh!" said Miss Paisley. "I see!"

Miss Paisley shut the door. She dressed and prinked with more care than usual. She remembered trying to pick up the knife, remembered sitting down in an ecstasy of self-contempt, then groping in a mental fog that enveloped time and place. But there were beacons in the fog. *"Get in under and strike UP!"* was one beacon, the slogan accompanied by a feeling of intense pride. And wasn't there another beacon? A vague memory of slinking, like a cat, in the shadows—to the river. Why the river? Of rinsing her hands in cold water. Of returning to her chair. Return. *£1 Reward for Return.* Her head spinning. Anyhow, "someone cut 'is throat for 'im in the night."

So far from feeling crushed, Miss Paisley found that she had recovered the power to pray.

"I have committed murder, so I quite see that it's absurd to ask for anything. But I really must keep calm for the next few hours. If I may be helped to keep calm, please, I can manage the rest myself."

At the local police station Miss Paisley gave an able summary of events leading to the destruction of her cat, and her own subsequent actions, "while in a state of trance."

The desk sergeant stifled a yawn. He produced a form and asked her a number of questions concerning her identity and occupation, but no questions at all about the murder. When he had finished writing down answers, he read them aloud.

"And your statement is, Miss Paisley, that it was you who killed William Rinditch, in—in a state of trance you said, didn't you?"

Miss Paisley assented, and signed her statement.

"Just at present the inspector is very busy," explained the sergeant, "so I must ask you to take a seat in the waiting room."

Miss Paisley, who had expected the interview to end with "hangcuffs," clung to her calm and sat in the waiting room, insultingly unguarded, for more than an hour. Then she was grudgingly invited to enter a police car, which took her to county headquarters.

Chief Inspector Green, who had served his apprenticeship at Scotland Yard, had dealt with a score or more of self-accusing hysterics. He knew that about one in four would claim to have committed the murder while in a trance—knew, too, that this kind could be most troublesome if they fancied they were treated frivolously.

"Then you believe Rinditch killed your cat, Miss Paisley, because Jenkins told you so?"

"By no means!" She described the cat's collar and the method of killing, which necessitated the removal of the collar. She added details about the wastepaper basket.

"Then the collar is still in that basket, if Jenkins was telling the truth?"

But investigation on the spot established that there was no cat's collar in the wastepaper basket, nor anywhere else in the apartment. Miss Paisley was astonished—she knew she had seen it in that basket.

The interview was resumed in her flatlet, where she asserted that she had intended to kill Mr. Rinditch when he returned at 10:30, but was insufficiently prepared at that time. She did not know what time it was when she killed him, but knew that it was not later than a quarter to three in the morning. The weapon had been the knife which she used exclusively for cutting the cat's special meat.

"I have no memory at all of the act itself, Inspector. I can only say that it was fixed in my mind that I must get in close and strike upwards."

The inspector blinked, hesitated, then tried another line.

"It was after 10:30, anyhow, you said—after he had locked up for the night. How did you get in?"

"Again, I can't tell. I can't have hammered on his door, or someone would have heard me. I might have—I must have—got in by his window. I regret to confess that on one occasion I did enter his apartment that way in order to remove my cat, which would not come out when I called it."

"How did you get into the yard? That door is locked at night."

"Probably Jenkins left the key in it—he is very negligent."

"So you have no memory at all of the crime itself? You are working out what you think you must have done?"

Miss Paisley remembered that she had prayed for calm.

"I appreciate the force of your remark, Inspector. But I suggest that it would be a little unusual, to say the least, for a woman of my antecedents and habits to accuse herself falsely for the sake of notoriety. I ask you to believe that I sat in that chair at about 10:30, that my next clear memory is of being in the chair at a quarter to 3. Also, there were other signs—"

"Right! We accept that you got out of that chair—though you don't remember it. You may have done other things, too, but I'll show you that you *didn't* kill Rinditch. To begin with, let's have a look at the murder knife."

Miss Paisley went to the cupboard.

"It isn't here!" she exclaimed. "Oh, but of course! I must have—I mean, didn't you *find* the knife?"

Inspector Green was disappointed. He could have settled the matter at once if she had produced the knife—which had indeed been found in the body of the deceased. A knife that could be bought at any ironmonger's in the country, unidentifiable in itself.

"If you had entered Rinditch's room, you'd have left fingerprints all over the place—"

"But I was wearing leather riding gloves—"

"Let's have a look at 'em, Miss Paisley."

Miss Paisley went back to the cupboard. They should be on the top shelf. They were not.

"I can't think where I must have put them!" she faltered.

"It doesn't matter!" sighed Green. "Let me tell you this, Miss Paisley. The man—or, if you like, woman—who killed Rinditch couldn't have got away without some pretty large stains on his—or her—clothes."

"It wouldn't have soaked through the lumber jacket," murmured Miss Paisley.

"What lumber jacket?"

"Oh! I forgot to mention it—or rather, I didn't get a chance. When I sat down in that chair at 10:30 I was wearing a green suede lumber jacket. When I came to myself in the small hours, I was not wearing it."

"Then somewhere in this flatlet we ought to find a ladies' lumber jacket, heavily bloodstained. I'll look under everything and you look inside."

When the search had proved fruitless, Miss Paisley turned at bay.

"You don't believe me!"

"I believe you believe it all, Miss Paisley. You felt you had to kill the man who had killed your cat. You knew you couldn't face up to a job like murder, especially with a knife. So you had a brainstorm, or whatever they call it, in which you kidded yourself you had committed the murder."

"Then my meat knife, my old riding gloves, and my lumber jacket have been hidden in order to deceive you?" shrilled Miss Paisley.

"Not to deceive me, Miss Paisley. To deceive yourself! If you want my opinion, you hid the knife and the gloves and the jacket because they were *not* bloodstained."

Miss Paisley felt a little giddy.

"You don't need to feel too badly about *not* killing him," he said, smiling to himself. "At 7 o'clock this morning a constable found Jenkins trying to sink a bag in the river. That bag was Rinditch's, which was kept under the bed o' nights. And Jenkins had 230-odd quid in cash which he can't account for."

Miss Paisley made no answer.

"Maybe you still sort of feel you killed Rinditch?" Miss Paisley nodded assent. "Then remember this. If the brain can play one sort of trick on you, it can play another—same as it's doing now."

Inspector Green had been very understanding and very kind, Miss Paisley told herself. It was her duty to abide by his decision—especially as there was no means of doing otherwise—and loyally accept his interpretation of her own acts. The wretched Jenkins—an abominable man—would presumably be hanged. Things, reflected Miss Paisley, had a way of coming right . . .

After a single appearance before the magistrate, Jenkins was committed on the charge of murder and would come up for trial in the autumn at the Old Bailey. Miss Paisley removed her interest.

One evening in early autumn Miss Paisley was sitting in her armchair, reviving the controversy as to whether her father had made a mistake about the croquet lawn. In her eagerness she thrust her hands between the folds of the upholstery. Her fingers encountered a hard object. She hooked it with her finger and pulled up her dead cat's collar.

She held it in both hands while there came a vivid memory of her peering through Mr. Rinditch's window, Jenkins beside her, and seeing the collar in the wastepaper basket . . . The buckle was still fastened. The leather had been cut, as if with a razor. She read the inscription: her own name and address and—*£1 Reward for Return*.

"I took it out of that basket—*afterwards!*" She relived the ecstatic moment in which she had killed Rinditch. Every detail was now clear cut. Strike *UP!*—as the cat had struck—then leap to safety. She had pulled off a glove, to snatch the collar from the basket and thrust the collar under the neck of her jumper; then she had put the glove on again before leaving the room and making her way to the river. Back in her chair she had retrieved the collar.

Gone was the exaltation which had sustained her in her first approach to the police. She stood up, rigid, as she had stood in the hall while listening to the scratching on the panel, refusing to accept an unbearable truth. Once again she had the illusion of being locked up, aware now that there could be no escape from herself.

There remained the collar—evidence irrefutable, but escapable.

"If I keep this as a memento, I shall soon get muddled and accuse myself of murder all over again! What was it that nice inspector said—'if the brain can play one trick on you it can play another'."

She smiled as she put the collar in her handbag, slipped on a coat and walked—by the most direct route, this time—to the Seventeenth-Century bridge. She dropped the collar into the river, knowing that it would sink under the weight of its metal—unlike the bloodstained lumber jacket and the riding gloves which, Miss Paisley suddenly remembered, she had weighted with stones scratched from the soil of the old cemetery . . .

Fred Hamlin

ARNOLD

I hear the first police car Saturday morning as I am driving back from the drugstore on an emergency run for aspirin and cat food. The aspirin is for me. The cat food is for Arnold, who talks. He has trouble with consonants, and a distinct Siamese accent, but he definitely talks. His favorite word is "chaoowww" which helps to explain why Arnold weighs seventeen pounds, and why I am making an emergency run for cat food.

The aspirin is because the going away party held last night at our apartment building for Sam Archibald was a considerable success. It is a Southern California apartment building, which is to say two stories and U-shaped around a swimming pool, with two palm trees, a tropical name, and frequent parties. I moved in two years ago, right out of college. Sam's party was even noisier than most, and his last official act of residence was a front one-and-a-half off my balcony into the pool. In truth it was a one-and-three-eighths, but he had absorbed enough wine to come up laughing. Sam will be missed. In the meantime, my eyelids ache.

This condition fails to improve when the black-and-white goes by with siren in full shriek. I am relieved to discover that the sound isn't coming from inside my head, a possibility that must not be ruled out. When the second squad car goes by, I try the radio, but am only able to get a rock band that sounds in my present condition like a series of trays being dropped in a restaurant.

As I turn the corner two blocks away from the apartment, I see both of the squad cars, plus two more, forming a rough roadblock between myself and my apartment building. I am waved to a stop. "I'm sorry, sir, this street is temporarily closed to through traffic," says the officer. He has clear eyes, a thirty-dollar haircut and military creases in his tailored uniform shirt.

Sir is not something I'm called very often, and it has a mildly palliative effect on my head.

"I live down at Tropical Towers. Apartment 24."

"Can I see your driver's license, please?"

I dig it out. "What seems to be the problem, officer?"

"An armed robbery at the Palm Paradise Savings and Loan. Witnesses saw the man headed this way. He shot a guard on his way out, so we know he's armed. The guard will live, but we have to be careful. We have the area sealed off."

"Does this mean I can't get to my apartment? I've got Arnold's breakfast, and he turns nasty if he misses a meal."

"Look, mister, I don't know Arnold, but nasty is what we're dealing with here. Our guy has a .44 revolver, armed and dangerous. Yes, you can go through, but be careful, and if you see anything strange, please call us at once. The suspect is about five nine, medium weight. He's wearing jeans and a denim jacket, and had a black watch cap when last seen. Blond hair, thin face. He's also kind of jumpy, probably drugs of some kind. If you see anyone like that, don't take any chances. We'll be coming through to search the area in a few minutes. Here's your license. Remember, call us if you see anything."

I park my van in the regular spot and head up to the apartment, where Arnold is by now probably sitting by his dish yelling, "Naaooww!" With luck he will not be venting his hostility by ripping the grass paper off the walls, a not uncommon form of protest on his part. If cats played football, Arnold would be Dick Butkus.

I open the apartment door and Arnold is hunkered down under the coffee table, with his ears flat against his head, and his tail twice normal size. His eyes look like a couple of solid onyx marbles.

"Knock it off, Arnold," I say, "you are overreacting. Food is forthcoming."

Arnold tends to be moody, no doubt due to kittenhood trauma. I agreed to keep him nine months ago when his former owner went over to Las Vegas for a weekend with her boyfriend. They wound up getting married and she moved into his no-pets-no-kids apartment. I have had Arnold ever since. Neither Arnold nor I am sure who he belongs to. There is the depressing possibility that I belong to Arnold, which he tends to assume.

I put the bag with the cat food cans and aspirin down on the kitchen counter. The open sliding door to the balcony has aired out the worst of the cheap-wine-and-stale-smoke atmosphere that I woke up to. The Formica dinette table that came with the apartment is still littered with glasses from last night, none of which are clean. I dig out the aspirin and head for the bathroom off my bedroom where there may be a clean glass. Arnold glowers from under the coffee table and makes a noise like he's sucking his teeth. Only the noise comes from the bedroom.

I later recreate my thought process at this juncture. First, maybe Arnold does ventriloquism. Second, there probably isn't anyone in the bedroom. Third, even if there is someone in the bedroom it may be a leftover from last night's party—it was too late to check the closets before I went to bed. Fourth, and here's a great mind in high gear, *the cop on the corner said to call*. Ergo, the phone is in the bedroom, and I have to go in there to call anyway. As I say, we gave Sam a significant party.

The first thing I notice when I go in the bedroom is not that there is anyone there. The first thing I notice is the gun. More specifically the open end of the barrel of the gun, which is level with and about three feet away from my left eye. Forty-four does not begin to describe it. It is more like looking into a railway tunnel that goes straight down, into which I am about to fall.

The railway tunnel shifts slightly, as if moved by a small earthquake, and the sense of vertigo eases somewhat. The gun is held by a pair of hands with white knuckles, and the hands are attached to a person. Give them credit, the police have a very accurate description. I can now add that he is about my age, mid-twenties, and has watery blue eyes and ears that stand out from his head, as if to keep the knit cap from falling over his face. There is something about the eyes that does not quite connect with reality. It occurs to me that Sam's eyes looked a bit like that when he started up to the balcony last night. This is not encouraging.

"Freeze. Don't move. Stay where you are." The voice is somewhere between a croak and a quaver, and I am still not reassured.

He has not asked me to raise my hands, but it couldn't hurt, so I do. Actually, it is a sort of reflex action like the kid's trick where you press the backs of your hands against the inside of a door frame, and then your arms float up by themselves.

"One move, man, and you're wasted. I mean that."

"Okay. Take it easy. I see the gun."

"One move or one sound, dig it? I already wasted one guy today." His eyes are flicking all around the room, almost independently of each other, but one or the other manages to stay on me. He reaches around me and pushes the door nearly closed.

"What's going on out there?"

"There are a lot of cops in the neighborhood. They seem to be looking for somebody."

"You got it, man. How many of them?"

"I don't know. I saw four cars, but there may be more."

"Too many, man, too many. I shouldn't a wasted that guy."

He is shifting from one foot to the other, and the eyes are still doing the pinwheel routine.

"Gotta think, man, gotta be cool. Hey, is this the only phone in here?"

"The only one. It's on an answering machine right now, so anybody who calls gets a message that I'm out."

"That's cool. No, wait, man, pull the plug on it. Pull the jack."

"'If I do that and somebody I know calls, they'll know something's wrong. I always leave the machine on when I'm out."

"Yeah, man, stay away from that jack or I'll blow you away."

I am aware of a slight noise and movement behind me, and my new pal crab-hops to one side and drops into a firing crouch with the gun on the door, which is slowly opening. Sweat pops out on his forehead so suddenly you can almost hear it squeak, and his eyes more or less manage to focus on the doorway.

It's Arnold, and we resume breathing. Arnold strolls over and gives the guy's leg a long affectionate rub. Because he is leaning on the guy's leg, the kick he gets in return lacks real force.

"Goddam cat."

"Cloowwwn," says Arnold and dives under the bed. Arnold has not yet learned how to swear convincingly.

The gun is back in my direction again.

"Is there a back way outta here?"

"Not really. Just the front door and the balcony, and that's one floor up."

"I gotta get outta here, dig?"

Needless to say, I am in favor of this, but no suggestions immediately come to mind.

At this point we hear official-sounding footsteps coming up the stairs out front, and shortly a heavy rap on the first apartment door; mine is the third one along. We both figure out what is happening at the same time.

"Okay, dig. When those guys get here you don't know nothing. You seen nobody. I stay here in the bedroom, but the gun is on you all the time. If you try anything funny, you're wasted. If I go down, you go down. Dig it?"

I nod, and we can both hear them move to the second apartment and bang on the door. From there it's close enough to hear them calling into the apartment. "Open up, police."

The foot-to-foot hopping starts up again, and the eyes are slipping in all directions. I am contemplating how large the end of the gun barrel looks, and imagine a hole that size in my back. I do not find this a pleasant fantasy.

"Okay, man, get out there and get rid of them. Fast."

I walk into the living room. The bedroom door is on a wall that runs front-to-back in the apartment, and the door swings into the bedroom. He leaves this open about two inches and is standing a foot or so back, next to the wall. He can't be seen, and like they say at the National Guard meetings, his field of fire is unimpaired.

I hear the footsteps and the banging on my door.

"Open up, police."

It is the same cop I talked to down at the barricade, and he remembers me. He has a partner with him who goes to the same barber.

"Hello again. We're checking the neighborhood. I don't suppose you've seen anything since you got back."

"I've seen nobody," I say, having my lines down pat, "and I'll give you a call if I do. Have a nice day."

"That must be Arnold," the cop says, remembering the name, and at about the same time I feel a familiar rubbing on my ankle.

This is not good news. First, Arnold could not have fit through the two-inch gap. Ergo, the door is open wider than it was, which means that the cop may be able to see into the bedroom. It also means that my pal back there has a bigger gap to shoot through. A trickle of sweat starts down my spine. It will no doubt stain a perfect bull's-eye on the back of my shirt.

The cop is bent over scratching Arnold's ears. "Did you get your breakfast, big fellow?"

"Noooooo," says Arnold.

"Arnold," I say, "shut up."

Arnold has rolled over on his back and is getting his stomach rubbed. He is smirking.

"He looks like an Arnold," says the cop. "Palmer, maybe. Or Schwarzenegger."

"Benedict," I say. "Look, don't let me hold you up. I know you want to get your man."

"Right. Remember, call if you see anything unusual. We should be through the neighborhood in a couple of hours. We'll find him. But be careful till we do."

I close the door and look around, but Arnold is out of retribution range under the coffee table. He is looking smug. The bedroom door swings open and my pal comes out.

"You did fine, man, but that cat almost got you killed. And those cops, too. I already wasted one guy."

I don't need to be reminded.

"Listen, maybe the guy isn't dead. Maybe this isn't as bad as you think it is."

"With this piece?" He is waving the gun in my face. "Man, this piece don't make mistakes, and I popped him twice."

I am looking down the barrel again and decide not to press the point.

"You got a car, man?"

"Right. If you would like to borrow it, the keys are right here in my pocket. You could be on your way and . . ."

"Do I look stupid, man? I take your car and you're on the phone the minute I'm out the door."

"So tie me up before you go. Put a gag in my mouth." I am not into bondage as a general rule, but there are always exceptions.

"No, man. I got a better idea. The cop said they would be through the neighborhood in a couple of hours, right? Okay, you and me we just sit tight here until they get it done. Then we both get in your car and just ease out of here. What kind of car you got?"

"It's a VW van."

"Okay, when we drive out of here I'm on the floor in the back and the gun is right behind your spine, dig? And if we run into anyone on the way to the van, the gun is in your neck. That way if we run into any cops they can't shoot without hitting you." His eyes have escalated from pinwheel to Roman candle. He is thinking very hard.

I am in no way enamored of his train of thought.

"So then what happens?"

"If everything stays cool, everything stays cool. I got no argument with you, man. You got rid of the cop. I could probably just let you go after a while."

It occurs to me that "probably" is a key word in this sentence. I am not sure I want to know what alternatives are under consideration.

Still, we now have an agenda and the atmosphere is marginally less tense. The eyes are back to low-grade shifty, and I remember where this whole mess started. I realize I am still holding the aspirin bottle.

"Would you like an aspirin?" I ask. "I could sure use one myself."

"No thanks, man," he says. "I've got my own stuff."

He digs a handful of miscellaneous capsules out of his pocket and swallows them and then follows me into the bathroom. I manage four aspirin, a dosage which seems appropriate.

"Do you mind if I feed the cat? He hasn't eaten since last night."

"Okay, man, but stay away from that window. And nothing cute." The eyes are speeding up again, and the movements are jerkier.

The phone rings, and he bounces about eight inches into the air. The answering machine kicks in.

"This is Arnold," my taped message says, "and the guy I live with is out right now. If you will leave your number at the tone . . ."

It gets no further than this because my visitor has ripped the jack out of the wall. When he turns back, the gun hand is downright shaky.

"One more trick like that, man, you're dead." I sense that a logical explanation may not help the situation, and also that the glue that is holding him together has begun to melt.

We proceed to the kitchen area with the gun acting as a sort of hyphen between us. He comes past the dinette table and stops at the counter that divides the cooking area from the small dining space. I go around the counter and dig out a can of cat food, stick it in the electric can opener, and push the lever down.

This sound is to Arnold as the bell is to Pavlov's pup. He is out of the living room in full feeding frenzy and leaps for the kitchen table on his way to the counter. He realizes too late that the glassware from last night is in the way, and his claws scrabble desperately for traction on the slick Formica.

"Whoa-oowwww," he yells, which is promptly drowned out by a blast of crashing glass.

This in turn is drowned out by the thunderclap of the .44 as my houseguest spins and unloads a couple of rounds at the empty air behind him.

By the time he turns back to where I was, I am through the sliding door and airborne over the railing. I hear two more shots before I hit the pool. Sensing a disturbance, the cops are through the front door of my apartment with guns drawn before I come up for air. My houseguest is still trying to figure out what happened. He has also emptied his gun.

A neighbor later tells me my form was better than Sam's, but that I lost points on degree of difficulty. I attribute this to inadequate planning and preparation and consider it a moral victory.

It's another hour or so before all of the questions are answered and the dust has settled and the cops have hauled their guy away. I get into dry clothes and the first order of business is to get Arnold fed. Fair is fair.

"Sorry for the delay, Arnold. It's been a busy morning."

"Surrrrrrrrrrrre," he says. If there's anything I can't stand, it's a sarcastic cat.

Nancy Schachterle

CALL TO WITNESS

The police captain himself came to see Allison. That pleased her immensely; but it's only right, she thought. The Ryder name still means something in this town, even if the last survivor is an old maid of eighty-three. Secretly she had been afraid that she had been in the backwater of age for so long that most people, if they thought about her at all, had decided that she must be long since dead.

Everett Barkley, he told her his name was. He was tall and well-built, filling his uniform to advantage, with little sign of the paunch that so many men his age allowed to develop.

Barkley helped himself to her father's big leather chair, slumping comfortably to accommodate his frame to its rump-sprung curves. Allison started toward a straight-backed chair suited to the erect posture of her generation, then yielded to the pleading of well-aged bones and lowered herself carefully into her familiar upholstered armchair.

The policeman surveyed the piecrust table at his elbow, laden with silver-framed photographs. Gingerly he reached out and picked up Dodie's picture.

"Mrs. Patrick. She must have been very young when this was taken."

"Nineteen. She sat for that four years ago." And she had watched, not an hour ago, Allison recalled, as they carried Dodie to the ambulance with a blanket entirely covering her.

"Did you know her well? As you probably know, I've been in town less than a year and I had never seen her before the . . . before this morning."

Allison shuddered slightly. Automatically her hand went to her lap to caress Snowball, to seek comfort in the warm, silky fur, and the pulsations of the gentle, almost silent, purr. With a start she remembered that she had let him out in the early hours of the morning, and he hadn't yet returned. Worry nagged at her.

What had Captain Barkley asked? Yes—about Dodie. *Did I know her well?*

"She came toddling up my front steps one day when she was about two, and we've been fast friends ever since. At that time she lived just up the hill, in the next block."

"And since they were married they've lived next door to you?"

"That's right."

"Miss Ryder. . ." The policeman shifted his position, slightly ill at ease. "Would you tell me something about Dodie? Anything you like. Just your mental picture of her."

Allison reached to take the photograph from him. "This shows her spirit well, those laughing, sparkling eyes. She was a happy girl. She used to come running up those steps—she never walked, always running—and she looked so full of life. Vital is the word that comes to my mind. Dancing, tennis, swimming, golf, singing—that was Dodie."

Allison looked down at the gray old hands that held the picture, with their knotted veins and their liver spots. Dodie had been the youth she herself had lost.

"I can see her right now, sitting on the porch railing, swinging those long, tanned legs. 'Frank finally asked me to the dance, Miss Ryder,' she told me. She was leaning so far out to look down the street that I was afraid she'd fall into my sweet william. 'Here he comes now. 'Bye. See you.' And she was gone, laughing and waving to him."

She had been pleased about Dodie and Frank, Allison remembered. All she knew of Frank Patrick was a dark, goodlooking boy with a quick grin and a cheery wave. She didn't know then that he was one of those helpless, hopeless creatures who feed on hurt. His charm swept up people like lilting dance music. Then, when they were dizzy from his gift of pleasure with themselves, he launched his barb and sucked at the wound. As his victims shriveled, Frank swelled with a grotesque satisfaction. Given the choice between kind and cruel, legal and illegal, moral and immoral, he'd rather go the lower path each time.

Allison handed the picture back to Captain Barkley. Carefully he placed it back among the dozen or so others that crowded the little table.

"Nieces and nephews, and their children," Allison remarked. "I even have one great-great," she told him, with visible pride. "But Dodie was closer to me than any of them."

The policeman shifted his cap between his fingers in a broken, shuffling motion as if he were saying the rosary on it.

"Miss Ryder," he said, lifting his eyes to meet hers, "it'll be out soon, so I might as well tell you, the doctor is virtually certain it was an overdose, probably of her sleeping pills. We'll know for sure after the autopsy. What I'm trying to do now is get a picture of her, of her husband, of her life. Now, the Patrick house and yours are very close, can't be much more than fifteen or twenty feet apart, and their bedroom is on this side. I noticed the window was open about eight inches at the bottom. Knowing how easily sound travels on these warm, summer nights, I wondered . . ." He paused, waiting for Allison to volunteer the ending to his sentence. She was wearing a look of polite attention, but said nothing.

"Well," he continued, "I just wondered whether you might have heard anything."

Absently Allison's hand reached again for Snowball's head. Where could he be? She had heard him yowling his love songs on the back fence about three this morning, so she knew he was near home. Then she shook herself mentally, and tried to remember what the officer had been saying. Oh, yes. *Did I hear anything?*

"My bedroom is on the far side of the house from the Patricks'. I'm afraid I can be of no help to you, Captain . . . Barkley, isn't it?"

Allison shrank into herself a little, half expecting a bolt of chastening lightning from above. But she hadn't lied, she decided. Her bedroom was indeed on the far side. She needn't tell him that most nights she didn't sleep well, and it was cooler out on the screened porch, practically outside Dodie's open window.

Barkley nodded, musing. "I understand Mrs. Patrick was a complete invalid for the past couple of years. Can you tell me anything about that?"

Allison sat a little more upright, legs crossed at the ankles and hands quiet in her lap. Absurdly, a seventy-year-old picture flashed into her memory of the class at Miss Van Renssalaer's Academy for Young Ladies absorbing the principles of being prim and proper. What did any of it matter now, she wondered, after all these years? It was people, and what they did to each other, that mattered. Dodie, too, had gone to a private school, and see what happened to her.

"She went out driving by herself one night," she told Barkley, "and . . . had an accident. Her spinal cord was crushed, and she was paralyzed from the waist down."

Allison remembered that night much too clearly. The stifling heat had been emphasized by the heartless cheerfulness of crickets. About eleven o'clock, Allison had prepared a glass of lemonade for herself, and moved to the old wicker lounge on the screened porch. It seemed cooler with the light off, so she sat in the dark, sipping the tart drink and resting. At first the voices had been muted, simply alto and baritone rhythms, then they had swelled and she caught phrases rising in passionate tones. Finally, there was no effort to hush their voices, and Dodie's anguish had cried across the night to Allison: "She's going to have a baby, and you expect me to be calm? How could you betray me so, and with a . . . a creature like that?"

Frank's voice had resounded with mocking laughter. "You can't be that much of an innocent! Do you honestly think your simple charms could be enough for a man like me? Susie wasn't the first, and you can be damned sure she won't be the last. Come on now, Dodie. You're a sweet kid, and your family's been real helpful in getting me where I want to go, but you just can't tie a man down."

Allison cringed, remembering Dodie's wounded cry. It had been followed by the slam of the screen door, then footsteps pounding across the porch and down the steps. The car door slammed and the engine roared to life. Gravel spurted as Dodie took off into the darkness.

Only Dodie knew whether the smashup truly was an accident. Perhaps she had simply tried to numb the pain with speed—but she had been twenty-one and she never walked again.

The policeman cleared his throat. "Miss Ryder?"

"Yes?"

"I hope you'll excuse me for asking you so much about your friends and neighbors, but you see . . . well, it's all going to come out eventually, and I'm sure you'll be discreet. There are only three possibilities to account for Mrs. Patrick's death. Crippled as she was, she had no access to the supply of sleeping pills. They were kept in the bathroom and her husband gave them to her whenever she needed them. It may be that she hoarded her pills, hiding them from her husband somehow, until she had enough for a lethal dose, and took them herself. Or it could be that Mr. Patrick was careless—criminally careless—and she received an accidental overdose. Or . . ." and he paused, while Allison's eyes searched his. "Well, you realize, we must consider the, uh, possibility that . . . perhaps the overdose wasn't accidental. Mr. Patrick wouldn't be the first man burdened by a crippled wife who took the wrong way out."

"Captain Barkley," Allison said. "There was no reason in the world for Dodie to kill herself. What does Frank say happened?"

"He insists she must have taken them herself. According to him she suffered a great deal of pain. He claims she must have saved up the sleeping pills, which rules out any chance of an accident. This is why I wanted to talk to you. You were very close to Mrs. Patrick. Was she in much pain?"

Allison's fingers unconsciously pleated the plum-colored fabric of the dress over her lap. Her head went a little higher, and an imperious generation spoke through her.

"I have already told you, there was no reason in the world for Dodie to kill herself. To my certain knowledge she was seldom, if ever, in pain. In fact, I can give you the names of three or four ladies who could confirm that fact, out of Dodie's own mouth. We'd often gather on the Patricks' front porch in the afternoon, so Dodie could be part of the group, and not a week ago we were discussing that case in the papers—you remember, the man who shot his wife because she was dying of cancer? Dodie was most upset. She was a dreadfully sympathetic child. She was torn between her distress at his immoral action and her sympathy with his concern for his wife's suffering. 'Perhaps I might judge differently,' she said, 'if I were in pain myself. I'm one of the fortunates, suffering only from the

72

handicap. But even if I were in pain, I don't believe that anyone but God has a right to take a life.' The other ladies will bear me out on this, captain."

Yes, she said to herself, we were discussing the case. Maybe nobody else noticed, it was so skillfully done, but Dodie herself was the one who maneuvered the conversation around to mercy killing. *I didn't know then, Dodie, but I can see now what you were doing.*

"Mrs. Patrick said herself that she was in no pain? Ever?"

"At the time of the accident, and for several months afterward, yes, she did have pain. But not recently. I never once heard her complain."

There now, Allison, she realized, you did tell a lie; you can't wiggle out of that one. The same night as that get-together you told him about, remember?—and Sunday night—and last night . . .

The scene had been the same all three nights, and the script had followed the same lines. Allison had been in her comfortable corner on the porch, Snowball's faint purrs pulsing against her caressing hand, the creaking wicker of the lounge cool against her bare arms. That first night it had rained earlier, breaking the heat, and the lilac leaves had whispered wetly to each other in the dark. Gentle dripping from the eaves seemed to deepen the quiet, rather than break it. Dodie's blind had been pulled down only to the level of the raised window. The muted voices were carried across to her by the force of their intensity.

"Please, Frank! Please!" Never had Allison heard such pleading in Dodie's voice.

"I've told you, I just can't," he'd said. "If the pain's so bad, let me get a shot for you, or something. But you don't know what you're talking about, wanting to kill yourself."

"What good am I to anybody like this? And the pain—I just can't stand it anymore." Her voice had risen with a startling anguish.

Allison, listening in spite of herself, had held herself tense, wondering. Just that afternoon Dodie had denied pain, yet now . . . Hot tears had welled in Allison's eyes as she listened to the tortured voice.

If she hadn't hated Frank so much for what he had done to Dodie, she might have been able to pity him as his voice broke with indecision. "Dodie, I can't do it! Don't ask me to. Even if you're ready to die, think of the position you'd put me in. They'd say I killed you. Think of me, Dodie! They'd give me the chair!"

The argument had gone on. Three different nights Dodie had hammered away. Then last night, while Allison, hypnotized, watched the shadows shifting on the drawn blind, Dodie had played out her drama. She had won. Frank gave her the pills.

Allison had no longer felt the heat of the night. Chilled with horror, she had fought her own battle. Her throat had throbbed with a scream to that silent window. She couldn't let Dodie do this! But a thin hand to her lips cut off that scream before it sounded. What right did she have to interfere? Dodie must hate with an unsuspected fury to die for her revenge. She wouldn't thank Allison for stopping her now.

Allison had sat quietly. Soon the Patricks' light went out. Only then did she rise stiffly and plod to her bedroom, where no one could hear her poorly stifled sobs.

The white cat had followed her to the bedroom. One soft, easy leap settled him beside the tired, sorrowing old lady. Allison remembered the day Dodie had brought him to her.

"Frank says he's allergic to cats, Miss Ryder. He won't have one in the house. But he's such a darling!" The vibrant face had gone quiet as she crooned over the kitten. "Snowball'd be a good name, don't you think? If you kept him, I could see him often. I could help groom him, and things. It wouldn't hurt so much if I knew you had him."

So Allison had kept Snowball, but Dodie had never visited him in his new home. The accident came only days later. That's what Allison resolutely called it, although she was very much afraid it was something else. Through those harrowing days the kitten grew, and comforted Allison. He was full-grown by the time Dodie left the hospital.

Please come home, Snowball, Allison begged in her head, forgetful of the waiting policeman. I need you so. There's not much left for an old lady. I had Dodie and I had you. Now Dodie's gone. Snowball, don't you know how much I need you?

A tear that couldn't be restrained by a lifetime of self-discipline slipped down the wrinkled, gray cheek.

Captain Barkley, tactfully clearing his throat again, bought Allison back to the present. This policeman and his questions! Allison was weary. Please, no more decisions . . .

Barkley hoisted himself out of the deep leather chair. "Well, Miss Ryder, I think you've told us what we need to know. One thing—when you get the chance, could you just write down the names of those other ladies you mentioned, who heard Mrs. Patrick say she suffered no pain? I won't trouble you now. I'll send a man by later today for it."

Dodie wins, Allison thought, but she felt no elation. Yes, Frank had killed Dodie, killed her youth and killed her innocence, and pummeled her spirit until she wanted to die. Yet, did Dodie, or did Allison, have the right to sentence him? Heedless of the waiting policeman, Allison closed her eyes momentarily, yielding to the grief that closed around her like a gray fog. Dodie was gone—but Allison didn't have to decide. All she had to do was let things go ahead without her, and all those other people would have to decide.

Allison struggled out of her chair. Captain Barkley rushed to help her, but she waved him aside. "Thank you, young man, but I have to do things by myself nowadays."

Yes, Allison, she mused, you have to do things by yourself. Once you make this decision, don't fool yourself that somebody else sent Frank to the electric chair. They still execute murderers in this state, you know, and rightly speaking, Frank did not murder Dodie. For eighty-three years you've known right from wrong. You've faced up to the truths, whether you liked the result or not. Now . . .

"Captain . . ." she started. Then her taut nerves jerked her like a marionette as the doorbell shrilled.

"I'll get it," the policeman offered.

It was another policeman, a close-shaven young man too big for his uniform, who bobbed his head respectfully to her, then turned to the captain, "Morrison says to tell you they're all finished over there, any time you're ready to go back to the station."

Captain Barkley glanced in speculation at Allison. Her expression told him nothing.

"I'll be out to the car in a minute." He held the door open for the younger man.

"Oh, and I thought I'd mention that we don't have to worry none about that big white cat the neighbors said was yowling early this morning. We found it in the Patricks' trash can. Somebody'd wrung its neck."

The captain nodded and turned back toward Allison where she stood by her overstuffed armchair, one hand lightly touching the back for support. Dodie smiled at him from the piecrust table.

"You were about to say . . . ?"

Allison reached to pick a white cat hair off of the chair beside her. "Yes . . . I was going to say I'll start on that list you wanted right away. You can send someone over for it in about half an hour. Good morning, captain."

Head erect, shoulders straight, she shuffled resolutely across the room to close the door behind him.

Lilian Jackson Braun

THE SIN OF MADAME PHLOI

From the very beginning Madame Phloi felt an instinctive distaste for the man who moved into the apartment next door. He was fat, and his trouser cuffs had the unsavory odor of fire hydrant.

They met for the first time in the decrepit elevator as it lurched up to the tenth floor of the old building, once fashionable but now coming apart at the seams. Madame Phloi had been out for a stroll in the city park, chewing city grass and chasing faded butterflies, and as she and her companion stepped on the elevator for the slow ride upward, the car was already half filled with the new neighbor.

The fat man and the Madame presented a contrast that was not unusual in this apartment house, which had a brilliant past and no future. He was bulky, uncouth, sloppily attired. Madame Phloi was a long-legged, blue-eyed aristocrat whose creamy fawn coat shaded into brown at the extremities.

The Madame deplored fat men. They had no laps, and of what use is a lapless human? Nevertheless, she gave him the common courtesy of a sniff at his trouser cuffs and immediately backed away, twitching her nose and breathing through the mouth.

"*Get* that cat away from me," the fat man roared, stamping his feet thunderously at Madame Phloi. Her companion pulled on the leash, although there was no need—the Madame with one backward leap had retreated to a safe corner of the elevator, which shuddered and continued its groaning ascent.

"Don't you like animals?" asked the gentle voice at the other end of the leash.

"Filthy, sneaky beasts," the fat man said with a snarl. "Last place I lived, some lousy cat got in my room and et my parakeet."

"I'm sorry to hear that. Very sorry. But you don't need to worry about Madame Phloi and Thapthim. They never leave the apartment except on a leash."

"You got *two*? That's just fine, that is! Keep 'em away from me, or I'll break their rotten necks. I ain't wrung a cat's neck since I was fourteen, but I remember

76

how."

And with the long black box he was carrying, the fat man lunged at the impeccable Madame Phloi, who sat in her corner, flat-eared and tense. Her fur bristled, and she tried to dart away. Even when her companion picked her up in protective arms, Madame Phloi's body was taut and trembling.

Not until she was safely home in her modest but well-cushioned apartment did she relax. She walked stiff-legged to the sunny spot on the carpet where Thapthim was sleeping and licked the top of his head. Then she had a complete bath herself—to rid her coat of the fat man's odor. Thapthim did not wake.

This drowsy, unambitious, amiable creature—her son—was a puzzle to Madame Phloi, who was sensitive and spirited herself. She didn't try to understand him; she merely loved him. She spent hours washing his paws and breast and other parts he could easily have reached with his own tongue. At dinnertime she chewed slowly so there would be something left on her plate for his dessert, and he always gobbled the extra portion hungrily. And when he slept, which was most of the time, she kept watch by his side, sitting with a tall, regal posture until she swayed with weariness. Then she made herself into a small bundle and dozed with one eye open.

Thapthim was lovable, to be sure. He appealed to other cats, large and small dogs, people, and even ailurophobes in a limited way. He had a face like a beautiful flower and large blue eyes, tender and trusting. Ever since he was a kitten, he had been willing to purr at the touch of a hand—any hand. Eventually he became so agreeable that he purred if anyone looked at him across the room. What's more, he came when called; he gratefully devoured whatever was served on his dinner plate; and when he was told to get down, he got down.

His wise parent disapproved this uncatly conduct; it indicated a certain lack of character, and no good would come of it. By her own example she tried to guide him. When dinner was served, she gave the plate a haughty sniff and walked away, no matter how tempting the dish. That was the way it was done by any self-respecting feline. In a minute or two she returned and condescended to dine, but never with open enthusiasm.

Furthermore, when human hands reached out, the catly thing was to bound away, lead them a chase, flirt a little before allowing oneself to be caught and cuddled. Thapthim, sorry to say, greeted any friendly overture by rolling over, purring, and looking soulful.

From an early age he had known the rules of the apartment:

No sleeping in a cupboard with the pot and pans.
Sitting on the table with the inkwell is permissible.
Sitting on the table with the coffeepot is never allowed.

The sad truth was that Thapthim obeyed these rules. Madame Phloi, on the other hand, knew that a rule was a challenge, and it was a matter of integrity to violate it. To obey was to sacrifice one's dignity. . . . It seemed that her son would never learn the true values in life.

To be sure, Thapthim was adored for his good nature in the human world of inkwells and coffeepots. But Madame Phloi was equally adored—and for the correct reasons. She was respected for her independence, admired for her clever methods of getting her own way, and loved for the cowlick on her white breast, the kink in her tail, and the squint in her delphinium-blue eyes. She was more truly Siamese than her son. Her face was small and perky. By cocking her head and staring with heart-melting eyes, slightly crossed, she could charm a porterhouse steak out from under a knife and fork.

Until the fat man and his black box moved in next door, Madame Phloi had never known an unfriendly soul. She had two companions in her tenth-floor apartment—genial creatures without names who came and went a good deal. One was an easy mark for between-meal snacks; a tap on his ankle always produced a spoonful of cottage cheese. The other served as a hot-water bottle on cold nights and punctually obliged whenever the Madame wished to have her underside stroked or her cheekbones massaged. This second one also murmured compliments in a gentle voice that made one squeeze one's eyes in pleasure.

Life was not all love and cottage cheese, however. Madame Phloi had her regular work. She was official watcher and listener for the household.

There were six windows that needed watching, for a wide ledge ran around the building flush with the tenth-floor windowsills, and this was a promenade for pigeons. They strutted, searched their feathers, and ignored the Madame, who sat on the sill and watched them dispassionately but thoroughly through the window screen.

While watching was a daytime job, listening was done after dark and required greater concentration. Madame Phloi listened for noises in the walls. She heard termites chewing, pipes sweating, and sometimes the ancient plaster cracking; but mostly she listened to the ghosts of generations of deceased mice.

One evening, shortly after the incident in the elevator, Madame Phloi was listening, Thapthim was asleep, and the other two were quietly turning pages of books, when a strange and horrendous sound came from the wall. The Madame's ears flicked to attention, then flattened against her head.

An interminable screech was coming out of that wall, like nothing the Madame had ever heard before. It chilled the blood and tortured the eardrums. So painful was the shrillness that Madame Phloi threw back her head and complained with a piercing howl of her own. The strident din even waked Thapthim. He looked about in alarm, shook his head wildly, and clawed at his ears to get rid of the offending noise.

The others heard it, too.

"Listen to that!" said the one with the gentle voice.

"It must be that new man next door," said the other. "It's incredible."

"I can't imagine anyone so crude producing anything so exquisite. Is it Prokofiev he's playing?"

"No, I think it's Bartók."

"He was carrying his violin in the elevator today. He tried to hit Phloi with it."

"He's a nut. . . . Look at the cats—apparently they don't care for violin."

Madame Phloi and Thapthim, bounding from the room, collided with each other as they rushed to hide under the bed.

That was not the only kind of noise which emanated from the adjoining apartment in those upsetting days after the fat man moved in. The following evening, when Madame Phloi walked into the living room to commence her listening, she heard a fluttering sound dimly through the wall, accompanied by highly conversational chirping. This was agreeable music, and she settled down on the sofa to enjoy it, tucking her brown paws neatly under her creamy body.

Her contentment was soon disturbed, however, when the fat man's voice burst through the wall like thunder.

"Look what you done, you dirty skunk!" he bellowed. "Right in my fiddle! Get back in your cage before I brain you."

There was a frantic beating of wings.

"*Get* down off that window, or I'll bash your head in."

This threat brought only a torrent of chirping.

"Shut up, you stupid cluck! Shut up and get back in that cage, or I'll . . ."

There was a splintering crash, and after that all was quiet except for an occasional pitiful "Peep!"

Madame Phloi was fascinated. In fact, when she resumed her watching the next day, pigeons seemed rather insipid entertainment. She had waked the family that morning in her usual way—by staring intently at their foreheads as they slept. Then she and Thapthim had a game of hockey in the bathtub with a Ping-Pong ball, followed by a dish of mackerel, and after breakfast the Madame took up her post at the living-room window. Everyone had left for the day but not before opening the window and placing a small cushion on the chilly marble sill.

There she sat—Madame Phloi—a small but alert package of fur, sniffing the welcome summer air, seeing all, and knowing all. She knew, for example, that the person who was at that moment walking down the tenth-floor hallway, wearing old tennis shoes and limping slightly, would halt at the door of her apartment, set down his pail, and let himself in with a passkey.

Indeed, she hardly bothered to turn her head when the window washer entered. He was one of her regular court of admirers. His odor was friendly, although it suggested damp basements and floor mops, and he talked sensibly— indulging in none of that falsetto foolishness with which some people insulted the Madame's intelligence.

"Hop down, kitty," he said in a musical voice. "Charlie's gotta take out that screen. See, I brought you some cheese."

He held out a modest offering of rat cheese, and Madame Phloi investigated it. Unfortunately, it was the wrong variety, and she shook one fastidious paw at it.

"Mighty fussy cat," Charlie laughed. "Well, now, you set there and watch Charlie clean this here window. Don't you go jumpin' out on the ledge, because Charlie ain't runnin' after you. No sir! That old ledge, she's startin' to crumble. Some day them pigeons'll stamp their feet hard, and down she goes! . . . Hey, lookit the broken glass out here. Somebody busted a window."

Charlie sat on the marble sill and pulled the upper sash down in his lap, and while Madame Phloi followed his movements carefully, Thapthim sauntered into the room, yawning and stretching, and swallowed the cheese.

"Now Charlie puts the screen back in, and you two guys can watch them crazy pigeons some more. This screen, she's comin' apart, too. Whole buildin' seems to be crackin' up."

Remembering to replace the cushion on the cool, hard sill, he then went on to clean the next window, and the Madame resumed her post, sitting on the very edge of the cushion so that Thapthim could have most of it.

The pigeons were late that morning, probably frightened away by the window washer. It was while Madame Phloi patiently waited for the first visitor to skim in on a blue-gray wing that she noticed the tiny opening in the screen. Every aperture, no matter how small, was a temptation; she had to prove she could wriggle through any tight space, whether there was a good reason or not.

She waited until Charlie had limped out of the apartment before she began pushing at the screen with her nose, first gingerly and then stubbornly. Inch by inch the rusted mesh ripped away from the frame until the whole corner formed a loose flap, and Madame Phloi slithered through—nose and ears, slender shoulders, dainty Queen Anne forefeet, svelt torso, lean flanks, hind legs like steel springs, and finally proud brown tail. For the first time in her life she found herself on the pigeon promenade. She gave a delicious shudder.

Inside the screen the lethargic Thapthim, jolted by this strange turn of affairs, watched his daring parent with a quarter inch of his pink tongue hanging out. They touched noses briefly through the screen, and the Madame proceeded to explore. She advanced cautiously and with mincing step, for the pigeons had not been tidy in their habits.

The ledge was about two feet wide. To its edge Madame Phloi moved warily, nose down and tail high. Ten stories below there were moving objects but nothing of interest, she decided. Walking daintily along the extreme edge to avoid the broken glass, she ventured in the direction of the fat man's apartment, impelled by some half-forgotten curiosity.

His window stood open and unscreened, and Madame Phloi peered in politely. There, sprawled on the floor, lay the fat man himself, snorting and heaving his immense paunch in a kind of rhythm. It always alarmed her to see a human on the floor, which she considered feline domain. She licked her nose apprehensively and stared at him with enormous eyes, one iris hypnotically off-center. In a dark corner of the room something fluttered and squawked, and the fat man waked.

"SHcrrff! *Get* out of here!" he shouted, struggling to his feet.

In three leaps Madame Phloi crossed the ledge back to her own window and pushed through the screen to safety. Looking back to see if the fat man might be chasing her and being reassured that he wasn't, she washed Thapthim's ears and her own paws and sat down to wait for pigeons.

Like any normal cat, Madame Phloi lived by the Rule of Three. She resisted every innovation three times before accepting it, tackled an obstacle three times before giving up, and tried each new activity three times before tiring of it. Consequently she made two more sallies to the pigeon promenade and eventually convinced Thapthim to join her.

Together they peered over the edge at the world below. The sense of freedom was intoxicating. Recklessly Thapthim made a leap at a low-flying pigeon and landed on his mother's back. She cuffed his ear in retaliation. He poked her nose. They grappled and rolled over and over on the ledge, oblivious of the long drop below them, taking playful nips of each other's hide and snarling guttural expressions of glee.

Suddenly and instinctively Madame Phloi scrambled to her feet and crouched in a defensive position. The fat man was leaning from his window.

"Here, kitty, kitty," he was saying in one of those despised falsetto voices, offering some tidbit in a saucer. The Madame froze, but Thapthim turned his beautiful trusting eyes on the stranger and advanced along the ledge. Purring and waving his tail cordially, he walked into the trap. It all happened in a matter of seconds: the saucer was withdrawn, and a long black box was swung at Thapthim like a ball bat, sweeping him off the ledge and into space. He was silent as he fell.

When the family came home, laughing and chattering, with their arms full of packages, they knew at once something was amiss. No one greeted them at the door. Madame Phloi hunched moodily on the windowsill staring at a hole in the screen, and Thapthim was not to be found.

"Look at the screen!" cried the gentle voice.

"I'll bet he got out on the ledge."

"Can you lean out and look? Be careful."

"You hold Phloi."

"Do you see him?"

"Not a sign of him! There's a lot of glass scattered around, and the window's broken next door."

"Do you suppose that man . . . ? I feel sick."

"Don't worry, dear. We'll find him. . . . There's the doorbell! Maybe someone's bringing him home."

It was Charlie standing at the door. He fidgeted uncomfortably. "'Scuse me, folks," he said. "You missin' one of your kitties?"

"Yes! Have you found him?"

"Poor little guy," said Charlie. "Found him lyin' right under your windows—where the bushes is thick."

"He's dead!" the gentle one moaned.

"Yes, ma'am. That's a long way down."

"Where is he now?"

"I got him down in the basement, ma'am. I'll take care of him real nice. I don't think you'd want to see the poor guy."

Still Madame Phloi stared at the hole in the screen and waited for Thapthim. From time to time she checked the other windows, just to be sure. As time passed and he did not return, she looked behind the radiators and under the bed. She pried open the cupboard door where the pots and pans were stored. She tried to burrow her way into the closet. She sniffed all around the front door. Finally she stood in the middle of the living room and called loudly in a high-pitched, wailing voice.

Later that evening Charlie paid another visit to the apartment.

"Only wanted to tell you, ma'am, how nice I took care of him," he said. "I got a box that was just the right size. A white box, it was. And I wrapped him up in a piece of old blue curtain. The color looked real pretty with his fur. And I buried the little guy right under your window behind the bushes."

And still the Madame searched, returning again and again to watch the ledge from which Thapthim had disappeared. She scorned food. She rebuffed any attempts at consolation. And all night she sat wide-eyed and waiting in the dark.

The living-room window was now tightly closed, but the following day the Madame—after she was left by herself in the lonely apartment—went to work on the bedroom screens. One was new and hopeless, but the second screen was slightly corroded, and she was soon nosing through a slit that lengthened as she struggled out onto the ledge.

Picking her way through the broken glass, she approached the spot where Thapthim had vanished. And then it all happened again. There he was—the fat man—reaching forth with a saucer.

"Here, kitty, kitty."

Madame Phloi hunched down and backed away.

"Kitty want some milk?" It was that ugly falsetto, but she didn't run home this time. She crouched there on the ledge, a few inches out of reach.

"Nice kitty. Nice kitty."

Madame Phloi crept with caution toward the saucer in the outstretched fist, and stealthily the fat man extended another hand, snapping his fingers as one would call a dog.

The Madame retreated diagonally—half toward home and half toward the dangerous brink.

"Here, kitty. Here, kitty," he cooed, leaning farther out. But muttering, he said, "You dirty sneak! I'll get you if it's the last thing I ever do. Comin' after my bird, weren't you?"

Madame Phloi recognized danger with all her senses. Her ears went back, her whiskers curled, and her white underside hugged the ledge.

A little closer she moved, and the fat man made a grab for her. She jerked back a step, with unblinking eyes fixed on his sweating face. He was furtively laying the saucer aside, she noticed, and edging his fat paunch farther out the window.

Once more she advanced almost into his grasp, and again he lunged at her with both powerful arms.

The Madame leaped lightly aside.

"This time I'll get you, you stinkin' cat," he cried, and raising one knee to the windowsill, he threw himself at Madame Phloi. As she slipped through his fingers, he landed on the ledge with all his weight.

A section of it crumbled beneath him. He bellowed, clutching at the air, and at the same time a streak of creamy brown flashed out of sight. The fat man was not silent as he fell.

As for Madame Phloi, she was found doubled in half in a patch of sunshine on her living-room carpet, innocently washing her fine brown tail.

Edward D. Hoch

THE NILE CAT

Professor Bouton had never killed a man before, and so was not at all prepared for the blood which spurted from Henry Yardley's shattered head. He was still standing above the bludgeoned body, trying to think how to get the blood from his clothes, when the night security guard walked into the Egyptian Room and found him. After that, there was no point in denying it.

The detective lieutenant, a man named Fritz, was calm and professional, but with tired eyes. He sat across the table from Professor Bouton and spoke to him quietly, as if this sort of murder happened every day in the week. "You admit killing Henry Yardley?" he asked, after checking to make certain the stenographer was ready.

"Oh, yes. I admit it. If that was the poor fellow's name."

"You didn't know his name?"

"I didn't know *him*. I never saw him before in my life."

Lieutenant Fritz looked blank, but only for a moment. "His name was Henry Yardley and he was a graduate student at the University, working for his master's degree in archeology. Does that help you?"

"I told you—I never saw him or heard of him before."

Fritz picked up a pencil and began to play with it. "We're not getting anywhere, Professor Bouton. You've admitted the crime—you might as well tell us the motive. Did you two have an argument, a fight?"

"No. We never spoke to each other."

"There are only a limited number of motives for murder—hate, fear, revenge—"

"It was nothing like that."

"—gain—"

"Not really—not gain in your sense of word."

"This Yardley, was he a queer or something?"

"I have no idea. He was doing nothing, had done nothing to me in the past. As I told you, I had never seen the man, never even heard his name spoken."

The detective put down the pencil and sighed. "You mean, he just walked into the room and you killed him?"

"Exactly."

"Then you must be nuts!"

Professor Bouton was still able to smile, however slightly. "Perhaps all murderers are insane. I am no more so than the rest."

"You had a motive for killing him? And you expected to get away with it?"

"I had a motive, yes. And I did expect somehow to get away with it. Though I must admit I had no plan beyond the murder itself."

"It was premeditated?"

"Yes, within the legal meaning of the word. I thought about it for some minutes before I acted. And now that I'm arrested, nothing is changed. In fact, it may actually be better that it's happening this way."

"Better for whom? Is there a woman involved?"

Professor Bouton smiled once again. "Perhaps I should tell you the entire story, from the beginning. I think you would understand my motive then . . ."

My name—my full name—is Patrick J. Bouton. I have been associated with the University for the past twenty years, most recently as Professor of Middle Eastern Civilizations. One of my duties, and increasingly a chief one, has been to act as curator of the Egyptian Room at the University Museum. This is hardly the British Museum with its room after room of mummies and sarcophagi, but we have a nice little collection. Mainly small statues, Coptic crosses, and a really fine group of scarabs.

The prize of the collection, and the only art object in the entire museum to achieve world-wide renown, is of course the Nile Cat. It's one of several representations of Bastet, Goddess of Joy, whose shrine was at Bubastis, in lower Egypt. The statue was found back in the 1920's near the banks of the Nile, and is part of a loan collection belonging to Cadmus Verne, the investment banker.

The Nile Cat is a beautiful thing, twelve inches high and made of bronze, with large ruby eyes set deep into the head. Some art critics have called it the most important single piece of early Egyptian art ever uncovered. The owner has it insured for a quarter of a million dollars, and it's easily worth that amount.

My entire collection—the pieces acquired under my direction—has been built around the Nile Cat, which occupies the largest display case in the Egyptian Room. So you can imagine that what happened two weeks ago was quite a shock to me. Cadmus Verne had given us the loan of the statue for his lifetime, with the provision that his heirs continue the arrangement for as long as they owned the

Cat. When Verne died a few months back at the age of 81, I was saddened but not particularly surprised. He had led a full and good life.

No, it was not until two weeks ago that the blow fell. His daughter, a middle-aged matron with no interest in Egyptology, came and told me the news. I'm Mrs. Constance Clark, she said. Cadmus Verne was my father. Oh, yes, it's about the statue—the Nile Cat. My husband and I have decided to withdraw it from your collection and sell it.

Sell it? I suppose my face must have revealed my dismay at her words. Sell it to whom? Where?

The French government has made an offer of $250,000 for the statue, she told me. They want it as the main exhibit in their new museum, opening next month.

Next month! Do you mean—?

I'll be selling it to them in a few weeks, she said. And that was it. There was no appeal from her decision. There could not even be a delay in the negotiations, because the new French museum also had in mind a head of Nefertiti from the National. If the Nile Cat was not available by their opening next month, the offer to Mrs. Clark would be withdrawn and they would buy the head of Nefertiti instead.

She said it and she was gone, leaving me alone with my thoughts. You must realize what those thoughts were. You must realize that I have no other interests in this world but my work. My wife has been dead for many years, and we had no children. Even my hobbies, such as they are, center around this museum and its contents. After years of building it, of making it an important part of the University, I was on the verge of losing my prize exhibit.

Well, I determined not to go down without a fight. By the terms of Verne's will, the statue had to remain with us unless it was sold. And I knew that the French offer was a once-in-a-lifetime thing. The Nile Cat might be important to me, and to a new French museum, but there were very few others who would pay that price for it. They didn't need to—the big museums have their own treasures.

One week ago, I finally got in touch with the French museum's representative in New York. I pleaded with him, begged him, but to no avail. The statue would be purchased from Mrs. Clark and flown to Paris for the opening. I came back home a broken man.

I think it was then that I decided to murder Mrs. Clark.

Yes, murder. The idea can come to the mildest of men, if the provocation is sufficient. I would kill her and save my precious statue.

But it was not that easy. For one thing, she was traveling now somewhere in the west. For another, her death would accomplish exactly nothing. The statue would still be sold, by her husband, by her family. A quarter of a million dollars is a great deal of money.

I hit upon a second plan, which in many ways was more fantastic than the first. I would buy the statue from her myself, borrowing the money against my salary of $12,000 a year. But of course the bank only laughed at that. I am only six years from compulsory retirement. Where, the bank asked, would I earn the money to repay the loan in six years? Especially with the interest.

So where did that leave me? Last night I walked out to the Egyptian Room and stood for a long time staring at the Nile Cat. I thought of stealing it, of hiding it somewhere until the French offer was withdrawn. But then it would still be gone from my museum, which was where it belonged. And could I ever return it? Mrs. Clark would have collected the insurance, and my problems would have multiplied. Besides, she would immediately guess that I had taken it, and send the police to search my house. I could never bring myself to destroy it, and I lacked the skill to find a really clever hiding place. I do not have a criminal mind.

She called me today from the West Coast and said the men would come for it tomorrow morning. This was to be my last night with the beautiful Nile Cat in my museum. I appealed to her again, but of course it was useless. Nothing could be done to save the Nile Cat. Nothing.

I thought about it for a long time. I thought about Cadmus Verne and his middle-aged daughter. I thought about the French museum half a world away. But mostly I thought about the Cat, and how to keep it here.

And then I guess it came to me. Tonight. Just a little while ago. I walked into the Egyptian Room and there was only one person in sight—this fellow Yardley. I went over to the display case and unlocked it and took out the Nile Cat and smashed his skull with it . . .

"You see now why I did it?" Professor Bouton asked, looking up from his hands.

"I guess I do," the detective said, very softly.

"My beloved Nile Cat is now a murder weapon—Exhibit A in an investigation and trial. Just the investigation alone would delay its release for weeks. Now that you have me for trial, it will be months before the statue can be returned to this museum. By the time Mrs. Clark can get her hands on it, the French sale will have collapsed. The Nile Cat will rest in my museum forever."

"Yes," the detective said. He motioned to the stenographer and pressed a buzzer on his desk.

"And even though I've confessed, the laws of this state require a plea of Not Guilty in a first-degree murder case. I'll be tried in some months—perhaps I might even appeal my conviction. It could be years before the Nile Cat gets back to her. It could be years . . ."

Mary Reed

CAT'S-PAW

"**W**ell, the only way I can think of for doing away with someone by way of a cat is to bash them on the head with a stuffed one!" Neil, resident wit at the Goat and Gamp, downed the remains of his pint at one swallow.

As if on cue, in walked Colin, carrying a box. Everyone propping up the bar-counter burst out laughing, and his normally sallow face flushed scarlet with confusion. Joyce, our buxom and very blonde hostess, leaned over the mahogany expanse of the counter to ask him, with that often-misunderstood easy familiarity of the English barmaid, what it would be. Colin, putting his burden onto the bar, pushed his hair out of his eyes, gave a grateful smile, and ordered the usual. A light scratching sound came from the box as Joyce set down a foaming tankard in front of him and raised fine-penciled eyebrows.

"Present for the wife," Colin said, wiping foam from his upper lip. "A kitten."

He looked startled at the gale of merriment his innocent reply provoked.

Taking pity on his obvious bewilderment, I moved a couple of feet along the bar and explained. He listened carefully, nose buried in the tankard. Poor old devil, I thought, he's always finding himself in unfortunate juxtapositions of unlikely circumstances. His very name, Colin Andrew Thompson, for example. It rolls off the tongue nicely, and sounds properly imposing for an Executive Insurance Director, which is what it says on the nameplate on his office door, but then he went and married a breeder of Calico Persians, so of course, between that and his initials, the local wags had a field day. He had scarcely set foot in the pub after his honeymoon when he was met with a barrage of jokes about cataloguing catastrophic losses from cat burglary, living in a cathouse (bucolic humor can be very coarse), and so on. But he never said much, just kept on pushing his hair out of his eyes and smiling at all and sundry over his nightly pint. He wasn't what you'd call a drinking man, by any means. A couple of refills would last him all night, and Neil often voiced the opinion that Colin only came in every evening to feast his eyes on Joyce.

Joyce and Gerald, the long-suffering landlord of the Goat and Gamp, had been courting for years. People in the village used to say "when Joyce and Gerry get wed" much as others might say "in a blue moon." Neil was always saying that one day someone—with a meaningful glance in Colin's direction—was going to come and sweep Joyce away, right from under Gerry's nose, and then he'd be sorry for procrastinating for so long. Colin just smiled, never rising to the bait, and said nothing.

Anyhow, the rather bizarre discussion we'd been having when Colin arrived that particular evening had arisen in the somewhat convoluted way pub conversations will. It had started when Gerry, leaning on the cash till, mentioned reading about a wealthy local spinster leaving all her money to her pet Pekinese. Needless to say, the grieving relatives were contesting the will, and he asked me what I thought the ruling might be.

As a solicitor myself, I hedged a bit, pointing out that litigation might well drag on for some time, because it would, so far as I could tell, hinge upon whether or not the deceased was of sound mind when she drew up the will. And that was a circumstance that might, at this late date, be a little difficult to prove one way or the other. But offhand, and speaking off the record, I guessed that the will would be proved legal, and thus valid, no matter how odd its bequest.

Neil inquired if I had come across any odd wills myself, but Joyce, polishing a glass, pointed out that I could hardly discuss such confidential matters as that, could I? Then she said: "But the wills you read about fair give you the creeps. What about that woman who left all her money to her husband, as long as she was above ground? Of course, he got round that by putting her into one of them fancy mausoleums. And do you remember that fellow in London who wanted to be stuffed?"

When things quietened down a bit, Ned, a local farmer who only happened to be at the Goat and Gamp that evening because it had been market day and he returned home this way, piped up, saying he had actually seen a photograph of the geezer Joyce mentioned. "It gave me a fair turn, I can tell you," he said, signaling Gerry to refill his glass. "Mind, that were years back, before folk got used to all them horror films and such."

Ned being a well known prankster, his supposed recollection of seeing such a photograph provoked some argument. I knew who he was talking about—it was, in fact, a true case—but held my peace. In the end, Neil was dispatched to the ladies' snug across the corridor to consult Marjory, the village librarian. She was a notorious gossip, but she also knew her business, and he returned with confirmation of the story—and, chortling to himself, he stood everyone a pint on the strength of it.

Neil raised his pint to Ned. "Cheers," he said, taking a big gulp, and then continuing: "Well, I don't know about queer wills or odd bequests, but from what you read in the papers it seems like more folk than ought to get themselves ideas about hastening the reading of the will, if you get my drift. Not but what it usually benefits them very much."

This latter gloomy statement was met with more hilarity. It was common knowledge in the village that for years Neil had been anticipating a small remembrance from his grandmother. When, cantankerous to the last, the old girl had died at the age of ninety-something, it turned out to be just that—a small remembrance. To wit, ten pounds and a lecture on the evils of intemperance. Neil spent the lot on standing everyone drinks. I remember we toasted his granny with them. He was never one to bear a grudge, was Neil.

Joyde was wiping the bar absentmindedly. "Yes, but the problem is, Neil, there's few ways you can help folk out of the world undetected, so to say, and get away with it. I mean, there's no such thing as an undetectable poison, like, and guns and knives are so gruesome—and easy to trace, anyhow, aren't they?" Joyce was a great lover of mystery novels, and the more convoluted the better. "Then there's your alibi. You got to be miles away when the murder is committed, don't you? And you can't pay anyone else to do it—there's always a chance of blackmail, right?"

"Well," Gerry commented, "if you can't use someone else, what about *something* else? Like that there Hound of the Basketballs or that Sprinkled Hand? One of them poisonous snakes, it was."

His patrons' general opinion was that poisonous snakes—as well as tarantulas and scorpions—were hard to come by in our neck of the woods. Nor did we have any lonely moors with quicksands over which a devilish dog could hound hapless landowners to death. Though there were several suggestions as to suitable landowners who might be selected for that particular honor, of course. Then someone suggested escaping zoo animals of the fiercer kind, such as tigers, say, or lions.

Surprisingly, it was Ned, the farmer, who addressed that one. "Big cats, you mean," he said from the end of the bar. "Actually, I was once almost frit to death by a small cat. I was having this nightmare about being crushed to death with these huge blocks—like the kind they used to build the Pyramids. It was probably the wife's cooking—her puddings tend to lie a bit heavy, like. Anyhow, I woke up in a bit of a sweat and there *was* this terrible weight on my chest. And when I opened my eyes, there were these huge green ones staring right at me.

"Well, you know how it is when you're coming out of a nightmare—you're not sure if you're here or there, so to speak. It was our Tommy, of course. I reckon he were trying to get his revenge on me for having him fixed."

Neil, evidently not a cat lover, suggested putting poison on a cat's claws as a method of poisoning its owner, but Gerry pointed out that the cat would probably scratch itself first, or lick its claws, die, and give the game away. To which Neil made his retort about bashing someone on the head with a stuffed cat, just as Colin made his entrance . . .

Funnily enough, just as Colin walked in, I'd been thinking about his wife, Penelope. We didn't see much of her at the Goat and Gamp. For one thing, she was a martyr to asthma, as well as being allergic to cigarette smoke—or so we understood. Besides which, she was just out of hospital after breaking her leg. This she had managed to do by slipping on one of her numerous cats' many toys, at the top of a darkened stairwell, en route to rendering aid to her oldest cat, Queenie. Fortunately, given the severity of the fall and the length of the stairs, Penelope had come out of it relatively unscathed.

Neil, needless to say, had been quick to talk about cats with nine lives, though, give him his due, he didn't say it in front of Colin. This Queenie was positively ancient by feline standards, something like twenty-three years old, and the daughter of one of the first blue-ribbon winners Penelope bred. Penelope is, in fact, quite famous in the cat-breeding world, as Marjory was telling me the last time I went in to change my library book.

However, it was from my wife Marie that I learned Penelope is hypersensitive to short-hairs. This seems unfortunate, because they form the bulk of your everyday domestic-cat population and must be a major handicap in Penelope's chosen profession. Not that I want you to think we spend our time discussing our neighbors. Marie mentioned it because she goes to the monthly sewing-circle meetings at the vicarage and when Penelope joined them, not long after she and Colin moved to Yew Lodge, the vicar's cat, which rejoiced in the name of Ezekiel, was banned from the meetings. Marie said she felt sorry for the cat, which is unusually friendly for a Siamese, and that she thought Penelope was turning into a professional invalid.

Anyhow, back to Colin explaining that there was a kitten in the box and it was a present for Penelope.

"Oh, yes?" Joyce said. "What a nice thought, especially with poor old Queenie dying last month."

Colin reddened again. I never knew a man who blushed so easily.

"As a matter of fact," he confessed, "I'm sort of responsible for that. I was the one that bought the bad fish, you see. We were going to have it for supper, but as my wife was feeling a bit off-color with her allergies she just gave a bit to Queenie for a treat and put the rest in the fridge for the following day." Pointing out how easily the fish might have made them ill didn't seem very tactful, because Penelope had broken her leg going downstairs to see to the cat the night it was taken sick. I wondered if she was speaking to Colin again yet.

"What sort is the kitten?" Joyce was cooing. "Can I see it?"

Colin opened the box and we all crowded around to look. The kitten reminded me a bit of those cats you see on Egyptian tomb-paintings, only with blue eyes and rather large ears.

"Hey, it looks a bit like Ezekiel," Gerry remarked, leaning over the bar with his nose almost in the box.

"No, this is an Abyssinian—the vicar's is a Siamese," Colin replied, stroking the kitten's head. It was certainly a handsome little thing. Even Neil the cat hater was charmed.

"Not bad-looking, is it?" he said, leaning over the box and breathing beer fumes over the hapless kitten. "So that's why you were borrowing the A-E section of the encyclopedia. And all those cat books. Wanted to surprise the wife, eh?"

Colin shot him a look of real dislike. "Not much chance of that if the whole village knows, is there?"

"Oh, go on, who's going to tell her what you've been reading in your spare time?" Neil cackled. "Besides, our Marjory only happened to notice because she wanted to look up a few things and you had the A-E volume. Anyhow, you'll be giving her her present tonight, right? Then the cat will *really* be out of the bag, won't it?" He chortled at his own joke.

Colin put the lid back on the box and finished his drink just as Gerry called ten minutes to time and there was the usual rush to the bar to order the last drinks of the evening. Colin left not long afterward, and I walked part of the way with him.

We strolled along in silence, past the school and across the green, skirting the war memorial. Our paths parted at the bottom of Church Lane, his taking him left through the ornate iron gates of Yew Lodge, mine bearing right, up the darkened lane. It was a fine, dear night, very quiet. Walking up the hill, I could hear Colin's fading footsteps as he crunched over the gravel in the Lodge forecourt.

But going home, I got to thinking. Abyssinians are short-haired cats, and I remembered not only Ezekiel's banishment from the sewing circle but also the time Ned's youngest got stung by a bee. He had an allergic reaction that was so bad he had to be rushed to the County Hospital, where it was really touch and go for a time. And A-E might include Abyssinian and Cat, but it also covered Allergies. The tainted fish that did for Queenie. The fall in the dark. The way Colin stared at Joyce when he thought no one was looking. Penelope's hypersensitivity to short-haired cats and her current immobilization in a plaster cast.

But the whole thing was quite fantastic, wasn't it? At least, that's what I tried to tell myself as I approached the house. I hoped Colin wasn't contemplating anything foolish. For one thing, he'd never get away with it. For another, as his wife's solicitor, I had seen the terms of her new will, drawn up while she was still in the hospital. It left the bulk of her not inconsiderable estate to the local humane society. To be sure, there was a small legacy for Colin, but it wasn't much. Not enough to keep Yew Lodge, for one thing. And her estate would pay it for only as long as he looked after the cats.

Frances & Richard Lockridge

CAT OF DREAMS

Ann Notson was nine years old; she had eyes which in certain lights looked green; there was a kind of glow in her soft brown hair. Her mother had had such eyes and hair, and so Philip Notson, when he looked at his daughter, must often—too often—have been reminded of his wife.

Ann Notson was an imaginative child—a "very" imaginative child, her teacher in Van Brunt District School had written, underlining the word "very." This, decided Captain M. L. Heimrich of the New York State Police, meant that Ann sometimes saw things which were not there or, perhaps, saw what was there in a more interesting form than was entirely real.

There was, however, no doubt of the very ugly reality of what she saw at about eight thirty of a bright, cold Saturday morning in mid-December—saw behind the garage of her father's house on Brickhouse Road in the town of Van Brunt, County of Putnam. She had gone out of the house to find a "kitty." "May I be excused, please?" she said to her father, who was lingering over breakfast coffee, as a man may on Saturday morning. "I want to go out and see if the kitty is all right."

"Um-mm," Philip Notson said. "Bundle up, kitten."

He heard the front door slam and stopped, coffee cup halfway between saucer and lips, and expression drained out of his eyes. It was the little, meaningless things which now were the worst things. Jean had always closed doors more firmly than necessary. . . . He wrenched his mind from memory.

What "kitty" did Ann expect to find? A cat of dreams, probably, since they had no cat; a "kitty" who frisked, chased his tail, only in a child's quick mind.

He picked up the newspaper. He made himself read it.

The door slammed again. She hadn't stayed long. No kitty to be found, he supposed. However imaginative a child . . .

"Daddy," Ann said, almost before she was in the dining room. "Daddy!

There's a man out there. Lying right on the ground. Is he asleep, Daddy? Because it's cold. It's—*awful* cold."

There was urgency in the clear voice; there was something—fear? shock?—in the child's greenish eyes. Philip Notson said, "Where?" and, on being told, went to see. The man who lay on the ground behind the garage, between it and the bank which broke sharply down from the field above, was not asleep.

Captain Heimrich, whose chief concern is with murder, drove up the driveway from Brickhouse Road to Philip Notson's white and gray house at a little after nine. Fortunately he had been nearby.

There were police cars already in the driveway and in the turnaround in front of the garage. He went around the garage and looked down at the body of Malcolm Arthur Bell.

Just two days before, on Thursday, Heimrich had heard Bell called "a very fortunate man" by County Judge Davies, who had just accepted a verdict of Not Guilty from a jury in the Carmel courthouse. Not guilty, that was, of manslaughter in connection with the death of one Jean Notson, thirty-one years old, at about one thirty-five o'clock on the morning of Sunday, the twenty-first of September. Bell's luck had now run out.

"Oh," Philip Notson said to Heimrich. "I see how it looks. He killed my wife. The jury says he's not guilty of anything. And—I said some bitter things and was heard saying them. I see how it looks. All the same—"

All the same, he knew nothing of Bell's death. Murder, if they were so sure it was that. He himself had thought that Bell had stumbled on the rough steps leading down from the upper field, pitched headlong and landed on a rock. Which, he said with some savagery, would have been appropriate.

Heimrich, a notably solid man, sat and watched and listened to Philip Notson—a slim, quick man, tall and with just a suggestion of the tall man's stoop. Notson walked back and forth in the living room and made quick motions with his hands. He was in his middle thirties; his hair was beginning to recede a little; the summer's tan had not quite faded from his mobile face.

"No," Heimrich said, "he didn't fall, Mr. Notson. He was struck. Several times, probably with an iron bar. Sometime yesterday evening. Between five and nine, at a guess—a wide guess, admittedly. He would have come that way, coming here?"

"Across the field? Yes. They used to. He and his wife. Not since Jean died. Since—he killed her."

But it had not been like that—not as Phil Notson said it now, looking down, his eyes angry, at Heimrich. The jury had said it was an accident—an accident in the early hours of a Sunday morning, after a dance.

"Come on and ride in a real car," Mal Bell had said to Jean Notson, a pretty, slender woman in a gray-green party dress, and patted the hood of his sports car. "Just try it and you'll make old stick-in-the-mud get you one."

They had all laughed, not that there was anything especially funny, but because they were young enough, and gay, and had had a good time at the country club dance.

They had all had drinks, but nobody—and specifically, of course, Malcolm Bell—had had too many. Bell said that it was a blown front tire that sent the hurrying little car into a tree, and Jean out of the car—far, far out of it, until a stone fence stopped her diving flight.

"As to yesterday evening, Mr. Notson," Heimrich said. "You got home about when?"

"A little after seven."

Heimrich raised his eyebrows and waited. Van Brunt is an express-train hour from Grand Central. Most commuters manage to make the 5:06.

Notson had missed the usual train, he told Heimrich. He had telephoned Mrs. Billings, who was the housekeeper, and caught the 5:58. Heimrich could ask Mrs. Billings. "Oh," Heimrich said. "Yes, naturally. You came home, had dinner. Then?"

"Read to my daughter. Saw she got to bed—about eight thirty. Read a little longer and went to bed myself. Didn't take time out to kill Mal Bell."

Heimrich said, "Now, Mr. Notson," and then Sergeant Forniss opened the door from the hall and made a motion with his head. Heimrich went out into the hall and closed the door behind him.

A little girl, with very wide greenish eyes and very soft brown hair and wearing a snow suit, was sitting on the third step of the stairs which led up from the hall, and looking out through the front door.

Heimrich smiled at her and Ann Notson said, "I saw a man." She had, Heimrich knew. That she would forget seeing him, after time enough, Heimrich hoped. He said, "Yes, dear," and listened to Forniss.

Then he smiled again at the little girl and went back into the living room, and told Philip Notson that the people across the road had seen the floodlight come on at the Notson place about nine o'clock the previous evening, and said that it had stayed on for about a quarter of an hour. Could Mr. Notson—

"Oh," Phil Notson said, and was very quick in speaking. "That. People looking for the Blakes. Live on Van Brunt Lane, the Blakes do. Next road up. They'd turned off too soon. Told them how to get there."

He looked at Heimrich with challenge. Heimrich told Philip Notson that he saw.

"No reason we would have heard anything," Notson said. "Unless Bell shouted. Maybe not even then. We'd have been in the dining room, the kitten—Ann,

95

that is—and I, and Mrs. Billings in the kitchen."

"No," Heimrich said. "Killing that way doesn't make a lot of noise. Well—"

"You know about the Perkins kid?" Notson said. "What Perkins said he'd do?"

"I know," Heimrich said. "We'll talk to Mr. Perkins."

"Kid of twelve," Notson said. "Crippled now. Who knows when he'll walk again? Because a louse doesn't look where he's going, where he's driving his car. The kid was a pitcher."

"I know," Heimrich said. But he also knew, and supposed that Philip Notson knew—but a bitter mind cannot be predicted—that Bell had not been at fault that time, either; that Jimmy Perkins had been on a bicycle, and had wobbled into the road too far, and that Bell had been driving within the limit, which was forty, through the place they called The Flats, and had done all that could be expected of a driver. (Except, possibly, to drive below the posted speed, which was too high, considering the number of kids, and dogs, on the highway where it ran through The Flats.)

The boy's father, a short and powerfully built man who was a yardman for the Van Brunt Supply Company, had said a lot of things which, it was to be presumed, he hadn't meant. At any rate, that had been a year ago and Perkins had not done anything. Except, of course, to collect a modest sum—modest since Bell had done all that could, officially, be asked—from Bell's insurance company.

Heimrich said, "Well, thanks, Mr. Notson," and went out into the hall. Forniss raised his eyebrows in inquiry and Heimrich shrugged in answer.

The little girl was still on the third step. She said, "You're a policeman, aren't you?"

"Yes, Ann," Heimrich said and smiled down at the little girl—the pretty little girl who, they said, looked so much like her mother. "I'm a policeman."

"I saw a man," Ann said. "When I turned the lights on. He was running. And a kitty."

"Yes," Heimrich said, but sat down on his heels so that he was level with the little girl. "Running?"

"A funny man," Ann said. "Thick. He ran funny. Why don't you wear clothes like the other policemen?"

Heimrich explained about that. He said, "When did you see the funny man, Ann?"

She had seen him the previous evening. When it was time for Daddy to come home—Mrs. Billings had said he was going to be late, but you couldn't tell—she turned on the floodlights over the garage. "It's my—perogative." She stopped and looked at Heimrich with doubt. He nodded his head. "Since Mamma went away," Ann said. "So Daddy won't bump into anything."

She had turned the light on at ten minutes after six—"precisely" —and she had seen the funny man running away from the house, toward the road. (He was funny, Heimrich decided, because he was a grown person and was running. Which was quite reasonable.) Ann didn't know who he was. He wasn't Mr. Bell. Of course she knew Mr. Bell. He wasn't Daddy. "Don't be so silly."

"And," Ann Notson said, "there was a kitty. Just where the light stops. It had shiny eyes. Like tail lights."

That was unexpected. In semidarkness, but with light on them, the eyes of cats shine—shine green, shine yellow.

"Like tail lights?" Heimrich said. "How like tail lights, dear?"

"Red," Ann said. "Red as anything. Like in the fireplace sometimes."

"Oh," Heimrich said. "Did you tell Daddy about the kitty with red eyes? And about the man?"

"Of course," Ann said. "He said I shouldn't make up things. *Every*body says that." She paused. "All the *time*," she said. "He said cats never have red eyes. But this—"

Heimrich touched the soft brown hair, smiled at her, stood up, and supposed that people did, all the *time*, tell Ann not to make things up.

A man running.

A red-eyed cat.

For a moment Heimrich wished that, just this once at any rate, a cat's eyes would glow red in semidarkness, with a light on them, instead of green or yellow; that such a glow, and a man running, would prove not to be merely things a little girl had made up. It would be bad for the soft-haired child if something happened to Daddy . . .

Things are collected, are put together. This takes time, since the collection must extend to byways. It takes more men than two. A trooper had been sent to talk to James Perkins, and by no means only to carry out Heimrich's assurance to Philip Notson.

Perkins was to be asked—was asked—whether he still had borne a grudge against the man who had maimed his son. He was also to be asked—was asked—where he had been the previous evening . . . between the hours of five, say, and nine.

The trooper had found Perkins loading sand into a burlap bag in the yard of the Van Brunt Supply Company. Perkins stuck his shovel in the sand and said that, hell, he bore no grudge, hadn't since he had had time to think it over. A kid on a bicycle—well, Perkins drove a car himself. Things happen before you know it; things you can't do anything about. Bell had been decent enough about it—or his insurance company had.

As for the previous evening, Perkins had got home from work a little after five, had had dinner around six and had stayed home until bedtime, looking at TV. And they could ask his wife. His wife had been asked; had said he certainly had. Wives have been known to alibi for husbands. And it could not be denied that Perkins might, by a child, well be called a "thick" man.

But Malcolm Bell's body had not been found in Perkins's back yard. It had been found behind Philip Notson's garage. So Heimrich and Sergeant Forniss concentrated, most logically, on Bell himself and on Philip Notson.

Bell, on the last day of his life, had driven his wife to New York and put her on a plane for Palm Beach. He had driven back and had a drink at the Old Stone Inn, and told a friend he met there he was thinking about going around to see old Phil Notson and try to get things straightened out.

Half a dozen men had got off the 5:58 local-express at Van Brunt, and one of them might have been Notson, but they had not proved it by late afternoon.

Nobody had seen Notson on the 5:06, and since that was his regular train he probably would have been noticed and spoken to if he had been on it. Which did not prove much, since the most likely thing was that Notson had turned the garage floodlight on at a little after nine to see who had come to the door, and when he found out, killed him . . .

Nobody had showed up at the Blake house on Van Brunt Lane to say that they had had to stop to ask directions. Of course, the prospective droppers-in might merely have changed their minds . . . Ann's teacher said the poor little thing was a dear, but that she was a *most* imaginative child.

And—the eyes of cats do not shine red when light strikes them out of darkness. Heimrich had been sure of that, but all the same—since a policeman can never be too sure of anything—he had talked to an eye specialist he knew. "Nope," the ophthalmologist said, "not that I ever heard of. Oh—I suppose an albino cat's might. No pigment on the tapetum lucidum."

"The what?"

"Layer in the chorioid," the eye man said. "Back part of the eye. What reflects light. Good many mammals have it. We don't, more's the pity."

"Are there," Heimrich asked, "many albino cats?"

"One in a million, at a guess. I never saw one. Never met anybody who had seen one. They'd have pink eyes, of course. White cats with pink eyes."

A cat like that would be noticeable, Heimrich thought, and he asked around. Nobody had ever seen one. Not around there or anywhere else. So—Ann had not seen a red-eyed cat. A million to one she hadn't. And hence—not a man running, either, since the two things went together—went together in a child's imagination.

Heimrich turned his car off NY 11-F into Brickhouse Road. It was time to get to work on Philip Notson—to get really to work on him. It was dusk, then.

Heimrich switched the headlights on—and jammed his brakes on; and Sergeant Forniss, sitting beside him, put hands out to brace himself and said, "What the *hell?*"

"Look," Heimrich said, and they both looked—looked at two tiny lights by the road's edge; lights which glowed like coals in a fireplace, like the twin tail lights of a car. Red lights.

The little red lights went out. But then they were glowing from the top of a stone fence. They went out again, but by then Heimrich had the car off the road and they were out of it at a driveway.

There was enough light to see a cat streak toward a house. A woman stood on the porch. The woman called, *"Boots! Here,* Boots. *Here—"* and then said to the arriving cat. *"You!* Again. *Again!"*

The woman was Mrs. Burnett—Mrs. Harry Burnett. Of course the cat belonged to her. "Come here, Boots," she said again, and Boots came to prove it.

"Oh," Heimrich said, and looked at Boots, who was certainly not a white cat with pink eyes; he was a cat with a black face and deep blue eyes and a black tail. "Oh," Heimrich said. "Siamese. We were looking for an albino cat." He could not remember that, as a policeman, he had ever made a sillier remark. "A cat with red eyes," he added, and felt sillier than ever, looking down at the blue-eyed cat.

"With red—" Mrs. Burnett said. "Oh—you mean with a light on them? Of course. They always are. Siamese eyes, I mean. Because Siamese are part albino, you know. Even if you'd never guess it to look at them."

It proved fortunate for Philip Notson—and for a little girl with greenish eyes and an imagination not quite, this time, as fervid as people were always saying— that Boots was a cat who led a somewhat circumscribed life; was a young female who, particularly at the moment, had her own idea about things, and hence was not let roam at large. But a cat who got out anyway, now and again, as she had this Saturday evening, but only for a few minutes.

The night before, however, Boots had got out at five thirty in the evening, Mrs. Burnett confided, and had been gone for an hour or more, and goodness knew where, and one could only hope.

Since two things were linked in the mind of a child, Heimrich and Forniss did not go on to the Notson house, but drove the other way—drove to The Flats and, with not much trouble, found a "thick" man standing at the bar of the Three Oaks Tavern.

James Perkins did not seem surprised to see them, but then James Perkins was drunk now—mumbling drunk.

He mumbled a good deal about a so-and-so who thought he could get away with anything, and about bought-off so-and-sos who would let him. And about that so-and-so Bell, who knew better now, knew you couldn't cripple a kid and get off for a few measly dollars. Some drunken men talk a lot.

If Perkins talked enough, Heimrich thought, they might never have to ask a little girl if this was the man—the thick man—she had seen running.

But he would, he thought, some day make a point of telling a little girl that some cats do too have red eyes.

Theodore Sturgeon

THE ABOMINABLE HOUSE GUEST

Ransome lay in the dark and smiled to himself, thinking about his hostess. Ransome was always in demand as a house guest, purely because of his phenomenal abilities as a raconteur. Said abilities were entirely due to his being so often a house guest, for it was the terse beauty of his word pictures of people and their opinions of people that made him the figure he was. And all those clipped ironies had to do with the people he had met last week-end. Staying a while at the Joneses, he could quietly insinuate the most scandalously hilarious things about the Joneses when he week-ended with the Browns the following fortnight. You think Mr. and Mrs. Jones resented that? Ah, no. You should hear the dirt on the Browns! And so it went, a two-dimensional spiral on the social plane.

This wasn't the Joneses or the Browns, though. This was Mrs. Benedetto's ménage; and to Ransome's somewhat jaded sense of humor the widow Benedetto was a godsend. She lived in a world of her own, which was apparently set about with quasi-important ancestors and relatives, exactly as her living room was cluttered up with perfectly unmentionable examples of Victorian rococo.

Mrs. Benedetto did not live alone. Far from it. Her very life, to paraphrase the lady herself, was wound about, was caught up in, was owned by and dedicated to her baby. Her baby was her beloved, her little beauty, her too darling my dear, and—so help me—her boobly wutsi-wutsikins. In himself he was quite a character. He answered to the name of Bubbles, which was inaccurate and offended his dignity. He had been christened Fluffy, but you know how it is with nicknames. He was large and he was sleek, that paragon among animals, a chastened alley cat.

Wonderful things, cats. A cat is the only animal which can live like a parasite and maintain to the utmost its ability to take care of itself. You've heard of little lost dogs, but you never heard of a lost cat. Cats don't get lost, because cats don't belong anywhere. You wouldn't get Mrs. Benedetto to believe that. Mrs.

100

Benedetto never thought of putting Fluffy's devotion to the test by declaring a ten-day moratorium on the canned salmon. If she had, she would have uncovered a sense of honor comparable with that of a bedbug's.

Knowing this—Ransome pardoned himself the pun—categorically, Ransome found himself vastly amused. Mrs. Benedetto's ministrations to the phlegmatic Fluffy were positively orgiastic. As he thought of it in detail, he began to feel that perhaps, after all, Fluffy was something of a feline phenomenon. A cat's ears are sensitive organs; any living being that could abide Mrs. Benedetto's constant flow of conversation from dawn till dark, and then hear it subside in sleep only to be replaced by resounding snores—well, that *was* phenomenal.

And Fluffy had stood it for four years. Cats are not renowned for their patience. They have, however, a very fine sense of values. Fluffy was getting something out of it—worth considerably more to him than the discomforts he endured, for no cat likes to break even.

Ransome lay still, marveling at the carrying power of the widow's snores. He knew little of the late Mr. Benedetto, but he gathered now that he had been either a man of saintly patience, a masochist, or a deaf-mute. A noise like that from just one stringy throat must be an impossibility, and yet, there it was.

Ransome liked to imagine that the woman had calluses on her palate and tonsils, grown there from her conversation, and it was these rasping together that produced the curious dry-leather quality of her snores. He tucked the idea away for future reference. He might use it next week-end. The snores were hardly the gentlest of lullabies, but any sound is soothing if it is repeated often enough.

There is an old story about a lighthouse tender whose lighthouse was equipped with an automatic cannon which fired every fifteen minutes, day and night. One night, when the old man was asleep, the gun failed to go off. Three seconds after, the old fellow was out of his bed and flailing around the room, shouting, "What was that?" And so it was with Ransome.

He couldn't tell whether it was an hour after he had fallen asleep, or whether he had not fallen asleep at all. But he found himself sitting on the edge of the bed, wide awake, straining every nerve for the source of the—what was it?—sound?—that had awakened him.

The old house was as quiet as a city morgue after closing time, and he could see nothing in the tall dark guestroom but the moon-silvered windows and the thick blacknesses that were drapes. Any old damn thing might be hiding behind those drapes, he thought uncomfortingly. He edged himself back on the bed and quickly snatched his feet off the floor. Not that anything was under the bed, but still—

A white object puffed along the floor, through the moonbeams, toward him. He made no sound, but tensed himself, ready to attack or defend, dodge or retreat.

Ransome was by no means an admirable character, but he owed his reputation, and therefore his existence, to this particular trait—the ability to poise himself, invulnerable to surprise.

The white object paused to stare at him out of its yellow-green eyes. It was only Fluffy—Fluffy looking casual and easy-going and not at all in a mood to frighten people. In fact, he looked up at Ransome's gradually relaxing hulk and raised a longhaired, quizzical eyebrow, as if he rather enjoyed the man's discomfiture.

Ransome withstood the cat's gaze with suavity, and stretched himself out on the bed with every bit of Fluffy's own easy grace. "Well," he said amusedly, "you gave me a jolt! Weren't you taught to knock before you entered a gentleman's boudoir?"

Fluffy raised a velvet paw and touched it pinkly with his tongue. "Do you take me for a barbarian?" he asked.

Ransome's lids seemed to get heavy, the only sign he ever gave of being taken aback. He didn't believe for a moment that the cat had really spoken—this was, of course, someone's idea of a joke.

Good God—it has to be a joke!

"You didn't say anything, of course," he told the cat, "but if you did, what was it?"

"You heard me the first time," said the cat, and jumped up on the foot of his bed.

Ransome inched back from the animal. "Yes, I thought I did. You know," he said, with an attempt at jocularity, "you should, under these circumstances, have written me a note before you knocked."

I refuse to be burdened with the so-called social amenities," said Fluffy. His coat was spotlessly clean, and he looked like an advertising photograph for eiderdown, but he began to wash carefully. "I don't like you, Ransome."

"Thanks," chuckled Ransome, surprised. "I don't like you either."

"Why?" asked Fluffy.

Ransome told himself silently that he was damned. He held tight to a mind that would begin to reel on slight provocation, and, as usual when bemused, he flung out a smoke screen of his own variety of glib chatter.

"Reasons for not liking you," he said, "are legion. They are all included in the one phrase—'You are a cat!' "

"I have heard you say that at least twice before," said Fluffy, "except that you have now substituted 'cat' for 'Woman.' "

"Your attitude is offensive. Is any given truth any the less true for having been uttered more than once?"

"No," said the cat with equanimity. "But it is just that more clichéd."

Ransome laughed. "Quite aside from the fact that you can talk, I find you most refreshing. No one has ever criticized my particular variety of repartee before."

"No one was ever wise to you before," said the cat. "Why don't you like cats?"

A question like that was, to Ransome, the pressing of a button which released ordered phrases. "Cats," he said oratorically, "are without doubt the most self-centered, ungrateful, hypocritical creatures on this or any other earth. Spawned from a mésalliance between Lilith and Satan—"

Fluffy's eyes widened. "Ah! An antiquarian!" he whispered.

"—they have the worst traits of both. Their best qualities are their beauty of form and of motion, and even these breathe vile. Women are the ficklest of bipeds, but few women are as fickle as, by nature, any cat is. Cats are not true. They are impossibilities, as perfection is impossible. No other living creature moves with utterly perfect grace. Only the dead can so perfectly relax. And nothing—simply nothing at all—transcends a cat's incomparable insincerity."

Fluffy purred.

"Pussy! Sit-by-the-fire and sing!" spat Ransome. "Smiling up, all bearers of liver and salmon and catnip! Soft little puffball, bundle of joy, playing with a ball on a string, making children clap their soft hands to see you, while your mean little brain is viciously alight with the pictures your play calls for you. Bite it to make it bleed; hold it till it all but throttles; lay it down and step about it daintily; prod it with a gentle silken paw until it moves again, and then pounce. Clasp it in your talons then, lift it, roll over with it, sink your cruel teeth into it while you pump out its guts with your hind feet. Ball on a string! Play-actor!"

Fluffy fawned. "To quote you, that is the prettiest piece of emotional claptrap that these old ears have ever heard. A triumph in studied spontaneity. A symphony in cynicism. A poem in perception. The unqualified—"

Ransome grunted. He deeply resented this flamboyant theft of all his pet phrases, but his lip twitched nevertheless. The cat was indeed an observant animal.

"—epitome of understatement," Fluffy finished smoothly. "To listen to you, one would think that you would like to slaughter earth's felinity."

"I would," gritted Ransome.

"It would be a favor to us," said the cat. "We would keep ourselves vastly amused, eluding you and laughing at the effort it cost you. Humans lack imagination."

"Superior creature," said Ransome ironically, "why don't you do away with the human race, if you find us a bore?"

"You think we couldn't?" responded Fluffy. "We can outthink, outrun, and outbreed your kind. But why should we? As long as you act as you have for these last few thousand years, feeding us, sheltering us, and asking nothing from us but our presence for purposes of admiration—why then, you may remain here."

Ransome guffawed. "Nice of you! But listen—stop your bland discussion of the abstract and tell me some things I want to know. How can you talk, and why did you pick me to talk to?"

Fluffy settled himself. "I shall answer the question socratically. Socrates was a Greek, and so I shall begin with your last question. What do you do for a living?"

"Why I—I have some investments and a small capital, and the interest—" Ransome stopped, for the first time fumbling for words.

Fluffy was nodding knowingly. "All right, all right. Come clean. You can speak freely."

Ransome grinned. "Well, if you must know—and you seem to—I am a practically permanent house guest. I have a considerable fund of stories and a talent for telling them. I look presentable and act as if I were a gentleman. I negotiate, at times, small loans—"

"A loan," said Flufy authoritatively, "is something one intends to repay."

"We'll call them loans," said Ransome airily. "Also, at one time and another, I exact a reasonable fee for certain services rendered—"

"Blackmail," said the cat.

"Don't be crude. All in all, I find life a comfortable and engrossing thing."

"Q. E. D.," said Fluffy triumphantly. "You make your living being scintilliant, beautiful to look at. So do I. You help nobody but yourself; you help yourself to anything you want. So do I. No one likes you except those you bleed; everyone admires and envies you. So with me. Get the point?"

"I think so. Cat, you draw a mean parallel. In other words, you consider my behavior catlike."

"Precisely," said Fluffy through his whiskers. "And that is both why and how I can talk with you. You're so close to the feline in everything you do and think; your whole basic philosophy is that of a cat. You have a feline aura about you so intense that it contacts mine; hence we find each other intelligible."

"I don't understand that," said Ransome.

"Neither do I," returned Fluffy. "But there it is. Do you like Mrs. Benedetto?"

"No!" said Ransome immediately and with considerable emphasis. "She is absolutely insufferable. She bores me. She irritates me. She is the only woman in the world who can do both those things to me at the same time. She talks too much. She reads too little. She thinks not at all. Her mind is hysterically hidebound. She has a face like the cover of a book that no one has ever wanted to read. She is built like a pinch-type whiskey bottle that never had any whiskey in it. Her voice is monotonous and unmusical. Her education was insufficient. Her family background is mediocre, she can't cook, and she doesn't brush her teeth often enough."

"My, my," said the cat, raising both paws in surprise. "I detect a ring of sincerity in all that. It pleases me. That is exactly the way I have felt for some years. I have never found fault with her cooking, though; she buys special food for me. I am tired of it. I am tired of her. I am tired of her to an almost unbelievable extent. Almost as much as I hate you."

"Me?"

"Of course. You're an imitation. You're a phony. Your birth is against you, Ransome. No animal that sweats and shaves, that opens doors for women, that dresses itself in equally phony imitations of the skins of animals, can achieve the status of a cat. You are presumptuous."

"You're not?"

"I am different. I *am* a cat, and have a right to do as I please. I disliked you so intensely when I saw you this evening that I made up my mind to kill you."

"Why didn't you? Why—don't you?"

"I couldn't," said the cat coolly. "Not when you sleep like a cat . . . No, I thought of something far more amusing."

"Oh?"

"Oh, yes." Fluffy stretched out a foreleg, extended his claws. Ransome noticed subconsciously how long and strong they seemed. The moon had gone its way, and the room was filling with slate-gray light.

"What woke you," said the cat, leaping to the window sill, "just before I came in?"

"I don't know," said Ransome. "Some little noise, I imagine."

"No, indeed," said Fluffy, curling his tail and grinning through his whiskers. "It was the *stopping* of a noise. Notice how quiet it is?"

It was, indeed. There wasn't a sound in the house—oh, yes, now he could hear the plodding footsteps of the maid on her way from the kitchen to Mrs. Benedetto's bedroom, and the soft clink of a teacup. But otherwise—suddenly he had it. "The old horse stopped snoring!"

"She did," said the cat.

The door across the hall opened, there was the murmur of the maid's voice, a loud crash, the most horrible scream Ransome had ever heard, pounding footsteps rushing down the hall, another scream, silence.

"What the—"

Ransome bounced out of bed.

"Just the maid," said Fluffy, washing between his toes, but keeping the corners of his eyes on Ransome. "She just found Mrs. Benedetto."

"Found—"

"Yes. I tore her throat out."

"Good God! Why?"

Fluffy poised himself on the window sill. "So you'd be blamed for it," he said, and laughing nastily, he leaped out and disappeared in the gray morning.

Lilian Jackson Braun

PHUT PHAT CONCENTRATES

Phut Phat knew, at an early age, that humans were an inferior breed. They were unable to see in the dark. They ate and drank unthinkable concoctions. And they had only five senses—the two who lived with Phut Phat could not even transmit their thoughts without resorting to words.

For more than a year, ever since he had arrived at the townhouse, Phut Phat had been attempting to introduce his system of communication, but his two pupils had made scant progress. At dinnertime he would sit in a corner, concentrating, and suddenly they would say, "Time to feed the cat," as if it were their own idea.

Their ability to grasp Phut Phat's messages extended only to the bare necessities of daily living, however. Beyond that, nothing ever got through to them, and it seemed unlikely that they would ever increase their powers.

Nevertheless, life in the townhouse was comfortable enough. It followed a fairly dependable routine, and to Phut Phat routine was the greatest of all goals. He deplored such deviations as tardy meals, loud noises, unexplained persons on the premises, or liver during the week. He always had liver on Sunday.

It was a fashionable part of the city in which Phut Phat lived. His home was a three-story brick house furnished with thick rugs and down-cushioned chairs and tall pieces of furniture from which he could look down on questionable visitors. He could rise to the top of a highboy in a single leap, and when he chose to scamper from first-floor kitchen to second-floor living room to third-floor bedroom, his ascent up the carpeted staircase was very close to flight, for Phut Phat was a Siamese. His fawn-colored coat was finer than ermine. His eight seal-brown points (there had been nine before that trip to the hospital) were as sleek as panne velvet and his slanted eyes brimmed with a mysterious blue.

Those who lived with Phut Phat in the townhouse were a pair, identified in his consciousness as One and Two. It was One who supplied the creature comforts—beef on weekdays, liver on Sunday, and a warm cuddle now and then. She also fed his vanity with lavish compliments and adorned his throat with jeweled collars taken from her own wrists.

Two, on the other hand, was valued chiefly for games and entertainment. He said very little, but he jingled keys at the end of a shiny chain and swung them back and forth for Phut Phat's amusement. And every morning in the dressing room he swished a necktie in tantalizing arcs while Phut Phat leaped and grabbed with pearly claws.

These daily romps, naps on downy cushions, outings in the coop on the fire escape, and two meals a day constituted the pattern of Phut Phat's life.

Then one Sunday he sensed a disturbing lapse in the household routine. The Sunday papers, usually scattered all over the library floor for him to shred with his claws, were stacked neatly on the desk. Furniture was rearranged. The house was filled with flowers, which he was not allowed to chew. All day long, One was nervous and Two was too busy to play. A stranger in a white coat arrived and clattered glassware, and when Phut Phat went to investigate an aroma of shrimp and smoked oysters in the kitchen the maid shooed him away.

Phut Phat seemed to be in everyone's way. Finally he was deposited in his wire coop on the fire escape, where he watched sparrows in the garden below until his stomach felt empty. Then he howled to come indoors.

He found One at her dressing table, fussing with her hair and unmindful of his hunger. Hopping lightly to the table, he sat erect among the sparkling bottles, stiffened his tail, and fastened his blue eyes on One's forehead. In that attitude he concentrated—and concentrated—and concentrated. It was never easy to communicate with One. Her mind hopped about like a sparrow, never relaxed, and Phut Phat had to strain every nerve to convey his meaning.

Suddenly One darted a look in his direction. A thought had occurred to her.

"Oh, John," she called to Two, who was brushing his hair in the dressing room, "would you ask Millie to feed Phuffy? I forgot his dinner until this very minute. It's after five o'clock and I haven't fixed my hair yet. You'd better put your coat on—people will start coming soon. And please tell Howard to light the candles. You might stack some records on the stereo, too.—No, wait a minute. If Millie is still working on the canapes, would you feed Phuffy yourself? Just give him a slice of cold roast."

At this, Phut Phat stared at One with an intensity that made his thought waves almost visible.

"Oh, John, I forgot," she corrected. "It's Sunday, and he should have liver. Cut it in long strips or he'll toss it up. And before you do that, will you zip the back of my dress and put my emerald bracelet on Phuffy? Or maybe I'll wear the emerald myself and he can have the topaz. John! Do you realize it's five-fifteen? I wish you'd put your coat on."

"And I wish you'd simmer down," said Two. "No one ever comes on time.

Why do you insist on giving big parties, Helen, if it makes you so nervous?"

"Nervous? I'm not nervous. Besides, it was *your* idea to invite my friends and your clients at the same time. You said we should kill a whole blasted flock of birds with one stone. Now, *please*, John, are you going to feed Phuffy? He's staring at me and making my head ache."

Phut Phat scarcely had time to swallow his meal, wash his face, and arrange himself on the living-room mantel before people started to arrive. His irritation at having the routine disrupted had been lessened somewhat by the prospect of being admired by the guests. His name meant "beautiful" in Siamese, and he was well aware of his pulchritude.

Lounging between a pair of Georgian candlesticks, with one foreleg extended and the other exquisitely bent under at the ankle, with his head erect and gaze withdrawn, with his tail drooping nonchalantly over the edge of the marble mantel, he awaited compliments.

It was a large party, and Phut Phat observed that very few of the guests knew how to pay their respects to a cat. Some talked nonsense in a falsetto voice. Others made startling movements in his direction or, worse still, tried to pick him up.

There was one knowledgeable guest, however, who approached the mantel with a proper attitude of deference and reserve. Phut Phat squeezed his eyes in appreciation. The admirer was a man, who leaned heavily on a shiny stick. Standing at a respectful distance, he slowly held out his hand with one finger extended, and Phut Phat twitched his whiskers in polite acknowledgement.

"You are a living sculpture," said the man.

"That's Phut Phat," said One, who had pushed through the crowded room toward the fireplace. "He's the head of our household."

"He is obviously a champion," said the man with the shiny cane, addressing his hostess in the same dignified manner that had charmed Phut Phat.

"Yes, he could probably win a few ribbons if we wanted to enter him in shows, but he's strictly a pet. He never goes out, except in his coop on the fire escape."

"A coop? That's a splendid idea," said the man. "I should like to have one for my own cat. She's a tortoiseshell long-hair. May I inspect this coop before I leave?"

"Of course. It's just outside the library window."

"You have a most attractive house."

"Thank you. We've been accused of decorating it to complement Phut Phat's coloring, which is somewhat true. You'll notice we have no breakable bric-a-brac. When a Siamese flies through the air, he recognizes no obstacles."

"Indeed, I have noticed you collect Georgian silver," the man said in his courtly way. "You have some fine examples."

"Apparently you know silver. Your cane is a rare piece."

"Yes, it is an attempt to extract a little pleasure from a sorry necessity." He hobbled a step or two.

"Would you like to see my silver collection downstairs in the dining room?" asked One. "It's all early silver—about the time of Wren."

At this point, Phut Phat, aware that the conversation no longer centered on him, jumped down from the mantel and stalked out of the room with several irritable flicks of the tail. He found an olive and pushed it down the heat register. Several feet stepped on him. In desperation, he went upstairs to the guest room, where he discovered a mound of sable and mink and went to sleep.

After this upset in the household routine, Phut Phat needed several days to catch up on his rest—so the ensuing week was a sleep blur. But soon it was Sunday again, with liver for breakfast, Sunday papers scattered over the floor, and everyone sitting around being pleasantly routine.

"Phuffy! Don't roll on those newspapers," said One. "John, can't you see the ink rubs off on his fur? Give him the *Wall Street Journal*—it's cleaner."

"Maybe he'd like to go outside in his coop and get some sun."

"That reminds me, dear. Who was that charming man with the silver cane at our party? I didn't catch his name."

"I don't know," said Two. "I thought he was someone you invited."

"Well, he wasn't. He must have come with one of the other guests. At any rate, he was interested in getting a coop like ours for his own cat. He has a long-haired torty. And did I tell you the Hendersons have two Burmese kittens? They want us to go over and see them next Sunday and have a drink."

Another week passed, during which Phut Phat discovered a new perch. He found he could jump to the top of an antique armoire—a towering piece of furniture in the hall outside the library. Otherwise, it was a routine week, followed by a routine weekend, and Phut Phat was content.

One and Two were going out on Sunday evening to see the Burmese kittens, so Phut Phat was served an early dinner and soon afterward he fell asleep on the library sofa.

When the telephone rang and waked him, it was dark and he was alone. He raised his head and chattered at the instrument until it stopped its noise. Then he went back to sleep, chin on paw.

The second time the telephone started ringing, Phut Phat stood up and scolded it, arching his body in a vertical stretch and making a question mark with his tail. To express his annoyance, he hopped on the desk and sharpened his claws on Webster's Unabridged. Then he spent quite some time chewing on a leather bookmark. After that he felt thirsty. He sauntered toward the powder room for a drink.

No lights were burning and no moonlight came through the windows, yet he moved through the dark rooms with assurance, side-stepping table legs and stopping to examine infinitesimal particles on the hall carpet. Nothing escaped him.

Phut Phat was lapping water, and the tip of his tail was waving rapturously from side to side, when something caused him to raise his head and listen. His tail froze. Sparrows in the backyard? Rain on the fire escape? There was silence again. He lowered his head and resumed his drinking.

A second time he was alerted. Something was happening that was not routine. His tail bushed like a squirrel's, and with his whiskers full of alarm he stepped noiselessly into the hall, peering toward the library.

Someone was on the fire escape. Something was gnawing at the library window.

Petrified, he watched—until the window opened and a dark figure slipped into the room. With one lightning glide, Phut Phat sprang to the top of the tall armoire.

There on his high perch, able to look down on the scene, he felt safe. But was it enough to feel safe? His ancestors had been watchcats in Oriental temples centuries before. They had hidden in the shadows and crouched on high walls, ready to spring on any intruder and tear his face to ribbons—just as Phut Phat shredded the Sunday paper. A primitive instinct rose in his breast, but quickly it was quelled by civilized inhibitions.

The figure in the window advanced stealthily toward the hall, and Phut Phat experienced a sense of the familiar. It was the man with the shiny stick. This time, though, his presence smelled sinister. A small blue light now glowed from the head of the cane, and instead of leaning on it the man pointed it ahead to guide his way out of the library and toward the staircase. As the intruder passed the armoire, Phut Phat's fur rose to form a sharp ridge down his spine. Instinct said, Spring at him! But vague fears held him back.

With feline stealth, the man moved downstairs, unaware of two glowing diamonds that watched him in the blackness, and Phut Phat soon heard noises in the dining room. He sensed evil. Safe on top of the armoire, he trembled.

When the man reappeared, he was carrying a bulky load, which he took to the library window. Then he crept to the third floor, and there were muffled sounds in the bedroom. Phut Phat licked his nose in apprehension.

Now the man reappeared, following a pool of blue light. As he approached the armoire, Phut Phat shifted his feet, bracing himself against something invisible. He felt a powerful compulsion to attack, and yet a fearful dismay.

111

Get him! commanded a savage impulse within him.

Stay! warned the fright throbbing in his head.

Get him! Now—now—*now!*

Phut Phat sprang at the man's head, ripping with razor claws wherever they sank into flesh.

The hideous scream that came from the intruder was like an electric shock. It sent Phut Phat sailing through space—up the stairs—into the bedroom—under the bed.

For a long time he quaked uncontrollably, his mouth parched and his ears inside-out with horror at what had happened. There was something strange and wrong about it, although its meaning eluded him. Waiting for Time to heal his confusion, he huddled there in darkness and privacy. Blood soiled his claws. He sniffed with distaste and finally was compelled to lick them clean. He did it slowly and with repugnance. Then he tucked his paws under his warm body and waited.

When One and Two came home, he sensed their arrival even before the taxicab door slammed. He should have bounded to meet them, but the experience had left him in a daze, quivering internally, weak and unsure.

He heard the rattle of the front door lock, feet climbing the stairs and the click of the light switch in the room where he waited in bewilderment under the bed.

One instantly gave a gasp, then a shriek. "John! Someone's been in this room. We've been robbed!"

Two's voice was incredulous. "What! How do you know?"

"My jewel case. Look! It's open—and empty!"

Two threw open a closet door. "Your furs are still here, Helen. What about money? Did you have any money in the house?"

"I never leave money around. But the silver! What about the silver? John, go down and see. I'm afraid to look. No! Wait a minute!" One's voice rose in panic. "Where's Phut Phat? What's happened to Phut Phat?"

"I don't know," said Two with alarm. "I haven't seen him since we came in."

They searched the house, calling his name—unaware, with their limited senses, that Phut Phat was right there under the bed, brooding over the upheaval in his small world, and now and then licking his claws.

When at last, crawling on their hands and knees, they spied two eyes glowing red under the bed, they drew him out gently. One hugged him with a rocking embrace and rubbed her face, wet and salty, on his fur, while Two stood by, stroking him with a heavy hand. Comforted and reassured, Phut Phat stopped trembling. He tried to purr, but the shock had constricted his larynx.

One continued to hold Phut Phat in her arms—and he had no will to jump down—even after two strange men were admitted to the house. They asked questions and examined all the rooms. "Everything is insured," One told them, "but the silver is irreplaceable. It's old and very rare. Is there any chance of getting it back, Lieutenant?" She fingered Phut Phat's ears nervously.

"At this point it's hard to say," the detective said. "But you may be able to help us. Have you noticed any strange incidents lately? Any unusual telephone calls?"

"Yes," said One. "Several times recently the phone has rung, and when we answered it there was no one on the line."

"That's the usual method. They wait until they know you're not at home."

One gazed into Phut Phat's eyes. "Did the phone ring tonight while we were out, Phuffy?" she asked, shaking him lovingly. "If only Phut Phat could tell us what happened! He must have had a terrifying experience. Thank heaven he wasn't harmed."

Phut Phat raised his paw to lick between his toes, still defined with human blood.

"If only Phuffy could tell us who was here."

Phut Phat paused with toes spread and pink tongue extended. He stared at One's forehead.

"Have you folks noticed any strangers in the neighborhood?" the lieutenant was asking. "Anyone who would arouse suspicion?"

Phut Phat's body tensed and his blue eyes, brimming with knowledge, bored into that spot above One's eyebrows.

"No, I can't think of anyone," she said. "Can you, John?"

Two shook his head.

"Poor Phuffy," said One. "See how he stares at me? He must be hungry. Does Phuffy want a little snack?"

Phut Phat squirmed.

"About these bloodstains on the window sill," said the detective. "Would the cat attack an intruder viciously enough to draw blood?"

"Heavens, no!" said One. "He's just a pampered little house pet. We found him hiding under the bed, scared stiff."

"And you're sure you can't remember any unusual incident lately? Has anyone come to the house who might have seen the silver or jewelry? Repairman? Window washer?"

"I wish I could be more helpful," said One, "but, honestly, I can't think of a single suspect."

Phut Phat gave up!

Wriggling free, he jumped down from One's lap and walked toward the door with head depressed and hind legs stiff with disgust. He knew who it was. He knew! The man with the shiny stick. But it was useless to try to communicate. The human mind was closed so tight that nothing important would ever penetrate. And One was so busy with her own chatter that her mind—

The jingle of keys caught Phut Phat's attention. He turned and saw Two swinging his key chain back and forth, back and forth, and saying nothing. Two always did more thinking than talking. Perhaps Phut Phat had been trying to communicate with the wrong mind. Perhaps Two was really number one in the household and One was number two.

Phut Phat froze in his position of concentration, sitting tall and compact with tail stiff. The key chain swung back and forth, and Phut Phat fastened his blue eyes on three wrinkles just underneath Two's hairline. He concentrated. The key chain swung back and forth, back and forth. Phut Phat kept concentrating.

"Wait a minute," said Two, coming out of his puzzled silence. "I just thought of something. Helen, remember that party we gave a couple of weeks ago? There was one guest we couldn't account for. A man with a silver cane."

"Why, yes! The man was so curious about the coop on the fire escape. Why didn't I think of him? Lieutenant, he was terribly interested in our Georgian silver."

Two said, "Does that suggest anything to you, Lieutenant?"

"Yes, it does." The detective exchanged nods with his partner.

"This man," One volunteered, "had a very cultivated voice and a charming manner."

"We know him," the detective said grimly. "We know his method. What you tell us fits perfectly. But we didn't know he was operating in this neighborhood again."

One said, "What mystifies me is the blood on the window sill."

Phut Phat arched his body in a long, luxurious stretch and walked from the room, looking for a soft, dark, quiet place. Now he would sleep. He felt relaxed and satisfied. He had made vital contact with a human mind, and perhaps—after all—there was hope. Someday they might learn the system, learn to open their minds and receive. They had a long way to go before they realized their potential—but there was hope.

Patricia Moyes

THE FAITHFUL CAT

The fact that Hubert Withers decided one Thursday morning not to murder his wife after all should not be ascribed to kindness, change of heart, nor any moral scruples, but to a mixture of squeamishness and cowardice, plus the realization that he could get what he wanted by other means. Hubert was a small man and had always shrunk from violence of any kind. The thought of actually killing Caroline made him feel quite nauseous. Also, there was the risk of being caught. However ingenious his plan, a husband who stood to inherit his wife's fortune would automatically be Suspect Number One.

Nevertheless, he had to have money—and very soon. It would be nice, of course, to have Caroline permanently out of the way and to come into his inheritance—but he now saw that the matter might be dealt with in a less drastic manner. If he could get her removed for even a short while and get a Power of Attorney to act on her behalf—that is, to sign checks and draw cash—all would be well.

It wasn't that Hubert particularly disliked Caroline. She wasn't a bad old thing at all really, although of course he had married her strictly for her money. She was the plain, shy daughter (and only child) of a widower who had made a fortune in the construction business in Washington, D.C., and she stood to pick up the lot when the old man died.

During her life, Caroline Todman had made few friends. At school—an extremely expensive private establishment where all the girls were by definition heiresses—her only real friend had been another girl, also plain but less shy, called Annabel: but Annabel had married the impoverished younger son of a British nobleman and was now Lady Fairley, living in a very grand Elizabethan manor house in southern England—bought with Annabel's money, naturally. Several times Annabel had written suggesting that Caroline should visit England and stay with her and her husband, but Caroline had felt too shy to make the trip alone.

Despite her plainness and shyness, Caroline had had plenty of suitors, as any girl in her position was bound to have, but old Todman, her father, swore he could pick out a fortune hunter at a hundred yards. Even Caroline herself got to be quite good at it, and this tended to increase her timidity and to put her off young men. Thus she had remained unmarried until the age of thirty.

Hubert Withers appeared to be the only man who had ever wanted her for herself alone. He, too, appeared to be very shy, and although he was reasonably good-looking he disguised the fact by wearing unbecoming steel-rimmed spectacles and a wispy moustache. He had been observing Caroline Todman's movements, and so cleverly contrived to meet her for the first time in the Georgetown Public Library. They started talking about books, and he shyly invited her out for a cup of coffee at a cheap cafe, apparently quite unaware of who she was.

Caroline was enchanted, and even old Todman grunted his approval. The young man appeared pleasant enough and seemed stupefied the first time Caroline invited him home to the family mansion, which stood in a couple of acres of garden in superfashionable Georgetown. Hubert had stammered out that he'd had no idea she was the daughter of *the* Arnold Todman. It was an excellent performance—Hubert should really have been an actor.

As it was, however, he confided frankly—but shyly—to his prospective father-in-law that he was simply an impecunious student, several years younger than Caroline, and without any means of visible support except his student grant. He was working, he said, on a definitive thesis on the impact of witchcraft on medieval European thought. As a matter of fact, it was a subject which interested him mildly, and he knew enough about it to talk convincingly to a millionaire who had started life as an unskilled building laborer.

Todman gave his consent—but on one condition. The very condition for which Hubert had been hoping. That young Withers should consign his interest in historical research to the status of a hobby and take a job with The Firm.

"Start at the bottom, my boy, as I did. You'll soon make good."

One look at Hubert had decided Arnold Todman that for this frail intellectual the bottom of the construction industry did not mean a job as a builder's laborer. Instead, Hubert was allotted a place in the more comfortable and less strenuous side of the bottom of the business—a glorified office boy, who happened to be married to the daughter of the boss.

This might have worked out very well, except for one fact. It became painfully obvious within a few months that Hubert was simply no good. It was probably just as well that Arnold Todman dropped dead of a heart attack before any of his senior staff had plucked up the courage to tell him that Hubert was, and always would be, hopeless. Arnold died happy, knowing that Caroline was married and that his son-in-law would soon make his way in The Firm. He left everything he had—including his controlling share in the business—to Caroline.

Caroline herself knew very little about The Firm, except that it provided a handsome income. She took the advice of the senior executives of the company and soon began to get a sound grasp of the business. She suggested tactfully to Hubert that since they no longer needed the extra money he should quit his so-called job and go back to the research on which he had always been so keen. Hubert agreed, with relief. His satisfaction with the situation was tempered only by the fact that Caroline, although as plain and shy as ever, kept a tight hold on the family purse-strings.

In the Todman mansion, where they now lived, the magnificent library had been handed over to Hubert for his research work and space cleared on the shelves for his books of reference. Caroline organized the house, dealt with all finances, and kept in touch with The Firm. Hubert spent lonely and frustrated hours in the library. He was regarded with great deference by the household staff.

"The Master is working on his book," the butler would say with great severity to a giggling maid or a clumsy kitchen boy. "Don't you know that he needs complete quiet?"

So Hubert got complete quiet, and it nearly drove him mad. In fact, what saved his sanity was that he began to fill in his Saharan hours by gambling on horses.

Naturally, as the husband of Caroline (nee Todman), his credit with bookmakers was excellent. Nevertheless, the fact remained that all he had was the pin-money doled out in cash by his wife—"After all, darling, you can charge everything, can't you?"—and matters had now reached a point where his creditors were demanding payment, and that without delay. He had stalled them for a while by quietly selling a valuable picture from the Blue Morning Room—a place Caroline seldom visited—but that was only a sop to the wolves. Soon the crunch must come.

As Hubert saw it, he had two alternatives. He could confess the whole thing to Caroline, who would undoubtedly pay his debts for the sake of family honor: but thenceforth his life would be untenable. Or he could kill her.

The fact that he had a third choice came to him, as has been remarked, on a Thursday morning in spring. Caroline, who had been complaining of internal pains, had been taken to the hospital for tests and observation on the Wednesday, and on Thursday Hubert was telephoned by Dr. Edwards—an old family friend as well as the Todman medical adviser.

"I'm afraid," the doctor said, "that Mrs. Withers must be operated on immediately."

"What is it?" asked Hubert, hoping he sounded suitably worried, for his heart had given an upward leap.

He was quickly disillusioned. "Oh, nothing dangerous, now that we've discovered it in time," the doctor reassured him. "She has a large but happily not malignant growth on her womb. This is undoubtedly why she hasn't had any children. I would like to think it can be removed without a complete hysterectomy, but—"

"A complete what?" said Hubert, who knew little of medical matters.

"Removal of the womb and ovaries," explained Dr. Edwards. "Not a dangerous operation—but I'm very much afraid, old man, that you'll have to face the fact that Caroline will never be able to have a baby."

This suited Hubert fine, but he made appropriate noises of regret. It was then that Dr. Edwards produced his life-saving bombshell.

"I must impress upon you, Mr. Withers," he said, "that although relatively simple medically, this operation can have quite serious mental aftereffects on a woman. The surgeon, you see, is doing in half an hour what nature does gradually over a period of many years. The result is that some women suffer severe postoperative depression. I don't want to frighten you, but sometimes they may have delusions and even become slightly unbalanced for a while. So I want you to be especially kind and considerate to your wife when she comes home from the hospital."

"Of course," said Hubert.

"The best thing," the doctor went on, "is for the woman to get a pet of some sort—a surrogate child, if you like. She may well transfer to it the pent-up affection for the child she now knows she can never have."

"Caroline has a pet already," said Hubert. "A Siamese cat." He tried to keep the dislike out of his voice. He had always hated the creature, with its steady blue eyes and supercilious manner.

"And she's fond of it?" pursued Dr. Edwards.

"She dotes on it," said Hubert. "She's even found a Siamese name for it—Pakdee, which means the faithful cat."

"Then it's splendid," said the doctor. "The cat will probably be able to do more for her than either you or I can."

A plan was forming in Hubert's mind. He said, "I was just thinking—when she's strong enough, it might be a good thing for her to take a vacation."

"Excellent. Excellent."

"I won't be able to get away myself," said Hubert, "but Caroline has an old school-friend who is married and lives in England. Lady Annabel Fairley. Annabel has been begging her to go and visit."

"A most satisfactory scheme, if Caroline agrees," said the doctor. "I wouldn't have liked her to go to some hotel on her own, but a visit to a friend and a complete change of scene—yes, by all means."

*   *   *

So in a couple of weeks, Caroline was back from the hospital and recovering rapidly. She appeared to suffer from none of the ill effects the doctor had predicted, but this didn't prevent Hubert's fertile imagination from inventing them.

Each time the doctor called—for even today doctors will pay house calls on people like Caroline—Hubert managed to have a word with him alone before he left.

"Our patient seem to be making excellent progress," the doctor would say.

"Well—yes and no, Doctor."

"How do you mean?"

"Of course you wouldn't notice it just visiting, but you did warn me, and I think you ought to know that the thing is becoming an obsession."

"Thing? What thing, Mr. Withers?"

"This business of the Siamese cat. She won't let him out of her sight." Indeed, Pakdee had been snuggled up with Caroline on the daybed where she was resting when the doctor arrived. Hubert went on, "She even has this crazy idea that somebody is out to harm the cat. I can't help feeling it's not healthy for somebody to be so wrapped up in a mere animal."

"I told you, Mr. Withers, it's quite natural." Dr. Edwards was reassuring. "It will pass."

A few days later, while Benson, the butler, was serving cocktails, Hubert suggested to Caroline that she might visit the Fairleys in England. Caroline was enthusiastic. Since her marriage and her involvement with the business, she had become much more self-reliant. "What a good idea, Hubert. I'll call her tomorrow. You'll come, too, won't you?"

"I wish I could, darling," said Hubert, "but I've had a word with Bentinck"—Bentinck was The Firm's managing director—"and he doesn't feel we should both be out of the country at the same time. Besides, I've never even met Annabel. You'll have much more fun on your own."

"Yes, perhaps I will," said Caroline cheerfully. "I wish I could take Dee-Dee, but one can't, with the silly British quarantine regulations. Still, you'll look after him for me, won't you, Hubert?"

Dee-Dee was Caroline's pet-name for Pakdee. It revolted Hubert almost as much as the cat's parlor trick, which he would perform for nobody but Caroline. Every time Caroline returned home after an outing, she would stand in the hallway and call "Dee-Dee!" in a particular tone of voice. Wherever the cat might be, he would come hurtling at the sound and with one leap would be in Caroline's arms, his dark-brown front legs embracing her and his face buried in the hollow of her neck. The whole thing made Hubert feel slightly sick.

Now, however, all that he said was "Of course I will, darling, you know that."

Soon he was able to report to Dr. Edwards that Caroline seemed much better and had agreed to go and visit her friend in England.

It was on the morning of the doctor's final checkup visit, while Caroline was sitting on the sofa with Pakdee on her lap, that Hubert said, "So it's all fixed? You go to England on the twentieth?"

"That's right," said Caroline. "The agency has made me a first-class booking on the lunchtime flight."

In the same pleasant, even tone, Hubert said, "I may as well tell you now that as soon as you've gone I intend to get rid of that cat."

"It should be—" Caroline did a double-take. "You intend to *what?*"

"Get rid of Pakdee," said Hubert. "I shall have him destroyed. Make no mistake about that, my dear." He left the room.

Dr. Edwards found his patient in near-hysterical tears. As far as he could make out, her husband had threatened to have the cat destroyed as soon as she left for England. She absolutely refused to go. Nothing would make her. Hubert must have gone mad. When the doctor suggested that she might have misunderstood her husband, Caroline clasped the cat even more firmly to her heart and sobbed that the doctor was as bad as Hubert and probably in league with him. Dr. Edwards persuaded her to take a sedative and went in search of Hubert.

Hubert sighed deeply. "Oh, dear," he said. "So it's started all over again. How very distressing. I suppose it's the idea of going abroad that's upset her. She's seemed so much more rational lately."

Edwards cleared his throat. "I don't suppose, Mr. Withers, that you might inadvertently have made any remark that might have led her to think—"

"Of course not!" Hubert was suitably indignant. "Why, only the other day I assured her I would do everything to care for the cat while she was away. I believe Benson was there, serving drinks. He must have heard me. I'll ring for him now."

The doctor was deeply embarrassed. "My dear Mr. Withers, there's no need. Of course I believe what you say."

Hubert, however, was adamant. "No, no, I insist." His finger was already on the bell. "This is all so worrying in its implications that I think you should feel convinced about poor Caroline's delusions."

Benson appeared, and dutifully confirmed what Hubert had said. Of course, he added, in answer to the doctor's questions, the cat was Madam's, and Madam had a special affection for him. On the other hand, he had never known the Master to be other than most kind and considerate to the animal. When he saw him, that was. Madam and the cat spent most of their time together.

The cat was not allowed in the kitchen, but Madam always fed him herself in the butler's pantry. While Madam was away, he, Benson, would be happy to undertake this duty personally. Benson was an English butler of the old school, inherited with the house from Arnold Todman, and he had known and been fond of Caroline since her childhood. In listing Caroline's scant number of friends, Benson should have been included.

"Well," said Dr. Edwards when Benson had withdrawn, "this is, as you say, a sad setback. I feel it more important than ever that she should get away for a vacation. On the other hand, since she can't take the cat with her, we must somehow convince her that she simply imagined your threat. Shall we talk to her together?"

They talked to Caroline together, and they talked to her separately. Hubert protested over and over again that he would cherish Pakdee. Benson promised to hand-feed him and to let Caroline know at once by telephone if anything seemed to be the matter with him.

Finally, Caroline was convinced. In fact, she was more than convinced, she was frightened—for she now truly believed she had been suffering from delusions. It's always a little scary to feel that one may be going slightly mad.

Dr. Edwards, speaking privately to Hubert, said that he had high hopes that Caroline's vacation in England would put an end to any further symptoms, especially when she returned to find her cat in good health. However, he added, changing to a more somber vocal gear, if delusions still persisted on her return, it might be necessary for her to take a cure in a quiet nursing home for a few weeks.

Hubert saw Caroline off at Dulles Airport, making all the right gestures and saying all the right things. Just as the doors were closing on the mobile lounge which was to take London-bound passengers to their waiting jumbo jet, he said, softly and pleasantly, "I shall have Pakdee destroyed this evening. Goodbye, darling. Have a wonderful time."

Caroline cried all the way to London, despite—or perhaps because of—the excellent champagne with which the air hostess plied her, hoping to cheer her up. As soon as she arrived at Fairley Hall, which was after midnight by British time, she insisted on telephoning home and speaking to Benson. He assured her that Pakdee was hale and hearty and enjoying his supper—it was seven o'clock in the evening, Washington time.

"I'm delighted you had a smooth journey, Madam," said Benson. "I'll fetch the Master to speak to you right away."

"No. No, don't do that, Benson," said Caroline. "Don't tell him I called." She rang off.

* * *

121

Early next morning, Hubert said to Benson, "I've been looking up Pakdee's health card. He's due for his yearly shots very soon."

"Yes, sir," said Benson. "Madam was remarking the same thing only the other day."

"Well, no time like the present. Call the Animal Hospital, will you, and make an appointment for this morning? Then find me the cat basket and I'll take him along."

So a couple of hours later Hubert drove to the Animal Hospital with a surly, silent Pakdee glaring from his wicker basket on the passenger seat of the Jaguar. The cat was duly given his inoculations and the details entered on his health card. On the way home, however, Hubert took a side street, doubled back, and drove to an entirely different address. It was that of a veterinarian he'd never met but had picked from the Yellow Pages on account of the fact that he lived in an outlying suburb to the south of the city, in Virginia. His name was Michaelson, and Hubert—identifying himself as Mr. Robinson—had made an appointment with him from a public phone booth before leaving Dulles Airport the previous day.

Dr. Michaelson was a tall, thin man with a long, slightly vague face and long-fingered, sensitive hands. Pakdee calmed down as soon as he got into the surgery and allowed himself to be lifted out of the basket.

"Well," said Michaelson admiringly, "you sure have a beautiful and valuable cat here, Mr. Robinson. He seems in fine fettle. Is anything wrong, or does he just need shots?"

"He needs more than shots," said Hubert. "He's to be destroyed."

"You can't mean that, Mr. Robinson."

"Oh, it's nothing to do with me," said Hubert crossly. "It's my wife. She bought him as a toy and now she's tired of him. He's got to go."

"And there's nothing the matter with him?"

"Not that I know of."

The vet looked thoughtful. He said, "I never like to destroy a young, healthy animal. Especially such a fine specimen. Are you sure you wouldn't like me to find a good home for him?"

"I want to see that cat killed," said Hubert with unattractive firmness. "I'm paying you to do it. The cat is mine, and I can do as I like with him. Come on, get it over with."

"You're absolutely adamant, Mr. Robinson?"

"Absolutely. And I want to see it done."

Michaelson sighed. "Very well," he said. He went to a cupboard and began to prepare a syringe. "Do you want to take the body away with you?"

"Certainly not."

"Some people," said Michaelson, gently ironic, "care enough about their pets to bury them in their gardens. However, if you wish me to dispose of him—"

"Yes I do. Do what you like—just get rid of him."

"Very well." Michaelson stroked Pakdee gently. "Come on then, old fellow. This won't hurt."

Hubert tried not to look as the needle went in, but somehow he couldn't keep his eyes off the cat. Pakdee turned his head with his last strength and gave Hubert such a look of concentrated hatred from his deep-blue eyes that Hubert took an instinctive step backward. Then Pakdee keeled over and lay still.

Hubert pulled himself together. Averting his eyes from the body, he said, "Well, that's that. Thank you. What do I owe you?"

Michaelson said, "Nothing, Mr. Robinson. I never make a charge for destroying animals—whether it's to put them out of their misery or whether they're in perfect health." The tone of his voice exactly matched Pakdee's dying stare.

Hubert picked up the basket and made his escape. As he passed through the waiting room, he felt acutely conscious of the empty basket he was carrying. The only occupant waiting to see the doctor was a severe-faced middle-aged lady who also held a cat basket, which was occupied by a nondescript tabby.

"I'm sorry to see you've had to leave your cat with the doctor," she remarked. "Is it something serious or is he just boarding?"

Hubert muttered something about just boarding and hurried out to the car. He didn't for the moment feel up to anything more than finding a bar and having a stiff drink. Everywhere he looked, he seemed to see Pakdee's eyes. It was unfortunate that in the course of his so-called research he had just been reading a book on the connection between cats and witchcraft. Perhaps Caroline was a witch and Pakdee had been her familiar spirit. He ordered another drink and told himself not to be a fool. After all, his plan was only half complete. Pakdee had gone forever, but there was the question of his successor.

After an hour or so, Hubert felt strong enough to resume his journey, with the empty cat basket as passenger. This time he drove around the Beltway and off into the northernmost Maryland suburbs to another address he'd found in the Yellow Pages. This was a private humane society, which he'd picked as being as far as possible distant from the Michaelson surgery. The society, which announced in its advertisement that it never destroyed a healthy animal, acted as a lost-and-found agency and a sort of adoption society for cats. Hubert had also telephoned them from Dulles, giving his name as Mr. Green. His wife, he said, had set her heart on having a seal-point Siamese cat, having just lost her elderly but much-loved one. Did they have any for adoption?

"We don't have any kittens at the moment." Hubert had been surprised to hear a masculine voice on the line. He had always supposed that these places were run by cranky old ladies.

"Oh, we don't want a kitten," said Hubert quickly. "We want an adult cat. About two years old."

"Ah, then I think we can help you. Adult animals are always more difficult to place. Seal-point Siamese, you said? Yes, we have no less than three."

"I'll be along after lunch tomorrow," Hubert said.

He lunched in a small Maryland restaurant where he knew he wouldn't be recognized, and then drove to the Society's address, which turned out to be a small suburban house with half an acre of garden.

The whole place seemed to Hubert to be swarming with cats of all ages, sizes, and colors—some in spacious wire runs, some roaming freely. A covey of them were gently shooed away by the benign elderly gentleman who opened the front door, introducing himself as Mr. O'Donnell.

"Ah, Mr. Green," he beamed. "So nice to see you. Please come in. I'll take you to the drawing room—that's the one place cats are not allowed." He ushered Hubert into a small, shabbily furnished room. "I daresay you find this a rather strange establishment, but it's very worthwhile work. Makes a contribution, you know."

Hubert felt sure that he, too, would be expected to make a contribution. He had the money with him.

Mr. O'Donnell was still talking. "A seal-point Siamese, I think you said. About two years old."

"That's right," said Hubert. "A neutered male."

"A neutered male? You didn't mention that. That cuts down the choice a little, but, yes, we do have two. I'll fetch them and you can choose."

Left alone, Hubert ran over his plan in his mind. It seemed to him a good one. All Siamese cats, in his view, looked very much alike—except perhaps to the eye of love. Certainly none of the domestic staff—not even Benson—knew Pakdee well enough to be able to identify him positively. Dr. Edwards had only seen the cat on a couple of fleeting occasions. Only Caroline would accept no substitutes—especially in view of the fact that the new cat would certainly not respond to her call with Pakdee's parlor-trick. He knew—because he'd been listening in—about Caroline's call to Benson the previous evening, and guessed that a similar call would be made daily. Benson would be uniformly reassuring. So when Caroline returned and claimed that the cat in the house was not her cat—well, Dr. Edwards would certainly prescribe the quiet nursing home, which would enable Hubert to get the Power of Attorney he needed. Even a couple of weeks would be long enough.

He was aroused from his reverie by the return of Mr. O'Donnell, carrying a cat under each arm. "There we are," he said, putting the animals down on the floor. "Delightful creatures, both of them. Take your choice."

There was never any doubt. One of the cats was noticeably larger than Pakdee, and his points were a much lighter shade of brown. The other, however, was perfectly possible. True, his whole coat was paler than Pakdee's, fluffier and less sleek, and his eyes were not only lighter blue, but mild and amiable. However, he was just about the right size and Hubert felt sure he would fool everybody except Caroline.

"There's no charge for the cat, of course," Mr. O'Donnell assured him, "but any little donation you feel inclined to make—"

Hubert made his donation and popped the counterfeit Pakdee into the basket, where he sat purring, his gentle eyes half shut. In fact, by the time Hubert had reiterated to Mr. O'Donnell that they had owned a Siamese before and therefore did not require the leaflets on care and feeding the Society provided, the cat had curled up in Pakdee's basket and was sound asleep.

Benson met Hubert at the front door and took the basket from him. "I hope the little fellow is quite all right, sir," he said. "We were a mite worried when you didn't return for luncheon."

"Sorry about that, Benson," said Hubert. "Matter of business I had to attend to, which involved lunching out." He hesitated. "Pakdee seems a little lethargic," he added. "Probably the effect of the shots. But the doctor says he's in excellent health. Just give him a light meal tonight."

"As you say, sir."

Hubert had been right. Caroline telephoned again that evening and spoke to Benson. When she heard that Pakdee had been taken to the hospital for shots, she panicked again—to the consternation of her friend Annabel. Only after she had phoned her veterinarian at his home and learned from him that Mr. Withers had indeed brought Pakdee in that morning for his inoculations did Caroline calm down. Annabel had a word with her husband and together they decided to write to Hubert and tell him they were worried about Caroline's nerves and her apparent obsession about her cat.

The letter arrived the day before Caroline's return, and was even more than Hubert could have hoped for. He called Dr. Edwards at once—he had intended to do so, anyway, but this gave him a God-sent opportunity. He suggested that the doctor should arrange to be at the house to welcome Caroline home and see her reunion with her beloved cat. The doctor agreed.

During Caroline's absence, Hubert had barely set eyes on the Siamese, who had been entirely in Benson's care. He had taken pains, however, to inquire frequently about the cat's well being and had been assured by Benson that the little fellow was fine, eating well and quite his old self. Very satisfactory.

On the day Caroline was due back, Hubert entertained the doctor to lunch and left him to his postprandial coffee as he went off to Dulles to meet his wife.

Caroline was looking remarkably well. She inquired at once about Pakdee and Hubert assured her that he was in good form. "He missed you, of course, darling," he said, "but Benson and I tried to make it up to him. He'll be thrilled to see you."

On the drive back down the lovely George Washington Parkway, Caroline chattered happily about England and her friends. Hubert was silent. He was bracing himself, with a mixture of emotions, for the scene that would shortly follow. It was bound to be unpleasant, and he disliked unpleasantness. There would be hysterics, and he disliked hysterics. Nevertheless, his plan would work. It couldn't fail. And Dr. Edwards himself would be there to see it.

Benson heard the car in the drive and had the front door open before Caroline had reached the top step.

"Welcome home, Madam!"

"Oh, Benson, it's nice to be back." Caroline came into the big hallway as the doctor came out of the drawing room. "Why, Dr. Edwards, I didn't know you'd be here! How very kind of you! Yes, I feel splendid—I had a marvelous vacation!" She put down her handbag and as Hubert came in through the front door she called, "Dee-Dee! I'm home, Dee-Dee!"

The cat must have been waiting on the stairs, on the landing where there was a window overlooking the front door. He came down the last flight like a flying bomb and leapt into Caroline's arms, purring his delight. And, as Caroline caressed him, he looked at Hubert over her shoulder. The old hard-blue eyes now gleaming with triumph. The old sleek coat. Pakdee.

"My Dee-Dee," Caroline was murmuring, "my Pakdee! My faithful cat."

It was Hubert who spent the next few weeks in the quiet nursing home. Soon after his release from it, he and Caroline were divorced. When last heard of, Hubert was in California, looking for another heiress. He was somehow managing to live on the meager allowance Caroline's lawyers sent him every month. The allowance would have been much larger—for Caroline was a generous soul—had Hubert not, in his frenzy, declared that she was a witch and that he had seen Pakdee die with his own eyes.

Dr. Edwards tried to put in a good word for Hubert. "He was mentally deranged, Mrs. Withers. How could he possibly have seen the cat die when it was obviously alive and well? I think you must make allowances."

"He had the intention," said Caroline. "That is what matters."

Funnily enough, it was only a few days after Caroline's return that Dr. Michaelson visited the private humane society in Maryland, bringing with him half a dozen delightful kittens for adoption.

"By the way," be said, "I suppose you had no difficulty in finding a home for that beautiful Siamese?"

"Which one?" asked Mr. O'Donnell.

"Oh," said Mrs. O'Donnell, her severe face softening into a very sweet smile, "John means the one I picked up from his surgery. Some miserable man had brought him in to be destroyed because he said his wife was tired of him—the cat, I mean."

"I suppose I should have destroyed him," said John Michaelson, "but he was an absolute beauty, and in perfect health. I took no money and got Robinson's permission to dispose of the cat as I wished. By that tune I'd given him a pre-operation anesthetic shot and the man went away convinced he was dead. I knew Grace was in the waiting room and could bring him back here right away."

"That's right," said Grace O'Donnell. "I gave him a bath and blow-dry—he emerged several shades lighter, I can tell you—and some eyedrops I thought he needed. Then I went out shopping and, believe it or not, by the time I came back Patrick had found a home for him with a—a Mr. Green, wasn't it, Patrick?"

"Yes, my dear. A nice guy, he seemed. Had had Siamese before. Wanted this one as a present for his wife, who'd just lost hers."

"Mr. Green seems to have a much nicer wife than Mr. Robinson," said Grace O'Donnell. "I'm sure the poor creature is in a very happy home now."

He is, Mrs. O'Donnell. He is.

A.H.Z. Carr

A CASE OF CATNAPPING

The biggest fee I ever got was for finding a cat. That's the way it goes. I have solved murders and traced stolen jewels, but the only time anybody ever paid me 5,000 smackers, it was for a cat. I grant you, not an ordinary cat. This was the great Dizzy.

The funny part of it was that before there was even a case, the wife and I had been to the Orpheum just to see that act. *Dizzy—The World's First Performing Cat—With Dave Knight*—that's the way they billed it. My wife is a nut about cats—we have two of our own—and when she saw this publicity story in the newspaper, she read it to me.

It told how this Dave Knight had been a small-time entertainer, with a corny routine of comedy, tap-dancing, and ventriloquism—not very good at any of them, and pretty near down and out—when one night on the street this kitten rubs against his leg. It is just a handful of skin, bones, fleas, and miaows, and he does not care much about cats, but he says, "O.K., some milk," puts her in his pocket, and takes her to his little walk-up apartment in Greenwich Village. He feeds her and cleans her up, and the next thing you know, he has a cat, for he cannot bring himself to kick her out.

She turns out to be a kind of genius—as smart as any trained dog or chimpanzee—smarter, even. The article tells how Knight named her Dizzy when he noticed her doing somersaults while she played with a piece of string. Little by little he taught her tricks, until she would do them even on a stage and was not frightened by the lights and noise, as long as Knight was there.

Vaudeville was coming back just then, and when the booking agents looked over the act, they realized it was something new. Knight and Dizzy crashed the big time, touring all over the country. It says in the article there are supposed to be ten million house cats in the world, but Dizzy is unique—the only cat that ever got into the upper tax brackets. A thousand a week Knight was making, and he had Dizzy's life insured for $100,000.

The wife said she had to see it before she would believe it, and the next thing I knew we had our coats on and were headed for the Orpheum. We came in during an act called *The Three Graces—and the Disgrace* (a comedy dance team, and good too)—three girls, one a redhead, one a blonde, and the third a brunette, and a guy with a very funny dance routine. Next was *McIntyre, the Irish Magician,* who had a midget dressed as a leprechaun, and who did a lot of neat magic— mind-reading, card tricks, sword tricks, disappearances—the works. But it was Dizzy that wowed the audience.

Quite a cat. She had long silky gray fur, crossed with tigerish black stripes, a white bib and ruff, white boots, and a tail like a silver fox. Then there was her face. Most cats look pretty much alike, but this one had big golden eyes, long white whiskers, and an eager, innocent, gentle expression that made my wife coo.

She was the whole act. Knight is just a freckle-faced kid with a friendly grin—the college type, with a crew-cut and glasses—and smart enough not to compete with Dizzy. He started very easy, making her sit up, lie down, and play dead, like a dog. Anything a dog could do, he said, Dizzy could do better. She stood on her hind legs, with little boxing gloves on her front paws, and hit a little punching bag that he rigged up, in time to music. Then she did a series of somer-saults and back flips, and jumped through three moving hoops. The orchestra played a rhumba, and they did a dance—very cute—with Knight tapping, and Dizzy moving around on her hind legs, with a little wiggle that made the audience roar.

The ventriloquist stunt was good, too. She sat on his knee, like a dummy, and he made her seem to speak in a high-pitched, miaowing voice, opening and shutting her mouth at the same time. At the end of the act he set up a contraption that looked like a little xylophone, with thin strips of metal hanging down loose. When she would hit one of the strips with her paw, it struck a note; and believe it or not, she jumps around, bangs the strips, and out comes *Home, Sweet Home.*

The audience loved it, and my wife couldn't talk about anything else for a week. So when my phone rang next Sunday morning and a fellow says, "Are you Jack Terry? This is Dave Knight," I knew who he was. He said the manager of the Orpheum—Eddie Thompson, who I went to School with—had suggested that he get in touch with me, and could he see me right away.

I told him sure, meet me at my office. When he showed up, there was a girl with him, and he introduced her as Miss Maribeth Lewis. I recognized her—one of The Three Graces—the dark-haired one. Very young, with one of these wide-mouthed, attractive faces, and a figure right out of a dream, as I knew from seeing her on the stage. Both of them were looking pale and worried, and Knight got right down to business.

"Dizzy is gone," he said. "I want you to find her."

"Look," I said. "I'm a detective, just an ordinary private eye, as they call them on TV. What you want is the SPCA or something. I'm sorry your cat is gone, but I wouldn't know how to begin to find a cat."

Knight was no dope. He did not argue. He just said, "I will pay you five thousand dollars if you find her. That's every cent I have saved so far, but you can have it."

"That's a lot of money," I said. "But suppose she has been hit by a truck or something."

Knight looked like *he* had been hit by the truck, and the girl, Maribeth, said, "Please don't say that, Mr. Terry!"

"Look," I said, "I don't want to scare you, but you know how it is when a cat is loose on city streets, with the traffic and all. Anything can happen. Besides, it isn't like she would be a total loss. How about that hundred grand you get if she is dead?"

"You don't understand," said Knight. "That cat is part of me. I wouldn't sell her for a million bucks. As far as the insurance goes, it only covers death under certain conditions. It does not apply if she is lost."

"Is she lost?"

"I don't know. I can't understand it." He kept running his hand through his thatch of sandy hair. "You don't know how I watch over that cat. She is hardly ever out of my sight. She sleeps in my bed, and we even eat together."

"Maybe she's just taking a day off," I said, trying to encourage him. "We've got a female cat, and she likes to go out on the town now and then."

"Dizzy has never done that," said Knight, shaking his head.

I said, "Have you thought about offering a reward?"

"There is a tag on Dizzy's collar," he explained, "giving my name and offering five hundred dollars to anyone who finds her if she is lost and returns her to me or to the police. And I have checked with the police—they are keeping a lookout for her."

I had been sizing him up. He did not strike me as the type who would get rid of his cat for the insurance. I knew my wife would never forgive me if I did not try to find Dizzy for him, so although I was not hopeful, I said, "Let's leave it like this. If I find her alive and in good shape, we can talk about a bonus. If she is dead, I get only my regular fee and expenses. Okay? Now tell me exactly what happened. How did you lose her?"

Knight said, "It was last night, in the theater. I was waiting in the wings for McIntyre the Magician to finish. I always stand there for maybe ten minutes before I go on, with Dizzy in my arms, so she can get used to the noise and lights."

He was pretty emotional, you could tell, but he gave me the facts straight and fast. "Then Barton—that's Bill Barton, he's the Disgrace in Maribeth's act—he called to me. He wanted to show me a loose piece of rope that was hanging down just over where Dizzy does her hoop act. He was afraid it might make her nervous. You couldn't see it from where I was standing, so I put Dizzy in her box and walked back to where Bill was."

"Wait a second. Did you leave the box open?"

"No, I latched it. It is really a big leather traveling case that I had specially built for her. She couldn't get out. Not unless somebody opened the box."

"Then somebody did," I said. "Well, go on."

"Bill was right. The rope was swaying just enough so it might have distracted Dizzy. I went after a stagehand and got him to go up and pull the rope out of the way."

"If you were on the stage," I said, "how come the audience couldn't see you?"

"McIntyre does the first part of his act before a close backdrop. I was behind the backdrop."

"How long were you away from Dizzy's box, all told?" I asked him.

"Not more than three minutes. At first I thought maybe some busybody had unlatched the box to look at her."

Maribeth said, "People are always trying to pet her."

"But," said Knight, "if Dizzy had jumped out of the box, she would have come to me. She always does. She just wasn't around. We searched everywhere—backstage, the wings, the dressing rooms. I called to her—she always comes running when I call, but she didn't show up. After McIntyre finished his act, I had to tell Mr. Thompson I couldn't go on. He explained to the audience what had happened, and asked them to let us know if any of them saw the cat—thinking it might have got out front somehow. But nobody had seen it."

I said, "You figure she was taken out of the box deliberately—stolen, is that it?"

"That's what must have happened," Knight said. "But who would do a thing like that? Everybody in the theater loves that cat, and is my friend. And where could they have hidden her? How could they have got her out of the theater without somebody noticing? It just doesn't make sense."

I chewed that over for a minute, and then I said, "Excuse me for getting personal—but did you and Miss Lewis just happen to come here at the same time?"

They looked at each other, and Knight said, "It's no secret. We're engaged. At least—" He stopped.

"Dave!" said Maribeth. "You know perfectly well we could make out." She turned to me. "We're going to get married when we finish our current bookings. But now he keeps saying that without Dizzy he doesn't amount to anything in the profession, and he has no right to ask me to team up with him. As if a cat—even

Dizzy—should be allowed to decide how people should live their lives. Isn't that ridiculous, Mr. Terry?"

"Ridiculous," I agreed, looking her over—a really sumptuous dish. "How long have you known each other?"

"Oh," she said, "for several months. We have been traveling on the same circuit. It was in New Orleans that we really knew—wasn't it, darling?"

Knight nods, and says, "Yesterday the world looked wonderful. Today—" He didn't finish.

"Well," I said, "let me think aloud for a minute, and don't hold it against me if I say something wrong. I'm just groping, you understand. You really love that cat, don't you? You think about her as if she was human."

"She is practically human. Of course I love her."

I put a cigar in my mouth, and lighted it, thinking hard. Then I said, "My wife once made me read a novel by a Frenchwoman—Colette, her name was—where a dame is so jealous of her husband's cat that she tries to kill it."

A second went by before Knight reacted. Then he exploded. "I thought you had some sense. You're crazy!"

But it was Maribeth I was watching. Her big, dark eyes flashed, but she only said, very quiet, "Mr. Terry, you're wrong. I love Dizzy, and I love Dave, and I'm not a murderess—or a kidnapper."

"Just testing," I said. I figured she was O.K. A woman who would consider killing a cat murder wouldn't kill it—or kidnap it. "Excuse it, please. Now let's get back to the facts. Knight, when you were standing in the wings with Dizzy, did you see anyone hanging around?"

"Not a soul. Nobody came near us."

"After you told the stagehand to take care of the rope, you went back to the box. You still didn't see anybody nearby?"

He shook his head.

"Everybody was backstage. They were just lifting the backdrop for the last part of McIntyre's act. The only person I could see from where I stood was McIntyre."

Something clicked in my mind. "How about the midget? The leprechaun? Doesn't he go offstage a couple of times?"

"Little Pat? Wait. You're right. He does go off once or twice to bring in little props for McIntyre. I suppose he must have passed Dizzy's box a couple of times. I guess I was so used to him, I didn't pay any attention."

"But surely," said Maribeth, "Pat wouldn't steal the cat."

This seemed like a good chance to make like Sherlock Holmes, which always impresses the clients, so I said, "When you have eliminated the impossible, that which remains—no matter how improbable—must be the truth. The way I see it, Pat the midget is it. He was near the cat's box. He could have stooped down, unlatched the box, and taken the cat out."

"But what would he have done with it?" Knight asked. "He had to be back on stage in a minute."

I cleared my throat—for my big idea. "Doesn't McIntyre put the leprechaun in a cabinet and make him disappear, the last part of his act?"

Knight jerked up straight. "You're right!" he said,

"Look at the facts. You are off looking for a stagehand. The cabinet that McIntyre uses for the disappearance trick is behind the backdrop—out of sight of the audience, and out of your sight, too. Nobody is around. It probably wouldn't take Pat more than a couple of seconds to carry the cat to the cabinet and put her inside. Let's say he knows how to work the trick. The cat disappears. Then he simply picks up his prop and goes onstage again with McIntyre."

Maribeth said, "But in that case, wouldn't Dizzy have come out when McIntyre opened the cabinet?"

Knight jumped to his feet. "No, that trick is just a new version of an old gag—works with a trapdoor. I've seen it. The trap goes down to a room in the basement. That's what must have happened!"

He was starting for the door. "Take it easy," I said. "Do you know where we could find the midget now?"

"I saw him in the hotel this morning," said Maribeth. "And—oh! I just thought of something. He had a piece of sticking plaster on his face. I thought he had cut himself shaving."

"That does it," I said. "Let's go."

"The hell with the midget," said Knight. "Let's find Dizzy. She may still be down in that basement."

I agreed we should go to the theater first, and we piled into my car. There was a watchman on duty at the theater, and he let us in. Knight was so impatient he wanted to run. Right under the stage there was a big room with several ladders leading to trapdoors above. It was empty, though.

There was one window in the room, at the back, and it was open. Knight swore and looked sick. "She could have got out that way," he said.

The window opened on a narrow alley. We went out there and walked up and down, while Knight called, "Dizzy! Dizzy, baby!" No use. Not a sign of a cat. "This is terrible," he said. "Somebody must have taken her away. If she was loose, she would still be here. She has a wonderful homing sense."

I said, "Let's go to the hotel. I want to talk to the little leprechaun."

We found Pat in the Coffee Shop of the hotel, having lunch alone. Steak, no less. He was only about three feet high, and dressed very dapper. Sure enough, he had a big piece of adhesive on his face.

I didn't waste any time. "Pat," I said, "what's under the plaster?"

He turned pale and said in his piping voice, "A cut. I cut myself."

"Mind if I look?" I said.

He tried to get away, but Knight held him, and I pulled off the tape. There was no mistaking the mark—three short parallel scratches, deep enough to draw blood. Dizzy was evidently a lady who didn't like to be roughhoused.

At first, Pat clammed up—wouldn't say a word. So, sitting there at the luncheon table, I reconstructed what must have happened—everything he had done, step by step. "You don't even have to tell us who put you up to it," I said.

"McIntyre," Knight said, real grim.

"No," I said. "Your friend Bill Barton. How much did he pay you, Pat?"

The midget called Barton several words, and said, "He talked!"

Maribeth and Knight looked stunned. She said, "I can't believe it."

"Obvious, my dear Watson," I said, "from the first. Barton got Knight out of the way with that prearranged business about the rope while Pat made the snatch. And Barton has a motive. If you marry Knight, you break up his act. And maybe," I added, "he has other ideas about who you ought to marry, Miss Lewis."

Her face showed she thought I was right.

"He said," squeaked the midget, opening up at last and talking to Knight, "he just wanted to keep the cat for a little while to get you out of his hair. So you couldn't finish your bookings. He thought if Maribeth didn't see you for a while, he might be able to beat your time."

"We'll see you later," I told the midget. "Enjoy your ill-gotten steak while you can. Do you know the penalty for kidnapping? And don't try to tell me it was only catnapping."

We had Maribeth call Barton on the hotel house phone to make sure he was in his room. She didn't say we were with her. When he opened his door to her knock and saw the three of us, he didn't like it. On stage, he had been made up as a bum, but standing there in his dressing gown he looked very distinguished—one of the tall, dark, and handsome boys.

Knight didn't stand on ceremony. He pushed Barton into a chair and stood over him, yelling, "You skunk, give me back my cat or I'll break your neck."

It took Barton only a few seconds to realize there was no use trying to lie out of it. Either he delivered the cat, I told him, or we would put him behind bars. That reached him. "I haven't got her," he said. "Believe me, I haven't. It was just a wild impulse. I'm in love with Maribeth, too. And I had to try to protect my act. You know the old saying—all's fair in love and war."

I hate guys who talk like that. "All right," I said, "then this is war." With that I cuffed him, hard, on the side of his head. "Spill it," I said. "Where's the cat?"

He rubbed his head and said, "She got away."

"What do you mean she got away?" Knight shouted.

Barton told us that after Pat had dropped the cat through the trapdoor under the magic cabinet, and Knight had gone to look for a stagehand, he had rushed down to the basement to get Dizzy. It was his idea to smuggle her out of the theater and keep her somewhere for a while. But she wasn't there. Somebody had left the basement window open, and she had got out. He had never seen her.

I believed him, and so did Knight, who started running his hand through his hair again. "Something must have happened to her," he groaned. "Otherwise she would have been reported by now."

Maribeth said, "Oh, Dave, darling," and he put his arms around her. I thought that was a good moment to give Barton a brief description of his ancestry and his future. Then we left him sitting there, crushed, and went back to the theater. I asked Knight again about his insurance policy. The way it was written, the company wasn't responsible if the cat was stolen or ran away while unguarded. Technically, that was what had happened, so it didn't seem as if Knight had a chance to collect. The only thing that could help him was to find Dizzy—pronto.

I didn't see much that I could do, but I felt I ought to try to earn my day's pay. When we reached the alleyway next to the theater, I stopped and said, "What we need now is psychology—cat psychology. Where would a cat go that jumped out of that basement window? I am assuming Dizzy is alive and able to navigate. Then she must be at a place where she is out of sight—because otherwise someone would have found her and brought her back for the reward. And it is probably a place that she likes—because otherwise she would have tried to come back to the theater and to Knight."

Knight nodded. "Yes," he said. "That makes sense." He was so eager to hope, it was pathetic.

"Now," I said, "what is it that would attract a cat like Dizzy so much that she would be content to stay away?"

"Could it be food?" Maribeth said.

"No," said Knight. "She is a dainty eater, and always gets her meals on schedule, and she never lets anybody else feed her. You couldn't keep her away just with food—not even caviar, which she loves."

"Look," I said. "She may have aristocratic tastes, but she is still a cat. What is the main interest of a female cat—especially one that has never had a boy friend?"

"Of course!" Maribeth said. "I bet that's it."

"I don't believe it," said Dave.

"You're just jealous," said Maribeth. "What could be more natural? I'm female myself. I know."

"Tomcats like alleys," I pointed out. "And if they are off somewhere holding paws, that would explain why nobody has seen her. I have noticed that cats like to keep to themselves at such times."

"But that would be ruinous!" said Knight.

"What's so terrible about it? It goes on all the time," I said.

"You don't understand," he said. "I had a talk with a cat authority about it. He said Dizzy's unusual intelligence shows that the ordinary cat instincts are not fully developed in her. He said if she were to—uh—have an affair with a male cat, she would probably revert to type, and then would not respond to me the way she does now."

"Maybe not," I said. "But you still want to find her, don't you?"

"Of course I do. Even if she never acts again, I've got to find her," he said.

"Then my hunch," I said, "I mean my deduction, is to look for a tomcat. And where would you be likely to find a tomcat in a business section like this? There are no homes around here. And stray cats do not often come into streets full of traffic. No—the chances are that any cat you would see in this alley comes from some store or restaurant."

I looked down the alley. A few buildings beyond the theater was a door with a few crates stacked outside. "We'll start there," I said.

It was the back door of a restaurant called The Rendevous. "This is the most likely place," I said, "because it's the closest. Let's go around front."

I got hold of the proprietor—a fat, friendly Italian named Pirelli—and asked him if he had a cat.

"Yes," he said, looking around. "Somewhere. Maybe in the kitchen. Maybe in the cellar. Maybe outside. He comes. He goes. What do you want with my cat?"

I said, "Look. This is important. We are trying to find a girl-cat who has got lost. We have an idea that she may be hiding out with some tomcat in this neighborhood. Could we look around your place for your cat, just in case the other one has sneaked in here too?"

When Pirelli got the idea, he laughed, and said, "Why, sure. My cat, Tommy, he is a great one with the ladies. You should hear the noise sometimes in the alley. Go ahead, look. I will go with you."

Tommy wasn't in the dining room or the kitchen. "Only one other place," Pirelli said. "Maybe down cellar."

Down cellar we went. When he switched on a light, we heard a miaow. Out from behind some barrels came a big, black, tough-looking tom, and rubbed against Pirelli's legs. Pirelli said, "Hello, Tommy. You got a lady friend down here, maybe?"

The tomcat looked at him and miaowed deeply. From behind the barrels came another, more musical miaow, and Dave Knight yelled, "Dizzy!"

There she was, stretched out on an old piece of burlap. Knight picked her up and kissed her, and Maribeth made a big fuss over her, too. They both told me

I was the greatest detective in the world, which is probably an exaggeration, and Pirelli congratulated us, while the tomcat and Dizzy miaowed. All of a sudden, Dizzy jumped out of Knight's arms, went to the tom, and rubbed against him.

"Aha!" said Pirelli. "You see? He is a great one with the ladies, that Tommy."

It was pretty plain that Dizzy thought so, too. When Knight reached for her, she drew back and spat at him. He stared at her in horror. Then she touched noses with Tommy. He licked himself, the way cats do when they are embarrassed by people looking at them. Finally, Dizzy turned around three times, and lay down on her side, stretching out her paws, purring like a little steam engine, and looking at Tommy with big, soulful eyes.

Knight looked absolutely crushed, and I didn't blame him. Dizzy had ceased to be a trained performing cat. She was just a female in love, and nobody could come between her and her mate—not even the man she had been sleeping with.

Maribeth said, "Dave, perhaps if the tom came along."

His face lighted up. "That's an idea," he said. "Mr. Pirelli, will you sell me your cat?"

Pirelli did not like it and held out for a while, but $25 finally convinced him. We got a big box, put both cats into it, loaded it into a taxi, and got it up to Knight's apartment in the hotel. The cats didn't seem to mind—they were so wrapped up in each other, a mere change of residence hardly mattered. Knight looked at the tom the way an outraged father might look at the scoundrel who has seduced his daughter, but what could he do?

What he wanted to know, of course, was whether Dizzy would do her tricks. He played a recording and tried to get her to dance and jump through a hoop, but all she did was turn her back, miaow, and sidle up to Tommy. When we put the tom out of the room, she scratched at the door and yelled until we had to let him in again.

Knight gave up. "Well," he said, "I have lost my meal ticket, but anyway, I've got my cat back."

"You have got your girl, too, in case you have forgotten," said Maribeth. "And don't think you can shake me with any excuse about poverty. Look at Dizzy and Tommy. You don't see them worrying about the future, do you?"

Knight kissed her. Finally I coughed and said, "Well, I guess the case is closed. I'll be going along."

They remembered me then, and began to shake my hand and thank me. Knight said, "About that five thousand. You've earned it. I haven't got it all in the bank, but I'll give you a check for a thousand right now, and the rest in a couple of days. Okay?"

"No," I said. "Forget it. What kind of a heel do you think I am? If Dizzy was still worth a thousand a week to you it might be different. This way, you will be needing all the money you have. This has been good fun, and you owe me exactly one day's pay—fifty dollars. The other four thousand, nine hundred and fifty is my wedding present to the two of you. Now don't argue about it!"

And that's the way we left it. When I asked Knight what we wanted to do about Barton and the midget, he said, "What's the use of making trouble? Their punishment won't get Dizzy to perform again—and the publicity would hurt McIntyre and Maribeth's sisters, who are innocent."

He was a good kid. So was Maribeth. They went to New York to try to work up a husband-and-wife act, and I didn't hear from them for more than two months. Then a postcard came from Maribeth, saying they were happy, and still hopeful of getting somewhere with their act. Also, Dizzy had produced six adorable kittens— three like herself, two like Tommy, and one white one that they couldn't account for. They had named the white one Terry, after me.

She sounded as if they were having a struggle, but not minding it too much. A few more months went by. Then, just yesterday, I got a letter from them. When I opened it, a check fell out. It was for $4,950.

The letter said:

> About this check. It is not your wedding present to us. No, we have been living on that, and blessing you for it. This is something else again. It is what we owe you, according to our original agreement, and if we did not pay it we would never feel right. So please take it—because we can afford it now. Besides, our agent says we can charge it off on our income tax.
>
> You see, some time back we went into the little room where Dizzy was playing with her kittens. There she was, turning somersaults again. And then it happened. *One after another, all of the kittens turned somersaults, too!*
>
> Inherited aptitude, they call it. We spent endless hours making sure, and training them. Today we signed a contract, with a big advance, for a full season's bookings and movie and television appearances. Fifteen hundred a week. We're going to be rich.
>
> We open at the Palace. The act is terrific. We have got a trapeze number with all six kittens flying through the air at the same time while Dizzy stands there like a ringmaster, with a little whip in her paw. There is no doubt about it. Every one of those kittens is a genius, just like Dizzy. Tommy, of course, is not in the act. But he does not have to do tricks. He has other gifts.
>
> We're billed as *Those Wonderful Cats—and the Knights*. When we come your way, there will be tickets at the box office for you and Mrs. Terry. Bless you.
>
> Love from Dave, Maribeth, Dizzy, Tommy, and The Six.

My wife can hardly wait to see the act. As a matter of fact, neither can I.

Barbara Owens

WHO KILLED WEE WINKY?

The contestants on *One in a Million* were being introduced as Mrs. Martin settled happily in front of her little black and white set with her breakfast tea and toast. The host, Rod Rooney, already had the studio audience in a fine mood. Mrs. Martin watched hopefully as Rod prepared to ask his first question. Would he do it today?

Yes. Just as the camera moved in for a closeup of his face, Rod looked directly at her and smiled. Mrs. Martin glowed, flushing warm all over.

"Did you see that, Wink? That was just for me. Today will be a good day."

The big orange tomcat stretched beside her on the sofa flicked an ear at the sound of his name but did not open his eyes. Mrs. Martin sighed, stroking him. She liked it when her day began so pleasantly.

Mrs. Martin had lived alone for a very long time. Sometimes she could scarcely remember Leonard and what life had been like when he was alive. It was just as well. Those earlier years held nothing but ugly memories—never enough money; an endless succession of cheap, dark, too-small apartments; and the smell. Oh, that smell. Leonard had hauled beer for a living. It had taken Mrs. Martin months after he was gone to get rid of the stink of beer in her home.

She had never stopped trying to convince Leonard to better himself, and she had devoted years to protecting Carol from the poverty and shame that he provided. And what good had it done? Carol ran away at seventeen to get married. Now she lived in California and in twenty years had never once invited her mother to visit. She rarely even wrote. No appreciation at all for the sacrifices her mother had made. Sometimes Mrs. Martin idly wondered if she'd recognize Carol today.

It was all Leonard's doing. Then he had taken sick at fifty and lingered three long years. She'd had to wait on him night and day, while his medicine and operations ate away at their pitiful savings. The savings went long before Leonard did. And he'd actually had the nerve to cry at the end and beg her to say just once that she loved him. Mrs. Martin had sniffed and turned away.

So she'd been reduced to living out her years in this dismal two-room apartment. In a big ugly building that squatted like a toad in a run-down Chicago neighborhood. She rarely went out except to market, and she had nothing to do with her trashy neighbors. They were always playing nasty tricks on her, although the various building managers never believed it. Her imagination, they said. Ha!

But she had forced herself to find small contentments. She lived on the meager benefits Leonard left her. She had her TV family who had become close friends. And, of course, she had Wee Winky. Such a tiny wink he'd been when she found him crying in an alley six years ago. Now he was the center of her life. Mrs. Martin had never loved anyone or anything the way she loved Wee Winky.

Twice during her morning TV shows he went to the back door asking to go out, but Mrs. Martin couldn't tear herself away from the set.

"In a little while, darling," she cooed to him. "We'll go out soon."

Right in the middle of a wonderful scene on *Let Us Live*, while Laura was at the hospital trying to find out if Michael had pulled through the operation, someone knocked at the front door. As usual, Mrs. Martin ignored it, but the knocking continued, accompanied by a persistent voice.

"Hey, Mrs. Martin, I know you're in there. It's Bob Singleton."

Annoyed, she rose and backed slowly to the door, keeping her eyes on poor anguished Laura until the last possible moment. The building manager's narrow face with its silly walrus moustache looked at her through the crack in the door.

"Open up," he said. "You been complaining about a leaky faucet. Well, I'm here to take a look at it."

Pursing her lips distastefully, Mrs. Martin took the chain off the door. Just as Bob Singleton started through it an orange streak shot across the room and between his bowed legs, and before either of them could move, Winky was down the hall, around the corner, and out of sight.

Bob blinked after him. "What the hell was that?"

Mrs. Martin's hands flew to her face and she let out a little scream. "Winky! Oh, now see what you've done! Go after him! My Winky—Winky, come back here!"

Bob Singleton sighed. "All right, don't get all upset. I'll get him."

He lumbered away down the hall with Mrs. Martin pattering right behind him. At the landing she leaned over and called after him, "Don't you scare him! He's not used to strangers. Winky? Come back, sweetheart."

Bob appeared on the landing below. "Don't see him," he said.

"He has to be there!" Mrs. Martin insisted in a shrill voice. "I saw him go down the stairs!"

Bob shrugged. "Well, he can't get out of the building. I'll find him."

But an hour of searching produced no cat. Mrs. Martin, wringing her hands and calling frantically, finally demanded that they canvass the building. Bob reluctantly agreed.

Unaware that she still wore her bedroom slippers, Mrs. Martin stood at his shoulder while they went door-to-door. Some residents were out, some barely understood English, and some were not at all pleased at being disturbed. It was almost lunchtime when they reached a door on the sixth floor labeled Diaz. Bob Singleton shuffled in front of it.

"Listen, I know this lady works nights. She's probably sleeping. I'll come back to her later."

"Certainly not!" Mrs. Martin cried. "You don't understand! Winky's never been outside the apartment alone. We have to find him!"

The woman who finally answered the door was round and rumpled from sleep. When Bob finished his little explanation, she stared at him in disbelief. "A cat? You wake me up for a cat?" She seemed ready to unleash a torrent, but when she caught sight of Mrs. Martin's tearful face, her own softened. "Lady," she said, "I been asleep. I don't see your cat. I see him, I tell you, okay?" And she closed the door.

"That's the last apartment," Bob said.

"He's gone. My Winky's gone." Mrs. Martin clasped her hands prayerfully.

"Aw, he'll come back, especially when he gets hungry. Look, Mrs. Martin, I got to get back to work. Maybe that old cat's waiting for you downstairs right now."

But he wasn't, and after a few quiet sniffles, Mrs. Martin phoned the police. The officer who answered sounded surprised at first, but he was courteous, and he wrote down all the information she gave him, reading it back at her insistence.

After she hung up, Mrs. Martin filled Winky's little dish with fresh liver that Mr. Vitale chopped special for her every day and sat with it on the back walkway, calling to him, until it got too cold and dark to stay outside.

The tiny apartment seemed huge and empty. She cuddled Winky's pillow while she ate a bowl of soup and watched *Tuesday Night Theater* on TV. It was a sad story, and soon Mrs. Martin's tears mingled freely with the chicken noodle. At the end the poor wretched woman on the screen was left alone, sobbing pitifully into the fadeout, "No one cares. No one cares."

Mrs. Martin blew vigorously into a tissue. "You are so right, my dear. None of them—they don't care."

All through the long sleepless night she rocked in her rocking chair, holding Winky's pillow. She peered frequently through the frosted back door, but the liver in Winky's dish remained untouched, slowly turning dark and hard.

When the first rays of morning sun began to lighten the room, Mrs. Martin stirred in her chair and blinked red-rimmed eyes. "Well, he's dead," she announced sadly to the empty room. "My Winky's dead and no one cares. One of them caught and killed him just to spite me. I'm an old woman. What can I do?"

After breakfast she tidied up the room and called the police station. The officer told her no, he didn't have any word on a missing orange cat.

"Of course not!" Mrs. Martin snapped. "What do you care?"

Bob Singleton's sloppy wife said he was on the fourth floor fixing a jammed door and wouldn't have time today to go chasing after a cat. Feeling like a thundercloud, Mrs. Martin sat down with a cup of tea to watch *One in a Million*.

The contestants were so silly and stupid today that poor Rod forgot to give her his special smile. Mrs. Martin's mind began to wander.

But it came back to her with a snap. "—one in a million!" Rod was shouting. Lights were flashing, horns trumpeting, and the music broke into the song it played when someone won the bank. A woman screamed off-camera, and Rod was grinning close up. "She did it! She did it!" Suddenly his eyes looked directly into Mrs. Martin's and he repeated with emphasis, *"Mrs. Diaz did it!"*

Mrs. Martin sat for several long minutes wrapped in cold white silence. Could she believe her ears? Rod had never spoken directly to her before. But he was her friend. Why would he lie?

"Mrs. Diaz?" Mrs. Martin whispered finally. "Killed my Winky? Why, Rod? Tell me why!"

She squinted desperately at the screen, but the show was proceeding normally and Rod would not look at her again.

Mrs. Martin stared briefly into her teacup, her mind ascramble. Finally she rose and left her apartment, creeping down the back stairs to her storage locker in the basement.

At 4:00 A.M. on the following morning, Doris Diaz finished her shift at the all-night market and drove the few short blocks home. It was cold, and she hurried up the back steps of her building, anxious for her soft, warm bed. The fifth-floor landing light was out, and as Doris rounded the corner in the dark, something rose up out of the shadows—a shapeless form wearing a man's heavy coat and a wide-brimmed hat pulled down over the ears.

Doris Diaz had lived on Chicago's west side all her life, and her mouth opened instinctively on a scream. But her foot slid off the edge of an icy step and she stumbled backward into the old wooden railing. A hand appeared from the shape to cover her gaping mouth, pushing the scream down her throat and adding just enough impetus to send her backward over the rail. She made a ripe, squashing sound when she hit the parking lot five stories below.

Later that morning, Mrs. Martin was washing her breakfast dishes when she heard voices in the hall outside her front door. Through her small spying crack she saw Bob Singleton with a big man in a police uniform.

Mrs. Martin widened the crack. "Are you here about my cat?"

The officer turned to look at her. "Ma'am?"

He was very young. He had a big open face covered with freckles and his smile was pleasant. He looked very much like her beloved brother Dennis.

She opened the door still wider. "My cat, Winky. Have you found him? I think he's dead."

Before the officer could speak, Bob Singleton interrupted. "There's been a little accident here, Mrs. Martin."

She narrowed the crack. "What kind of accident?"

"You remember Mrs. Diaz on the sixth floor?"

Mrs. Martin nodded dumbly.

"Looks like she took a fall from one of the top floors," the nice young man spoke up. "Sorry to tell you, she's dead. I don't suppose you heard anything?"

"Oh my," Mrs. Martin said. "This awful old building isn't safe to live in. Do you think she'd been drinking? They all do."

The officer looked startled. "Well, I'm sorry we bothered you. Don't let it upset you." The two men turned to go.

"Wait!" Mrs. Martin said. "What is your name?"

"Officer Burdick, ma'am," he said, turning back.

"What about my cat?"

He looked thoughtful. "You've lost a cat, Mrs. Martin?"

"I thought you'd know. I made a report. His name is Wee Winky, a lovely orange tom. I'm so worried. He's never been out alone and he's all I have left in this world."

She managed an effective quaver in her voice, but her heart ached at having to pretend. She knew Wink was dead, and she knew who'd killed him, but the officer must never know that.

Officer Burdick smiled kindly. "Well, that's too bad. I'll sure keep an eye out for him." Again, he turned to go.

"Would you like to come in for a cup of tea?"

As soon as she said it, she was astounded at herself. No one but a succession of building managers had put a foot through her door in years. But this young man was very appealing.

"I'd like to, ma'am," he said. "But I'm on duty. I'm sorry." And he sounded like he was. "Good morning to you."

"You can't mistake Wee Winky," she called after him. "He has a white moustache right under his nose." Officer Burdick waved.

Mrs. Martin closed her door. "Well," she said. "Well, well, well." She settled on the sofa with Wink's pillow, smoothing it sadly while her old set warmed up.

Rod Rooney avoided looking directly at her during his show today, but several times she caught him looking at her from the corner of his eye. Mrs. Martin nodded to show him that she had gotten his message and taken care of things.

As soon as *Let Us Live* began, it was obvious that Laura had received bad news. Her eyes shone with tears, and as the camera pulled away from her face, Mrs. Martin saw that she was sitting in the hospital waiting room with Michael's mother sobbing and clinging to her hand. Mrs. Martin's own eyes misted. "Oh no," she whispered. "Not Michael."

The camera panned to the hallway and the figure of a doctor walking slowly toward them. When Laura saw him, she sprang to her feet.

"There!" she cried, pointing to him. "He's responsible!" Her stricken face filled the screen. "He's the one!" Her streaming eyes looked directly into Mrs. Martin's. "The butcher! The butcher!!" The screen blanked out to a commercial.

Mrs. Martin felt faint. She rose on tottering legs and turned off the set. Confusion filled her aching head.

"Mr. Vitale?" she murmured incredulously. "But I thought—Rod said—Why would Mr. Vitale—"

Was that why Rod had avoided looking at her this morning? Had he made a mistake? Mrs. Martin's eyes widened. Or, worse yet, was he playing a trick on her?

"Mr. Vitale!" she said aloud. Then, "Oh dear. Poor Mrs. Diaz."

She was up early the following morning after another sleepless night. The day was gray and dreary; frost rimmed the kitchen window. Mrs. Martin dressed warmly in coat, hat, and gloves.

Mr. Vitale's butcher shop was only a short walk, but her nose was quite cold by the time she reached it. The shop was not open yet, but Mrs. Martin could see him at the slicer. She rapped smartly on the glass.

"Not open yet!" he shouted without looking up. Mrs. Martin tapped again. "Come back pretty soon!"

Mrs. Martin pressed her face against the glass. Mr. Vitale looked at her, cast his eyes to heaven, and came to open the door a slit.

"Mrs. Martin, I'm not open yet, you see that?"

Mrs. Martin smiled sweetly. "I'm so sorry, Mr. Vitale. I'm hungry for a nice little lamb chop for my supper. I had to be out anyway. I didn't think you'd mind if I slipped in."

"Not ready yet," he grumbled, still blocking the door. "You come back."

Mrs. Martin placed her hand against the door as if to steady herself, pushing it against him. "Oh, it's so cold this morning. I feel quite weak."

Mr. Vitale sighed gustily. "Come in, Mrs. Martin, come in."

She followed close at his heels as he crossed the small shop. She had looked closely, but she'd seen no hint of guilt at what he'd done. He was an evil man. All the years of chopping liver special for Winky and now her poor darling could be hanging in his frozen storage room. She had to close her eyes at the thought.

"Today's lamb is still in the back," Mr. Vitale said. "I give you some from yesterday, special price."

"Oh no." Mrs. Martin shook her head. "Day-old lamb just won't do. I'll have the fresh, if you don't mind."

He minded. He pressed his lips together and rolled his eyes. "I'm a busy man today, Mrs. Martin, all alone. My son takes his wife to the doctor. Lamb from yesterday be fine if you cook it right." He repeated heavily, "Special price."

Mrs. Martin's chin began to quiver. "I've been your customer for years, Mr. Vitale. Have I ever asked for a favor before?"

With a final tragic look he turned and stalked into the meat locker at the rear of the shop. Mrs. Martin, right behind him, slammed the door, wrestling home the special burglar bolt that his son had insisted upon installing recently. Ignoring the sound of the panic buzzer and Mr. Vitale's pounding on the door, she tore a length of butcher paper from its roll and lettered it carefully in grease pencil: CLOSED. SICK TODAY. She taped it to the front door as she went out, taking care to be certain that the door locked behind her.

As she walked home she looked and called into every alley and alcove, just in case. Oh, Wink, I'm only a poor helpless old woman. What can I do?

Early the next morning someone knocked at the door.

"Sorry to bother you again, Mrs. Martin," Officer Burdick said through the crack she opened. "And I'm sorry, but it's not about your cat."

He looked surprised when she opened the door wide. "Good morning. Won't you come in for a cup of tea?"

The young policeman looked cold and tired. "I can't, ma'am. I'm here on police business."

"I see," Mrs. Martin murmured. "Still that Mrs. Diaz?"

"No, ma'am. I'm afraid we've had a murder. We're questioning everyone in the area."

Mrs. Martin gasped. "Murder! In the building? Why, they're all killing each other out there, aren't they?"

"No, ma'am. It's a Mr. Vitale. He owned the meat market down the street. Have you seen any suspicious characters in the neighborhood lately?"

Mrs. Martin managed to look shocked. "Why, I've known Mr. Vitale for years. Suspicious, you say? They all look suspicious to me. Was it a robbery?"

"Now, don't you worry," Officer Burdick reassured her. "We think it might have been a grudge killing. Someone locked Mr. Vitale in his freezer."

"Oh my. No one is safe anymore. It's very frightening, I can tell you, for an old woman alone like me."

The officer closed his notebook. "You just stay inside and keep your doors locked. You'll be all right."

145

"Are you sure you wouldn't like a cup of tea? It's so cold outside." She was getting much better at quavering. "I'm so lonely now without my Winky."

Officer Burdick's smile was gentle. "I'm sure you are. I'm watching out for him, like I said. I'll bet he turns up."

Mrs. Martin felt a surprising surge of real emotion. "You're a very nice young man. You remind me of my dear dead brother Dennis."

The freckled face blushed. "You know, I was just thinking you remind me of my grandma. You take care now." And he clumped off down the hall.

Mrs. Martin closed her door with satisfaction. "Well," she said with relish, "finally that is that."

Let Us Live featured Helen and Barney today instead of Laura. Their troubles continued with their wayward daughter, Liz. Afterwards, Mrs. Martin took a small bundle of washables to the basement laundry room. It was warm and deserted at this hour, so she stationed herself in a quiet corner to daydream about happier days with Winky. In a few minutes she heard steps outside in the hallway. Bob Singleton and another man. They went past the laundry-room door without seeing her and into the storage-locker room. She could hear their voices quite clearly.

"—wife said you was around the other day with that loony old woman looking for her cat. That what they pay you for nowadays?"

Bob's answer was muffled, the other man said something, then they both laughed loudly.

"How'd you guess?" Bob said. Then, in falsetto, "Okay, officer, I confess. I overdosed him on fleas. I know I'll get the chair."

More laughter, then the other man carried a box back past the door. Mrs. Martin didn't know him, just another one of the swarthy ones who had gradually taken over the building.

She sat very still, having trouble finding air to breathe. Of course. Bob Singleton. He had picked Winky up when he first followed him down the stairs—hidden him somewhere until they had finished searching the building. Mrs. Martin closed her tired eyes. Winky would have been afraid. He probably cried for her. Then Bob had killed him just to spite her. Rod and Laura must have been in on it, too. She shook her sad head. Mrs. Diaz and Mr. Vitale had died by mistake. It had been Bob Singleton all along, and he had pretended to help her, pretended to care.

She slipped stealthily into the storage room. Bob was kneeling with his back to her, working on one of the compartment locks.

"Mr. Singleton?" she said right at his ear.

He started violently, dropping the lock and cracking his head against the door. "Mrs. Martin! You scared the hell out of me!"

"I'm so sorry. I was just wondering if you'd heard anything about my Winky."

He didn't even have the grace to blush or look away. Instead, he rubbed his head gingerly. "Nope. Don't give up, though. I still think he'll show up."

"Well," she said, lowering her eyes demurely, "I've been meaning to thank you for helping me look for him. Would you like to come up for a cup of tea?"

She'd never noticed before what a mean little face he had. "Well, thanks," he said, "but I'm pretty busy. I ain't much of a tea drinker anyway."

"I can make coffee then," she offered earnestly. Again she lowered her eyes. "But maybe you'd rather not. You probably think I'm just a silly old woman." She produced a tear and wiped it away.

"Uh," Bob said. Mrs. Martin waited patiently. "Tell you what. Maybe I could stop by in the morning for a few minutes. Would ten o'clock be okay?"

"Oh yes, ten will be fine. Thank you." Mrs. Martin smiled to herself all the way upstairs.

Back in her kitchen, she climbed on a chair to search the high back shelf of her cupboard until she located the container of rat poison. It was almost full.

By 9:30 the next morning there were fresh homemade cookies and a pot of steaming coffee laid out on her little dining table. The empty poison container had been dropped discreetly down a neighbor's garbage chute. Mrs. Martin waited, sipping a cup of tea and humming a happy little tune.

When a knock came at her door she jumped, hands flying to her throat. Her heart gave a couple of sharp ugly slaps. Then two deep breaths and she was able to go to the door and open it, a smile forming prettily on her lips.

"Hi!" Officer Burdick said with a grin that stretched his freckles to their limit. "You'll never guess what I found."

Mrs. Martin faltered, her eyes moving from his big cheerful face down to the crook of his arm where he held—dirty, bedraggled, but unmistakably—"Winky!" Mrs. Martin cried. "Oh, it's—you've—little Winky!"

She reached out blindly. Burdick placed the cat gently into her arms and watched her fold it to her breast.

"Found him in an alley just a few blocks from here, white moustache and all. I brought him right over. He sure looks sorry, doesn't he?"

Tears fell helplessly. "Oh, I thought he was—how can I ever thank you— oh, my Winky's home and you—"

Burdick thought she looked like she was going to fall. He placed a strong hand on her elbow. "Sure looks like he could use something to eat."

"Oh yes, of course. I—a little warm milk—oh, Winky, I missed you, it's just been terrible—"

Officer Carl Burdick stood tall in the center of the tiny room, watching her fly around warming milk and crooning to the cat. Bless her old soul, she'd forgotten he was there.

A plate of cookies and a pot of hot coffee sat invitingly on a small table across the room. He eyed the spread thoughtfully. She'd been after him to come in and he'd kept turning her down. What the hell, a few minutes wouldn't make any difference. Poor thing was lonely. Made him feel good just watching her and the cat. He stepped up to the table, poured himself a cup of coffee, and selected two large cookies.

Yessir, it was worth it. After all the dirt he was forced to deal with on the streets out there, moments like this made it all worthwhile.

Manly Wade Wellman

THE WITCH'S CAT

Old Jael Bettiss, who lived in the hollow among the cypresses, was not a real witch.

It makes no difference that folk thought she was, and walked fearfully wide of her shadow. Nothing can be proved by the fact that she was as disgustingly ugly without as she was wicked within. It is quite irrelevant that evil was her study and profession and pleasure. She was no witch; she only pretended to be.

Jael Bettiss knew that all laws providing for the punishment of witches had been repealed, or at the least forgotten. As to being feared and hated, that was meat and drink to Jael Bettiss, living secretly alone in the hollow.

The house and the hollow belonged to a kindly old villager, who had been elected marshal and was too busy to look after his property. Because he was easy-going and perhaps a little daunted, he let Jael Bettiss live there rent free. The house was no longer snug; the back of its roof was broken in, the eaves drooped slackly. At some time or other the place had been painted brown, before that with ivory black. Now both coats of color peeled away in huge flakes, making the clapboards seem scrofulous. The windows had been broken in every small, grubby pane, and mended with coarse brown paper, so that they were like cast and blurred eyes. Behind was the muddy, bramble-choked backyard, and behind that yawned the old quarry, now abandoned and full of black water. As for the inside—but few ever saw it.

Jael Bettiss did not like people to come into her house. She always met callers on the old cracked doorstep, draped in a cloak of shadowy black, with gray hair straggling, her nose as hooked and sharp as the beak of a buzzard, her eyes filmy and sore-looking, her wrinkle-bordered mouth always grinning and showing her yellow, chisel-shaped teeth.

The nearby village was an old-fashioned place, with stone flags instead of concrete for pavements, and the villagers were the simplest of men and women. From them Jael Bettiss made a fair living, by selling love philters, or herbs to cure sickness, or charms to ward off bad luck. When she wanted extra money, she would wrap her old black cloak about her and, tramping along a country road, would stop at a cowpen and ask the farmer what he would do if his cows went dry. The farmer, worried, usually came at dawn next day to her hollow and bought a good-luck charm. Occasionally the cows would go dry anyway, by accident of nature, and their owner would pay more and more, until their milk returned to them.

Now and then, when Jael Bettiss came to the door, there came with her the gaunt black cat, Gib.

Gib was not truly black, any more than Jael Bettiss was truly a witch. He had been born with white markings at muzzle, chest, and forepaws, so that he looked to be in full evening dress. Left alone, he would have grown fat and fluffy. But Jael Bettiss, who wanted a fearsome pet, kept all his white spots smeared with thick soot, and underfed him to make him look rakish and lean.

On the night of the full moon, she would drive poor Gib from her door. He would wander to the village in search of food, and would wail mournfully in the yards. Awakened householders would angrily throw boots or pans or sticks of kindling. Often Gib was hit, and his cries were sharpened by pain. When that happened, Jael Bettiss took care to be seen next morning with a bandage on head or wrist. Some of the simplest villagers thought that Gib was really the old woman, magically transformed. Her reputation grew, as did Gib's unpopularity. But Gib did not deserve mistrust—like all cats, he was a practical philosopher, who wanted to be comfortable and quiet and dignified. At bottom, he was amiable. Like all cats, too, he loved his home above all else; and the house in the hollow, be it ever so humble and often cruel, was home. It was unthinkable to him that he might live elsewhere.

In the village he had two friends—black-eyed John Frey, the storekeeper's son, who brought the mail to and from the county seat, and Ivy Hill, pretty blonde daughter of the town marshal, the same town marshal who owned the hollow and let Jael Bettiss live in the old house. John Frey and Ivy Hill were so much in love with each other that they loved everything else, even black-stained, hungry Gib. He was grateful; if he had been able, he would have loved them in return. But his little heart had room for one devotion only, and that was given to the house in the hollow.

One day, Jael Bettiss slouched darkly into old Mr. Frey's store, and up to the counter that served as a post office. Leering, she gave John Frey a letter. It was directed to a certain little-known publisher, asking for a certain little-known book. Several days later, she appeared again, received a parcel, and bore it to her home.

In her gloomy, secret parlor, she unwrapped her purchase. It was a small,

150

drab volume, with no title on cover or back. Sitting at the rickety table, she began to read. All evening and most of the night she read, forgetting to give Gib his supper, though he sat hungrily at her feet.

At length, an hour before dawn, she finished. Laughing loudly and briefly, she turned her beak-nose toward the kerosene lamp on the table. From the book she read aloud two words. The lamp went out, though she had not blown at it. Jael Bettiss spoke one commanding word more, and the lamp flamed alight again.

"At last!" she cried out in shrill exultation, and grinned down at Gib. Her lips drew back from her yellow chisels of teeth. "At last!" she crowed again. "Why don't you speak to me, you little brute? . . . Why don't you, indeed?"

She asked that final question as though she had been suddenly inspired. Quickly she glanced through the back part of the book, howled with laughter over something she found there, then sprang up and scuttled like a big, filthy crab into the dark, windowless cell that was her kitchen. There she mingled salt and malt in the palm of her skinny right hand. After that, she rummaged out a bundle of dried herbs, chewed them fine, and spat them into the mixture. Stirring again with her forefinger, she returned to the parlor. Scanning the book to refresh her memory, she muttered a nasty little rhyme. Finally she dashed the mess suddenly upon Gib.

He retreated, shaking himself, outraged and startled. In a corner he sat down, and bent his head to lick the smeared fragments of the mixture away. But they revolted his tongue and palate, and he paused in the midst of this chore, so important to cats; and meanwhile Jael Bettiss yelled, "Speak!"

Gib crouched and blinked, feeling sick. His tongue came out and steadied his lips. Finally he said: "I want something to eat."

His voice was small and high, like a little child's, but entirely understandable. Jael Bettiss was so delighted that she laughed and clapped her bony knees with her hands, in self-applause.

"It worked!" she cried. "No more humbug about me, you understand? I'm a real witch at last, and not a fraud!"

Gib found himself able to understand all this, more clearly than he had ever understood human affairs before. "I want something to eat," he said again, more definitely than before. "I didn't have any supper, and it's nearly—"

"Oh, stow your gab!" snapped his mistress. "It's this book, crammed with knowledge and strength, that made me able to do it. I'll never be without it again, and it'll teach me all the things I've only guessed at and mumbled about. I'm a real witch now, I say. And if you don't think I'll make those ignorant sheep of villagers realize it—"

Once more she went off into gales of wild, cracked mirth, and threw a dish at Gib. He darted away into a corner just in time, and the missile crashed into blue-and-white china fragments against the wall. But Jael Bettiss read aloud from her book an impressive gibberish, and the dish re-formed itself on the floor; the bits crept together and joined and the cracks disappeared, as trickling drops of water form into a pool. And finally, when the witch's twiglike forefinger beckoned, the dish floated upward like a leaf in a breeze and set itself gently back on the table. Gib watched warily.

"That's small to what I shall do hereafter," swore Jael Bettiss.

When next the mail was distributed at the general store, a dazzling stranger appeared.

She wore a cloak, an old-fashioned black coat, but its drapery did not conceal the tall perfection of her form. As for her face, it would have stirred interest and admiration in larger and more sophisticated gatherings than the knot of letter-seeking villagers. Its beauty was scornful but inviting, classic but warm, with something in it of Grecian sculpture and oriental allure. If the nose was cruel, it was straight; if the lips were sullen, they were full; if the forehead was a suspicion low, it was white and smooth. Thick, thunder-black hair swept up from that forehead, and backward to a knot at the neck. The eyes glowed with strange, hot lights, and wherever they turned they pierced and captivated.

People moved away to let her have a clear, sweeping pathway forward to the counter. Until this stranger had entered, Ivy Hill was the loveliest person present; now she looked only modest and fresh and blonde in her starched gingham, and worried to boot. As a matter of fact, Ivy Hill's insides felt cold and topsy-turvy, because she saw how fascinated was the sudden attention of John Frey.

"Is there," asked the newcomer in a deep, creamy voice, "any mail for me?"

"Wh-what name, ma'am?" asked John Frey, his brown young cheeks turning full crimson.

"Bettiss. Jael Bettiss."

He began to fumble through the sheaf of envelopes, with hands that shook. "Are you," he asked, "any relation to the old lady of that name, the one who lives in the hollow?"

"Yes, of a sort." She smiled a slow, conquering smile. "She's my—aunt. Yes. Perhaps you see the family resemblance?" Wider and wider grew the smile with which she assaulted John Frey. "If there isn't any mail," she went on, "I would like a stamp. A one-cent stamp."

Turning to his little metal box on the shelf behind, John Frey tore a single green stamp from the sheet. His hand shook still more as he gave it to the customer and received in exchange a copper cent.

There was really nothing exceptional about the appearance of that copper cent. It looked brown and a little worn, with Lincoln's head on it, and a date—1917. But John Frey felt a sudden glow in the hand that took it, a glow that shot along his arm and into his heart. He gazed at the coin as if he had never seen its like before. And he put it slowly into his pocket, a different pocket from the one in which he usually kept change, and placed another coin in the till to pay for the stamp. Poor Ivy Hill's blue eyes grew round and downright miserable. Plainly he meant to keep that copper piece as a souvenir. But John Frey gazed only at the stranger, raptly, as though he were suddenly stunned or hypnotized.

The dark, sullen beauty drew her cloak more tightly around her and moved regally out of the store and away toward the edge of town.

As she turned up the brush-hidden trail to the hollow, a change came. Not that her step was less young and free, her figure less queenly, her eyes dimmer, or her beauty short of perfect. All these were as they had been; but her expression became set and grim, her body tense, and her head high and truculent. It was as though, beneath that young loveliness, lurked an old and evil heart, which was precisely what did lurk there, it does not boot to conceal. But none saw except Gib, the black cat with soot-covered white spots, who sat on the doorstep of the ugly cottage. Jael Bettiss thrust him aside with her foot and entered.

In the kitchen she filled a tin basin from a wooden bucket, and threw into the water a pinch of coarse green powder with an unpleasant smell. As she stirred it in with her hands, they seemed to grow skinny and harsh. Then she threw great palmfuls of the liquid into her face and over her head, and other changes came. . . .

The woman who returned to the front door, where Gib watched with a cat's apprehensive interest, was hideous old Jael Bettiss, whom all the village knew and avoided.

"He's trapped," she shrilled triumphantly. "That penny, the one I soaked for three hours in a love philter, trapped him the moment he touched it!" She stumped to the table, and patted the book as though it were a living, lovable thing.

"You taught me," she crooned to it. "You're winning me the love of John Frey!" She paused, and her voice grew harsh again. "Why not? I'm old and ugly and queer, but I can love, and John Frey is the handsomest man in the village!"

The next day she went to the store again, in her new and dazzling person as a dark, beautiful girl. Gib, left alone in the hollow, turned over in his mind the things that he had heard. The new gift of human speech had brought with it, of necessity, a human quality of reasoning; but his viewpoint and his logic were as strongly feline as ever.

Jael Bettiss's dark love that lured John Frey promised no good to Gib. There would be plenty of trouble, he was inclined to think, and trouble was something that all sensible cats avoided. He was wise now, but he was weak. What could he do against danger? And his desires, as they had been since kittenhood, were food and warmth and a cozy sleeping place, and a little respectful affection. Just now

153

he was getting none of the four.

He thought also of Ivy Hill. She liked Gib, and often had shown it. If she won John Frey despite the witch's plan, the two would build a house all full of creature comforts—cushions, open fires, probably fish and chopped liver. Gib's tongue caressed his sootstained lips at the savory thought. It would be good to have a home with Ivy Hill and John Frey, if once he was quit of Jael Bettiss. . . .

But he put the thought from him. The witch had never held his love and loyalty. That went to the house in the hollow, his home since the month that he was born. Even magic had not taught him how to be rid of that cat-instinctive obsession for his own proper dwelling place. The sinister, strife-sodden hovel would always call and claim him, would draw him back from the warmest fire, the softest bed, the most savory food in the world. Only John Howard Payne could have appreciated Gib's yearnings to the full, and he died long ago, in exile from the home he loved.

When Jael Bettiss returned, she was in a fine trembling rage. Her real self shone through the glamor of her disguise, like murky fire through a thin porcelain screen.

Gib was on the doorstep again and tried to dodge away as she came up, but her enchantments, or something else, had made Jael Bettiss too quick even for a cat. She darted out a hand and caught him by the scruff of the neck.

"Listen to me," she said, in a voice as deadly as the trickle of poisoned water. "You understand human words. You can talk, and you can hear what I say. You can do what I say, too." She shook him, by way of emphasis. "Can't you do what I say?"

"Yes," said Gib weakly, convulsed with fear.

"All right, I have a job for you. And mind you do it well, or else—" She broke off and shook him again, letting him imagine what would happen if he disobeyed.

"Yes," said Gib again, panting for breath in her tight grip. "What's it about?"

"It's about that little fool, Ivy Hill. She's not quite out of his heart. Go to the village tonight," ordered Jael Bettiss, "and to the house of the marshal. Steal something that belongs to Ivy Hill."

"Steal something?"

"Don't echo me, as if you were a silly parrot." She let go of him and hurried back to the book that was her constant study. "Bring me something that Ivy Hill owns and touches—and be back here with it before dawn."

Gib carried out her orders. Shortly after sundown he crept through the deepened dusk to the home of Marshal Hill. Doubly black with the soot habitually smeared upon him by Jael Bettiss, he would have been almost invisible, even had anyone been on guard against his coming. But nobody watched; the genial old man sat on the front steps, talking to his daughter.

"Say," the father teased, "isn't young Johnny Frey coming over here tonight, as usual?"

"I don't know, daddy," said Ivy Hill wretchedly.

"What's that, daughter?" The marshal sounded surprised. "Is there anything gone wrong between you two young 'uns?"

"Perhaps not, but—oh, daddy, there's a new girl come to town—"

And Ivy Hill burst into tears, groping dolefully on the step beside her for her little wadded handkerchief. But she could not find it.

For Gib, stealing near, had caught it up in his mouth and was scampering away toward the edge of town, and beyond to the house in the hollow.

Meanwhile, Jael Bettiss worked hard at a certain project of wax modeling. Any witch, or student of witchcraft, would have known at once why she did this.

After several tries, she achieved something quite interesting and even clever—a little female figure, that actually resembled Ivy Hill.

Jael Bettiss used the wax of three candles to give it enough substance and proportion. To make it more realistic, she got some fresh, pale-gold hemp, and of this made hair, like the wig of a blonde doll, for the wax head. Drops of blue ink served for eyes, and a blob of berry juice for the red mouth. All the while she worked, Jael Bettiss was muttering and mumbling words and phrases she had gleaned from the rearward pages of her book.

When Gib brought in the handkerchief, Jael Bettiss snatched it from his mouth, with a grunt by way of thanks. With rusty scissors and coarse white thread, she fashioned for the wax figure a little dress. It happened that the handkerchief was of gingham, and so the garment made all the more striking the puppet's resemblance to Ivy Hill.

"You're a fine one!" tittered the witch, propping her finished figure against the lamp. "You'd better be scared!"

For it happened that she had worked into the waxen face an expression of terror. The blue ink of the eyes made wide round blotches, a stare of agonized fear; and the berry-juice mouth seemed to tremble, to plead shakily for mercy.

Again Jael Bettiss refreshed her memory of goetic spells by poring over the back of the book, and after that she dug from the bottom of an old pasteboard box a handful of rusty pins. She chuckled over them, so that one would think triumph already hers. Laying the puppet on its back, so that the lamplight fell full upon it, she began to recite a spell.

"I have made my wish before," she said in measured tones. "I will make it now. And there was never a day that I did not see my wish fulfilled." Simple, vague—but how many have died because those words were spoken in a certain way over images of them?

155

The witch thrust a pin into the breast of the little wax figure and drove it all the way in, with a murderous pressure of her thumb. Another pin she pushed into the head, another into an arm, another into a leg; and so on, until the gingham-clad puppet was fairly studded with transfixing pins.

"Now," she said, "we shall see what we shall see."

Morning dawned, as clear and golden as though wickedness had never been born into the world. The mysterious new paragon of beauty—not a young man of the village but mooned over her, even though she was the reputed niece and namesake of that unsavory old vagabond, Jael Bettiss—walked into the general store to make purchases. One delicate pink ear turned to the gossip of the house-wives.

Wasn't it awful, they were agreeing, how poor little Ivy Hill was suddenly sick almost to death; she didn't seem to know her father or her friends. Not even Doctor Melcher could find out what was the matter with her. Strange that John Frey was not interested in her troubles; but John Frey sat behind the counter, slumped on his stool like a mud idol, and his eyes lighted up only when they spied lovely young Jael Bettiss with her market basket.

When she had heard enough, the witch left the store and went straight to the town marshal's house. There she spoke gravely and sorrowfully about how she feared for the sick girl, and was allowed to visit Ivy Hill in her bedroom. To the father and the doctor, it seemed that the patient grew stronger and felt less pain while Jael Bettiss remained to wish her a quick recovery; but, not long after this new acquaintance departed, Ivy Hill grew worse. She fainted, and recovered only to vomit.

And she vomited—pins, rusty pins. Something like that happened in old Salem Village, and earlier still in Scotland, before the grisly cult of North Berwick was literally burned out. But Doctor Melcher, a more modern scholar, had never seen or heard of anything remotely resembling Ivy Hill's disorder.

So it went, for three full days. Gib, too, heard the doleful gossip as he slunk around the village to hunt for food and to avoid Jael Bettiss, who did not like him near when she did magic. Ivy Hill was dying, and he mourned her, as for the boons of fish and fire and cushions and petting that might have been his. He knew, too, that he was responsible for her doom and his loss—that handkerchief that he had stolen had helped Jael Bettiss to direct her spells.

But philosophy came again to his aid. If Ivy Hill died, she died. Anyway, he had never been given the chance to live as her pensioner and pet. He was not even sure that he would have taken the chance—thinking of it, he felt strong, accustomed clamps upon his heart. The house in the hollow was his home forever. Elsewhere he'd be an exile.

Nothing would ever root it out of his feline soul.

*　　*　　*

On the evening of the third day, witch and cat faced each other across the tabletop in the old house in the hollow.

"They've talked loud enough to make his dull ears hear," grumbled the fearful old woman—with none but Gib to see her, she had washed away the disguising enchantment that, though so full of lure, seemed to be a burden upon her. "John Frey has agreed to take Ivy Hill out in his automobile. The doctor thinks that the fresh air, and John Frey's company, will make her feel better—but it won't. It's too late. She'll never return from that drive."

She took up the pin-pierced wax image of her rival, rose, and started toward the kitchen.

"What are you going to do?" Gib forced himself to ask.

"Do?" repeated Jael Bettiss, smiling murderously. "I'm going to put an end to that baby-faced chit, but why are you so curious? Get out, with your prying!"

And, snarling curses and striking with her clawlike hands, she made him spring down from his chair and run out of the house. The door slammed, and he crouched in some brambles and watched. No sound, and at the half-blinded windows no movement; but, after a time, smoke began to coil upward from the chimney. Its first puffs were dark and greasy-looking. Then it turned dull gray, then white, then blue as indigo. Finally it vanished altogether.

When Jael Bettiss opened the door and came out, she was once more in the semblance of a beautiful dark girl. Yet Gib recognized a greater terror about her than ever before.

"You be gone from here when I get back," she said to him.

"Gone?" stammered Gib, his little heart turning cold. "What do you mean?"

She stooped above him, like a threatening bird of prey.

"You be gone," she repeated. "If I ever see you again, I'll kill you—or I'll make my new husband kill you."

He still could not believe her. He shrank back, and his eyes turned mournfully to the old house that was the only thing he loved.

"You're the only witness to the things I've done," Jael Bettiss continued. "Nobody would believe their ears if a cat started telling tales, but anyway, I don't want any trace of you around. If you leave, they'll forget that I used to be a witch. So run!"

She turned away. Her mutterings were now only her thoughts aloud:

If my magic works—and it always works—that car will find itself idling around through the hill road to the other side of the quarry. John Frey will stop there. And so will Ivy Hill—forever.

Drawing her cloak around her, she stalked purposefully toward the old quarry behind the house.

Left by himself, Gib lowered his lids and let his yellow eyes grow dim and deep with thought. His shrewd beast's mind pawed and probed at this final wonder and danger that faced him and John Frey and Ivy Hill.

He must run away if he would live. The witch's house in the hollow, which had never welcomed him, now threatened him. No more basking on the doorstep, no more ambushing woodmice among the brambles, no more dozing by the kitchen fire. Nothing for Gib henceforth but strange, forbidding wilderness, and scavenger's food, and no shelter, not on the coldest night. The village? But his only two friends, John Frey and Ivy Hill, were being taken from him by the magic of Jael Bettiss and her book. . . .

That book had done this. That book must undo it. There was no time to lose.

The door was not quite latched, and he nosed it open, despite the groans of its hinges. Hurrying in, he sprang up on the table.

It was gloomy in that tree-invested house, even for Gib's sharp eyes. Therefore, in a trembling fear almost too big for his little body, he spoke a word that Jael Bettiss had spoken, on her first night of power. As had happened then, so it happened now; the dark lamp glowed alight.

Gib pawed at the closed book, and contrived to lift its cover. Pressing it open with one front foot, with the other he painstakingly turned leaves, more leaves, and more yet. Finally he came to the page he wanted.

Not that he could read; and, in any case, the characters were strange in their shapes and combinations. Yet, if one looked long enough and levelly enough— even though one were a cat, and afraid—they made sense, conveyed intelligence.

And so into the mind of Gib, beating down his fears, there stole a phrase: *Beware of mirrors. . . .*

So that was why Jael Bettiss never kept a mirror—not even now, when she could assume such dazzling beauty.

Beware of mirrors, the book said to Gib, *for they declare the truth, and truth is fatal to sorcery. Beware also, of crosses, which defeat all spells.*

That was definite inspiration. He moved back from the book, and let it snap shut. Then, pushing with head and paws, he coaxed it to the edge of the table and let it fall. Jumping down after it, he caught a corner of the book in his teeth and dragged it to the door, more like a retriever than a cat. When he got it into the yard, into a place where the earth was soft, he dug furiously until he had made a hole big enough to contain the volume. Then, thrusting it in, he covered it up.

Nor was that all his effort, so far as the book was concerned. He trotted a little way off to where lay some dry, tough twigs under the cypress trees. To the little grave he bore first one, then another of these, and laid them across each other, in the form of an **X**. He pressed them well into the earth, so that they would be hard to disturb. Perhaps he would keep an eye on that spot henceforth, after he had done the rest of the things in his mind, to see that the cross remained. And, though he acted thus only by chance reasoning, all the demonologists, even the Reverend Montague Summers, would have nodded approval. Is this not the way to foil the black wisdom of the *Grand Albert*? Did not Prospero thus inter his grimoires, in the fifth act of *The Tempest*?

Now back to the house once more and into the kitchen. It was even darker than the parlor, but Gib could make out a basin on a stool by the moldy wall, and smelled an ugly pungency: Jael Bettiss had left her mixture of powdered water after last washing away her burden of false beauty.

Gib's feline nature rebelled at a wetting; his experience of witchcraft bade him be wary, but he rose on his hind legs and with his forepaws dragged at the basin's edge. It tipped and toppled. The noisome fluid drenched him. Wheeling, he ran back into the parlor, but paused on the doorstep. He spoke two more words that he remembered from Jael Bettiss. The lamp went out again.

And now he dashed around the house and through the brambles and to the quarry beyond.

It lay amid uninhabited wooded hills, a wide excavation from which had once been quarried all the stones for the village houses and pavements. Now it was full of water, from many thaws and torrents. Almost at its lip was parked John Frey's touring car, with the top down, and beside it he lolled, slack-faced and dreamy. At his side, cloak-draped and enigmatically queenly, was Jael Bettiss, her back to the quarry, never more terrible or handsome. John Frey's eyes were fixed dreamily upon her, and her eyes were fixed commandingly on the figure in the front seat of the car—a slumped, defeated figure, hard to recognize as poor sick Ivy Hill.

"Can you think of no way to end all this pain, Miss Ivy?" the witch was asking. Though she did not stir, or glance behind her, it was as though she had gestured toward the great quarry pit, full to unknown depths with black, still water. The sun, at the very point of setting, made angry red lights on the surface of that stagnant pond.

"Go away," sobbed Ivy Hill, afraid without knowing why. "Please, please!"

"I'm only trying to help," said Jael Bettiss. "Isn't that so, John?"

"That's so, Ivy," agreed John, like a little boy who is prompted to an unfamiliar recitation. "She's only trying to help."

Gib, moving silently as fate, crept to the back of the car. None of the three human beings, so intent upon each other, saw him.

"Get out of the car," persisted Jael Bettiss. "Get out, and look into the water. You will forget your pain."

"Yes, yes," chimed in John Frey mechanically. "You will forget your pain."

Gib scrambled stealthily to the running board, then over the side of the car and into the rear seat. He found what he had hoped to find. Ivy Hill's purse—and open.

He pushed his nose into it. Tucked into a little side pocket was a hard, flat rectangle, about the size and shape of a visiting card. All normal girls carry mirrors in their purses; all mirrors show the truth. Gib clamped the edge with his mouth, and struggled to drag the thing free.

"Miss Ivy," Jael Bettiss was commanding, "get out of this car, and come and look into the water of the quarry."

No doubt what would happen if once Ivy Hill should gaze into that shiny black abyss; but she bowed her head, in agreement or defeat, and began slowly to push aside the catch of the door.

Now or never, thought Gib. He made a little noise in his throat, and sprang up on the side of the car next to Jael Bettiss. His black-stained face and yellow eyes were not a foot from her.

She alone saw him; Ivy Hill was too sick, John Frey too dull. "What are you doing here?" she snarled, like a bigger and fiercer cat than he; but he moved closer still, holding up the oblong in his teeth. Its back was uppermost, covered with imitation leather, and hid the real nature of it. Jael Bettiss was mystified, for once in her relationship with Gib. She took the thing from him, turned it over, and saw a reflection.

She screamed.

The other two looked up, horrified through their stupor. The scream that Jael Bettiss uttered was not deep and rich and young; it was the wild, cracked cry of a terrified old woman.

"I don't look like that," she choked out, and drew back from the car. "Not old—ugly—"

Gib sprang at her face. With all four claw-bristling feet he seized and clung to her. Again Jael Bettiss screamed, flung up her hands, and tore him away from his hold; but his soggy fur had smeared the powdered water upon her face and head.

Though he fell to earth, Gib twisted in midair and landed upright. He had one glimpse of his enemy. Jael Bettiss, no mistake—but a Jael Bettiss with hooked beak, rheumy eyes, hideous wry mouth and yellow chisel teeth—Jael Bettiss exposed for what she was, stripped of her lying mask of beauty!

And she drew back a whole staggering step. Rocks were just behind her. Gib saw, and flung himself. Like a flash he clawed his way up her cloak, and with both forepaws ripped at the ugliness he had betrayed. He struck for his home that was forbidden him—Marco Bozzaris never strove harder for Greece, or Stonewall Jackson for Virginia.

Jael Bettiss screamed yet again, a scream loud and full of horror. Her feet had slipped on the edge of the abyss. She flung out her arms, the cloak flapped from them like frantic wings. She fell, and Gib fell with her, still tearing and fighting.

The waters of the quarry closed over them both.

Gib thought that it was a long way back to the surface and a longer way to shore. But he got there, and scrambled out with the help of projecting rocks. He shook his drenched body, climbed back into the car and sat upon the rear seat. At least Jael Bettiss would no longer drive him from the home he loved. He'd find food some way, and take it back there each day to eat. . . .

With tongue and paws he began to rearrange his sodden fur.

John Frey, clear-eyed and wide awake, was leaning in and talking to Ivy Hill. As for her, she sat up straight, as though she had never known a moment of sickness.

"But just what did happen?" she was asking.

John Frey shook his head, though all the stupidity was gone from his face and manner. "I don't quite remember. I seem to have wakened from a dream. But are you all right, darling?"

"Yes, I'm all right." She gazed toward the quarry, and the black water that had already subsided above what it had swallowed. Her eyes were puzzled, but not frightened. "I was dreaming, too," she said. "Let's not bother about it."

She lifted her gaze, and cried out with joy. "There's that old house that daddy owns. Isn't it interesting?"

John Frey looked, too. "Yes. The old witch has gone away—I seem to have heard she did."

Ivy Hill was smiling with excitement. "Then I have an inspiration. Let's get daddy to give it to us. And we'll paint it over and fix it up, and then—" She broke off, with a cry of delight. "I declare, there's a cat in the car with me!"

It was the first she had known of Gib's presence.

John Frey stared at Gib. He seemed to have wakened only the moment before. "Yes, and isn't he a thin one? But he'll be pretty when he gets through cleaning himself. I think I see a white shirt front."

Ivy Hill put out a hand and scratched Gib behind the ear. "He's bringing us good luck, I think. John, let's take him to live with us when we have the house fixed up and move in."

"Why not?" asked her lover. He was gazing at Gib. "He looks as if he was getting ready to speak."

But Gib was not getting ready to speak. The power of speech was gone from him, along with Jael Bettiss and her enchantments. But he understood, in a measure, what was being said about him and the house in the hollow. There would be new life there, joyful and friendly this time. And he would be a part of it, forever, and of his loved home.

He could only purr to show his relief and gratitude.

Charles Peterson

THE CAT IN THE BAG

I am sitting on a park bench minding my own business, which at the moment consists of the study of some passing statistics like 5'6", 120 pounds, 34-26-34, when this little bimbo in the grey fedora and pencil mustache sits down next to me, hems and haws a bit, then says, "Are you by any chance Kit the Cat Burglar?"

I perform a sitting high jump of eighteen and a quarter inches—a new intramural record.

True, on the date of this park bench episode, I am still in the burgling business. Nowadays, of course, I am plain Augie Augenblick, having paid my debt to society—at least as much of it as they could tag me with—but even at the time whereof I speak I am not anxious to have my business advertised in the public parks. So I murmur, "Excuse me!" and prepare to leave a large void in the immediate area.

Grey Fedora hauls me back by the jacket sleeve. "Because if you are," he goes on, "I have a five-grand proposition for you."

The words "five grand" induce a certain immobility, and though I am prompt with many disclaimers, in case he is concealing a tape recorder and police badge about his person, I express curiosity to hear what this proposition may be, supposing (ho! ho!) that I am this Kit what's-his-name.

"I want you to steal a cat," says Grey Fedora.

"You have a very perverted idea of what cat burglars do," I say, frowning. "Excuse me again."

Again he hauls me back, and this time he presses a business card into my hand. It is so heavily embossed as to be readable in Braille and says

RENFREW T. SNYDE, JR.
Senior Account Executive
Snyde, Fingle and Chatsworthy, Advertising.

162

"You have no doubt heard of Scat Cat Food. The Feast for Finicky Felines?" he begins, with a hopeful expression.

I look blank. "No, but I've heard of Sweetums Cat Cuisine."

Mr. Snyde sighs and twitches his mustache. "That's the problem. Everybody knows about Sweetums; nobody knows about Scat. It's those dratted television commercials starring Sweetums."

"The cat with the $25,000 diamond-studded collar?"

"Hah!" Mr. Snyde's mustache quivers mirthlessly. "People who believe in cats that wear $25,000 diamond collars generally believe in tooth fairies, too. But Sweetums *is* the problem. We've learned that Muckley and Swerge, the agency for Sweetums Cat Cuisine, is about to begin production of a new series of commercials."

A light begins to dawn. "And you want me to steal Sweetums beforehand."

"Precisely!" says Mr. Snyde.

Once Mr. Snyde and I have formalized the arrangements, I begin my preparations. Ordinarily, I prefer an ad lib approach to purloinment, but this being a commissioned assignment I feel impelled to plan rather carefully, and among the first steps is that of checking out the establishment where Sweetums lives when not on camera or opening shopping centers. It is an oldish house standing by itself in the middle of a couple of acres—doubtless an elementary business precaution for an outfit whose stock in trade come with yaps, yips, barks, howls, growls and yowls that could raise eyebrows in the typical suburb. There is a chain-link fence, behind which are dog runs and kennels, but the place appears not much more difficult to get into than, say, your average used car lot. I manage to catch several of Sweetums' TV spots, and can see why Mr. Snyde's client has problems. Most cats can give you a disdainful look that makes you feel you have gravy spots on your necktie, but Sweetums is positively uncanny. When she stares at you over that diamond collar and suggests that your cat deserves Sweetums Cat Cuisine, you get this strange urge to trot out and buy the stuff even if you must then buy a cat to feed it to.

But the commercials give me an idea of what to look for, and a feature story in a recent TV magazine even tells me where—Sweetums' own room toward the back of the house, with a balcony that might have been designed with a burglar's ease and convenience in mind.

With a few other details taken care of, it is a dark and moonless night suitable for stratagems, spoils and cat-nappings when I approach the McGurk Animal Farm, that being Sweetums' formal address. I am anticipating, and prepared for, a certain amount of what-the-helling to erupt when the dogs scent an intruder. But all is quiet. As I tiptoe by, I find that the Dobermans are in dreamland, the Schnauzers are snoring, the beagles are blissfully blank and the German Shepherds counting sheep.

I pause to mull this over. If I didn't know better, I would think that someone kindly disposed to burglars had slipped each of them a mickey, just as I had planned to do. It is odd, to say the least, and I wonder briefly if perhaps I should scrub the mission. But, finding nothing else to cause alarm, I pull the black knit hood over my head, clamber over the chain-link fence and scamper up a handy trellis to the balcony with no more uproar than a marshmallow falling into tapioca pudding. Another few moments and I have the window open (a bit of noise there, but unavoidable) and am entering the house.

At the same time, I hear the sound of a window being softly closed somewhere else.

Curiouser and curiouser, I think, freezing.

I haven't thawed appreciably when the sound of soft footsteps approaching congeals the bloodstream once more. Then a door opens and a figure slips through, so close that I can reach out and touch him.

Except that he happens to touch me first, at which there are symptoms of sudden paralysis in both of us, and the yelp that emerges from the other is so high-pitched that I realize he is really a she.

"Good grief!" she says, making a quick recovery. "You nearly scared me to death! I didn't expect you so soon," she continues, in a low whisper. "I was just checking to see that everything was all set."

"Um!" I say, feeling that some comment is called for but unwilling to contribute anything that might be misinterpreted. There is a stab of light from a tiny flash. "No lights!" I gasp.

"Sorry!" says the girl. "I never met a burglar before. I'm Jennifer Potter, junior account executive for Muckley and Swerge. And you're—?"

"No names, no K.P.," I respond, thinking that this situation is growing goofier by the minute. She evidently thinks so, too, for she giggles. "Right! I keep forgetting. You have a very nice voice for a burglar."

"I'm a very nice burglar."

"I'm glad. Sweetums doesn't take to everybody, you know, and I was kind of worried that—well—" briskly—"let's get on with it, shall we? You're here to kidnap Sweetums, so let's go."

"H-How did you know?"

"It was my idea to begin with," says Jennifer Potter, proudly, "of course, I just figured we'd hide Sweetums away for a few days, but Mr. Muckley thought we should stage a real kidnapping. That way, we could legitimately call in the police and get some great publicity—just as, by an odd coincidence, we're about to announce the new broccoli-flavored Sweetums Cat Cuisine. Then, according to the plan, Sweetums will be rescued at risk of life and limb and *voila!*—TV coverage, newspaper stories, features in all the magazines, America's most beloved feline restored to the bosom of her adoring public . . . here you are," says Miss Potter, guiding my hand to some kind of cushioned wicker basket. "Go ahead—kidnap away!"

"One small problem."

"Oh?"

"There's no cat to kidnap."

"You're kidding!"

The penlight snaps on again and a finger of light probes the basket, which I now see is painted gold with a red velvet cushion and the name "Sweetums" picked out in rhinestones on the back.

"She must be here!" insists Miss Potter who, now that I have enough light to see her by, turns out to be worth considerably more wattage. She has soft brown hair that tumbles fetchingly over her eyes, and a tilted little nose over a rather wide, humorous mouth—only right now it is not looking humorous at all. Her flash sweeps the room, which is pretty sparsely furnished at best, but even more sparsely furnished with cats.

"I thought I heard a window closing as I came in," I offer. "That one, probably."

We look and find that the catch has been snapped from the outside, where there is another balcony—the twin of the one I climbed in on. And the light reveals a muddy footprint on the floor.

"That's not mine," I point out.

Jennifer Potter stiffens. "Good grief! Somebody beat us to Sweetums! Mr. Muckley's going to kill me!"

She may have company, I learn when I report to Mr. Snyde the following A.M. He is sitting on the park bench, reading the morning paper, and standing nearby—at first I take it for an outcropping of rock—is a very large person whose face looks as though it had been thrown together by a Mother Nature anxious to break for lunch. Mr. Snyde chuckles and I am sure he is reading the front page feature on the disappearance of Sweetums.

"Well, I see you were successful," he says.

"Not so's you could notice it," I reply.

He glances up sharply. "What's that supposed to mean?"

"I don't have the cat. Somebody got there first." I explain about the Muckley and Swerge kidnap plot and how J. Potter evidently confused me with the hired heister.

Mr. Snyde gives me a long look, and I sense a sudden cold front passing by. "Cut the clowning," he says. "Where's the cat?"

"Cross my heart and hope to die—" I begin, before thinking this is perhaps an unfortunate choice of words, as Mr. Snyde crooks a finger and says, "Humbert!"'

The nearby monolith stirs and lumbers forward. "Yus, Mr. S.?"

"Humbert," says Mr. Snyde, "I want you to take a good look at this gentleman."

Hurnbert turns a beady little eye on me. The effect is akin to that of an elephant examining a peanut of suspicious antecedents.

"It is now nine-thirty," notes Mr. Snyde. "In the event that he fails to bring us a cat named Sweetums by six this evening, I want you to turn him inside out and play tunes on his ribs like a xylophone."

"Yus, Mr. S."

"Following which, you may push his nose so far around his head that he'll have to smell the flowers through the back of his neck."

"Yus, Mr. S."

"Following which, you may chastise him severely."

"Yus, Mr. S.," Humbert replies, registering a lively approval of the scenario.

"As for you," Mr. Snyde says, turning to me, "I don't know what your game is, but if you're thinking of holding me up for more dough, forget it. Humbert and I will expect you here at six. With cat. Understood?"

"Yus, Mr. S.," I say.

I have not, up to this point, taken much time to analyze the situation, but it is amazing how the prospect of being taken apart like a Tinkertoy by Humbert tends to concentrate the mind. For the first time, I give some thought to the following points:

A. Somebody, using a modus operandi very much like that of Kit the Cat Burglar, has made off with Sweetums.

B. It wasn't Kit the Cat Burglar.

C. Therefore, who? Or is it whom?

There are only three possible candidates I can think of; "Nervous" Sam Purvis, who is presently on sabbatical up at the state pen; "Easy Eddie" Magruder, who hasn't been heard from since he inadvertently robbed the wife of the local mob boss and is rumored to be part of the sub-base of the interstate highway; and Frank "Fingers" Fenster.

It has to be Frank, but he is not all that evident, either, and it takes hours of running down leads before I find myself, late that afternoon, about to rap on the door of a third floor room on the east side. Odd noises and muffled curses emanate from behind the door, to cease abruptly as I knock. A wary voice says, "Whozat?"

"This is Mr. Muckley," I reply, in the commanding tone I imagine an advertising agency account executive might employ.

"Waitaminnit!" There are more noises, followed by the unmistakable sound of a cat being stuffed into a bag, before the door opens.

"Hey, you ain't Muckley!" says Fingers, recoiling and preparing to slam the door.

"True, but I thought you might not let me in if I said I was the Avon lady. May I?" Since I have taken the precaution of sticking a .32 in his midriff, he invites me in. I wave him to a chair as I close the door, and he sits down, looking humble.

He also looks as though he has recently gone feet first through some sort of shredding machinery, or perhaps an agricultural combine. His hair is awry, one sleeve is ripped, his face is dotted with bits of adhesive tape and there are more bits speckling his hands.

"I understand you have a cat here," I begin.

"Hah!" says Fingers, bitterly. "What I have here is a cross between a buzzsaw and an octopus!" He nods toward a burlap bag that is writhing in a corner and expressing feline outrage. "And how come you know so much?" A gleam of comprehension appears in his eye. "Say! Was that you comin' in as I was goin' out last night? Hey, you must be Kit the Cat burglar!"

I acknowledge this and Fingers looks at me with mingled awe and admiration. "Say, that was a slick job of slippin' that catch! I didn't hear a thing until you was almost in the room!"

"Well, I hardly heard you leaving, either."

Fingers shrugs modestly. "Aw, I do my best, but—"

"You did fine. Leaving that footprint, though—that wasn't too neat."

"That Muckley guy—it was his idea," says Fingers, defensively. "Said he needed some evidence for the fuzz. Say, could I have your autograph before you go?"

The amenities satisfied, Fingers relaxes and resumes binding up his wounded digits and I am about to return to the subject of Sweetums when I am startled to hear a voice crying, "Get me out! Get me out!" Then I realize this must be Sweetums' version of "Meow!" And although I am not quite sure why I'm doing it, I start untying the bag. Fingers reacts with terror as he notices what I'm doing.

"Don't let her out!" he pleads. "She'll wreck the joint!"

But it is too late. A blur emerges at high speed from the bag, orbits the room several times, causing Fingers to leap behind a chair, then finally comes to rest as an orange-colored cat clad in a diamond collar. The face that launches thousands of bags of Sweetums Cat Cuisine wears the kind of expression you might surprise on Queen Victoria, had she just slipped on a banana peel, and it sweeps over

Fingers like a laser beam. He winces, picks up his chair and assumes a lion-tamer's stance as Sweetums takes a step toward him, hissing. Then, surprisingly, she dismisses him with a sniff, her fur subsides, and she walks over and starts rubbing against my leg. I pick her up and darned if she doesn't start purring as if I am a long lost buddy who just turned up to repay a loan. Fingers is goggle-eyed, and remarks that he never woulda believed it.

"Jennifer Potter said she doesn't take to everybody," I explain.

"She with the ad agency? I only met Muckley—and I wish he had mentioned that before I took on this job. I didn't plan on getting skinned alive for a lousy five bills!"

"Is that all you're getting? Fingers, old pal, I think we have the makings of a mutual assistance pact here!"

He is somewhat dubious at first, but when I tell him I have a customer for Sweetums who is willing to lay out $5000—which I propose to split with him—his eyes light up like Fourth of July sparklers and he is even willing to gift-wrap Sweetums for me, provided he can do it from ten feet away with tongs. The upshot of the negotiations is that I am speeding on my way to rendezvous with Mr. Snyde and Humbert with minutes to spare before the six o'clock deadline. Looking as though canaries wouldn't melt in her mouth, a docile Sweetums is seated beside me, grooming herself and occasionally looking at me with those unsettling green eyes. I have the odd impression that she is suppressing a grin, as though she were getting a big charge out of this variation in the routine. I admonish her to be on her best behavior as we approach Mr. Snyde.

"Ah!" he breathes, as we come into view. "I knew I could count on you. Didn't I say so, Humbert?" 'Kit the Cat Burglar is a man of his word,' I said! You may put the brass knuckles away for now, Humbert."

"Yus, Mr. S.," says Humbert, masking his disappointment.

"And now," says Mr. Snyde, unclasping the diamond collar from Sweetums' neck, "I'll just remove this little item. . . . "

"I thought you told me that was a fake," I say. "What do you want that for?"

"Because, my poor chump," says Mr. Snyde, "it's not a fake—as you might have found, had you done your homework as I did. The whole point of this exercise was to get you to steal it for us, since neither Humbert nor I are really qualified."

"For a fee of five thousand dollars," I remind him.

Mr. Snyde looks astonished. "Five thousand dollars? Did I say anything that sounded like five thousand dollars, Humbert?"

"No, Mr. S."

"I thought not. Humbert never forgets."

"And I haven't forgotten the name of your advertising agency, either."

"Oh, that!" Mr. Snyde fans out a bunch of business cards, all with different names and companies on them. "You'd be surprised how easy it is to set yourself up in business. All you need is a supply of pasteboard and a friendly printer."

"So it's all a scam? You weren't planning to stash the cat away someplace to spike some TV commercials?"

"Oh, we'll stash the cat someplace, all right," says Mr. Snyde. "The lagoon in this park seems a convenient spot. Do you have a sack and a rock handy, Humbert?"

"Yus, Mr. S."

Humbert looms menacingly as I utter an exclamation of protest, and Mr. Snyde says. "You weren't thinking of making a fuss, I trust?"

Baffled, I can only watch as Humbert grabs Sweetums by the scruff of the neck despite her yowl of indignation, and prepares to insert her into the sack he produces from a back pocket. Then all at once a look of agony and alarm spreads over his face. His nose twitches. His eyes begin to water. His face turns the color of a Hawaiian sunset. He struggles with a series of strangled gasps, then goes, "ATCHOOOO!" in a blast that shakes leaves from the trees, sends the park pigeons into hysterics and registers on Richter scales for miles around.

"ATCHOO!" he erupts again. And again. As Sweetums seizes the opportunity to clout him a good one across the chops, he adds, "OW!" and continues in this vein, dropping the sack, dropping Sweetums—who vanishes in the underbrush— and, in an especially violent paroxysm, stepping on Mr. Snyde's foot, thereby adding the latter's yelps of anguish to what is fast developing into a localized debacle. "Cats bake be sdeeze!" Humber explains apologetically, between explosions.

"Come on, you oaf!" snarls Mr. Snyde, hopping on one foot. He throws me a poisonous look. "Forget the cat! Let's get out of here!"

Humbert's sneezes grow fainter as the two of them leg it across the park, Mr. Snyde limping to keep up, and presently Sweetums reappears from under a bush with a regal air, as though she has just been off reviewing the troops. I pick her up and she cries, "My hero!" At least, that's what it sounds like, though on further reflection I realize it is only another "Meow!"

I am not anxious to return to Fingers and confess that the deal has fallen through, as I foresee a bit of difficulty in convincing him that I really didn't collect the five grand, and that consequently he and I have a fifty-fifty split of zero. With some trepidation I give his door the code knock we'd agreed on earlier, and the feeling grows when, upon entering, I find three additional persons seated around Fingers' table, all giving me looks that could bore holes in a bank vault. One of them is Jennifer Potter, and I assume even before Fingers' introductions that the others are Messrs. Muckley and Swerge. They are wearing dark three-piece suits, Muckley being stocky, swarthy and forceful-looking while Swerge is tall and thin, with big eyeglasses giving him the appearance of an agitated stork.

There is a lot of "Aha!"-ing as I heave into view, and the initial relief at finding Sweetums unharmed is succeeded by a storm of vituperation. I gather that Fingers and I are going to be strung up by the thumbs as soon as they find a rope and a stout lamppost, and Muckley is expanding on this topic, explaining how delighted he will be, personally, to turn us over to the authorities, when Fingers looks alarmed.

"Hey, waitaminnit!" he protests. "You hired me!"

"And you tried to double-cross us!"

"I'll tell everybody it was all a publicity stunt!"

"Who's going to believe you?"

"What kind of a deal is this?" demands Fingers, rhetorically.

"Rawr!" says Sweetums, but no one pays any attention to her except Jennifer, in whose lap she is sitting, and me. The cat gives me a long look, slowly winks one eye, and cocks her head toward the cupboard in the pullman kitchen. I follow her glance—toward her food and water dishes.

"Sorry you feel that way," I remark. "We'd hoped to settle things peacefully, but I guess we'll have to mention it."

"Mention what?" says Swerge, blinking behind his spectacles.

"Oh, nothing. Just a kind of amusing sidelight, that's all."

"What's amusing?" asks Muckley, suspiciously.

"The fact that all the while we had Sweetums, she refused to eat anything but Scat, The Feast for Finicky Felines." They follow my gaze to the bag of cat food in the kitchen and the room falls suddenly silent.

"I beg your pardon?" says Muckley.

"I beg your pardon?" says Swerge.

"I beg your pardon?" says Jennifer, making it a clean sweep.

"Scat, The Feast for Finicky Felines," I repeat. "You've heard of it, I suppose? Sweetums seemed to think it was caviar—couldn't get enough. I'm sure her fans would be interested in knowing."

Muckley and Swerge exchange looks. "Er—do you have to mention it?"

"I'm afraid so."

"It—er—could embarrass our client."

"Think how embarrassed Fingers and I will be, serving terms in the slammer."

A hint of perspiration beads Swerge's brow. "Perhaps we've been a bit hasty. After all, it's not as though Mr. Kit here actually profited from this—this . . . "

"It seems to me," says J. Potter, firmly, "that we owe these two a vote of

170

thanks for recovering America's favorite cat from a band of ruthless criminals, who are doubtless still being pursued by the police, the F.B.I. and Interpol, with arrests expected momentarily."

Muckley and Swerge consider this. "Well," they respond, "when you look at it *that* way . . ."

And that is how Fingers and I wind up splitting the reward for Sweetums' return—under different names, of course—and I am sufficiently pleased with the outcome to overlook Mr. Snyde's slurs on my planning abilities. Because, after all, I *had* checked out that ad agency of his and found there was no such outfit— which sort of made me wonder what he was really after, if not to sabotage some competitive TV spots. It could only have been the diamond collar, so one of my preparatory moves involved having a duplicate made by a friend who specializes in such things. That was the one Snyde got. And then, just in case it might cause a stir if Sweetums came back minus her famous collar, I had my friend make me another. That was the one Muckley and Swerge got.

As to who got the real diamond collar, well, I'm afraid that's a secret between Sweetums and me, and Sweetums isn't talking. Although I'm not at all sure she couldn't, if she felt like it.

Edward D. Hoch

THE CAT AND FIDDLE MURDERS

The strange chain of events that carried Sir Gideon Parrot and myself to England in the autumn of last year need not be recounted here. Suffice it to say that upon completion of the business at hand we were invited to spend a few days at a little island off the Devon Coast. Our host was to be Archibald Knore, the department-store heir who'd spent ten years and countless thousands of pounds assembling a private zoo for the amusement of himself and his friends.

"How do you happen to know Knore?" I asked Gideon as we made our way across the strip of water that separated the mainland from Placid Island. Knore's was one of the largest department-store chains in Britain, and the invitation to spend a few days in such illustrious company was most impressive.

"I did the man a favor once," Gideon explained. "It's not the sort of favor one mentions in polite conversation, and I doubt if he will do so. He was visiting a young lady of dubious reputation and I helped him escape just before her apartment was raided by the police. But this was years ago. I dare say Archibald has settled down now and devotes his full energies to this private zoo of his."

Right on cue there came a loud trumpeting from the island just ahead. The little mail boat bucked in the water as if startled by the noise and I fastened a grip on Gideon's arm. "What was that?"

"Sounded like an elephant to me. We'll see soon enough—there's the dock straight ahead."

I'd expected Archibald Knore himself to be waiting for us at dockside, but although he wasn't there it was no disappointment. In his stead was as lovely a young woman as I'd ever had the pleasure to meet since leaving New York. She reached down a firm hand to help us onto the dock, then introduced herself with a sunny smile. "I'm Lois Lanchester, Mr. Knore's secretary. Welcome to Placid Island."

"What a nice name for it," Gideon said, bowing to kiss her hand.

She laughed and tossed her mane of yellow hair with one hand. "During the winter storms we sometimes suspect the prior owners chose that name to enhance its value as real estate."

"This is a year-round home, then?" I asked.

She turned, as if noticing me for the first time, and Gideon hurried to introduce me. "Yeah," she said. "Mr. Knore devotes his full time to the zoo these days. The family business is handled by others."

She led the way up to the house, the fit of her designer jeans over her perfectly formed hips snug. When the great house itself came into full view, my gaze was distracted elsewhere. It was a magnificent place, a sprawling English country house that seemed oblivious to its somewhat cramped island setting. And on the lawn to greet us was a strutting peacock, its iridescent tail-feathers erect.

"He's quite a sight," I remarked.

"King Jack is our official greeter. But you'll be seeing more animals soon." As if to confirm her words the trumpet of the distant elephant sounded again.

We entered the house and passed down an oak-paneled corridor to a grimly masculine study where Archibald Knore awaited us. I'd seen newspaper pictures of him once or twice, but they hadn't prepared me for the overwhelming presence of the man himself. He was tall and large without seeming overweight, and his voice seemed to boom across the room. "Sir Gideon! A pleasure to see you again! Come right in!"

He shook my hand vigorously as Gideon introduced me. "He spent a great deal of time in your London store this week," Gideon said.

Knore smiled broadly. "Spending money, I hope. These animals seem to eat more every year."

"We're anxious to see your zoo," I told him. "But isn't a private zoo unusual these days?"

"No. There are privately owned wildlife habitats in several countries. My friend Gerald Durrell, the author, has a very fine zoo on the island of Jersey. Only government regulation prevents many others from existing. I firmly believe that the task of preserving certain rare species could be carried out much more efficiently in private hands. As long as zoos remain dependent upon public funds, those funds are often the first items to be cut in a budget crunch. The point that feeding people is more important than feeding animals is too easily made."

"Why don't I get you two settled," Lois Lanchester suggested, "and then we can show you around?"

"Do that, Lois," Archibald Knore agreed, "and then bring them back downstairs to meet the other guests for cocktails."

On the way up to our rooms Gideon asked about the other guests. "Mr. Knore often has weekend visitors," Lois said. "This weekend it's a cousin, Bertie

Foxe, his wife, and a close friend of theirs, the Czech violinist Jan Litost."

Our adjoining rooms were all we could have desired, with comfortable beds and leaded glass windows looking out on the sea. I was thankful the zoo itself was on the other side of the house where the nocturnal noises of the animals were less likely to disturb our sleep.

We'd barely had time to unpack when Lois Lanchester was tapping on our doors with all the exuberance of a shipboard cruise director. "If you're ready I can give you a quick look at the zoo before cocktails," she told us. "Sylvia Foxe wants to come along too."

"It will be a pleasure," Gideon said. "I've always had a great love for animals."

We met the wife of Knore's cousin in the downstairs hall. She was a tall dark-haired woman dressed in riding britches and leather boots. She had no doubt been pretty once but middle age had turned her face hard and stern. "Are there bridle paths on the island?" I asked after Lois had introduced us.

"No," Sylvia replied. "I simply find this costume more suitable for prowling around the animals. I wouldn't want some little creature taking a bite out of my leg."

"There's no danger of that," Lois told her sweetly.

We left the house by a rear door and followed a covered walkway to a low cinder-block building. Already the scent of animals was heavy in the air, but Lois explained that only the smallest creatures and most dangerous species of snake were kept indoors.

Never having been one for snakes, I passed quickly by the glass cages with their traditional tree branch upon which a serpent lay sunning itself beneath the artificial light from above. The lizards I found a bit more interesting, especially when they were in motion. "The temperature is kept at eighty degrees for the reptiles," Lois explained as she walked us through. "Over there is the bird house with its new penguin pond. But let me show you some of the big cats first."

The lions and tigers were kept in large open pits, with plenty of space to roam about and trees for climbing. "In the coldest weather we take them indoors," Lois said.

"Who takes care of the animals?" Gideon Parrot asked, his eyes on a large tiger that seemed to be feasting on its afternoon meal.

"We have a full-time zookeeper on the staff. His name is Taupper. You'll meet him later. He—" She paused, watching the tiger now, along with Gideon. "My god! That looks like a human body in the tiger pit!"

"It most certainly does," Gideon confirmed. "You'd better call for help."

We were above it now, and as the tiger rolled it over with one powerful paw Sylvia Foxe gasped, "It's Jan! It's our friend Jan Litost!"

A burly man in work clothes I took to be the zookeeper came running in answer to Lois's summons. While he was lowering a ladder into the pit Gideon pulled me aside and pointed to a large sheet of paper that had been tacked to a nearby tree. In large childlike letters were printed some familiar words: HIGH DIDDLE, DIDDLE, THE CAT AND THE FIDDLE.

"He was murdered," Archibald Knore said some twenty minutes later. "There's no doubt in my mind."

"Murdered by someone on this island?" Lois Lanchester asked.

We were back at the main house, gathered about the big stone fireplace where cocktails were to have been served. Sylvia Foxe's husband Bertie had joined us, a slender man with thinning hair. "It *can't* be murder," he insisted. "Who on this island could have any possible motive for killing Jan?"

"The back of his skull was crushed," Knore argued. "He was hit very hard with a blunt instrument of some sort. And there are spots of blood on the railing surrounding the tiger pit. Someone killed him and dumped him in there. As to who would have a motive, that's for the police to discover."

"Have they been summoned?" Gideon asked.

"I'll do that now."

But his telephone call to the mainland didn't bring the prompt response we desired. The local constable informed Knore that all the boats were tied up with a rescue mission down the coast and with the winds increasing as darkness approached the police helicopter couldn't make the flight over to the island until morning. "Don't touch anything," his voice crackled. "We'll be there first thing in the morning."

Archibald Knore slammed down the telephone. "The old fool! If there's a murderer loose on this island we could all be dead by morning!"

"The winds are picking up outside," Sylvia Foxe said. "It looks like a storm."

"No storm," the zookeeper said. "The animals aren't that restless." It was the first time Peter Taupper had spoken since he'd lifted the body of Jan Litost from the pit. He was a burly, unkempt man with tufts of gray hair protruding from his ears. I wondered if Knore paid him as much as a municipal zoo would, though I had no idea what good public or private zookeepers earned.

At this point Gideon Parrot cleared his throat and the room fell silent. "In the absence of the official police I may be of some service," he announced. "I was invited here as a guest, but Archibald knows I've had some experience in matters of this nature. I propose we take a few moments to examine the facts."

"What facts?" Lois asked.

"Well, if someone on this island is a murderer we need to know exactly how many people are here."

"That's easy," she responded, counting them off on her fingers. "You two, myself, Mr. Knore, Mrs. Knore—"

"Wait a minute," Gideon interrupted. "Is your wife on the island, Archibald?"

"Dora has been crippled for some years now. She never leaves her room."

"I see. Go on, please, Miss Lanchester."

"O.K. Mrs. Knore, Mr. and Mrs. Foxe, Peter Taupper, his assistant Milo Lune who also tends to the gardening, and of course the butler, the maid, and the cook. There is also a nurse who tends to Mrs. Knore, but this is her day off."

"Then there are twelve people on the island at the present time, not counting the unfortunate Mr. Litost."

"That's correct."

"Who tends to Mrs. Knore when the nurse is away?"

Knore answered the question. "The maid does. She's quite efficient."

"Mr. and Mrs. Foxe," Gideon said. "You brought the victim to this island. Suppose you tell me a bit about him."

Bertie Foxe snorted. "No one has to be told about Jan Litost. He was one of Europe's foremost violinists—he wasn't yet forty yeas old! It's a terrible loss to the world of music!"

"Had he a wife? A lover?"

"I believe he was married in his youth, but he'd been alone for many years. We met him in London last season and became fast friends. It was I who suggested he might want to visit Archibald's private zoo."

"When did you arrive?"

"Yesterday afternoon."

Gideon turned to Mrs. Foxe. "And how is it you hadn't viewed the animals until today?"

"I was indisposed when we arrived," Sylvia Foxe explained. "It was a rough crossing by boat just after lunch—my stomach was unprepared for it."

"But your husband and the late Mr. Litost had toured the zoo?"

"I took them around yesterday," Knore volunteered, "and Peter showed them the giraffe and the zebras this morning. They're kept farther out, away from the house."

Another man in work clothes, somewhat younger than Taupper, entered during the conversation. Taupper introduced him to Gideon and me. "This is my assistant, Milo Lune."

The man seemed unusually shy. He rubbed his dirty hands against the legs of his work pants as he answered Gideon's questions. "Did I see Mr. Litost this morning? No—well, yes, I think I did spot him strolling by the monkey cages but only at a distance. I didn't speak with him."

"Is something the matter?" Gideon asked. "You seem nervous."

"No, no—it's just I'm worried about the animals is all."

Gideon next produced the crudely printed note he'd discovered tacked to the tree. "Did any of you see this before? I found it on a tree near the scene."

"It looks like the work of a child," Lois Lanchester said.

"Are there any children on Placid Island?"

"No."

Archibald Knore came forward to study the message. "A child's nursery rhyme. What does it mean?"

"The cat and the fiddle could refer to the tiger and Jan Litost."

"The rhyme is believed to be a reference to Queen Elizabeth the First," Bertie Foxe said. "I've made a study of nursery rhymes."

"Notice the location of the commas in the message," Gideon said, holding it up again.

HIGH DIDDLE, DIDDLE, THE CAT AND THE FIDDLE,

"What about it?" Lois asked.

"Not many persons would place commas between those two 'diddles,' yet that is the correct version of the rhyme. The person who wrote this was no child. Note too the comma at the end of the line. What does that tell us?"

"That there's more to come," Lois answered quietly.

There was always the possibility of another person on the island, perhaps an escaped convict who'd come out by boat from the mainland and remained hidden back there among the animals. Knore suggested a search party be organized and I readily agreed to be part of it. Gideon, who walked slowly at best, decided to stay behind and question the servants about anything unusual they might have seen.

I found myself with Bertie Foxe, Peter Taupper, and Milo Lune, making a sweep of the far end of the island. There was a dense wooded area here, with only a high fence to indicate the outer limits of the zoo itself. "No one's here," Milo Lune said. "I'm back here a few days a week and nothing's been disturbed. We're wasting our time."

"We should split up," Foxe suggested. "We'd cover the ground much quicker."

The zookeeper, Taupper, agreed readily enough. "Why don't we spread out and keep walking in a counter-clockwise direction? Then meet back at the house?"

I found myself on the far right of the sweep, close to the rocky shoreline with a view of the water. The others were out of sight within minutes and I eyed the setting sun uncertainly, hoping I'd make it back before dark. But the island wasn't as large as I'd feared and it took me only a quarter of an hour to circle around, following the shoreline until the big house was in sight once more.

But now there were only three of us.

Taupper's assistant, Milo Lune, was missing.

"Where the hell is he?" Taupper demanded, and tried shouting his name. There was no reply.

"Shall we go back?" Foxe suggested. "It'll be dark soon."

"He'll show up," Taupper said, a bit uncertainly.

We were standing, uncertain of our next move, when a window high in the house opened and Sylvia Foxe's head appeared. "There's someone in the elephant enclosure!" she shouted. "I can see him from here!"

I took a deep breath and followed quickly after the others. When we reached the elephant enclosure I saw at once what Sylvia had spotted from her window. Milo Lune was crumpled near the fence of the enclosure while one of the smaller elephants nudged the body with its trunk. The back of his head was battered and bloody, but I was beyond blaming the injury on an elephant's hoof. I wasn't even surprised a few minutes later when Gideon Parrot joined us and snatched another message off a nearby tree.

"THE COW JUMP'D OVER THE MOON," he read.

After a dinner eaten quickly in gloomy silence, we gathered in Archibald Knore's study to sort out what few facts we had in our possession. Knore himself had tried to reach the mainland again, but without success. "The phone is dead," he reported. "It may be because of the heavy winds, or—"

"Or the line may have been cut," Sylvia Foxe supplied. "God, we're trapped on this island with a madman!"

"We must all stay together," Knore agreed. He toward Gideon Parrot and said, "I think you and your friend had better double up for the night. Bertie and Sylvia will be together and I will be with my wife." He paused, trying to puzzle out the rest of it. "Lois, you'd better share a room with the maid and cook. And, Peter, you can sleep with the butler."

"Old Oakes?" the zookeeper snorted. "He snores so loud he keeps the animals awake! I'll take my chances alone, thanks!"

We'd already been over the timing of Milo Lune's killing and everyone agreed that either Bertie or Peter Taupper could have done it—or even myself, for that matter. But it was just as likely that someone from the house, or a hidden stranger, could have surprised him with that terrible blow to the head.

"But how could he let anyone approach him with a club or anything after what happened to Jan Litost?" Lois asked. "It doesn't make sense."

"The killer might have been well hidden and struck before he was seen," Gideon suggested.

"But he'd have to push the body into the elephant enclosure," I pointed out.

"With the rest of us in the area, someone would be sure to see him."

"But no one did," Gideon replied. "So apparently it wasn't such a risk, after all." He turned to Sylvia Foxe. "You were watching from your window. Did you see anything?"

She shook her head. "Not until I noticed the body. But I wasn't at the window for very long. I'd just come up from downstairs. I went to see if Bertie was in sight anywhere and I spotted what looked like a body."

Gideon turned to Archibald Knore. "Where were you during this time?"

"Alone here in the study. You certainly can't suspect *me* of killing them!"

"I suspect everyone. It's the only way. In fact, I must ask you the same question, Miss Lanchester."

Lois flushed prettily and stammered a bit. "Well, I—well, I was using one of the upstairs bathrooms. My stomach's been in knots since Jan's body was found. I wasn't feeling well."

"Perfectly understandable," Gideon agreed.

Knore came out from behind his desk. "The killer is no one here. It's some madman who murders whoever he finds alone. Jan and Milo were simply unlucky."

But Gideon shook his head, like a professor correcting a wayward student. "No, they were the intended victims. We know that from the nursery rhyme. The cat was the tiger, and the fiddle was a reference to the violinist, Jan Litost."

"But how," Knore asked, "does this latest message pertain to Lune and the elephants?"

"Lune is the French word for moon, of course. I noticed some smaller elephants in that enclosure." He turned to the zookeeper. "Mr. Taupper, if male elephants are called bulls, what are the females called?"

"Cows," Taupper answered quietly. "Everyone knows that."

"Thus, the cow jumped over the moon—and crushed his skull while doing it."

"What's the rest of the rhyme?" Bertie Foxe asked after a moment's silence. "Nothing about foxes in it, is there?"

"No," Gideon answered seriously. "In its earliest version the verse reads, High diddle, diddle, The Cat and the Fiddle, The Cow jump'd over the Moon; The little Dog laugh'd To see such Craft, And the Dish ran away with the Spoon."

"You remember all that?" Lois asked.

"During this afternoon's search I looked it up in *The Oxford Dictionary of Nursery Rhymes*. There's a copy in the library."

"Where anyone else could have looked it up too," I observed. "That's how they got the punctuation right."

"Perhaps."

"The little Dog laugh'd To see such Craft," Knore repeated. "I don't see how that can apply to anyone here. And there are no dogs on the island."

"We can't have them," Taupper explained. "They'd upset the animals with their barking."

"Then maybe the chain will be broken," Lois said. "Maybe the killer's work is finished."

Gideon Parrot said nothing. He was staring at a photograph on Knore's desk, obviously a portrait of Knore and his wife when they were much younger. "I think we must speak with Mrs. Knore," he said quietly.

"She knows nothing," Knore protested. "She never leaves her room."

"But things can be seen from a window. Sylvia Foxe saw a body from her window. Your wife might have seen the killer."

Archibald Knore was silent for a moment. Finally he said, "Very well. You and your friend can see her. But only for a few minutes. I'll take you up."

The upper reaches of the house seemed unusually dark, with only a dim bulb at the top of the stairs to light the way. The maid who'd been sitting with Dora Knore rose as we entered and Archibald dismissed her with a wave of his hand.

The woman in the bed seemed about Knore's age but she was very thin and rather feeble in her gestures. "You've brought me visitors, Archie," she said in a soft voice. "How nice."

"This is Sir Gideon Parrot, dear. He's investigating the trouble I told you about."

"The killings?"

"Yes."

"Terrible things! We moved here to get away from crime in the cities. After my accident I couldn't walk anymore—"

"Might I ask what caused it?" Gideon asked her.

"An auto crash. Archie was driving and the car went off the road. I think he was dozing a bit but I've never blamed him for what happened."

"Mrs. Knore," Gideon began, keeping his voice soft to match hers, "I was wondering if you might have seen anything today from your window at about the time either of those men was killed."

"Oh, no. I never get out of bed. The nurse or Winifred—the maid—tells me what I need to know, which is very little. The weather makes no impact on my life and the animals are Archie's hobby, not mine."

"So you saw or heard nothing?"

"Not a thing."

Her eyes closed for a moment and Knore took that as a signal she was tiring. "That's all," he said.

When we were in the hall Gideon asked, "Wouldn't she be more comfortable in a wheelchair, with the rest of us?"

"No, no," her husband said. "She's fine as she is. She wants it this way."

Back downstairs, plans were again made for the sleeping arrangements. Everyone would be safe through the remainder of the night. And in the morning the police would come.

That, at least, is what we thought.

But in the morning, as Gideon and I were arising before breakfast, Peter Taupper brought news of the latest outrage. The island's only boat had been scuttled at its dock and now lay in eight feet of water. Tacked to one of the mooring posts was the expected message: THE LITTLE DOG LAUGH'D TO SEE SUCH CRAFT,

The telephone was still dead and the winds were still high. We were cut off from the mainland with a killer who showed no sign of stopping.

Over breakfast Archibald Knore said, "At least no one was killed this time."

"No," Lois Lanchester murmured. "Not yet. But there's still one line of the nursery rhyme to go." She was helping to serve the breakfast and, taking a sip of Knore's hot porridge with a spoon before she placed the bowl in front of him, she said, "Tastes good."

The Foxes were together at the end of the table, looking unhappy, and Taupper stood in the doorway with a cup of coffee, explaining how he'd happened to find the damaged boat. "I went down to the dock to see if any boats were coming over from the mainland. That's when I saw her sunk in the water. Somebody whacked the side of it with an ax—below the water line, near as I could tell. It was probably done last night, before we all went to bed."

"But what sense does the message make?" Bertie Foxe asked. "I understand that the craft refers to the boat, but there's still no dog on the island."

"Nor anyone whose name sounds like dog," Sylvia chimed in.

Knore looked unhappy. "My wife Dora. *Dora* and *dog* start with the same two letters, but that's a bit farfetched."

"It certainly is," Lois agreed. "Your wife is the one person on the island who *can't* be involved. She never leaves her *room*."

"It's obvious the killer intends to complete the verse," Gideon said. "It's important that we anticipate his actions and beat him to it."

"What is it? *And the Dish ran away with the Spoon?* What could that possibly mean?" I asked.

"I think we're worrying needlessly," Taupper said. "As soon as the winds die down, the helicopter will be over from the mainland."

"Can the boat be repaired?" Knore asked.

"Certainly. Anything can be repaired."

"Can it be repaired by you?"

"I think so. I can patch it and pump out the water."

"Then do it, man! Quickly!"

Sylvia Foxe cleared her throat. "Might I suggest that someone should go with him? If he's down there alone the killer might get ideas."

"Good thinking," her husband said.

"Lois, how about you?" Sylvia suggested. "Or would you rather I go?"

Lois Lanchester finished her morning coffee and stubbed out her cigarette. "I'll be glad to go, but I don't know that I'll be of much help. What say, Peter? Do you need me?"

Taupper grinned. "You can hold my tools. Come along."

After they'd left, Gideon and I went for a walk outside. The unsettled weather had made the animals restless, and the camels shied away as we approached their pen. Over beyond it the zoo's young giraffe was romping in the tall grass and two zebras grazed nearby. "A peaceful place," Gideon said. "The peaceable kingdom—even with a killer loose."

"Gideon," I said, "I've got a theory. Suppose the animals really did kill Litost and Lune. Suppose those crazy notes were written afterward by Taupper to protect his precious animals."

"An interesting theory, but hardly a practical one. The rhyme doesn't fit the events perfectly, but there is some connection. It could hardly have been a spur-of-the-moment idea in the first case, and the coincidence of a second killing accidentally fitting the pattern is out of the question."

"What now?"

He'd turned to stare up at the great old house. "I think we should speak to Bertie Foxe."

We found Bertie and his wife upstairs in their room where they'd gone after breakfast. It was a big sunny bedroom, larger than the one Gideon and I were now sharing but similarly furnished. Bertie sat on the bed smoking while Sylvia stared out the window at the animals.

"I want to know more about Jan Litost," Gideon said. "He was the first victim and the key to this puzzle must lie with him."

"Jan was extremely talented," Bertie Foxe said, taking a long drag on his cigarette. "We'd been friends for years and it seemed a natural thing to accept Archibald's kind invitation to visit the zoo after the London concert."

"Did the three of you travel together frequently?"

"Quite frequently," Sylvia answered from the window.

"You'll forgive me but I must ask this next question. Was there any sort of romantic involvement between yourself and Jan, Mrs. Foxe, which might have made your husband jealous?"

"See here!" Bertie barked, jumping to his feet.

But Sylvia answered calmly, "Certainly not. Bertie and I are happily married and always have been."

"There was nothing between them!" Bertie growled, stepping forward. "Take your dirty little thoughts elsewhere, Parrot!"

Gideon walked to the window and stared out across the tiled roof of the zoo building. He seemed to be looking at the tops of the elephants' heads, barely visible in their enclosure, as he said, "We're all like those animals at times. We meet, and mate, and sometimes kill. It's human nature, or the animal side of human nature, for the males to clash over a female—"

His words were interrupted by a sharp scream from somewhere downstairs.

"Come on!" I shouted, breaking for the door.

We found Archibald Knore at the foot of the stairs, holding onto the maid, Winifred. "What is it?" Gideon demanded as we hurried down to join them.

"I lost my head," Knore muttered, releasing the girl at once. "I was questioning her and she told me a lie. When I grabbed her she screamed."

"A lie about what?"

Winifred was sobbing softly. "He accused me of wantin' to run off with Mr. Oakes, the butler. I never would do a thing like that, sir."

"They've been carrying on behind my back. I know they have!"

"*And the Dish ran away with the Spoon,*" Gideon quoted. "You thought it referred to your butler and maid."

"What else could it refer to?" Knore said. "They did it and now they're going to run off."

"You think the butler did it?" I asked in amazement.

"You have books on nursery rhymes in the library. Let's check them," Gideon suggested to Knore, "and let this young woman be about her work."

The library, next to Knore's study, was a pleasant room with books reaching from floor to ceiling and the odor of leather bindings in the air. It took Gideon only a few moments' search to find what he sought. "See here—the same theory that links the rhyme to Queen Elizabeth says that the Dish was a courtier honored by being assigned to carry golden dishes into the state dining room."

"A butler, in other words," Knore insisted.

"Or a custodian of something valuable, at least. And the Spoon was a beautiful young woman at court who was taster at the royal meals, insuring that the king or queen had not been poisoned."

"I know all that," Knore grumbled. "It still adds up to butler and maid in this household."

"If you'll pardon me," said Gideon, "the maid, Winifred, could hardly be described as beautiful. And the duties of taster seen more closely to resemble your secretary, Lois. In fact, I saw her taste the breakfast porridge just a few minutes ago."

"That's right!" I agreed.

"Lois?" Knore repeated, frowning with puzzlement.

The Foxes had come back downstairs, and as we left the library I saw Sylvia emerge from the kitchen carrying a rolled-up newspaper in her gloved hand. "I'm going outside for a little reading," she said. "Call me if anything happens, Bertie."

Bertie Fox grunted and said to us, "How do you suppose Taupper's coming along with the boat repairs?"

"Want me to take a look?" I said. But Gideon ignored the question. His mind was still on the problem of the rhyme.

"If the Spoon referred to Lois Lanchester, couldn't the Plate refer not to the butler but to the custodian of your most valuable property, Archibald?"

Knore looked puzzled. "I have no gold."

"The animals, man! Peter Taupper is the custodian of your animals! He is the Plate of the rhyme!"

"Taupper and Lois?" I asked. "You think they're running away together?"

"That's the only way the rhyme can work out," Gideon answered grimly. "Come quickly—there's not a moment to lose."

He led the way, with Knore, Bertie, and me following along. We hurried out of the house and down the path toward the boat dock. I was vaguely aware that the morning's strong winds had let up, but right now we were concerned with more important matters than the weather.

It was the note that stopped us, at the final turn before the boat landing. It had been tacked to a tree like the others, and it read AND THE DISH RAN AWAY WITH THE SPOON. This time the period was firmly in place at the end of the line. A finish had been reached.

"We're too late," I said.

"Maybe not!" Gideon plunged on and I followed, outdistancing the others.

The first thing we saw was Peter Taupper's body sprawled by the dock, and then Lois struggling with Sylvia Foxe. Sylvia's newspaper lay near Taupper. As Gideon and I hurried to pull them apart I said, "What happened? Did Sylvia come upon them as they were about to get away?"

"That's what it was," Sylvia gasped, struggling in my grip. "Turn me loose!"

But Gideon cautioned, "Hang onto her! She was about to add two more victims to her list! Sylvia Foxe is our nursery-rhyme murderess!"

*   *   *

Peter Taupper had only been stunned by the blow, and he and Lois were able to confirm the attack by Sylvia. She'd used the rolled-up newspaper, which she had soaked in water and put into the kitchen freezer until it froze into a dub of ice. The victims never suspected a thing when they saw her walking toward them with a newspaper. All she needed was a reasonable amount of strength behind that ice club to crush their skulls. And the weapon could be dropped anywhere unnoticed.

"I *saw* her coming out of the kitchen with the paper," I confirmed. "But why did she want to kill them all?"

"I expect Bertie can tell us about the first murder," Gideon said.

Bertie Foxe hung his head. "I always suspected Jan was having an affair with my wife. I spoke to him about it back in London, man to man, and I had the impression he was going to break it off."

"I imagine he tried to," Gideon agreed. "That's why she killed him. Then when she saw Milo Lune working nearby she must have feared he'd seen her. So he had to die too. The fact that Litost was a violinist and Lune's name means 'moon' must have suggested the nursery rhyme to her as a means of putting us off the track. But in truth it put us *on* the track. In the original rhyme and in her messages, there were eight words beginning with capital letters besides the first word in each line. They are Cat, Fiddle, Cow, Moon, Dog, Craft, Dish, and Spoon. She gave each one the meaning of a person, animal, or thing. Cat was the tiger, Fiddle was Litost, Cow was the female elephant, Moon was Lune, Craft was the sunken boat, Dish was Taupper, for reasons I've explained, and Spoon was Lois."

"What about Dog?" I asked.

"It was a clue to her own identity. A fox is indeed a member of the dog family, and when no other meaning presented itself I saw what she meant—*The little Dog laugh'd*, just as Sylvia Foxe herself must have laughed when the boat sank."

"She was going to kill Taupper and Lois just to finish the rhyme?" Knore asked.

"I imagine she would have weighted their bodies and pushed them off the dock. If they had seemed to run away, as in the rhyme, we would have blamed them for the prior killings."

Lois Lanchester still couldn't believe it. "And you knew all this just because a fox is a member of the dog family? Why couldn't the killer have been Bertie Foxe instead of Sylvia?"

"There were other things," Gideon admitted. "It was Sylvia who persuaded you to accompany Taupper to the dock, where she could kill you both. And remember yesterday when Sylvia called down from her window that she saw Lune's body up against the fence in the elephant enclosure? When I stood at that same window this morning I could barely see the tops of the elephants' heads. The zoo building blocked the view. She could only have known about the body if she'd put it there herself a few minutes earlier."

There was a throbbing in the sky and we looked up to see the police helicopter coming in for a landing. Out beyond the big house one of the elephants trumpeted a greeting.

Ingram Meyer

PROFESSOR KRELLER'S SECRET

They were walking single file along the uneven rocky path. Large cottonwood trees grew on both sides, the branches spreading umbrella-like above their heads. The lake would be just a hundred yards or so to their left. Pixy, carrying a high, aluminum-framed backpack, walked in front. He was completely hidden; only his legs showed from behind. The backpack was bright red, and his corduroys dark green.

"A giant walking tomato," thought Grandma. "What a funny little man." And not for the first time did she wonder why on earth she had ever gone into partnership with that small, ridiculous detective. She pulled her large beat-up vinyl suitcase on casters by a leather grasp. It wasn't an easy feat, either, on this awful hikers' trail. Her arm was getting sore.

"You all right, Gran?" called Pixy from behind his backpack.

"Yeah, great. This miserable suitcase is like a big fat dog, jumping and dipping behind me. How much farther is that blasted house?"

"Must be coming up soon. Mooshi said it was a mile from the highway.—There! There it is now."

And there it was. Both detectives stopped, mouths open.

"THIS is Mooshi Winthrop's hideaway?" Grandma cried. "THIS is where she writes all those wonderful love stories? It's a terrible place!"

Pixy had to admit that it was one of the worst houses he had ever seen. It was an ugly old place, originally a brown clapboard house but now mended all over with odd pieces of plywood and shingles. The roof was overgrown with thick, brownish moss, and the chimney was crumbly. There was an outhouse to the right. It wouldn't be haunted, would it? Oh man, he hoped not! If there was one thing that he, Pixy, was afraid of, it was the supernatural. He looked up at the four small windows, two on either side of the entrance, and thought that on the whole it wasn't the kind of place that ghosts would choose to occupy. Shabby and unattractive it was, but not especially creepy.

187

Grandma sat down on her suitcase.

"That thing will snap open," warned Pixy, but she didn't bother to answer. Instead she asked, "Did you know that rich and famous Mooshi Winthrop, author of over two hundred romantic novels, lived in a cheap ramshackle like this? You were the one who went to her hotel to negotiate the contract."

"Well, yes and no." Pixy was leaning against a craggy dead tree trunk, easing the weight of his backpack.

"What kind of an answer is that, Pixy!" She got up from her suitcase—it had creaked dangerously, for she was a large person—and took off her heavy tweed jacket.

Pixy almost laughed aloud. Good heavens, what a sight she was. Smart navy skirt and lace-trimmed white blouse, a beautiful cameo pin at her throat, silver hair coiled all around her head and held by a large glittering mother-of-pearl clip.—And then there were the legs! Thick crinkly cotton stockings, shabby faded sneakers with knotted laces and holes in the toes. That was Grandma all right. Not his granny, not anybody's granny, but for some reason or other called so by half their hometown because of her several ex-husbands and accordingly other ex-this-and-thats. Ten years ago she had finally decided to become something other than a housewife for a change. She had looked all over for an important and glamorous job to do, then decided that her next door neighbor Pixy was really the only person she knew who led a fairly exciting life. She had bought a partnership in his business, and Grandma had become a private detective.

"What does 'yes and no' mean, Pixy?" she asked again, sharply.

"Well, Gran, it's like this. Mooshi told me her hideaway was quaint and rustic—"

Grandma sniffed. "Quaint and rustic, my foot! This is an awful place to send a person detecting. Outhouse in the yard, for goodness sake! I haven't seen such a thing since I married my first husband."

"Mooshi writes about olden times," said Pixy. "This setting probably inspires her stories about—"

"—knights in shining armor? Handsome, charming young gentlemen asking for the hand of beautiful aristocratic maidens?" laughed Grandma. "Well, one never knows. Writers are said to be strange people. Let's unlock the door and see what the house looks like on the inside."

"I promised Mooshi we'd stay here for a few days. Do you think we'll be able to find out what's behind all those strange happenings in her neighbor Professor Kreller's cabin? It would be located a little farther along this trail, but the trees seem way too dense to get a view of it from here."

"Well, we sure as hell can't see anything from this place. And to tell you the truth, Pixy, I for one don't fancy creeping through these woods and spying on

188

someone else's house. But, as always, we're damned short on money. Sleuthing is a poor man's occupation." Grandma sighed deeply.

"Mooshi is loaded. Regardless of her funny taste in living quarters and all, that lady is *rich*. We solve this mystery, and the rent will get paid once again." Pixy stuck the large cast iron key into the lock, whistling. And Grandma pulled up her suitcase, and she too was in good spirits once again.

On the inside the house was quite clean and cosy, albeit tacky. There were only two big rooms. On the left was a bedroom, with a kingsize bed, a stool, a large mirrored dresser, and a cedar trunk. And on the right was the combination kitchen and living room, with a huge black woodburning stove, a modern refrigerator with a cat on top, a round maple table with four chairs, a brown saggy sofa, and three big overstuffed armchairs, none of them matching. Then there was a rather lovely corner china cabinet, which also had a cat on top.

"Oh, how cute!" cried Grandma. "Look at the darling beautiful grey Persian cats. Here, kitty, kitty!" She left her suitcase by the door and dashed over to the one on the fridge. She reached up and tried to grab it. But the cat stood up, leaned on its hindlegs, flattened its ears—and hissed.

"Gee, if you want to be like that, then I'll talk to your friend!" Grandma was insulted. She was a cat lover, and she seldom met a feline who didn't fall instantly in love with her. She stood on her toes and tried to get the other cat, but this one went almost berserk. It flew over to the sofa, jumped on the table, and landed with a thud behind the big stove. It growled and spat and wagged its bushy tail furiously. Grandma was in shock.

"Maybe they've got rabies," said Pixy. He stood pressed against the bedroom door, shaking. Cats weren't his favorite animals under any circumstances.

"They don't look sick to me. They're just unfriendly. How Mooshi Winthrop can keep such badly behaved pets is beyond me."

She grabbed a broom from a hook beside the door and swatted at them. Pixy held the front door wide open, but the cats wouldn't budge. They had flattened themselves under the stove, and four yellowish-green eyes squinted nastily at Grandma and Pixy.

"Oh well," said Grandma. "They aren't very nice, are they? But if we leave the door open, they'll probably go outside eventually. Let's unpack our stuff and get settled. I get the bedroom, and you get the couch."

Oh sure, he, Pixy, would get the saggy sofa!

Grandma had percolated a pot of coffee, and they were sitting in wooden armchairs in front of the house. Pixy had put on bluejeans and a grey T-shirt with a large green alligator on it. Grandma had also changed. She now wore a pale yellow caftan, with big orange and brown flowers.

"This *is* nice!" she sighed contentedly. "I can almost see how one can write romantic novels in this setting."

"I don't know about romantic, Gran. Seems more a setting for a nice murder story. It's deserted here. House is crooked, trees are high."

Grandma had to laugh. She stirred a little more sugar into her coffee, tried it, put in half a spoonful more. Then she said, "How about a Dracula thing? There are apt to be oodles of bats around."

"Bats! Here?"

"Well, of course. Where else do you think they'd live? Bats live in attics and under eaves, especially in old houses. They also love hollow tree trunks—like those over there by the outhouse. Just wait until twilight. You'll see them swarming all over the place."

"Stop it, Gran! You give me the creeps. You were just kidding, huh? We're not going outside at night, are we?" Pixy had, all of a sudden, visions of hundreds of shadowy, soundless bats descending on everything. Horrible!

"We won't have to work at night, will we?" he asked again. "We can't see anything in the dark anyhow."

Grandma just looked at him. How that little chicken had ever solved all those so-called unsolvable crimes he had to his credit was beyond her. But then again, those had been bright-light downtown things. You put her partner into isolated lonely places, especially older houses, and Pixy became a coward. Grandma knew darn well that he believed in ghosts. It was almost laughable, but it was a nuisance nevertheless.

"I only hope we won't get in trouble for snooping around Mooshi's neighbor," she said.

"She was awfully upset when I talked to her. I mean," said Pixy, "who wouldn't be upset when people start disappearing into thin air just like that. And with the police shrugging the whole thing off as nonsense."

"Can't blame them, though. Nobody ever officially reported any of those people missing in the first place." Grandma drank the last of her coffee. "Want some more?"

He shook his head. "Two cups are my limit."

She went on. "Maybe there's a sea monster in the lake, and it gobbles them all up."

For a minute Pixy thought Grandma was serious, then decided she was teasing him once more. He sighed. This just wasn't his sort of case. But of course with business being so slow these days, they had to accept any kind of detective work. And, as his partner had pointed out, they could more or less look on this job as a paid vacation. If Mooshi Winthrop wanted to throw away her money for such a silly thing, who were they to argue? Writing fiction day in and day out probably made her imagination run wild in every other respect as well. Disappearing guests at the Kreller cabin, for goodness sake!

"You think that maybe they drowned in the lake?" he asked. "Maybe their bodies got caught on something on the bottom."

"I don't think anything. Mooshi lost a few of her marbles, living here in the woods all by herself. Just look at her crazy cats. Even they aren't normal. You told me Mooshi admitted that Kreller had laughed off the whole thing anyhow. Said that nobody was missing at all, and for her to keep her nose out of his business. And to tell you the truth, Pixy, I'm inclined to agree with him. She really must have snooped around his cabin a lot, for how else could she know that his guests did-n't leave by boat? It's a big lake."

"There is that. But she insists that only Professor Kreller himself left by the trail last week. And the two old ladies, his guests, weren't anywhere around here. Mooshi looked everywhere for them. The cabin was locked and the boat moored securely. And that wasn't the only time something strange has happened over there. Last November Professor Kreller came along this trail, past Mooshi's house, with two middle-aged men dressed in hunting gear. They were a noisy bunch, too. At nights she heard them laugh and carry on raucously. And—okay, she spied on them—they were drinking whisky and playing cards almost the whole time. And then at the end Professor Kreller was the only one who left. Mooshi went over to his cabin, but it was all boarded up for the winter. His boat was on blocks up on land. She was especially annoyed because he had left his cats behind to fend for themselves while he was gone. They were shy and Mooshi just left them alone." Pixy got up from the hard chair, stretching himself.

Grandma picked up the empty coffee cups. "Why don't we take a little stroll over to Kreller's place now," she said. "He's supposed to have a guest there again this week. We can just walk right up to the cabin and say hi. We'll tell them we're here on holiday."

The professor's cabin was a beautiful A-frame building, with a balcony on top and a large porch in front. It was painted sky blue with white trim.

"No outhouse here," said Pixy. "What a smart weekend cottage!"

"Yes, it *is* lovely. That little separate thing over there must be for an electric pump." Grandma went over to it—it was a miniature of the main house—and tried the door but it was locked. They then went to the front door and knocked, but there was no answer.

"Must be fishing. Let's go down to the lake," said Grandma.

The lake was fifty yards or so behind the house. The grounds in between had been cleared and beautifully landscaped, with a luscious green lawn and flowers and shrubs bordering it. The embankment by the lake was turned into a rockery; steps made of large granite chips led down to a wooden landing. There a small white and blue boat was moored, its outboard motor tipped upwards.

"Don't seem to be around here, either. Probably went for a walk in the woods," said Grandma.

They were going back around the house when Pixy whispered, "There is someone inside the house. I just saw a curtain move."

The detectives stopped. Sure enough, the curtain did twitch. Grandma hollered, "Hello there!" The curtain fell into place, but no one opened the front door.

"What an unfriendly neighbor," said Pixy. "No wonder Mooshi says the professor is weird."

They had just turned their backs to the house again when a terrific noise came from inside. There was crashing and banging. There was hissing and screeching, intermingled with long-drawn-out meowing.

"Damned cats!" exclaimed Pixy. "They seem to be especially crazy in these parts of the woods."

Later Pixy chopped wood for the stove while Grandma peeled potatoes, cut up carrots and broccoli, and prepared T-bone steaks. Mooshi's freezer and refrigerator were filled with goodies, and the two hungry detectives weren't going to save on food during their stay. Grandma loved her food—her figure showed it—and it wouldn't hurt to put a few pounds on her skinny little partner. She decided to make a vanilla pudding and bake a chocolate cake for dessert. Maybe a small pie for a bedtime snack would be a good idea as well. She had seen a package of frozen blueberries in the freezer.

She also put a bowl of canned milk and some cut-up pieces of smoked ham out for the cats. Then she pushed the bowls under the sofa where they were hiding now.

It was a hot evening. They were sitting in the twilight, in the wooden garden chairs again. Grandma used a plastic fly swatter and Pixy a small leafy tree branch to hit at the pesky mosquitoes and gnats. Pixy looked suspiciously at the black birds flying above. Or were they bats? He didn't feel too good but he was not going to admit his discomfort to his partner.

Over at the Kreller cabin, they seemed to be having a lot of fun. The loud laughter of two men, one voice deep, the other scratchy, drifted periodically over to the Winthrop house.

The detectives had finished their blueberry pie and sweet tea when Grandma said, "You know, Pixy, I feel like a little walk. Let's go over and have a look at the other place again."

"Now?! In the dark, with the ba—, er, things flying—"

"Sure. We'll just follow the trail again. It's not very far. Come on." Grandma was already at the corner of the house. Pixy followed reluctantly. Bats wouldn't come down to his level, he hoped. He put his hands into his pockets and he stooped.

Through gaps in the foliage they had a fairly clear view of Professor Kreller's front porch. A large, elderly man with a mane of white hair and a bushy mustache was just pouring red wine from a gallon jug into two big goblets. He was apparently telling a very funny story, for the other man, a tallish Oriental-looking person, was laughing so hard that he had to wipe tears from his eyes. From inside the house came jazzy music.

Pixy started to snap his fingers in tune, but Grandma shushed him.

"Let's go up and introduce ourselves," whispered Pixy. "They seem to have lots of wine."

"We do not drink!" Grandma shot back at him. Honestly, if she didn't watch over him almost every minute of his life, her young partner would go to the dogs. Boozing it up, for heaven's sake. She had weaned him of that the day she became his partner.

Pixy shrugged his shoulders, and the two detectives went back to their own place.

They were cooking breakfast, Grandma making the waffles and Pixy scrambling eggs, when they heard someone go past the house. Grandma opened the door.

"Good morning! You must be Miss Winthrop's neighbor, Professor Kreller."

"Morning to you, too." The professor stopped, shook back his long white hair, and came over. "Looks like we're in for another hot day."

"It does that. Won't you come in for a cup of freshly percolated coffee? Miss Winthrop kindly lent us her house for a little vacation." Grandma wiped her hands on her apron. Pixy came and stood beside her.

"No, no," the professor said. "But thank you ever so much anyway. I'm in quite a hurry to get to the university."

"Perhaps your guest would like to come over for a visit," said Pixy. "He might get lonely all by himself."

"Guest? What guest?" Professor Kreller looked astonished. "I've been working most of the week, all by myself, on the book I'm writing. Well, nice to have met you. Give my regards to Miss Winthrop." And with that he disappeared among the cottonwood trees.

Grandma and Pixy looked at each other, then rushed inside the house. They took the food off the stove and hurried down the trail towards Kreller's cabin. Grandma was remarkably quick for such a big person, and her partner could hardly keep up with her.

Both front door and back door were locked. They tried to look through the windows, but all the curtains were drawn. It was uncommonly quiet everywhere. Grandma tried the doorknob of the pumphouse. It turned, and the door opened inwards. An earsplitting shriek filled the air, and a furious Siamese cat came flying out. It jumped right over Pixy and sped around the cabin.

"My goodness," exclaimed Grandma. "Professor Kreller locked one of his poor cats in here by mistake."

"Are you sure it was by mistake!" cried Pixy. "Gran, it was an Oriental cat!"

"So?"

"The guest. The guest who wasn't—but whom *we* know was."

"Pixy! You are not seriously suggesting—no, even you wouldn't!" But she did take a look inside the pumphouse. There was nothing in it but a galvanized tank with a couple of valves and switches. "Come, let's get back to Mooshi's house and get on with another couple of days' vacation. We haven't even eaten our breakfast yet."

"What *about* the guest, Gran? We know there was one here last night. We both saw him with our own eyes. I mean, we are being paid for finding out about these disappearing guests," said Pixy uneasily. "Where could that man be?"

"Left by boat most likely. Come on, don't worry, Pixy. Mooshi Winthrop is a fool. And of course the professor had a guest."

"He denies it, though."

"Oh, well. You heard him say he's writing a book. So the logical explanation for his denying having anybody here is that he has hired a ghost writer. Many a good book has been written by hired professional writers. Famous people, like movie stars and politicians, use them all the time."

"But, Gran, he's a university professor."

"Sure. Probably professor of something funny. Perhaps he has some very interesting things to say but no talent for writing them down."

The partners spent most of the afternoon down by the lake. Pixy went swimming, and Grandma sat on a big flat rock and dangled her bare feet in the cool water. Then they went back to the house, where she fried a whole chicken and cooked the rice, and he prepared the salad. They ate outside, balancing their plates on their knees. This was the good life! Later Grandma washed and Pixy dried the dishes, and the kitchen corner was neat again in no time. The cats had gotten a plate with scraps.

The detectives had just decided to take yet another little walk, this time into the woods opposite the lake, when they heard branches snapping and the sound of rolling pebbles from the direction of the trail. After a moment Mooshi Winthrop came puffing and stumbling out from among the trees.

"Oh, thank goodness you're still around!" she cried, then sank exhausted into the nearest garden chair. Her pepper and salt hair was tousled, and her blouse had crept out of her skirt. She was perspiring.

"My, am I ever glad to find you alive and well!"

Grandma had rushed into the house and come out again with a tall glass of orange juice.

"You get cooled off first, Mooshi. Then tell us why you are so surprised that we're still here." Grandma took the only other chair, and Pixy perched on a nearby tree stump. "Pixy did tell you we'd stay for several days." Oh boy, she hoped the owner of this house wouldn't immediately look into either her fridge or her freezer. Grandma had sort of a bad conscience about all the food she and her partner had already consumed.

Mooshi drank half the juice in one gulp. "Yes, it was so silly of me to worry about you two. But with those people going missing and all, and then the professor's strange death this noon—"

"Death? Professor Kreller is *dead*?" cried Pixy.

"But we just talked to him this morning!" Grandma was just as shocked. "He came by here on his way to the university."

"Yes, and on his way there he dropped dead. Seems that one minute he was walking along the sidewalk in front of the university library, the next he was dead in the bushes. Was supposed to have some nasty scratches on his arms, but otherwise they think he just died of old age." Mooshi drank the last of her juice. "I got the whole story from my nephew who was one of Professor Kreller's students.— Biology, you know."

Grandma and Pixy told Mooshi then about their strange encounter with the professor. Pixy tried to elaborate on Kreller's cats, but the women just looked funny at him. That is, Mooshi shrugged it off until Grandma said, "Oh, by the way, I fed your two cats. Guess they aren't used to strangers, though."

"Cats?" asked Mooshi.

"Yes, your beautiful long-haired grey ones. They seem to love sitting on top of your china cabinet. They don't go outside much, do they?"

"But I have no cats!" cried Mooshi. She rushed into the house and looked wildly around. Grandma and Pixy followed, and they too were shocked, for now there were other cats here as well. In fact, cats seemed to be everywhere. Green and yellow eyes were peeking from under the sofa, from atop the refrigerator and the china cabinet, from behind the armchairs.

"I can count five now," said Grandma. "At supper time there were only two here. Whose could they be? The professor's?"

"There's the Siamese one from Kreller's pumphouse." Pixy moved toward it, but it hissed.

Mooshi was in tears. How was she going to get them out of her place? She wasn't fond of cats, and now here were all these full-grown ones in her dear little house. She sniffled.

"And what is going to happen to the professor's book now?" asked Pixy. "I wonder what it's about. Cats, maybe? It's probably still in his cabin. Perhaps it even has something to do with disappearing people." And seeing Grandma's disapproving looks, he added quickly, "Maybe it has nothing at all to do with those things— should we take another look at the cabin?"

They had walked up to the Kreller place. The front door stood wide open now, but otherwise all seemed empty and quiet. It was rapidly getting dark, and the place didn't look all that inviting anymore.

"It seems as dead as its owner. The cats must have felt it, too. You think they opened the door themselves?" asked Pixy as he switched on the lights.

They looked uneasily around. It was a man's room, but very cosy. There was a large desk, a fireplace, dark brown vinyl upholstered armchairs, and low bookshelves all along the walls.

Pixy went over to the desk. An inch-high stack of typed papers, probably *the* manuscript, lay beside a covered typewriter. There was a pile of reference and technical books, a dictionary, and several thin cardboard folders on it. One of the folders had slipped down to the floor, and Pixy picked it up. It had scratches on it, as if one of the cats had tried to sharpen its claws there. Inside the folder were several newspaper clippings, some with pictures. Mooshi came over and looked at a couple of them, then exclaimed, "Oh my, oh my—I recognize those people in the photos! Please, let's go over to my house and take these clippings with us. I can't stand this place another minute!"

Back at the Winthrop house Pixy riffled through the newspaper clippings, with Grandma and Mooshi looking over his shoulder. Nobody said a word. The five cats sat side by side on top of the china cabinet, their eyes big and round and much friendlier. Their loud purring filled the room.

First they inspected the pictures of two middle-aged, bearded men. The headline read: "MacDonald Brothers Acquitted in Hotel Murders for Lack of Evidence."

"They look exactly like the two hunters Professor Kreller brought to his cabin last November," whispered Mooshi.

Pixy pulled out the next clipping. It was a very clear photo of two sweet-looking elderly ladies, with neat white curls around their faces and lace around their throats. The caption said: "Retired Teachers Acquitted in Murder of Millionaire Cousin."

"Those by any chance the two little old ladies who were Kreller's guests a couple of weeks ago?" asked Grandma.

Mooshi could only nod her head. Everything was horrid. She glanced at the cats. Oh dear, would they stay here now? Could she, Mooshi Winthrop, actually get used to those creatures—five of them yet! She shuddered. How could one write romantic novels under those circumstances? Maybe she should try her hand at something different? Maybe ghost stories?

They came to the last clipping, the one of a tall, slim, Oriental-looking young man.

" 'Suspect in Holdup Killing Released for Lack of Evidence,'" Pixy read aloud. "That was Professor Kreller's last guest, huh?"

Mooshi shivered. And from the top of the china cabinet the Siamese cat let out a shrill, drawn-out cry.

They were walking single file back along the uneven rocky path, Pixy in front with his backpack and Grandma following with her rolling suitcase.

"Got the check in your purse, Gran?" called Pixy.

"Oh yes. And a nice one it is, too," she answered. "Funny she should have paid us, seeing we didn't really solve the mystery of the missing people. You didn't believe the thing about the cats by any chance, did you, Pixy? About the professor being a one-man law enforcer, luring the murder suspects to his remote cabin and turning them into—"

"Who, me?!" It was a good thing Grandma couldn't see her partner's face behind his high backpack, as Pixy blushed.

For Pixy believed indeed that Professor Kreller had been some sort of magician.

Lael J. Littke

A FELINE FELONY

Jerome Kotter looked like a cat. However, this did not bring him any undue attention from his schoolmates since almost all of them had an unusual quality or two. Beverly Baumgartner had a laugh like a horse. Bart Hansen was as rotund as an elephant. Carla Seaver's long neck resembled that of a giraffe. And Randy Ramsbottom always smelled remarkably like a dog on a rainy day.

The only person who worried about Jerome's unusual appearance was his father, who quietly set about arming his son to face a world in which he was a bit different. He taught Jerome gentle manners, assuring him that no matter how different he looked he would always get along fine if he acted right. He taught him to recite all the verses of "The Star-Spangled Banner" by heart. He encouraged him to read the Bible. And he taught him to sing the songs from the best-known Gilbert and Sullivan operettas. He felt Jerome was well equipped to face the world.

When Jerome got to high school he became the greatest track star that Quigley High had ever produced, although he had to be careful because the coaches from rival schools cried foul when Jerome resorted to running on all fours.

Altogether, Jerome's school years would have been quite happy—if it hadn't been for Benny Rhoades.

Whereas Jerome was tall, polite, studious, and well groomed with silken fur and sparkling whiskers, Benny was wizened, unkempt, rude, and sly. His face was pinched and pointed and his hair stuck up in uneven wisps. He hated anyone who excelled him in anything. Almost everybody excelled him in everything, and since Jerome surpassed him in the one thing he did do fairly well—running—he hated Jerome most of all. When Jerome took away his title of champion runner of Quigley High, Benny vowed he would get even if it took him the rest of his life.

One of Benny's favorite harassments was to tread on Jerome's tail in study hall, causing him to yowl and thereby incurring the wrath of the monitor. Benny tweaked Jerome's whiskers and poured honey in his fur. He did everything he

198

could think of to make Jerome's life miserable.

When it came to Benny Rhoades, Jerome found it hard to follow the admonitions of his father—that he should love his enemies and do good even to those who used him spitefully. He looked forward to the day when he would finish school and get away, for he had to admit in his heart that he loathed the odious Benny. It rankled him to think that Benny was the only person who could make him lose his composure and caterwaul in public, thus making people notice that despite his suave manner and intellectual conversation he was a bit different. To keep his temper he took to declaiming "The Star-Spangled Banner" or passages from the Bible. Once he got all the way through the "begats" in Genesis before he took hold of himself and regained his composure.

Just before Jerome was graduated from college, Benny stole all the fish from Old Man Walker's little fish cart and deposited them in Jerome's car, after which he made an anonymous phone call to the police. The police, who had always regarded Jerome as the embodiment of what they would like all young men to be, preferred to believe his claim of innocence; but then again, looking as he did, it was natural for them to believe that he might have swiped a mess of fish.

People began to whisper about Jerome when he passed on the street. They pointed out that although his manners were perfect, he did have those long sword-like claws, and they certainly wouldn't want to be caught alone with him in any alley on a dark night. And wasn't there a rather feline craftiness in his slanted eyes?

Jerome left town after graduation enveloped in an aura of suspicion and an aroma of rotting fish which he never could dispel completely from his car.

Jerome decided to pursue a career as a writer of advertising copy in New York, reasoning that what with all the strange creatures roaming about in that city no one was apt to notice anything a bit different about him. He was hired at the first place he applied, Bobble, Babble, and Armbruster, Inc., on Madison Avenue. Mr. Armbruster had been out celebrating his fourteenth wedding anniversary the night before and had imbibed himself into near oblivion trying to forget what devastation those fourteen years had wrought. When Jerome walked into his office he naturally figured him to be related to the ten-foot polka-dot cobra that had pursued him the night before, and thought he would fade with the hangover. After ducking behind his desk for a little hair of the dog, he hired Jerome. By the time Mr. Armbruster had fully recovered from his celebration, Jerome had proved himself capable at his job and affable with the other employees, so he was allowed to stay. Mr. Armbruster naturally put him on the cat-food account.

Before long Jerome fell in love with his secretary, Marie, a shapely blonde, who thought Jerome's sleek fur and golden eyes sexy. He wanted to ask her for a date, but first, in all fairness, he thought he should find out how she felt about him.

"Marie," he said one day as he finished the day's dictation, "do you like me as a boss?"

"Oh, yes," breathed Marie. "Gee, Mr. Kotter, you're the swellest boss I ever had. You're so different."

Jerome's heart sank. "Different? In what way, Marie?"

"Well," said Marie, "Mr. Leach, my old boss, used to pinch me sometimes. And he used to sneak up behind me and kiss me." She peered coyly at Jerome from under her lashes. "You're a perfect gentleman, Mr. Kotter. You're real different."

Jerome was enchanted and wasted no further time asking her out to dinner.

For several weeks everything was wonderful. Then, unexpectedly, Benny Rhoades turned up. Jerome looked up from his desk one day to see his nemesis standing in the doorway.

"Man," said Benny, "if it ain't Jerome Kotter." He grinned.

"Benny Rhoades," exclaimed Jerome. "What are you doing here?"

"Man, you're the most," said Benny softly. "I work in the mail room, man. You're gonna see a lot of me, Jerome."

Jerome's tail twitched.

"Why did you come here?" he asked. "Why don't you leave me alone?"

Offended innocence replaced the calculating look on Benny's pasty face.

"Why, man, I ain't done a thing. A man's got to work. And I work here." He lounged against the doorjamb. "I hear you're a real swingin' cat around here. I wonder how long that's gonna last."

"Get out," said Jerome.

"Sure, Mr. Kotter, sir. Sure. Think I'll drop by your secretary's desk. Quite a dish, that Marie."

"You stay away from her." Jerome could feel the fur around his neck rising. His whiskers bristled.

Benny smiled and glided away like an insidious snake.

From that time on Benny did what he could to torment Jerome. He held up his mail until important clients called the bosses to complain about lack of action on their accounts. He slammed Jerome's tail in doors, usually when some VIP was visiting the office. Worst of all, he vexed Marie by hanging around her desk asking for dates and sometimes sneaking up to nibble at her neck. Marie hated him almost as much as Jerome did.

Jerome didn't know quite what he could do about it without jeopardizing his job, of which he had become very fond. The other people at the agency liked him, although they regarded him as a trifle eccentric since he always insisted on sampling the cat food he wrote about. But then, everyone to his own tastes, they said.

Things came to a head one evening when Jerome invited Marie to his apartment for a fish dinner before going out to a show. They were just sitting down to eat when the doorbell rang.

It was Benny.

"Cozy," he murmured, surveying the scene. He slammed the door shut behind him.

"A real swingin' cat," he said sidling into the room. He produced a small pistol from his pocket.

"Are you out of your mind, Benny?" said Jerome. "What do you think you're doing?"

"I lost my job," smiled Benny.

"What's that got to do with me?"

"Marie complained that I bothered her. They fired me."' Benny's small eyes glittered. "I'll repay her for the favor, then I'll take care of you, Jerome. I'll fix it so they'll think you shot her for resisting your charms, and then shot yourself. Everybody knows a big cat like you could go berserk anytime."

"You're a rat," said Marie. "You're a miserable, blackhearted little rat."

Jerome stepped protectively in front of her.

"Sticks and stones may break my bones but names will never hurt me," chanted Benny gleefully.

Jerome was looking at Benny thoughtfully. "A rat," he said. "That's what he is. A rat. Funny it never occurred to me before." His tail twitched nervously.

Benny didn't like the look on Jerome's face. "Stay away from me, man. I'll shoot."

Before Benny could aim, Jerome leaped across the room with the swift, fluid motion of a tiger. He knocked Benny to the floor and easily took the gun from him.

"A rat," repeated Jerome softly.

Benny looked at Jerome's face so close to his own. "What are you going to do?" he squeaked, his own face pinched and white and his beady eyes terror-stricken. "What are you going to do?"

Jerome ate him.

It took a long time to get the police sergeant to take the matter seriously. Marie had urged Jerome to forget the whole thing, but Jerome felt he must confess.

"You say you ate this guy Benny?" the sergeant asked for the twentieth time.

"I ate him," said Jerome.

"He was a rat," said Marie.

The sergeant shook his head. "We get all kinds," he muttered. "Go home. Sleep it off." He sighed. "Self-defense, you say?"

"Benny was going to shoot both of us," said Marie.

"Where's the body?" asked the sergeant.

Jerome shook his head. "There is no body. I ate him."

"He was a rat," said Marie.

"There's no body," said the sergeant. "We sent a coupla men up to your apartment and there's no body and no sign of anybody getting killed. We even called this Benny's family long distance to find out if they knew where he is, but his old man said as far as they are concerned he died at birth. So go home."

"I ate him," insisted Jerome.

"So you performed a public service. I got six kids to support, buddy. I don't want to spend the next two years on a headshrinker's couch for trying to make the Chief believe I got a six-foot cat here who ate a guy. Now go home, you two, before I get mad."

Jerome remained standing in front of the desk.

"Look," said the sergeant. "You ate a guy."

"A rat," corrected Marie.

"A rat," said the sergeant. "So how do you feel?"

"Terrible," said Jerome. "I have a most remarkable case of indigestion."

"You ate a rat," said the sergeant. "Now you've got a bellyache. That's your punishment. Remember when you ate green apples as a kid?" He sighed. "Now go home."

As they turned to leave, Jerome heard the sergeant muttering to himself about not having had a vacation in four years.

Despite his indigestion, Jerome felt marvelous. "Let the punishment fit the crime," he said with satisfaction. He took Marie's arm in a courtly fashion and sang softly as they walked along. "My object all sublime, I shall achieve in time, to let the punishment fit the crime, the punishment fit the crime. . . ."

"Gee, Mr. Kotter," said Marie, gazing up at him in admiration. "You're so different from anyone else I ever went with."

"Different?" asked Jerome. "How, Marie?"

"Gee," said Marie, "I never went out before with anybody who quoted poetry."

Hugh B. Cave

THE LADY WORE BLACK

Ignoring the familiar rustle of leather being dragged over the living room carpet, eighty-year-old Emma Bell continued to watch the six o'clock evening news on television. A cat's harness was dropped at her feet, and the bearer gazed up at her with demanding blue eyes.

Without even looking down, Emma stubbornly wagged her head. "Not this evening, Tai-Tai. My arthritis is acting up."

The cat, a Siamese blue point, replied with an indignant meow that, if translated—and, of course, Emma could always translate—clearly said, "This can't go on! It's been three days now and we need our exercise, all three of us!"

"No, Tai-Tai."

Tai-Tai looked toward the bedroom doorway and summoned the old lady's other companion, a much younger Siamese seal point. Yum-Yum, named by Emma after the character in her favorite Gilbert and Sullivan operetta, obediently appeared from that room with *her* harness, and dropped it beside the one at Emma's feet.

Both cats—the large blue-gray and white one with lavender ears, and the smaller, light brown one with a chocolate-colored face and paws—then sat like statues in front of Emma's sofa, gazing relentlessly at her. And would continue to sit, the old lady knew, until they had their way.

"Oh, all right, my darlings. If you insist. But only a short one because I really do hurt."

They understood her—they always did—and meowed in unison.

At eighty, Emma Bell had been without a husband for nine years, but having had Tai-Tai for eight years and Yum-Yum for five, she no longer suffered acutely from loneliness. She had loved her husband dearly, though, and still always wore black, and vowed she always would.

They lived, the three of them, in total harmony in a small cottage in rural South Carolina. What they lived on was the monthly social security check Emma received as a widow, plus the interest from a modest nest egg lodged in the local bank. That paid the taxes and bought food for the three of them.

It also financed the daily sip of brandy Emma's aging doctor had prescribed to help her endure the pain of her arthritis.

The harnesses buckled and leashes attached, Emma led the cats out the front door, transferring both leashes to her left hand so she could make sure the door locked itself behind her. It was certainly not a crowded neighborhood, but there had been a number of break-ins of late. "We have to be extra careful, darlings."

At the end of the driveway she turned to the right, along a road that curled attractively through pine woods, with shallow ditches on either side. In some places the ditches held water, and water harbored frogs that filled the evening with their throaty music. The clean country air smelled of wild honeysuckle and pine needles. Tai-Tai walked sedately on one side of her and Yum-Yum strained to accelerate the pace on the other.

The younger Siamese was always the more impetuous. Looking down at her, the old lady wagged her head in mild reproach. "Can't you see I'm limping? Please, darling, have a little consideration." The cat actually stopped straining. "There, that's better. Thank you."

At the first intersection Emma, as always, carefully looked both ways before starting across. Her eyes were still sharp; she wore glasses only when reading; but her aging legs grew stiffer every day, it seemed. Of course, with so few houses around, there was not much danger from cars. But the neighborhood was home to one young man, the son of the town's police chief, who seemed to think he owned every road he raced his pickup over. Twice in the past month neighborhood dogs had been run down and killed by someone. If not by him, then by whom?

The young man in question was not driving his pickup this evening, however. When Emma and her companions approached his house, he was seated on his front porch steps with a bourbon bottle in one hand. His slack face twisted into a grin under its shock of blond hair. He flapped his empty hand in a salute. "Evenin', Mrs. Bell. Out for your conshatutional?"

Emma politely nodded. "Good evening, Maynard." One must always do the proper thing. But to her cats, after they were past, she said with a frown, "Did you see that, darlings? Always a bottle. Always. He even drives his truck with a bottle or a beer can in one hand. And he uses drugs, too; I'm sure he does. I don't know what kind, but he uses them. He's dangerous, that young man is."

The cats meowed to let her know they were being attentive.

"And he's the one breaking into people's houses around here, too," Emma declared. "I'm sure of *that*. Where else would he get all the money he must spend on his drugs and drinking? He never does a lick of honest work, and his folks wouldn't be giving him money to ruin his life with, you can be certain. If they know what-all he does, of course. Maybe they don't."

Tai-Tai and Yum-Yum declared their agreement. The walk continued.

"All right," the old lady announced at the next crossroad. "We'll go down here and back home along Linden because I don't want to have to say 'good evening' to that man again. Come, darlings." And so she added a quarter mile to the length of the return journey, pleasing her two companions enormously but increasing her own torment.

Because she had difficulty sleeping, Emma usually stayed up and watched television at night, at least until the eleven o'clock news ended. If the programs happened to be of interest to Tai-Tai and Yum-Yum, they too sat on the living room sofa, one on each side of her, and watched with her. If they were bored with what they saw, they left her and went to bed. All three used the same double bed, the two cats sleeping outside the covers, at Emma's feet.

Tonight, tired and in more pain than usual from her unwise walk, the old lady stayed up late. It was after midnight when she at last turned off the TV and shuffled into the kitchen for her ounce of brandy, then went to the bedroom. The cats were already there.

Gazing down at them for a moment, she thought how fortunate she was to have two such loyal and loving creatures to keep her company. Then, knowing she would not sleep and would have to walk about from time to time to ease the pain, she simply lay down on the bed in her black dress and closed her eyes.

But she could not even doze. From ankle to hip, her left leg ached like an infected tooth. No matter how she turned, seeking a position of relief, the ache persisted.

The luminous, snail-slow hands of the electric clock on the chest of drawers near the bed stood nearly at two A.M. when she heard a door creak open.

In the whole house there was but one door that creaked. It led from the back yard into the small laundry room off the kitchen, and it had been creaking now for at least two years, in spite of her oiling the hinges. It must be warped, the man at the local hardware store had said. At the bottom of it was a small swinging gate by which the cats went in and out. But the gate didn't creak; the door itself did.

A glance at the foot of the bed assured the old lady the cats were still with her. Unafraid but puzzled, she wriggled painfully off the bed and went padding through the house to the kitchen.

There stood the intruder at the sink—the same young man she had spoken to earlier when passing the police chief's house. He had the cupboard door above the sink open and was reaching for the bottle of brandy she kept there.

How had he known she kept it there? Had he watched her at times through the sliding glass doors leading to the back porch when she poured her bedtime drink? Even tonight, perhaps?

Emma jerked to a halt and put her hands on her hips. "Young man, what do you think you're doing?"

He took the bottle from the shelf anyway, before turning to face her. His features, all slack, took on the unwholesome gray of spoiled liver and shaped themselves into something one might find in an ape-house at a zoo. His white shirt was almost as gray with grime. His khaki pants were urine-stained. His bare feet were as nasty as the rest of him.

Drunk, Emma decided. And probably high on drugs, as well. That was the word they used, wasn't it? High? She fixed him with her gaze. "So you *are* the one who's been breaking into houses." Not very often did her voice go shrill like that. "Well, you won't get away with it this time, even if your father *is* the chief of police! You'll have *me* to deal with."

Something brushed against her ankle and she glanced down. It was the blue point, Tai-Tai, rubbing against her but peering warily at the intruder. Suddenly Yum-Yum appeared from the bedroom, too.

The cat with the chocolate-colored face and paws voiced a shrill meow of disapproval and launched herself like a furry rocket at the intruder's chest. It was ever thus with the seal point. Act on instinct; think later.

Too tardily the old lady cried, "No, Yum-Yum, no!"

The leer on the thief's face widened as he swung the bottle by its neck. There was a crunch as the weapon made contact with the cat's head. Deflected in mid leap, Yum-Yum must have been dead before she crashed into the refrigerator door. At least, she uttered no cry but simply fell to the floor, a twisted brown ball with a shattered head or broken neck or both, while Emma Bell stood there gazing down at her in horror.

"You beast! You filthy beast!" Emma screamed, and with arms outflung and fingers twitching, hurled *her* frail body at the intruder.

He lashed out with the bottle again. Again there was a dull crunch, but with a difference. As her legs melted under her and she slumped to the floor, Emma moaned and put her hands to her head.

The young man took one look at what he had accomplished and sucked in a sputtering breath. The bottle, falling from his hand, struck Emma on the hip and rolled onto the floor without shattering. He retrieved it. Clutching it by the neck again, he backed slowly out of the room and into the laundry, where he had left open the door to the yard. On reaching that, he wheeled and ran stumbling into the night.

Emma Bell somehow succeeded in turning her head a few inches, looking for the cat that was still alive. The blue point was in a crouch ten feet away, ready to leap. Her quivering tail was twice as bushy as usual. Her shoulders were coiled springs. Her haunches had never looked more powerful. But she seemed uncertain of what to do, and her gaze flicked back and forth, back and forth, from the old lady to the crumpled body of Yum-Yum.

"Tai-Tai." Emma's voice was barely audible, not even a whisper. "Come here."

The cat crawled to her with nostrils twitching, and sniffed at the ooze of blood now coloring Emma's face. She peered into the woman's glazed eyes, her own bright ones only inches away.

The old lady struggled to move one arm and at last, with a tremendous effort, she touched the cat with her fingertips. "Did you . . . did you see what he did to our Yum-Yum?" she breathed. "He killed her, Tai-Tai. Oh, darling, make him pay!"

"Mrrreeoouw!"

The eyes of Emma Bell closed then. Her fingertips were still. But the blue point remained there for another hour or so, peering into her dead face, before departing.

Knowing he had killed the old woman, Maynard Albro did not return home by way of the road. He took to the pine woods instead. This was not exactly his style; he was more used to driving hell-for-leather along that road in his pickup. As a consequence, when he finally emerged from the woods into his own back yard, he was exhausted. Dragging his feet, he staggered to the back door and clawed it open.

He had not locked the house on leaving it, even though he was temporarily alone in it. His parents had gone that morning to the state capital, where his father was to attend a seminar for police chiefs. They would be away for several days.

Once in the house, however, he did lock the back door behind him, then went to the front and locked that. Then he went to the windows and secured those. Finally, in the living room, he slumped into a chair with Emma Bell's bottle of brandy and drank deeply from the bottle and reflected on what he had done.

Stupid . . . he shouldn't have left the old lady there on the kitchen floor. Sooner or later someone was bound to wonder where she was, and investigate. "You dumb jerk, Albro, what's the matter with you? Go back there and clean up!"

He went back through the pine woods, still carrying the bottle because he guessed he would need it. Along with the brandy he carried a long-handled shovel, and before going into the house, the back door of which was still open as he had left it, he groped his way into Emma Bell's flower garden and began to dig a grave.

Fortunately, the earth there was soft enough for even a drunken man to handle with ease. First Emma's beloved husband, then Emma herself had lovingly grown flowers there. In half an hour the grave was ready, and he went into the house for the body, with an eye peeled for the big gray and white cat lest it attack him as the smaller one had done.

The cat was not in the kitchen, however. Either it was someplace else in the house—he wasn't about to look—or it had ducked out. To hell with it. Lifting the old lady, he carried her to the garden, marveling at how light she was. Then he returned for the cat he had killed, and laid it beside her.

After filling the grave, he put back the clumps of zinnias, petunias, and marigolds he had carefully removed before digging it. No one would ever in the world suspect a body was laid to rest there. "You're pretty smart, Albro, you know that? And you done it in the dark, with only a quarter moon up there to see by. So finish up now and clear out, you hear?"

Back in the kitchen he pulled a strip of paper towels off a roll above the counter, wet it under a tap, and on hands and knees rubbed up every last spot of blood from the woman and cat. Then with the towels in his pants pocket and the brandy bottle in one hand again, he departed.

Twice on the way home he tipped the bottle to his mouth and deeply drank. When he got there and slumped again into his chair in the living room, he drank more. Earlier that evening, on the porch steps, he had emptied a nearly full bottle of bourbon. Now the room's off white walls and green curtains began to spin, and he closed his eyes to keep from spinning with them, and reviewed what he had done.

It was okay. Nobody would look for a grave in the old lady's flower garden. Folks would think she just wandered off somewhere. Plenty of people thought she was a little crazy anyway, still wearing black for a husband that died all that long ago.

Miserable old black-dress widow woman, why hadn't she been asleep like she ought to've been, instead of causing all this trouble?

He heard his mother's antique clock, on the bookcase, chime thrice. Then with his eyes closed against the undulations of the room, he slept.

When he awoke, the lamp by his chair was still on and the clock's hands stood at ten past seven. It had to be ten past seven in the evening because there was no daylight at the windows.

At one of the windows something was scratching.

Not only scratching; it was meowing. And even more than meowing. *Howling.* Where had he heard a sound like that before? He remembered. It was the night he went to the local graveyard to swipe some fresh flowers off a grave, to give to Mom next day for her birthday. There'd been a high wind wailing through the big trees there. And among the stones. Now it was a cat.

The lamp beside his chair had a three-way bulb. He turned it up bright, and the cat's image appeared behind the window pane as if by magic. *Her* cat, the gray and white one, the one he hadn't killed.

The light touched its eyes and they were like Fourth of July sparklers. The howling increased to an accusation that lanced his eardrums and filled him with fear.

"Shut up!" He stormed to the window and banged on the glass almost hard enough to break it. "Shut up, damn you! Get out of here!"

The cat leaped from the sill and disappeared into the dark of the yard.

Maynard Albro returned to his chair. The pounding in his head was all but unbearable, and so was the wrenching cramp in his gut. He shouldn't have hit the booze so hard after so many joints of pot; the combination was stupid. It wasn't his fault, though, was it? What the hell had they expected, leaving him alone like this with no one to fix a meal for him, no one for him to talk to, no one even to nag him for drinking too much. He lifted the brandy bottle and gulped another long drink. The cat was back.

"Mrrreeoouw!" God, that howl! It was enough to tear a man's scalp off.

Up from his chair, he went reeling into his parents' bedroom. No way was any stupid cat going to drive him out of his mind while there was a shotgun in the house. Even if it was only a cheap twelve-gauge single-shot his miserly old man had owned for years. It would damn well blow a cat away.

With the weapon in his hands he staggered back through the living room, accompanied by a chorus of cat-screams from the thing at the window. Stealthily he unlocked the front door.

But when he lurched out onto the wooden front porch, he stumbled over something there, and before he could regain his balance, he crashed into the porch railing. When he recovered from that and went plunging down the steps and around the house to the window where the cat was, the cat had disappeared again.

Cursing his own clumsiness, Albro returned to the porch and sought the thing that had tangled his feet and tripped him. Picking it up in anger, he saw by the light from the living room that it was a dress. A black dress. In a hand that wouldn't stay steady he held it away from him and walked into the living room. Halting by the lamp, he looked at it.

A black dress. The same dress the old lady was wearing when he buried her. It was damp all over and blotchy with earth. Pine needles and bits of dead leaves clung to the fabric. As if she had crawled here in it.

Dropping it on the carpet, he sank into his chair and sat there staring at it like one hypnotized. Not for half an hour did he stop shaking. Even then his eyes stayed bigger than normal and his heart continued its scary pounding.

That cat did not come back. But the dress was there at his feet and he had to do something with it. Had to get rid of it. Leaning from his chair, he gingerly picked it up, then rose and walked very slowly with it, holding it at arm's length, through the kitchen to the back door and out into the yard. At the end of the yard was a concrete incinerator his father had built to burn rubbish in. But the dress was too damp to catch fire when he held matches to it.

After using up half a book of paper matches and growing more panicky with each failure, he forced himself to stop. "Use your head, stupid. Get some newspaper!" That morning's paper lay on the kitchen table, still in its plastic wrapper. It had been tossed onto the front lawn by the carrier after his folks left for the capital, and he had brought it in. He hadn't looked at it, of course. He never messed with newspapers.

The paper did it. The dress caught and burned, and he stood there watching it. The smoky orange light flickered on his face and the terror slowly faded from his eyes. But had he looked beyond the incinerator to where the yard merged into the pine woods, he would have seen other eyes watching him, close to the ground.

Under the influence of alcohol and marijuana, Maynard Albro slept most of the following day. Because he'd been afraid to take off his soiled clothes and crawl into bed properly, he did his sleeping on top of the covers. On waking just before dark, he fed himself from the refrigerator with cold meatloaf his mother had left, a raw egg in beer, and half a loaf of bread layered with peanut butter.

Then, feeling better and convinced he no longer had anything to fear, he looked for the brandy bottle and finished what was left in it.

Not enough. A three-mile ride in the pickup carried him to the town's only liquor store, where he spent his last few dollars on two more bottles. Not brandy this time. The cheapest on-sale whisky the store had to offer.

They knew him in this town where his father was chief of police. The young woman who took his money looked with unconcealed distaste at his stubbled face and filthy clothes, but offered no comment.

On his way home he drank from the bottle, arriving there just after dark. Ten minutes later, while sprawled in his living room chair, he heard the cat at the window again.

"Mrrreeoouw!"

"Oh no you don't, damn you! Not tonight!" The nearest weapon at hand was the bottle he was drinking from, on the lamp table beside his chair. Lurching to his feet, he seized and hurled it. It exploded against the wall a foot from the window and fell to the floor in a rain of shattered glass. The cat did not even leap from the sill, but continued to peer in at him.

"Mrrreeoouw!"

This time he wasn't drunk, he told himself. He would know how to be stealthy. The shotgun was leaning in the corner by the front door, where he had left it last night after his unsuccessful attempt to kill the cat. Elaborately pretending he was not even aware of the cat's keening, he strolled to the door. One hand reached for the weapon; the other silently pushed the door open.

But he did not step out. On the porch in front of him, right where the other had been, was a second black dress. Or was it the same black dress? Anyway, it was hers, the one he had buried her in. Like the first, it lay there in a soggy heap and was smeared with earth, as though she had crawled here in it.

He didn't pick this one up. His hands, his whole body, shook so hard he couldn't. Like something made of wooden parts and activated by springs and gears, he backed away from it and jerked up the twelve-gauge and squeezed the trigger.

The black dress moved a foot or so toward the porch steps, leaving a jagged rent in the porch flooring.

Scarcely able to breathe, Albro slammed the door shut. Then he ran with the gun into his bedroom and slammed that door, too.

Seated on the bed, staring wide-eyed at a blank wall, he told himself the old woman couldn't have crawled here. Not tonight, not last night. There was no *way* she could have done such a thing. She was dead. Dead, dead, dead. In the ground. Rotting.

But the dress. How had it *got* here?

A scratching sound behind him made him turn his head in panic. That wall was not blank; it was an outside wall with two windows. At one of them something gray and white, on the sill, peered in at him and scratched the glass with sharp claws.

"Mrrreeoouw!"

His hands still gripped the shotgun. They jerked it up and again he squeezed the trigger, but nothing happened. He had not reloaded it. The cat looked in at him with what had to be a sneer, its face clearly visible in the light from the lamp on his dresser. Then, with languid lack of haste, it leaped from the sill and vanished.

All right, the dress. No matter how it had got here, he had to get *rid* of it. And this time he would make *sure*.

He went to the front porch and gingerly picked it up. Walked around to the back yard with it. In the toolhouse there his father kept a container of gasoline for the lawn mower. He carried that to the incinerator and this time soaked the garment after dropping it in. Then he returned the can to the toolhouse because everything had to be done right.

Returning to the incinerator, he stood a few feet away from it and held a lighted match to a crumpled ball of newspaper. When the paper caught fire, he tossed it onto the fuel-soaked dress.

No question this time. After the first big *whoof* of flame and smoke, the dress burned brightly until nothing was left but ash. Even though drunk he couldn't be mistaken. This time it would not reappear.

Still, there was no real reprieve in store for him tonight. Every few minutes, hour after hour, that accusing meow pursued him. Though the doors and windows were again locked, no matter where he went in the house he heard it. Living room, kitchen, his bedroom, his parents' bedroom, there was no escaping it anywhere. And whenever he heard it, it reminded him of the sound in the cemetery the night he had swiped the flowers.

A cat cry but not *only* a cat cry. Something more. Something meant to drive him crazy.

It was after four in the morning when he at last succeeded in drinking himself to sleep.

His room was dark when he again struggled up from the depths of his liquor haze into a murky kind of awareness. The light was on. In fact, all the lights in the house were on, he discovered when he went stumbling about in an effort to orient himself. He must have turned them on last night when the cat was trying to get to him, and left them on when he finally hit the bed. Well, okay. With the lights on he felt safer. What time was it, anyway?

He peered at the watch on his wrist. He'd neglected to wind it. There was a battery wall clock in the kitchen, he vaguely remembered. He blinked up at it. Seven forty.

Something was scratching at the kitchen door. A *door* this time, not a window.

"Mrrreeoouw!"

"I'll *kill* you!" The gun. Where had he put the gun? For hours last night he'd carried it around with him while he prowled the house, hoping to see the damned thing at a window and get a shot at it. The gun must be *somewhere*.

He searched the house. Found the weapon at last under his bed. Loading it, he went back to the kitchen. But the scratching at the door had ceased.

A drink. He had to have a drink. Where was the bottle?

He had bought two, he distinctly remembered. Had killed one last night before falling asleep. The other had to be around somewhere.

No. He'd hurled one at the window where the cat was, and missed, and watched it explode against the wall. He was out of liquor. Out of money, too. And anyway, he wouldn't dare leave the house now and drive to the store.

He licked his dry lips and began sobbing. Then heard a scratching sound at the *front* door.

This time, by God . . . !

212

Shotgun in hand, he stole through the living room and jerked the door open. And despite a backward leap, the old lady's gray-white cat was a perfect target, facing him halfway across the porch with only another of those damned black dresses between them. The gun was loaded. All he had to do was fire it.

But a town police car was at the foot of the front walk, by the mailbox, and its door was open, and one of his father's cops, Andy Cramer, was stepping out of it. With a triumphant "Mrrreeoouw!" the old lady's cat fled into the night.

The cop strode up the walk, climbed the steps, and scowled at the shotgun in Albro's hands. He was a man of forty or so, with long arms and big shoulders. "You fixin' to *shoot* that cat, Maynard?"

"I—no, I—well, it was drivin' me crazy!"

"Drivin' you crazy, Maynard? I know that cat well. Belongs to old Emma Bell down the road, and it's a purebred Siamese, one of the best-behaved cats you'll ever meet. What you talkin' about, drivin' you crazy? You drunk again?"

Reaching out, he took the shotgun from Albro's hands and checked it. Removing the shell, he handed the weapon back. Then, stooping to pick up the black dress on the porch floor between them, he said, scowling, "What's this?"

Maynard Albro took a backward step and began shaking again. His hands were so unsteady, the barrel of the gun beat a tattoo against the doorframe.

"A dress?" Andy Cramer's gaze lifted to the youth's face again. "What's a dress doin' here on your porch?"

"I—dunno."

"By God, it's one of *hers*." Andy turned to peer into the dark of the yard, where Tai-Tai had disappeared. "What's goin' on here, Maynard? Her cat, her dress, you with a gun this time of night . . . Looks like it's a good thing I stopped. Wouldn't have, except I seen all the lights on and knew your folks was away. Are you stoned?"

Albro's mouth uncontrollably twitched now. "N-n-no, I'm n-n-not."

"What's this dress doin' here, then? Tell me!" Andy held the garment up between them by its shoulders. "It's hers, all right. She never wears anything different. Why's it here on your porch, all wet and dirty like this?"

"I d-d-don't know."

"Get in the car, Maynard. I think we better call on that little lady and see what you been up to."

It was at Emma Bell's house that Maynard Albro broke down. Two reasons. One: when they got into the car, the cop thrust the black dress at him, saying, "Here, *you* hold this," and of course to Maynard it was like being ordered to hold *all* of what he had buried. And two: when they were almost to Emma's house, he couldn't help but look toward the back yard flower garden, and there where he had dug the grave he saw the gray and white cat again. It was just sitting there in the light of the quarter moon, its eyes aglow, watching as the car slowed down to make the turn into the driveway.

He confessed in the driveway, so instead of going into the house or even the garden, Andy Cramer drove him to the police station. But a little while later, with another man from the station, Andy did go into Emma's house to complete his investigation.

In Emma's bedroom closet he found three black dresses hanging, all identical to the one he had discovered on the Albros' porch. Alongside them was an empty hanger, and under that, on the floor, were two more hangers that must have fallen from the same rod.

Shaking his head at this discovery, Andy said to his companion, "These dresses are what she always wore, and it looked like she had quite a few of them, all alike. I can see how finding one on his front porch three nights running would scare young Albro into talking. But how do you suppose those dresses got from here to there, Joe?"

The man spoken to merely stared at the dresses in the closet and shrugged his shoulders.

Andy struggled to answer his own question. "They were all wet and dirty, the kid said. So was the one I seen. There's plenty of bare ground between here and there, and water in some of those roadside ditches. If some animal was to drag a thing like a dress from here to there and didn't want to be seen, it wouldn't travel on the road, either, would it?"

Silent for a moment, he tugged at an ear while concentrating on the problem. Then with a frown he said, "Joe, you suppose that cat of Emma's . . . ? It's a whole heap smarter'n most cats, you know. I swear it understood everything the old lady said to it—always."

Theodore Sturgeon

HELIX THE CAT

Did you see this in the papers?

BURGLAR IS CAT
Patrolman and Watchman
Shoot "Safe-cracker"

It was a strange tale that George Murphy, night watchman for a brokerage firm, and Patrolman Pat Riley had to tell this morning.

Their report states that the policeman was called from his beat by Murphy, who excitedly told him that someone was opening the safe in the inner office. Riley followed him into the building, and they tip-toed upstairs to the offices.

"Hear him?" Murphy asked the policeman. The officer swears that he heard the click of the tumblers on the old safe. As they gained the doorway there was a scrambling sound, and a voice called out of the darkness, "Stand where you are or I plug you!"

The policeman drew his gun and fired six shots in the direction of the voice. There was a loud feline yowl and more scrambling, and then the watchman found the light switch. All they saw was a big black cat thrashing around—two of Riley's bullets had caught him. Of the safe-cracker there was no sign. How he escaped will probably always remain a mystery. There was no way out of the office save the door from which Riley fired.

The report is under investigation at police headquarters.

I can clear up that mystery.

It started well over a year ago, when I was developing my new flexible glass. It would have made me rich, but—well, I'd rather be poor and happy.

That glass was really something. I'd hit on it when I was fooling with a certain mineral salt—never mind the name of it. I wouldn't want anyone to start fooling with it and get himself into the same kind of jam that I did. But the idea was that if a certain complex sulphide of silicon is combined with this salt at a certain temperature, and the product carefully annealed, you get that glass. Inexpensive, acid-proof, and highly flexible. Nice. But one of its properties—wait till I tell you about that.

The day it all started, I had just finished my first bottle. It was standing on the annealer—a rig of my own design; a turntable, shielded, over a ring of Bunsen burners—cooling slowly while I was turning a stopper from the same material on my lathe. I had to step the lathe up to twenty-two thousand before I could cut the stuff, and Helix was fascinated by the whine of it. He always liked to watch me work, anyway. He was my cat, and more. He was my friend. I had no secrets from Helix.

Ah, he was a cat. A big black tom, with a white throat and white mittens, and a tail twice as long as that of an ordinary cat. He carried it in a graceful spiral—three complete turns—and hence his name. He could sit on one end of that tail and take two turns around his head with the other. Ah, he was a cat.

I took the stopper off the lathe and lifted the top of the annealer to drop it into the mouth of the bottle. And as I did so—*whht!*

Ever hear a bullet ricochet past your ear? It was like that. I heard it, and then the stopper, which I held poised over the rotating bottle, was whipped out of my hand and jammed fast on the bottle mouth. And all the flames went out—*blown* out! I stood there staring at Helix, and noticed one thing more:

He hadn't moved!

Now you know and I know that a cat—any cat—can't resist that short, whistling noise. Try it, if you have a cat. When Helix should have been on all fours, big yellow eyes wide, trying to find out where the sound came from, he was sitting sphinxlike, with his eyes closed, his whiskers twitching slightly, and his front paws turned under his forelegs. It didn't make sense. Helix's senses were unbelievably acute—I knew. I'd tested them. Then—

Either I had heard that noise with some sense that Helix didn't possess, or I hadn't heard it at all. If I hadn't, then I was crazy. No one likes to think he is crazy. So you can't blame me for trying to convince myself that it was a sixth sense.

Helix roused me by sneezing. I took his cue and turned off the gas.

"Helix, old fellow," I said when I could think straight, "what do you make of this? Hey?"

Helix made an inquiring sound and came over to rub his head on my sleeve. "Got you stopped too, has it?" I scratched him behind the ear, and the end of his tail curled ecstatically around my wrist. "Let's see. I hear a funny noise. You don't.

Something snatches the stopper out of my hand, and a wind comes from where it's impossible for any wind to be, and blows out the burners. Does that make sense?" Helix yawned. "I don't think so either. Tell me, Helix, what shall we do about this? Hey?"

Helix made no suggestion. I imagine he was quite ready to forget about it. Now, I wish I had.

I shrugged my shoulders and went back to work. First I slipped a canvas glove on and lifted the bottle off the turntable. Helix slid under my arm and made as if to smell the curved, flexible surface. I made a wild grab to keep him from burning his nose, ran my bare hand up against the bottle, and then had to make another grab to keep it off the floor. I missed with the second grab—the bottle struck dully, bounced, and—landed right back on the bench? Not only on it, but in the exact spot from which I had knocked it!

And—get this, now—when I looked at my hand to see how big my hypothetical seared spot might be, it wasn't there! That bottle was *cold*—and it should have been hot for hours yet! My new glass was a very poor conductor. I almost laughed. I should have realized that Helix had more sense than to put his pink nose against the bottle if it were hot.

Helix and I got out of there. We went into my room, closed the door on that screwy bottle, and flopped down on the bed. It was too much for us. We would have wept aloud purely for self-expression, if we hadn't forgotten how, years ago, Helix and I.

After my nerves had quieted a bit, I peeped into the laboratory. The bottle was still there—but it was *jumping*! It was hopping gently, in one place.

"Come on in here, you dope. I want to talk to you."

Who said that? I looked suspiciously at Helix, who, in all innocence, returned my puzzled gaze. Well, I hadn't said it. Helix hadn't. I began to be suspicious as hell of that bottle.

"Well?"

The tone was drawling and not a little pugnacious. I looked at Helix. Helix was washing daintily. But—Helix was the best watchdog of a cat that ever existed. If there had been anyone else—if he had *heard* anyone else—in the lab, he'd have let me know. Then he hadn't heard. And I had. "Helix," I breathed—and he looked right up at me, so there was nothing wrong with his hearing—"we're both crazy."

"No, you're not," said the voice. "Sit down before you fall down. I'm in your bottle, and I'm in to stay. You'll kill me if you take me out—but just between you and me I don't think you can get me out. Anyway please don't try . . . what's the matter with you? Stop popping your eyes, man!"

"Oh," I said hysterically, "there's nothing the matter with me. No, no, no. I'm nuts, that's all. Stark, totally, and completely nuts, balmy, mentally unbalanced, and otherwise the victim of psychic loss of equilibrium. Me, I'm a raving lunatic. I hear voices. What does that make me, Joan of Arc? Hey, Helix. Look at me. I'm Joan of Arc. You must be Bucephalus, or Pegasus, or the great god Pasht. First I have an empty bottle, and next thing I know it's full of djinn. Hey, Helix, have a li'l drink of djinn . . ." I sat down on the floor and Helix sat beside me. I think he was sorry for me. I know I was—very.

"Very funny," said the bottle—or rather, the voice that claimed it was from the bottle. "If you'll only give me a chance to explain, now—"

"Look," I said, "maybe there is a voice. I don't trust anything anymore—except you, Helix. I know. If you can hear him, then I'm sane. If not, I'm crazy. Hey, Voice!"

"Well?"

"Look, do me a favor. Holler 'Helix' a couple of times. If the cat hears you, I'm sane."

"All right," the voice said wearily. "Helix! Here, Helix!"

Helix sat there and looked at me. Not by the flicker of a whisker did he show that he had heard. I drew a deep breath and said softly, "Helix! Here, Helix!"

Helix jumped up on my chest, put one paw on each shoulder, and tickled my nose with his curving tail. I got up carefully, holding Helix. "Pal," I said, "I guess this is the end of you and me. I'm nuts, pal. Better go phone the police."

Helix purred. He could see I was sad about something, but what it was didn't seem to bother him any. He was looking at me as if my being a madman didn't make him like me any the less. But I think he found it interesting. He had a sort of quizzical look in his glowing eyes. As if he'd rather I stuck around. Well, if he wouldn't phone the law, I wouldn't. I wasn't responsible for myself any more.

"Now, *will* you shut up?" said the bottle. "I don't want to give you any trouble. You may not realize it, but you saved my life. Don't be scared. Look. I'm a soul, see? I was a man called Gregory—Wallace Gregory. I was killed in an automobile accident two hours ago—"

"You were killed two hours ago. And I just saved your life. You know, Gregory, that's just dandy. On my head you will find a jeweled turban. I am now the Maharajah of Mysore. Goo. Da. And flub. I—"

"You are perfectly sane. That is, you are right now. Get hold of yourself and you'll be all right," said the bottle. "Yes, I was killed. My body was killed. I'm a soul. The automobile couldn't kill that. But They could."

"They?"

"Yeah. The Ones Who were chasing me when I got into your bottle."

"Who are They?"

"We have no name for Them. They eat souls. There are swarms of them.

Anytime They find a soul running around loose, They track it down."

"You mean—anytime anyone dies, his soul wanders around, running away from Them? And that sooner or later, They catch it?"

"Oh, no. Only some souls. You see, when a man realizes he is going to die, something happens to his soul. There are some people alive today who knew, at one time, that they were about to die. Then, by some accident, they didn't. Those people are never quite the same afterward, because that something has happened. With the realization of impending death, a soul gets what might be called a protective covering, though it's more like a change of form. From then on, the soul is inedible and undesirable to Them."

"What happens to a protected soul, then?"

"That I don't know. It's funny . . . people have been saying for millennia that if only someone could come back from death, what strange things he could relate . . . well, I did it, thanks to you. And yet I know very little more about it than you. True, I died, and my soul left my body. But then, I only went a very little way. A protected soul probably goes through stage after stage . . . I don't know. Now, I'm just guessing."

"Why wasn't your soul 'protected'?"

"Because I had no warning—no realization that I was to die. It happened so quickly. And I haven't been particularly religious. Religious people, and free-thinkers if they think deeply, and philosophers in general, and people whose work brings them in touch with deep and great things—these may all be immune from Them, years before they die."

"Why?"

"That should be obvious. You can't think deeply without running up against a realization of the power of death. 'Realization' is a loose term, I know. If your mind is brilliant, and you don't pursue your subject—*any* subject—deeply enough, you will never reach that realization. It's a sort of dead end to a questing mind—a *ne plus ultra*. Batter yourself against it, and it hurts. And that pain is the realization. Stupid people reach it far easier than others—it hurts more, and they are made immune easier. But at any rate, a man can live his life without it, and still have a few seconds just before he dies for his soul to undergo the immunizing change. I didn't have those few seconds."

I fumbled for my handkerchief and mopped my face. This was a little steep. "Look," I said, "this is—well, I'm more or less of a beginner. Just what *is* a soul?"

"Elementally," said the bottle, "it is matter, just like everything else in the universe. It has weight and mass, though it can't be measured by earthly standards. In the present stage of the sciences, we haven't run up against anything like it. It usually centers around the pineal gland, although it can move at will throughout the body, if there is sufficient stimulus. For example—"

219

He gave me the example, and it was very good. I saw his point.

"And anger, too," the bottle went on. "In a fit of fury, one's soul settles momentarily around the adrenals, and does what is necessary. See?"

I turned to Helix. "Helix," I said, "we're really learning things today." Helix extended his claws and studied them carefully. I suddenly came to my senses, realizing that I was sitting on the floor of my laboratory, holding a conversation with an empty glass bottle; that Helix was sitting in my lap, preening himself, listening without interest to my words, and *not hearing* those from the bottle. My mind reeled again. I had to have an answer to that.

"Bottle," I said hoarsely, "why can't Helix hear you?"

"Oh. That," said the bottle. "Because there is no sound."

"How can I hear you?"

"Direct telepathic contact. I am not speaking to you, specifically, but to your soul. Your soul transmits my message to you. It is functioning now on the nerve centers controlling your hearing—hence you interpret it as sound. That is the most understandable way of communication."

"Then—why doesn't Helix get the same messages?"

"Because he is on a different—er—wavelength. That's one way of putting it, though thoughtwaves are not electrical. I can—that is, I believe I can—direct thoughts to him. Haven't tried. It's a matter of degree of development."

I breathed much easier. Astonishing, what difference a rational explanation will make. But there were one or two more things—

"Bottle," I said, "what's this about my saving your life? And what has my flexible glass to do with it?"

"I don't quite know," said the bottle. "But, purely by accident, I'm sure, you have stumbled on the only conceivable external substance which seems to exclude—Them. Sort of an insulator. I sensed what it was—so did They. I can tell you, it was nip and tuck for a while. They can really move, when They want to. I won, as you know. Close. Oh, yes, I was responsible for snatching the stopper out of your hand. I did it by creating a vacuum in the bottle. The stopper was the nearest thing to the mouth, and you weren't holding it very tightly."

"Vacuum?" I asked. "What became of the air?"

"That was easy. I separated the molecular structure of the glass, and passed the air out that way."

"What about Them?"

"Oh, They would have followed. But if you'll look closely, you'll see that the stopper is now fused to the bottle. That's what saved me. Whew!—Oh, by the way, if you're wondering what cooled the bottle so quickly, it was the vacuum formation. Expanding air, you know, loses heat. Vacuum creation, of course, would create intense cold. That glass is good stuff. Practically no thermal expansion."

"I'm beginning to be glad, now that it happened. Would have been bad for you . . . I suppose you'll live out the rest of your life in my bottle."

"The rest of my life, friend, is—eternity."

I blinked at that. "That's not going to be much fun," I said. "I mean—don't you ever get hungry, or—or anything?"

"No. I'm fed—I know that. From outside, somehow. There seems to be a source somewhere that radiates energy on which I feed. I wouldn't know about that. But it's going to be a bit boring. I don't know—maybe someday I'll find a way to get another body."

"What's to prevent your just going in and appropriating someone else's?"

"Can't," said the bottle. "As long as a soul is in possession of a body, it is invulnerable. The only way would be to convince some soul that it would be to its advantage to leave its body and make room for me."

"Hmm . . . say, Bottle. Seems to me that by this time you must have experienced that death-realization you spoke about a while back. Why aren't you immune from Them now?"

"That's the point. A soul must draw its immunity from a body which it possesses at the time. If I could get into a body and possess it for just one split second, I could immunize myself and be on my way. Or I could stay in the body and enjoy myself until it died. By the way, stop calling me Bottle. My name's Gregory—Wallace Gregory."

"Oh. Okay. I'm Pete Tronti. Er—glad to have met you."

"Same here." The bottle hopped a couple of times. "That can be considered a handshake."

"How did you do that?" I asked, grinning.

"Easy. The tiniest of molecular expansion, well distributed, makes the bottle bounce."

"Neat. Well—I've got to go and get some grub. Anything I can get for you?"

"Thanks, no, Tronti. Shove along. Be seeing you."

Thus began my association with Wally Gregory, disembodied soul. I found him a very intelligent person; and though he had cramped my style in regard to the new glass—I didn't fancy collecting souls in bottles as a hobby—we became real friends. Not many people get a break like that—having a boarder who is so delightful and so little trouble. Though the initial cost had been high—after all, I'd almost gone nuts! the upkeep was negligible. Wally never came in drunk, robbed the cash drawer, or brought his friends in. He was never late for meals, nor did he leave dirty socks around. As a roommate, he was ideal, and as a friend, he just about had Helix topped.

One evening about eight months later I was batting the wind with Wally while I worked. He'd been a great help to me—I was fooling around with artificial rubber synthesis at the time, and Wally had an uncanny ability for knowing exactly what was what in a chemical reaction—and because of that, I began to think of his present state.

"Say, Wally—don't you think it's about time that we began thinking about getting a body for you?"

Wally snorted. "That's about all we can do—think about it. How in blazes do you think we could ever get a soul's consent for that kind of a transfer?"

"I don't know—we might try kidding one of them along. You know—put one over on him."

"What—kid one along when he has the power of reading every single thought that goes through a mind? Couldn't be done."

"Now, don't tell me that every soul in the universe is incapable of being fooled. After all, a soul is a part of a human being."

"It's not that a soul is phenomenally intelligent, Pete. But a soul reasons without emotional drawbacks—he deals in elementals. Any moron is something of a genius if he can see clearly to the roots of a problem. And any soul can do just that. That is, if it's a soul as highly developed as that of a human being."

"Well, suppose that the soul isn't that highly developed? That's an idea. Couldn't you possess the body of a dog, say, or—"

"Or a cat . . . ?"

I stopped stirring the beakerful of milkweed latex and came around the table, stopping in front of the bottle. "Wally—not Helix. Not that cat! Why, he's—he's a friend of mine. He trusts me. We *couldn't* do anything like that. My gosh, man—"

"You're being emotional," said Wally scornfully. "If you've got any sense of values at all, there'll be no choice. You can save my immortal soul by sacrificing the life of a cat. Not many men have that sort of an opportunity, especially at that price. It'll be a gamble. I haven't told you, but in the last couple of months I've been looking into Helix's mentality. He's got a brilliant mind for a cat. And it wouldn't do anything to him. He'd cease to exist—you can see that. But his soul is primitive, and has been protected since he was a kitten, as must be the case with any primitive mentality. Man needs some powerful impetus to protect his soul, because he has evolved away from the fear of death to a large degree—but a cat has not. His basic philosophy is little different from that of his wild forebears. He'll be okay. I'd just step in and he'd step out, and go wherever it is that good cats go when they die. You'd have him, in body, the same as you have now; but he'd be motivated by my soul instead of his own. Pete, you've *got* to do it."

"Gosh, Wally . . . look, I'll get you another cat. Or . . . say! How's about a monkey?"

"I've thought about all that. In the first place, a monkey would be too notice-able, walking around by himself. You see, my idea is to get into some sort of a body in which I can go where I please, when I please. In the second place, I have a headstart with Helix. It's going to be a long job, reconditioning that cat to my needs, but it can be done. I've been exploring his mind, and by now I know it pretty well. In the third place, you know him, and you know me—and he knows me a little now. He is the logical subject for something which, you must allow, is going to be a most engrossing experiment."

I had to admire the way Wally was putting it over. Being dissociated from emotionalism like that must be a great boon. He had caused me to start the con-versation, and probably to put forward the very objections to which he had pre-pared answers. I began to resent him a little—but only a little. That last point of his told. It *would* be a most engrossing experiment—preparing a feline body and mind to bear a human soul, in such a way that the soul could live an almost nor-mal life . . . "I won't say yes or no, Wally," I said. "I want to talk it over a little. . . . Just how would we go about it, in case I said yes?"

"Well—" Wally was quiet a minute. "First we'd have to make some minor changes in his physique, so that I could do things that are impossible for a cat—read, write, speak and memorize. His brain would have to be altered so that it could comprehend an abstraction, and his paws would have to be made a little more manageable so that I could hold a pencil."

"Might as well forget the whole thing, then," I told him. "I'm a chemist, not a veterinary surgeon. There isn't a man alive who could do a job like that. Why—"

"Don't worry about that. I've learned a lot recently about myself, too. If I can once get into Helix's brain, I can mess around with his metabolism. I can stimulate growth in any part of his body, in any way, to any degree. I can, for instance, atro-phy the skin between his toes, form flesh and joints in his claws. Presto—hands. I can—"

"Sounds swell. But how are you going to get in there? I thought you could-n't displace his soul without his consent. And—what about Them?"

"Oh, that will be all right. I can get in there and work, and his soul will pro-tect me. You see, I've been in contact with it. As long as I am working to increase the cat's mental and physical powers, his soul won't object. As for getting in there, I can do it if I move fast. There are times when none of Them are around. If I pick one of those times, slide out of the bottle and into the cat, I'll be perfectly safe. My one big danger is from his soul. If it wants me out of there, it can bring a tremen-dous psychic force into play—throw me from here to the moon, or farther. If that happened—that will finish me. They wouldn't miss a chance like that."

"Golly . . . listen, friend, you'd better not take the chance. It's a swell idea, but I don't think it's worth it. As you are now, you're safe for the rest of time. If something goes wrong—"

"Not worth it? Do you realize what you're saying, man? I have my choice between staying here in this bottle forever—and that's an awful long time, if you can't die—or fixing up Helix so that he can let me live a reasonable human existence until he dies. Then I can go, protected, into wherever it is I should go. Give me a break, Pete. I can't do it without you."

"Why not?"

"Don't you see? The cat has to be educated. Yes, and civilized. You can do it, partly because he knows you, partly because that is the best way. When we can get him speaking, you can teach him orally. That way we can keep up our mental communication, but he'll never know about it. More important, neither will his soul. Pete, can't you see what this means to me?"

"Yeah. Wally, it's a shabby trick on Helix. It's downright dirty. I don't like it—anything about it. But you've got something there . . . all right. You're a rat, Wally. So am I. But I'll do it. I'd never sleep again if I didn't. How do we start?"

"Thanks, Pete. I'll never be able to thank you enough . . . First, I've got to get into his brain. Here's what you do. Think you can get him to lick the side of the bottle?"

I thought a minute. "Yes. I can put a little catnip extract—I have some around somewhere—on the bottle. He'll lick it off . . . Why?"

"That'll be fine. See, it will minimize the distance. I can slip through the glass and be into his brain before one of Them has a chance at me."

I got the little bottle of extract and poured some of it on a cloth. Helix came running when he smelled it. I felt like a heel—almost tried to talk Wally out of it. But then I shrugged it off. Fond as I was of the big black cat, Wally's immortal soul was more important.

"Hold it a minute," said Wally. "One of Them is smelling around."

I waited tensely. Helix was straining toward the cloth I held in my right hand. I held him with the other, feeling smaller and smaller. He *trusted* me!

"Let 'er go!" snapped Wally. I slapped the cloth onto the side of the bottle, smeared it. Helix shot out of my grip, began licking the bottle frantically. I almost cried. I said, "May God have mercy on his soul . . ." Don't know why . . .

"Good lad!" said Wally. "I made it!" After a long moment, "Pete! Give him some more catnip! I've got to find out what part of his brain registers pleasure. That's where I'll start. He's going to enjoy every minute of this."

I dished up the catnip. Helix, forgive me!

Another long pause, then, "Pete! Pinch him, will you? Or stick a pin in him."

I chose the pinch, and it was a gentle one. It didn't fool Wally. "Make him holler, Pete! I want a real reaction."

I gritted my teeth and twisted the spiral tail. Helix yowled. I think his feelings were hurt more than his caudal appendage.

And so it went. I applied every possible physical and mental stimulus to Helix—hunger, sorrow, fright, anger (that was a hard one. Old Helix just wouldn't get sore!), heat, cold, joy disappointment, thirst and insult. Hate was impossible. And Wally, somewhere deep in the cat's mind, checked and rechecked; located, reasoned, tried and erred. Because he was tireless, and because he had no side-tracking temptations to swerve him from his purpose, he made a perfect investigator. When he finally was ready to emerge, Helix and I were half dead from fatigue. Wally was, to hear him talk, just ready to begin. I got him back into his bottle without mishap, using the same method; and so ended the first day's work, for I absolutely refused to go on until the cat and I had had some sleep. Wally grumbled a bit and then quieted down.

Thus began the most amazing experiment in the history of physiology and psychology. We made my cat over. And we made him into a—well, guess for yourself.

Inside of a week he was talking. I waited with all the impatience of an anxious father for his first word, which was, incidentally, not "Da-da" but "Catnip." I was so tickled that I fed him catnip until he was roaring drunk.

After that it was easy; nouns first, then verbs. Three hours after saying "Catnip" he was saying "How's about some more catnip?"

Wally somehow stumbled onto a "tone control" in Helix's vocal cords. We found that we could give him a loud and raucous voice, but that by sacrificing quantity to quality, something approximating Wally's voice (as I "heard" it) could be achieved. It was quiet, mellow and very expressive.

After a great deal of work in the anterior part of Helix's brain, we developed a practically perfect memory. That's one thing that the lower orders are a little short on. The average cat lives almost entirely in the present; perhaps ten minutes of the past are clear to him; and he has no conception of the future. What he learns is retained more by muscular or neural memory than by aural, oral or visual memory, as is the case with a schoolchild. We fixed that. Helix needed no drills or exercises; to be told once was enough.

We hit one snag. I'd been talking to Wally the way I'd talk to anyone. But as Helix came to understand what was said aloud, my long talks with no one began to puzzle and confuse him. I tried hard to keep my mouth shut while I talked with Wally, but it wasn't until I thought of taping my mouth that I succeeded. Helix was a little surprised at that, but he got used to it.

And we got him reading. To prove what a prodigy he was, I can say that not one month after he started on his ABC's he had read and absorbed the Bible, Frazer's *Golden Bough* in the abridged edition, *Alice in Wonderland* and four geography texts. In two months he had learned solid geometry, differential calculus, the fourteen basic theories of metempsychosis, and every song on this week's Hit Parade. Oh, yes; he had a profound sense of tone and rhythm. He used to sprawl for hours in front of the radio on Sunday afternoons, listening to the symphony broadcasts; and after a while he could identify not only the selection being played and its composer, but the conductor as well.

I began to realize that we had overdone it a bit. Being a cat, which is the most independent creature on earth, Helix was an aristocrat. He had little, if any, consideration for my comparative ignorance—yes, ignorance; for though I had given him, more or less, my own education, he had the double advantage of recent education and that perfect memory. He would openly sneer at me when I made a sweeping statement—a bad habit I have always had—and then proceed to straighten me out in snide words of one syllable. He meant me no harm; but when he would look over his whiskers and say to me, "You don't really know very much, do you?" in that condescending manner, I burned. Once I had to go so far as to threaten to put him on short rations; that was one thing that would always bring him around.

Wally would spring things on me at times. He went and gave the cat a craving for tobacco, the so-and-so. The result was that Helix smoked up every cigarette in the house. I had a brainstorm, though, and taught him to roll his own. It wasn't so bad after that. But he hadn't much conception of the difference between "mine" and "thine." My cigarettes were safe with Helix—as long as he didn't feel like smoking.

That started me thinking. Why, with his mental faculties, couldn't he learn not to smoke my last cigarette? Or, as happened once, eat everything that was on the table—my dinner as well as his—while I was phoning? I'd told him not to; he couldn't explain it himself. He simply said, "It was there, wasn't it?"

I asked Wally about it, and I think that he hit the right answer.

"I believe," he told me, "that it's because Helix has no conception of generosity. Or mercy. Or any of those qualities. He is completely without conscience."

"You mean that he's got no feeling toward me? That bringing him up, feeding him, educating him, has done nothing to—"

Wally sounded amused. "Sure, sure. He likes you—you're easy to get along with. Besides, as you just said, you're the meal ticket. You mustn't forget, Tronti, that Helix is a cat, and until I take possession, always will be. You don't get implicit obedience from any cat, no matter how erudite he may be, unless he damn well pleases to give it to you. Otherwise, he'll follow his own sweet way. This whole process has interested him—and I told you he'd enjoy it. But that's all."

"Can't we give him some of those qualities?"

"No. That's been bothering me a little. You know, Helix has a clever and devious way of his own for going about things. I'm not quite sure how he—his soul—stands on this replacement business. He might be holding out on us. I can't do much more than I've done. Every attribute we have developed in him was, at the beginning, either embryonic or vestigial. If he were a female, now, we might get an element of mercy, for instance. But there's none in this little tiger here; I have nothing to work on." He paused for a moment.

"Pete, I might as well confess to you that I'm a little worried. We've done plenty, but I don't know that it's enough. In a little while now he'll be ready for the final stage—my entrance into his psyche. As I told you, if his soul objects, he can sling mine out of the solar system. And I haven't a chance of getting back. And here's another thing. I can't be sure that he doesn't know just why we are doing this. If he does—Pete, I hate to say this, but are you on the level? Have you told Helix anything?"

"Me?" I shouted. "Why, you—you ingrate! How could I? You've heard every single word that I've said to that cat. You never sleep. You never go out. Why, you dirty—"

"All right—all right," he said soothingly. "I just asked, that's all. Take it easy. I'm sorry. But—if only I could be sure! There's something in his mind that I can't get to . . . Oh, well. We'll hope for the best. I've got a lot to lose, but plenty to gain—everything to gain. And for heaven's sake don't shout like that. You're not taped up, you know."

"Oh—sorry. I didn't give anything away, I guess," I said silently. "But watch yourself, Gregory. Don't get me roiled. Another crack like that and I throw you and your bottle into the ocean, and you can spend the rest of eternity educating the three little fishies. *Deve essere cosi.*"

"In other words, no monkey business. I took Italian in high school," sneered the voice from the bottle. "Okay, Pete. Sorry I brought it up. But put yourself in my place, and you'll see what's what."

The whole affair was making me increasingly nervous. Occasionally I'd wake up to the fact that it was a little out of the ordinary to be spending my life with a talking bottle and a feline cum laude. And now this friction between me and Wally, and the growing superciliousness of Helix—I didn't know whose side to take. Wally's, Helix's, or, by golly, my own. After all, I was in this up to my ears and over. Those days were by no means happy ones.

One evening I was sitting morosely in my easy chair, trying to inject a little rationality into my existence by means of the evening paper. Wally was sulking in his bottle, and Helix was spread out on the rug in front of the radio, in that hyper-perfect relaxation that only a cat can achieve. He was smoking sullenly and making passes at an occasional fly. There was a definite tension in the air, and I didn't like it.

"Helix," I said suddenly, hurling my paper across the room, "what ails you, old feller?"

"Nothing," he lied. "And stop calling me 'old feller.' It's undignified."

"Ohh! So we have a snob in our midst! Helix, I'm getting damn sick of your attitude. Sometimes I'm sorry I ever taught you anything. You used to show me a little respect, before you had any brains."

"That remark," drawled the cat, "is typical of a human being. What does it matter where I got anything I have? As long as any talents of mine belong to me, I have every right to be proud of them, and to look down on anyone who does not possess them in such a degree. Who are you to talk? You think you're pretty good yourself, don't you? And just because you're a member of the cocky tribe of"—and here his words dripped the bitterest scorn—"Homo sapiens."

I knew it would be best to ignore him. He was indulging in the age-old pastime of the cat family—making a human being feel like a fool. Every inferiority complex is allergic to felinity. Show me a man who does not like cats and I'll show you one who is not sure of himself. The cat is a symbol of aloneness superb. And with man, he is not impressed.

"That won't do you any good, Helix," I said coldly. "Do you realize how easy it would be for me to get rid of you? I used to think I had a reason for feeding you and sheltering you. You were good company. You certainly are not now."

"You know," he said, stretching out and crushing his cigarette in the rug because he knew it annoyed me, "I have only one deep regret in my life. And that is that you knew me before my little renaissance. I remember little about it, but I have read considerably on the subject. It appears that the cat family has long misled your foolish race. And yet the whole thing is summed up in a little human doggerel:

I love my dear pussy, his coat is so warm,
And if I don't hurt him, he'll do me no harm.

"There, my friend and"—he sniffed—"benefactor, you have our basic philosophy. I find that my actions previous to your fortuitous intervention in my mental development led you to exhibit a sad lack of the respect which I deserve. If it were not for that stupidity on my part, during those blind years—and I take no responsibility on myself for that stupidity; it was unavoidable—you would now treat me more as I should be treated, as the most talented member of a superlative race.

"Don't be any more of a fool than you have to be, Pete. You think I've changed. I haven't. The sooner you realize that, the better for you. And for heaven's sake stop being emotional about me. It bores me."

"Emotional?" I yelled. "Damn it, what's the matter with a little emotion now and then? What's happening around here, anyway? Who's the boss around here? Who pays the bills?"

"You do," said Helix gently, "which makes you all the more a fool. You wouldn't catch me doing anything unless I thoroughly enjoyed it. Go away, Pete. You're being childish."

I picked up a heavy ashtray and hurled it at the cat. He ducked it gracefully. "Tsk tsk! *What* an exhibition!"

I grabbed my hat and stormed out, followed by the cat's satiric chuckle.

Never in my life have I been so completely filled with helpless anger. I start to do someone a favor, and what happens? I begin taking dictation from him. In return for that I do him an even greater favor, and what happens? He corrupts my cat. So I start taking dictation from the cat too.

It wouldn't matter so much, but I had loved that cat. Snicker if you want to, but for a man like me, who spends nine-tenths of his life tied up in test tubes and electrochemical reactions, the cat had filled a great gap. I realized that I had kidded myself—Helix was a conscienceless parasite, and always had been. But I had loved him. My error. Nothing in this world is quite as devastating as the realization of one's mistaken judgment of character. I could have loved Helix until the day he died, and then cherished his memory. The fact that I would have credited him with qualities that he did not possess wouldn't have mattered.

Well, and whose fault was it? Mine? In a way; I'd given in to Wally in his plan to remake the cat for his use. But it was more Wally's fault. Damn it, had I asked him to come into my house and bottle? Who did he think he was, messing up my easy, uncomplicated life like that? . . . I had someone to hate for it all, then. Wallace Gregory, the rat.

Lord, what I would have given for some way to change everything back to where it was before Gregory came into my life! I had nothing to look forward to now. If Wally succeeded in making the change, I'd still have that insufferable cat around. In his colossal ego there was no means of expressing any of the gentler human attributes which Wally might possess. As soon as he fused himself with the cat, Helix would disappear into the cosmos, taking nothing but his life force, and leaving every detestable characteristic that he had—and he had plenty. If Wally couldn't make it, They would get him, and I'd be left with that insufferable beast. What a spot!

Suppose I killed Helix? That would be one way . . . but then what about Wally? I knew he had immense potentialities; and though that threat of mine about throwing him into the ocean had stopped him once, I wasn't so sure of myself. He had a brilliant mind, and if I incurred his hatred, there's no telling what he might do. For the first time I realized that Wally Gregory's soul was something of a menace. Imagine having to live with the idea that as soon as you died, another man's soul would be laying for you, somewhere Beyond.

I walked miles and hours that night, simmering, before I hit on the perfect solution. It meant killing my beloved Helix; but, now that would be a small loss. And it would free Wallace Gregory. Let the man's soul take possession of the cat, and then kill the cat. They would both be protected then; and I would be left alone. And, by golly, at peace.

I stumbled home after four, and slept like a dead man. I was utterly exhausted and would have slept the clock around. But that would not have suited Helix. At seven-thirty that morning he threw a glass of ice water over me. I swore violently.

"Get up, you lazy pig," he said politely. "I want my breakfast."

Blind with fury, I rolled out and stood over him. He stood quite still, grinning up at me. He was perfectly unafraid, though I saw him brace his legs, ready to move forward or back or to either side if I made a pass at him. I couldn't have touched him, and he knew it, damn him.

And then I remembered that I was going to kill him, and my throat closed up. I turned away with my eyes stinging. "Okay, Helix," I said when I could speak. "Comin' up."

He followed me into the kitchen and sat watching me while I boiled us some eggs. I watched them carefully—Helix wouldn't eat them unless they were boiled exactly two minutes and forty-five seconds—and then took his out and cut them carefully in cubes, the way he liked them. And then I put a little shot of catnip extract over them and dished them up. Helix raised his eyebrows at that. I hadn't given him any catnip for weeks. I'd only used it as a reward when he had done especially well. Recently I hadn't felt like rewarding him.

"Well!" he said as he wiped his mouth delicately, "I see that little session of ambulating introspection in which you indulged after your outbreak last night did you good. There never need be any friction between us, Pete, if you continue to behave this way. I can overlook almost anything but familiarity."

I choked on a piece of toast. Of all the colossal gall! He thought he had taught me a lesson! For a moment I was tempted to rub him out right then and there, but managed to keep my hands off him. I didn't want him to be suspicious.

Suddenly he swept his cup off the table. "Call this coffee?" he said sharply. "Make some more immediately, and this time be a little careful."

"You better be careful yourself," I said. "I taught you to say 'please' when you asked for anything."

"'Please' be damned," said my darling pet. "You ought to know by this time how I like my coffee. I shouldn't have to tell you about things like that." He reached across the table and sent my cup to the floor too. "Now you'll have to make more. I tell you, I won't stand for any more of your nonsense. From now on

230

this detestable democracy is at an end. You're going to do things *my* way. I've taken too much from you. You offend me. You eat sloppily, and I never did care particularly for your odor. Hereafter keep away from me unless I call. And don't speak unless you are spoken to."

I drew a deep breath and counted to ten very, very slowly. Then I got two more cups out of the closet, made more coffee, and poured it. And while Helix was finishing his breakfast, I went out and bought a revolver.

When I got back I found Helix sleeping. I tiptoed into the kitchen to wash the dishes, but found them all broken. His idea of a final whimsical touch. I ground my teeth and cleaned up the mess. Then I went into the laboratory and locked the door. "Wally!" I called.

"Well?"

"Listen, fella, we've got to finish this up now—today. Helix has gotten it into his head that he owns the place, me included. I won't stand for it, I tell you! I almost killed him this morning, and I will yet if this nonsense keeps up. Wally, is everything ready?"

Wally sounded a little strained. "Yes . . . Pete, it's going to be good! Oh, God, to be able to walk around again! Just to be able to read a comic strip, or go to a movie, or see a ball game! Well—let's get it over with. What was that about Helix? Did you say he's a little—er—intractable?"

I snorted. "That's not the word for it. He has decided that he is a big shot. Me, I only work here."

"Pete, did he say anything about—about me? Don't get sore now, but—do you think it's safe? If what you say is true, he's asserting his individuality; I would-n't like that to go too far. You know, They have a hunch that something's up. The last time you got me into Helix's mind, there were swarms of Them around. When they sensed that I was making a change, They all drew back as if to let me get away with it. Pete, They have something up Their sleeve, too."

"What do you mean, 'too'?" I asked quickly.

"Why nothing. Helix is one, They are another. Too. What's the matter with that?"

It didn't relieve me much. Wally probably knew I was planning to kill the cat as soon as he made the change, thus doing him out of several years of fleshly enjoyment before he went on his way. He wasn't saying anything, though. He had too much to lose.

I took the bottle out of the laboratory into the kitchen and washed it, just by way of stalling for a minute. Then I set it down on the sink and went and got my gun, loaded it and dropped it into a drawer in the bench. Next I set the bottle back on the bench—I was pretty sure Wally hadn't known about the gun, and I didn't want him to—and went for Helix.

I couldn't find him.

The cushion where he had been sleeping was still warm; what was he up to now?

I hunted feverishly all through the apartment, without success. This was a fine time for him to do a blackout! With an exasperated sigh I went back into the laboratory to tell Wally.

Helix was sitting on the bench beside the bottle, twirling his whiskers with his made-over right paw and looking very amused. "Well, my good man," he greeted me, "what seems to be the trouble?"

"Damn it, cat," I said irritably, "where have you been?"

"Around," he said laconically. "You are as blind as you are stupid. And mind your tone."

I swallowed that. I had something more important to think about. How was I going to persuade him to lick the bottle? Mere catnip wouldn't do it, not in his present frame of mind. So—

"I suppose," Helix said, "that you want me to go through the old ritual of bottle-cataglottism again. Pardon the pun."

"Why, yes," I said, surprised but trying not to show it. "It's to your benefit, you know."

"Of course." said the cat. "I've always known that. If I didn't get something out of it, I'd have stopped doing it long ago."

That was logical, but I didn't like it. "All right," I said. "Let's go!"

"Pete!" Wally called. "This time, I want you to hold him very firmly, with both hands. Spread your fingers out as far as possible, and if you can get your forearms on him too, do it. I think you'll learn something—interesting."

A little puzzled, I complied. Helix didn't object, as I thought he might. Wally said, "Okay. They're drawing away now. Get him to lick the bottle."

"All right, Helix," I whispered tightly.

The pink tongue flashed out and back. The bottle tipped the tiniest bit. Then there was a tense silence.

"I . . . think . . . I'll . . . make it . . ."

We waited, Helix and I.

Suddenly something deep within me wrenched sickeningly. I almost dropped with the shock of it. And there was a piercing shriek deep within my brain—Wally's shriek, dwindling off into the distance. And faintly, then, there was a rending, tearing sound. It was horrible.

I staggered back and leaned against the lathe, gasping. Helix lay unmoving where I had left him. His sides were pumping in and out violently.

Helix shook himself and came over to me. "Well," he said, looking me straight in the eye, "they got your friend."

"Helix! How did you know about that?"

"Why must you be so consistently stupid, Pete? I've known about that all along. I'll give you a little explanation, if you like. It might prove to you that a human being is really a very, very dull creature."

"Go ahead," I gulped.

"You and I have just been a part of a most elaborately amusing compound double cross." He chuckled complacently. "Gregory was right in his assumption that I could not overhear his conversations with you—and a very annoying thing it was, too. I knew there was something off-color somewhere, because I didn't think that you were improving me so vastly just out of the goodness of your heart. But—someone else was listening in, and knew everything."

"Someone else?"

"Certainly. Have you forgotten Them? They were very much interested as to the possibilities of getting hold of our mutual friend Mr. Gregory. Being a lower order of spirit, They found it a simple matter to communicate with me. They asked me to toss Mr. Gregory's soul out to Them." He laughed nastily.

"But I was getting too much out of it. See what a superior creature I am! I told Them to stand by; that They would have a chance at Gregory when I was through using him, and not before. They did as I said, because it was up to me to give what They wanted. That's why They did not interfere during the transfers."

"Why, you heel!" I burst out. "After all Wally did for you, you were going to do that?"

"I wouldn't defend him, if I were you," the cat said precisely. "He was double-crossing you too. I know all about this soul-replacement business; needn't try to hide that from me. He was sincere, at first, about using my body, but he couldn't help thinking that yours would suit his purpose far better. Though why he'd prefer it to mine—oh, well. No matter. However, his idea was to transfer himself from the bottle to me, and then to you. That's why he told you to hold me firmly—he wanted a good contact."

"How—how the devil do you know that?"

"He told me himself. After I had reached a satisfactory stage of development, I told him that I was wise. Oh, yes, I fooled him into developing a communication basis in me! He thought it was a taste for alcohol he was building up! However, he caught wise in time to arrest it, but not before it was good enough to communicate with him. If he'd gone a little farther, I'd have been able to talk with you that way too. At any rate, he was a little dampened by my attitude; knew he'd never get a chance to occupy me. I suggested to him, though, that we join forces in having him possess *you*."

"*Me!*" I edged toward the drawer in the bench. "Go on, Helix."

"You can see why I did this, can't you?" he asked distantly. "It would have been embarrassing to have him, a free soul, around where he might conceivably undo some of the work he had done on me. If he possessed you, you would be out of the way—They would take care of that—and he would have what he wanted. An ideal arrangement. You had no suspicion of the plan, and he had a good chance of catching your soul off-guard and ousting it. He knew how to go about it. Unfortunately for him, your soul was a little too quick. It was *you* who finally killed Wallace Gregory, not I. Neat. eh?"

"Yes," I said slowly, pulling the gun out of the drawer and sighting down the barrel, right between his eyes. "Very neat. For a while I thought I'd be sorry to do this. Now, I'm not." I drew a deep breath; Helix did not move. I pulled the trigger four times, and then sagged back against the bench. The strain was too much.

Helix stretched himself and yawned. "I knew you'd try something like that," he said. "I took the trouble of removing the bullets from your gun before the experiment. Nice to have known you!"

I hurled the gun at him but I was too slow. In a flash he was out of the laboratory, streaking for the door. He reached for the knob, opened the door, and was gone before I could take two steps.

There was a worrisome time after that, once I had done all the hysterical things anyone might do—pound out, run left, run right, look up and back and around. But this was a *cat* I was chasing, and you don't catch even an ordinary cat that does not in some way want to be caught.

I wonder why he decided to crack a safe.

No, I don't. I know how his head works. Worked. He had plans for himself—you can be sure of that, and unless I'm completely wrong, he had plans for all of us, ultimately. There have been, in human history, a few people who had the cold, live-in-the-present, me-first attitude of a cat, and humanity has learned a lot of hard lessons from them. But none of them was a cat.

Helix may have made a try or two to get someone to front for him—I wouldn't know. But he was smart enough to know that there was one tool he could use that would work—money. Once he had that, who knows how he would have operated? He could write, he could use a telephone. He would have run a lethal and efficient organization more frightening than anything you or I could imagine.

Well—he won't do it now. As for me, I'll disappear into research again. Flexible glass would be a nice patent to own and enjoy, but thank you, I'm glad to pass on that one.

But Helix . . . damn him, I miss him.

P. G. Wodehouse

DEATH AT THE EXCELSIOR

The room was the typical bedroom of the typical boardinghouse, furnished, insofar as it could be said to be furnished at all, with a severe simplicity. It contained two beds, a pine chest of drawers, a strip of faded carpet, and a wash basin. But there was that on the floor which set this room apart from a thousand rooms of the same kind. Flat on his back, with his hands tightly clenched and one leg twisted oddly under him and with his teeth gleaming through his gray beard in a horrible grin, Captain John Gunner stared up at the ceiling with eyes that saw nothing.

Until a moment before, he had had the little room all to himself. But now two people were standing just inside the door, looking down at him. One was a large policeman, who twisted his helmet nervously in his hands. The other was a tall gaunt old woman in a rusty black dress, who gazed with pale eyes at the dead man. Her face was quite expressionless.

The woman was Mrs. Pickett, owner of the Excelsior boardinghouse. The policeman's name was Grogan. He was a genial giant, a terror to the riotous element of the waterfront, but obviously ill at ease in the presence of death. He drew in his breath, wiped his forehead, and whispered, "Look at his eyes, ma'am!"

Mrs. Pickett had not spoken a word since she had brought the policeman into the room, and she did not do so now. Constable Grogan looked at her quickly. He was afraid of Mother Pickett, as was everybody else along the waterfront. Her silence, her pale eyes, and the quiet decisiveness of her personality cowed even the tough old salts who patronized the Excelsior. She was a formidable influence in that little community of sailormen.

"That's just how I found him," said Mrs. Pickett. She did not speak loudly, but her voice made the policeman start.

He wiped his forehead again. "It might have been apoplexy," he hazarded.

Mrs. Pickett said nothing. There was a sound of footsteps outside, and a young man entered, carrying a black bag.

"Good morning, Mrs. Pickett. I was told that—good Lord!" The young doctor dropped to his knees beside the body and raised one of the arms. After a moment he lowered it gently to the floor and shook his head in grim resignation.

"He's been dead for hours," he announced. "When did you find him?"

"Twenty minutes back," replied the old woman. "I guess he died last night. He never would be called in the morning. Said he liked to sleep on. Well, he's got his wish."

"What did he die of, sir?" asked the policeman.

"It's impossible to say without an examination," the doctor answered. "It looks like a stroke, but I'm pretty sure it isn't. It might be a coronary attack, but I happen to know his blood pressure was normal, and his heart sound. He called in to see me only a week ago and I examined him thoroughly. But sometimes you can be deceived. The inquest will tell us."

He eyed the body almost resentfully. "I can't understand it. The man had no right to drop dead like this. He was a tough old sailor who ought to have been good for another twenty years. If you want my honest opinion—though I can't possibly be certain until after the inquest—I should say he had been poisoned."

"How would he be poisoned?" asked Mrs. Pickett quietly.

"That's more than I can tell you. There's no glass about that he could have drunk it from. He might have got it in capsule form. But why should he have done it? He was always a pretty cheerful sort of man, wasn't he?"

"Yes, sir," said the constable. "He had the name of being a joker in these parts. Kind of sarcastic, they tell me, though he never tried it on me."

"He must have died quite early last night," said the doctor. He turned to Mrs. Pickett. "What's become of Captain Muller? If he shares this room he ought to be able to tell us something?"

"Captain Muller spent the night with some friends at Portsmouth," said Mrs. Pickett. "He left right after supper, and hasn't returned."

The doctor stared thoughtfully about the room, frowning.

"I don't like it. I can't understand it. If this had happened in India I should have said the man had died from some form of snake bite. I was out there two years, and I've seen a hundred cases of it. The poor devils all looked just like this. But the thing's ridiculous. How could a man be bitten by a snake in a Southampton waterfront boardinghouse? Was the door locked when you found him, Mrs. Pickett?"

Mrs. Pickett nodded. "I opened it with my own key. I had been calling to him and he didn't answer, so I guessed something was wrong."

The constable spoke, "You ain't touched anything, ma'am? They're always very particular about that. If the doctor's right and there's been anything up, that's the first thing they'll ask."

"Everything's just as I found it."

"What's that on the floor beside him?" the doctor asked.

"Only his harmonica. He liked to play it of an evening in his room. I've had some complaints about it from some of the gentlemen, but I never saw any harm, so long as he didn't play it too late."

"Seems as if he was playing it when—it happened," Constable Grogan said. "That don't look much like suicide, sir."

"I didn't say it was suicide."

Grogan whistled. "You don't think—"

"I'm not thinking anything—until after the inquest. All I say is that it's queer."

Another aspect of the matter seemed to strike the policeman. "I guess this ain't going to do the Excelsior any good, ma'am," he said sympathetically.

Mrs. Pickett shrugged.

"I suppose I had better go and notify the coroner," said the doctor.

He went out, and after a momentary pause the policeman followed. Constable Grogan was not greatly troubled with nerves, but he felt a decided desire to be where he could not see the dead man's staring eyes.

Mrs. Pickett remained where she was, looking down at the still form on the floor. Her face was expressionless, but inwardly she was tormented and alarmed. It was the first time such a thing as this had happened at the Excelsior, and, as Constable Grogan had suggested, it was not likely to increase the attractiveness of the house in the eyes of possible boarders. It was not the threatened pecuniary loss which was troubling her. As far as money was concerned, she could have lived comfortably on her savings, for she was richer than most of her friends supposed. It was the blot on the escutcheon of the Excelsior, the stain on its reputation, which was tormenting her.

The Excelsior was her life. Starting many years before, beyond the memory of the oldest boarder, she had built up a model establishment. Men spoke of it as a place where you were fed well, cleanly housed, and where petty robbery was unknown.

Such was the chorus of praise that it is not likely that much harm could come to the Excelsior from a single mysterious death, but Mother Pickett was not consoling herself with that.

She looked at the dead man with pale grim eyes. Out in the hallway the doctor's voice further increased her despair. He was talking to the police on the telephone, and she could distinctly hear his every word.

The offices of Mr. Paul Snyder's Detective Agency in New Oxford Street had grown in the course of a dozen years from a single room to an impressive suite bright with polished wood, clicking typewriters, and other evidences of success.

237

Where once Mr. Snyder had sat and waited for clients and attended to them himself, he now sat in his private office and directed eight assistants.

He had just accepted a case—a case that might be nothing at all or something exceedingly big. It was on the latter possibility that he had gambled. The fee offered was, judged by his present standards of prosperity, small. But the bizarre facts, coupled with something in the personality of the client, had won him over. He briskly touched the bell and requested that Mr. Oakes should be sent in to him.

Elliott Oakes was a young man who both amused and interested Mr. Snyder, for though he had only recently joined the staff, he made no secret of his intention of revolutionizing the methods of the agency. Mr. Snyder himself, in common with most of his assistants, relied for results on hard work and common sense. He had never been a detective of the showy type. Results had justified his methods, but he was perfectly aware that young Mr. Oakes looked on him as a dull old man who had been miraculously favored by luck.

Mr. Snyder had selected Oakes for the case in hand principally because it was one where inexperience could do no harm, and where the brilliant guesswork which Oakes preferred to call his inductive reasoning might achieve an unexpected success.

Another motive actuated Mr. Snyder. He had a strong suspicion that the conduct of this case was going to have the beneficial result of lowering Oakes's self-esteem. If failure achieved this end, Mr. Snyder felt that failure, though it would not help the agency, would not be an unmixed ill.

The door opened and Oakes entered tensely. He did everything tensely, partly from a natural nervous energy, and partly as a pose. He was a lean young man, with dark eyes and a thin-lipped mouth, and he looked quite as much like a typical detective as Mr. Snyder looked like a comfortable and prosperous stockbroker.

"Sit down, Oakes," said Mr. Snyder. "I've got a job for you."

Oakes sank into a chair like a crouching leopard and placed the tips of his fingers together. He nodded curtly. It was part of his pose to be keen and silent.

"I want you to go to this address"—Mr. Snyder handed him an envelope—"and look around. The address is of a sailors' boardinghouse down in Southampton. You know the sort of place—retired sea captains and so on live there. All most respectable. In all its history nothing more sensational has ever happened than a case of suspected cheating at halfpenny nap. Well, a man has died there."

"Murdered?" Oakes asked.

"I don't know. That's for you to find out. The coroner left it open. 'Death by Misadventure' was the verdict, and I don't blame him. I don't see how it could have been murder. The door was locked on the inside, so nobody could have got in."

"The window?"

"The window was open, granted. But the room is on the second floor. Anyway, you may dismiss the window. I remember the old lady saying there were bars across it, and that nobody could have squeezed through."

Oakes's eyes glistened. "What was the cause of death?" he asked.

Mr. Snyder coughed. "Snake bite," he said.

Oakes's careful calm deserted him. He uttered a cry of astonishment. "Why, that's incredible!"

"It's the literal truth. The medical examination proved that the fellow had been killed by snake poison—cobra, to be exact, which is found principally in India."

"Cobra!"

"Just so. In a Southampton boardinghouse, in a room with a door locked on the inside, this man was stung by a cobra. To add a little mystification to the limpid simplicity of the affair, when the door was opened there was no sign of any cobra. It couldn't have got out through the door, because the door was locked. It couldn't have got out through the window, because the window was too high up, and snakes can't jump. And it couldn't have got up the chimney, because there was no chimney. So there you have it."

He looked at Oakes with a certain quiet satisfaction. It had come to his ears that Oakes had been heard to complain of the infantile nature of the last two cases to which he had been assigned. He had even said that he hoped someday to be given a problem which should be beyond the reasoning powers of a child of six. It seemed to Mr. Snyder that Oakes was about to get his wish.

"I should like further details," said Oakes, a little breathlessly.

"You had better apply to Mrs. Pickett, who owns the boardinghouse," Mr. Snyder said. "It was she who put the case in my hands. She is convinced that it is murder. But if we exclude ghosts, I don't see how any third party could have taken a hand in the thing at all. However, she wanted a man from this agency, and was prepared to pay for him, so I promised her I would send one. It is not our policy to turn business away."

He smiled wryly. "In pursuance of that policy I want you to go and put up at Mrs. Pickett's boardinghouse and do your best to enhance the reputation of our agency. I would suggest that you pose as a ship's chandler or something of that sort. You will have to be something maritime or they'll be suspicious of you. And if your visit produces no other results, it will, at least, enable you to make the acquaintance of a very remarkable woman. I commend Mrs. Pickett to your notice. By the way, she says she will help you in your investigations."

Oakes laughed shortly. The idea amused him.

"It's a mistake to scoff at amateur assistance, my boy," said Mr. Snyder in the benevolently paternal manner which had made a score of criminals refuse to believe him a detective until the moment when the handcuffs snapped on their wrists. "Crime investigation isn't an exact science. Success or failure depends in a large measure on applied common sense and the possession of a great deal of special information. Mrs. Pickett knows certain things which neither you nor I know, and it's just possible that she may have some stray piece of information which will provide the key to the entire mystery."

Oakes laughed again. "It is very kind of Mrs. Pickett," he said, "but I prefer to trust to my own methods." Oakes rose, his face purposeful. "I'd better be starting at once," he said. "I'll send you reports from time to time."

"Good. The more detailed the better," said Mr. Snyder genially. "I hope your visit to the Excelsior will be pleasant. And cultivate Mrs. Pickett. She's worthwhile."

The door closed, and Mr. Snyder lighted a fresh cigar. Dashed young fool, he thought and turned his mind to other matters.

A day later Mr. Snyder sat in his office reading a typewritten report. It appeared to be of a humorous nature, for, as he read, chuckles escaped him. Finishing the last sheet he threw his head back and laughed heartily. The manuscript had not been intended by its author for a humorous effect. What Mr. Snyder had been reading was the first of Elliott Oakes's reports from the Excelsior. It read as follows:

> "I am sorry to be unable to report any real progress. I have formed several theories which I will put forward later, but at present I cannot say that I am hopeful.
>
> "Directly I arrived I sought out Mrs. Pickett, explained who I was, and requested her to furnish me with any further information which might be of service to me. She is a strange silent woman, who impressed me as having very little intelligence. Your suggestion that I should avail myself of her assistance seems more curious than ever now that I have seen her.
>
> "The whole affair seems to me at the moment of writing quite inexplicable. Assuming that this Captain Gunner was murdered, there appears to have been no motive for the crime whatsoever. I have made careful inquiries about him, and find that he was a man of 55; had spent nearly 40 years of his life at sea, the last dozen in command of his own ship; was of a somewhat overbearing disposition, though with a fund of rough humour; he had travelled all over the world, and had been a resident of the Excelsior for about ten months. He had a small annuity, and no other money at all, which disposes of money as the motive for the crime.
>
> "In my character of James Burton, a retired ship's chandler, I have mixed with the other boarders, and have heard all they have to say about the affair. I gather that the deceased was by no means popular. He appears to have had a bitter tongue, and I

have not met one man who seems to regret his death. On the other hand, I have heard nothing which would suggest that he had any active and violent enemies. He was simply the unpopular boarder—there is always one in every boardinghouse—but nothing more.

"I have seen a good deal of the man who shared his room—another sea captain named Muller. He is a big silent person, and it is not easy to get him to talk. As regards the death of Captain Gunner he can tell me nothing. It seems that on the night of the tragedy he was away at Portsmouth. All I have got from him is some information as to Captain Gunner's habits, which leads nowhere.

"The dead man seldom drank, except at night when he would take some whisky. His head was not strong, and a little of the spirit was enough to make him semi-intoxicated, when he would be hilarious and often insulting. I gather that Muller found him a difficult roommate, but he is one of those placid persons who can put up with anything. He and Gunner were in the habit of playing draughts together every night in their room, and Gunner had a harmonica which he played frequently. Apparently he was playing it very soon before be died, which is significant, as seeming to dispose of any idea of suicide.

"As I say, I have one or two theories, but they are in a very nebulous state. The most plausible is that on one of his visits to India—I have ascertained that he made several voyages there—Captain Gunner may in some way have fallen foul of the natives. The fact that he certainly died of the poison of an Indian snake supports this theory. I am making inquiries as to the movements of several Indian sailors who were here in their ships at the time of the tragedy.

"I have another theory. Does Mrs. Picket know more about this affair than she appears to? I may be wrong in my estimate of her mental qualities. Her apparent stupidity may be cunning. But here again, the absence of motive brings me up against a dead wall. I must confess that at present I do not see my way clearly. However, I will write again shortly."

Mr. Snyder derived the utmost enjoyment from the report. He liked the substance of it, and above all he was tickled by the bitter tone of frustration which characterized it. Oakes was baffled, and his knowledge of Oakes told him that the sensation of being baffled was gall and wormwood to that high-spirited young man. Whatever might be the result of this investigation, it would teach him the virtue of patience.

He wrote his assistant a short note:

"Dear Oakes,

"Your report received. You certainly seem to have got the hard case which, I hear, you were pining for. Don't build too much on plausible motives in a case of this sort. Fauntleroy, the London murderer, killed a woman for no other reason than that she had thick ankles. Many years ago I myself was on a case where a man murdered an intimate friend because of a dispute about a bet. My experience is that five murderers out of ten act on the whim of the moment, without anything which, properly speaking, you could call a motive at all.

Yours very cordially,

Paul Snyder

P.S. I don't think much of your Pickett theory. However, you're in charge. I wish you luck."

Young Mr. Oakes was not enjoying himself. For the first time in his life that self-confidence which characterized all his actions seemed to be failing him. The change had taken place almost overnight. The fact that the case had the appearance of presenting the unusual had merely stimulated him at first. But then doubts had crept in and the problem had begun to appear insoluble.

True, he had only just taken it up, but something told him that, for all the progress he was likely to make, he might just as well have been working on it steadily for a month. He was completely baffled. And every moment which he spent in the Excelsior boardinghouse made it clearer to him that that infernal old woman with the pale eyes thought him an incompetent fool. It was that, more than anything, which made him acutely conscious of his lack of success.

His nerves were being sorely troubled by the quiet scorn of Mrs. Pickett's gaze. He began to think that perhaps he had been a shade too self-confident and abrupt in the short interview which he had had with her on his arrival.

As might have been expected, his first act, after his brief interview with Mrs. Pickett, was to examine the room where the tragedy had taken place. The body was gone, but otherwise nothing had been moved.

Oakes belonged to the magnifying-glass school of detection. The first thing he did on entering the room was to make a careful examination of the floor, the walls, the furniture, and the window sill. He would have hotly denied the assertion that he did this because it looked well, but he would have been hard put to it to advance any other reason.

If he discovered anything, his discoveries were entirely negative and served only to deepen the mystery. As Mr. Snyder had said, there was no chimney, and nobody could have entered through the locked door.

There remained the window. It was small, and apprehensiveness, perhaps, of the possibility of burglars had caused the proprietress to make it doubly secure with two iron bars. No human being could have squeezed his way through.

It was late that night that he wrote and dispatched to headquarters the report which had amused Mr. Snyder . . .

Two days later Mr. Snyder sat at his desk, staring with wide unbelieving eyes at a telegram he had just received. It read as follows:

HAVE SOLVED GUNNER MYSTERY.
RETURNING. OAKES.

Mr. Snyder narrowed his eyes and rang the bell.

"Send Mr. Oakes to me directly he arrives," he said.

He was pained to find that his chief emotion was one of bitter annoyance. The swift solution of such an apparently insoluble problem would reflect the highest credit on the agency, and there were picturesque circumstances connected with the case which would make it popular with the newspapers and lead to its being given a great deal of publicity.

Yet, in spite of all this, Mr. Snyder was annoyed. He realized now how large a part the desire to reduce Oakes's self-esteem had played with him. He further realized, looking at the thing honestly, that he had been firmly convinced that the young man would not come within a mile of a reasonable solution of the mystery. He had desired only that his failure would prove a valuable educational experience for him. For he believed that failure at this particular point in his career would make Oakes a more valuable asset to the agency.

But now here Oakes was, within a ridiculously short space of time, returning to the fold, not humble and defeated, but triumphant. Mr. Snyder looked forward with apprehension to the young man's probable demeanor under the intoxicating influence of victory.

His apprehensions were well grounded. He had barely finished the third of the series of cigars which, like milestones, marked the progress of his afternoon, when the door opened and young Oakes entered. Mr. Snyder could not repress a faint moan at the sight of him. One glance was enough to tell him that his worst fears were realized.

"I got your telegram," said Mr. Snyder.

Oakes nodded. "It surprised you, eh?" he asked.

Mr. Snyder resented the patronizing tone of the question, but he had resigned himself to be patronized, and managed to keep his anger in check.

"Yes," he replied, "I must say it did surprise me. I didn't gather from your report that you had even found a clue. Was it the Indian theory that turned the trick?"

Oakes laughed tolerantly. "Oh, I never really believed that preposterous theory for one moment. I just put it in to round out my report. I hadn't begun to think about the case then—not really think."

Mr. Snyder, nearly exploding with wrath, extended his cigar case. "Light up and tell me all about it," he said, controlling his anger.

"Well, I won't say I haven't earned this," said Oakes, puffing away. He let the ash of his cigar fall delicately to the floor—another action which seemed significant to his employer. As a rule his assistants, unless particularly pleased with themselves, used the ashtray.

"My first act on arriving," Oakes said, "was to have a talk with Mrs. Pickett. A very dull old woman."

"Curious. She struck me as rather intelligent."

"Not on your life. She gave me no assistance whatever. I then examined the room where the death had taken place. It was exactly as you described it. There was no chimney, the door had been locked on the inside, and the one window was too high up. At first sight it looked extremely unpromising. Then I had a chat with some of the other boarders. They had nothing of any importance to contribute. Most of them simply gibbered. I then gave up trying to get help from the outside and resolved to rely on my own intelligence."

He smiled triumphantly. "It is a theory of mine, Mr. Snyder, which I have found valuable, that in nine cases out of ten remarkable things don't happen."

"I don't quite follow you there," Mr. Snyder interrupted.

"I will put it another way, if you like. What I mean is that the simplest explanation is nearly always the right one. Consider this case. It seemed impossible that there should have been any reasonable explanation of the man's death. Most men would have worn themselves out guessing at wild theories. If I had started to do that, I should have been guessing now. As it is—here I am. I trusted to my belief that nothing remarkable ever happens, and I won out."

Mr. Snyder sighed softly. Oakes was entitled to a certain amount of gloating, but there could be no doubt that his way of telling a story was downright infuriating.

"I believe in the logical sequence of events. I refuse to accept effects unless they are preceded by causes. In other words, with all due respect to your possibly contrary opinions, Mr. Snyder, I simply decline to believe in a murder unless there was a motive for it. The first thing I set myself to ascertain was—what was the motive for the murder of Captain Gunner? And after thinking it over and making every possible inquiry, I decided that there was no motive. Therefore, there was no murder."

Mr. Snyder's mouth opened, and he obviously was about to protest. But he appeared to think better of it and Oakes proceeded: "I then tested the suicide theory. What motive was there for suicide? There was no motive. Therefore, there was no suicide."

This time Mr. Snyder spoke: "You haven't been spending the last few days in the wrong house by any chance, have you? You will be telling me next that there wasn't any dead man."

Oakes smiled. "Not at all. Captain John Gunner was dead, all right. As the medical evidence proved, he died of the bite of a cobra. It was a small cobra which came from Java."

Mr. Snyder stared at him. "How do you know?"

"I do know, beyond any possibility of doubt."

"Did you see the snake?"

Oakes shook his head.

"Then, how in heaven's name—"

"I have enough evidence to make a jury convict Mr. Snake without leaving the box."

"Then suppose you tell me this. How did your cobra from Java get out of the room?"

"By the window," replied Oakes impassively.

"How can you possibly explain that? You say yourself that the window was too high up."

"Nevertheless, it got out by the window. The logical sequence of events is proof enough that it was in the room. It killed Captain Gunner there and left traces of its presence outside. Therefore, as the window was the only exit, it must have escaped by that route. Somehow it got out of that window."

"What do you mean—it left traces of its presence outside?"

"It killed a dog in the back yard behind the house," Oakes said. "The window of Captain Gunner's room projects out over it. It is full of boxes and litter and there are a few stunted shrubs scattered about. In fact, there is enough cover to hide any small object like the body of a dog. That's why it was not discovered at first. The maid at the Excelsior came on it the morning after I sent you my report while she was emptying a box of ashes in the yard. It was just an ordinary stray dog without collar or license. The analyst examined the body and found that the dog had died of the bite of a cobra."

"But you didn't find the snake?"

"No. We cleaned out that yard till you could have eaten your breakfast there, but the snake had gone. It must have escaped through the door of the yard, which was standing ajar. That was a couple of days ago, and there has been no further tragedy. In all likelihood it is dead. The nights are pretty cold now, and it would probably have died of exposure."

"But I just don't understand how a cobra got to Southampton," said the amazed Mr. Snyder.

"Can't you guess it? I told you it came from Java."

"How did you know it did?"

"Captain Muller told me. Not directly, but I pieced it together from what he said. It seem that an old shipmate of Captain Gunner's was living in Java. They corresponded, and occasionally this man would send the captain a present as a mark of his esteem. The last present he sent was a crate of bananas. Unfortunately, the snake must have got in unnoticed. That's why I told you the cobra was a small one. Well, that's my case against Mr. Snake, and short of catching him with the goods, I don't see how I could have made out a stronger one. Don't you agree?"

It went against the grain for Mr. Snyder to acknowledge defeat, but he was a fair-minded man, and he was forced to admit that Oakes did certainly seem to have solved the impossible.

"I congratulate you, my boy," he said as heartily as he could. "To be completely frank, when you started out, I didn't think you could do it. By the way, I suppose Mrs. Pickett was pleased?"

"If she was, she didn't show it. I'm pretty well convinced she hasn't enough sense to be pleased at anything. However, she has invited me to dinner with her tonight. I imagine she'll be as boring as usual, but she made such a point of it I had to accept."

For some time after Oakes had gone, Mr. Snyder sat smoking and thinking, in embittered meditation. Suddenly there was brought the card of Mrs. Pickett, who would be grateful if he could spare her a few moments. Mr. Snyder was glad to see Mrs. Pickett. He was a student of character, and she had interested him at their first meeting. There was something about her which had seemed to him unique, and he welcomed this second chance of studying her at close range.

She came in and sat down stiffly, balancing herself on the extreme edge of the chair in which a short while before young Oakes had lounged so luxuriously.

"How are you, Mrs. Pickett?" said Mr. Snyder genially. "I'm very glad that you could find time to pay me a visit. Well, so it wasn't murder after all."

"Sir?"

"I've been talking to Mr. Oakes, whom you met as James Burton," said the detective. "He has told me all about it."

"He told *me* all about it," said Mrs. Pickett dryly.

Mr. Snyder looked at her inquiringly. Her manner seemed more suggestive than her words.

"A conceited, headstrong young fool," said Mrs. Pickett.

It was no new picture of his assistant that she had drawn. Mr. Snyder had often drawn it himself, but at the present juncture it surprised him. Oakes, in his hour of triumph, surely did not deserve this sweeping condemnation.

"Did not Mr. Oakes's solution of the mystery satisfy you, Mrs. Pickett?"

"No."

"It struck me as logical and convincing," Mr. Snyder said.

"You may call it all the fancy names you please, Mr. Snyder. But Mr. Oakes's solution was not the right one."

"Have you an alternative to offer?"

Mrs. Pickett tightened her lips.

"If you have, I should like to hear it."

"You will—at the proper time."

"What makes you so certain that Mr. Oakes is wrong?"

"He starts out with an impossible explanation and rests his whole case on it. There couldn't have been a snake in that room because it couldn't have gotten out. The window was too high."

"But surely the evidence of the dead dog?"

Mrs. Pickett looked at him as if he had disappointed her. "I had always heard *you* spoken of as a man with common sense, Mr. Snyder."

"I have always tried to use common sense."

"Then why are you trying now to make yourself believe that something happened which could not possibly have happened just because it fits in with something which isn't easy to explain?"

"You mean that there is another explanation of the dead dog?" Mr. Snyder asked.

"Not *another*. What Mr. Oakes takes for granted is not an explanation. But there is a common-sense explanation, and if he had not been so headstrong and conceited he might have found it."

"You speak as if you had found it," said Mr. Snyder.

"I have." Mrs. Pickett leaned forward as she spoke, and stared at him defiantly.

Mr. Snyder started. "*You* have?"

"Yes."

"What is it?"

""You will know before tomorrow. In the meantime try and think it out for yourself. A successful and prosperous detective agency like yours, Mr. Snyder, ought to do something in return for a fee."

There was something in her manner so reminiscent of the schoolteacher reprimanding a recalcitrant pupil that Mr. Snyder's sense of humor came to his rescue. "We do our best, Mrs. Pickett," he said. "But you mustn't forget that we are only human and cannot guarantee results."

Mrs. Pickett did not pursue the subject. Instead, she proceeded to astonish Mr. Snyder by asking him to swear out a warrant for the arrest of a man known to them both on a charge of murder.

Mr. Snyder's breath was not often taken away in his own office. As a rule he received his clients' communications calmly, strange as they often were. But at her words he gasped. The thought crossed his mind that Mrs. Pickett might be mentally unbalanced.

Mrs. Pickett was regarding him with an unfaltering stare. To all outward appearances she was the opposite of unbalanced. "But you can't swear out a warrant without evidence," he told her.

"I have evidence," she replied firmly.

"Precisely what kind of evidence?" he demanded,

"If I told you now you would think that I was out of my mind."

"But, Mrs. Pickett, do you realize what you are asking me to do? I cannot make this agency responsible for the arbitrary arrest of a man on the strength of a single individual's suspicions. It might ruin me. At the least it would make me a laughingstock."

"Mr. Snyder, you may use your own judgment whether or not to swear out that warrant. You will listen to what I have to say, and you will see for yourself how the crime was committed. If after that you feel that you cannot make the arrest I will accept your decision. I know who killed Captain Gunner," she said. "I knew it from the beginning. But I had no proof. Now things have come to light and everything is clear."

Against his judgment Mr. Snyder was impressed. This woman had the magnetism which makes for persuasiveness.

"It—it sounds incredible." Even as he spoke, he remembered that it had long been a maxim of his that nothing was incredible, and he weakened still further.

"Mr. Snyder, I ask you to swear out that warrant."

The detective gave in. "Very well," he said.

Mrs. Pickett rose. "If you will come and dine at my house tonight I think I can prove to you that it will be needed. Will you come?"

"I'll come," promised Mr. Snyder.

Mr. Snyder arrived at the Excelsior and shortly after he was shown into the little private sitting room where he found Oakes, the third guest of the evening unexpectedly arrived.

Mr. Snyder looked curiously at the newcomer. Captain Muller had a peculiar fascination for him. It was not Mr. Snyder's habit to trust overmuch to appearances. But he could not help admitting that there was something about this man's aspect, something odd—an unnatural aspect of gloom. He bore himself like one carrying a heavy burden. His eyes were dull, his face haggard. The next moment the detective was reproaching himself with allowing his imagination to run away with his calmer judgment.

The door opened and Mrs. Pickett came in.

To Mr. Snyder one of the most remarkable points about the dinner was the peculiar metamorphosis of Mrs. Pickett from the brooding silent woman he had known to the gracious and considerate hostess.

Oakes appeared also to be overcome with surprise, so much so that he was unable to keep his astonishment to himself. He had come prepared to endure a dull evening absorbed in grim silence, and he found himself instead opposite a bottle of champagne of a brand and year which commanded his utmost respect. What was even more incredible, his hostess had transformed herself into a pleasant old lady whose only aim seemed to be to make him feel at home.

Beside each of the guest's plates was a neat paper parcel. Oakes picked his up and stared at it in wonderment. "Why, this is more than a party souvenir, Mrs. Pickett," he said. "It's the kind of mechanical marvel I've always wanted to have on my desk."

"I'm glad you like it, Mr. Oakes," Mrs. Pickett said, smiling. "You must not think of me simply as a tired old woman whom age has completely defeated. I am an ambitious hostess. When I give these little parties, I like to make them a success. I want each of you to remember this dinner."

"I'm sure I will."

Mrs. Pickett smiled again. "I think you all will. You, Mr. Snyder." She paused. "And you, Captain Muller."

To Mr. Snyder there was so much meaning in her voice as she said this that he was amazed that it conveyed no warning to Muller. Captain Muller, however, was already drinking heavily. He looked up when addressed and uttered a sound which might have been taken for an expression of polite acquiescence. Then he filled his glass again.

Mr. Snyder's parcel revealed a watch charm fashioned in the shape of a tiny candid-eye camera. "That," said Mrs. Pickett, "is a compliment to your profession." She leaned toward the captain. "Mr. Snyder is a detective, Captain Muller."

He looked up. It seemed to Mr. Snyder that a look of fear lit up his heavy eyes for an instant. It came and went, if indeed it came at all, so swiftly that he could not be certain. "So?" said Captain Muller. He spoke quite evenly, with just the amount of interest which such an announcement would naturally produce.

"Now for yours, Captain," said Oakes. "I guess it's something special. It's twice the size of mine, anyway."

It may have been something in the old woman's expression as she watched Captain Muller slowly tearing the paper that sent a thrill of excitement through Mr. Snyder. Something seemed to warn him of the approach of a psychological moment. He bent forward eagerly.

There was a strangled gasp, a thump, and onto the table from the captain's hands there fell a little harmonica. There was no mistaking the look on Muller's face now. His cheeks were like wax, and his eyes, so dull till then, blazed with a panic and horror which he could not repress. The glasses on the table rocked as he clutched at the cloth.

Mrs. Pickett spoke. "Why, Captain Muller, has it upset you? I thought that, as his best friend, the man who shared his room, you would value a memento of Captain Gunner. How fond you must have been of him for the sight of his harmonica to be such a shock."

The captain did not speak. He was staring fascinated at the thing on the table. Mrs. Pickett turned to Mr. Snyder. Her eyes, as they met his, held him entranced.

"Mr. Snyder, as a detective, you will be interested in a curious and very tragic affair which happened in this house a few days ago. One of my boarders, Captain Gunner, was found dead in his room. It was the room which he shared with Mr. Muller. I am very proud of the reputation of my house, Mr. Snyder, and it was a blow to me that this should have happened. I applied to an agency for a detective, and they sent me a stupid boy, with nothing to recommend him except his belief in himself. He said that Captain Gunner had died by accident, killed by a snake which had come out of a crate of bananas. I knew better. I knew that Captain Gunner had been murdered. Are you listening, Captain Muller? This will interest you, as you were such a friend of his."

The captain did not answer. He was staring straight before him, as if he saw something invisible in eyes forever closed in death.

"Yesterday we found the body of a dog. It had been killed, as Captain Gunner had been, by the poison of a snake. The boy from the agency said that this was conclusive. He said that the snake had escaped from the room after killing Captain Gunner and had in turn killed the dog. I knew that to be impossible, for if there had been a snake in that room it could not have made its escape."

Her eyes flashed and became remorselessly accusing. "It was not a snake that killed Captain Gunner. It was a cat. Captain Gunner had a friend who hated him. One day, in opening a crate of bananas, this friend found a snake. He killed it, and extracted the poison. He knew Captain Gunner's habits. He knew that he played a harmonica. This man also had a cat. He knew that cats hated the sound of a harmonica. He had often seen this particular cat fly at Captain Gunner and scratch him when he played. He took the cat and covered its claws with the poison. And then he left the cat in the room with Captain Gunner. He knew what would happen."

Oakes and Mr. Snyder were on their feet. Captain Muller had not moved. He sat there, his fingers gripping the cloth. Mrs. Pickett rose and went to a closet. She unlocked the door. "Kitty!" she called. "Kitty! Kitty!" A black cat ran swiftly out into the room. With a clatter and a crash of crockery and a ringing of glass the table heaved, rocked, and overturned as Muller staggered to his feet. He threw up his hands as if to ward something off. A choking cry came from his lips. "Gott! Gott!"

Mrs. Pickett's voice rang through the room, cold and biting. "Captain Muller, you murdered Captain Gunner!"

The captain shuddered. Then mechanically he replied, "Gott! Yes, I killed him."

"You heard, Mr. Snyder," said Mrs. Pickett. "He has confessed before witnesses."

Muller allowed himself to be moved toward the door. His arm in Mr. Snyder's grip felt limp. Mrs. Pickett stopped and took something from the debris on the floor. She rose, holding the harmonica.

"You are forgetting your souvenir, Captain Muller," she said.

Phyllis Bentley

MISS PHIPPS AND THE SIAMESE CAT

"Original plus two copies, double spacing, margins twelve and twenty-two, fresh page for each chapter, French words underlined—" began Miss Phipps.

"Punctuation to be followed exactly," concluded Mrs. Norton with a prim cough.

"Just so."

"It's a long time since you've visited the Norton Agency for typing, Miss Phipps," said Mrs. Norton, her tone slightly acid. "I thought perhaps you'd obtained a permanent secretary again."

"Oh, I have. A very nice girl. Very accurate. But at the moment she's *hors de combat*. Having a baby."

"Married, I hope," said Mrs. Norton with a sniff.

"Of course," replied Miss Phipps staunchly. "Now when can I have my finished typescript, please?"

"Well, you can't."

How she enjoys saying that, thought Miss Phipps, vexed. "Shall I take it elsewhere, then?" she said coolly, rising.

"No, no! I mean you can't have it done by me until the week after next."

"Oh, dear," fretted Miss Phipps.

"There's Maureen, however, or Bertha."

"Who's Maureen? Who's Bertha?"

"Bertha is my senior girl. Maureen did your last one."

"Oh, well, her work was satisfactory."

"Maureen, come here a moment."

A small slender girl with remarkably long golden hair rose from one of the desks in the crowded room a-clatter with typewriters. Miss Phipps noted with pleasure that this golden mane was beautifully brushed.

"You've nearly finished that report, Maureen?" said Mrs. Norton in a voice which would have frozen a polar bear.

"On the last page, Mrs. Norton."

"We'd better just look at your work together," suggested Mrs. Norton, holding out a hand to Miss Phipps for the script. "Is it a full-length novel, dear?"

"Just a short children's book," deprecated Miss Phipps, blushing and feeling embarrassed and inferior, as she always did when her writing was mentioned.

She reluctantly laid the script on the table in its folder, which she had tied round with string two ways to keep the pages within from slipping. If asked, Miss Phipps would have admitted frankly that while all the literary work on the script was as good as she could make it, the outside appearance was not altogether prepossessing, the folder being slightly dirty and dog-eared and the string knotted in several places.

Mrs. Norton, with her rather pompous little cough, advanced long-nailed fingers toward it, with an air of trying, for friendship's sake, not to show disdain. Miss Phipps hated to see those mercenary hands take hold of her precious writing—But that's not fair, she rebuked herself. She's a professional in her own line and proud of it, just as I am in mine.

While Miss Phipps was thinking this, the group had been joined by a new member. A Siamese cat, slim, brownish, young and handsome, had leaped onto the table and was now devoting tooth and claw to the dismemberment of the folder's string.

"No, no," said Miss Phipps mildly, gently laying aside a smooth brown paw. The cat promptly scratched her.

"I don't mind a scratch or two," said Miss Phipps. "But not the string, please. *PLEASE!* No, pussy! No. I shall be cross!"

"She doesn't understand," purred Mrs. Norton. "She lives here, you see. This office is her home and she thinks she can do as she pleases. Now, Edith, dear."

"Who is Edith?" inquired Miss Phipps, looking interrogatively at Maureen, who was standing patiently by the table.

"The cat, of course. Called after my aunt, who gave her to me."

"Edith!" said Miss Phipps sternly. "Paws off, please!"

Edith bit the bow of the string, rolled over with that beautiful feline grace which is the admiration and despair of humans, and lying on her back, waving a couple of paws, seemed to invite praise. Since she had contrived to untie the string and wind it about herself in complex trails, Miss Phipps did not feel the slightest bit laudatory.

"You're a naughty cat, Edith," Miss Phipps said, snatching the precious folder from the table.

Edith scowled ferociously from yellow eyes.

"Well, really!" exclaimed Mrs. Norton. "Don't blame the cat! Maureen spoils her."

Indeed Maureen, smiling, had extended loving arms toward Edith.

"*You'd* better take her, Bertha," commanded Mrs. Norton.

A rather handsome girl, tall, with a composed face and a stack of fair curls piled up on her head, approached from her front-row desk with dignity, raised the bestringed Edith distastefully into her arms, and walked away.

"Let Bertha finish that report, Maureen," instructed Mrs. Norton, having flicked Miss Phipps's pages. "Begin Miss Phipps's script at once. I know she's always in a hurry."

Bertha, having detached the string, put Edith outside the door of the room, closed the door, and came back, walking with measured tread. Meanwhile Maureen retrieved Miss Phipps's script. She handled it respectfully, and Miss Phipps felt somewhat mollified.

"I'll give you a ring when it's done," offered Mrs. Norton.

They parted on cool but friendly terms.

The Norton Typing Agency occupied an office-apartment on the first floor of a large Victorian house. Outside the room Miss Phipps found Edith, glowering, seated at the head of the steps leading to the street. Miss Phipps was not at all disposed to let the cat approach within range of her typescript, so she took some pains to close the office door promptly. Edith tripped down the steps gracefully in front of her and sat at the foot, still glowering.

"Beautiful animal," conceded Miss Phipps. "Fine coat."

At the foot of the steps, leaning against the wall, was Geoffrey, Mrs. Norton's son, now an engineer apprentice. Mrs. Norton was a widow, and Geoffrey could have used a father, Miss Phipps thought, surveying his beads and style of dress. She had known Geoffrey since he was an infant, and greeted him in familiar tones.

"Hullo, Geoff. You've grown a good deal lately, I see."

"Hullo, Miss Phipps. Edith doesn't seem to like you, I see."

"We had a bit of a tiff upstairs," admitted Miss Phipps, noting the cat's still furious glaring and the lashing of her slender tail. "She's vexed."

"Well, wouldn't you be vexed if *you* were thrown out on your paws?"

"She wasn't exactly thrown out," objected Miss Phipps.

"That's what you think," said Geoffrey. "Now purr nicely for Miss Phipps, Edith."

Edith, in the haughty manner peculiar to cats, raised her head and stalked slowly off in the opposite direction.

Miss Phipps and Geoffrey laughed together. "Cats know how to administer the snub direct," said Geoff.

"None better. How's life, Geoff?"

"*Comme ci, comme ça*," said Geoff without enthusiasm, scowling.

"If only all this hoo-ha nowadays made the young happier, I shouldn't mind," reflected Miss Phipps, moving toward a bus. "But it doesn't seem to, you know."

Three days later Miss Phipps, hearing the bell ring in her flat one evening, found Geoffrey, Maureen, and a neatly packed parcel at her door.

"Your script. Miss Phipps," said Maureen meekly, offering the parcel.

"Come in, come in!" exclaimed Miss Phipps, delighted. "Have some coffee." She tore off the wrapping hastily and gloated over the neat, professionally typed script. "You type very well, Maureen," she said with pleasure.

She was particularly enthusiastic because she thought Maureen looked rather downcast, indeed almost ready to cry. Of course it was obvious these children were madly in love with each other. They were both good-looking, even handsome. Geoffrey with fine dark eyes and masses of thick dark curls—pity he didn't cut them! And Maureen with that really glorious golden hair. A sweet face, too. They sat down. Miss Phipps gave them coffee. Nobody spoke.

"Is anything wrong?" asked Miss Phipps at length.

Maureen at once burst into tears. Geoffrey blushed.

"Oh, dear, oh, dear, I'm terribly sorry," apologized Miss Phipps.

"It's Mother," said Geoffrey with disgust. "She doesn't want us to get married."

"Aren't you perhaps a little—young?"

"Why should we waste all these years?" demanded Geoffrey, almost savagely.

"Well," began Miss Phipps. But on thinking it over, she couldn't find a particularly good reason, so she said nothing.

"Will you say a word to Mother? Persuade her?" urged Geoffrey.

"I don't think your mother would like that, Geoffrey," said Miss Phipps nervously.

"Oh, yes, she would."

"She thinks the world of you, Miss Phipps," said Maureen. "She's proud of typing your stories and all that. Isn't she, Geoffrey?"

"Yes. I don't read them myself, of course," said Geoffrey flatly.

Somehow this touch of honesty cheered Miss Phipps.

"When will you be out of your apprenticeship, Geoffrey?" she inquired.

"Next spring."

"Why not wait till then?"

"Yes, if we can have a firm promise from Mum for then. But to go on just hanging around isn't good enough. And she seems set against it. She prefers Bertha," concluded Geoffrey in a tone of disgust.

"The trouble is, you see," said Maureen sadly, "Mrs. Norton thinks I'm a bad worker—careless, you know—and so I should be a careless unreliable wife for Geoff. But I wouldn't," she protested, weeping again.

"Look, Maureen," said Miss Phipps, kind but firm. "You've just said two things to me. Since they contradict each other, one of them must be untrue."

Maureen looked up, horrified. "Oh, Miss Phipps! I wouldn't say anything untrue to you, truly, I wouldn't."

"You said Mrs. Norton is proud of typing my stories, and you said she thinks you're a careless worker. But she gives my stories to you to type. Don't you see? Either she doesn't care a button about me, or she doesn't think you're a careless worker."

"I'm not a careless person, Miss Phipps," said Maureen raising her head, with spirit.

"I believe you."

"Will you come and see Mum and put in a word for us, then?" pleaded Geoff.

"Perhaps."

"Tomorrow?"

"Well—I'll see."

As it turned out, the next morning Miss Phipps visited the Norton Typing Agency, but in a very different mood and on a very different errand. She raged up to Mrs. Norton's table, threw down the parcel of typing, and shouted, "That abominable cat!"

"What do you mean, Miss Phipps?" asked Mrs. Norton in her most genteel voice.

"If you will examine my original script, pages thirty through thirty-six, chapter four, and then examine your own typed version of chapter four, you will see that pages thirty through thirty-six have been omitted in your version. I have marked the passage with strips of paper."

"Maureen!" cried Mrs. Norton. Miss. Phipps with regret could not help but detect an undercurrent of satisfaction in Mrs. Norton's voice. Maureen, pale and anguished, approached. "The carelessness can easily be remedied," said Mrs. Norton stiffly.

"It can, if my original pages are not lost," said Miss Phipps.

"What are you suggesting, Miss Phipps?"

"That abominable Edith tore them to shreds."

To Miss Phipps's astonishment Mrs. Norton burst into tears.

"I never typed those pages," said Maureen quickly. "I noticed they weren't there. But some writers make gaps, you know. It was the end of one section and the beginning of another, so I thought—"

Mrs. Norton continued to weep.

"Well, never mind, don't cry. I must rewrite that chapter, that's all. It's tiresome, but I daresay I can manage," said Miss Phipps, furious.

"You don't understand," wept Mrs. Norton.

"She's lost," whispered Maureen in Miss Phipps's ear. "Edith, I mean. She's disappeared. Last night—she wasn't here this morning. We've searched the whole house. It's awful. Come with me."

She led the mystified Miss Phipps to the communal bathroom-cum-lavatory in the rear of the agency. The sash window was slightly raised. The bath was spattered with splashes of red oily liquid which Miss Phipps observed with horror.

"We don't like to clear it away," murmured Maureen. "Mrs. Norton doesn't know whether to send for the police."

"You don't think—" began Miss Phipps, aghast.

"Well, yes, we do really. Edith has vanished. She used to go down to the housekeeper in the basement, you see, at night, but the housekeeper hasn't seen her."

"But, my dear child—" began Miss Phipps. She wanted to ask where, if these were splashes of Edith's blood, was Edith's body? Nerving herself to a great effort of courage, she bent over the bathtub, dipped one finger in a crimson splash, and raised the finger to her nose. Then, to Maureen's exclamation of horror, she actually put the stained finger in her mouth.

"This, my dear Maureen," she announced triumphantly, "is cough medicine. It probably comes," she went on, raising her eyes to the glass shelves in the corner, "from that bottle up there."

"But how—but why—but where is she now?" objected Maureen, accepting the bottle of sticky red medicine as the obvious but still mysterious explanation.

"She was shut in here and was frightened and leaped about and knocked over the bottle."

"How could she get shut in here?"

"That is what we must find out."

"Where is Edith now?"

Miss Phipps strode to the window, threw up the sash, and gazed out. The landscape visible from this back window, as is true so often in central London, consisted of an architectural chaos—walls, mostly blank, roofs, chimneys, houses, snug little secret yards, with here and there one or two lean but courageous trees. Edith was not visible.

"She wriggled out of the window and fell down there."

"We must ask at every house in that back street, Miss Phipps," urged Maureen. "Come along."

As they proceeded down the street, building by building, Miss Phipps was struck by the kindliness and good humor shown to them. Some of the buildings were occupied by offices filled with clerks, some were still private homes. All the inhabitants looked rather cross when first summoned from their occupations to seek a lost cat, but then Miss Phipps had an inspiration.

"You see, the cat belongs to the mother of this young lady's boyfriend," she explained.

They all melted at once, perceiving the romantic importance of the cat to Maureen. They smiled sympathetically. "Really!" they said. "Well, come in, dear. She may be in the backyard, you know. We don't often go out there."

And that was just where Edith was, when at last they found her. In a corner of a dismal little yard, surrounded by high windowless walls, Edith lay on her front, with her paws neatly tucked in beneath her. The moment she saw Maureen, she sprang toward her, and safe in the girl's arms nestled against her neck, kneading her over and over with her paws and giving her loud, raucous purr.

"Fond of you, I daresay," said the elderly clerk with them.

"I hope so."

"She'll be hungry, poor thing. I'll get a drop of milk. I wonder how she got down here, I must say."

"She fell out of our bathroom window, I expect, and then made her way along, looking for a way out."

"That'll be it. Here you are, pussy. Lap this up."

"But how did Edith get shut into the bathroom?" queried Mrs. Norton, stroking the cat with the passion of a lonely woman. "I suppose the door must have slammed."

"I think Bertha slammed the door," said Miss Phipps, giving Bertha an accusing look.

"Why should I lock up Edith?" demanded Bertha.

"You destroyed my pages, you wanted Edith to be blamed for that, and Maureen to be blamed for allowing it to happen. For obvious reasons," added Miss Phipps.

"Nonsense," snapped Bertha. But she had crimsoned.

"Edith was frightened and rushed round the bathroom and upset the cough-mixture bottle. *You* recorked the bottle and replaced it on the upper shelf. *After* you had contrived that she fell out of the window."

"I didn't mean her any harm," cried Bertha. "She wriggled suddenly out through the open part of the window. I couldn't stop her. You know how quick cats are."

"Some cats I know are rather too clever for their own good," said Miss Phipps.

"If you don't care for cats, Bertha, you had perhaps better give your notice at once," said Mrs. Norton coldly. "I must get your replacement settled in before Maureen leaves to get married, in the spring."

"I should like to continue working for you after our marriage, Mrs. Norton," said Maureen mildly.

"Very well, dear," agreed Mrs. Norton.

Kristine Kathryn Rusch

LITTLE MIRACLES

We found the cat just as we were about to seal off the house. Its throat had been slit, and its coat was matted with blood. Some instinct made me crouch down to touch it. Its skin was warm, and its body struggled with shallow breaths. Life among the carnage.

I snapped my fingers for the paramedics. They glanced at each other and didn't move.

"Gentlemen, kindly get your asses over here," I said.

"But, sir, it's a cat."

"And it's still breathing. Get over here."

They crouched over the cat, placed a bandage over its neck, and did something to ease its breathing. I directed them to a veterinarian down the street, then returned my attention to the bloodbath before me. In the kitchen, a woman's body, curled in a fetal hug, clutching a knife in what appeared to have been self-defense. In the bedroom, two children, slaughtered. And in the master bathroom, a man collapsed over the bathtub, also dead. In the living room, the TV stand was empty. The door to the empty stereo cabinet in the dining room stood open, and pictures were missing from the walls.

It looked like a desperate act of a startled burglar. But the cat was the clue. Sliced on the way out for the pleasure of the act. Cats don't bark. They don't threaten killers. Cats hide from frightening circumstances. The killer flushed the cat and slit its throat just to see the blood.

Wrote up the preliminary report and went home, washed the blood-stink off my skin. It was raining. Felt like it was always raining. Oregon: land of the nonexistent sun.

The house was a mess—dishes in the sink, dirty clothes tumbling out of the closet. No time to clean, not even now, with another crazy on the loose. I opened the fridge, searching for a beer, and heard Delilah's voice. *I don't know how you*

259

can come home and assume you lead a normal life, as if nothing happened to you all day. In the early days, she had liked that, the way I could leave my job behind me. But she never could. She always wanted to know the details, relishing the jargon as if it was a new language. *Was there high velocity blood?* she would have asked about this case.

All over the house, I would have replied. *Especially the bathroom and the kitchen. The man must have gone first, but the woman put up quite a fight.*

I would never have told her about the blood's odd trajectory, indicating that the killer used a sharp weapon, knife perhaps, but not a normal kitchen knife. I would never have trusted her that far.

I closed the refrigerator door without the beer. I never did leave the work at the office. It was always there, one corner of the brain assessing the evidence, searching for the clue that would lead us to the creep of the week. Maybe that was why Delilah left. Maybe her words had always been sarcasm, her questions medicine to draw out the poison.

Grabbed the car keys and let myself out the back door. The car, the only thing she left me, a 1988 Saab, drove itself. We stopped in the slanted parking lot at the vet's, a place I hadn't been since her dog nearly died chewing a steak bone. Pulled open the door, stepped into the scent of disinfectant, matted fur, and frightened animals. The woman behind the reception desk didn't recognize me, which was fine, since I didn't remember seeing her before.

I flashed my badge. "Some of my paramedics brought a cat in earlier."

She shuddered delicately. Just once, but enough for me to notice. "What an awful thing to do to an animal," she said.

You should have seen what happened to the people, I nearly said, but since the paramedics had followed procedure and not said anything, I wouldn't either. "I was wondering if you folks had ever seen the cat before."

"I haven't, but let me check with the doctor." She got up, a tidy woman in a green dress, her age nearly impossible to determine. I glanced around the room. Empty now, but I had seen it filled with worried people hovering over their animals as if the animals were as precious as children. Something in the back set off the dogs, and one of them howled, followed by another. She returned with the vet, the man I remembered, a big-boned redhead with a touch that even the most skittish animal trusted.

"Frank," he said, and held out a well-scrubbed hand. I shook it.

"Doug." We have never socialized, only saw each other in this small building, but the familiarity put me at ease when I hadn't even realized I was uncomfortable. "Ever see the cat before?"

"No," the vet said. "And he's got distinctive markings. I would have remembered."

"Family named Torgenson, lived just down the block. Ever treat their animals?"

He nodded, looking thoughtful, too polite to ask why Torgenson. They had a dog, died of old age a month ago. He always brought the dog in. She was allergic to cats. They both came to put the dog down, and she was a mess by the time they left even though we keep this place as dander-free as modern technology allows."

The news startled me. The cat had been found beside her.

"He's awake. Want to see him?"

It took me a moment to realize that the vet was talking about the cat. "Sure," I said, feeling more than a bit uncomfortable. I'd lived through this scene a number of times in hospitals, seeing the survivor, asking preliminary questions. But I couldn't ask the cat why he'd been there, what he'd seen.

The vet led me through the narrow hallway into a large room filled with steel tables. In the back, rows of cages lined the walls. Cats, in various stages of distress, stared at me. I didn't see any dogs, figured they must be kept elsewhere.

The vet showed me a cage on the far side of the wall. A white cat with an orange mustache stared at us through the mesh. His eyes were still wide with the effect of the drug. A gauze bandage had been taped in place around his neck. He saw me and rolled on his back, paws kneading the empty air.

"Amazing, huh?" the vet said. "I've never seen such a friendly cat. Especially one drugged and wounded."

"He'll live?"

"He probably used up eight of his nine lives, but yeah, he'll make it." The vet opened the door, reached in, and scratched the cat's stomach. "What do you plan to do with him?"

I hadn't realized I had given the cat any thought. "Take him home," I said.

The station was a dingy gray. The walls were made of steel and concrete, built during the Vietnam era when everything had to be bombproof. The ventilation was poor, and the place smelled of old cigarettes, stale coffee, and sweat. My desk was the only spotless one among the detectives, mostly because I shoved everything in drawers. When I arrived the morning after the killings, though, files were piled five inches high on the top.

I sat down and sorted through them. Autopsies, blood analyses, request forms for DNA scans, forensics results, photos of the house's contents . . . amazing how much reading could be generated in one night. I pulled out the autopsy reports and the photographs of the crime scene.

All night I had been thinking about the cat. Hell, I even stopped at the grocery store and bought litter, a litter pan, and food dishes. The vet said he would give me food when Rip—that's what they were calling the little guy—was ready to go home.

But that wasn't all I was thinking about. I was thinking about the kind of person who would slit a cat's throat. I was thinking about the woman dead on the kitchen floor. I was thinking about the knife in her hand.

It would have been easy enough for her to surprise her husband in the bathroom. A bit of a struggle and he would be down, then attack the sleeping children. In the kitchen, a quick slash across the throat of a stray cat, and then the final act— a knife to her own gut, enough times to bleed to death.

A domestic tragedy, something I had seen so often it no longer turned my stomach. The papers would play it up, and the D.A.'s office would look into her life just enough to give her a motive before the case closed completely.

I pulled out the pictures, studied them, realized my theory was wrong. No wounds on Mrs. Torgenson's chest, face, or neck. All in the back. She had been stabbed in the back, surprised in her own kitchen, knife in hand. Not self-defense as I had earlier thought. Surprised chopping an onion for the family dinner.

And Rip, blood matted on his fur, running down his front as it should in a neck wound, but no pool beneath his body. Blood on his back, his tail, his ears. Someone else's blood. I picked up the pictures, turned them. Handprints. He had been moved.

I set the photos down, put my face in my hands. Amazing the details I had missed. I used to approach a crime scene as if it were a complete jigsaw puzzle. All the clues were there; I just had to notice them and arrange them in the correct order. That way each detail went into the brain, from the day-old cigarette stub on the driveway to the pattern of the bloodstains on the wall. In those days, I would have seen the onions on the sideboard, noticed her shredded back, commented on the handprints covering Rip.

Ceramic clanged against the metal surface of my desk, and the aroma of fresh coffee hit me. "Breakfast, Frank?"

Denny, one of the few men who had been in the station as long as I have. Fifteen years sounds like a long time, but I could remember the days when we were enthusiastic about our work, when we concentrated on catching the creeps and then having a few brews after a rough day. We hadn't spent time together in I couldn't remember how long.

I brought my hands down casually, as if I had been resting my eyes instead of berating myself. He had put a cup of coffee on one of my files. I took it, sipped.

"Tough case, huh?" He half-sat, half-leaned on my desk. "I hate seeing kids sliced up like that."

I stared at him, seeing instead the little girl clutching her stuffed bunny, eyes still closed as if she were asleep. Her older sister, eyes wide with terror . . .

Rip had bothered me more than they had. But Rip had been the anomaly at the crime scene.

"Yeah," I said.

Denny looked at me strangely. Once he pulled me off a perp who'd been caught molesting a five-year-old girl. The murder case I'd busted my ass working on because I knew the mother had tried to strangle her daughters and I didn't want her to regain custody of them.

"You okay?" he asked.

"No different than I've been."

He nodded once, as if my comment ended the conversation, and disappeared around the corner to his own desk. When Delilah left, he invited me over for dinner for weeks until it became clear that I would never go. I didn't want to see him and Sheila, perfect examples of conjugal bliss. I didn't want to socialize with anyone.

I sighed, pulled out my legal pad. Options: The killer was (1) someone they knew; (2) some sicko creep just starting; (3) some sicko creep with a pattern; (4) a burglar, caught in the act; (5) a family member.

I pushed the list aside, filled out the DNA forms, sent a notice of the killing across the wire to see if anyone else picked up a pattern. Then I read the files, crossed off the family member—since, with that bloodbath, the entire family died—and assigned one of my men to monitor the fences in town. I was preparing a list of interviews when McRooney stopped.

"Frank, my office."

I set my pen down and followed him through the maze of desks to the only walled-off office in the place. McRooney had a large glass door through which he saw damn near everything. Fake plants hung from the fluorescents, and filing cabinets stood like soldiers behind his desk.

He pulled the blinds on he door.

"Sit," he said.

I did as I was told. McRooney was an okay guy—political, ambitious, people-savvy. I remember when he was a green kid, puking at the scene of his first murder. Long time ago.

"Hear you missed some things at the Torgenson house."

"Too damn much," I said. No use lying to the man. He knew.

"Crime lab boys caught some of it. Forensics more. You're usually ahead of the game, Frank."

"I know," I said.

"You've been slipping these past six months. You didn't take time when the wife left. You need to."

"When the case is wrapped."

"Now," McRooney sat behind his desk, looking like a politician in a thirties movie. "I'm going to reassign. This kind of thing is too important."

"To trust to a guy who's screwing up."

"Your words, Frank." He pulled out a sheet of paper, stamped it, and slid it toward me. "A leave with pay. As much time as you need. Your heart's gone."

I ignored the paper. "I'll just sit at home and get sloshed. Gimme a week. If I haven't got the case wrapped by then, I'll go."

"It'll be cold then."

"If I continue to screw up, you mean?"

"You never used to be so defensive." He leaned back in his chair. It groaned under his weight.

"I never used to notice my own mistakes, either." I sighed, adjusted my trouser legs. "I don't think staying home is the way for me. I got a glimmer in this case, first interest I've felt in a while. Let me try."

He pulled the paper back, looked at it, crumpled it. Missed the hook shot to the garbage can. "Three days. That way we don't lose too much ground."

Three days. As if he expected nothing from my work. I stood. I wouldn't expect much from my work, either. I grabbed the doorknob.

"Frank?"

Stopped, waited, head down, not turning.

"Is she worth all this?"

Friend. The comment of a concerned friend. I let my breath out slowly, feeling truth come with it. "I don't think it's her. I think it's been building for a long time. Her going was just a symptom."

"Studen is a good shrink."

Flush rose on my cheeks—anger canceling truth. "You gave me three days," I said, and let myself out.

Not so much as a half-formed fingerprint by five. Neighbors heard nothing. No, the family was quiet, kept to themselves. Dog was loud, but it died months ago.

Called the vet. Rip was doing better. Could go home in a few days. Quite the survivor, huh?, a comment I took to mean that the vet had seen the papers, understood what happened to the cat.

A little miracle, I replied as I hung up.

Closed the files, went down to the Steelhead for a beer and a burger. The inside was crowded, but not too, just enough so that I had to take a table instead of a booth. Three screens played the news, and the music blared country-western, unusual for a yuppie bar. Glanced at the menu, glanced at the microbrews being sipped at the tables around me. Three days. And day one nearly gone.

When the waitress showed, I ordered a bacon-cheddar burger, fries, and a coffee nudge without the nudge. I'd get more work done with caffeine as the drug of choice.

Woman sat across from me, alone. Blonde, leggy, nail polish, and lip gloss. Not usually my type. She smiled, I smiled back, and it felt good. But the burger arrived before I could pick myself up and sit beside her. Then the boyfriend showed, three-piece suit and silk tie, and I leaned back, outclassed.

Not that I was too disappointed. I'd picked up too many women in that bar, both before and after Delilah, never for conversation, always for exercise and sometimes not enough of that. Couldn't imagine bringing a woman to my place now, with its ancient dishes and unwashed sheets. Guess it had been a long time. I did the laundry just after Delilah left, months ago.

The burger settled me, the coffee buzzed me. I wandered back to the station, half wishing the cat had died so we could have sent his body to the lab to check for prints. Uncharitable thought—remembering the little guy on his back, trusting paws kneading the air, the cat box at the house, waiting. We'd had cats at home, barn cats who sat on my shoulders while I milked the cows at five in the morning. Two cats, both killed one morning when they got loose in the cow pen. I cried until my momma shamed me.

Men don't cry, she said. They get mad.

Yeah, Momma, I thought. What happens when the anger goes, too, and you're just a big hulking shell?

She would have no answer for that. I squinted, wondered when we last spoke. Wasn't even sure if I'd told her Delilah was gone.

Opened the door to the station, stepped into the familiar noise and stink. Place never changed, day to night, always busy, always crazy. Problems everywhere, even in a small city like this one.

Three new files on my desk: fax-sent cases, one from Washington, one from California, one from Utah. Sat down and read. Perp never caught. One scene left a dog, thought to be a stray, throat slit. Another a cat, belonged to the neighbors, throat slit. Yet another cat, black, purchased from a pet store, throat slit.

California, skipped Nevada, Utah, skipped Idaho, Washington, and now Oregon. New pattern? Or getting sloppy? Hard to tell with a random crazy.

I put my head on my desk. A random crazy. The worst kind.

Typed up a new report, flagged it for McRooney, and reminded him to notify the FBI. The case was theirs now, not that I couldn't work on it, too.

On the drive home, found myself wondering what the crazy would think if he knew the cat lived. First survivor. The thought gave me a pang, made me half-swerve to head for the vet's, then forced myself to continue the drive home. Silly idea. The cat was safe. As if it mattered.

Opened the door, turned on the lights, blared Tchaikovsky on the CD, and dug into the dishes. Grunge work for relaxation. Had to get the case out of my mind. The best detecting happened in the subconscious—comparing details, fitting pieces. The subconscious still worked, I knew that. The path to the conscious was blocked. I'd seen everything at the murder site but couldn't remember it until something jogged me. Not good. Not good at all.

Left the dishes to soak, went into the living room, and flopped on the couch. Closed my eyes and walked through the Torgenson house again.

First thing: stale-death reek of blood, even before we walked through the door. Into the sunken living room, done in modular white, with chrome lamps, decorative books. An unused room. And nothing, except a little mud leading up the stairs. Half-moon pattern. Man's shoe.

Den. Sloppy with toys, half-read books, another stereo still there. Television cabinet empty, VCR gone. No evidence of search, of a mess other than the intentional one.

Into the formal dining. Stereo cabinet door open, equipment gone. Nothing else touched. No prints on the cabinet glass.

Kitchen. Blood-spattered. Woman on her side, fetal position, knife in her hand. Onions chopped on the sideboard, eggs unbeaten in a mixing bowl, meat burned on the stove. The smell of hamburger mixed with fresh blood. Cat left like a calling card beside the back door. Blood pattern on the carpeted steps—dripping blood, spatters on the rug, not the wall.

Follow the stairs twisting to the second story. No handprints, no marks at all on the white walls. Odd for people with children. Fresh paint?

Blood trail leads to the bathroom. Man doubled over the tub, throat slit, blood pouring down the drain. (Drain cleaned? Something else hiding in there? Some missing evidence?) High velocity blood patterned on the mirror around the sink and onto the toilet. Why couldn't he see perp in mirror? Mirror has unusually high placement. Perp too short? Or too quick? With throat slit, man unable to scream. First victim, then. The children might have screamed, at least the second girl. Woman didn't hear—why?

Back to the kitchen, searching, searching, realized the answer in the dining room, now missing. Stereo probably blaring. How, then, could the children sleep? And why was she cooking?

Onions, hamburger, eggs on the sideboard. She was making breakfast.

Back up stairs. Master bedroom, again in white. King-sized bed, made army style—by him, retired colonel, probably his last act. More decorative books in wall cases. Television propped near headboard. Another VCR, more movies. Didn't have to look to guess the kind. Television still there, as is VCR. Half-moon footprints leading to the bathroom, mud plus blood leading out. Confirmed: killer stopped here first. Knew the morning routine well enough to avoid the woman, get the man, the children, and finally her in the kitchen, alone and terrified.

Followed prints to the girls' room. Took the youngest first, nearest the door. Quick slash, throat again, killed her before she could wake. Blood trickles off the bed onto the floor. No prints. Went around to kill her sister. Awake, eyes open, body curled. Sister tried to escape, got caught in the man's arms, watched him kill her. . . .

Opened my eyes, took a deep sigh, body shaking. Relieved to be in my own living room, *Marche Slav* repeating over and over on the CD. Picked up the remote and shut the music off, deciding silence was more amenable than the noise.

He arrived early morning, interrupted the routine, just as he had in the other states. They thought he was a nighttime killer, but he wasn't. He had a set time for attack, and a set plan, and he carried it through. Letting Rip live was no accident. He was trying to get caught. Each set of deaths more dangerous than the last, as if he were searching for the final adrenaline rush, the final opportunity . . .

I leaned over the couch's arm, picked up the phone, and ordered the forensics squad to return to the house, check the drain, the prints. Hung up and remembered the details from the other reports. Each place he had taken something large, something different. Microwave from California, computer from Utah, china and silver in Washington. He wasn't fencing, or even masquerading as a burglar. He was furnishing his home. Souvenirs.

And Rip. Not a calling card, but a clue. A stray dog, a neighbor's cat. Animals didn't belong to the perp, but were associated with him, somehow. A job, maybe, that took him into certain neighborhoods at particular times of the morning? Allowed him to travel, and to watch patterns. Not animal welfare. Those were city jobs, stable because they paid well, not likely to take a drifter. Vet? Perhaps, but again, stability was the key. Needing to build a practice, to get good references.

Vet. Finally the light bulb went off. I picked up the phone, called the station again, asked Vinnie to doublecheck the files. Yes, a vet close to each murdered family.

Thumbed through the phone book, found Doug the vet's home address, grabbed my coat and shield, and left. Ten o'clock might be too late to go visiting in some neighborhoods, but not in mine.

Took five minutes after I knocked for him to come to the door. Out of his smock, he looked younger—aided, I think, by his tousled hair. I half-expected a female voice to query, an admonition not to wake the kids. Instead got a shirtless, sleepy man clutching a beer, TV blaring in the background, cats emerging from all parts of the house, and a quiet dog padding its way to the door.

"Frank?" Doug—he didn't seem like a vet anymore to me—ran his hand over his face. "You got a problem? There's an emergency vet on Walker."

"Need to talk to you about the Torgenson case. Got a minute?"

"Sure." Rubbing the sleep from his eyes, pushing back a cat with his foot. "Come on in."

The place smelled like home. Unwashed dishes piled in the kitchen, blanket on the couch. He tossed a cat off the recliner, bade me sit, used the remote to shut off the TV. "Sorry about the mess. Wife left a few weeks ago, and I can't bring myself to clean."

Vets have lives, too. "It's been six months for me, and I've been thinking about hiring a service."

"Thing is," Doug said, sitting on the couch, feet propped on the coffee table, "I always thought I did a lot of chores."

I nodded. Recognition that my situation was not unique warmed me. "Sorry to bother you so late. Just need a few questions answered. You hire anyone new in the last few months?"

He shook his head. "I haven't hired anyone for two years. Got college kids cleaning the cages—they've been with me since they started school. One's a junior, the other'll graduate in spring. My receptionist has been there for nearly two years, and the lab techs since I started."

The air left me, as a feeling of failure grew. Somehow I'd assumed that his night attendants, cage cleaners, would be the ones. Transient, short-term jobs—

Then felt a flood of relief. If that were true, Rip would have died the first night. "Who else comes through?"

He closed his eyes. I liked his concentration. Most folks always wanted to know why I needed the information. "Medical supply people like any doctor's office, deliveries—"

"Any in the morning?"

"Cat food, sometimes, about once a month. Arrives seven A.M. sharp, and gets annoyed if no one's at the door to let him in. But he's not new, either. Been servicing us as long as I can remember."

"But only once a month?"

"Sometimes not even that. Got quite a route. Heard him brag to Sally—that's my receptionist. He can cover six states in thirty days if he has to, although he runs Oregon, Nevada, usually, picking up supplies in California as he drives through."

"Don't like him much." No need to make that a question. I could feel the animosity in Doug's every word.

Doug opened his eyes, looked at me, hand on a black cat that decided to stare at me from his lap. "No, I don't. He's odd. Animals don't like him, but they come because he smells like food. Animals always know."

Strays. The neighbor's cat. Food.

"Remember his name?"

Doug gently eased the cat away, got up. "No, but I've got his card around here, somewhere, if I can find my wallet." He walked barefoot over to a desk mounded with open envelopes, pushed them aside, and picked up a leather wallet, thumbed through it, and produced a card. I took it. Black lettering on white.

Jonathan Kivy.

Had him.

I still sweated it. FBI wanted to make the collar—allowed them to take him anywhere they needed to. They found him in southern Oregon, TV, VCR, stereo, and paintings in the back of his truck, and radioed, promised to bring him in to me.

All night I'd dreamed about Rip walking up to him, trusting but nervous, hoping that a man who smelled like food would provide him with some. Saw the arm flash down, the quick throat slash, the one-handed bloody carry into the Torgensons' kitchen, dumped by the door like a single sack of cat food.

Woke up, tears on my cheeks, anger in my gut, repeating *it doesn't matter, it doesn't matter*. Remembered nights like that, Delilah's arms around me, soothing, dreams of dead children, bodies in the river, perps with guns, perps with knives. She'd tell me it was over. I knew it would never be over, so all I could do was drown the tears, let the anger serve. Repeating *it doesn't matter, it doesn't matter*, until it didn't anymore.

They showed up about eleven A.M., two men in black suits with regulation haircuts, leading a small man, hands in cuffs. I started shivering, anger running through my body, looking for an escape. One leap across the desk, fingers against his throat, showing him how it felt to be small and helpless and dying . . .

But I didn't move. Clasped my hands under the desk, waited for them to stop. McRooney left his office, watched me. He said he'd abide by my decision.

They brought him to my desk. Stared at his hands, long slender fingers, strong. Pictured Rip in them, then the little girl, gripped by the hair, head pulled back—

It didn't matter.

But it did.

—throat slashed, one quick movement, her sister screaming. . . .

"He's yours, if you want him, detective," Adams, one of the FBI men, said. They had praised me the night before for saving them so much headache.

I looked at the perp's eyes. Cold, black, reflecting only my face. How close had I gotten to that empty stare?

"Extradite him. Utah. They have a death penalty there, and they're not afraid to use it. Tell them I'll cooperate in any way I can." The words came out angry, so forceful that I almost spit at him.

The perp's face didn't change. I didn't so much care about the death penalty as the trial. Oregon's prisons were overcrowded, good reason, sometimes, to opt for an insanity defense. I didn't want the perp's abusive childhood—if he had one—or an anti-social personality disorder, which he did have, to get in the way of his punishment.

They led him into McRooney's office to prepare the paperwork, perhaps allow him a phone call. I leaned back, wondering why he did it, and then realizing that it didn't matter. He would have some reason, some crazy rationale, but it would just mask the compulsion. I read a lot on serial killers in the early days. Random crazies, triggered by an unknown mechanism. Human, but not human, threatening us all.

I stood up, staggered with the force of released emotion. Denny stopped by my desk, concern on his face. "You okay?"

Reached up, found wet cheeks. Odd that the tears would come now. "Fine," I said.

McRooney had left his office, coming to pat me on the back. I didn't want him to touch me, didn't want anyone to touch me just then. I swallowed, made the lump disappear. "I'm going to take that leave," I said. "Starting now."

McRooney watched, slight frown on his face. To his credit, he didn't comment on my appearance. "You deserve it, Frank. We'll set the details later. Good work on this."

"Thanks," I said. Grabbed my jacket, and half-ran from the station, knowing that on the leave, I would have to think about my future, too. Maybe homicide was no longer for me. Maybe being a cop was no longer for me.

The thought sobered the weird elation building in my gut. Doug said I could get Rip today, and I would. Funny. A cat started my emotional lockup, and a cat undid it. Because he was an anomaly, the only living thing I had not trained my emotions to hide from at a crime scene. I remembered him on his back, paws kneading the air. Like a little child. Delilah used to say pets brought out the parenting instinct. Fine. I needed something to mother, to take the attention from myself.

I got in the car, wondering how Rip would like the drive. Wondering if I could clean the house in an afternoon. Wondering if Doug would drop by after work for a brew. A man without a wife, without conjugal bliss. We could complain about women, get royally sloshed, laugh and cry until we were sure the emotions ran both hot and cold.

Had to clear the ice water from my veins.

Whoa, body, heat wave moving in.

I shivered one last time.

The heat would feel good.

Lee Somerville

THE BLACK CAT

She was an old cat, coal black, lean and ugly. Her right ear had been chewed and her old hide showed scars, but she had a regal look when she sat under the rosebushes in the plaza and surveyed us with yellow-green eyes.

If the witch cat had a name, we never knew it. Miss Tessie fed it, as she fed other strays. She even let the old cat sleep in her store in rainy weather. But mostly the cat slept under the rosebushes in our plaza in Caton City, Texas. We have a pretty little plaza, or square, here in the center of town. It has a fountain and a statue of a tired Confederate soldier facing north, ready to defend us from Northern invaders, and a bit of grass and lots of rosebushes.

Nobody dared to pet the old cat. People gave the cat scraps of bread and meat from hamburgers and hot dogs. She accepted this placidly, as a queen accepts homage from peons. Now and then a stray dog came through our small dusty town, saw the cat, and made a lunge at it. The cat would retreat to the base of the fountain, turn, lash with a razor-sharp claw that sliced the poor dog's nose. The dog would run howling while townspeople laughed. Our dogs, having learned the hard way, left that cat alone.

When I was fourteen, my mother's jailbird distant relative, Cousin Rush, came to live with us. My little brother Pete and I had to give up our room to this scruffy relative, but that wasn't the only reason I disliked him. I despised his dumpy figure and his smelly cigars and his scaly bald head and his way of looking at me with beady small eyes and nodding and winking.

Mama told me to show Cousin Rush the town, and I had to do it. This was the day before Halloween, and half the town was in the theater across the street from the plaza, rehearsing for the Heritage Festival we have every Halloween night. Miss Tessie was in the front of the theater, selling plastic masks of Cajun Caton and Davy Crockett. We have this play about Cajun Caton and a Delaware Indian, Chief Cut Hand, saving the town from Comanches on a Halloween night in the early

1800s. It ends with Cajun Caton, town hero, leaving his eight children and one wife later on and going off with Davy Crockett and getting killed in the Alamo during the Texas Revolution against Mexico in 1836.

Cousin Rush bought a mask from Miss Tessie. He smiled and flirted and talked of the Importance of History. His face smiled, but his eyes remained cold and scornful, and I could tell he thought this heritage business was hillbilly country foolishness. He'd already told me Caton City was a hick town filled with stupid people. It didn't compare with real towns.

As we started walking across the plaza, the black cat jumped from the rosebushes and ran in front of us.

To keep walking in a straight direction would have meant bad luck. I side-stepped, made a little circle, and prevented bad luck. I'm not superstitious, not really, but no use taking chances.

Cousin Rush laughed at me. Then, to show his scorn of superstition and black cats, he did a fat-legged little hop and skip and kicked that cat in the stomach.

The old cat doubled up on Cousin Rush's sharp-toed shoe. She clawed at his sock, then bounced into a rosebush. She landed on her feet, stood there, weaving, hurt. Cousin Rush kicked again, and she dodged. She ran into the street, stopped, looked at Cousin Rush with yellow-green eyes. As he popped his hands together, making a threatening noise, she stood her ground for a moment, then ran into Miss Tessie's store.

"You didn't have to do that," I said.

Cousin Rush stood there, the October sun beating down on his bald head and his cigar sticking out of his fat face. "You country bumpkins don't have to act ignorant, but you do. The only way to deal with a black cat running across your path is to kick the manure out of the cat. It's a callous world, Brian, and the only way to deal with it is to skin your buddy before he skins you."

"We don't act that way here," I disagreed.

"You are fools," he stated. He blew cigar smoke and looked at people milling around in front of the theater, talking and being friendly. "Now, tell me about this Heritage Festival you'll have tomorrow night. As I understand it, half the town is in the play, including the sheriff and his deputy. The other half—and that includes a lot of people that make this a sort of homecoming—will buy tickets and make cash contributions to the historical society. I understand this crazy old maid, this Miss Tessie, has collected a neat bit of cash."

"She's raising money for a historical marker to honor her ancestor, Cajun Caton."

"Yes. That's the idiot the town is named for."

"He was not an idiot. Caton and Davy Crockett were both killed in the

Alamo, and they were Texas heroes."

Cousin Rush blew more smoke. "And there are at least a hundred people in this town descended from Caton. I understand that during the finale of this play, which Miss Tessie wrote, it has become a custom for every man in the audience to put on a mask to honor Cajun Caton or Davy Crockett? Hmmm."

I didn't like the sudden suspicion I had. I'd heard Mama and Dad talking in whispers, telling that Rush had served time in a Texas penitentiary for small-time robbery. I didn't like the cold, greedy look on my cousin's face.

I could have reported my suspicion to Sheriff Mitchell or to Deputy Haskins except for one thing—my mother was an Adams. Every Adams is intensely loyal to other Adamses, and don't you forget it. Cousin Rush was Rushid E. Sarosy, and his daddy had been a shoe salesman in Dallas, but his mama was Verney Adams to start with. Verney was a hot little blonde who was born with a female urge and grew up around it. She left Caton County fifty-six years ago for the big city, but she was still an Adams.

I had a suspicion, from the calculating look on his face, that Cousin Rush would burglarize some place tomorrow night when everybody was in the theater, or he'd rob the box office at the theater, wearing a mask like everybody else would wear.

I couldn't talk to Mama about my suspicions. If I was wrong and Cousin Rush didn't do anything bad, she'd say I was disloyal to the name of Adams.

As we left the Plaza, the old black cat that Cousin Rush had kicked came out of Miss Tessie's store and looked at us as if she were casting a spell. I shivered.

I still wonder if what happened that night was just coincidence.

My little brother Pete had been unsuccessfully baiting that animal trap for a week. The trap was in the back yard. Here in Caton City, which is in northeast Texas, just south of Oklahoma and not far from Arkansas between the Red River and the Sulphur River, things were different. Coyotes and raccoons and possums and other animals came into town at night to raid garbage cans. Pete had been baiting that animal trap, actually a cage, for a week with cornbread, beans, cabbage, and such, hoping to catch a raccoon and make a pet of it. On this night, with a big moon beaming down, he had jerry-rigged a Rube Goldberg device that would turn on a light if the trap door was triggered.

Cousin Rush had our room now, so we slept in beds on our big screened-in back porch. About midnight the signal light came on to show the trap door had slammed down. Pete got out of bed in his underwear and ran barefoot to the trap, waving a flashlight.

He came back in a hurry. "Brian, we got trouble!"

I sat up, sniffed. "I smell it." The smell of skunk was not all that strong, showing the animal was fairly content, but it was definitely skunk.

"You got to shoot it."

"Hell, no! If you shoot that skunk, it'll make a smell that will wake up the town," I cautioned. "It has plenty of food and water and room to move around in that cage-trap. After it eats, it will probably go to sleep, won't it?"

Pete thought this over. "I guess so, unless it's disturbed."

"Okay. I'll make sure the yard gates are closed, so no dogs or other animals can disturb that skunk. We'll figure what to do after it gets daylight tomorrow. Let sleeping skunks sleep, that's my motto."

After Pete had gone back to bed, I lay awake, thinking. I could take a long fishing pole, hold the cage as far from me as possible, and move gently. I'd have to get that skunk out of our back yard somehow. . . .

I finally went to sleep and dreamed that Cousin Rush robbed Miss Tessie of all the Heritage Festival money. He got by with it because he was wearing a mask and all the men in the crowd he joined afterward wore masks. Nobody knew which masked man had the money. I woke up. Then I went to sleep again and this time I dreamed Cousin Rush didn't get away with it after all. He came out of the theater with the money still in his hands, and the old black cat cast a spell on him and made him throw the money in the air.

And I dreamed the old cat was really a witch in disguise.

When I woke up, it was Halloween Day and I still didn't know what to do about Cousin Rush. Maybe I was suspicious of him because I didn't like him.

But later in the day, as I listened to him talk with Miss Tessie, I became more alarmed. Oh, it was just general talk, discussion of the fact that Cajun Caton wasn't really a cajun. He was from Henry County, Tennessee, and he had picked up that nickname in Louisiana in what Miss Tessie described as an "indiscreet house."

I watched as Cousin Rush got his Oldsmobile filled with gas and the tires and oil checked. Looked like he was planning for a trip. He couldn't go to Houston, because police would arrest him if he went back there. He'd have trouble with his fourth wife in Dallas, and was wanted on charges there. But the way he was fussing around his car, it looked as if he would go somewhere in a hurry.

Long before the Heritage Play started that night, he parked his car on the north side of the plaza near the biggest rosebush. Then he went into the theater early, carrying a cape and a mask as some other men were doing.

I stood looking across the plaza, worried. The black cat came from the rosebushes, sat on the base of the fountain, and stared back at me. Darkness came, and a full moon rose. Stars shone.

Looking at that cat, I knew what I had to do. Maybe it wouldn't work, but maybe it would. I had to try.

After the play was well under way, with everyone except me in the theater,

I got a long fishing pole and some cord. Cautiously, holding my breath at times, I carried that animal cage-trap the three blocks to the plaza. The skunk, his belly full of cornbread and cabbage and beans, slept most of the time.

I learned later that during the last two minutes of the play a man wearing a mask and a cape went inside the box office where Miss Tessie was counting money. He didn't speak a word, but he pushed a small pistol in Miss Tessie's face and motioned for her to sit down. He tied her to the chair. She opened her mouth to scream, and he jammed a handkerchief in it. Nobody would have heard if she had screamed because the audience and the cast were singing the finale.

The man put his pistol inside his cape, took handfuls of the paper money she'd been sorting. He stuffed money in his pockets and inside the cape pockets, and left with some money in his hands.

He walked out of the theater as the townspeople, wearing capes and masks, also walked out.

I knew which one was Cousin Rush. I could tell by the prissy walk and the dumpy figure.

A couple of kids ran ahead of him across the plaza, but I pulled the cord I had rigged to the trap door. With that door open, and with all the noise, the skunk would come out. He would not be disturbed or afraid, because skunks are not usually afraid. Even a grizzly bear would tippy-toe around a skunk.

The two kids apparently saw him, hollered, "Uh-oh," detoured slightly, and kept running. Cousin Rush paid them no attention.

Then Miss Tessie's old black cat ran out of the rosebushes, ran right in front of Cousin Rush, ran back into the bushes.

Cousin Rush slowed in his fast walk to the Oldsmobile. It was a beautiful night, bright as day with white moonlight and black shadows. Just as Cousin Rush got near his car, a small black animal came out of the rosebushes again, right in front of him.

If he had climbed in his car without noticing, he would have gotten away with robbery. Being Cousin Rush and being naturally mean, and probably thinking this was Miss Tessie's old black cat, he kicked the skunk.

Then he bent over, ready to kick again. He got that spray full in his face. He staggered back, threw both arms in the air, hands spread wide. Money fluttered high, caught the wind, and blew all over the plaza. Cousin Rush fought for breath, ran into the monument, bounced off, stumbled against the fountain, coughed, gasped, vomited, waved his hands again.

He tore off his mask and cape, and money came from the pockets inside the cape and swirled in the air. People stood watching, wondering.

Somebody found Miss Tessie bound and gagged and cut her loose. She ran into the street, screaming she'd been robbed.

With all those dollar bills and five-dollar bills and ten-dollar bills floating in the air around Cousin Rush, he became the Prime Suspect. Nobody went near him for a while, though. The smell was nauseating.

Finally Sheriff Mitchell spoke firm words to Deputy Haskins. Haskins looked reluctant, but Mitchell gave the orders. Don't take him to our clean jail, he said. Take him to the old county stables and lock him up for the night.

The skunk got away in all the excitement. Nobody would have touched him anyway. I knew I would pick up the cage-trap when everybody left, or I'd be incriminated. I didn't want Mama to know I'd had anything to do with trapping Cousin Rush.

Citizens picked up the money that was blowing around and put it in a well-ventilated place for the night. Then people left for the American Legion Barbecue and Dance. Some of those who had gotten close to skunk smell while picking up the money might have to stay outside the Legion Hall, but they'd eat barbecue and drink Blanton Creek bourbon and they'd survive.

As the crowd left the plaza, and as Deputy Haskins started Cousin Rush walking twenty feet ahead of him to the stables, I saw Miss Tessie's old black cat sitting on the base of the fountain. Her eyes glinted in the Halloween moonlight, and I'll swear that cat was laughing.

Gene DeWeese

CAT BURGLAR

"Come on, Uncle Clay, you're the sheriff," the twenty-four-year-old voice on the phone whined. "Mom will listen to *you*."

"If she listened to me, Jerry," Clayton Barlow said, resisting an almost overwhelming urge to shout, "she and your stepfather would've cut you off cold a year ago. If you think I'm going to help you milk them for even *more* money—"

"But if my car gets repossessed, how can I get to work?"

"You live in the big city. Springfield has bus service. And *you* had feet the last time I looked. According to your mother, you live only a mile and a half from your job. Now if there's nothing else, things are busy around here."

"I'm sorry." The boy's voice was suddenly filled with sympathy and insincerity. "Any idea who the burglar is yet? Mom said you'd been getting pressure from the mayor."

"No, no idea, but we'll get him. He'll make a mistake, they always do."

"I hope so, Uncle Clay. But look, about what we were talking about, maybe if I drove down this evening so I could explain my situation to everyone all at once—are you all having dinner at the usual place?"

"Yes, we are, and you stay away. I mean it, Jerry. Stay away!"

Slamming the receiver down, Barlow leaned back in the swivel chair and pulled in a deep breath, hoping he could get rid of the knot of anger in his stomach before the monthly ritual of dinner with his sister and her husband. All he needed was for his ulcer to start acting up at the restaurant. Claudia would want to know what was wrong, and he'd have to either lie or tell her about Jerry's call, and that would just start the same old argument all over again. Not as bad as if Jerry showed up himself, but bad enough. She'd say he was her son and she had to see him through this latest self-generated crisis, and Clayton would tell her she was just making things worse, that the boy would never learn to stand on his own two feet as long as she kept bailing him out every time he came to her with a new sob story.

Grimacing, he checked his shirt pocket to be sure he had a full packet of antacid tablets.

To his relief, he didn't need them. The rash of burglaries—a dozen in the last month and a half—was all Claudia and her husband Martin wanted to talk about. Each time it looked as if they were about to start on something else, someone else would stop by the table and start it all up again by asking Barlow how the investigation was going.

It wasn't until they were in Martin's air-conditioned car on the way home that Jerry's name was mentioned. "You'll never guess the stunt he pulled the last time he was down," Martin said, ignoring Claudia's fluttering efforts to shush him. "He purposely let Mordecai out. We were lucky it was so warm and Jeff next door had his car windows down. You know how Mordecai loves cars."

Smiling in spite of himself, Barlow remembered how he'd found the cat two winters before in an abandoned car a few miles outside town. The car—and probably Mordecai—had been there at least a month before a farmer had called about having it towed away. Mordecai had obviously once been someone's pet and, unlike the feral cats the department occasionally got calls about, was on his best behavior when Barlow pried open the door. The cat had jumped down from the seat, next to the hole in the floorboards through which he had doubtless entered, and waited, apprehensive but not frightened. When Barlow had tentatively reached out, the animal, instead of retreating, had come forward and started rubbing against his outstretched fingers.

After that, it had been only a matter of showing the cat to Claudia, and when it took to her as quickly as it had to him, the matter was all settled, The only problem was, the cat refused to quit thinking of cars as homes away from home and was as likely to hop into the first one he found as he was to come back to the house. This made taking him to the vet a cinch, but it also made it impossible to let him outside. If he got into the wrong car, he could be miles away before the driver noticed him, curled up and sleeping in the back seat.

"Now, Martin," Claudia objected, "he didn't do it on purpose. The screen door just didn't close all the way."

"Oh, he did it on purpose all right," Martin said, shaking his head. "The little freeloader's jealous."

"Martin, please! You mustn't talk about the boy that way. And he's getting better. He hasn't asked for a cent for at least a month now."

"Face it, Claudia. I've seen the way he looks at the cat. And I've heard—we've both heard—the cracks he makes about how soft a life he has."

"But he's just *joking*, Martin."

"He wants you to *think* he's joking, that's all. I'll give you ten to one that behind that twinkly little smile of his, he's deadly serious."

Sighing, Clayton settled back for the rest of the drive. At the house, after turning down Claudia's half-hearted invitation to come in out of the muggy evening air for a while, he walked to his squad car, still at the curb where he'd left it three hours before. He was just getting in when Claudia came running across the lawn.

"Clay! The house—someone's broken in!"

His instant reaction was to smile and tell her not to let her imagination run away with her. All the burglaries had been in the middle of the night, not the evening, and in houses where the owners were out of town for at least the night, not just out for dinner at a local restaurant. But when he got inside, he saw it was real, and except for the odd timing, it was identical to all the others. Entry through a basement window, nothing disturbed or torn up, VCR and TV sets missing along with Martin's laptop computer and Claudia's few pieces of jewelry.

Barlow was just hanging up after phoning his office when Claudia let out an anguished shriek. "Mordecai!"

Hurrying to the kitchen, he found his sister on the back steps looking frantically around the yard in the harsh glare of the outdoor lights.

"The back door was open," Claudia almost wailed. "He's gone."

Barlow blinked, remembering Martin's words about his stepson's latest stunt. Suddenly it all made sense. The different time, the fact that Claudia and Martin hadn't been out of town, the fact that Jerry hadn't mooched any money recently.

And especially that seemingly pointless call—the boy wasn't stupid enough to think he could talk Barlow into pleading his case with his mother. He had simply called to verify that she and Martin would be out of the house for the evening.

And he hadn't been able to resist leaving the door ajar so Mordecai could get out. In all the other houses, the door had been carefully closed, so that everything would seem perfectly normal from the outside.

"A couple of deputies will be here in a few minutes, sis," he said. "I have somewhere to go."

Without waiting for a reply, he stalked to his squad car. Forty-five minutes later, he was jabbing the bell at the front door of his nephew's ten-unit apartment building. The boy's car, its hood still warm, sat at the curb in front of the squad car a few yards away.

"Who is it?" Jerry's voice came tinnily through the intercom.

"Your uncle. Open up."

"Uncle Clay? What are *you* doing here?"

"Open up and I'll tell you."

There was no reply.

"Open up, Jerry!"

"No."

"I haven't told the Springfield police yet, Jerry, but I will if you don't open up—now!"

"The police? Why would you—"

"Because you just burglarized your parents' house—and probably a dozen others the last six weeks."

For a moment there was only silence, but then the voice came back, harsh and filled with infuriating confidence. "You're out of your jurisdiction, Uncle Clay, and even if you weren't, you'd need a warrant."

"I'll get one, and—"

"You need evidence for that. Probable cause, they call it, or something like that. Now beat it."

The crackle of the intercom died. Barlow jabbed at the button again, but there was no response.

Swearing under his breath, he turned from the door, realizing the boy was right. With nothing more than a sudden hunch, compounded by dislike, he'd never get a judge to sign a warrant.

And by the time he got proof—*if* he got proof—it would be too late. Now that the boy knew Barlow was onto him, he'd ditch whatever was still in the apartment. If only he'd waited, acted more calmly. If only—

As he walked angrily past Jerry's car, something meowed.

Stiffening, he glanced around.

It meowed again. This time, listening, he caught the direction it was coming from. Leaning close and cupping his hands on either side of his eyes, he looked through the closed back window of the car.

"Mordecai!"

The cat, apparently searching the floorboards for a nonexistent exit, looked up, saw Clayton, and hopped up on the seat.

Clayton laughed suddenly as he turned to glance up at the lighted windows of his nephew's apartment.

"You want probable case, Jerry," he breathed grimly as he walked to the squad car, "you got probable cause—unless you can think of some way a cat could cover thirty miles on his own in less than four hours."

Taking the microphone from its clip under the dash, he switched to the channel used by the Springfield police.

Edward D. Hoch

THE THEFT OF THE MAFIA CAT

Nick Velvet had always harbored a soft spot for Paul Matalena, ever since they'd been kids together on the same block in the Italian section of Greenwich Village. He still vividly remembered the Saturday afternoon when a gang fight had broken out on Bleecker Street, and Paul had yanked him out of the path of a speeding police car with about one inch to spare. He liked to think that Paul had saved his life that day, and so, being something of a sentimentalist, Nick responded quickly to his old friend's call for help.

He met Paul in the most unlikely of places—the Shakespeare garden in Central Park, where someone many years ago had planned a floral gathering which was to include every species of flower mentioned in the works of the Bard. If the plan had never come to full blossom, it still produced a colorful setting, a backdrop for literary discussion.

"'There's rosemary, that's for remembrance,'" Paul quoted as they strolled among the flowers and shrubs. "'And there is pansies, that's for thoughts.'"

Nick, who could hardly be called a Shakespeare scholar, had come prepared. "'A rose by any other name would smell as sweet,'" he countered.

"You've gotten educated since we were kids, Nick."

"I'm still pretty much the same. What can I do for you, Paul?"

"They tell me you're in business for yourself these days. Stealing things."

"Certain things. Those of no great value. You might call it a hobby."

"Hell, Nick, they say you're the best in the business. I been hearing about you for years now. At first I couldn't believe it was the same guy."

Nick shrugged. "Everyone has to earn a living somehow."

"But how did you ever get started in it?"

The beginning was something Nick rarely thought about, and it was something he'd never told another person. Now, strolling among the flowers with his boyhood friend, he said, "It was a woman, of course. She talked me into helping her with a robbery. We were going to break into the Institute for Medieval Studies over in New Jersey and steal some art treasures. I got a truck and helped her remove a stained-glass window so we could get into the building. While I was inside she drove off with the window. That was all she'd been after in the first place. It was worth something like $50,000 to collectors."

Paul Matalena gave a low whistle. "And you never got any of it?"

Nick smiled at the memory. "Not a cent. The girl was later arrested, and the window recovered, so perhaps it's just as well. But that got me thinking about the kind of objects people steal. I discovered there are things of little or no value that can be worth a great deal to certain people at certain times. By avoiding the usual cash and jewelry and paintings I'm able to concentrate on the odd, the unusual, the valueless."

"'They say you get $20,000 a job, and $30,000 for an especially dangerous one."

Nick nodded. "My price has been the same for years. No inflation here."

"Would you do a job for me, Nick?"

"I'd have to charge you the usual rate, Paul."

"I understand. I wasn't asking for anything free."

"Some say you're a big man in the Mafia these days. Is that true?"

Matalena shot him a sideways glance. "Sure, it's true. I'm right up with the top boys. But we don't usually talk about it."

"Why not? I'm an Italian-American just like you, Paul, and I think it's wrong to act as if organized crime doesn't exist. What we should do is admit it, and then go on to stress the accomplishments of other Italian-Americans—men like Fiorello LaGuardia, John Volpe, and John Pastore in government, Joe DiMaggio in sports, and Gian Carlo Menotti in the arts."

"I stay out of policy matters, Nick. I've got me a nice laundry business that covers restaurants and private hospitals. Brings me in a nice fat income, all legit. In the beginning I had to lean on some of the customers, but when they found out I was Mafia they signed up fast. And no trouble with competition."

"You must be doing well if you can afford my price. What do you want stolen?"

"A cat."

"No problem. I once stole a tiger from a zoo."

"This cat might be tougher. It's Mike Pirrone's pet."

Nick whistled softly. Pirrone was a big man in the Syndicate—one of the biggest still under 50. He lived in a country mansion on the shore of a small New Jersey lake. Not many people visited Mike Pirrone. Not many people wanted to.

"The cat is on the grounds of his home?"

Matalena nodded. "You can't miss it. A big striped tabby named Sparkle. Pirrone is always being photographed with it. This is from a magazine."

He showed Nick a picture of Mike Pirrone standing with an older, white-haired man identified as his lawyer. The Mafia don was holding the big tabby in his arms, almost like a child. Nick grunted and put the picture in his pocket. "First time I ever saw Pirrone smiling."

"He loves that cat. He takes it with him everywhere."

"And you want to kidnap it and hold it for ransom?"

Matalena chuckled. "Nick, Nick, these wild ideas of yours! You haven't changed since schooldays."

"All right. It's not my concern, as long as your money's good."

"This much on account," Matalena said, slipping an envelope to Nick. "I need results by the weekend."

They strolled a bit longer among the flowers, talking of old times, then parted. Nick caught a taxi and headed downtown.

Mike Pirrone's mansion was a sprawling ranch located on a hill overlooking Stag Lake in northern New Jersey. It was a bit north of Stag Pond, in an area of the state that boasted towns with names like Sparta and Athens and Greece. It was fishing country, and the man at the gas station told Nick, "Good yellow perch in these lakes."

"Might try a little," Nick admitted. "Got my fishing gear in back. How's Stag Lake?"

"Mostly private. If you come ashore at the wrong spot it could mean trouble."

Nick thanked him and drove on, turning off the main road to follow a rutted lane that ran along the edge of the Pirrone estate. The entire place was surrounded by a wall topped by three strands of electrified wire. As he passed the locked gates and peered inside, he saw the large sprawling house on its hill about two hundred feet back. The lake lay at the end of the road, and a chain-link fence ran from the end of the wall into the water. Mike Pirrone was taking no chances on uninvited guests.

Nick was studying the layout when a girl's voice spoke from very close behind him. "Thinking of doing some fishing?"

He turned and saw a willowy blonde in white shorts and a colorful print blouse standing by the back of his car. He hadn't heard her approach and he wondered how long she'd been watching him. "I might try for some yellow perch. I hear they're biting."

"It's mostly private property around here," she said. Her face was hard and tanned, with features that might have been Scandinavian and certainly weren't Italian.

"I noticed the wall. Who lives there—Howard Hughes?"

"A man named Mike Pirrone. You probably never heard of him."

"What business is he in?"

"Management."

"It must be profitable."

"It is."

"You know him?"

She smiled at Nick and said, "I'm his wife."

After his unexpected encounter with Mrs. Pirrone, Nick knew there was no chance for a direct approach to the house. He rented a boat in mid-afternoon and set off down the lake, trolling gently along the shoreline. No one was more surprised than Nick when he hooked a large fish almost at once. It could have been a yellow perch, but he wasn't sure. Fishing was not his sport.

The boat drifted down to a point opposite the Pirrone estate, and Nick checked the shoreline for guards. No one was visible, but through his binoculars he could see a group of wire cages near the main house. Since the cat Sparkle could be expected to sleep indoors, the cages seemed to indicate dogs—probably watchdogs that prowled the grounds after dark.

Working quickly, Nick filled his jacket pockets with fishhooks, lengths of nylon leader, and a folded and perforated plastic bag. A few other items were already carefully hidden on his person, but the binoculars and fishing pole would have to be abandoned. He used a small hand drill to bore a tiny hole in the bottom of the boat, then watched while the water began to seep in. He half stood up in the boat, giving an image of alarm to anyone who might have been watching, then threw the drill overboard and quickly headed the boat toward shore. In five minutes he was beached on the Pirrone estate; the boat was half full of water.

For a few minutes he stood by it as if pondering his next move. Then he looked up toward the house on the hill and started off for it, carrying his fish. Almost at once he heard the barking of dogs and suddenly two large German shepherds were racing toward him across the expanse of lawn. Nick broke into a run, heading for the nearest tree, but as the dogs seemed about to overtake him they stopped dead in their tracks.

Nick leaned against the tree, panting, and watched a white-haired man walking across the lawn toward him. It was the man in the picture—Pirrone's lawyer—and he held a shiny silver dog whistle in one hand.

"They're well trained," Nick said by way of greeting.

"That they are. You could be a dead man now, if I hadn't blown this whistle."

"My boat," Nick said, gesturing helplessly toward the water. "It sprang a leak. I wonder if I could use your phone?"

The man was well dressed, in the sporty style of the town and country gentleman. He eyed Nick up and down, then nodded. "There's a phone in the gardener's shed."

Nick had hoped to make it into the house, but he had no choice. As the lawyer led the way, Nick held up his fish and said, "They're really biting today."

The man grunted and said nothing more. He led Nick to a small shack where tools and fertilizer were stored and pointed to the telephone on the wall. Nick put down his fish and dialed information, seeking the number of a taxi company. He'd just got the operator when the fish by his foot gave a sudden lurch. He looked down to see a large striped tabby cat pulling at it with a furry paw.

"Sparkle," Nick whispered. "Here, Sparkle."

The cat lifted its head in response to the name. It seemed to be awaiting some further conversation. Nick bent to stroke it under the chin and saw the legs of a man in striped slacks and golf shoes. His eyes traveled upward to a broad firm chest and the familiar beetle-browed face above. It was Mike Pirrone, and he wasn't smiling. In his hand he held a snubnosed revolver pointed at Nick's face.

"To what do I owe this pleasure, Mr. Velvet?"

The house was fit for a don, or possibly a king, with a huge beamed living room that looked out over the lake. The furniture was expensive and tasteful, and Pirrone's blonde wife fitted the setting perfectly. She was much younger than her husband, but seeing them together one quickly forgot the difference in ages. Pirrone was approaching 50 gracefully, with a hint of youth that occasionally broke through the dignified menace of his stony face.

"He's the fisherman I told you about," Mrs. Pirrone said as they entered. Her eyes darted from Nick to her husband.

"Yes," Pirrone said softly. "It seems he was washed up on our shore, and I recognized him. His name is Nick Velvet."

"The famous thief?"

"None other."

Nick smiled. He still held the fish at the end of a line in one hand. "You have me at a disadvantage. I don't believe we've ever met."

"We met. A long time ago at a political dinner. I never forget a face, Velvet. It costs money to forget faces. Sometimes it costs lives. I'm Mike Pirrone, as you certainly know. This is my wife, Frieda, and my lawyer, Harry Beaman."

The white-haired man nodded in acknowledgment and Nick said deliberately, "I thought he was your dog trainer."

Mike Pirrone laughed softly and Beaman flushed. "He does have a way with the dogs," Pirrone said. "He's trained them well. But they only guard the place. I'm a cat fancier myself." As if to illustrate he bent and cupped his arms. Sparkle took a running leap and landed in them. "This cat goes everywhere I go."

"Beautiful animal," Nick murmured.

Pirrone continued to stroke the cat for a few moments, then put it down. "All right, Velvet," he said briskly. "What do you want here?"

"Merely to use the phone. My boat sprang a leak."

"You're no fisherman," Pirrone said, pronouncing the words like a final judgment.

"Here's my fish," Nick countered, holding it up; but the don was unimpressed.

"You scouted my place and you managed to get inside. What for?"

"Even a thief needs a vacation now and then."

"You don't take vacations, Velvet. I investigated you quite closely a few years back, when I almost hired you for a job. I know your habits and I know where you live. Who hired you, and why?"

"I didn't even know this was your place till I met your wife this morning."

"I heard you call my cat by name, out in the shed."

Nick hesitated. Mike Pirrone was no fool. "Everybody knows Sparkle. You're always photographed with him."

"Her. Sparkle is a her."

Harry Beaman cleared his throat. "What do you plan to do with him, Mike? If you try to hold him against his will it could be a serious legal matter. So far you've been within your rights to treat him as a trespasser, but that could change."

Pirrone threw up his hands. "Lawyers! Things were simple in the old days— right, Velvet?"

"I wouldn't know."

A maid appeared with cocktails and Pirrone waved his hand. "You're a guest here, Velvet. You arrived in time for the cocktail hour." He took a glass himself and went off to an adjoining study to make some phone calls. Nick wondered what Pirrone had in mind for him.

Frieda Pirrone rose from the sofa and came to sit by him. "You should have told me you wanted to meet my husband. I could have arranged it much more easily. Are you really a thief?"

"I steal women's hearts, among other things."

Her eyes met his for just an instant. "It would take a brave man—or an idiot—to steal anything from Mike Pirrone."

"I'm neither of those." He watched Sparkle move slowly across the carpet, stalking some imaginary prey.

"Just what sort of thief are you?"

"Sometimes I'm a cat burglar."

"Really? You mean one of those who climbs across rooftops?"

Before he could answer, Pirrone returned and handed his lawyer a sheaf of papers. "Business can be a bore at times, Velvet. I'm being a poor host."

"Perfectly all right. Your drinks are very good."

The dark-browed don nodded. "My chauffeur will be driving Harry to the train shortly. You're free to leave with them."

"Thank you."

"But one word of advice. If anything turns up missing from this house—now or later—I'll know just where to look. I'll send somebody for you, Velvet, and it'll be just like the old days. Understand?"

"I understand."

"Good! Whoever paid you, tell them the deal is off."

Nick nodded. He needed to be careful now. There would be no other chance to enter the Pirrone domain. Whatever the risk, he had to take Sparkle out of the house with him. He glanced at his watch. It was just after five. "Could I use your bathroom?"

Mike Pirrone nodded. "Go ahead. The maid will show you." Then, as Nick started to follow her, the don called out, "Taking your fish with you? Now I've seen everything!"

The maid waved him into a large tiled bathroom and departed. Nick checked his watch again. He had perhaps three minutes before they would grow suspicious. Quickly he crossed to the door and opened it. As he'd hoped, Sparkle had followed the trail of the fish and was hovering in the hall. With a bit of coaxing Nick had her in hand. He only hoped Pirrone wouldn't come looking for her right away.

Close up, Sparkle was a handsome feline, uniquely spotted and with a curious expression all her own. Perhaps that was why Pirrone liked her—because she was one of a kind. Nick held her firmly and injected a quick-acting sleeping drug. Sparkle gave one massive yawn and curled up on the floor. Then, working fast, he wrapped the disposable syringe in a tissue and put it in his pocket. He lifted Sparkle's limp body and slipped it into the perforated plastic bag.

Carrying the cat in one hand, Nick opened the bathroom door again and glanced down the hall toward the living room. No one was in sight. He crossed the hall quickly, entering a spare bedroom which he hoped was the room he sought. From the road he'd observed the telephone line running up the hill to the house and he thought it reached the wall just outside this room. Opening the window he saw that he'd been correct. The phone wire was just above his head, about a foot beyond the window.

He removed two fishhooks from his pocket and attached one to each end of a length of nylon leader. Reaching up he looped the fishing leader over the telephone wire and left it dangling there while he lifted the plastic-bagged cat. The fishhooks snagged two of the perforations in the bag and held it dangling beneath the telephone wire.

Nick tested it for weight, drew a deep prayerful breath, then gave the bag a shove. It began to slide slowly down the phone line, across the wide side yard, and finally over the wall to the telephone pole by the road. Near the pole the bag came to a stop, but by carefully tugging on his end of the wire Nick was able to propel it over the last few feet.

He sighed and closed the window. The whole operation had taken him four minutes—one minute more than he'd planned. He went back to the living room, still carrying his fish, and saw at once that Pirrone and Frieda and the lawyer were waiting for him. A large man in a chauffeur's uniform stood by the door.

Mike Pirrone smiled slightly and brought out the snubnosed revolver once more. "I hope you'll excuse the precaution, Velvet, but we don't want you leaving with anything that doesn't belong to you. Search him, Felix."

Nick raised his arms and the chauffeur ran quick firm hands over his body. After a few seconds he yanked one hand away; it was bleeding. "Damn! What's he got in there?"

"Fishhooks," Nick answered with the trace of a smile. "I should have warned you."

Felix cursed and finished the search. "He's clean, Mr. Pirrone."

"All right." The don put away his gun. "You can go now, Velvet."

"Thanks," Nick said, and started to follow the chauffeur and Beaman to the car.

He was halfway down the front walk when he heard Pirrone ask his wife, "Where's Sparkle?"

Nick kept walking steadily, glancing across the wall at the distant telephone pole and its hanging plastic bag. "I think she went outside," Frieda answered.

Suddenly Pirrone called, "Velvet! Hold it!"

Nick froze. The chauffeur, Felix, had turned toward the don, waiting for instructions. "What is it?" he asked as Pirrone came down the walk.

"That fish—let me have it. You could have hidden something small inside it. And if you didn't it'll make a nice supper for Sparkle."

Nick handed it over with feigned reluctance, then climbed into the car with Beaman. On the drive into town the white-haired lawyer tried to smooth things over. "You have to understand Mike. He's a real gentleman, with a heart of gold, but he lives in constant fear of rivals trying to take over what he's spent his life building."

"I assumed he had something to fear when I saw the gun," Nick said, nodding.

Beaman went on, "Frieda doesn't like it. She doesn't like anything connected with his old life, but Mike has to be careful."

"Of course."

Beaman dropped him at the marina and went on to the station. Shortly after dark Nick drove back to the Pirrone estate, climbed the telephone pole outside the wall, and removed the perforated plastic bag from the overhead wire. The cat was still sleeping peacefully. From inside the wall Nick could hear one of the servants calling for Sparkle.

Paul Matalena was overjoyed. "Nick, I never thought you could do it!" He stroked the cat on his lap and listened to it purr. "How in hell did you manage it?"

"I have my methods, Paul."

"Here's the rest of your money. And my thanks."

"You realize that Sparkle is a unique cat. She's been photographed with Pirrone a hundred times, and could hardly be mistaken for anyone else's pet. When people see it they'll know it's Pirrone's."

"That's exactly the idea, Nick."

"If you're planning to hold Sparkle for ransom you're playing with dynamite."

"It's nothing like that. In fact, I only want the cat for a meeting tomorrow afternoon. Then you can have her back. If Pirrone recovers his pet within a day, the whole thing shouldn't upset him too much."

"You mean you only want Sparkle for one day?"

"That's right, Nick." Matalena went to the phone and started making calls. The hour was late, but that didn't seem to bother him. Sparkle watched for a time, then ran over to Nick and rubbed against his leg. Suddenly, listening to Paul's words on the telephone, Nick knew why his old schoolmate was willing to pay $20,000 to have Sparkle for one day. He looked at Paul Matalena and chuckled.

"What's so funny, Nick?"

"Paul, you always were something of a phony, even back in school."

"What?"

Nick got to his feet and headed for the door. "Good luck to you."

The following evening, as Nick sat on his front porch drinking a beer, Gloria called to him. "Telephone for you, Nicky."

He went in, setting down his beer on the table near the phone. She grabbed it up at once and wiped away the damp ring. Grinning, he said, "You're acting more like a wife every day."

The voice on the phone was soft and feminine. "Nick Velvet?"

"Yes."

"This is Frieda Pirrone. My husband is on his way to kill you. He thinks that somehow you stole Sparkle."

"Thanks for the warning."

"I don't want him to go back to killing, back to the way it used to be."

"Neither do I," Nick said. He hung up and turned to Gloria.

"Trouble, Nicky?"

"Just a little business problem." He bit his lip and pondered. "Look, Gloria, I've got a man coming over to see me. Why don't you go to a movie or something?"

"That was no man on the phone, Nicky."

"Come on," he grinned. "Ask no questions and I'll buy you that little foreign sports car you've been wanting."

"Will you, Nicky? You really mean it?"

"Sure I mean it."

When she'd gone he turned out all the lights in the house and sat down to wait. Just before ten o'clock a big black limousine pulled up and parked across the street. Nick had always considered his home to be forbidden territory, away from the dangers of his career; but this time it was different. Two men left the car and crossed the street to his house. One was the chauffeur, Felix. The other was a burly hood Nick didn't recognize. Mike Pirrone would be waiting in the car.

As they reached the porch Nick opened the door. Felix's hand dived into his pocket and the hood grabbed Nick, who didn't resist when they forced him back into the house. "I want to see Pirrone," Nick said.

"You'll see him." While the hood pinioned Nick, Felix went to the door and signaled across the street. Mike Pirrone left the car and came slowly up the walk, studying the house and the tree-lined street.

"Nice little place you have here, Velvet."

"Good to see you again so soon."

"Did you think you wouldn't?" He stepped close to Nick. "Did you think I'd let you get away with Sparkle?"

"No. Not really."

"Where is she?"

"Right here—I'll get her."

"No tricks." Pirrone had drawn his gun again, and this time he looked as if he meant to use it.

"No tricks," Nick agreed. He stepped into the kitchen with Felix at his side and called, "Sparkle!"

The big striped tabby came running at the sound of her name, rubbed briefly against Nick's leg, then bounded into Pirrone's waiting arms. He put away the gun and stroked her fur while he carefully examined her.

"All right," he said quietly. "Sparkle is all right, so I'll let you live. But Felix and Vic here are going to teach you a little lesson about stealing from me."

"Wait!" Nick said, holding up his hand. "Can't we talk this over?"

"There's no need for talk. You were warned, Velvet."

"At least let me tell you a story first. It's about the man who hired me to steal Sparkle."

"Tell me. We'll want to pay him a visit, too."

Nick started to talk fast. "You might almost call this a detective story in reverse. Instead of discovering a guilty person, I found one who's innocent."

"What are you talking about, Velvet?" Pirrone's patience was wearing thin.

"The man who hired me, who shall be nameless, runs a highly profitable business in New York City. He was able to establish the business, and maintain it profitably for years, mainly by convincing both his customers and his competitors that he is an important member of the Mafia."

Mike Pirrone frowned. "You mean he isn't one?"

"Exactly," Nick said. "He is not a member of the Mafia, never has been. He's a simple hard-working guy who took advantage of his Italian name and the fact that many people are willing to believe that any Italian in business must be in the Mob. By fostering the idea that he had important Syndicate connections, he got a lot of business from people who were afraid to go elsewhere.

"But recently some of his customers began to have doubts. The word started circulating that he wasn't a big Mafia man at all. Faced with the loss of his best customers he decided to call a meeting to keep them in line. Ideally, he would have liked someone like Mike Pirrone with him at the meeting. But since he didn't even know Mike Pirrone he settled for the next best thing—Mike Pirrone's cat."

"What?" Pirrone's mouth hung open. "You mean he had the cat stolen so he could con people into thinking he was a friend of mine?"

Nick Velvet smiled. "That's right. It was worth my fee of $20,000 to keep his customers in line. He showed up at the meeting today with Sparkle in his arms. Naturally, in an audience like that, all of them knew the cat by sight—and they knew that Mike Pirrone couldn't be far away. It convinced them."

"Didn't he think I'd hear about something like that?"

"Possibly. But by that time you'd have Sparkle back safe and sound, and you'd probably be reluctant to admit the theft to anyone."

"Tell me this guy's name."

"So you can beat him up or kill him? Where's your sense of humor? You have Sparkle back and the man has his customers back. No one's been harmed, and there's a certain humor in the situation. At a time when the Mafia is taking great pains to deny its existence, here is someone cashing in on the false story that he belongs to the Mafia. In fact, it was his open talking about it that made me suspicious in the first place. The real dons don't brag about it."

Felix shifted position. "What should I do, Mr. Pirrone?"

Pirrone studied Nick for a moment, then smiled slightly. "Let him go, Felix.

You've got one hell of a nerve, Velvet—you and the guy who hired you." He started out of the house, but then paused by the door. "How did you do it? How did you get Sparkle out of my house?"

"Sorry. That's a trade secret. But I'll give you a tip about something else."

"What sort of tip?"

"Your watchdogs have been well trained by Harry Beaman."

Pirrone shrugged. "He likes them, I guess."

"He called them off me, and he could call them off his friends, too, if they happened to come visiting you late some night."

"I trust Harry," Pirrone said quickly, but his eyes were thoughtful.

"Think it over. You might live a few years longer."

Pirrone took a step forward and shook Nick's hand. "You've got a brain, Velvet. I could use someone like you in the organization."

Nick smiled and shook his head. "Organizations aren't for me. But remember me if you ever need anything stolen. Something odd or unusual"—Nick grinned—"or valueless."

Bruce Bethke

SPECTRE IN BLUE DOUBLEKNIT

As his eyes adjusted to the darkness, he found Richard and Louisa sprawled on the bed, asleep. Quietly, so as not to disturb them, he stepped out of the bedroom and wandered through the apartment, correlating.

The tattered green easy chair, the cigarette-scarred sofa; the disorganized heap of textbooks on the coffee table; good. The pint mason jar of marijuana, the pyramid of empty Schmidt "Sportspak" beer cans, the cold half-cup of coffee etching a ring on the top of the stereo speaker; all was exactly as he had pictured it. He headed for the kitchen, for the final test.

Blue mercury streetlight spilled through the uncurtained windows, allowing him to clearly read the date of the *Tribune* sports section lying on the radiator. May 6, 1975. Perfect. He'd manifested right on target.

He stepped back into the bedroom, and took a gentle moment to compare the dozing man to himself. The sleeper had a full head of thick, curly, brown hair, a smooth, clear, untroubled face, and a trim, muscular, one-hundred-seventy-pound physique. His own body was another story; his hairline had receded clear back to the crown of his head, his ulcer was developing a resistance to Maalox, and he couldn't keep his weight under two forty on a bet.

A small twinge of sympathy passed through him as he looked down at the man on the bed. Twenty-two-year-old Richard Luck had such *possibilities* ahead of him. And he was about to toss them all away . . . That thought choked off the sympathy. He leapt up on the bed and kicked young Richard hard in the ribs.

His foot passed right through, of course.

With a modest sigh of disappointment, he lay down through the sleeper and started insinuating himself into the dream.

Richard and Carynne go to Marty's Deli for lunch, and as soon as they get inside the door he sees Louisa working behind the counter. He yells, "I can explain!" but she picks up that enormous knife she uses to slice the French bread, so he grabs Carynne's hand and starts running.

They run across the street, jump the fence, and start through the railroad tunnel, but when they get about halfway he sees his mother coming from the other end. "It's okay, Mom," he says, "I know what I'm doing." She just stands there blocking the end of the tunnel (which has become so narrow he's got to stoop to stand in it), and he can hear Louisa coming up behind, so he turns and drags Carynne down a side passage he hadn't noticed before. They emerge into the corridor by the physics classrooms in the basement of North Hall and round the corner to find the stairwell door locked from the other side, so Carynne pulls him into one of the dark classrooms and—my God, how'd she get to be so naked?—and pulls him tight against her smooth, cool skin, and pulls him down, and pulls him—

The fluorescent lights flare on; he and Carynne are entwined, naked, on the sofa in his parents' basement, and his father is standing there scowling. Except it isn't his father, it's the pudgy guy in the navy blue doubleknit suit! The pudgy guy walks over, picks up Richard's jeans off the floor, throws them at him, and says, "Wake up, dirtball. We need to talk."

"Dammit, you again? Bug off!"

"You can chase wet dreams later. This is important."

"Who *are* you?" Richard demands. "What are you doing here?" Carynne has vanished.

"Is it bigger than a breadbox?" the pudgy guy mocks him. "What do you *think* I'm doing here? This is a premonition. I'm you from twenty years in the future."

"I'm going to look like *that* when I'm forty?" Richard wakes with a start, and finds himself drenched in cold sweat.

No, as Richard lay in the dark thinking about it, maybe he hadn't waked up. He was in his bedroom for sure, in his bed, staring at the ceiling; everything *seemed* real enough, but he was utterly unable to move. He believed the woman sleeping next to him was Louisa, but an effort to roll over and confirm that got him nowhere.

And then there was this curious sense of *detachment*, he felt. He was lying on the bed, and at the same time lying under the bed among the old sneakers and dust bunnies, and sitting perched like a cat on the windowsill, and gently floating up near the ceiling, noting that the lintel moldings hadn't been cleaned in years. He thought his eyes were open, but the multiple viewpoints cast some doubt on that.

Deep in the back of his head, his rational daytime self panicked and started screaming something about being dead or paralyzed or at the very least psychotic, but Richard ignored the noise. His windowsill self (which was looking more like a cat with every passing moment) had spotted a sort of umbilical cord between his bedded and ceiling selves, and ambled over to investigate. The thought occurred to him then that if he could just get a window open, he'd be able to fly his ceiling self like a kite.

Whatever state his mind was in, it certainly wasn't awake.

"It's called lucid sleep," someone suggested, helpfully. "Your forebrain is awake, but your voluntary nervous system doesn't know that yet."

Richard managed to round up most of his attention and become aware of another presence in the room. A presence sitting on the foot of his bed, to be exact.

"Hello!" the spectre in the blue polyester suit said cheerfully.

With an unpleasant lack of startle reflex, Richard's eyes didn't snap open. "Omigod," Richard . . . *said*, for lack of a better word. His lips barely moved, no sound came out, and yet the thought was expressed. "Naw. Don't hallucinate like this from pot. Must be still dreaming." He turned his attention out to graze and tried to slide back into deep sleep.

"Stop it!" said the apparition. "Don't drag me back into dreamstate again."

"Give me two good reasons," Richard mumbled.

"Lucid sleep is the only state I can reliably communicate with you in. If you go back to normal sleep I'm just a nightmare."

"A nightmare with lousy timing," Richard corrected. "I was finally going to score with Carynne."

"You want to go back to sleep? Never see me again?"

"Who, *me*?" Richard said, as sarcastically as possible. "Did *I* say that?"

The apparition leaned in close to bedded Richard's face. "Well, then get *this* through your little pea-sized brain, boy! You won't be rid of me until you hear me out. You don't know *half* the nightmare I can be!"

With the equivalent of a resigned sigh, Richard turned back from deep sleep. "Okay. Accepting—just for the moment—that this isn't some bizarre twist in the dream, how do you do it? I mean, you've been invading my sleep all week."

"Sympathetic resonance. My consciousness resonates inside your empty head."

"Insults from hallucinations I don't need," Richard snarled. The tiny flare of anger led to a twitch in his leg, which disturbed Louisa. She rolled a bit, *mmphed* something, and put an arm across Richard's chest.

The apparition bit his lip. "I'm pre-memory, okay? I'm an up-town projection of your own future consciousness. Look, it's all in the Muldoon book; read about it later. I can only hyperdynamize like this for about thirty minutes, so you'll excuse me if I get to the point."

"Aha!" Richard gleefully seized an idea. "*I* know where you come from. It's that silly parapsychology course, isn't it? I skipped the readings and now my sub-conscious is punishing me for it." He wished he were awake enough to resolutely cross his arms. "Well, I don't care if I get a Z-minus on the final. I got a B on the mid-term and an A on my paper, so I pass no matter what. I am *not* going to read any more of that garf; I've got a marketing final to worry about."

"Gah!" The pudgy spectre slapped himself on the forehead. "You *jerk*! Sure, there's so much fluff in the course it says *Do Not Remove Tag Under Penalty of Law* in the syllabus. Some of it is still true. If you—but no, all *you* can think about is Louisa's breasts and Carynne's tight jeans. *I* had to start studying projection all over again when I was thirty-five because *you* took such lousy notes. It took me six years to get here."

Louisa dragged an arm up, pushed a few strands of her long brown hair out of her face, and whimpered, "Whasmatter honey?" before nodding off again.

Richard focused on her, then on the spectre sitting across his knees. "Can she hear?" he whispered.

The pudgy man paled. "Jeez, I hope not. I'm supposed to be manifesting to you only. Maybe there's some spillover."

"Well, try to keep it down, will you?"

"Okay." They stared at each other in uneasy silence until Richard realized the older man was composing himself to deliver a lecture, just as Richard's father used to.

Richard quickly spoke first. "So you're my future, huh? How's IBM doing?" It had the desired effect; he totally blew away the older man's composure. "Y'see, I figure I can borrow another three grand at two points on my tuition loan and invest—"

"Kid!" the older man barked. "I came here to prevent the biggest mistake in your life. Not to turn a few lousy bucks."

"Slack off, okay?" Richard said defensively. "I mean, I'm having some trouble dealing with this, y'know? It's not every day my future pops in for a chat." Richard let his viewpoint drift back to the cat. He felt comfortable being a cat. "But I do know that if this were *really* happening, I wouldn't miss an opportunity like this. You sure you're my future?" The man just glared.

"Okay. Accepting for the sake of argument that you're who you say you are, don't you know that coming back is absurd? If you convince me to change my future, then the thing you say you came back to warn me about doesn't happen, so you don't—"

"I'm trying to save his life," the older man growled under his breath, "and he wants to argue jerk-off philosophy with me." He pointed at Richard and raised his voice. "Look, kid, every time you say causality paradox I'll say branching alternate time-line. Personally, I think you get premonitions from unchosen futures all the time; you're just too dimwitted to notice them. It took me five tries to get you lucid."

"But if this works, won't you disintegrate or something?"

"I don't know. And frankly I don't care."

Richard whistled low. "That bad, huh?" and watched as the pudgy man slowly, portentously, nodded. "There you go, getting all ominous again. You came *back* from the future, didn't you? That means the world doesn't get nuked into slag in the next twenty years. Hey, I feel better already!"

"Worse things can happen than the end of the world."

"You out of a job?" Richard suggested. "Economy collapse in the late eighties like Greenburg says it will?"

The older man angrily dug his ghost fingers into sleeping Richard's leg. "Is that all you want from the future? Money? Kid, your priorities are *all* screwed up. 'Am I successful?' Sure, I'm successful. I'm national sales manager for IMDC; I make—"

Richard interrupted. "Who?"

"Integrated Micro Data Corp. They don't exist yet."

"Damn." Cat/Richard twitched his tail with vexation. "And how much did you say you earn?" His interest perked up.

"For chrissakes, what difference does it make?!"

"I only ask," Richard pointed out, "because I want to know why a successful man wears such an ugly suit."

"It's part of the projection," the older man explained, patience struggling with exasperation. "I'm not physically here, of course. I can only travel by avatar—symbol—and my avatar is a sweaty guy in a cheap suit. It's not a true image; in the real world I wouldn't be caught dead wearing white patent leather loafers and a matching vest."

"*Sure,*" said the cat, dubiously, "and—"

"Dammit, stop changing the subject! I'm trying to tell you about real happiness!"

"Ah," Richard said, with dawning comprehension. "Now we come to the point. You advise choosing spiritual fulfillment over material success, right? Thanks, I'll think it over, good night."

"Louisa's a nice girl. Marry her."

Richard licked a paw, rubbed his ear, and then sat in thoughtful silence. At last he spoke. "You traveled twenty years to tell me *that*?"

"She's a sweet kid. The two of you could be very happy."

"That's *it*?"

"No, there's one thing more. You're so worried about this marketing final, you've talked Carynne Reichmann into giving you some coaching this weekend.

Break the date."

"But if I do that," Richard protested, "I'll flunk. And if I flunk marketing, how do I get to be a national sales manager?"

"Come off it," the older man said, annoyed. "You've had the hots for Carynne all year; this is just an excuse to take one last crack at her before she graduates."

Richard looked chagrined. "Okay, I admit I was dreaming about her. But hey, she's the original Snow Queen. Nothing will happen."

"Dickie boy," the older man said, clucking his tongue, "You forget who you're lying to. I *remember* what you're thinking. And right now, you're thinking that if you were getting somewhere with Carynne you'd toss Louisa out the door in a minute." The older man suddenly grabbed cat/Richard roughly by the neck, held him nose-to-nose, and spoke in low, dark tones. "*So get this straight, pinhead!* This Saturday, Carynne not only coaches you for the exam, but she also invites you into her bed. You'll come dragging your lethargic ass home Sunday at six in the morning to find Louisa already packed."

The cat stopped squirming. "Oh?"

"Of all the things you could possibly do in this universe, I promise you, you do *not* want to do that."

"Are you out of your mind?" Richard shrieked. "Carynne's beautiful! Brilliant! Everything I ever wanted in a woman!"

"Including selfish? Demanding? Manipulative?"

Richard fastened on an idea. "That's it. You're right about alternate time-lines; I'm the wrong past for you. *My* Carynne's nothing like—"

"Of course she isn't. Now."

Richard paused. "Okay, tell you what. If it turns out you're right, I'll dump her in a few years."

"Idiot!" the older man thundered, "in six months you marry her! In a year she pushes you into going back to school full-time—while holding down a full-time job—to get your MBA. In five years she's into leased BMW's and semiannual vacations in the Virgin Islands, neither of which you can afford; by the time you're thirty your hairline's back *here*," the older man karate-chopped himself on the crown of his head, "your stomach's in real trouble, and Carynne has realized you aren't half as ambitious as she is."

"So? Lots of people survive divorce."

"You, unfortunately, stay married. Always hoping things will improve, and always getting affection from her the same way Muffy gets dog yummies: only when you roll over and beg."

"*Muffy?*"

The older man dropped the cat on the bed. "Her Lhasa apso."

"You mean one of those small, yapping . . ? Eesh," said Richard, disgusted.

He jumped down to the floor, sniffed at his self lying under the bed, then looked at the older man and cocked his head quizzically. Somehow, no matter how hard he tried, he found it hard to accept such grim portents from a caricature of a salesman. "So it won't work, huh?"

"It can't work," the spectre explained. "You two are incompatible at the most primal level. I mean—look, you've got three avatars now, right? That's 'cause your life path isn't decided yet.

"That inert spud under the bed—that's *me*. Or rather what Carynne will make out of me. And that one up there," he gestured at the Richard floating near the ceiling, "I don't know what future he represents.

"But right now, your primary manifestation is as a cat. That's your favorite avatar; the tomcat.

"She can't stand cats unless they're neutered, declawed, and kept in the house. Even then she prefers docile, obedient, nearly asexual dogs. You're a cat person. She's a dog person. It's that basic."

Richard began pacing back and forth between the bed and the radiator, twitching his tail anxiously. "Look, there's got to be something redeeming about the marriage. Kids?" he suggested, hopefully.

"Two daughters who are carbon copies of their mother. They're into horses. You have any idea how much a ten-year-old who wants a horse can whine?"

"Friends, then?"

"Hers. Frank and Gordy are too plebeian for her tastes and you won't see them again after '77."

Richard looked up, into the older man's face. There was tremendous bitterness and inner-directed anger there, eating away at the man like a cancer. And yet, there was something else. A soft—wistfulness? Ignoring the cat for the moment, the older man had turned and was watching Louisa sleep. Hesitantly, tenderly, he reached out a ghost hand and touched her leg. She didn't stir. Quickly, as if she were a delicate treasure he feared his rude touch would ruin, he pulled his hand away and turned around, to find the cat looking straight into his eyes.

"Anyway, that's what I came here to tell you," the older man said softly. "It's your decision now." He turned to look at Louisa again. "I'll be snapping back to my own time in a minute or two."

That, at last, was what touched cat/Richard. For all the bluster, it was the brief unguarded slice of tenderness that convinced Richard the older man was telling the truth. Unable to think of anything more comforting, he rubbed up against the man's legs. Older Richard noticed, reached down to scratch him behind the ears, and whispered, "Take good care of her, okay?" Before cat/Richard could answer, older Richard and suddenly sat up straight, blanched white with pain, and clamped his fists to the sides of his head.

"What's wrong?" the cat mewed. "Can I help?"

"Weird!" gasped the older man "Like—*hot maggots* in my brain! Snapback never felt like this be . . ." In that instant, both of them became aware of another presence in the room.

"I thought I'd find you here."

"Carynne!" older Richard shouted. Cat/Richard spun around to find a thin, deeply wrinkled, ascetic old woman wearing an elegant white dress and sitting stiffly erect in a Louis Quatorze armchair (which she had apparently brought with her), holding a Lhasa apso in her lap. "And your little dog, too!" At that moment the dog spotted cat/Richard and, with a pugnacious yap, jumped out of the woman's arms.

"Muffy the fourth!" she commanded. "Heel!"

Instinctively, cat/Richard leapt up onto the bed, turned to face the dog, and let out his most vile and gutttural hiss. The dog stopped short, considered the *very* sharp claws Richard had extended, and dutifully trotted back to Carynne. "I'm sorry," she said, addressing the cat. "Muffy's so excitable." She lifted the dog into her lap, then turned to older Richard. "Now, if you're done lying to this young man . . ."

"You can't be here!" older Richard gasped.

"Don't look so surprised, dear," the woman said. "If you can learn projection, I can."

"But—time transference only works between the same mind!"

"Dickie," she admonished, "as usual you're too stubborn to admit you're wrong. I *am* here; therefore I *can* be." She glanced at cat/Richard. "I only hope I'm in time."

"In time for what?" cat/Richard asked, suspiciously.

"I don't know what he's told you so far," Carynne explained, smiling, "but Dickie was going through a premature mid-life crisis when he started this projection business. Seems he had a habit of picking up teenage bimbos on his sales trips, and when his weight hit two fifty they started laughing in his face. Gave his poor little male ego a terrible shock."

Cat/Richard turned sharply on older Richard, forming the question.

"She isn't *my* Carynne," older Richard protested.

"I certainly am!" she countered.

"But you're so—"

"Old?" she completed. "Did you think you had a monopoly on projecting into your past? All this—" she pointed a long, polished fingernail at older Richard, "including *your* present, is *my* past!"

"How did you—"

"You hid your notes well, Dickie. I didn't find out about this projection nonsense until I went through your papers after you died."

"Died!" cat/Richard yowled.

"Don't listen to her," the older man said quickly. "She's trying to get you rattled."

"And so I've come back to provide some balance," Carynne continued, addressing the cat. "Not that it really matters what he tells you. He can't possibly succeed—causality paradox, you know—I'm just disappointed that he spent years trying."

"Kid?" the older man prompted, panic rising in his voice. Cat/Richard found himself wishing Carynne had flown in, cackling, on a broomstick; it would've made things so much easier. Instead, the glimpse of his own mortality had triggered a surge of guilt, and he was busy remembering just how convincingly he could lie to himself when he wanted something. "Listen, she's . . ." older Richard started, then paused when he saw the way the cat was glaring, first at him, then at Carynne.

"He's trying to decide who to believe," Carynne observed.

Older Richard turned on her. "You'll ruin *everything*!" he hissed. "You weren't satisfied with making *my* life miserable; you're trying to screw up all my *possible* lives." Closing his eyes, he sat up rigidly and grimaced with fierce concentration. "I won't let you do it," he whispered. "I'll force you out."

"Really, Dickie dear," Carynne said, shaking her head slowly, "I should think by now you'd know better than to try a contest of wills with me."

"I am restructuring the projection . . ." he muttered.

"And I'm still here," she said nonchalantly. "At the risk of reminding you of our sex life: are you finished?"

With a gasp, older Richard broke concentration and staggered to his feet, defiantly facing Carynne. "You think you've won, don't you?" he snarled. "I'll be back!"

"No, you won't," Carynne stated flatly.

"Stop me!"

Carynne shrugged. "If you insist. Dickie dear, do you understand how dreamstate time is purely subjective? I can control my projections far better than you ever could." She rapped her knuckles on the arm of the chair for emphasis. "In a month of real time I can haunt you for the rest of your sad little life, if you force it on me."

"No!" shouted cat/Richard. "Don't give in, Dickie!" He urgently tried to pull his selves together and focus all his awareness through the cat. "We can beat her! If we unite—"

"Goodbye, Dickie," Carynne smiled. A silvery umbilicus snaked down from somewhere and started entwining older Richard. Cat/Richard leapt at it, claws flailing, but the cord was unyielding as cold marble. It fell about older Richard in heavy loops; he struggled briefly, but when the end dropped down and the whole mass began constricting, he gave up.

"Dickie?" the cat screamed.

"I'm sorry," came a muffled voice from inside the coils. "I can't hold off snap-back any longer." In the space of a few seconds, the coils tightened to a mass the size of a fist and then abruptly vanished, leaving a momentary pucker in the air.

On the night of June 27th, 1995, Richard Luck woke up at two A.M. with a start so sudden it disturbed his wife, Carynne.

"What's the matter, Dickie?" she asked.

"Oh . . . just had a *weird* dream."

"That's all right," she mumbled. Pulling him close, she gave him a peck on the cheek, then rolled over and turned her back to him. "Go back to sleep, dear. And no more dreaming about Louisa."

He was awake for hours, wondering.

"My, that was easy," Carynne said smugly. "Now, as for you," she took a step towards cat/Richard, who crouched low, raised his hackles, and bared his teeth. "Oh, very well. Go ahead and have your little tantrum; you won't escape me, dear." She lifted the Lhasa apso into her arms and began spinning the same glossy cord about herself, slipping into the coils with practiced ease. "See you Saturday!" she called out gaily.

Cat/Richard frantically nudged at his sleeping self, trying to wake up. He had a feeling it was critically urgent that he wake up; he desperately needed to tell the whole story to his rational daytime self, which was still asleep. If he could just remember every detail; if he could just see Carynne with his waking eyes before she vanished—

As she spun the last loops about herself, Carynne cocked her head at Louisa's sleeping form. "Dickie dear, you always had such cheap taste in women. Whatever do you see in *her*?"

Cat/Richard was getting through. Slowly, his sleeping self was beginning to rouse. Slowly, *very* slowly, his daytime mind was grinding into gear. And then—

Carynne vanished. Richard sat up straight in bed. The disturbance woke Louisa. She rolled over, brushed a few strands of her long brown hair out of her face, and mumbled, "Whasmatter, honey? How come you're awake?"

"Damn cat was licking my face."

"Don't *have* a cat," Louisa noted.

"Then we'll get one. I want a cat."

"Silly boy," Louisa murmured. Richard realized that, as was often the case, when he woke up in the middle of the night, he needed to go to the bathroom.

He slid out of bed.

"Honey?" Louisa called out as he pulled on the terrycloth bathrobe they shared. "Come back to bed?"

"In a minute." He had this odd, nagging feeling in the back of his head, like there was something he needed to remember.

"Don't stay up late reading again. You need sleep, too."

"I know." Something *important*, and it was just beyond his grasp.

"Don't want to fall asleep during your marketing exam." He stopped short at the bedroom door. He *remembered*. Turning around, he came back to the bed, and kissed Louisa.

"Lou, sweetheart," he said gently, "I think it's time we talked about getting married."

"Inna morning, honey," she mumbled. Then, as the words soaked in, her eyes snapped wide open. "Did you say married?" she whispered. He nodded. Louisa threw her arms around Richard and hugged so hard his ribs ached. "I thought you'd *never* ask!"

Somewhere down the twisting braided streams of time, a different Richard began chuckling in his sleep again, which woke his wife one more time. It annoyed Carynne no end when it happened, but there was nothing she could do about it.

At that moment.

Joyce Harrington

THE OLD GRAY CAT

"I should kill her. I should really kill her."

"Yeah, yeah. But how, how?"

"I could find a way. I bet I could."

"Oh, sure."

"You don't think I could? I could put poison in her cocoa."

"What kind of poison?"

"Ah, you know, arsenic. Something like that."

"Sure. You gonna go down to the store, say, 'Gimme a pound of arsenic, something like that.' Nobody's gonna ask what you want to do with it?"

"I could push her down the stairs. She'd die."

"Maybe not. She could break all her bones and still live. She'd say, 'Ellie pushed me down the stairs.' Then what?"

"She lies. Everybody knows she tells lies."

"Somebody would believe her. A thing like that, why would she lie?"

"Everybody knows she hates me. She steals my things. Remember the time I had that box of chocolate-covered cherries and she took a bite out of every one and put them all back in the box? Even you said she was the one."

"Probably she was. But everybody knows you hate her right back."

"You think I shouldn't kill her? You think I should just let her get away with this?"

"I didn't say that, did I? You want to kill her, go ahead. Only be smart. Don't get caught."

"I don't care if I get caught."

"You'll care. If you have to spend the rest of your life in jail, you'll care all right."

"Is this better than a jail? Listen, if I get caught I'll play crazy. You think I can't play crazy? Watch this."

Ellie crossed her eyes, let her tongue loll out of her mouth, and waggled her head. "Glah-glah-glah," she said.

"Nobody would believe that for a minute. You need some lessons in playing crazy."

"That's funny. You know, you're really funny. Ha, ha, see how I'm laughing? You don't think I'm crazy enough. I suppose you think you're crazier than I am?"

"The whole world is crazy. Just act normal. Then everybody'll think you're crazy."

"Margo, you're my best friend. But you're wrong. Anyway, if I really do kill her, which maybe I won't, but if I do, nobody will know I did it. Not even you."

"Will you tell me?"

"I guess so. Maybe. I could put a deadly snake in her bed. I read that in a book once."

"Where would you get a deadly snake?"

"That's a problem."

A bell rang. The door banged open and Miss Swiss marched into the room.

"Lunchtime, girls," she announced. Her voice was brassy and her hair was the color of tarnished trumpets, stiff and shiny with hair spray. She wore a pink ruffled pinafore over a green nylon dress. The ruffles flapped over her bulging frontage lending a quivering vitality to the corseted flesh beneath.

"Put your games away," she blared. "Books and magazines back on the shelf. Let's keep this room tidy, girls." Her eyes swept the room like twin beacons, flashing malice.

Ellie picked up a fistful of marbles from the Chinese checkerboard that lay on the table between them. She aimed at the back of Miss Swiss's metallic coiffure. Margo grabbed her arm across the table.

"Don't be stupid," she whispered.

Miss Swiss turned. "Fighting again, girls? Margo, I'm surprised at you. Ellie, you've been warned before. I'll have to report you to the Director. No dessert for either one of you." She smiled widely, showing gold inlays. "It's apple brown Betty today."

"Damn your apple brown Betty!" Ellie shouted, throwing marbles onto the worn wine-colored carpet. "And damn you, you fat elephant!"

"Shut up, you dummy," Margo whispered more urgently.

"Language, Ellie. Shocking," said Miss Swiss with an even more complacent smile. "The Director will be terribly disappointed. Margo, leave the room. Ellie will stay and pick up all those marbles. She will get no lunch at all. She will go to her room and stay there until I tell her she may come out. After lunch there will be a movie. I believe it is a film about Hawaii. Move along, girls."

Margo joined the drift of others toward the door of the recreation room. The smell of over-baked fish and boiled potatoes crept in at the door as the group of

20 or so trickled out. In the doorway Margo turned and mouthed silently at Ellie, "I'll bring you some food later."

Ellie shook her head and blinked back tears. Suddenly she felt hungry. The food was usually tasteless but now that it was being withheld, she felt a gnawing in her stomach that could only be assuaged by large helpings of hot food.

"I'm hungry," she whined.

"You should have thought of that before," snapped Miss Swiss, no longer smiling. "Pick up those marbles."

Ellie hunkered down on her heels, her thin legs disappearing into the folds of her wrinkled cotton skirt. She dropped her head onto her bony knees and folded her arms over both.

"I'm really going to kill you," she muttered into the flower-printed fabric.

"What was that?" demanded Miss Swiss. And, "What did you say?" when she got no answer. "Look at me!"

Ellie said nothing and did not raise her head. She remained folded into an unresponsive mound on the floor.

Miss Swiss reached down and prodded Ellie's shoulder with a sharp forefinger. Her nails were filed into curving talons and were painted a frosted pink.

"Pick. Up. Those. Marbles." said Miss Swiss, forming each word as if it were a stone falling from her lips onto Ellie's head.

Ellie grunted and toppled over. She lay on the floor, amid the brightly colored marbles, gazing up with hatred at Miss Swiss.

"Where's the cat?" she said.

"What cat?" Miss Swiss stepped back, looking surprised. "You know we don't allow cats in here. Or dogs, for that matter."

"My old gray cat. That's what cat. The one that came to my room." Ellie knew that Miss Swiss was only pretending to be surprised. She knew Miss Swiss was somehow responsible for the non-appearance of the rangy gray tomcat who had the habit of leaping onto Ellie's window sill and wolfing down whatever tidbit she had left for him there, favoring her with a wicked leer and departing with an arrogant flirt of his crooked tail. All summer long the cat had appeared with the first morning light while Ellie lay sleepless, with no reason to get up and no company but her hatred for Miss Swiss.

"If you've had a cat in your room, you've been breaking the rule. I don't know what we're going to do with you, Ellie. You're a very disruptive influence on the other girls. Do you think I like to be always punishing you? Wouldn't you like to be friends?"

"What did you do to him? Did you poison him? Or did you send him to the A.S.P.C.A.? They put cats in gas chambers there. Did you know that? I'd like to put you in a gas chamber."

Ellie felt tears rising again and rolled over to hide her face from Miss Swiss's inquisitory stare. She felt a marble under her hip and concentrated on that small pain to keep the tears in check.

"Ellie, Ellie," said Miss Swiss, her voice wheedling now, placatory. "That's a terrible thing to say. But I won't hold it against you. I won't even report it to the Director. But you've really got to get up now and pick up those marbles. I'll help you. And then later on, when I take my break, you can come and have cocoa in my room and we'll talk about this cat."

Ellie sat up. So, she thought, she does know about the cat. She can't fool me. She's trying to get around me so I won't kill her. Fat chance, the fat slob. Ellie picked up a red marble and then a yellow one. Miss Swiss was on her hands and knees, her green rump in the air, gathering marbles.

"Maybe I can even save you some apple brown Betty," she said.

"With whipped cream," said Ellie. "I like whipped cream."

"We'll see," said Miss Swiss.

Ellie made a rude gesture toward Miss Swiss's backside . . .

Ellie waited in her room for Miss Swiss's summons. It wasn't much of a room, but as Miss Swiss often reminded her, it was one of the best in the house. It had a window that looked out over the little park across the street. The leaves were falling now from the spindly trees that dotted the shriveled grass, and a gusty wind blew the leaves in erratic spirals between the benches.

Ellie lay on her bed and let her mind drift. Her pillow smelled musty and the smell evoked a memory, not of an event, but of a life lived in a house where a dark closet under a staircase smelled just that way and fetching galoshes on a rainy day was an occasion for terror. But the tall woman with the soft brown hair and the long strong hands was there to dispel morbid fancies with raisin cookies, a song, and the certainty of love.

"Ma. Oh, Ma," Ellie sighed.

Ellie had no memory of the death of her mother; she had been too young. There was only the unbearable absence, the loss of love, the vacancy that could never be filled no matter how hard she tried. And she had tried.

The cat had been her latest attempt. Too well she realized that the cat's attachment to her had been cupboard love. His first visit had coincided with half a tuna sandwich smuggled into her room from the regular Sunday evening cold supper. She had wrapped it in a paper napkin and placed it on the window sill to eat later before she went to bed. But a quarrel over the television set had brought a scolding from Miss Swiss, and Ellie had gone to bed spurting wrathful tears. The tuna sandwich had been forgotten.

A rustling had awakened her to a gray dawn and a gray shape on the window sill. The cat, sensing her movement, had looked up from his feast and hissed a warning at her. Then he had resumed his marauding, ignoring her as the sandwich disappeared and the napkin fell, limp and shredded, from his claws.

From her bed, Ellie had watched the cat's thin sides heave in and out as he chomped voraciously. She'd heard a sound, not quite a purr, yet not a growl, as the cat broadcast his ownership of the food. As the light gradually increased, she saw his tattered ear, his patchy fur, a scab, a clouded eye. He's like me, she thought. Alone and hungry. He left abruptly, not stopping to preen as house cats do after eating.

After that she always left something on the window sill. And always the cat came in the still hour of dawn. After a few visits he permitted Ellie to approach the window, each time a little closer until, by midsummer, he presented his scruffy head to be scratched. Ellie scratched diligently. She fondled his torn ear and passed her fingers gently over the milky eye. The first time she did that, the cat moved swiftly, clamping her hand between sharp yellow teeth.

Ellie was startled, but she didn't flinch. The cat held on for a minute. Two minutes. Ellie stood very still, sweating in her thin nightgown. Then the cat released her hand and nuzzled it with his damp, scarred nose. It was as close as they ever became to each other. The cat would not permit himself to be picked up. Ellie never thought of a name for him. He was just "the old gray cat."

Ellie told no one about the cat. No one but Margo. After her transistor radio disappeared, Ellie had to talk to someone.

"Bet I know who took it," said Margo.

"You think she did? Ooh, I could kill her!"

"She took my Snoopy dog away, didn't she? Said I was too old for baby toys. I bet she has a closet full of stuff she's taken away from people here. She's bad news."

"Well," said Ellie proudly, "I've got something she can't take away from me." And she told Margo about the visits of the cat in the early morning.

"Of course," she added, "he's ugly as sin, and probably dirty and diseased. Nobody would want him but me, and she couldn't keep *him* in any closet. He'd scratch her eyes out." Ellie giggled. "Serve her right," she said.

"Be careful," Margo had warned her. "Don't let her find out. She'll figure out some way to spoil it for you. She's a genius that way."

Ellie had been careful. But somehow Miss Swiss had found out. The cat had been absent for over a week now. Almost ten days. At first she told herself that a tomcat might have gotten into a fight and gone away to heal himself. She waited and watched every morning, wishing he might feel safe enough with her to come and have his injuries tended. Then she thought he might have been hit by a car. She envisioned him lying stiff and bedraggled in a filthy gutter somewhere in the city. But that didn't feel right to her. The cat was too wary, too wise, to be the victim of an accident.

No, she decided, the cat had been intercepted on one of his morning visits. The cat had been on his way to her and had been trapped because of his faithfulness. Trapped and killed, and who would have been mean enough, ruthless enough, cruel enough to do such a thing? Only Miss Swiss.

Ellie rummaged in her bureau drawer and failing to find her embroidery scissors remembered she had loaned them to Margo. She crept out of her room and down the hall to Margo's room. Everyone was at the movie. Hawaii! All hula dancers and pineapples and surfing. As if any of them could ever hope to go there.

Margo's room was dark, even in the middle of the day, and it smelled bad. Margo wasn't very clean. And her window looked out on an alley where the garbage cans were kept. She found her scissors lying on the floor where Margo had been cutting up magazine pictures for a decoupage project. The floor was littered with scraps of paper and there were dollops of dried glue on the rug. Ellie hurried back to her own room, the embroidery scissors safe in her pocket.

Back in her room, she cast about for some other weapon against Miss Swiss. The embroidery scissors were sharply pointed, but short-bladed. Miss Swiss was thickly clothed in fat. The short blades might not be equal to the task. But search as she might, there was no other possibility in her room; no pills, potions, or powders. Certainly not a knife, and Ellie had never seen a real gun. She considered wrenching one of the iron railings from the foot of her bedstead, but knew without trying that she lacked the strength. Maybe there would be something lying about Miss Swiss's room, some innocuous object that she could use if the right moment came.

If the moment came. But it probably would not come. Ellie would drink cocoa in Miss Swiss's room and listen to the lecture that would accompany it. She would nod and smile and promise to be good, all the while thinking deadly thoughts at the pink and falsely smiling Miss Swiss. But thoughts, however deadly, couldn't kill. Ellie's hand groped in the folds of her skirt, pressing the hard sharp outline of the small scissors against her thigh.

There was no knock at the door. Miss Swiss never knocked. The doorknob turned and the door opened just wide enough to admit the stiff curls and the painted smirk.

"Come along now, Ellie. The cocoa's ready and that movie's good for another half hour. At least we'll have some privacy for our chat."

"Coming, Miss Swiss."

With her hand still pressing the scissors against her thigh, Ellie followed the fluttering pink pinafore down the hall. Miss Swiss had, undoubtedly, the best room in the house, if you discounted the Director's office on the second floor which was paneled in glowing rosewood and draped in burgundy velvet. But the Director didn't live on the premises and Miss Swiss did.

Miss Swiss opened the massive door and ushered Ellie into her sanctum.

"Take the rocking chair, Ellie, dear. Pull it right up to the table. I'll pour the cocoa. There's the dessert I saved for you. *And* a bowl of whipped cream. We can have some in our cocoa, too. Although I really shouldn't, should I? Not with my weight problem."

While Miss Swiss babbled on, Ellie glanced round the room appraisingly. There were china animals everywhere. Quaint mice were pursued by cunning cats who were chased in turn by winsome dogs across the top of a bookcase. A pyramid of owls perched wisely in a whatnot by the window. Beasts of prey were restricted to a bureau where lions, leopards, and bears indiscriminately stalked each other across a long lace doily. A barnyard group browsed placidly atop a console television set. Ellie sneered inwardly at Miss Swiss's execrable taste, while envying both her freedom and her privacy to indulge her whims.

"I see you're admiring my menagerie. I've been collecting them for years. I just love animals, don't you?"

"No," said Ellie, and shifted her gaze to the fireplace. More animals paraded across the mantel: elephants, deer, and a particularly ugly version of a camel complete with howdah.

"No? But I thought that was why we're here. Something about a cat. Help yourself to cream, dear."

Ellie did, and spooned dessert in her mouth before answering. "One cat," she said, while taking careful note of the brass andirons and the iron poker that stood beside the firescreen.

"Well? What about this cat? You know we can't allow you girls to keep animals."

"I wasn't keeping him. Nobody could keep him. He came to visit. He was my friend, and now you've gone and done something to him." Ellie continued spooning up cream and chunks of apple.

Miss Swiss sipped cocoa and licked chocolate foam from her plump pink lips. "But I never saw this cat, Ellie, dear. If I had, I could not have allowed you to continue having him in your room. I would have spoken to you about it. Fair is fair."

"Fair is fair," mocked Ellie. "You killed him, didn't you?" She finished her dessert and stuck her finger into the remaining cream in the bowl.

"Ellie," chided Miss Swiss, "don't eat with your fingers. Use a spoon. I most certainly did not kill your cat. I love animals. I understand how you feel. Suppose I give you one of these?"

She set down her cocoa mug and walked across to the bookcase.

"Now, which one shall it be? A Siamese? Or would you like to have this dear little fluffy white kitten? I can't give you the tabby. She's my absolute out-and-out favorite, given to me by a girl who left us seven years ago. But any of the others. You may take your pick."

While Miss Swiss stood fondling each china cat in turn, Ellie took a final swipe at the bowl of cream and noiselessly left the rocking chair. She felt that the moment had come. If she didn't do it now, she never would. And after all her talk to Margo, she felt obliged to carry out her intentions. She sidled closer to the fireplace. And closer.

Miss Swiss continued to hover lovingly over the glossy representations of cat antics. "Now here's a cutie. I call him my Manx cat because his tail broke off, but he looks so lifelike playing with his tiny ball of yarn."

Ellie picked up the poker. It dragged at her arm and she wondered if she would have the strength to raise it. Her heart pounded and her head felt as if it would float off her shoulders with excitement. She felt an odd drawing together in her stomach almost as though all her vital organs were gathering themselves for one enormous effort. With both hands she raised the poker over her head. Her feet started traveling across the braided rug.

Miss Swiss looked over her shoulder and screamed. The poker flew from Ellie's hands. Miss Swiss stepped to one side, quickly for a woman of her size and weight. The ruffles on her pinafore fluttered wildly and her normally pink face turned the color of used chewing gum. The poker smashed into the bookcase and devastated the prim line of smirking cats.

Ellie's hand fumbled in the folds of her skirt, but before she could find her pocket her knees buckled and she fell to the floor with a thump. She fought for breath and fought the pain that scuttled like a trapped animal through her body. She gritted her teeth and closed her eyes. Her hand found its way into her pocket and she clutched the cold steel scissors.

"My cat," she gasped. "I'll kill you for that."

And she died. Ellie died.

Miss Swiss had seen death before. She recognized its awful presence on Ellie's face, bluish now and set forever in a snarl. But never had she come so close to death herself. If she hadn't moved quickly, she might have been lying on the rug beside Ellie with her head smashed in. Shakily she tiptoed around the pitiful corpse and opened the heavy door.

In the hall wondering eyes stared at her.

"We heard a noise," said Margo. "Anyway, the movie's over. It wasn't any good."

"Ellie has suffered a collapse," said Miss Swiss in answer to their unspoken question. "I shall have to call the doctor and the Director. And that son of hers."

"Is she dead?" asked Margo.

"She is," said Miss Swiss softly, and then resuming her trumpet-like tone, "Go to your rooms, girls. This is no time to be wandering about."

Gray and white heads nodded and carpet-slippered feet shuffled away. There were a few disheartened whispers, but for the most part there was silence as each old woman reflected on the nearness of her own inescapable end.

Only Margo remained.

"Miss Swiss," she said. "May I have Ellie's room? I know this may not be the right time to ask, but it is a much nicer room than mine, and if I wait someone else might get it. So may I, please?"

"Yes, yes," said Miss Swiss. "Margo, you were her friend. Do you know why . . . ? No, never mind. Go along now."

Margo lurched down the hall, scarcely needing to lean on the cane that was never out of her hand these days. In her room she began hauling things out of her bureau drawers and piling them on her bed in preparation for moving into Ellie's room: flannel nightgowns, warm winter underwear, a transistor radio. Too bad about Ellie, she thought, but if she hadn't died she would have got herself tossed out one of these days.

When she came to the closet, she paused. The smell was getting rather bad. She groped on the floor of the closet and came up with a plastic bag. The bag sagged heavily and Margo handled it gingerly, holding it away from her body with stiff fingertips.

It had been so easy to lure the cat onto her own window sill. All it took was a morsel of greasy hamburger. So easy to pretend insomnia and get a sleeping capsule from Miss Swiss. One capsule taken apart and its contents mixed with the meat. The cat, disarmed by Ellie's kindness, had allowed Margo to come close. One swift blow with her cane, and then pop into the plastic bag. Margo never knew whether the cat had died from the capsule or from a crushed skull. Or whether he had suffocated inside the plastic bag. Maybe all three.

But now she had no further use for him. Ellie was dead, too. If Ellie hadn't died this afternoon, or at least provoked Miss Swiss into having her removed, Margo had one final scheme in mind. Early tomorrow morning she would have placed the dead cat on Ellie's window sill. That would surely have done the trick. Ellie would have gone on a rampage and they would have had to get rid of her. But none of that was necessary now.

Margo carried the reeking plastic bag to the open window and dropped it into a lidless garbage can below. Then she cheerfully set about removing her clothes from the closet.

It had been worth it. The best room in the house was now hers. Next to Miss Swiss's, of course.

Clark Howard

ANIMALS

As Ned Price got off the city bus at the corner of his block, he saw that Monty and his gang of troublemakers were, as usual, loitering in front of Shavelson's Drugstore. A large portable radio—they called it their "ghetto blaster"—was sitting atop a newspaper vending machine, playing very loud acid rock. The gang, six of them, all in their late teens, appeared to be arguing over the contents of a magazine that was circulating among them.

Ned started down the sidewalk. An arthritic limp made him favor his right leg. That, coupled with lumbago and sixty-two years of less than easy living, gave him an overall stooped, tired look. A thrift-shop sportcoat slightly too large didn't help matters. Ned could have crossed the street and gone around Monty and his friends, but he lived on this side of the street so he would just have to cross back again farther down the block. It was difficult enough to get around these days without taking extra steps. Besides, he figured he had at least as much right to walk down the sidewalk as they did to obstruct it.

When Ned got closer, he saw the magazine the gang was passing around was *Ring* and that their argument had to do with the relative merits of two boxers named Hector "Macho" Camacho and Ray "Boom Boom" Mancini. Maybe they'd be too caught up in their argument to hassle him today. That would be a welcome change. A day without having to match wits with this year's version of the Sharks.

But no such luck.

"Hey, old man, where you been?" Monty asked as Ned approached. "Down to pick up your check?" He stepped in the middle of the sidewalk and blocked the way.

Ned stopped. "Yes," he said, "I've been down to pick up my check."

"You're one of those old people who don't let the mailman bring their check, huh?" Monty asked with a smile. "You know there's too many crooks in this neighborhood. You're smart, huh?"

"No, just careful," Ned said. If I was smart, he thought, I would have crossed the street.

"Hey, lemme ask you something," Monty said with mock seriousness. "I seen on a TV special where some old people don't get enough pension to live on an' they eat dogfood and catfood. Do you do that, old man?"

"No, I don't," Ned replied. There was a slight edge to his answer this time. He knew several people who *did* resort to the means Monty had just described.

"Listen, old man, I think you're lying," Monty said without rancor. "I myself have seen you in Jamail's Grocery buying catfood."

"That's because I have a cat." Ned tried to step around Monty but the youth moved and blocked his way again.

"You got a cat, old man? Ain't that nice?" Monty feigned interest. "Wha' kind of cat you got, old man?"

"Just an ordinary cat," Ned said. "Nothing special."

"Not a Persian or a Siamese or one of them expensive cats?"

"No. Just an ordinary cat. A tabby, I think it's called."

"A tabby! Hey, that's really nice."

"Can I go now?" Ned asked.

"Sure!" Monty said, shrugging elaborately. "Who's stopping you, old man?"

Ned stepped around him and this time the youth did not interfere with him. As he walked away, Ned heard Monty say something in Spanish and the others laughed.

A regular Freddie Prinze, Ned thought.

As Ned entered his third-floor-rear kitchenette, he said, "Molly, I'm back." Double-locking the door securely behind him, he hung his coat on a wooden wall peg and limped into a tiny cluttered living room. "Molly!" he called again. Then he stood still and a cold feeling came over him that he was alone in the apartment. "Molly?"

He stuck his head in the narrow Pullman kitchen, then pushed back a curtain that concealed a tiny sleeping alcove.

"Molly, where are you?"

Even as he asked the question one last time, Ned knew he would not find her. He hurried into the bathroom. The window was open about three inches. Ned raised it all the way and stuck his head out. Three stories below, in the alley, some kids were playing Kick-the-Can. A ledge ran from the window to a backstairs landing.

"Molly!" Ned called several times.

Moments later, he was out in front looking up and down the street. Monty and his friends, seeing him, sauntered down to where he stood.

"What's the matter, old man?" Monty asked. "You lose something?"

314

"My cat," Ned said. He turned suspicious eyes on Monty and his friends. "You wouldn't have seen her, by any chance, would you?"

"Is there a reward?" Monty inquired.

Ned gave the question quick consideration. There was an old watch of his late wife's he could probably sell. "There might be, if the cat isn't harmed. Do you know where she is?"

Monty turned to the others. "Anybody see this old man's cat?" he asked with a total absence of concern. When they all shrugged and declared ignorance, he said to Ned, "Sorry, old man. If you'd let the mailman deliver your check, you'd have been home to look after your cat. See the price you pay for being greedy?" He strutted off down the street, his followers in his wake. Feeling ill, Ned watched them all the way to the corner, where they turned out of sight. Pain from an old ulcer began as acid churned in his stomach.

"Molly!" he called and started walking down the block. "Molly! Here, kitty, kitty."

He searched for her until well after dark.

Ned was up early the next morning and back outside looking. He scoured the block all the way to the corner, then came back the other way. In front of the drugstore, he encountered Monty again. The youth was alone this time, leaning up against the building, eating a jelly doughnut and drinking milk from a pint carton.

"You still looking for that cat, old man?" Monty asked, his tone a mixture of incredulity and irritation.

"Yes."

"Man, why don't you go in the alley and get another one? There must be a dozen cats back there."

"I want this cat. It belonged to my wife when she was alive."

"Hell, man, a cat's a cat," Monty said.

Shavelson, the drugstore owner, came out, broom in hand. "Want to make half a buck sweeping the sidewalk?" he asked Monty, who looked at him as if he were an imbecile, then turned away disdainfully, not even dignifying the question with an answer. Shavelson shrugged and began sweeping debris toward the curb himself. "You're out early," he said to Ned.

"My cat's lost," Ned said. "She may have got out the bathroom window while I was downtown yesterday."

"Why don't you go back in the alley—"

Ned was already shaking his head. "I want *this* cat."

"Maybe the pound got her," Shavelson suggested. "Their truck was all over this neighborhood yesterday."

The storekeeper's words sent a chill along Ned's spine. "The pound?"

315

"Yeah. You know, the city animal shelter. They have a truck comes around—"

"It was here yesterday? On this block?"

"Yeah."

"Where do they take the animals they catch?" Ned asked out of a rapidly drying mouth.

"The animal shelter over on Twelfth Street, I think. They have to hold them there seventy-two hours to see if anybody claims them."

Too distressed by the thought to thank Shavelson, Ned hurried back up the street and into his building. Five minutes later, he emerged again, wearing a coat, his city bus pass in one hand. Crossing the street, he went to the bus stop and stood peering down the street, as if by sheer will he could make a bus appear.

Monty, having finished his doughnut and milk, sat on the curb in front of Shavelson's, smoking a cigarette and reading one of the morning editions from the drugstore's sidewalk newspaper rack. From time to time he glanced over at Ned, wondering at his concern over a cat. Monty knew a few back yards in the neighborhood that were knee-deep in cats.

Presently it began to sprinkle light rain. Monty stood up, folding the newspaper, and handed it to Shavelson as the storekeeper came out to move his papers inside.

"You sure you through with it?" Shavelson asked. "Any coupons or anything you'd like to tear out?"

Monty's eyes narrowed a fraction. "Someday, man, you're gonna say the wrong thing to me," he warned. "Then you're gonna come to open up your store and you gonna find a pile of ashes."

"You'd do that for *me*?" Shavelson retorted.

The sprinkle escalated to a drizzle as the storekeeper went back inside. From the doorway, Monty looked over at the bus stop again. Ned was still standing there, his only concession to the rain being a turned-up collar. I don't believe this old fool, Monty thought. He goes to more trouble for this cat than most people do for their kids.

Tossing his cigarette into the gutter, he trotted down the block and got into an old Chevy that had a pair of oversize velvet dice dangling from the rearview mirror. Revving the engine a little, he listened with satisfaction to the rumble of the car's gutted muffler, then made a U-turn from the curb and drove to the bus stop.

"Get in, old man," he said, leaning over to the passenger window. "I'm going past Twelfth Street—I'll give you a lift."

Ned eyed him suspiciously "No, thanks. I'll wait for the bus."

"Hey, man, waiting for a bus in this city at your age ain't too smart. An old lady over on Bates Street *died* at a bus stop last week, she was there so long. Besides, in case you ain't noticed, it's raining." Monty's voice softened a touch. "Come on, get in."

Ned glanced up the street one last time, saw that there was still no bus in sight, thought of Molly caged up at the pound, and got in.

As they rode along, Monty lighted another cigarette and glanced over at his passenger. "You thought me and my boys did something with your cat, didn't you?"

"The thought did cross my mind," Ned admitted.

"Listen, I got better things to do with my time than mess with some cat. You know, for an old guy you ain't very smart."

Ned grunted softly. "I won't argue with you there," he said.

On Twelfth, Monty pulled to the curb in front of the animal shelter. "I got to go see a guy near here, take me about fifteen minutes. I'll come back and pick you up after you get your cat."

Ned studied him for a moment. "Is there some kind of Teenager of the Year award I don't know about?"

"Very funny, man. You're a regular, what's-his-name, Jack Albertson, ain't you?"

At the information counter in the animal shelter a woman with tightly styled hair and a superior attitude asked, "Was the animal wearing a license tag on its collar?"

"No, she—"

"Was the animal wearing an ID tag on its collar?"

"No, she wasn't wearing a collar. She's really an apartment cat, you see—"

"Sir," the woman said, "our animal enforcement officers don't go into apartments and take animals."

"I think she got out the bathroom window."

"That makes her a street animal, unlicensed and unidentifiable."

"Oh, I can identify her," Ned assured the woman. "And she'll come to me when I call her. If you'll just let me see the cats you picked up yesterday—"

"Sir, do you have any idea how many stray animals are picked up by our trucks every day?"

"Why, no, I never gave—"

"*Hundreds,*" he was told. "Only the ones with license tags or ID tags are kept at the shelter."

"I thought all animals had to be kept here for three days to give their owners time to claim them," Ned said, remembering what Shavelson had told him.

"You're not listening, sir. Only the animals with license or ID tags are kept at the shelter for the legally required seventy-two hours. Those without tags are

317

taken directly to the disposal pound."

Ned turned white. "Is that where they—where they—?" The words would not form.

"Yes, that is where stray animals are put to sleep." She paused a beat. "Either that or sold."

Ned frowned. "Sold."

"Yes, sir. To laboratories. To help offset the overhead of operating our department." Her eyes flicked over Ned's shabby clothing. "Tax dollars don't pay for *everything*, you know." But she had unknowingly given Ned an ember of hope.

"Can you give me the address of this—disposal place?"

The woman scribbled an address on a slip of paper and pushed it across the counter to him. "Your cat might still be there," she allowed, "if it was picked up late yesterday. Disposal hours for cats are from one to three. If it was a dog you'd be out of luck. They do dogs at night, eight to eleven, because there are more of them. That's because they're easier to catch. They trust people. Cats, they don't trust—"

She was still talking as Ned snatched up the address and hurried out.

Monty was waiting at the curb.

"I didn't think you'd be back this quick," Ned said, getting into the car.

"The guy I went to see wasn't there," Monty told him. It was a lie. All he had done was drive around the block.

"They've taken my cat to be gassed," Ned said urgently, "but if I can get there in time I might be able to save her." He handed Monty the slip of paper. "This is the address. It's way out at the edge of town, but if you'll take me there I'll pay you." He pulled out a pathetically worn billfold, the old-fashioned kind that zipped around three sides. When he opened it, Monty could see several faded cellophane inserts with photographs in them. The photographs were old, all in black-and-white except for a paler picture of June Allyson that had come with the billfold.

From the currency pocket Ned extracted some bills, all of them singles. "I don't have much because I haven't cashed my check yet. But I can at least buy you some gas."

Monty pushed away the hand with the money and started the car. "I don't *buy* gas, man," he scoffed, "I quit buying it when it got to a dollar a gallon."

"Where do you get it?" Ned asked.

"I siphon it. From police cars parked behind the precinct station. It's the only place where cars are left on a lot unguarded." He flashed a smile at Ned. "That's because nobody would *dare* siphon gas from a cop car, you know what I mean?"

They got on one of the expressways and drove toward the edge of the city. As Monty drove, he smoked and kept time to rock music from the radio by drumming his fingers on the steering wheel. Ned glanced at a scar down the youth's right cheek. Thin and straight, almost surgical in appearance, it had probably been put there by a straight razor. Ned had been curious about the scar for a long time. Now would be an opportune time to ask how he got it, but Ned was too concerned about Molly. She was such an old cat, nearly fourteen. He hoped she hadn't died of a stroke from the trauma of being captured and caged. If she was still alive, she was going to be so glad to see him Ned doubted she would ever climb out the bathroom window again.

After half an hour on the expressway, Monty exited and drove them to a large warehouselike building at the edge of the city's water-treatment center. A sign above the entrance read simply: *Animal Shelter—Unit F.*

F for final, Ned thought. He was already opening his door as Monty brought the car to a full stop.

"Want me to come in with you?" Monty asked.

"What for?" Ned wanted to know, frowning.

The younger man shrugged. "So's they don't push you around. Sometimes people push old guys around."

"Really?" Ned asked wryly.

Monty looked off at nothing. "You want me to come in or not?"

"I can handle things myself," Ned told him gruffly.

The clerk at this counter, a thin gum-chewing young man with half a dozen ballpoints in a plastic holder in his shirt pocket, checked a clipboard on the wall and said, "Nope, you're too late. That whole bunch from yesterday was shipped out to one of our lab customers early this morning."

Ned felt warm and slightly nauseated. "Do you think they might sell my cat back to me?" he asked. "If I went over there?"

"You can't go over there," the clerk said. "We're not allowed to divulge the name or address of any of our lab customers."

"Oh." Ned wet his lips. "Do you suppose you could call them for me? Tell them I'd like to make some kind of arrangements to buy back my cat?"

The clerk was already shaking his head. "I don't have time to do things like that, mister."

"A simple phone call," Ned pleaded. "It'll only take—"

"Look, mister, I said no. I'm a very busy person."

Just then someone stepped up to the counter next to Ned. Surprised, Ned saw that it was Monty. He had his hands on the counter, palms down, and was smiling at the clerk.

"What time you get off work, Very Busy Person?" he asked.

The clerk blinked rapidly. "Uh, why do you want to know?"

"I'm jus' interested in what kind of hours a Very Busy Person like you keeps." Monty's smile faded and his stare grew cold. "You don't have to tell me if you don't want to. I can wait outside and find out for myself."

The clerk stopped chewing his gum; the color disappeared from his face, leaving him sickly pale. "Why, uh—why would you do that?"

"'Cause I ain't got nothing better to do," Monty replied. "I *was* gonna take this old man here to that lab to try and get his cat back. But if he don't know where it is, I can't do that. So I'll just hang around here." He winked at the clerk without smiling. "See you later, man."

Monty took Ned's arm and started him toward the door.

"Just—wait a minute," the clerk said.

Monty and Ned turned back to see him rummaging in a drawer under the counter. He found a sheet of paper with three names and addresses mimeographed on it. With a ballpoint from the selection in his shirt pocket, he circled one of the addresses. Monty stepped back to the counter and took the sheet of paper.

"If it turns out they're expecting us," Monty said, "I'll know who warned them. You take my meaning, man?"

The clerk nodded. He swallowed dryly and his gum was gone.

At the door, looking at the address circled on the paper, Monty said, "Come on, old man. This here place is clear across town. You positive one of them cats in the alley wouldn't do you?"

On their way to the lab, Ned asked, "Why are you helping me like this?"

Monty shrugged. "It's a slow Wednesday, man."

Ned studied the younger man for a time, then observed, "You're different when your gang's not around."

Monty tossed him a smirk. "You gonna, what do you call it, analyze me, old man? You gonna tell me I got 'redeeming social values' or something like that?"

"I wouldn't go quite that far," Ned said dryly. "Anyway, sounds to me like you've *been* analyzed."

"Lots of times," Monty told him. "When they took me away from my old lady because it was an 'unfit environment,' they had some shrink analyze me then. When I ran away from the foster homes I was put in, other shrinks analyzed me. After I was arrested and was waiting trial in juvenile court for some burglaries, I was analyzed again. When they sent me downstate to the reformatory, I was analyzed. They're very big on analyzing in this state."

"They ever tell you the results of all that analyzing?"

"Sure. I'm incorrigible. And someday I'm supposed to develop into a sociopath. You know what that is?"

"Not exactly," Ned admitted.

Monty shrugged. "Me neither. I guess I'll find out when I become one."

They rode in silence for a few moments and then Ned said, "Well, anyway, I appreciate you helping me."

"Forget it," Monty said. He would not look at Ned; his eyes were straight ahead on the road. After several seconds, he added, "Jus' don't go telling nobody about it."

"All right, I won't," Ned agreed.

Their destination on the other side of the city was a large square two-story building on the edge of a forest preserve. It was surrounded by a chain-link fence with an entrance gate manned by a security guard. A sign on the gate read: *Consumer Evaluation Laboratory*.

Monty parked outside the gate and followed Ned over to the security-guard post. Ned explained what he wanted. The security guard took off his cap and scratched his head. "I don't know. This isn't covered in my guard manual. I'll have to call and find out if they sell animals back."

Ned and Monty waited while the guard telephoned. He talked to one person, was transferred to another, then had to repeat his story to still a third before he finally hung up and said, "Mr. Hartley of Public Relations is coming out to talk to you."

Mr. Hartley was a pleasant but firmly uncooperative man. "I'm sorry, but we can't help you," he said when Ned had told him of Molly's plight. "We have at least a hundred small animals in there—cats, dogs, rabbits, guinea pigs—all of them undergoing scientific tests. Even the shipment we received this morning has already been processed into a testing phase. We simply can't interrupt the procedure to find one particular cat."

"But it's *my* cat," Ned insisted. "She's not homeless or a stray. She belonged to my late wife—"

"I understand that, Mr. Price," Hartley interrupted, "but the animal *was* outside with no license or ID tag around its neck. It was apprehended legally and sold to us legally. I'm afraid it's just too late."

As they were talking, a bus pulled up to the gate. Hartley waved at the driver, then turned to the security guard. "These are the people from Diamonds-and-Pearls Cosmetics, Fred. Pass them through and then call Mr. Draper. He's conducting a tour for them."

As the bus passed through, Hartley turned back to resume the argument with Ned, but Monty stepped forward to intercede.

"We understand, Mr. Hartley," Monty said in a remarkably civil tone. "We're sure you'd help us if you could. Please accept our apology for taking up your time." Monty offered his hand.

"Quite all right," Hartley said, shaking hands.

Ned was staring incredulously at Monty. Macho had suddenly become Milquetoast.

"Come along, old fellow," Monty said, putting an arm around Ned's shoulders. "We'll go to a pet store and buy you a new kitty."

Ned allowed himself to be led back to the car, then demanded, "What the hell's got into you?"

"You're wasting your time with that joker," Monty said. "He's been programmed to smile and say no to whatever you want. We got to find some other way to get your cat."

"What other way?"

Monty grinned. "Like using the back door, man."

Driving away from the front gate, Monty found a gravel road and slowly circled the fenced-in area of the Consumer Evaluation laboratory. On each side of the facility, beyond its fence, were several warehouses and small plants. In front, beyond a feeder road, was a state highway. Growing right up to its rear fence was the forest preserve: a state-protected wooded area.

Monty made one full circuit of the complex occupied by the laboratory and its neighbors, then said, "I think the best plan is to park in the woods, get past the fence in back, and sneak in that way."

"You mean slip in and *steal* my cat?" Ned asked.

Monty shrugged. "They stole her from you," he said.

Ned stared at him. "I'm sixty-two years old," he said. "I've never broken the law in my life."

"So?" said Monty, frowning. He did not see any relevance. The two men, one young, one old, each so different from the other, locked eyes in a silent stare for what seemed like a long time.

They were parked on the shoulder of the gravel road, the car windows down. The air coming into the car was fresh from the morning rain. Ned detected the scent of wet earth. Some movement a few yards up the road caught his eye and he turned his attention away from Monty. The movement was a gray squirrel scurrying across the road to the safety of the nearby woods. Watching the little animal, wild and free, made Ned think of the animals in the laboratory that were not free—the dogs and rabbits and guinea pigs.

And cats.

"All right," he told Monty. "Let's go in the back way."

Monty parked in one of the public picnic areas. From the trunk, he removed a pair of chain cutters and held them under his jacket with one hand.

"What do you carry those things for?" Ned asked, and realized at once that his question was naive.

322

"To clip coupons with, man," Monty replied. "Coupons save you money on everyday necessities."

The two men made their way through the trees to the rear of the laboratory's chain-link fence. Crouching, they scrutinized the back of the complex. Monty's eyes settled immediately on a loading dock served by a single-lane driveway coming around one side of the building. "We can go in there," he said. "Overhang doors are no sweat to open. But first let's see if there's any juice in this fence." Keeping his hands well on the rubber-covered handles, he gently touched the metal fence with the tip of the chain cutters. The contact drew no sparks. "Nothing on the surface," he said. "Let's see if there's anything inside. Some of these newer chain-links have an insulated circuit running through them." Quickly and expertly, he spread the cutters and snipped one link of the metal. Again there were no sparks. "This is going to be a breeze."

With a practiced eye, he determined his pattern and quickly snipped exactly the number of links necessary to create an opening large enough for them to get through. Then he gripped the cut section and bent it open, like a door, about eight inches. The chain cutters he hid nearby in some weeds.

"Now here's our story," he said to Ned. "We was walking through the public woods here and saw this hole cut in the fence, see? We thought it was our civic duty to tell somebody about it, so we came inside looking for somebody. If we get caught, stick to that story. Got it?"

"Got it," Ned confirmed.

Monty winked approval. "Let's do it, old man."

They eased through the opening and Monty bent the cut section back into place. Then they started toward the loading dock, walking upright with no attempt at hurrying or hiding. Ned was nervous but Monty remained very cool; he even whistled a soft little tune. When he sensed Ned's anxiety, he threw him a grin.

"Relax, old man. It'll take us forty, maybe fifty seconds to reach that dock. The chances of somebody seeing us in that little bit of time are so tiny, man. And even if they do, so what? We got our story, right?"

"Yeah, right," Ned replied, trying to sound confident.

But as Monty predicted, they reached the loading dock unobserved and unchallenged. Once up on the dock, Monty peered through a small window in one of the doors. "Just a big room with a lot of work tables," he said quietly. "Don't look like nobody's around. Hey, this service door's unlocked. Come on."

They moved inside into a large room equipped with butcher-block tables fixed to a tile floor. A number of hoses hung over each table, connected to the ceiling. As the two men stood scrutinizing the room, they suddenly heard a voice approaching. Quickly they ducked behind one of the tables.

An inner door opened and a man led a group of people into the room, saying, "This is our receiving area, ladies and gentlemen. The animals we purchase are delivered here and our laboratory technicians use these tables to wash and delouse them. They are then taken into our testing laboratory next door, which I will show you next. If you would, please take a smock from the pile there, to protect your clothes from possible contact with any of the substances we use in there."

Peering around the table, Ned and Monty watched as the people put on smocks and regrouped at the door. As they were filing out, Ned nudged Monty and said, "Come on."

Monty grinned. "You catching on, old man."

The two put on smocks and fell in at the rear of the group. They followed along as it was led through the hall and into a much larger room. This one was set up with a series of aisles formed by long work counters on which stood wire-grille cages of various sizes. Each cage was numbered and had a small slot containing a white card on its door. In each cage was a live animal.

"Our testing facility, we feel, is the best of its kind currently in existence," the tour guide said. "As you can see, we have a variety of test animals: cats, dogs, rabbits, guinea pigs. We also have access to larger animals, if a particular test requires it. Our testing procedures can be in any form. We can force-feed the test substance, introduce it by forced inhalation, reduce it to a dermal form and apply it directly to an animal's shaved skin, or inject it intravenously. Over here, for instance, are rabbits being given what is known as a Draize test. A new hairspray is being sprayed into their very sensitive eyes in order to gauge its irritancy level. Just behind the rabbits you see a group of puppies having dishwashing detergent introduced directly into their stomachs by a syringe with a tube attached to a hand pump. This is called an Internal LD-50 test; the LD stands for lethal dose and the number fifty represents one-half of a group of one hundred animals on which the test will be conducted. When half of the test group has died, we will have an accurate measurement of the toxicity level of this product. This will provide the company marketing the product with evidence of safety testing in case it is later sued because some child swallows the detergent and dies. During the course of the testing, we also learn exactly how a particular substance will affect a living body, by observing whatever symptoms the animal exhibits: convulsions, paralysis, tremors, inability to breathe, blindness as in the case of the rabbits there—"

Ned was staring at the scene around him. As he looked at the helpless, caged, tortured animals, he felt his skin crawl. Which were the animals, the ones in the cages, or the ones outside the cages? Glancing at Monty, he saw the younger man reacting the same way—his eyes were wide, his expression incredulous, and his hands were curled into fists.

"We can test virtually any substance or product there is," the guide continued. "We test all forms of cosmetics and beauty aids, all varieties of detergents and other cleaning products, every food additive, coloring, and preservative, any new chemical or drug product—you name it. In addition to servicing private business, we test pesticides for the Environmental Protection Agency, synthetic substances for the Food and Drug Administration, and a variety of products for the Consumer Product Safety Commission. Our facility is set up so that almost no lead time is required to service our customers. As an example of this, a dozen cats brought in this morning are already in a testing phase over here—"

Ned and Monty followed the group to another aisle where the guide pointed out the newly arrived cats and explained the test being applied to them. Ned strained to see beyond the people in front of him, trying to locate Molly.

Finally the tour guide said, "Now, ladies and gentlemen, if you'll follow me, I'll take you to our cafeteria, where you can enjoy some refreshments while our testing personnel answer any questions you have about how we can help Diamonds-and-Pearls Cosmetics keep its products free of costly lawsuits. Just drop your smocks on the table outside the door."

Again Ned and Monty ducked down behind a workbench to conceal themselves as the people filed out of the room. When the door closed behind the group, Ned rose and hurried to the cat cages. Monty went over to lock the laboratory door.

Ned found Molly in one of the top cages. She was lying on her side, eyes wide, staring into space. The back part of her body had been shaved and three intravenous needles were stuck in her skin and held in place by tape. The tubes attached to the needles ran out the grille and up to three small bottles suspended above the cage. They were labeled: FRAGRANCE, DYE, and POLYSORBATE 93.

Ned wiped his eyes with the heel of one hand. Unlatching the grille door, he reached in and stroked Molly. "Hello, old girl," he said. Molly opened her mouth to meow, but no sound came.

"Dirty bastards," Ned heard Monty whisper. Turning, he saw the younger man reading the card on the front of Molly's cage. "This is some stuff that's going to be used in a hair tint," he said. "This test is to see if the cat can stay alive five hours with this combination of stuff in her."

"I can answer that," Ned said. "She won't. She's barely alive now."

"If we can get her to a vet, maybe we can save her," Monty suggested. "Pump her stomach or something." He bobbed his chin at the back wall. "We can get out through one of those windows—they face our hole in the fence."

"Get one open," Ned said. "I'll take Molly out."

Monty hurried over to the window while Ned gently unfastened the tape and pulled the hypodermic needles out of Molly's flesh. Once again the old cat looked at him and tried to make a sound, but she was too weak and too near death. "I know, old girl," Ned said softly. "I know it hurts."

Near the window, after opening it, Monty noticed several cages containing puppies that were up and moving around, some of them barking and wagging their tails. Monty quickly opened their cages, scooped them out two at a time, and dropped them out the window.

"Lead these pups to the fence, old man," he said as Ned came over with Molly.

"Right," Ned replied. He let Monty hold the dying cat as he painfully got his arthritic legs over the ledge and lowered himself to the ground. "What about you?" he asked as Monty handed down the cat.

"I'm gonna turn a few more pups loose, an' maybe some of those rabbits they're blinding. You head for the fence—I'll catch up."

Ned limped away from the building, calling the pups to follow him. He led them to the fence, bent the cut section open again and let them scurry through. As he went through himself, he could feel Molly becoming ever more limp in his hands. By the time he got into the cover of the trees, her eyes had closed, her mouth had opened, and she was dead. Tears coming again, he knelt and put the cat up against a tree trunk and covered her with an old red bandanna he pulled out of his back pocket.

Looking through the fence, he saw that Monty was still putting animals out the window. Two dozen cats, dogs, rabbits, and guinea pigs were moving around tentatively on the grass behind the laboratory. He's got to get out of there or he'll get caught, Ned thought. Returning through the opening in the fence, he hurried back to the window.

"Come on," he urged as the younger man came to the window with a kitten in each hand.

"No—" Monty tossed the kittens to the ground "—I'm going to turn loose every animal that can stand!"

Old man and young man fixed eyes on each other as every difference there had ever been between them faded.

"Give me a hand up, then," Ned said.

Monty reached down and pulled him back up through the window.

As they worked furiously to open more cages and move their captives out the window, they became aware of someone trying the lab door and finding it locked. Several moments later, someone tried it again. A voice outside the door mentioned a key. The two inside the lab worked all the faster. Finally, a sweating Monty said, "I think that's all we can let go. The rest are too near dead. Let's get out of here!"

"I'm going to do one more thing first," Ned growled.

Poised by the open window, Monty asked, "What?"

Ned walked toward a shelf on which stood several plastic gallon jugs of isopropyl alcohol. "I'm going to burn this son-of-a-bitch down."

Monty rushed over to him. "What about the other animals?"

"You said yourself they were almost dead. At least this will put them out of their misery without any more torture." He opened a jug and started pouring alcohol around the room. After a moment of indecision, Monty joined him.

Five minutes later, just as someone in the hall got the lab door open and several people entered, Ned and Monty dropped out the open window and tossed a lighted book of matches back inside.

The laboratory became a ball of flame.

While the fire spread and the building burned, Ned and Monty managed to get the released animals through the fence and into the woods. Sirens of fire and police emergency vehicles pierced the quiet afternoon. There were screams and shouts as the burning building was evacuated. Monty retrieved the chain cutters and ran toward the car. Ned limped hurriedly after him, but stopped when he got to where Molly was lying under the red bandanna. I can't leave her like that, he thought. She had been a good, loving pet to Ned's wife, then to Ned after his wife died. She deserved to be buried, not left to rot next to a tree. Dropping to his knees, he began to dig a grave with his hands.

Monty rushed back and saw what he was doing. "They gonna catch you, old man!" he warned.

"I don't care."

Ned kept digging as Monty hurried away.

He had barely finished burying Molly a few minutes later when the police found him.

Ned's sentence, because he was a first offender and no one had been hurt in the fire, was three years. He served fourteen months. Monty was waiting for him the day he came back to the block.

"Hey, old man, ex-cons give a neighborhood a bad reputation," Monty chided.

"You ought to know," Ned said gruffly.

"You get the Vienna sausages and crackers and stuff I had sent from the commissary?"

"Yeah." He did not bother to thank Monty; he knew it would only embarrass him.

"So how you like the joint, old man?"

Ned shrugged. "It could have been worse. A sixty-two-year-old man with a game leg, there's not much they could do to me. I worked in the library, checking books out. Did a lot of reading in between. Mostly about animals."

"No kidding?" Monty's eyebrows went up. "I been learning a little bit about animals, too. I'm a, what do you call it, volunteer down at the A.S.P.C.A. That's American Society for the Prevention of Cruelty to Animals."

"I know what it is," said Ned. "Good organization. Say, did that Consumer Evaluation Laboratory ever rebuild?"

"Nope," Monty replied. "You put 'em out of business for good, old man."

"Animal shelter still selling to those other two labs?"

"Far as I know."

"Still got their addresses?"

Monty smiled. "You bet."

"Good," Ned said, nodding. Then he smiled, too.

Frances & Richard Lockridge

THE SEARCHING CATS

The cat appeared soundlessly on the open window sill—the window which had been forced open. The cat was spotlessly black and for a moment, poised there, he looked around the room with unblinking yellow eyes.

The cat looked at M. L. Heimrich, captain, New York State Police, a man most often concerned with homicide, and now so concerned. The cat looked away again, dismissing the man. The cat dropped to the polished tile floor of the living room. Then he spoke, once, on a note which seemed to Heimrich to have a curious insistence. The cat seemed to wait for an answer.

When there was no answer, the cat began to move—to glide around the floor, nose close to the floor. The cat's progress was erratic; the cat circled among chairs and under tables; now and then the cat paused and Heimrich could see his nostrils quiver. But always he went on again, engrossed and, it seemed to the watching man, impelled. Heimrich had never before seen a cat behave so—search so. Search, Heimrich decided after a time, for something he would never find again.

"It's no good, fellow," Heimrich said, and the cat paused and looked up, as if he had understood the words and waited to be told more. (Which was, of course, absurd.) "Your man's dead, fellow," Heimrich said, and the cat still seemed to wait. "Murdered," Heimrich told him. The cat waited a moment longer and then went back to sniffing the green tile floor.

Heimrich, having other things to do, walked across the living room, ignored by the black cat, and out of the small, pleasant, country house. It was about four o'clock, then, in the afternoon.

At a few minutes after four, Russell Ashby circled his white farmhouse and sounded the horn of the pickup truck to tell Jane he was home. He ran the truck into the shed which served as a garage and walked back to the house—a tall man in slacks and a jacket with suede-patched elbows. He took long strides on the path

329

to the house and, when he saw Jane standing in the doorway, began to nod his head and smile at her.

It was a kind of pantomime of triumph. But the set expression—was it of anxiety?—on his wife's young face did not alter, and then Ashby slapped his left hip pocket, where his wallet was, to make what should have been evident, clearer yet. But still her face did not brighten.

He walked up on the porch, his footsteps emphatic on the boards. She stepped out onto the porch to meet him and there was an odd rigidity in her slender body, matching the rigidity of her face—a rigidity unbecoming to so lovely a face.

"Got it," Russell Ashby said. "All I had to do was . . ." He stopped; her eyes stopped his words. "What's the matter, baby?" he said, in a very different tone.

"Russ," she said, "where have you been?"

"Been?" he said. "What's the matter, Jane? You knew—" He broke off. "Oh," he said, "afterward. That's it. Think I'd got run over? Went to look at Jenkins's north field. See if it's worth haying. Took longer than—"

"Russ," Jane Ashby said, and her young voice shook. "Russ—Mr. Bailey's dead. They say—Russ, they say somebody killed him. Broke into the house and—killed him. Russ—somebody from the police called. Wanted—"

She did not go on. He held her close and could feel her body trembling. Over her head he looked, flatly, at nothing. And waited. After a time, stumbling on the words, she told him what everybody around East Belford had known for an hour or more. "Everybody but me," Russell Ashby said, his voice steady, uninflected.

Thwaite Bailey, the richest man around, had been found dead by his daughter, who had walked the hill path from the "big" house to her father's house at about three o'clock. She had telephoned him first and got no answer, and had been worried and walked the quarter of a mile which separated the original Bailey house from the low, contemporary house Bailey had built for week ends when he turned the old house—too big for anybody, the old house was—over to his daughter and Sidney Combe, her husband.

Margaret Combe had found her father dead in the doorway of his bedroom, his head crushed. She had found the little house, which had so much glass it glittered like a jewel in its green valley, ransacked.

"They think he was taking a nap," Jane Ashby said, sitting straight in her living room. "That somebody broke in, thinking he wouldn't be there in the middle of the week. And that whoever it was made a noise that wakened Mr. Bailey and then—killed him. Russ . . ."

"Yes?" Russell Ashby said.

"Russ—Sid says Mr. Bailey had a lot of money in the house. A—a thousand dollars. That he always had. And—it isn't there, Russ. *It isn't there!*"

"No," Russ Ashby said. "It's in my pocket."

She put hands over her eyes—the biggest ever, he thought. The brownest ever.

"Hold it, baby," Russ said. "Like we planned—I said did he want to invest in an outfit that needed a push over a hump. Because of the way he and Dad felt about each other. I made a pitch, Jane. And—look." He took his billfold from his hip pocket and they both looked—looked at twenty fifty-dollar bills. "I said a check would be just as good but he said, 'Here, son. Take it.' It was—a gesture, I guess. He was always a little like that."

Thwaite Bailey had been like that, as a good many people knew. It was a quirk. Rich men—and men as generous in service as with money—are entitled to quirks.

"Russ," she said, "when were you there?"

"About two," he said.

"He'd been dead about an hour," Jane Ashby said, "when Marge found him. They say that . . . Russ, did anybody see you? There, I mean? Because . . ."

He looked at her strangely. "You mean," he said, "because of that other thing?"

She did not answer. That was good enough, or bad enough. "It was a long time ago," Russ Ashby said, slowly.

It had been—long before Clint Ashby had died and left his son a dairy farm which was now—in spite of everybody's advice—an Aberdeen Angus breeding farm; long before Russ went to Korea in the Marines. It had been before Russ Ashby grew up; when he was a "wild kid." With other wild kids he had broken into a closed country house. "For the hell of it." But Russell Ashby had been the one caught—and booked. Clinton Ashby had made good and the charges had been dropped. But . . .

"Sid was walking his dog," Russell Ashby, the grown-up Russell Ashby, said now. He spoke slowly. "On the hill. He was going away when I saw him—his back was to me. Swinging that squire's walking stick of his. I left the truck on Shady Lane and cut across by the path . . ."

Someone knocked at the front door. The knocking was not loud. There was no threat in it.

"Russ," Jane said, in a very low voice, a hurried voice. "Russ—I'm scared. *Terribly scared.* They won't believe . . ."

Russell Ashby went to the door and let in two large, solid men—men not in uniform; Captain M. L. Heimrich and Sergeant Charles Forniss, of the New York State Police.

Heimrich said, "Mr. Ashby?" and then, "We'd like to ask you a couple of questions." Heimrich and Forniss did not wait for more, but went on into the living room. "Oh," Heimrich said. "Mrs. Ashby?" She was a remarkably pretty young woman, he thought; she looked frightened. Which was reasonable. She nodded her head, standing, fear in her face. "Sit down," Heimrich said, and then, "You, too, Mr. Ashby." He waited until they sat down. Then he sat on a straight chair. Forniss remained near the door, standing, looking very large.

"Mr. Thwaite Bailey was killed this afternoon," Heimrich said. "About the time you were there, Mr. Ashby."

Heimrich closed bright blue eyes. And waited. And Jane Ashby, fear rioting in her eyes, waited, too.

Waiting, she held her breath. That was evident to Heimrich—the cessation, utter if momentary, of breath movement in her body. Heimrich looked at Russell Ashby and Ashby looked only at his wife—and looked as if he listened. Heimrich saw Ashby's chest rise, slowly. It seemed a long time before Russell Ashby spoke.

"I was there," Ashby said. "He was all right when I went in—when he let me in. He was all right when I left."

"Yes," Heimrich said, "you were there. Your fingerprints are there. On the desk drawer."

"Maybe," Ashby said. "I don't know what I touched. I've said I was there. Mr. Bailey was an old friend of father's. Of mine, too. I dropped by to see him now and then. He—"

"Your prints are on record," Heimrich said. "From the other time. You know what I mean?"

Again Russell Ashby and his wife looked at each other—looked quickly, then away again. Ashby said, "I know what you mean."

"The same thing," Heimrich said. "Except—murder, this time. A window forced. But this time—a man killed."

"I was a kid then," Ashby said. "A long time ago, when I was a kid."

"Yes," Heimrich said. "Mr. Combe—Sidney Combe—says you were carrying something when you left the house. He couldn't make out what it was. He was taking a walk—walking his dog. It was about two o'clock, he says. You went out of the house and around it toward the path that leads down to Shady Lane. Walking very fast, Mr. Combe says."

"Most of the time," Russ Ashby said, "I walk fast. Most of the time I take the path. I wasn't carrying anything. Sid's wrong about that."

"Better show him, Charley," Heimrich said, and Forniss went out the door. He came back almost at once. He carried a stick of firewood—a stick about three feet long and a little over two inches in diameter; a stick like a club. "Found it halfway down the path," Heimrich said. "To where you parked your car in the lane. And—there's blood on this, Mr. Ashby. Not a lot. Didn't bleed much, Mr. Bailey

332

didn't. But—enough."

"I don't know anything about it," Ashby said. "You claim this was what I was carrying? You claim it's got my prints on it?

"Now, Mr. Ashby," Heimrich said. "Rough wood. Wouldn't take prints worth anything, naturally. It was used to force the window. The way you and the other kids forced the other window. Then—to kill Mr. Bailey." Heimrich paused.

"Mr. Combe says his father-in-law had about a thousand dollars in the desk drawer. Says he kept it there as—as a kind of petty cash. Mr. Combe's term for it."

He watched. For a moment neither of the Ashbys spoke. Then—slowly, as if so simple a movement were incredibly difficult—Jane Ashby brought her hands from her eyes. Heimrich could see no expression in her eyes.

"He loaned it to us," she said, in a voice which was blank like her eyes. "Show them, Russ."

Russell Ashby looked at her for a long moment. Then he showed them. Heimrich took the crisp bills out of Ashby's billfold, riffled them, put them back, then put the billfold in his own pocket.

"We'll give you a receipt for this, Mr. Ashby," Heimrich said. "At the station house."

They left Jane Ashby then—left her sitting in a chair, with her face buried in her hands again, her slender body shaking again. "I'll be back," Russell Ashby said, and she did not seem to hear him.

That was about five o'clock. At a quarter after seven, Heimrich went into the taproom of the Maples Inn, on the main street of East Belford, and ordered a before-dinner drink. He sipped the drink and thought of murder—and of the tall young man at the police station, still denying murder. A stubborn young fool, Russell Ashby was, to deny what was so obvious.

Heimrich sighed. He thought of Ashby's dark-haired wife—was she still sitting so, with hands hiding her face, shutting out a world which had crumbled? There was no good in thinking of that.

He thought, instead, of Margaret Combe, who had gone through a bright afternoon to invite her father over for tea. If it was necessary to think of such things, think of *her* white face, *her* blank eyes. With nobody better, stronger, than Sidney Combe to stand with her.

Combe, the country squire—Ashby had called him that, bitterly, but, Heimrich thought, with reason. Tweeds and walking stick and dog on rawhide leash—and with the seven forty-three to catch five mornings a week to a job in town which wasn't much more than a clerk's job. Well, Combe wouldn't have to go back from this two-week vacation. He could spend the rest of his life walking his dog. He—

Heimrich, who had been looking at nothing, found he was looking at another cat. This cat was yellow. Another tom, from the shape of the forelegs—a big yellow cat standing in the doorway of the taproom and looking at Heimrich, and looking away again. I don't, Heimrich thought, seem to interest cats. The cat came into the taproom and began to sniff the floor. Two cats in one day, sniffing intricate patterns around a floor. Yellow cat and black cat, both searching. Yellow cat and—

"Marty," Heimrich said, through the service window of the bar, "what's he doing that for?"

The bartender looked at the cat.

"Smells something," Marty said. "Mrs. Latham's peke, most likely. Brought it in with her, while back. If he bothers you—"

"Not me," Heimrich said, and watched the cat's systematic sniffing of the floor, watched the yellow cat follow the scent where the little dog had gone. "Does he smell around after people?" Heimrich asked, and Marty shook his head. He said that cats don't care much how people smell. Only other cats, and dogs—

"You don't want dinner?" Marty said, because Heimrich stood up abruptly.

"Not now," Heimrich said, and went to his car, and drove toward the old Bailey house a few miles out of East Belford—toward the house, and a white-faced woman and a rather strutting man, who wouldn't have to catch the seven forty-three anymore, now that his wife had inherited a few million dollars; toward a man who would be free, now, to walk his boxer on a leash any day he chose—and to take him along on leash when he went to call on people. Toward a man, at any rate, who had planned on that freedom, and might have got it but for a cat who followed a dog's scent around a room. A persistent cat, following a scent.

"I've come to have a look at that walking stick of yours," Heimrich told Sidney Combe, at the door of the old house—told a tweedy Sidney Combe, with his boxer sitting behind him, attentive, in the hall. Combe merely looked at Heimrich. "To see if there are blood traces on it," Heimrich said. "Hard to get blood off things, the lab boys tell me—"

Combe was a fool—but a frightened man maybe—to try to slam the door on Heimrich. Heimrich had a foot in it.

"Now, Mr. Combe," Heimrich said. "That's no good. Where would you go? Your mind was working better earlier. When you smeared a little of Mr. Bailey's blood on the club, for example. And planted it on the path. When you took advantage of the fact that Ashby went around for a loan, and you saw him. When you tried to make it all look like a robbery, because Ashby broke into a place when he was a kid. Disappointed not to find the money, Mr. Combe? Mr. Bailey had given it to Ashby. But that worked out all right, too, or looked like working—"

Combe gave up trying to close the door. He said he didn't know what

Heimrich was talking about.

"Now, Mr. Combe," Heimrich said. "A black cat, among other things. Cats can't testify, naturally. But I watched the cat and—I can testify, you know."

Combe really didn't know what Heimrich was talking about, then. Heimrich told him, later, about the cat—told him after he had got the East Belford substation on the telephone and said to let Russell Ashby go and come pick Sidney Combe up. Heimrich followed the police car which had Combe in it only as far as the Maples Inn. He stopped off there to finish his dinner. He started into the taproom but stopped at the door.

Russell and Jane Ashby were sitting at a corner table, with food in front of them, and no great interest in food. They were looking at each other as if, to the other, each was new. They wouldn't want to see him, Heimrich thought. They had each other to look at—and a whole future to talk about.

A future, Heimrich thought, that a past might have ruined, but fortunately had not. Thanks, in large part, to a dead man's cat—inquisitive, as cats are notoriously. And, Heimrich thought, as policemen have need to be, however obvious the truth seems.

Lillian de la Torre

THE HIGHWAYMAN'S HOSTAGE

A Story of the Detector's Cat
(as told by James Boswell)

A golden harvest moon was rising that evening when I donned my bloom-coloured breeches and my gold-laced three-cornered hat and set forth to pay my devoirs to my philosophical friend Dr. Sam: Johnson, detector of crime and chicane, at his lodgings in Waterfield Square. There I found Frank, his dark domestick, lounging by the doorpost.

"Is Dr. Johnson within?" said I. Frank was looking sour. "He is, sir. You will find him in the kitchen," (wryly adding) "opening oysters." Curious to see the great philosopher at such a labour of Hercules, thither I hastened. There I found him, sure enough, hunkered down on his massive hams, opening oysters with a rusty knife.

As fast as he released a bivalve, he offered it to a large tiger-striped grey tomcat, whose little pink mouth quickly made away with it. There sat the tomcat, erect as a grenadier, accepting his meed of oysters with stately condescension.

"That's a fine cat, sir," I remarked. "Oh," said Dr. Johnson carelessly, "I have had much finer cats than this one." Then, as if perceiving that the creature was put about by so cavalier a dismissal, he added hastily, "But Hodge is a fine cat, Hodge is a very fine cat."

He regarded his pet with that smile of benevolence that always softened the harsh lines of his rugged face, with its scars of the king's evil, and let the warm good will of the sage shine through, drawing to him man and cat alike.

Rising from among his oyster shells, with his own grave stately courtesy, he made me welcome.

"You come in good time, Bozzy. Do but stay and take a dish of tea with me and I will make you acquainted with the prettiest young lady in London."

"With all my heart, sir. How comes it that you have acquired so valuable an acquaintance?"

"Easily. You must know, sir, that my humble lodgings lie jig-by-jowl with the town house of his Majesty's judge. My Lord Stanfield."

"Stanfield, eh?" said I. "It is all the talk among the benchers that within the week Stanfield will have Natty Jack in the dock and must sentence him to the gallows."

"A notorious highwayman!" said Dr. Johnson. "Stanfield will not spare him."

"Speaking of Stanfield," said I, "here he comes now."

I had glimpsed the judge's party approaching. To a frequenter of the criminal courts, the judge's hawk's profile was unmistakeable, and his women-folk proved their quality by their fashionable attire. Hastily polishing up at the scullery tap, we soon were making them welcome in the above-stairs withdrawing room.

Dr. Johnson had not exaggerated. Miss Bess was the daintiest little porcelain figurine it had been my good fortune to encounter in many a year. Long black lashes shadowed a pair of melting violet eyes. And little white teeth smiled from the shapely red mouth like snow-flakes in the heart of a rose. She bore in the crook of her arm a little creature as dainty as herself, a snow-white cat, with sea-blue eyes, which she set down at her feet, saying, "I present my friend, Powder Puff."

"Bess!" said Lady Stanfield sharply, glaring at Hodge. "Take up Powder Puff, we are among rakes!"

Across the room, Hodge had stiffened to attention, his green eyes intent upon Powder Puff. Powder Puff simpered and returned his gaze.

As I eyed Miss Bess, I felt a fellow feeling for the grey tomcat. With a cat's uncanny instinct for recognizing an unfriend to cats, Hodge now asserted himself.

He suddenly ascended my Lady's French silk stocking, planted himself on her purple-velvet lap, and fell to "kneading biscuits" with his sharp little claws on her fashionable knee. My Lady screamed and cast him from her, and the tea party broke up in confusion.

I watched them depart, my Lord handing Lady Jean, Miss Bess carrying Powder Puff.

The last I saw of the little cortege, passing homewards along the square, was the long grey tail, erect as a lance, of Hodge, escorting his new lady friend home.

Peace descended on Waterfield Square.

But not for long.

"Great heavens!" I cried suddenly. "What is that? A banshee?" "What, Bozzy," smiled Dr. Johnson, "have you never an amorous tomcat at Auchinleck?" "Yes, sir," I replied with a conscious grin, "but I don't yowl like that."

"Sir, it is no laughing matter," replied my moral mentor. "No, sir," I replied meekly. The yowling was broken off suddenly by a yip of pain. A moment later a frantic clawing shook the kitchen door, and Dr. Johnson hastened to open up. In shot Hodge, hackles bristling, tail distended, and flattened himself among the oyster shells under the kitchen table. A figure of wrath followed close upon him—the judge, brandishing his silver-shod staff in fury.

"Pray be seated, my Lord," said Dr. Johnson easily. "You honour my domestick offices with an informal visit. You will find the fireside settle not too uncomfortable." "Humph, that disturber of the peace is yours?" the judge countered, jerking his staff at Hodge, who flattened his ears and shewed his teeth.

"Yes, sir, what then?"

"Then I desire you'll keep him at home and away from my daughter's lapcat Powder Puff. He is making night hideous with his caterwaulering."

"I grant you that Hodge is no Italian soprano," said Dr. Johnson, "but consider, my Lord, the same passions inflame the hearts of beast and man. Hodge here is protesting his attachment to his fair inamorata in his own way, as it were in Shakespeare's own immortal words, 'Shall I compare thee to a summer's day?'"

"Twaddle!" snapped the judge. "Sir," said Johnson sternly, "the words of immortal Shakespeare are not twaddle." "Hodge's protestations are becoming a publick nuisance," snapped Judge Stanfield, "and I demand that they be put an end to." "They shall be so, my Lord," said my friend.

The episode ended with mutual courtesies and Hodge, deprived of his oyster, moping under the kitchen table.

Calling in Waterfield Square the next morning, I was shocked to receive bad news. Miss Bess had been stolen away out of her bed by ill-intentioned persons! They had taken her up in her blanket, together with Powder Puff, who slept in her arms. The town was abuzz with the news, and it soon transpired that the kidnappers were Natty Jack's robber crew.

I saw aghast the paper they had pinned to the judge's door:

BLOODY STANFIELD

If Natty Jack hangs, so will Miss Bess. Wee got her hid safe whare you ull never find her til shee is a swinging.

"BANDY-LEGGED BART"

"Natty Jack's second-in-command, another dangerous scoundrel," commented Dr. Johnson. "The Bow Street men have searched in vain every evil den in their vicinity. Miss Bess must be found and fast. Come, Boswell, we must hasten to the judge to offer our services."

We were admitted by the liveried butler with his long face even longer than ever.

In the withdrawing room, we found the judge and his Lady in anguished consultation. "If you condemn Natty Jack," milady was sobbing out, "then you condemn your own daughter!" "God help me," groaned my Lord, "I can do no otherwise." "Alack, what are we to do?" cried Lady Jean.

"Be patient, milady, the law will protect her," I said in a vain attempt to console. "How can they protect her," said milady angrily, "when they can not even find her?"

"I'll send to Auchinleck for the cleverest couple of hounds on the estate and we will soon have her back," I cried. "Good of you, Boswell," said the judge without hope.

"She shall be found, milady, I pledge you my word on it," said Dr. Johnson. "Come, Boswell, there is no time to lose." He made a leg and we betook ourselves homeward. There we found Hodge still moping under the table.

Instructed by fast courier, my factor sent the dogs up by waggon—Flasher and Dasher, my smartest couple. The cart rattled up to Dr. Johnson's door as the sun was setting.

"Huzzah!" I cried. "The hounds are here."

"Hounds!" snorted Dr. Johnson. "What use are hounds?"

"You shall see, sir," I replied. "I'll fetch them from the cart." I opened the door. In a flash, Hodge was out and away.

"So," smiled Dr. Johnson, "the feline gets the start of the canine."

"Not by much," I smiled back, seizing my pair's sturdy leathern lead and steering a course for the mansion next door.

My heart was wrung as the judge put into my hand the tiny red-satin slipper. So small to be in such peril! Flasher and Dasher took in the new scent.

They barked all around the square, and then fell to yapping on the judge's doorstep. An irate householder across the square thrust his head out at window, bawling: "Be off or I'll call the watch!"

Flasher and Dasher pulled me hither and thither about the square wherever the little red shoes had trod. They caught a scent that interested them. With a jerk that set me on my breech, they were off Hell-for-leather. Loose cobble and brickbats told their tale on my posterior as my involuntary steeds dragged me wildly down to the foot of Water Lane Hill. They had treed a cat.

Unfortunately for us, the cat was Hodge. Before the skirmish was over, he had wounded Dasher's nose, ripped out Flasher's ear, and landed with all four feet, claws unsheathed, on my best gold-laced hat.

Over the hysterical yelping of the dogs, from somewhere above our heads rang out Hodge's song of victory. The love-notes of a courting cat ascended to the harvest moon.

A bulky shape crossed my vision. Twas Dr. Sam: Johnson, and he took up a stand under the back wall of a disreputable-looking tumbled-down house of resort. I picked myself up and hastened to his side.

"Mr. Boswell, can you climb?"

I considered the house wall above me. "Yes, sir, I can. You observe the window embrasures are like a flight of stairs. I can climb them."

"Are you armed?" "I wear a sword." "Then climb. There is a rushlight burning in the topmost chamber. The sash-window is open a crack. Slip through, draw your sword, and stand guard over the sleeper."

I began to climb, feeling like a knight of old saving a princess in a tower. The ground looked alarmingly far below me. I hastily adverted my gaze, to where I caught sight of a dusky shape legging it across the square in the moonlight.

Above my head, Hodge's victory song soared. There he sat on the window ledge, peering intently through the pane. Fending off Hodge, I eased open the window and slipped through. There she lay asleep, on her rude pallet. She wore a shift of sheer French gauze embroidered with strawberries, not redder than the tight little crimson rosebuds that tipped her white bosom. So precious was my charge! I drew my sword and took up my post beside the chamber door.

From the attick descended a bandy-legged man. He carried a dagger. With a lunge, I shewed him the bare steel of my rapier edge, and put him to flight. At the stair foot, a door burst open and I heard the feet of the Bow Street men. Then pandemonium erupted—curses and the sound of blows. I started down the stair, sword in hand, just as the constables had the villains laid by the heels.

A burly Bow Street man—no, it was Dr. Sam: Johnson—emerged from the chamber carrying the girl and Powder Puff in his arms.

At the foot of the stair, Dr. Johnson eased himself and his burden into the curve of the entry-way sofa, supporting the slight form against his sturdy shoulder. Miss Bess opened wide violet eyes upon her rescuer.

"Oh, Dr. Johnson," she breathed, "they kept moving us, Powder Puff and me—for I never let loose my hold on Powder Puff—they kept moving us from hiding place to hiding place." "Where?" Dr. Johnson asked. "I know not, sir," she replied. "They kept me under. I think they gave me a sleepy draft. In all of London, how did you ever find us?"

"Why, my dear," said the great detector, "it was Hodge who found you. Once a tomcat has his lady's perfume stuck fast in his nostrils, you may depend upon it, love will found out the way." "How true," said I.

"Thus it fell out, my dear," went on Dr. Johnson, "that Hodge found out Powder Puff, and by his song told me where she was. Thus it fell out that Mr. Boswell mounted the wall to where you were and guarded you at sword's point."

"Dear Mr. Boswell," breathed Miss Bess tenderly.

"And," concluded Dr. Johnson, "when my messenger had informed the Bow Street men, they did the rest."

"Hodge is a good cat," said Miss Bess, reaching down and caressing the velvet ears.

"Hodge is a very good cat," said Dr. Johnson. "He shall hereinafter be known as the 'Detector Cat.' We'll have a neat sign set up in the square curiously lettered: 'Johnson and Hodge, Detectors.'"

"And what about me?" I asked.

"So, Mr. Boswell, you would join the firm—in what capacity?"

"Write it thus: 'J. Boswell, Rapparee.'"

"Pray, Dr. Johnson, you are our lexicographer. What is a rapparee?" asked Miss Bess.

"A bully-huff, who wields a rapier."

"And how valiantly," exclaimed Miss Bess, clasping her hands, and regarding me much as Powder Puff was regarding Hodge.

I took out my tablets and, at Natty Jack's fireside escritoire, I sketched in the new sign.

I thought it looked well—so well that I resolved to affix it to the kitchen door as soon as sunrise gave light for the operation.

I created the new sign on a shingle with fireplace charcoal. Hodge, inquisitive like every cat, supervised my proceeding. When I nailed the shingle above the kitchen door, the unwanted din brought Dr. Johnson down in his shirtsleeves to see what was toward.

We were drinking our breakfast tea at the kitchen table, and Hodge was lapping his milk under it, when a thunderous rapping at the kitchen door broke the morning calm.

I hastened to open the door. Instantly Hodge scooted under the table.

It was our neighbour the judge, in slippers and purple brocaded morning gown. He carried a large covered basket. Seating himself on the kitchen doorstep, he uncovered his basket and fell to opening oysters. Allured by the rich fishy aroma, Hodge warily edged towards it, and a morsel of oyster in the judge's hand quickly won him over.

As man and cat sat amicably on the kitchen doorstep sharing oysters, the party-gate creaked and an apparition appeared, wearing a pink dimity pinafore over her dainty white ruffles. She seated herself beside Hodge and began to ply him with morsels of oyster as fast as her father pried them loose.

"A pretty sight," said Dr. Johnson, appearing beside me. He bent his warmest smile of loving kindness upon the group: the judge in his purple, his beautiful daughter rosy as the dawn, and handsome Hodge between them in amity.

And over all my sign:

JOHNSON & HODGE
DETECTORS

J. Boswell, Rapparee

Author's Note: It was inevitable that Dr. Sam: Johnson's favorite cat, Hodge, should play a part in his master's detections. This is his story.

Many people have made this story possible, and I thank them with a full heart.

To my nephew, Dr. José de la Torre-Bueno, I owe the concept of cat psychology that makes Hodge a "Detector Cat."

To my brother Theodore de la Torre-Bueno and his wife Evelyn and their fine cats Tuxedo and Leon, I owe the cat lore that rounds out Hodge's story.

I am indebted to my dear friend Jackie Bellmyer for all kinds of moral support, for her critical judgment, for her intimate knowledge of cats, and for putting together and typing a very patched-up manuscript.

To my valued long-time friend Vincent O'Brien, I owe my thanks for his knowledgeable criticism and much help and encouragement, and for reading Dr. Johnson onto tape with the most pungent sense of his character.

There are many other friends who gave me help and encouragement. To each and all I say, "Thank you, good friends."

Patricia Highsmith

MING'S BIGGEST PREY

Ming was resting comfortably on the foot of his mistress's bunk, when the man picked him up by the back of the neck, stuck him out on the deck and closed the cabin door. Ming's blue eyes widened in shock and brief anger, then nearly closed again because of the brilliant sunlight. It was not the first time Ming had been thrust out of the cabin rudely, and Ming realized that the man did it when his mistress, Elaine, was not looking.

The sailboat now offered no shelter from the sun, but Ming was not yet too warm. He leapt easily to the cabin roof and stepped on to the coil of rope just behind the mast. Ming liked the rope coil as a couch, because he could see everything from the height, the cup shape of the rope protected him from strong breezes, and also minimized the swaying and sudden changes of angle of the *White Lark*, since it was more or less the centre point. But just now the sail had been taken down, because Elaine and the man had eaten lunch, and often they had a siesta afterward, during which time, Ming knew, that man didn't like him in the cabin. Lunchtime was all right. In fact, Ming had just lunched on delicious grilled fish and a bit of lobster. Now, lying in a relaxed curve on the coil of rope, Ming opened his mouth in a great yawn, then with his slant eyes almost closed against the strong sunlight, gazed at the beige hills and the white and pink houses and hotels that circled the bay of Acapulco. Between the *White Lark* and the shore where people plashed inaudibly, the sun twinkled on the water's surface like thousands of tiny electric lights going on and off. A water-skier went by, skimming up white spray behind him. Such activity! Ming half dozed, feeling the heat of the sun sink into his fur. Ming was from New York, and he considered Acapulco a great improvement over his environment in the first weeks of his life. He remembered a sunless box with straw on the bottom, three or four other kittens in with him, and a window behind which giant forms paused for a few moments, tried to catch his attention by tapping, then passed on. He did not remember his mother at all. One day a young woman who smelled of something pleasant came into the place and

343

took him away—away from the ugly, frightening smell of dogs, of medicine and parrot dung. Then they went on what Ming now knew was an aeroplane. He was quite used to aeroplanes now and rather liked them. On aeroplanes he sat on Elaine's lap, or slept on her lap, and there were always titbits to eat if he was hungry.

Elaine spent much of the day in a shop in Acapulco, where dresses and slacks and bathing suits hung on all the walls. This place smelled clean and fresh, there were flowers in pots and in boxes out front, and the floor was of cool blue and white tiles. Ming had perfect freedom to wander out into the patio behind the shop, or to sleep in his basket in a corner. There was more sunlight in front of the shop, but mischievous boys often tried to grab him if he sat in front, and Ming could never relax there.

Ming liked best lying in the sun with his mistress on one of the long canvas chairs on their terrace at home. What Ming did not like were the people she sometimes invited to their house, people who spent the night, people by the score who stayed up very late eating and drinking, playing the gramophone or the piano—people who separated him from Elaine. People who stepped on his toes, people who sometimes picked him up from behind before he could do anything about it, so that he had to squirm and fight to get free, people who stroked him roughly, people who closed a door somewhere, locking him in. *People!* Ming detested people. In all the world, he liked only Elaine. Elaine loved him and understood him.

Especially this man called Teddie Ming detested now. Teddie was around all the time lately. Ming did not like the way Teddie looked at him, when Elaine was not watching. And sometimes Teddie, when Elaine was not near, muttered something which Ming knew was a threat. Or a command to leave the room. Ming took it calmly. Dignity was to be preserved. Besides, wasn't his mistress on his side? The man was the intruder. When Elaine was watching, the man sometimes pretended a fondness for him, but Ming always moved gracefully but unmistakably in another direction.

Ming's nap was interrupted by the sound of the cabin door opening. He heard Elaine and the man laughing and talking. The big red-orange sun was near the horizon.

"Ming!" Elaine came over to him. "Aren't you getting *cooked*, darling? I thought you were *in!*"

"So did I!" said Teddie.

Ming purred as he always did when he awakened. She picked him up gently, cradled him in her arms, and took him below into the suddenly cool shade of the cabin. She was talking to the man, and not in a gentle tone. She set Ming down in front of his dish of water, and though he was not thirsty, he drank a little to please her. Ming did feel addled by the heat, and he staggered a little.

Elaine took a wet towel and wiped Ming's face, his ears and his four paws. Then she laid him gently on the bunk that smelled of Elaine's perfume but also of the man whom Ming detested.

Now his mistress and the man were quarrelling, Ming could tell from the tone. Elaine was staying with Ming, sitting on the edge of the bunk. Ming at last heard the splash that meant Teddie had dived into the water. Ming hoped he stayed there, hoped he drowned, hoped he never came back. Elaine wet a bathtowel in the aluminum sink, wrung it out, spread it on the bunk, and lifted Ming on to it. She brought water, and now Ming was thirsty, and drank. She left him to sleep again while she washed and put away the dishes. These were comfortable sounds that Ming liked to hear.

But soon there was another *plash* and *plop*, Teddie's wet feet on the deck, and Ming was awake again.

The tone of quarrelling recommenced. Elaine went up the few steps on to the deck. Ming, tense but with his chin still resting on the moist bathtowel, kept his eyes on the cabin door. It was Teddie's feet that he heard descending. Ming lifted his head slightly, aware that there was no exit behind him, that he was trapped in the cabin. The man paused with a towel in his hands, staring at Ming.

Ming relaxed completely, as he might do preparatory to a yawn, and this caused his eyes to cross. Ming then let his tongue slide a little way out of his mouth. The man started to say something, looked as if he wanted to hurl the wadded towel at Ming, but he wavered, whatever he had been going to say never got out of his mouth, and he threw the towel in the sink, then bent to wash his face. It was not the first time Ming had let his tongue slide out at Teddie. Lots of people laughed when Ming did this, if they were people at a party, for instance, and Ming rather enjoyed that. But Ming sensed that Teddie took it as a hostile gesture of some kind, which was why Ming did it deliberately to Teddie, whereas among other people, it was often an accident when Ming's tongue slid out.

The quarrelling continued. Elaine made coffee. Ming began to feel better, and went on deck again, because the sun had now set. Elaine had started the motor, and they were gliding slowly towards the shore. Ming caught the song of birds, the odd screams, like shrill phrases, of certain birds that cried only at sunset. Ming looked forward to the adobe house on the cliff that was his and his mistress's home. He knew that the reason she did not leave him at home (where he would have been more comfortable) when she went on the boat was because she was afraid that people might trap him, even kill him. Ming understood. People had tried to grab him from almost under Elaine's eyes. Once he had been suddenly hauled away in a cloth bag and, though fighting as hard as he could, he was not sure he would have been able to get out if Elaine had not hit the boy herself and grabbed the bag from him.

Ming had intended to jump up on the cabin roof again but, after glancing at it, he decided to save his strength, so he crouched on the warm, gently sloping deck with his feet tucked in, and gazed at the approaching shore. Now he could hear guitar music from the beach. The voices of his mistress and the man had come to a halt. For a few moments, the loudest sound was the *chug-chug-chug* of the boat's motor. Then Ming heard the man's bare feet climbing the cabin steps. Ming did not turn his head to look at him, but his ears twitched back a little, involuntarily. Ming looked at the water just the distance of a short leap in front of him and below him. Strangely, there was no sound from the man behind him. The hair on Ming's neck prickled, and Ming glanced over his right shoulder.

At that instant, the man bent forward and rushed at Ming with his arms outspread.

Ming was on his feet at once, darting straight towards the man, which was the only direction of safety on the rail-less deck, and the man swung his left arm and cuffed Ming in the chest. Ming went flying backward, claws scraping the deck, but his hind legs went over the edge. Ming clung with his front feet to the sleek wood which gave him little hold, while his hind legs worked to heave him up, worked at the side of the boat which sloped to Ming's disadvantage.

The man advanced to shove a foot against Ming's paws, but Elaine came up the cabin steps just then.

"What's happening? *Ming!*"

Ming's strong hind legs were getting him on to the deck little by little. The man had knelt as if to lend a hand. Elaine had fallen on to her knees also, and had Ming by the back of the neck now.

Ming relaxed, hunched on the deck. His tail was wet.

"He fell overboard!" Teddie said. "It's true, he's groggy. Just lurched over and fell when the boat gave a dip."

"It's the sun. Poor *Ming!*" Elaine held the cat against her breast, and carried him into the cabin. "Teddie—could you steer?"

The man came down into the cabin. Elaine had Ming on the bunk and was talking softly to him. Ming's heart was still beating fast. He was alert against the man at the wheel, even though Elaine was with him. Ming was aware that they had entered the little cove where they always went before getting off the boat.

Here were the friends and allies of Teddie, whom Ming detested by association, although these were merely Mexican boys. Two or three boys in shorts called "Señor Teddie!" and offered a hand to Elaine to climb on to the dock, took the rope attached to the front of the boat, offered to carry "*Ming! —Ming!*" Ming leapt on to the dock himself and crouched, waiting for Elaine, ready to dart away from any other hand that might reach for him. And there were several brown hands making a rush for him, so that Ming had to keep jumping aside. There were laughs, yelps, stomps of bare feet on wooden boards. But there was also the reassuring voice of

Elaine warning them off. Ming knew she was busy carrying off the plastic satchels, locking the cabin door. Teddie with the aid of one of the Mexican boys was stretching the canvas over the cabin now. And Elaine's sandalled feet were beside Ming. Ming followed her as she walked away. A boy took the things Elaine was carrying, then she picked Ming up.

They got into the big car without a roof that belonged to Teddie, and drove up the winding road towards Elaine's and Ming's house. One of the boys was driving. Now the tone in which Elaine and Teddie were speaking was calmer, softer. The man laughed. Ming sat tensely on his mistress's lap. He could feel her concern for him in the way she stroked him and touched the back of his neck. The man reached out to put his fingers on Ming's back, and Ming gave a low growl that rose and fell and rumbled deep in his throat.

"Well, well," said the man, pretending to be amused, and took his hand away.

Elaine's voice had stopped in the middle of something she was saying. Ming was tired, and wanted nothing more than to take a nap on the big bed at home. The bed was covered with a red and white striped blanket of thin wool.

Hardly had Ming thought of this, when he found himself in the cool, fragrant atmosphere of his own home, being lowered gently on to the bed with the soft woollen cover. His mistress kissed his cheek, and said something with the word hungry in it. Ming understood, at any rate. He was to tell her when he was hungry.

Ming dozed, and awakened at the sound of voices on the terrace a couple of yards away, past the open glass doors. Now it was dark. Ming could see one end of the table, and could tell from the quality of the light that there were candles on the table. Concha, the servant who slept in the house, was clearing the table. Ming heard her voice, then the voices of Elaine and the man. Ming smelled cigar smoke. Ming jumped to the floor and sat for a moment looking out of the door towards the terrace. He yawned, then arched his back and stretched, and limbered up his muscles by digging his claws into the thick straw carpet. Then he slipped out to the right of the terrace and glided silently down the long stairway of broad stones to the garden below. The garden was like a jungle or a forest. Avocado trees and mango trees grew as high as the terrace itself, there were bougainvillaea against the wall, orchids in the trees, and magnolias and several camellias which Elaine had planted. Ming could hear birds twittering and stirring in their nests. Sometimes he climbed trees to get at their nests, but tonight he was not in the mood, though he was no longer tired. The voices of his mistress and the man disturbed him. His mistress was not a friend of the man's tonight, that was plain.

Concha was probably still in the kitchen, and Ming decided to go in and ask her for something to eat. Concha liked him. One maid who had not liked him had been dismissed by Elaine. Ming thought he fancied barbecued pork. That was what his mistress and the man had eaten tonight. The breeze blew fresh from the ocean, ruffling Ming's fur slightly. Ming felt completely recovered from the awful experience of nearly falling into the sea.

Now the terrace was empty of people. Ming went left, back into the bedroom, and was at once aware of the man's presence, though there was no light on and Ming could not see him. The man was standing by the dressing table, opening a box. Again involuntarily Ming gave a low growl which rose and fell, and Ming remained frozen in the position he had been in when he first became aware of the man, his right front paw extended for the next step. Now his ears were back, he was prepared to spring in any direction, although the man had not seen him.

"*Ssss-st!* Damn you!" the man said in a whisper. He stamped his foot, not very hard, to make the cat go away.

Ming did not move at all. Ming heard the soft rattle of the white necklace which belonged to his mistress. The man put it into his pocket, then moved to Ming's right, out of the door that went into the big living-room. Ming now heard the clink of a bottle against glass, heard liquid being poured. Ming went through the same door and turned left towards the kitchen.

Here he miaowed, and was greeted by Elaine and Concha. Concha had her radio turned on to music.

"Fish?—Pork. He likes pork," Elaine said, speaking the odd form of words which she used with Concha.

Ming, without much difficulty, conveyed his preference for pork, and got it. He fell to with a good appetite. Concha was exclaiming "Ah-eee-ee!" as his mistress spoke with her, spoke at length. Then Concha bent to stroke him, and Ming put up with it, still looking down at his plate, until she left off and he could finish his meal. Then Elaine left the kitchen. Concha gave him some of the tinned milk, which he loved, in his now empty saucer, and Ming lapped this up. Then he rubbed himself against her bare leg by way of thanks and went out of the kitchen, made his way cautiously into the living-room en route to the bedroom. But now Elaine and the man were out on the terrace. Ming had just entered the bedroom, when he heard Elaine call:

"Ming? Where are you?"

Ming went to the terrace door and stopped, and sat on the threshold.

Elaine was sitting sideways at the end of the table, and the candlelight was bright on her long fair hair, on the white of her trousers. She slapped her thigh, and Ming jumped on to her lap.

The man said something in a low tone, something not nice.

Elaine replied something in the same tone. But she laughed a little.

Then the telephone rang.

Elaine put Ming down, and went into the living-room towards the telephone.

The man finished what was in his glass, muttered something at Ming, then set the glass on the table. He got up and tried to circle Ming, or to get him towards the edge of the terrace, Ming realized, and Ming also realized that the man was drunk—therefore moving slowly and a little clumsily. The terrace had a parapet about as high as the man's hips, but it was broken by grilles in three places, grilles with bars wide enough for Ming to pass through, though Ming never did, merely looked through the grilles sometimes. It was plain to Ming that the man wanted to drive him through one of the grilles, or grab him and toss him over the terrace parapet. There was nothing easier for Ming than to elude him. Then the man picked up a chair and swung it suddenly, catching Ming on the hip. That had been quick, and it hurt. Ming took the nearest exit, which was down the outside steps that led to the garden.

The man started down the steps after him. Without reflecting, Ming dashed back up the few steps he had come, keeping close to the wall which was in shadow. The man hadn't seen him, Ming knew. Ming leapt to the terrace parapet, sat down and licked a paw once to recover and collect himself. His heart beat fast as if he were in the middle of a fight. And hatred ran in his veins. Hatred burned his eyes as he crouched and listened to the man uncertainly climbing the steps below him. The man came into view.

Ming tensed himself for a jump, then jumped as hard as he could, landing with all four feet on the man's right arm near the shoulder. Ming clung to the cloth of the man's white jacket, but they were both falling. The man groaned. Ming hung on. Branches crackled. Ming could not tell up from down. Ming jumped off the man, became aware of direction and of the earth too late, and landed on his side. Almost at the same time, he heard the thud of the man hitting the ground, then of his body rolling a little way, then there was silence. Ming had to breathe fast with his mouth open until his chest stopped hurting. From the direction of the man, he could smell drink, cigar, and the sharp odour that meant fear. But the man was not moving.

Ming could now see quite well. There was even a bit of moonlight. Ming headed for the steps again, had to go a long way through the bush, over stones and sand, to where the steps began. Then he glided up and arrived once more upon the terrace.

Elaine was just coming on to the terrace.

"Teddie?" she called. Then she went back into the bedroom where she turned on a lamp. She went into the kitchen. Ming followed her. Concha had left the light on, but Concha was now in her own room, where the radio played.

Elaine opened the front door.

The man's car was still in the driveway, Ming saw. Now Ming's hip had begun to hurt, or now he had begun to notice it. It caused him to limp a little.

Elaine noticed this, touched his back, and asked him what was the matter. Ming only purred.

"Teddie?—Where are you?" Elaine called.

She took a torch and shone it down into the garden, down among the great trunks of the avocado trees, among the orchids and the lavender and pink blossoms of the bougainvillaeas. Ming, safe beside her on the terrace parapet, followed the beam of the torch with his eyes and purred with content. The man was not below here, but below and to the right. Elaine went to the terrace steps and carefully, because there was no rail here, only broad steps, pointed the beam of the light downward. Ming did not bother looking. He sat on the terrace where the steps began.

"Teddie!" she said. *"Teddie!"* Then she ran down the steps.

Ming still did not follow her. He heard her draw in her breath. Then she cried: *"Concha!"*

Elaine ran back up the steps.

Concha had come out of her room. Elaine spoke to Concha. Then Concha became excited. Elaine went to the telephone, and spoke for a short while, then she and Concha went down the steps together. Ming settled himself with his paws tucked under him on the terrace, which was still faintly warm from the day's sun. A car arrived. Elaine came up the steps, and went and opened the front door. Ming kept out of the way on the terrace, in a shadowy corner, as three or four strange men came out on the terrace and tramped down the steps. There was a great deal of talk below, noises of feet, breaking of bushes, and then the smell of all of them mounted the steps, the smell of tobacco, sweat, and the familiar smell of blood. The man's blood. Ming was pleased, as he was pleased when he killed a bird and created this smell of blood under his own teeth. This was big prey. Ming, unnoticed by any of the others, stood up to his full height as the group passed with the corpse, and inhaled the aroma of his victory with a lifted nose.

Then suddenly the house was empty. Everyone had gone, even Concha. Ming drank a little water from his bowl in the kitchen, then went to his mistress's bed, curled against the slope of the pillows, and fell fast asleep. He was awakened by the *rr-rr-r* of an unfamiliar car. Then the front door opened, and he recognized the step of Elaine and then Concha. Ming stayed where he was. Elaine and Concha talked softly for a few minutes. Then Elaine came into the bedroom. The lamp was still on. Ming watched her slowly open the box on her dressing table, and into it she let fall the white necklace that made a little clatter. Then she closed the box. She began to unbutton her shirt, but before she had finished, she flung herself on the bed and stroked Ming's head, lifted his left paw and pressed it gently so that the claws came forth.

"Oh, Ming—Ming," she said.

Ming recognized the tones of love.

Edgar Allan Poe

THE BLACK CAT

For the most wild, yet most homely, narrative which I am about to pen, I neither expect nor solicit belief. Mad indeed would I be to expect it, in a case where my very senses reject their own evidence. Yet, mad am I not—and very surely do I not dream. But tomorrow I die, and today I would unburthen my soul. My immediate purpose is to place before the world, plainly, succinctly, and without comment, a series of mere household events. In their consequences, these events have terrified—have tortured—have destroyed me. Yet I will not attempt to expound them. To me they have presented little but horror—to many they still seem less terrible than *barroques*. Hereafter, perhaps, some intellect may be found which will reduce my phantasm to the commonplace—some intellect more calm, more logical, and far less excitable than my own, which will perceive, in the circumstances I detail with awe, nothing more than an ordinary succession of very natural causes and effects.

From my infancy, I was noted for the docility and humanity of my disposition. My tenderness of heart was even so conspicuous as to make me the jest of my companions. I was especially fond of animals, and was indulged by my parents with a great variety of pets. With these I spent most of my time, and never was so happy as when feeding and caressing them. This peculiarity of character grew with my growth, and, in my manhood, I derived from it one of my principal sources of pleasure. To those who have cherished an affection for a faithful and sagacious dog, I need hardly be at the trouble of explaining the nature or the intensity of the gratification thus derivable. There is something in the unselfish and self-sacrificing love of a brute which goes directly to the heart of him who has had frequent occasion to test the paltry friendship and gossamer fidelity of mere man.

I married early, and was happy to find in my wife a disposition not uncongenial with my own. Observing my partiality for domestic pets, she lost no opportunity of procuring those of the most agreeable kind. We had birds, goldfish, a fine dog, rabbits, a small monkey, and a cat.

This latter was a remarkably large and beautiful animal, entirely black, and sagacious to an astonishing degree. In speaking of his intelligence, my wife, who at heart was not a little tinctured with superstition, made frequent allusion to the ancient popular notion which regarded all black cats as witches in disguise. Not that she was ever *serious* upon this point—and I mention the matter at all for no better reason than that it happens, just now, to be remembered.

Pluto—this was the cat's name—was my favorite pet and playmate. I alone fed him, and he attended me wherever I went about the house. It was even with difficulty that I could prevent him from following me through the streets.

Our friendship lasted in this manner for several years, during which my general temperament and character—through the instrumentality of the Fiend Intemperance—had (I blush to confess it) experienced a radical alteration for the worse. I grew, day by day, more moody, more irritable, more regardless of the feelings of others. I suffered myself to use intemperate language to my wife. At length, I even offered her personal violence. My pets, of course, were made to feel the change in my disposition. I not only neglected but ill-used them. For Pluto, however, I still retained sufficient regard to restrain me from maltreating him, as I made no scruple of maltreating the rabbits, the monkey, or even the dog, when by accident, or through affection, they came in my way. But my disease grew upon me—for what disease is like Alcohol!—and at length Pluto, who was now becoming old and consequently somewhat peevish, even Pluto began to experience the effects of my ill-temper.

One night, returning home much intoxicated from one of my haunts about town, I fancied that the cat avoided my presence. I seized him—when, in his fright at my violence, he inflicted a slight wound upon my hand with his teeth. The fury of a demon instantly possessed me. I knew myself no longer. My original soul seemed at once to take its flight from my body and a more than fiendish malevolence, gin-nurtured, thrilled every fiber of my frame. I took from my waistcoat pocket a pen-knife, opened it, grasped the poor beast by the throat, and deliberately cut one of its eyes from the socket! I blush, I burn, I shudder, while I pen the damnable atrocity.

When reason returned with the morning—when I had slept off the fumes of the night's debauch—I experienced a sentiment half of horror, half of remorse, for the crime of which I had been guilty. But it was, at best, a feeble and equivocal feeling, and the soul remained untouched. I again plunged into excess, and soon drowned in wine all memory of the deed.

In the meantime, the cat slowly recovered. The socket of the lost eye presented, it is true, a frightful appearance, but he no longer appeared to suffer any pain. He went about the house as usual, but, as might be expected, fled in extreme terror at my approach. I had so much of my old heart left as to be at first grieved by this evident dislike on the part of a creature which had once so loved me, but this feeling soon gave place to irritation. And then came, as if to my final and irrevocable overthrow, the spirit of perverseness.

Of this spirit, philosophy takes no account. Yet I am not more sure that my soul lives than I am that perverseness is one of the primitive impulses of the human heart—one of the indivisible primary faculties, or sentiments, which give direction to the character of man. Who has not, a hundred times, found himself committing a vile or a silly action for no other reason than because he knows he should *not*? Have we not a perpetual inclination, in the teeth of our last judgment, to violate that which is law merely because we understand it to be such?

This spirit of perverseness, I say, came to my final overthrow. It was this unfathomable longing of the soul to *vex itself*—to offer violence to its own nature, to do wrong for the wrong's sake only—that urged me to continue and finally to consummate the injury I had inflicted on the unoffending brute. One morning in cold blood, I slipped a noose about its neck and hung it to the limb of a tree— hung it with the tears streaming from my eyes and with the bitterest remorse at my heart, hung it *because* I knew that it had loved me and *because* I felt it had given me no reason of offense, hung it *because* I knew that in so doing I was committing a sin—a deadly sin that would so jeopardize my immortal soul as to place it, if such a thing were possible, even beyond the reach of the infinite mercy of the Most Merciful and Most Terrible God.

On the night of the day on which this cruel deed was done, I was aroused from sleep by the cry of fire. The curtains of my bed were in flames. The whole house was blazing. It was with great difficulty that my wife, a servant, and myself made our escape from the conflagration. The destruction was complete. My entire worldly wealth was swallowed up, and I resigned myself thenceforward to despair.

I am above the weakness of seeking to establish a sequence of cause and effect, between the disaster and the atrocity. But I am detailing a chain of facts and wish not to leave even a possible link imperfect.

On the day succeeding the fire, I visited the ruins. The walls, with one exception, had fallen in. This exception was found in a compartment wall, not very thick, which stood about the middle of the house, and against which had rested the head of my bed. The plastering had here, in great measure, resisted the action of the fire—a fact which I attributed to its having been recently spread.

About this wall a dense crowd had collected, and many persons seemed to be examining a particular portion of it with very minute and eager attention. The words "strange!" "singular!" and other similar expressions excited my curiosity. I approached and saw, as if graven in bas-relief upon the white surface, the figure of a gigantic cat. The impression was given with an accuracy truly marvelous.

There was a rope about the animal's neck.

When I first beheld this apparition—for I could scarcely regard it as less—my wonder and my terror were extreme. But at length reflection came to my aid. The cat, I remember, had been hung in a garden adjacent to the house. Upon the alarm of fire, this garden had been immediately filled by the crowd—and some one by whom the animal must have been cut from the tree and thrown through an open window into my chamber. This had probably been done with the view of arousing me from sleep. The falling of the other walls had compressed the victim of my cruelty into the substance of the freshly spread plaster, the lime of which with the flames, and the ammonia from the carcass, had then accomplished the portraiture as I saw it.

Although I thus readily accounted to my reason, if not altogether to my conscience, for the startling fact just detailed, it did not the less fail to make a deep impression upon my fancy. For months I could not rid myself of the phantasm of the cat, and during this period there came back into my spirit a half sentiment that seemed, but was not, remorse. I went so far as to regret the loss of the animal, and to look about me, among the vile haunts which I now habitually frequented, for another pet of the same species, and of somewhat similar appearance, with which to supply its place.

One night as I sat, half stupefied, in a den of more than infamy, my attention was suddenly drawn to some black object reposing upon the head of one of the immense hogsheads of gin, or of rum, which constituted the chief furniture of the apartment. I had been looking steadily at the top of this hogshead for some minutes, and what now caused me surprise was the fact that I had not sooner perceived the object thereupon. I approached it, and touched it with my hands.

It was a black cat—a very large one—fully as large as Pluto, and closely resembling him in every respect but one. Pluto had not a white hair upon any portion of his body, but this cat had a large although indefinite splotch of white covering nearly the whole region of the breast.

Upon my touching him, he immediately arose, purred loudly, rubbed against my hand, and appeared delighted with my notice. This, then, was the very creature of which I was in search. I at once offered to purchase it of the landlord, but this person made no claim to it—knew nothing of it—had never seen it before.

I continued my caresses, and when I prepared to go home the animal evinced a disposition to accompany me. I permitted it to do so, occasionally stopping and patting it as I proceeded. When it reached the house, it domesticated itself at once, and became immediately a great favorite with my wife.

For my own part, I soon found a dislike to it arising within me. This was just the reverse of what I had anticipated, but—I know not how or why it was—its evident fondness for me rather disgusted and annoyed.

By slow degrees, these feelings of disgust and annoyance rose into the bitterness of hatred. I avoided the creature, a certain sense of shame and the remembrance of my former deed of cruelty preventing me from physically abusing it. I did not, for some weeks, strike or otherwise violently ill-use it but gradually—very gradually—I came to look upon it with unutterable loathing, and to flee silently from its odious presence as from the breath of a pestilence.

What added, no doubt, to my hatred of the beast was the discovery, on the morning after I brought it home, that, like Pluto, it also had been deprived of one of its eyes. This circumstance, however, only endeared it to my wife, who, as I have already said, possessed in a high degree that humanity of feeling which had once been my distinguishing trait, and the source of many of my simplest and purest pleasures.

With my aversion to this cat, however, its partiality for myself seemed to increase. It followed my footsteps with a pertinacity which it would be difficult to make the reader comprehend. Whenever I sat, it would crouch beneath my chair or spring upon my knees, covering me with its loathsome caresses. If I arose to walk, it would get between my feet and thus nearly throw me down, or, fastening its long and sharp claws in my dress, clamber in this manner to my breast. At such times, although I longed to destroy it with a blow, I was yet withheld from so doing, partly by a memory of my former crime but chiefly—let me confess it at once—by absolute *dread* of the beast.

This dread was not exactly a dread of physical evil and yet I should be at a loss how otherwise to define it. I am almost ashamed to own—yes, even in this felon's cell, I am almost ashamed to own—that the terror and horror with which the animal inspired me had been heightened by one of the merest chimeras it would be possible to conceive.

My wife had called my attention, more than once, to the character of the mark of white hair, of which I have spoken, and which constituted the sole visible difference between the strange beast and the one I had destroyed. The reader will remember that this mark, although large, had been originally very indefinite. But by slow degrees—degrees almost imperceptible, and which for a long time my reason struggled to reject as fanciful—it had, at length, assumed the rigorous distinctness of outline. It was now the representation of an object that I shudder to name—and for this, above all, I loathed and dreaded and would have rid myself of the monster had I dared—it was now, I say, the image of a hideous, of a ghastly thing—of the gallows! Oh, mournful and terrible engine of Horror and of Crime—of Agony and of Death!

And now I was indeed wretched beyond the wretchedness of mere humanity. And a brute beast—whose fellow I had contemptuously destroyed—a brute beast to work out for *me*, a man fashioned in the image of the High God—so much of insufferable woe! Alas, neither by day nor by night knew I the blessing of rest any more! During the former, the creature left me no moment alone and in the latter I started, hourly, from dreams of unutterable fear to find the hot breath of *the thing* upon my face, and its vast weight—an incarnate Nightmare that I had no power to shake off—incumbent eternally upon my heart!

Beneath the pressure of torments such as these, the feeble remnant of the good within me succumbed. Evil thoughts became my sole intimates—the darkest and most evil of thoughts. The moodiness of my usual temper increased to hatred of all things and of all mankind while, for the sudden, frequent, and ungovernable outbursts of a fury to which I now blindly abandoned myself—my uncomplaining wife, alas, was the most usual and the most patient of sufferers.

One day she accompanied me, upon some household errand, into the cellar of the old building which our poverty compelled us to inhabit. The cat followed me down the steep stairs, and, nearly throwing me headlong, exasperated me to madness. Uplifting an axe, and forgetting in my wrath the childish dread which had hitherto stayed my hand, I aimed at the animal a blow, which, of course, would have proved instantly fatal had it descended as I wished. But this blow was arrested by the hand of my wife.

Goaded by the interference into a rage more than demoniacal, I withdrew my arm from her grasp and buried the axe in her brain. She fell dead upon the spot, without a groan.

This hideous murder accomplished, I set myself forthwith, and with entire deliberation, to the task of concealing the body. I knew that I could not remove it from the house, either by day or by night, without the risk of being observed by the neighbors. Many projects entered my mind. At one period I thought of cutting the corpse into minute fragments and destroying them by fire. At another, I resolved to dig a grave for it in the floor of the cellar. Again, I deliberated about casting it in the well in the yard and then about packing it in a box, as if merchandise, with the usual arrangements, and so getting a porter to take it from the house. Finally I hit upon what I considered a far better expedient than any of these. I determined to wall it up in the cellar—as the monks of the Middle Ages are recorded to have walled up their victims.

For a purpose such as this, the cellar was well adapted. Its walls were loosely constructed and had lately been plastered throughout with a rough plaster, which the dampness of the atmosphere had prevented from hardening. Moreover, in one of the walls was a projection caused by a false chimney or fireplace that had been filled up and made to resemble the rest of the cellar. I made no doubt that I could readily displace the bricks, insert the corpse, and wall the whole up as before so that no eye could detect anything suspicious.

And in this calculation I was not deceived. By means of a crowbar, I easily dislodged the bricks and, having carefully deposited the body against the inner wall, I propped it in that position while with little trouble I relaid the whole structure as it originally stood.

Having procured mortar, sand, and hair, with every possible precaution I prepared a plaster which could not be distinguished from the old—and with this I very carefully went over the new brickwork. When I had finished, I felt satisfied that all was right. The wall did not present the slightest appearance of having been disturbed. The rubbish on the floor was picked up with the minutest care. I looked around triumphantly and said to myself, Here at least, then, my labor has not been in vain.

My next step was to look for the beast which had been the cause of so much wretchedness—for I had, at length, firmly resolved to put it to death. Had I been able to meet with it at that moment, there could have been no doubt of its fate—but it appeared that the crafty animal had been alarmed at the violence of my previous anger and forbore to present itself in my present mood.

It is impossible to describe or to imagine the deep, the blissful sense of relief the absence of the detested creature occasioned in my bosom. It did not make its appearance during the night—and thus for one night, at least, since its introduction into the house I soundly and tranquilly slept. Aye, *slept*, even with the burden of murder upon my soul!

The second and third day passed, and still my tormentor came not. Once again I breathed as a free man. The monster, in terror, had fled the premises forever! I should behold it no more! My happiness was supreme! The guilt of my dark deed disturbed me but little. Some few inquiries had been made, but these had been readily answered. Even a search had been instituted—but, of course, nothing was to be discovered. I looked upon my future felicity as secured.

Upon the fourth day of the assassination, a party of the police came very unexpectedly into the house and proceeded again to make rigorous investigation of the premises. Secure, however, in the inscrutability of my place of concealment, I felt no embarrassment whatever. The officers bade me accompany them in their search. They left no nook or corner unexplored. At length, for the third or fourth time, they descended into the cellar. I quivered not in a muscle. My heart beat calmly as that of one who slumbers in innocence. I walked the cellar from end to end. I folded my arms upon my bosom and roamed easily to and fro. The police were thoroughly satisfied and prepared to depart. The glee at my heart was too strong to be restrained. I burned to say if but one word by way of triumph, and to render doubly sure their assurance of my guiltlessness.

"Gentlemen," I said at last, as the party ascended the steps, "I delight to have allayed your suspicions. I wish you all health and a little more courtesy. By the by, gentlemen, this is a very well constructed house." (In the rabid desire to say something easily, I scarcely knew what I uttered at all.) "I may say an *excellently* well constructed house. These walls—are you going, gentlemen?—these walls are solidly put together." And here, through the mere frenzy of bravado, I rapped heavily with a cane, which I held in my hand, upon that very portion of the brickwork behind which stood the corpse of the wife of my bosom.

But may God shield and deliver me from the fangs of the Arch Fiend, no sooner had the reverberation of my blows sunk into silence than I was answered by a voice from within the tomb—by a cry, at first muffled and broken, like the sobbing of a child, and then quickly swelling into one long, loud, and continuous scream, utterly anomalous and inhuman—a howl, a wailing shriek, half of horror and half of triumph, such as might have arisen only out of hell, conjointly from the throats of the damned in their agony and of the demons that exult in the damnation!

Of my own thoughts it is folly to speak. Swooning, I staggered to the opposite wall. For one instant, the party upon the stairs remained motionless through extremity of terror and of awe. In the next, a dozen stout arms were toiling at the wall. It fell bodily. The corpse, already greatly decayed and clotted with gore, stood erect before the eyes of the spectators. Upon its head, with red extended mouth and solitary eye of fire, sat the hideous beast whose craft had seduced me into murder, and whose informing voice had consigned me to the hangman! I had walled the monster up within the tomb!

Leslie Meier

CHOCOLATE

Peering anxiously around her apartment door, Minnie Mittelstadt checked the hallway to see if he was there. Since that last dreadful episode, she had decided to take no chances. If he was there, she would simply duck back into her apartment, lock and bolt the door, secure the safety chain, and wait until he was gone.

She had never been so frightened, and she was certain she was lucky to have escaped with her life. Living in the big city held plenty of terrors for a single, middle-aged woman, but Minnie had lived in the Bronx all her life and she wasn't about to leave her pleasant cooperative apartment in the attractive neighborhood known as Riverdale.

Minnie simply took reasonable precautions to guarantee her safety, as she was doing today. She read all the advice the newspapers thoughtfully provided for single women, and carefully followed their suggestions to thwart muggers and purse snatchers. She stayed alert, she remained aware of who was around her, she carried her purse close to her body, and she only carried the cash she absolutely needed. Charge cards, or large amounts of money, she tucked securely into a dress or skirt pocket.

Minnie didn't worry too much about being mugged; the small amount of money she usually carried could easily be replaced. The threat of violence, especially rape, was something else, however. Dear Mama had brought her up believing that a woman must save herself for marriage. She realized she had been saving herself for quite a while, as she was now retired from her job at a downtown department store, but she was determined to preserve that which was most precious to her.

Minnie never got in an elevator with a stranger, she never spoke to strange men on the street, and she always checked her peephole before opening the door. If she didn't recognize the delivery man or the telephone man, she asked him to hold up his identification, and then she called the company and checked before allowing him to enter her apartment. Minnie didn't believe in taking unnecessary risks. In fact, she never even went out after dark.

That's why it was so frustrating to have this situation taking place right in her own apartment house. However could the members of the cooperative association have voted to allow that dreadful man to move in, and with a dog no less?

Minnie enjoyed the fact that the cooperative allowed pets, as she was the proud owner of a beautiful Siamese cat. King Tut was every bit as regal as his name implied, and he ruled the household with a velvet brown paw. Like all Siamese cats, Tut was stunningly attractive, sporting eight lovely chocolate brown points; one nose, two ears, one tail and four paws. His tail curved in a question mark, his sapphire blue eyes were crossed, and he loved to talk. "Meeyowww," he would yowl when Minnie returned from a shopping trip, "Where have you been and what have you brought me? I was so lonely without you," he would complain, or so it seemed to Minnie.

Breathtakingly agile and graceful, Tut could jump to the top of the refrigerator in one perfect leap. He loved to sleep up there, soothed by the slight vibration of the motor. He also enjoyed sitting on the cushion Minnie had placed on the window sill, where he could watch people passing in the street. But most of all, he liked to nap in Minnie's lap while she watched TV. He always began by curling up in a neat ball, sleeping like a baby while she gently stroked his silky champagne-beige tummy. Then Tut's purr would rumble with pleasure, and Minnie would think what a lovely little boy he was.

That creature living across the hall, owned by that monster of a man, was something else entirely. Minnie didn't really see why the association allowed dogs. They were messy and unruly, they scratched the woodwork when they jumped frantically begging for walkies, and they were noisy. Yipping, barking, and whining, that awful animal across the hall kept up a constant racket that disturbed poor Tut. And, thought Minnie with a sniff, even the best-trained dog seemed inevitably to have an accident in the hallway sooner or later.

Unpleasant as they might be, Minnie was prepared to tolerate dogs in the building if their owners were responsible. But that was not the case in 3A across the hall, as the incident last week so clearly indicated.

Minnie had been minding her own business, waiting for the elevator, with one or two bits of clothing over her arm that she was taking to the dry cleaner. Suddenly, the door of 3A had been thrown open, and the hideous beast ran out, his nails clicking furiously against the tile floor. Growling and snarling, he jumped up and began pulling at the clothes she was holding on her arm. She tried to snatch them away, but the dog bared his teeth at her and began savaging the garments. Frightened, terrified in fact, Minnie dropped her favorite skirt and cowered in the corner as the ferocious animal ripped and shredded it to bits.

"What's going on here?" shouted a deep, masculine voice, and Minnie shrank even farther into the corner as the occupant of 3A charged down the hall. O'Connor was his name, and Minnie couldn't help noticing he had a bristly red mustache and very large teeth, just like his apricot miniature poodle.

"I'm so sorry," said O'Connor, hooking a leash onto the naughty dog's collar. "Please allow me to replace your clothes," he told a horrified Minnie. "This will never happen again, I promise you."

"It had better not," replied Minnie indignantly, as she scuttled down the hall to the safety of her apartment.

Since that awful day, Minnie had been living as if she were under siege. Residents of Beirut and Belfast probably took fewer precautions to guarantee their safety than Minnie did. And it was all because of him, and that dog.

When she came to think about it, as she frequently did, Minnie realized that dogs have a lot of the same unpleasant characteristics as those other threatening animals, men. Like men, dogs are noisy, unruly, and unpredictable. They often have gross and disgusting habits; dogs sniff at everything and lift their legs, men tend to spit in the street. They are both impulsive and overeager, unable to delay gratification. Their animal appetites must be satisfied immediately.

When she remembered her childhood, Minnie recalled the companionable relationship she had enjoyed with dear Mama. Mama had been an excellent housekeeper, and their apartment had always been neat as a pin, and spotlessly clean as well. Mama also practiced home economy, and took pride in carefully managing the household money. She and Minnie often had a salad, or an omelet, for dinner. Such a meal was simple to prepare, easy to clean up, and inexpensive, too.

All that would change, however, when Papa was home. He was a merchant seaman, and away for months at a time. But when he returned, the placid way of life she and her mother enjoyed was turned topsy-turvy. His boots would be thrown down carelessly in the hall, his pea jacket tossed over a chair, and the scent of cigar smoke would fill the air. No matter how they tried, she and Mama couldn't keep the house properly tidy when Papa was home.

There were no more tasty cheese and egg meals, either. Men had to have meat, as her mother explained. The stench of cooking fat would linger in the kitchen, and Minnie would have to wash the greasy, blood-smeared plates and platters. The heavy meals would turn her stomach, but Papa loved his meat and potatoes. He also liked a bit of whiskey now and again, and would smack his lips in pleasure as he sipped the amber liquid. Often when Papa drank whiskey of an evening, Minnie would later hear strange bumps and moans coming from the room he shared with dear Mama. Minnie suspected it was a bit of a relief to Mama when Papa's ship sank off the coast of Greenland in an icy winter storm, taking all hands down with it. Poor Papa, Mama would often sigh, stepping back to admire a cushion she had just fluffed or a picture she had straightened.

It was a few days later that Minnie found the answer to her problem. She had just settled down on the couch with a cup of tea, anticipating a peaceful hour with *Better Living* magazine. Tut leaped gracefully up beside her, lowering his rear legs but holding his head and chest upright and occasionally twitching his tail. He watched attentively as she turned the pages, almost as if he could read.

Leafing through the magazine, Minnie was amused to see the cat examine each page intently. She was startled when he suddenly yowled and put his paw on a page, and she was amazed to see the title of the story. "CHOCOLATE," it said in large letters, and just below were the words, "The deadly treat for dogs."

As she read, Minnie was astonished to learn that eating even a small amount of chocolate can cause a severe reaction in a small dog. The most dangerous, the article informed her, was baking chocolate. As little as one half ounce of baking chocolate could be life-threatening to a small dog, such as a miniature poodle, thanks to the theobromine it contained.

In addition, she was interested to read, dogs are not very discriminating eaters and will apparently wolf down large amounts of chocolate. Even more interestingly, the symptoms might not appear for several hours, she learned.

"Aren't you the clever boy," Minnie told Tut. Tut remained quiet, but narrowed his eyes, and lifted his chin so Minnie could stroke it. As she ran her fingers back and forth under his chin, Minnie would have sworn Tut smiled.

Giving O'Connor's dog the fatal dose turned out to be easier than Minnie imagined. Meeting them in the hall one day, she listened patiently while O'Connor again offered his apologies and tried to pay her for the skirt.

"It's absolutely all right," Minnie assured him. "Just to show there are no hard feelings, let me give the dog a treat. It's chocolate, is that all right?"

"Sure, he loves everything as long as he's not supposed to have it."

That gave Minnie a bit of a start, but O'Connor didn't seem to mean anything by his comment, so she bravely offered the dog a square of baking chocolate. He seemed to enjoy it, and wagged his tail in thanks. Next time she saw O'Connor in the hallway, the dog wasn't with him.

"Where's your doggie?" she asked.

"He's dead. Darnedest thing. Just had a seizure and that was it. Too bad."

"What a shame," commiserated Minnie.

"Actually, he was getting on, and I wasn't all that fond of him. He was my wife's dog and when we got divorced and she went to California, she left him with me. I always felt a little silly walking him," confessed O'Connor.

"Really?" Minnie smiled politely.

"Yeah. So I got another dog, a real man's dog."

"Oh?"

"Wanna meet him? Hold on just a sec and I'll get him."

Minnie pushed the button for the elevator and prepared to wait. Hearing O'Connor's door open, she turned. A huge brown-and-black hound hurtled down the hall towards her, pulling O'Connor behind him. Even though the dog was leashed, the man could just barely control it.

"This is Brutus," panted O'Connor. "He's a Rottweiler. A real man's dog."

"He's certainly very large—I mean handsome," stammered a horrified Minnie, as the elevator doors slid open. "I just remembered, I forgot something in my apartment. Goodbye."

Employing great self-control, Minnie walked back down the hall. Her hands were shaking so that she had quite a struggle with the locks, but she finally gained the safety of her apartment. Once inside, she ran directly to the coffee table, and began scrabbling through the magazines, finally locating the article. Running her trembling finger down the chart so thoughtfully provided by the author, she found the listing for very large dogs, dogs weighing over seventy-five pounds.

"Oh, Tut," she wailed. "How will I ever get that dog to eat ten jumbo candy bars?"

James Holding

A VISITOR TO MOMBASA

Sergeant Harper of the Mombasa Police was daydreaming about Rebecca Conway when his telephone rang. He reached a long arm for the instrument on his desk. "Yes?"

"Constable Jenkins here, sir. Waterfront Detail."

"What is it, Jenkins?"

"I've got a queer one, sir. Probably nothing in it, but I thought I ought to report it." Jenkins was new to the job and anxious to play everything safe.

"What is it?" Harper repeated.

"Man named Crosby, sir. Works near the end of the causeway, a night watchman. He claims he saw a leopard sneaking across the causeway into town last night. Or this morning, rather. Just before dawn."

"A leopard!" Harper's voice held surprise.

"Yes, sir." Jenkins waited respectfully for Harper's reaction

It came promptly. "Fellow was drunk," Harper said.

"I thought of that, sir." Jenkins sounded worried now, but continued. "Crosby admits to a couple of pints on the job during the night. But he swears he saw a leopard. Walking across the causeway from the mainland, bold as brass. He couldn't see the cat's spots, it was too dark, but he says he could see the shape all right for just a moment, and he's sure it was a leopard."

Harper said, "We've had no sighting reports this morning from anyone. Which we surely would have by now, if a leopard's on the loose. Anyway, thanks, Jenkins. I'll look into it." He hung up.

Harper leaned back in his desk chair. He damned the sticky heat of his cramped office and the gullibility of all police recruits. A leopard in Mombasa—he snorted. Tsavo, Nairobi and Amboseli Parks weren't far away, of course, but no, the hell with it. He went back to picturing the bright Scandinavian beauty of Lieutenant Conway's wife.

Ten minutes later, his telephone rang again. The constable on switchboard duty said, "A lady calling about a leopard, sir. Insists on speaking to someone in authority."

Harper groaned. "Put her on."

The lady, a Mrs. Massingale, reported seeing a creature she was sure was a leopard at daybreak that morning.

"Where?" Harper asked.

"Right here in Mombasa, Sergeant!" Mrs. Massingale said indignantly. "The least we could expect in this godforsaken city, it seems to me, is protection against wild animals wandering freely about the streets!"

"I meant," explained Harper with exaggerated patience, "just where in Mombasa did you see this leopard?"

"On the old railway line near Mbaraki Creek. Our cottage isn't fifty feet from the line. I happened to look out a rear window this morning at daybreak and there was this black shadow slinking along the ties. I caught its silhouette quite clearly for a moment. It was a leopard."

"Thanks for reporting it, Mrs. Massingale," Harper said. "I'll look into the matter promptly."

"See that you do!" She hung up with a muted crash that made Harper grin.

Two reports. So perhaps there *was* a leopard in Mombasa, unlikely as it seemed. Harper stood up, a tall, solidly built man with a heavy black moustache and an air of general frustration which he made no attempt to conceal.

The frustration was easily explained, even understandable, in a man of his type. He had come late to police work after a long career as a white hunter in Tanganyika before *uhuru*. Now, after being mildly famous in East Africa, he found himself all at once a lowly sergeant of police, reduced to obeying the orders of Lieutenant Conway, a stuffy man, ten years his junior, who was married, damn his eyes, to the most beautiful woman in Mombasa.

Harper stepped two paces from his desk to the city map taped on his office wall. A leopard reported on the causeway just before dawn—he put a fingertip on the map at the end of the causeway. A leopard reported on the railway line near Mbaraki Creek at daybreak—he touched the spot with another fingertip, and regarded the space between his fingertips narrowly. Yes, he decided, it's quite possible.

Suddenly he felt a surge of cheerfulness. Dealing with a leopard was work he knew. Still looking at the wall map, he tried consciously to put himself inside the spotted skin and the narrow skull of a leopard, to think as the cat might think, to forecast the movements of the killer he had come to know so well on a hundred safaris.

Suppose, he mused, the leopard was an accidental fugitive from one of the nearby game reserves. The unexpected sight of a long bridge, deserted and comfortably dark, might well have aroused enough feline curiosity in the leopard to make it venture out upon the causeway. Once there, a drift of scent across the water from dockside cattle pens, perhaps, may have drawn it on in quest of meat. Harper could picture vividly the silent cat, padding cautiously across the causeway, nostrils twitching with finicky distaste at the odors of diesel fuel and rotting refuse that vied with the cattle smell over Kilindini Harbor.

Having crossed the bridge, finding no direct route to the cattle scent that drew him, and suddenly surrounded by the strange effluvia of a large city, the leopard would rapidly become confused and frightened, Harper theorized. The beast's curiosity and hunger would be forgotten in an instinctive urge to find cover quickly in this unfamiliar terrain.

The cat, Harper felt, would therefore turn aside from the wide vulnerable expanse of Makupa Road into the comparative seclusion of the deserted railway line, stepping delicately along the ties through the industrial section of town to Mbaraki Creek, where Mrs. Massingale had caught a fleeting glimpse of him. Thence, it seemed obvious from the map, the leopard might be expected to come out on the bluffs overlooking the sea at Azania Drive, footsore now, apprehension growing as the daylight strengthened, the need for cover reaching panic proportions.

Azania Drive; Harper tried to recall the configuration of the land just there where the railway line bisected the Drive. It was a bleak and lonely stretch of the seaside road, as he remembered it, meandering along the bluffs past an ancient Arab watchtower and bearing little resemblance to the fashionable Azania Drive which also yielded a view of the sea to the Oceanic Hotel, the golf club, and scores of comfortable residences beyond. At that place on Azania Drive, above the ferry, a grove of baobab trees stood, defying the sea winds, Harper remembered.

He nodded to himself, utterly intent, thinking with a sense almost of excitement that the thick twisted foliage of those baobab trees just possibly might offer welcome sanctuary to a frightened leopard.

He turned his back to the map. His next step was clear. He should delegate Constable Gordon in the squad room to go at once and check out the baobab trees on Azania Drive for a stray leopard. Gordon would welcome the action, and he was an excellent shot, too, Harper knew. Yet, after the stimulating exercise of mentally plotting the leopard's probable whereabouts in Mombasa, Harper was reluctant to turn the hunt over to somebody else before he, himself, had even sighted the game. He needn't be in at the kill, he told himself. On safari, he had always turned the final shot over to his clients—he was used to that—but he *did* want to mark down the target with certainty before yielding the kill to another. Aside from his thus far unsuccessful campaign to make Rebecca Conway unfaithful to her pompous husband, this city leopard hunt was the most exciting thing that had happened to Harper since he joined the police force.

Yielding to temptation, he reached for his hat, took field glasses from the shelf under his wall map, and strode into the squad room. "Back in a few minutes, Gordon," he told the constable in passing. "Take over until Lieutenant Conway gets in, will you?" Conway never showed for duty until nine o'clock. Yet who could blame him, Harper thought enviously, with the voluptuous Rebecca to keep him at home until the last moment?

He felt the sweat start the moment he stepped out of headquarters into the compound. He climbed into one of the two police cars parked there, a Land Rover. As he turned out of the police compound and headed for Azania Drive, the sun had already warmed the driver's seat so that the cushions burned him, even through his trousers.

A hundred and fifty yards short of the baobab trees on Azania Drive, he stopped the Land Rover, parked it beside the road and walked slowly toward the trees. The field glasses hung on their strap about his neck. It was still only a little after eight. Traffic was very light on Azania Drive.

He waited until the road was empty both ways before he stepped from it onto the springy turf that ran like a shaggy carpet along the landward side of the road, solidly covering the acre of ground under the baobab grove. He walked carefully to within thirty yards of the trees, then stopped and brought the glasses up to his eyes and examined carefully the twisted branches and tangled foliage of the baobabs. He saw nothing that looked even remotely like a leopard.

After five minutes, he moved across the road, still well clear of the trees, and walked another fifty yards to a position from which he could comb the grove from a different angle. He swept the glasses slowly from tree to tree, conscious of growing disappointment as they failed to find what he sought.

The glasses were trained on the last of the trees—a gnarled giant closer to the road than its neighbors—when suddenly, with the sense of electrical shock that accompanies an unexpected explosion, he found himself gazing through the magnifying lenses at two merciless yellow eyes which seemed disembodied in the tree's sun-dappled shade.

He breathed an exclamation that was part admiration for the magnificent cat, whose savage stare transfixed him, part satisfaction at his own astuteness in locating the beast.

Carefully he marked the tree and the cat's position in it. Then he withdrew to his Land Rover and drove away, whistling softly to himself and thinking he should have brought a rifle with him when he left headquarters. Still, he hadn't really expected there was a chance in ten that he'd find the leopard in the grove of baobab trees, he justified himself.

All the same, the cat was there!

Harper felt like celebrating, all at once, his frustrations temporarily forgotten. He had brought off a surprising feat, really: tracking a wild leopard . . . mentally . . . through several miles of sprawling city to a specific lair. His mood was one of exhilaration.

This is what I am good at, he reflected, this is what I *was* meant to do—not piddling along at a stinking little police job in a dirty city, but working with wild animals, somehow, somewhere, in free, open country, tracking them down and killing them, or working to preserve them from extinction, no matter which, so long as the job was useful and, yes, dangerous. He'd made a horrible mistake when he gave up hunting animals for hunting men. If he could only convince Rebecca Conway to go with him, he'd leave Mombasa tomorrow for Nairobi, Uganda, Australia, India, Alaska—anywhere away from the imperious beck and call of Rebecca's impossible, intolerable husband.

He'd asked her a dozen times to leave the fool she was married to and join him in a new free life somewhere else; but Rebecca only smiled at his pleading, kissed him lightly on the check like a sister, called him an aging Lothario (at forty-one!) and quoted Shakespeare at him about preferring to bear those ills she had than fly to others that she knew not of. She was flattered by his passion for her, of course, yet she was too fond of her idle, easy life in Mombasa as Conway's wife to risk it lightly.

Harper decided to drive back to headquarters by way of the center of town. That would give him a little extra time to savor his success with the leopard; to anticipate the soon-to-come thrill of squeezing off the perfectly aimed shot that would rid Mombasa of its dangerous visitor in the baobab tree. Fifteen minutes delay in finishing off the leopard would make no difference to anyone, so far as he could see. The leopard was treed well off the road. It was still frightened, edgy, and hungrier than ever, no doubt, yet posed no threat, Harper knew, to passersby on Azania Drive unless someone approached its tree.

His memory played back to him one of the warnings he had always issued to hunters on safari: remember that a treed leopard, if hungry, frightened, or wounded, will usually attack anything that moves beneath it. So why would anyone approach that baobab tree? Harper was the only person in the city who could possibly have any interest in it.

The high crenellated battlements of Fort Jesus loomed on his left above the crimson blossoms of a flame tree as he passed the Mombasa Club. In the center of the turn-about, the bust of King George caught the morning sunlight and seemed to wink at Harper as he tooled the Land Rover around the circle and into Prince Arthur Street.

At police headquarters, he remembered to park his car in the compound off the street, even though he intended to use the Land Rover again at once, as soon as he secured a rifle from the gun case in his office. That was one of Lieutenant Conway's silly rules, if you like: that the curb before headquarters must be kept clear and free at all times, so that if the wooden building ever caught fire, there would be ample space for the fire-fighting apparatus to park there!

Thinking of Lieutenant Conway and, inevitably, of Rebecca, Harper's leopard-inspired high spirits drained rapidly away. The exhilaration of ten minutes ago had turned to creeping depression by the time he reached his office; the elation of winning a guessing game with a leopard lost its edge. If Rebecca refused him one more time, he swore to himself, he'd throw up this bloody job, anyway, and go off without her.

He unlocked his gun cabinet and took down one of his old rifles, unused since his last safari five years ago. As a special favor, Lieutenant Conway had allowed him to keep this personal weapon as an addition to the headquarter's arsenal. Harper was glad of it now.

He put ammunition into his pocket, relocked the gun cabinet, and was turning for the door when his telephone rang. Impatiently he paused by his desk, scooped up the receiver and said, "Yes?"

"Some fellow wants the lieutenant," the switchboard man said.

"Then give him the lieutenant," snapped Harper. "I'm busy."

"Lieutenant's not in yet, sir." The constable was apologetic.

Harper glanced at his watch. It was not yet nine o'clock. "Who's calling the lieutenant?"

"He won't say, sir. Says it's confidential and urgent. Native, I believe, and he speaks Swahili."

"Put him on."

The caller's voice was male, low-pitched, sounded very young. "Who is this?" it asked.

Harper said, "Sergeant Harper. Lieutenant Conway is not here. What do you want?"

"The reward, sir," the young voice whispered. "The reward offered by your lieutenant."

"What reward?"

"For arrow poison, sir. For the names of Wakamba doctors who make arrow poison against the new law."

"Oh." Harper remembered that Conway had been trying for six months to discover which of the Wakamba witch doctors were still manufacturing arrow poison, and thus contributing to massive native slaughter of the game in the reserves. The arrow poison of the Wakamba was made from tree sap; it smelled like licorice; it left a black discoloration in the wound; and it was capable of killing a bull elephant in fifteen minutes.

369

Harper said, "Have you earned the reward?"

"Yes, sir. I have two names for Lieutenant Conway. "

"Who are they? I'll tell the lieutenant."

"No names," the young Wakamba murmured, "until the reward is given. Not until then."

Harper grinned. "Don't trust us, is that it?"

The boy was silent.

"We'll give you the reward first, in that case. All right? What's *your* name?"

"I have no name," said the young voice very formally. "I am risking death to give the lieutenant this information, sir. My own people will kill me if they learn of it."

Harper tried it another way. "Where are you calling from?"

"The Golden Key."

Harper knew the Golden Key, a disreputable bar immediately across the Nyalla Bridge. Used to be called the Phantom Inn because natives would dress up in sheets and act the ghost to startle customers. "You a houseboy there?" he asked.

"No, sir."

Harper hefted his rifle, impatient to go after his leopard. "How can we arrange to give you the reward if you won't tell us who you are?"

"Very simple, sir. I will meet the lieutenant in private. He brings me the reward. I give him the names of the poison makers."

Harper considered for a moment. "Where do you want the lieutenant to meet you?"

"Where no Wakamba can see me talking to a policeman." Simple and clear.

"When?" asked Harper.

"Today, sir, please. This morning, if possible. I need the reward very badly, sir. Otherwise, of course . . ." His voice, touched with desperation now, trailed off.

"All right, then," Harper said. "*I'll* meet you and bring the reward, since the lieutenant isn't here just yet. How much were you promised?"

"Ten pounds, sir." Eagerness now. "That will be good. Where shall I meet you?"

The Wakamba boy's simple question seemed to echo and reecho in a strange pervasive way inside Harper's head, and the idea that was born in his mind at that instant seemed to make his heart shift position in his chest. He sank into his desk chair, clutching the rifle on the desk before him with one hand.

He took a deep breath and said, "You know the old Arab watchtower, boy? Below Azania Drive near the ferry?"

"Yes, sir."

"I'll meet you there in an hour. Or Lieutenant Conway will, if he comes here soon enough. You can make it in an hour, can't you?"

"Yes. But remember, please, I dare not be seen, sir. Azania Drive is very public. Is there no private place we can meet?"

"That's private enough." Harper was brusque. "Don't use Azania Drive to get there, come up the shore line on the beach under the bluffs. No one will see you. No one ever goes there, to the tower."

"Very well," said the soft boyish voice. "I'll be there, sir. One hour."

"Good," Harper said. His hand was sweating on the rifle stock. After he hung up, he dried his palms on the jacket of his uniform. He glanced again at his watch: 9:10. Conway was later than usual today.

He rose and put the rifle back in the wall cabinet. Then, pretending to be busy over a stack of reports, he sat quietly at his desk until he heard Lieutenant Conway's fussy voice in the squad room, greeting Constable Gordon as he passed through to his office.

Harper waited a moment or so before walking into Conway's room.

"Morning, Sergeant," Conway said briskly. "Something on your mind?"

Harper told him about the telephone call from the young Wakamba informer who wouldn't give his name. "Now you're here, sir," he finished matter-of-factly, "I expect you'll want to meet the boy and get his information yourself, since it's your pigeon, so to speak."

"Of course." Conway rubbed his hands together in a gesture of satisfaction that Harper found extremely irritating. He was exultant, his high voice almost a crow of pleasure as he went on. "So the clever lad, whoever he is, has a couple of witch doctors' names for me, does he? Quite a feather in our cap, Sergeant, if we can clear up this arrow-poison business at last, eh? Where am I supposed to meet him?"

Harper said quietly, "At the Arab watchtower below Azania Drive. It's private enough to quiet the boy's fears of being seen, I thought, yet within easy reach for us. You know it, of course?"

"Certainly I know it. An admirable choice, Sergeant. There and back in fifteen minutes without unduly wasting the taxpayers' time, eh? There's an old track down the bluff to the tower's base as I remember it."

"Right, sir. You can park by the grove of the baobab trees on Azania Drive and go straight through under the trees to the cliff edge, where the track goes down."

"I must remember to take the boy's money. What time did you tell him you'd be there?"

"As soon as I could. He seemed anxious to get it over with. He's been at considerable risk, he claims."

"I'll leave at once." Lieutenant Conway stood up. "Take charge here, Sergeant." He strutted from the room, calling loudly to the cashier outside to give him ten pounds at once.

That was at 9:20. At 10:15 the call came.

"A motorist on Azania Drive just called in, sir," the switchboard man said. "Says he saw a fellow lying under a tree up there, covered with blood, as he was driving past. Stopped to see if he could help. Got to within fifty feet of the man under the tree and saw he was dead, so he called us."

"Dead!" Harper kept his voice level. "How could he tell from fifty feet away?"

"No face left, sir," the switchboard man said, as though he were reporting a shortage of beer in the commissary icebox. "Bundle of bloody flesh and shredded clothes, the motorist says. As though the fellow'd been mauled by a leopard, maybe." The constable cleared his throat. "Any chance, sir, it could have been the leopard the lady reported earlier?"

"Possible," Harper said. "Where'd he telephone from?"

"The nearest house. He'll stand by until one of our chaps gets there, he says."

"Fine. Hope he has enough sense to keep people out from under that tree where the dead man is. Where is it on Azania Drive?"

"Near the old Arab watchtower. There's a grove of baobab trees just there . . ."

"Right," Harper said. "I'm on my way. Better take a rifle, I guess. Give any calls for me to Constable Gordon."

Surprisingly, when he reached the baobab grove and drew up behind Conway's parked car, there was no one in view nearby save for the motorist, a man named Stacy, who had telephoned headquarters. Greeting Harper's arrival with obvious relief, he said he'd managed to send curiosity seekers—only a handful so far—quickly about their business by telling them there was a wild leopard loose in the grove.

"Good work," grunted Harper, stepping from his car. As though drawn by magnets, his eyes went to the ghastly figure lying asprawl under the nearest tree. Then, in a voice that sounded shocked even to him, he said, "From the looks of that poor chap under the tree, I'd say you were right about the leopard, Mr. Stacy."

Stacy swallowed hard. "I was sick in the ditch when I saw it," he said. "Then I ran like hell and called you.

Harper nodded and reached into the back of the Land Rover for the rifle. "So let's see what we can do about it," he said. "Get across the road, away from the trees, will you, Mr. Stacy, and handle anybody else who may stop to gawk?"

Stacy was more than glad to withdraw across the road.

Harper knew where his target was. For Stacy's benefit however, he was forced to carry on a pretended search of the baobab tree. He moved to various vantage points, left and right of the tree, the rifle held ready. At length, he suddenly raised a hand to Stacy and nodded vigorously, as though he had at last located the cat.

As indeed he had. Even without the field glasses, he had no trouble zeroing in on those blazing eyes turned unblinkingly toward him; and even without the field glasses, he could see quite plainly the streaks and spatters of blood on the savage muzzle. Lieutenant Conway's blood, he told himself with grim satisfaction.

He brought up the gun, steadied his sights on the small target and squeezed off his shot.

Instantly, a squalling cyclone of spotted hide and sheathed claws fell out of the tree, crashing through the baobab foliage. At the crack of the shot, a widow bird rose from the top of a neighboring tree and flapped slowly away, trailing its long black feathers. Harper wondered if that was sign. When the leopard struck the ground, only a few feet from its mangled victim, it was quite dead.

"You got him!" yelled Stacy from across the road, his voice thin from excitement, "Bravo!"

Harper didn't take his eyes off the leopard, holding the gun ready for a second shot, although he was quite sure the first had done its work thoroughly. He was remembering another of his white-hunter maxims: never approach downed game until you are certain it is dead.

At length he was satisfied. He motioned to Stacy to stay where he was, and stepping carefully on the rough turf, made his way to the baobab tree and the still figures under it. A glance showed him the leopard was quite dead; a head shot of which he could be proud.

He turned, then, toward Lieutenant Conway's corpse, his brain suddenly busy with a variety of thoughts. He must not forget to give the Wakamba boy at the watchtower his reward and settle the arrow-poison business, now that Conway was gone. He must inform Rebecca Conway of her husband's tragic end and console her as best he could. Would he be promoted now to lieutenant, and thus be able to offer Rebecca a continuation of the privileged life she seemed to find so enchanting in Mombasa? Given time, he was sure he could persuade her to marry him—and now, he thought, smiling a little, he had lots of time.

He was wrong. He didn't even have time to raise his eyes to the tree branch above him, or to bring up the rifle, still held loosely in his hand. In the last split second of his life, before pitiless teeth and talons tore his throat out, Harper had time for but a single flash of realization: there had been a *pair* of leopards visiting Mombasa!

Jimmy Vines

BETWEEN A CAT AND A HARD PLACE

This morning, as every morning, Charlie Wainwright woke up sneezing. His swollen and irritated eyes felt like lumps of wet sand that were beginning to dry and harden around the edges. At breakfast he rubbed his itching arms and neck, and tried to taste his Cheerios.

"Now don't forget," his wife Gerta said impatiently, "today's Thursday, time for Slyboots's weekly checkup!"

She kissed the big cat's mouth, then wiped lipstick off its furry chin. "That's right, Slyboots," she said lovingly, "you're going to see nice Dr. Feemer today!" Gerta was a heavy woman of fifty-eight in a blue dress that was too tight in the bosom and too loose everywhere else. She poured the cat out of her arms gently and it nuzzled her puffy ankles. "The appointment's at one o'clock. Don't be late. I will call the vet to make sure you've been there!"

Charlie started to mumble the obligatory, "Yes, dear," around a mouthful of cereal, but a sneeze took the words and sprayed them across the table as globs of mash and milk.

Gerta slammed the door and waddled up the driveway to her car. She had a very busy schedule, forever hurrying between church functions, the bridge club, and local cultural events, so Charlie was always left to take care of her adorable little Slyboots.

The instant Gerta backed her car into the road, Charlie hurled his spoon at the cat. His aim was bad: the spoon whacked the refrigerator. Slyboots scurried away before Charlie could throw anything else. The cat might just as well have walked slowly—because for a whole minute Charlie was immobilized by a harsh sneezing fit.

Charlie was sixty-nine, and he'd had two heart attacks in recent years. A specialist had warned that a third heart attack or even a stroke was very likely, so Charlie took it easy and stayed on his diet and medication. Until fourteen months ago, in spite of his heart problem, things were going fine for Charlie; he'd planned on living a long quiet life.

The turning point came that fine spring day Gerta brought the cat home. Charlie hadn't objected at first, because he didn't think he was allergic to cats. Since he'd never owned a cat, and since friends' cats didn't bother him, the possibility of a latent allergy never crossed his mind. Yet as it happened, something about this cat made Charlie sneeze ceaselessly.

And the sneezing hadn't started the first day; it was only after a couple of weeks, once the house was thoroughly permeated with shedded cat hairs, that Charlie's sinuses awoke and began giving him fits. But by that time Gerta was so attached to her pet that she wouldn't give it up.

Charlie's specialist told him sneezing was bad on the heart, but Charlie already knew that. He felt his heart stammer every time he had a sneezing bout.

Reasoning with Gerta proved futile. She refused to believe that her dear, darling little Slyboots was to blame for Charlie's suffering. She blamed the sneezing on everything else: dust, pollen, the spray deodorant that he used. Gerta would not be coerced into giving the cat away.

But Charlie, out of extreme discomfort and fear for his weak heart, decided to take control of the situation. The cat had to go! One afternoon, after an especially tiresome and fruitless argument about the cat, Gerta left the house to attend one of her various social functions. She'd be gone a few hours, Charlie knew. He put Slyboots outdoors. There was plenty of time for the cat to wander off and never be heard from again. Charlie waited. And waited. And much to his chagrin, the fat feline stayed on the porch, howling the whole time. That evening, when Gerta's car bounced up the driveway, Charlie quickly let the cat back inside before his wife found out what he'd done.

About a week later, after another lost battle of words, when Gerta left the house, Charlie drove the cat to the outskirts of the neighborhood and remorselessly let it out of his car by a thick wooded lot. That night he told Gerta that when he was taking out the trash, Slyboots had slipped past him. He said he'd chased the cat across three neighbors' yards but that Slyboots was just too fast for him, what with his weak heart and all. Gerta scoffed at the story. She accused Charlie of being responsible for the cat's disappearance, and Charlie vehemently denied it. But the crowning hideous thing happened later in a dark hour past midnight: just like one of those famous pets in *Reader's Digest*, the cat somehow found its way home and woke a teary-eyed Gerta with its wailing at the back door.

Now the possibility that the cat might "run away" was exhausted. After all, what's better proof of a pet's loyalty than its return after a twelve-hour absence? Suddenly Charlie was faced with the one alternative by which to restore an equilibrium to his life: he had to kill the cat. The way Charlie saw it, if he didn't kill the cat, the cat would kill him.

Taking a cat's life should be simple. But to keep Gerta from divorcing him, and to avoid a lawsuit from the Animal Rights people, Charlie had to make the little murder look as though his furry tormentor died of natural causes. He couldn't leave a mangled corpse. He had to do this carefully.

At ten o'clock one morning, about to take a shower, Charlie reached inside the linen closet for a big fluffy towel. He hadn't seen the cat since breakfast, and in the meantime his sneezing and itching had subsided a little.

Charlie took a towel and started to close the folding doors when a red-brown blur sprang from the shadowy depths of the closet with a *Yowwwwl*, swiping Charlie's arm loathsomely and scampering away.

"Goddamnit!" Charlie bellowed. The cat disappeared down the hallway with a twitch of its tail. Charlie shook all over, realizing his towel was contaminated with cat hair. He flung the towel down to the floor and kicked it after the cat.

Control, he reminded himself. Must keep control. His heart lost its rhythm, and he leaned against the closet doors until danger passed.

Suppressing rage, Charlie grabbed a towel down deep in the stack, one that the cat couldn't possibly have touched. He sneezed violently, and had to pause for a long ten-count before proceeding to the shower.

Over the months, Charlie had thought of many different ways of killing the cat that would position him so that his own innocence could not be doubted. All the methods he devised, except one, were slightly flawed for one reason or another. The plan that he'd finally settled on seemed perfect, and he was now ready to carry it out.

Today was the day.

His plan involved the veterinarian, Nathan Feemer.

The veterinarian was an old family friend. His private office was a small cedar-paneled room with potted plants in the windows and bright prints of well-bred dogs on the walls. With the door closed, the din of the animals in the kennel across the hall quieted to muffled background noise. Behind the desk sat Dr. Nathan Feemer, a solidly built man of sixty, writing something in a file.

"Well, Charlie! I'm happy to say that Slyboots is in tiptop shape. Really," he chuckled, "you ought to tell Gerta that weekly checkups aren't necessary. Don't get me wrong, I'm not trying to turn away business—but once every two months would be more than ample."

Charlie glanced down at the Kitty Kondo which housed Slyboots. He wiped his nose with a handkerchief which he replaced in the pocket of his rumpled brown sportscoat. His silver hair hung limply over his forehead, dangling in his bloodshot eyes. He looked miserable.

Dr. Feemer closed his file and smiled at Charlie.

Charlie squirmed. It suddenly seemed impossible. How could he tell his friend the vet, a man whose life's work was healing pets, that this cat must die? He opened his mouth to speak, but no sound came out.

"I'll bill you as usual," the vet said, blinking slowly behind his thick glasses.

Last week when Charlie had taken the cat for its checkup he wanted to explain the situation and reveal his plan. But instead, he'd stalled and pushed his thoughts to the back of his mind until he was out the door, hating his silence.

Now Charlie drew a breath, gathered his resolve. "I have a problem, Nate. And you're the only one I can turn to," he said. "I mean, this falls in your field of expertise."

The vet rubbed his chin, waited for Charlie to continue. His eyes registered puzzlement, with a hint of intrigue.

Charlie plucked at the hairs on the back of his hand and then blurted: "I've got to—"

The vet's eyes narrowed.

"I've got to kill my wife's cat!" He saw that his fists were clenched.

The vet was taken by surprise. "What did you say?"

"I'VE GOT TO KILL MY WIFE'S CAT!"

Nate seemed flustered. "*Kill* the—?" His eyes ticked about the room. "Whatever for? Why—why would anyone want to kill a dear pet?"

"Dear pet!" Charlie pulled out his handkerchief just in time, and sneezed into it. His face crimsoned; he felt hot all over. Irritably swiping cat hair from his lapels, he stood up and began pacing—and the whole story tumbled out.

Afterwards, in the silence that followed, Charlie groped for his chair and sat, a bewildered expression on his face, as if he'd just woken from a nap and didn't know quite where he was.

The vet cleared his throat and took a moment, and when he spoke it was with studied patience, as if he were explaining the game of Tic-Tac-Toe to an imbecile. "I can't just haul Slyboots into the operating room and make a mistake for you. It would jeopardize my whole practice."

"I wasn't suggesting that *you* kill him, Nate!"

"I'm sorry, I won't offer any advice on how to kill him either."

"I've thought it all out," Charlie said. "I've looked at it from every angle!" Charlie shoved the plastic Kitty Kondo with his foot. His voice dropped to nearly a whisper. "I can't shoot the cat—how would I explain the bloody little corpse? And besides, the bang of the pistol, even if I was prepared for it, might be too much for my heart. Can't poison his food because Gerta opens a fresh can of cat food for each of his meals. Strangling is no good because I'd get clawed and bitten, and might end up breaking his furry neck."

There was a pause. Slyboots scratched at the walls of his Kitty Kondo.

"You're my only hope." Charlie's hands fluttered helplessly. "You put animals to sleep all the time. You do it by injection, don't you?"

"I've already said I won't be party to this."

Charlie smacked his thigh once, hard. *"Don't you give a cat an injection to put it to sleep?"*

"Yes!" Now the vet's hands were fluttering. "But that is irrelevant because I'll not—"

"Give me a hypodermic!" Charlie was wild-eyed. "I'll do it myself, at home!"

The doctor stood abruptly. "Good day, Charles." He pointed to the door.

"Please! I'll pay you! I'll—"

"I said, good day!"

The office door opened, and a pretty young red-haired nurse leaned in. "The O.R.'s ready, Doctor."

Nathan Feemer's frosty eyes thawed at the sight of the young nurse.

Charlie noticed this, and then he listened closely for subtle nuances in the doctor's vocal tones.

"Yes, Suzanne," Feemer said, "I—I'll be with you in a moment." She withdrew, closing the door quietly. A fresh tantalizing trace of perfume lingered in the office. The veterinarian stared at the door, seemingly lost in thought, his eyes blank blue orbs.

Charlie swiveled in his chair. He made some quick calculations, and what he calculated made his blood run hot. He'd thought his old friend would understand and help him. But now he saw that Nate would have to be forced. In past visits Charlie noticed the intimacy with which Nate and his nurse spoke; but now, with the scent of her perfume fresh in his nostrils, Charlie was ready to explore the issue. It was Charlie's reserve ammunition, his last resort.

He stretched out, propping his feet on the Kitty Kondo, as if to stay awhile longer. Looking at his friend Nathan Feemer, he cackled.

The glassy look in the vet's eyes shattered.

Charlie then dealt his trump card, the one he'd held so close to his vest until just the right moment. He accused Nathan Feemer of marital infidelity.

Feemer was thrown. His chin jiggled as he blubbered a flimsy denial. The vet marched around his desk, jaw clenched. He jerked the door open and demanded that Charlie leave.

But like a swordsman who has disarmed his opponent and sent him sprawling on the flagstones, Charlie chuckled victoriously. Riding a swell of bravado, the same feeling that drives a swaggering swordsman to tickle the fallen man's throat with the blade until a trace of blood seeps forth, Charlie made it clear that he was not above planting seeds of evidence that would arouse a wife's suspicions.

At that moment the men were interrupted: the nurse's voice, light and pure-sounding, floated down the hall. "You coming, Nate?"

Nate whined, *whined*, down deep in his throat; checked himself. "Yes, yes, Nurse Summerton," he said. His voice was too even. "Just a moment." He shut the door and thrust fists in his pockets. "What do you want from me?"

"I already told you, Nate. A hypo. Simple little hypo. I know you've got one around here somewhere." Charlie pitched forward and sneezed.

Dr. Feemer turned to the wall, and then to Charlie, and then turned away again. He was quietly livid. "You don't honestly think I can be bribed."

YES! Charlie wanted to say, but he did not. What he said, after pursing his lips thoughtfully, was: "*Bribed?* A bad word choice, Nate. That cancels any doubts I might have had about your illicit little tete-a-tete with Nurse—Summerton, is it? Now, I'll have that hypo."

"This is criminal!"

Charlie smiled up at the veterinarian, and snuffed. "Since when is killing a cat against the law?" He rubbed his watery eyes.

The doctor paced a moment. He looked at Charlie; looked at the door. His shoulders drooped defeatedly. Then he took a key from his desk drawer. Pulling on his white lab coat, he mumbled, "Wait here."

When the vet returned to the office, Charlie was scratching under his collar, but he was a happy man. The vet produced a small clear hypodermic from a big pocket in his lab coat. "Won't she get another cat, Charlie? To replace the first?"

"No, I've already figured that out." Charlie's red-rimmed eyes sparkled when he spoke. His voice trembled enthusiastically. "I'll remind her psychologists say it's very unhealthy to get a pet that's even remotely similar to a recently deceased pet. We'll get a canary or something. A goldfish. I don't know. But we won't have a cat!"

Feemer held the syringe up to the light and looked through it. A protective plastic cap sheathed the needle. "You've obviously thought this through in every detail."

"Oh yes. Yes." Charlie Wainwright's face was that of a child's sitting on Santa's lap the day before Christmas. "I know what I want. Give me the needle."

"You didn't get this from me. I'll deny it to my last gasp."

"I know! I know!"

The vet was tense and pale. "Sodium pentobarbital. The best place to inject is in the abdomen, and deep. Too shallow and you put the poison in the fatty areas around its stomach. Takes longer to work that way—a minute or so. Push the needle to the hilt and it'll take just seconds."

"Okay. Okay," Charlie said, pocketing the hypo.

"And don't uncap the needle until you're ready to use it. You don't want to stick yourself, you know."

"Righto," Charlie said, grabbing the handle of the Kitty Kondo and heading for the door. Slyboots growled.

"Er—one more thing, Charlie," the doctor said shamefacedly, wringing his hands. "Is it—are we, Suzanne and I—really that obvious?"

"The secret is safe with me," Charlie said with a wink.

That night Charlie was in his favorite chair, a brown vinyl recliner to which cat hair would not cling, when Gerta came in the front door after an evening at the theater. She wore a maroon felt hat with a gigantic brim, a dark velvety dress, ropes of fake pearls, and an antique fox stole. She chattered noisily as she crossed the room. "The play was an *abomination*, Charles. Really, you should have seen it. When the poor dreadful actors weren't dropping props they were dropping lines. You ever heard anybody improvise Shakespeare?"

"Glad you had a nice time, dear," Charlie said behind his newspaper.

The cat ambled into the den from some other part of the house, fat and slow. It crossed between Gerta's ankles, rubbing against her vein-corded legs, shedding reddish brown hairs on her white stockings.

How hard it had been for Charlie not to launch the cat into eternity before Gerta got home! But if she'd come home to find the cat dead, no amount of feigned sorrow on Charlie's part would have been enough to fully convince her that he hadn't played a part in the cat's untimely demise. He'd stretched his willpower to the limit, reminding himself that it would be only a few hours. He would do the deed while Gerta—and supposedly he—was asleep.

"*Othello* was a torture! They had a Chinese woman playing the title part, of all things. Have you ever heard of such?" She flung her big hat and tiny clasp purse on the couch. "That's right, Slyboots."

Charlie grimaced at the sound of the cat's name.

Gerta buried her face in the cat's long red fur, and went to the kitchen. "Let's get you something to eat, and then you and Mommy are going beddiebye. I'll give you your dinner in bed. You like that, don't you, Slyboots? Hm?"

Charlie could picture the cat licking one of Gerta's many chins. And even as the thought came to him, he heard Gerta giggle.

"Stop that, Sly. You know I'm ticklish!"

A minute later, Gerta came through the den with an open can of cat food and a spoon. Slyboots, in her arms, batted at the nose of the dead fox that hung around Gerta's neck. "You coming with us?" Gerta asked her husband.

"In a little while, sweets," he said, reaching out and patting the cat between the ears.

"Come on, Sly," Gerta crooned, going down the hallway. "We'll have dinner and then you and Mommy will snuggle up and go to sleep . . ."

Charlie waited until her voice died away before he allowed himself to sneeze. He sneezed three times, each more explosive than the last. After it was over, he wiped his runny eyes and nose, and sat still as his heart whacked against his ribs. Willing himself to relax, he closed his eyes until his heart slowed to its normal pace.

Everything was perfect. He'd shown no antagonism toward the shedding red beast; he'd even been kind to it. He was sure Gerta noticed the gentle pat, and would remember it. This was just the position he wanted to be in before the cat's stiffening body was found in the morning.

Earlier today he'd taken a pair of gardening gloves from the tool room and stowed them in the very back of the linen closet, under plenty of towels. The gloves would afford protection from getting scratched in the process of plunging the needle into the cat. He didn't want to have to explain scratches in the morning.

Three hours passed. It usually took Gerta a long time to fall asleep. Charlie couldn't concentrate on the newspaper, but he dared not turn on the television. He didn't want the noise to bother Gerta or the cat and keep either from sleeping. He read the same comics page again and again, not taking in a word of it, not cracking a smile.

At two A.M. he rose slowly from the chair. His heart skipped along at a rather fast rate, but he didn't let it upset him. He simply stood in place until it slowed a fraction. Then he stepped into the dark hall and opened the doors of the linen closet.

Gloves on, hypodermic in hand, he advanced to the bedroom door. It was open, and the room was very dark. He let his eyes adjust. Blue moonlight through the gauzy drapes gave the room an otherworldly glow. Charlie stood at the foot of the bed looking at his wife, who was rolled into a comfortable ball on one side of the bed. Beside her, on the nightstand, Charlie saw the half-finished can of cat food which, as always, would be scraped down the garbage disposal in the morning. Under her arms, a lumpy form. The cat? How could he inject the cat if it was wrapped so intimately against its mother's bosom?

But on closer examination Charlie saw that Gerta was not holding the cat. It was a pillow she was suffocating in her sleep. Charlie moved around the foot of the bed, his eyes wide in search of the cat.

There, on a chair next to the bed, not a yard from the opened can of cat food, Charlie's eyes found the form they sought. The creature had assumed the pose of its mother, head tucked down, front legs wrapped under its chin, deep in a world of dreams.

Charlie's heart flopped and hung quiet for an instant too long. He shut his eyes and stood perfectly still until the moment passed. When he opened his eyes again, he checked Gerta; she was still in a knot on the bed. His victim hadn't moved either.

He went across the floor on his knees. The carpet whispered beneath him. For fear of waking the beast, he breathed shallowly. In one practiced motion he took the cap off the needle and placed it between his teeth. Now at the chair, he leaned in.

But Charlie recoiled suddenly, his back high, straight. He was going to sneeze. His free hand covered his nose, pinched it tight. The glove leather tickled his nostrils and he sneezed silently, keeping the sound deep inside his chest. Once. Twice. The needle shook in the moonlight. Had Gerta moved? Not an inch. The cat? Quiet as ever. Relieved, Charlie dropped his shoulders and hesitated, listening to his heart until it was regular, before leaning over the chair again.

Swiftly, surprising himself, Charlie clamped his hand over the cat's head to keep the mouth from opening with a screech as the hand with the needle swept into the beast from underneath—careful to avoid pinning the seat cushion by mistake—and pressed the plunger home. He shivered at the crucial moment, but he would not let himself be betrayed by his own body. He held the needle in place until he was calm again—had the cat kicked?—and froze for two minutes. Removing the drained hypo, he stood, a fine sheen of sweat on his forehead.

He backed away, glancing over his shoulder, careful not to bump into anything on his way out. Then he turned out of the room and walked down the hall, capping the needle with a trembling hand. Victory!

Charlie replaced the leather gloves in the linen closet for removal tomorrow, and went to the kitchen. In the trash can under the sink was the cardboard milk carton he'd emptied and placed there early in the evening. He dropped the syringe in the carton and closed the mouth of it. Rooting down into the mess of egg shells, coffee grinds, and cat food cans, Charlie interred the milk carton with its hidden evidence. He washed his hands under the faucet and dried them on the handtowel, making sure he left no bits of debris on the towel.

He stood at the counter awhile, quivering with an overwhelming happiness. The oven clock ticked in rhythm with his heartbeat. Though his heart had been through some terrible strains that night, Charlie wasn't going to take any more of his pills. He'd already had the prescribed daily dose, and besides, now that his work was accomplished, wouldn't he go to bed with a light heart? He already felt better than he had in a long, long time.

He took several deep relaxing breaths, and drank a glass of water. Then he went to the den and flopped down in his favorite chair to read the comics. He was sure they'd be funny this time. He'd enjoy himself a little before going to bed.

Charlie shook the paper to straighten it, and beamed at the antics of the cartoon characters. Where did those guys get their ideas? He laughed out loud, and then reminded himself to stay quiet. He'd go to bed soon.

And then suddenly the bottom edge of the newspaper crinkled, and a furry red form sprang into Charlie's lap. The cat! For a full four seconds he stared with horror and disbelief at the beast as it walked in circles looking for a place to sit. Charlie started to sneeze, but instead—he screamed.

The next day, as Gerta made her way through the group of mourners who'd assembled themselves in her living room, one of the ladies from church, a tiny twig of a woman, took Gerta aside to give her personal regards. She said how sorry she was that Charlie's heart gave out on him so suddenly, and how good Gerta looked in spite of everything.

Gerta smiled sadly, and hugged her cat Slyboots closer. "Yes," she said, "Charlie was a dear heart. We sure will miss him."

The twig woman commented on Gerta's fox stole, and wondered aloud why people didn't wear them much anymore.

Gerta said they were coming back in style, you just watch and see. Then, fingering the fox fur absently, she withdrew her hand and said, "Ugh! Looks like I've got to get this thing cleaned. Somehow the fur's gotten all damp and sticky!"

Patricia Highsmith

THE EMPTY BIRDHOUSE

The first time Edith saw it she laughed, not believing her eyes.

She stepped to one side and looked again; it was still there, but a bit dimmer. A squirrel-like face—but demonic in its intensity—looked out at her from the round hole in the birdhouse. An illusion, of course, something to do with shadows, or a knot in the wood of the back wall of the birdhouse. The sunlight fell plain on the six-by-nine-inch birdhouse in the corner made by the toolshed and the brick wall of the garden. Edith went closer, until she was only ten feet away. The face disappeared.

That was funny, she thought as she went back into the cottage. She would have to tell Charles tonight.

But she forgot to tell Charles.

Three days later she saw the face again. This time she was straightening up after having set two empty milk bottles on the back doorstep. A pair of beady black eyes looked out at her, straight and level, from the birdhouse, and they appeared to be surrounded by brownish fur. Edith flinched, then stood rigid. She thought she saw two rounded ears, a mouth that was neither animal nor bird, simply grim and cruel.

But she knew that the birdhouse was empty. The bluetit family had flown away weeks ago, and it had been a narrow squeak for the baby bluetits as the Masons' cat next door had been interested; the cat could reach the hole from the toolshed roof with a paw, and Charles had made the hole a trifle too big for bluetits. But Edith and Charles had staved Jonathan off until the birds were well away. Afterward, days later, Charles had taken the birdhouse down—it hung like a picture on a wire from a nail—and shaken it to make sure no debris was inside. Bluetits might nest a second time, he said. But they hadn't as yet—Edith was sure because she had kept watching.

And squirrels never nested in birdhouses. Or did they? At any rate, there were no squirrels around. Rats? They would never choose a birdhouse for a home. How could they get in, anyway, without flying?

While these thoughts went through Edith's mind, she stared at the intense brown face, and the piercing black eyes stared back at her.

"I'll simply go and see what it is," Edith thought, and stepped onto the path that led to the toolshed. But she went only three paces and stopped. She didn't want to touch the birdhouse and get bitten—maybe by a dirty rodent's tooth. She'd tell Charles tonight. But now that she was closer, the thing was still there, clearer than ever. It wasn't an optical illusion.

Her husband Charles Beaufort, a computing engineer, worked at a plant eight miles from where they lived. He frowned slightly and smiled when Edith told him what she had seen. "Really?" he said.

"I *may* be wrong. I wish you'd shake the thing again and see if there's anything in it," Edith said, smiling herself now, though her tone was earnest.

"All right, I will," Charles said quickly, then began to talk of something else. They were then in the middle of dinner.

Edith had to remind him when they were putting the dishes into the washing machine. She wanted him to look before it became dark. So Charles went out, and Edith stood on the doorstep, watching. Charles tapped on the birdhouse, listened with one ear cocked. He took the birdhouse down from the nail, shook it, then slowly tipped it so the hole was on the bottom. He shook it again.

"Absolutely nothing," he called to Edith, "not even a piece of straw." He smiled broadly at his wife and hung the birdhouse back on the nail. "I wonder what you could've seen? You hadn't had a couple of Scotches, had you?"

"*No.* I described it to you." Edith felt suddenly blank, deprived of something. "It had a head a little larger than a squirrel's, beady black eyes, and a sort of serious mouth."

"Serious mouth!" Charles put his head back and laughed as he came back into the house.

"A tense mouth. It had a grim look," Edith said positively.

But she said nothing else about it. They sat in the living room. Charles looking over the newspaper, then opening his folder of reports from the office. Edith had a catalogue and was trying to choose a tile pattern for the kitchen wall. Blue and white, or pink and white and blue? She was not in a mood to decide, and Charles was never a help, always saying agreeably, "Whatever you like is all right with me."

Edith was thirty-four. She and Charles had been married seven years. In the second year of their marriage Edith had lost the child she was carrying. She had lost it rather deliberately, being in a panic about giving birth. That was to say, her fall down the stairs had been rather on purpose, if she were willing to admit it, but the miscarriage had been put down as the result of an accident. She had never tried to have another child, and she and Charles had never even discussed it.

She considered herself and Charles a happy couple. Charles was doing well with Pan-Com Instruments, and they had more money and more freedom than several of their neighbors who were tied down with two or more children. They both liked entertaining, Edith in their house especially, and Charles on their boat, a thirty-foot motor launch which slept four. They plied the local river and inland canals on most weekends when the weather was good. Edith could cook almost as well afloat as on shore, and Charles obliged with drinks, fishing equipment, and the record player. He would also dance a hornpipe on request.

During the week-end that followed—not a boating week-end because Charles had extra work—Edith glanced several times at the empty birdhouse, reassured now because she *knew* there was nothing in it. When the sunlight shone on it she saw nothing but a paler brown in the round hole, the back of the birdhouse; and when in shadow the hole looked black.

On Monday afternoon, as she was changing the bedsheets in time for the laundryman who came at three, she saw something slip from under a blanket that she picked up from the floor. Something ran across the floor and out the door—something brown and larger than a squirrel. Edith gasped and dropped the blanket. She tiptoed to the bedroom door, looked into the hall and on the stairs, the first five steps of which she could see.

What kind of animal made no noise at all, even on bare wooden stairs? Or had she really seen anything? But she was sure she had. She'd even had a glimpse of the small black eyes. It was the same animal she had seen looking out of the birdhouse.

The only thing to do was to find it, she told herself. She thought at once of the hammer as a weapon in case of need, but the hammer was downstairs. She took a heavy book instead and went cautiously down the stairs, alert and looking everywhere as her vision widened at the foot of the stairs.

There was nothing in sight in the living room. But it could be under the sofa or the armchair. She went into the kitchen and got the hammer from a drawer. Then she returned to the living room and shoved the armchair quickly some three feet. Nothing. She found she was afraid to bend down to look under the sofa, whose cover came almost to the floor, but she pushed it a few inches and listened. Nothing.

It *might* have been a trick of her eyes, she supposed. Something like a spot floating before the eyes, after bending over the bed. She decided not to say anything to Charles about it. Yet in a way, what she had seen in the bedroom had been more definite than what she had seen in the birdhouse.

A baby yuma, she thought an hour later as she was sprinkling flour on a joint in the kitchen. A yuma. Now, where had that come from? Did such an animal exist? Had she seen a photograph of one in a magazine, or read the word somewhere?

Edith made herself finish all she intended to do in the kitchen, then went to the big dictionary and looked up the word yuma. It was not in the dictionary. A trick of her mind, she thought. Just as the animal was probably a trick of her eyes. But it was strange how they went together, as if the name were absolutely correct for the animal.

Two days later, as she and Charles were carrying their coffee cups into the kitchen, Edith saw it dart from under the refrigerator—or from behind the refrigerator—diagonally across the kitchen threshold and into the dining room. She almost dropped her cup and saucer, but caught them, and they chattered in her hands.

"What's the matter?" Charles asked.

"I saw it again!" Edith said. "The animal."

"What?"

"I didn't tell you," she began with a suddenly dry throat, as if she were making a painful confession. "I think I saw that thing—the thing that was in the birdhouse—upstairs in the bedroom on Monday. And I think I saw it again. Just now."

"Edith, my darling, there wasn't anything in the birdhouse."

"Not when you looked. But this animal moves quickly. It almost flies."

Charles's face grew more concerned. He looked where she was looking, at the kitchen threshold. "You saw it just now? I'll go look," he said, and walked into the dining room.

He gazed around on the floor, glanced at his wife, then rather casually bent and looked under the table among the chair legs. "Really, Edith—"

"Look in the living room," Edith said.

Charles did, for perhaps fifteen seconds, then he came back, smiling a little. "Sorry to say this, old girl, but I think you're seeing things. Unless, of course, it was a mouse. We might have mice. I hope not."

"Oh, it's much bigger. And it's brown. Mice are gray."

"Yep," Charles said vaguely. "Well, don't worry, dear, it's not going to attack you. It's running." He added in a voice quite devoid of conviction, "If necessary, we'll get an exterminator.'

"Yes," she said at once.

"How big is it?"

She held her hands apart at a distance of about sixteen inches. "This big."

"Sounds like it might be a ferret," he said.

"It's even quicker. And it has black eyes. Just now it stopped just for an instant and looked straight at me. Honestly, Charles." Her voice had begun to shake. She pointed to the spot by the refrigerator. "Just there it stopped for a split second and—"

"Edith, get a grip on yourself." He pressed her arm.

"It looks so evil. I can't tell you."

Charles was silent, looking at her.

"Is there any animal called a yuma?" she asked.

"A yuma? I've never heard of it. Why?"

"Because the name came to me today out of nowhere. I thought—because I'd thought of it and I'd never seen an animal like this that maybe I'd seen it somewhere."

"Y-u-m-a?"

Edith nodded.

Charles, smiling again because it was turning into a funny game, went to the dictionary as Edith had done and looked for the word. He closed the dictionary and went to the Encyclopedia Britannica on the bottom shelves of the bookcase. After a minute's search he said to Edith, "Not in the dictionary and not in the Britannica either. I think it's a word you made up." And he laughed. "Or maybe it's a word in *Alice in Wonderland*."

It's a real word, Edith thought, but she didn't have the courage to say so. Charles would deny it.

Edith felt done in and went to bed around ten with her book. But she was still reading when Charles came in just before eleven. At that moment both of them saw it: it flashed from the foot of the bed across the carpet, in plain view of Edith and Charles, went under the chest of drawers and, Edith thought, out the door. Charles must have thought so, too, as he turned quickly to look into the hall.

"You saw it!" Edith said.

Charles's face was stiff. He turned the light on in the hall, looked, then went down the stairs.

He was gone perhaps three minutes, and Edith heard him pushing furniture about. Then he came back.

"Yes, I saw it." His face looked suddenly pale and tired.

But Edith sighed and almost smiled, glad that he finally believed her. "You see what I mean now. I wasn't seeing things."

"No." Charles agreed.

Edith was sitting up in bed. "The awful thing is, it looks uncatchable."

Charles began to unbutton his shirt. "Uncatchable. What a word. Nothing's uncatchable. Maybe it's a ferret. Or a squirrel."

"Couldn't you tell? It went right by you."

"Well!" He laughed. "It *was* pretty fast. You've seen it two or three times and you can't tell what it is."

"Did it have a tail? I can't tell if it had or if that's the whole body—that length."

Charles kept silent. He reached for his dressing gown, slowly put it on. "I think it's smaller than it looks. It is fast, so it seems elongated. Might be a squirrel."

"The eyes are in the front of its head. Squirrels' eyes are sort of at the side."

Charles stooped at the foot of the bed and looked under it. He ran his hand over the tucked foot of the bed, underneath. Then he stood up. "Look, if we see it again—*if* we saw it—"

"What do you mean *if*? You did see it—you said so."

"I *think* so." Charles laughed. "How do I know my eyes or my mind isn't playing a trick on me? Your description was so eloquent." He sounded almost angry with her.

"Well—*if*?"

"If we see it again, we'll borrow a cat. A cat'll find it."

"Not the Masons' cat. I'd hate to ask them."

They had had to throw pebbles at the Masons' cat to keep it away when the bluetits were starting to fly. The Masons hadn't liked that. They were still on good terms with the Masons, but neither Edith nor Charles would have dreamed of asking to borrow Jonathan.

"We could call in an exterminator," Edith said.

"Ha! And what'll we ask him to look for?"

"What we saw," Edith said, annoyed because it was Charles who had suggested an exterminator just a couple of hours before. She was interested in the conversation, vitally interested, yet it depressed her. She felt it was vague and hopeless, and she wanted to lose herself in sleep.

"Let's try a cat," Charles said. "You know, Farrow has a cat. He got it from the people next door to him. You know, Farrow the accountant who lives on Shanley Road? He took the cat over when the people next door moved. But his wife doesn't like cats, he says. This one—"

"I'm not mad about cats either," Edith said. "We don't want to acquire a cat."

"No. All right. But I'm sure we could borrow this one, and the reason I thought of it is that Farrow says the cat's a marvelous hunter. It's a female nine years old, he says."

Charles came home with the cat the next evening, thirty minutes later than usual, because he had gone home with Farrow to fetch it. He and Edith closed the doors and the windows, then let the cat out of its basket in the living room. The cat was white with gray brindle markings and a black tail. She stood stiffly, looking all around her with a glum and somewhat disapproving air.

"Ther-re, Puss-Puss," Charles said, stooping but not touching her. "You're only going to be here a day or two. Have we got some milk, Edith? Or better yet, cream."

They made a bed for the cat out of a carton, put an old towel in it, then placed it in a corner of the living room, but the cat preferred the end of the sofa. She had explored the house perfunctorily and had shown no interest in the cupboards or closets, though Edith and Charles had hoped she would. Edith said she thought the cat was too old to be of much use in catching anything.

The next morning Mrs. Farrow rang up Edith and told her that they could keep Puss-Puss if they wanted to. "She's a clean cat and very healthy. I just don't happen to like cats. So if you take to her—or she takes to you—"

Edith wriggled out by an unusually fluent burst of thanks and explanations of why they had borrowed the cat, and she promised to ring Mrs. Farrow in a couple of days. Edith said she thought they had mice, but were not sure enough to call in an exterminator. This verbal effort exhausted her.

The cat spent most of her time sleeping either at the end of the sofa or on the foot of the bed upstairs, which Edith didn't care for but endured rather than alienate the cat. She even spoke affectionately to the cat and carried her to the open doors of closets, but Puss-Puss always stiffened slightly, not with fear but with boredom, and immediately turned away. Meanwhile she ate well of tuna, which the Farrows had prescribed.

Edith was polishing silver at the kitchen table on Friday afternoon when she saw the thing run straight beside her on the floor—from behind her, out the kitchen door into the dining room like a brown rocket. And she saw it turn to the right into the living room where the cat lay asleep.

Edith stood up at once and went to the living-room door. No sign of it now, and the cat's head still rested on her paws. The cat's eyes were closed. Edith's heart was beating fast. Her fear mingled with impatience and for an instant she experienced a sense of chaos and terrible disorder. The animal was in the room! And the cat was of no use at all! And the Wilsons were coming to dinner at seven o'clock. And she'd hardly have time to speak to Charles about it because he'd be washing and changing, and she couldn't, wouldn't mention it in front of the Wilsons, though they knew the Wilsons quite well. As Edith's chaos became frustration, tears burned her eyes. She imagined herself jumpy and awkward all evening, dropping things, and unable to say what was wrong.

"The yuma. The damned yuma!" she said softly and bitterly, then went back to the silver and doggedly finished polishing it and set the table.

The dinner, however, went quite well, and nothing was dropped or burned. Christopher Wilson and his wife Frances lived on the other side of the village, and had two boys, seven and five. Christopher was a lawyer for Pan-Com.

"You're looking a little peaked, Charles," Christopher said. "How about you and Edith joining us on Sunday?" He glanced at his wife. "We're going for a swim at Hadden and then for a picnic. Just us and the kids. Lots of fresh air."

"Oh—" Charles waited for Edith to decline, but she was silent. "Thanks very much. As for me—well, we'd thought of taking the boat somewhere. But we've borrowed a cat, and I don't think we should leave her alone all day."

"A cat?" asked Frances Wilson. "Borrowed it?"

"Yes. We thought we might have mice and wanted to find out," Edith put in with a smile.

Frances asked a question or two about the cat and then the subject was dropped. Puss-Puss at that moment was upstairs, Edith thought. She always went upstairs when a new person came into the house.

Later when the Wilsons had left, Edith told Charles about seeing the animal again in the kitchen, and about the unconcern of Puss-Puss.

"That's the trouble. It doesn't make any noise," Charles said. Then he frowned. "Are you *sure* you saw it?"

"Just as sure as I am that I ever saw it," Edith said.

"Let's give the cat a couple of more days," Charles said.

The next morning, Saturday, Edith came downstairs around nine to start breakfast and stopped short at what she saw on the living-room floor. It was the yuma, dead, mangled at head and tail and abdomen. In fact, the tail was chewed off except for a damp stub about two inches long. And as for the head, there was none. But the fur was brown, almost black where it was damp with blood.

Edith turned and ran up the stairs.

"Charles!"

He was awake, but sleepy. "What?"

"The cat caught it. It's in the living room. Come down, will you?—I can't face it, I really can't."

"Certainly, dear," Charles said, throwing off the covers.

He was downstairs a few seconds later. Edith followed him.

"Um. Pretty big," he said.

"What is it?"

"I dunno. I'll get the dustpan." He went into the kitchen.

Edith hovered, watching him push it onto the dustpan with a rolled newspaper. He peered at the gore, a chewed windpipe, bones. The feet had little claws.

"What is it? A ferret?" Edith asked.

"I dunno. I really don't." Charles wrapped the thing quickly in a newspaper. "I'll get rid of it in the ashcan. Monday's garbage day, isn't it?"

Edith didn't answer.

Charles went through the kitchen and she heard the lid of the ashcan rattle outside the kitchen door.

"Where's the cat?" she asked when he came in again.

He was washing his hands at the kitchen sink. "I don't know." He got the floor mop and brought it into the living room. He scrubbed the spot where the animal had lain. "Not much blood. I don't see any here, in fact."

While they were having breakfast, the cat came in through the front door, which Edith had opened to air the living room—although she had not noticed any smell. The cat looked at them in a tired way, barely raised her head, and said, "Mi-o-ow," the first sound she had uttered since her arrival.

"Good pussy!" Charles said with enthusiasm. "Good Puss-Puss!"

But the cat ducked from under his congratulatory hand that would have stroked her back and went on slowly into the kitchen for her breakfast of tuna.

Charles glanced at Edith with a smile which she tried to return. She had barely finished her egg, but could not eat a bite more of her toast.

She took the car and did her shopping in a fog, greeting familiar faces as she always did, yet she felt no contact between herself and other people. When she came home, Charles was lying on the bed, fully dressed, his hands behind his head.

"I wondered where you were," Edith said.

"I felt drowsy. Sorry." He sat up.

"Don't be sorry. If you want a nap, take one."

"I was going to get the cobwebs out of the garage and give it a good sweeping." He got to his feet. "But aren't you glad it's gone, dear—whatever it was?" he asked, forcing a laugh.

"Of course. Yes, God knows." But she still felt depressed, and she sensed that Charlie did, too. She stood hesitantly in the doorway. "I just wonder what it was." If we'd only seen the head, she thought, but couldn't say it. Wouldn't the head turn up, inside or outside the house? The cat couldn't have eaten the skull.

"Something like a ferret," Charles said. "We can give the cat back now, if you like."

But they decided to wait till tomorrow to ring the Farrows.

Now Puss-Puss seemed to smile when Edith looked at her. It was a weary smile, or was the weariness only in the eyes? After all, the cat was nine. Edith glanced at the cat many times as she went about her chores that week-end. The cat had a different air, as if she had done her duty and knew it, but took no particular pride in it.

In a curious way Edith felt that the cat was in alliance with the yuma, or whatever animal it had been—was or had been in alliance. They were both animals and had understood each other, one the enemy and stronger, the other the prey. And the cat had been able to see it, perhaps hear it too, and had been able to get her claws into it. Above all, the cat was not afraid as she was and even Charles was, Edith felt. At the same time she was thinking this, Edith realized that she disliked the cat. It had a gloomy, secretive look. The cat didn't really like them, either.

Edith had intended to phone the Farrows around three on Sunday afternoon, but Charles went to the telephone himself and told Edith he was going to call them. Edith dreaded hearing even Charles's part of the conversation, but she sat on with the Sunday papers on the sofa, listening.

Charles thanked them profusely and said the cat had caught something like a large squirrel or a ferret. But they really didn't want to keep the cat, nice as she was, and could they bring her over, say around six? "But—well, the job's done, you see, and we're awfully grateful . . . I'll definitely ask at the plant if there's anyone who'd like a nice cat."

Charles loosened his collar after he put the telephone down. "Whew! That was tough—I felt like a heel! But after all, there's no use saying we want the cat when we don't. Is there?"

"Certainly not. But we ought to take them a bottle of wine or something, don't you think?"

"Oh, definitely. What a good idea! Have we got any?"

They hadn't any. There was nothing in the way of unopened drink but a bottle of whiskey, which Edith proposed cheerfully.

"They did do us a big favor," Edith said.

Charles smiled. "That they did!" He wrapped the bottle in one of the green tissues in which their liquor store delivered bottles and set out with Puss-Puss in her basket.

Edith had said she did not care to go, but to be sure to give her thanks to the Farrows. Then Edith sat down on the sofa and tried to read the newspapers, but found her thoughts wandering. She looked around the empty, silent room, looked at the foot of the stairs and through the dining-room door.

It was gone now, the yuma baby. Why she thought it was a baby, she didn't know. A baby *what*? But she had always thought of it as young—and at the same time as cruel, and knowing about all the cruelty and evil in the world, the animal world and the human world. And its neck had been severed by a cat. They had not found the head.

She was still sitting on the sofa when Charles came back.

He came into the living room with a slow step and slumped into the armchair. "Well—they didn't exactly want to take her back."

"What do you mean?"

"It isn't their cat, you know. They only took her on out of kindness—or something—when the people next door left. They were going to Australia and couldn't take the cat with them. The cat sort of hangs around the two houses there, but the Farrows feed her. It's sad."

Edith shook her head involuntarily. "I really didn't like the cat. It's too old for a new home, isn't it?"

"I suppose so. Well, at least she isn't going to starve with the Farrows. Can we have a cup of tea, do you think? I'd rather have that than a drink."

And Charles went to bed early, after rubbing his right shoulder with liniment. Edith knew he was afraid of his bursitis or rheumatism starting.

"I'm getting old," Charles said to her. "Anyway, I feel old tonight."

So did Edith. She also felt melancholy. Standing at the bathroom mirror, she thought the little lines under her eyes looked deeper. The day had been a strain, for a Sunday. But the horror was out of the house. That was something. She had lived under it for nearly a fortnight.

Now that the yuma was dead, she realized what the trouble had been, or she could now admit it. The yuma had opened up the past, and it had been like a dark and frightening gorge. It had brought back the time when she had lost her child—on purpose—and it had recalled Charles's bitter chagrin then, his pretended indifference later. It had brought back her guilt. And she wondered if the animal had done the same thing to Charles? He hadn't been entirely noble in his early days at Pan-Com. He had told the truth about a man to a superior, the man had been dismissed—Charles had got his job—and the man had later committed suicide. Simpson. Charles had shrugged at the time. But had the yuma reminded him of Simpson? No person, no adult in the world, had a perfectly honorable past, a past without some crime in it . . .

Less than a week later, Charles was watering the roses one evening when he saw an animal's face in the hole of the birdhouse. It was the same face as the other animal's, or the face Edith had described to him, though he had never had such a good look at it as this.

There were the bright, fixed black eyes, the grim little mouth, the terrible alertness of which Edith had told him. The hose, forgotten in his hands, shot water straight out against the brick wall. He dropped the hose, and turned toward the house to cut the water off, intending to take the birdhouse down at once and see what was in it; but, he thought at the same time, the birdhouse wasn't big enough to hold such an animal as Puss-Puss had caught. That was certain.

Charles was almost at the house, running, when he saw Edith standing in the doorway.

She was looking at the birdhouse. "There it is *again!*"

"Yes." Charles turned off the water. "This time I'll see what it is."

He started for the birdhouse at a trot, but midway he stopped, staring toward the gate.

Through the open iron gate came Puss-Puss, looking bedraggled and exhausted, even apologetic. She had been walking, but now she trotted in an elderly way toward Charles, her head hanging.

"She's back," Charles said.

A fearful gloom settled on Edith. It was all so ordained, so terribly predictable. There would be more and more yumas. When Charles shook the birdhouse in a moment, there wouldn't be anything in it, and then she would see the animal in the house, and Puss Puss would again catch it. She and Charles, together, were stuck with it.

"She found her way all the way back here, I'm sure. Two miles," Charles said to Edith, smiling.

But Edith clamped her teeth to repress a scream.

Ellis Peters

THE TRINITY CAT

He was sitting on top of one of the rear gate-posts of the churchyard when I walked through on Christmas Eve, grooming in his lordly style, with one black leg wrapped round his neck, and his bitten ear at an angle of forty-five degrees, as usual. I reckon one of the toms he'd tangled with in his nomad days had ripped the starched bit out of that one, the other stood up sharply enough. There was snow on the ground, a thin veiling, just beginning to crackle in promise of frost before evening, but he had at least three warm refuges around the place whenever he felt like holing up, besides his two houses, which he used only for visiting and cadging. He'd been a known character around our village for three years then, ever since he walked in from nowhere and made himself agreeable to the vicar and the verger, and finding the billet comfortable and the pickings good, constituted himself resident cat to Holy Trinity church, and took over all the jobs around the place that humans were too slow to tackle, like rat-catching, and chasing off invading dogs.

Nobody knows how old he is, but I think he could only have been about two when he settled here, a scrawny, chewed-up black bandit as lean as wire. After three years of being fed by Joel Woodward at Trinity Cottage, which was the verger's house by tradition and flanked the lych-gate on one side, and pampered and petted by Miss Patience Thompson at Church Cottage on the other side, he was double his old size, and sleek as velvet, but still had one lop ear and a kink two inches from the end of his tail. He still looked like a brigand, but a highly prosperous brigand. Nobody ever gave him a name, but he wasn't the sort to get called anything fluffy or familiar. Only Miss Patience ever dared coo at him, and he was very gracious about that, she being elderly and innocent and very free with little perks like raw liver, on which he doted. One way and another, he had it made. He lived mostly outdoors, never staying in either house overnight. In winter he had his own little ground-level hatch into the furnace-room of the church, sharing his lodgings matily with a hedgehog that had qualified as assistant vermin-destructor

396

around the churchyard, and preferred sitting out the winter among the coke to hibernating like common hedgehogs. These individualists keep turning up in our valley, for some reason.

All I'd gone to the church for that afternoon was to fix up with the vicar about the Christmas peal, having been roped into the bell-ringing team. Resident police in remote areas like ours get dragged into all sorts of activities, and when the area's changing, and new problems cropping up, if they have any sense they don't need too much dragging, but go willingly. I've put my finger on many an astonished yobbo who thought he'd got clean away with his little breaking-and-entering, just by keeping my ears open during a darts match, or choir practice.

When I came back through the churchyard, around half-past two, Miss Patience was just coming out of her gate, with a shopping bag on her wrist, and heading toward the street, and we walked along together a bit of the way. She was getting on for seventy, and hardly bigger than a bird, but very independent. Never having married or left the valley, and having looked after a mother who lived to be nearly ninety, she'd never had time to catch up with new ideas in the style of dress suitable for elderly ladies. Everything had always been done mother's way, and fashion, music, and morals had stuck at the period when mother was a carefully-brought-up girl learning domestic skills, and preparing for a chaste marriage. There's a lot to be said for it! But it had turned Miss Patience into a frail little lady in long-skirted black or gray or navy blue, who still felt undressed without hat and gloves, at an age when Mrs. Newcombe, for instance, up at the pub, favored shocking pink trouser suits and red-gold hair-pieces. A pretty little old lady Miss Patience was, though, very straight and neat. It was a pleasure to watch her walk. Which is more than I could say for Mrs. Newcombe in her trouser suit, especially from the back!

"A happy Christmas, Sergeant Moon!" she chirped at me on sight. And I wished her the same, and slowed up to her pace.

"It's going to be slippery by twilight," I said. "You be careful how you go."

"Oh, I'm only going to be an hour or so," she said serenely. "I shall be home long before the frost sets in. I'm only doing the last bit of Christmas shopping. There's a cardigan I have to collect for Mrs. Downs." That was her cleaning lady, who went in three mornings a week. "I ordered it long ago, but deliveries are so slow nowadays. They've promised it for today. And a gramophone record for my little errand-boy." Tommy Fowler that was, one of the church trebles, as pink and wholesome looking as they usually contrive to be, and just as artful. "And one mustn't forget our dumb friends, either, must one?" said Miss Patience cheerfully. "They're all important, too."

I took this to mean a couple of packets of some new product to lure wild birds to her garden. The Church Cottage thrushes were so fat they could hardly fly, and when it was frosty she put out fresh water three and four times a day.

We came to our brief street of shops, and off she went, with her big jet-and-gold brooch gleaming in her scarf. She had quite a few pieces of Victorian and Edwardian jewelry her mother'd left behind, and almost always wore one piece, being used to the belief that a lady dresses meticulously every day, not just on Sundays. And I went for a brisk walk round to see what was going on, and then went home to Molly and high tea, and took my boots off thankfully.

That was Christmas Eve. Christmas Day little Miss Thomson didn't turn up for eight o'clock Communion, which was unheard of. The vicar said he'd call in after matins and see that she was all right, and hadn't taken cold trotting about in the snow. But somebody else beat us both to it. Tommy Fowler! He was anxious about that pop record of his. But even he had no chance until after service, for in our village it's the custom for the choir to go and sing the vicar an aubade in the shape of "Christians, Awake!" before the main service, ignoring the fact that he's been up for four hours, and conducted two Communions. And Tommy Fowler had a solo in the anthem, too. It was a quarter-past twelve when he got away, and shot up the garden path to the door of Church Cottage.

He shot back even faster a minute later. I was heading for home when he came rocketing out of the gate and ran slam into me, with his eyes sticking out on stalks and his mouth wide open, making a sort of muted keening sound with shock. He clutched hold of me and pointed back toward Miss Thomson's front door, left half-open when he fled, and tried three times before he could croak out:

"Miss Patience . . . She's there on the floor—she's bad!"

I went in on the run, thinking she'd had a heart attack all alone there, and was lying helpless. The front door led through a diminutive hall, and through another glazed door into the living-room and that door was open, too, and there was Miss Patience face-down on the carpet, still in her coat and gloves, and with her shopping bag lying beside her. An occasional table had been knocked over in her fall, spilling a vase and a book. Her hat was askew over one ear, and caved in like a trodden mushroom, and her neat gray bun of hair had come undone and trailed on her shoulder, and it was no longer gray but soiled, brownish black. She was dead and stiff. The room was so cold, you could tell those doors had been ajar all night.

The kid had followed me in, hanging on to my sleeve, his teeth chattering. "I didn't open the door—it was open! I didn't touch her, or anything. I only came to see if she was all right, and get my record."

It was there, lying unbroken, half out of the shopping bag by her arm. She'd meant it for him, and I told him he should have it, but not yet, because it might be evidence, and we mustn't move anything. And I got him of there quick, and gave him to the vicar to cope with, and went back to Miss Patience as soon as I'd telephoned for the outfit. Because we had a murder on our hands.

So that was the end of one gentle, harmless old woman, one of very many these days, battered to death because she walked in on an intruder who panicked. Walked in on him, I judged, not much more than an hour after I left her in the street. Everything about her looked the same as then, the shopping bag, the coat, the hat, the gloves. The only difference, that she was dead. No, one more thing! No handbag, unless it was under the body, and later, when we were able to move her, I wasn't surprised to see that it wasn't there. Handbags are where old ladies carry their money. The sneak-thief who panicked and lashed out at her had still had greed and presence of mind enough to grab the bag as he fled. Nobody'd have to describe that bag to me, I knew it well, soft black leather with an old-fashioned gilt clasp and a short handle, a small thing, not like the hold-alls they carry nowadays.

She was lying facing the opposite door, also open, which led to the stairs. On the writing-desk by that door stood one of a pair of heavy brass candlesticks. Its fellow was on the floor beside Miss Thomson's body, and though the bun of hair and the felt hat had prevented any great spattering of blood, there was blood enough on the square base to label the weapon. Whoever had hit her had been just sneaking down the stairs ready to leave. She'd come home barely five minutes too soon.

Upstairs in her bedroom, her bits of jewelry hadn't taken much finding. She'd never thought of herself as having valuables, or of other people as coveting them. Her gold and turquoise and funereal jet and true-lover's-knots in gold and opals, and mother's engagement and wedding rings, and her little Edwardian pendant watch set with seed pearls, had simply lived in the small top drawer of her dressing-table. She belonged to an honest epoch, and it was gone, and now she was gone after it. She didn't even lock her door when she went shopping. There wouldn't have been so much as the warning of a key grating in the lock, just the door opening.

Ten years ago not a soul in this valley behaved differently from Miss Patience. Nobody locked doors, sometimes not even overnight. Some of us went on a fortnight's holiday and left the doors unlocked. Now we can't even put out the milk money until the milkman knocks at the door in person. If this generation likes to pride itself on its progress, let it! As for me, I thought suddenly that maybe the innocent was well out of it.

We did the usual things, photographed the body and the scene of the crime, the doctor examined her and authorized her removal, and confirmed what I'd supposed about the approximate time of her death. And the forensic boys lifted a lot of smudgy latents that weren't going to be of any use to anybody, because they weren't going to be on record, barring a million to one chance. The whole thing stank of the amateur. There wouldn't be any easy matching up of prints, even if they got beauties. One more thing we did for Miss Patience. We tolled the dead-bell for her on Christmas night, six heavy, muffled strokes. She was a virgin. Nobody had to vouch for it, we all knew. And let me point out, it is a title of honor, to be respected accordingly.

We'd hardly gotten the poor soul out of the house when the Trinity cat strolled in, taking advantage of the minute or two while the door was open. He got as far as the place on the carpet where she'd lain, and his fur and whiskers stood on end, and even his lop ear jerked up straight. He put his nose down to the pile of the Wilton, about where her shopping bag and handbag must have lain, and started going round in interested circles, snuffing the floor and making little throaty noises that might have been distress, but sounded like pleasure. Excitement, any-how. The chaps from the C.I.D. were still busy, and didn't want him under their feet, so I picked him up and took him with me when I went across to Trinity Cottage to talk to the verger. The cat never liked being picked up, after a minute he started clawing and cursing, and I put him down. He stalked away again at once, past the corner where people shot their dead flowers, out at the lych-gate, and straight back to sit on Miss Thompson's doorstep. Well, after all, he used to get fed there, he might well be uneasy at all these queer comings and goings. And they don't say "as curious as a cat" for nothing, either.

I didn't need telling that Joel Woodward had had no hand in what had hap-pened, he'd been nearest neighbor and good friend to Miss Patience for years, but he might have seen or heard something out of the ordinary. He was a little, wiry fellow, gnarled like a tree-root, the kind that goes on spry and active into his nineties, and then decides that's enough, and leaves overnight. His wife was dead long ago, and his daughter had come back to keep house for him after her hus-band deserted her, until she died, too, in a bus accident. There was just old Joel now, and the grandson she'd left with him, young Joel Barnett, nineteen, and a bit of a tearaway by his grandad's standards, but so far pretty innocuous by mine. He was a sulky, graceless sort, but he did work, and he stuck with the old man when many another would have lit out elsewhere.

"A bad business," said old Joel, shaking his head. "I only wish I could help you lay hands on whoever did it. But I only saw her yesterday morning about ten, when she took in the milk. I was round at the church hall all afternoon, getting things ready for the youth social they had last night, it was dark before I got back. I never saw or heard anything out of place. You can't see her living-room light from here, so there was no call to wonder. But the lad was here all afternoon. They only work till one, Christmas Eve. Then they all went boozing together for an hour or so, I expect, so I don't know exactly what time he got in, but he was here and had the tea on when I came home. Drop round in an hour or so and he should be here, he's gone round to collect this girl he's mashing. There's a party somewhere tonight."

I dropped round accordingly, and young Joel was there, sure enough, shoulder-length hair, frilled shirt, outsize lapels and all, got up to kill, all for the benefit of the girl his grandad had mentioned. And it turned out to be Connie Dymond, from the comparatively respectable branch of the family, along the canal-side. There were three sets of Dymond cousins, boys, no great harm in 'em but worth watching, but only this one girl in Connie's family. A good-looker, or at least most of the lads seemed to think so, she had a dozen or so on her string before she took up with young Joel. Big girl, too, with a lot of mauve eyeshadow and a mother-of-pearl mouth, in huge platform shoes and the fashionable drab granny-coat. But she was acting very prim and proper with old Joel around.

"Half-past two when I got home," said young Joel. "Grandad was around at the hall, and I'd have gone round to help him, only I'd had a pint or two, and after I'd had me dinner I went to sleep, so it wasn't worth it by the time I woke up. Around four, that'd be. From then on I was here watching the telly, and I never saw nor heard a thing. But there was nobody else here, so I could be spinning you the yarn, if you want to look at it that way."

He had a way of going looking for trouble before anyone else suggested it, there was nothing new about that. Still, there it was. One young fellow on the spot, and minus any alibi. There'd be plenty of others in the same case.

In the evening he'd been at the church social. Miss Patience wouldn't be expected there, it was mainly for the young, and anyhow, she very seldom went out in the evenings.

"*I* was there with Joel," said Connie Dymond. "He called for me at seven, I was with him all the evening. We went home to our place after the social finished, and he didn't leave till nearly midnight."

Very firm about it she was, doing her best for him. She could hardly know that his movements in the evening didn't interest us, since Miss Patience had then been dead for some hours.

When I opened the door to leave the Trinity cat walked in, stalking past me with a purposeful stride. He had a look round us all, and then made for the girl, reached up his front paws to her knees, and was on her lap before she could fend him off, though she didn't look as if she welcomed his attentions. Very civil he was, purring and rubbing himself against her coat sleeve, and poking his whiskery face into hers. Unusual for him to be effusive, but when he did decide on it, it was always with someone who couldn't stand cats. You'll have noticed it's a way they have.

"Shove him off," said young Joel, seeing she didn't at all care for being singled out. "He only does it to annoy people."

And she did, but he only jumped on again, I noticed as I closed the door on them and left. It was a Dymond party they were going to, the senior lot, up at the filling station. Not much point in trying to check up on all her cousins and swains when they were gathered for a booze-up. Coming out of a hangover, tomorrow, they might be easy meat. Not that I had any special reason to look their way, they were an extrovert lot, more given to grievous bodily harm in street punch-ups than anything secretive. But it was wide open.

Well, we summed up. None of the lifted prints was on record, all we could do in that line was exclude all those that were Miss Thomson's. This kind of sordid little opportunist break-in had come into local experience only fairly recently, and though it was no novelty now, it had never before led to a death. No motive but the impulse of greed, so no traces leading up to the act, and none leading away. Everyone connected with the church, and most of the village besides, knew about the bits of jewelry she had, but never before had anyone considered them as desirable loot. Victoriana now carry inflated values, and are in demand, but this still didn't look calculated, just wanton. A kid's crime, a teen-ager's crime. Or the crime of a permanent teen-ager. They start at twelve years old now, but there are also the shiftless louts who never get beyond twelve years old, even in their forties.

We checked all the obvious people, her part-time gardener—but he was demonstrably elsewhere at the time—and his drifter of a son, whose alibi was nonexistent but voluble, the window-cleaner, a sidelong soul who played up his ailments and did rather well out of her, all the delivery men. Several there who were clear, one or two who could have been around, but had no particular reason to be. Then we went after all the youngsters who, on their records, were possibles. There were three with breaking-and-entering convictions, but if they'd been there they'd been gloved. Several others with petty theft against them were also without alibis. By the end of a pretty exhaustive survey the field was wide, and none of the runners seemed to be ahead of the rest, and we were still looking. None of the stolen property had so far showed up.

Not, that is, until the Saturday. I was coming from Church Cottage through the graveyard again, and as I came near the corner where the dead flowers were shot, I noticed a glaring black patch making an irregular hole in the veil of frozen snow that still covered the ground. You couldn't miss it, it showed up like a black eye. And part of it was the soil and rotting leaves showing through, and part, the blackest part, was the Trinity cat, head down and back arched, digging industriously like a terrier after a rat. The bent end of his tail lashed steadily, while the remaining eight inches stood erect. If he knew I was standing watching him, he didn't care. Nothing was going to deflect him from what he was doing. And in a minute or two he heaved his prize clear, and clawed out to the light a little black leather handbag with a gilt clasp. No mistaking it, all stuck over as it was with dirt and rotting leaves. And he loved it, he was patting it and playing with it and rubbing his head against it, and purring like a steam engine. He cursed, though, when I took it off him, and walked round and round me, pawing and swearing, telling me and the world he'd found it, and it was his.

It hadn't been there long. I'd been along that path often enough to know that the snow hadn't been disturbed the day before. Also, the mess of humus fell off it pretty quick and clean, and left it hardly stained at all. I held it in my handkerchief and snapped the catch, and the inside was clean and empty, the lining slightly frayed from long use. The Trinity cat stood upright on his hind legs and protested loudly, and he had a voice that could outshout a Siamese.

Somebody behind me said curiously: "Whatever've you got there?" And there was young Joel standing open-mouthed, staring, with Connie Dymond hanging on to his arm and gaping at the cat's find in horrified recognition.

"Oh, no! My gawd, that's Miss Thomson's bag, isn't it? I've seen her carrying it hundreds of times."

"Did *he* dig it up?" said Joel, incredulous. "You reckon the chap who—you know, *him*!—he buried it there? It could be anybody, everybody uses this way through."

"My gawd!" said Connie, shrinking in fascinated horror against his side. "Look at that cat! You'd think he *knows*. . . . He gives me the shivers! What's got into him?"

What, indeed? After I'd got rid of them and taken the bag away with me I was still wondering. I walked away with his prize and he followed me as far as the road, howling and swearing, and once I put the bag down, open, to see what he'd do, and he pounced on it and started his fun and games again until I took it from him. For the life of me I couldn't see what there was about it to delight him, but he was in no doubt. I was beginning to feel right superstitious about this avenging detective cat, and to wonder what he was to unearth next.

I know I ought to have delivered the bag to the forensic lab, but somehow I hung on to it overnight. There was something fermenting at the back of my mind that I couldn't yet grasp.

Next morning we had two more at morning service besides the regulars. Young Joel hardly ever went to church, and I doubt if anybody'd ever seen Connie Dymond there before, but there they both were, large as life and solemn as death, in a middle pew, the boy sulky and scowling as if he'd been press-ganged into it, as he certainly had, Connie very subdued and big-eyed, with almost no make-up and an unusually grave and thoughtful face. Sudden death brings people up against daunting possibilities, and creates penitents. Young Joel felt silly there, but he was daft about her, plainly enough, she could get him to do what she wanted, and she'd wanted to make this gesture. She went through all the movements of devotion, he just sat, stood, and kneeled awkwardly as required, and went on scowling.

There was a bitter east wind when we came out. On the steps of the porch everybody dug out gloves and turned up collars against it, and so did young Joel, and as he hauled his gloves out of his coat pocket, out with them came a little bright thing that rolled down the steps in front of us all and came to rest in a crack between the flagstones of the path. A gleam of pale blue and gold. A dozen people must have recognized it. Mrs. Downs gave tongue in a shriek that informed even those who hadn't.

"That's Miss Thomson's! It's one of her turquoise ear-rings! *How did you get hold of that, Joel Barnett?*"

How, indeed? Everybody stood staring at the tiny thing, and then at young Joel, and he was gazing at the flagstones, struck white and dumb. And all in a moment Connie Dymond had pulled her arm free of his and recoiled from him until her back was against the wall, and was edging away from him like somebody trying to get out of range of flood or fire, and her face a sight to be seen, blind and stiff with horror.

"You!" she said in a whisper. "It was you! Oh, my God, *you* did it—*you* killed her! And me keeping company—how could I? How could *you!*"

She let out a screech and burst into sobs, and before anybody could stop her she turned and took to her heels, running for home like a mad thing.

I let her go. She'd keep. And I got young Joel and that single ear-ring away from the Sunday congregation and into Trinity Cottage before half the people there knew what was happening, and shut the world out, all but old Joel who came panting and shaking after us a few minutes later.

The boy was a long time getting his voice back, and when he did he had nothing to say but, hopelessly, over and over: "I didn't! I never touched her, I wouldn't. I don't know how that thing got into my pocket. I didn't do it. I never. . . . "

Humans are not all that inventive. Given a similar set of circumstances they tend to come out with the same formula. And in any case, "deny everything and say nothing else" is a very good rule when cornered.

They thought I'd gone round the bend when I said: "Where's the cat? See if you can get him in."

Old Joel was past wondering. He went out and rattled a saucer on the steps, and pretty soon the Trinity cat strolled in. Not at all excited, not wanting anything, fed and lazy, just curious enough to come and see why he was wanted. I turned him loose on young Joel's overcoat, and he couldn't have cared less. The pocket that had held the ear-ring held very little interest for him. He didn't care about any of the clothes in the wardrobe, or on the pegs in the little hall. As far as he was concerned, this new find was a non-event.

I sent for a constable and a car, and took young Joel in with me to the station, and all the village, you may be sure, either saw us pass or heard about it very shortly after. But I didn't stop to take any statement from him, just left him there, and took the car up to Mary Melton's place, where she breeds Siamese, and borrowed a cat-basket from her, the sort she uses to carry her queens to the vet. She asked what on earth I wanted it for, and I said to take the Trinity cat for a ride. She laughed her head off.

"Well, *he's* no queen," she said, "and no king, either. Not even a jack! And you'll never get that wild thing into a basket."

"Oh, yes, I will," I said. "And if he isn't any of the other picture cards, he's probably going to turn out to be the joker."

A very neat basket it was, not too obviously meant for a cat. And it was no trick getting the Trinity cat into it, all I did was drop in Miss Thomson's handbag, and he was in after it in a moment. He growled when he found himself shut in, but it was too late to complain then.

At the house by the canal Connie Dymond's mother let me in, but was none too happy about letting me see Connie, until I explained that I needed a statement from her before I could fit together young Joel's movements all through those Christmas days. Naturally I understood that the girl was terribly upset, but she'd had a lucky escape, and the sooner everything was cleared up, the better for her. And it wouldn't take long.

It didn't take long. Connie came down the stairs readily enough when her mother called her. She was all stained and pale and tearful, but had perked up somewhat with a sort of shivering pride in her own prominence. I've seen them like that before, getting the juice out of being the center of attention even while they wish they were elsewhere. You could even say she hurried down, and she left the door of her bedroom open behind her, by the light coming through at the head of the stairs.

"Oh, Sergeant Moon!" she quavered at me from three steps up. "Isn't it *awful*? I still can't believe it! *Can* there be some mistake? Is there any chance it *wasn't* . . . ?"

I said soothingly, yes, there was always a chance. And I slipped the latch of the cat-basket with one hand, so that the flap fell open, and the Trinity cat was out of there and up those stairs like a black flash, startling her so much she nearly fell down the last step, and steadied herself against the wall with a small shriek. And I blurted apologies for accidentally loosing him, and went up the stairs three at a time ahead of her, before she could recover her balance.

He was up on his hind legs in her dolly little room, full of pop posters and frills and garish colors, pawing at the second drawer of her dressing-table, and singing a loud, joyous, impatient song. When I came plunging in, he even looked over his shoulder at me and stood down as though he knew I'd open the drawer for him. And I did, and he was up among her fancy undies like a shot, and digging with his front paws.

He found what he wanted just as she came in at the door. He yanked it out from among her bras and slips, and tossed it into the air, and in seconds he was on the floor with it, rolling and wrestling it, juggling it on his four paws like a circus turn, and purring fit to kill, a cat in ecstasy. A comic little thing it was, a muslin mouse with a plaited green nylon string for a tail, yellow beads for eyes, and nylon threads for whiskers, that rustled and sent out wafts of strong scent as he batted it around and sang to it. A catmint mouse, old Miss Thomson's last-minute purchase from the pet shop for her dumb friend. If you could ever call the Trinity cat dumb! The only thing she bought that day small enough to be slipped into her handbag instead of the shopping bag.

Connie let out a screech, and was across that room so fast I only just beat her to the open drawer. They were all there, the little pendant watch, the locket, the brooches, the true-lover's-knot, the purse, even the other ear-ring. A mistake, she should have ditched both while she was about it, but she was too greedy. They were for pierced ears, anyhow, no good to Connie.

I held them out in the palm of my hand—such a large haul they made— and let her see what she'd robbed and killed for.

If she'd kept her head she might have made a fight of it even then, claimed he'd made her hide them for him, and she'd been afraid to tell on him directly, and could only think of staging that public act at church, to get him safely in custody before she came clean. But she went wild. She did the one deadly thing, turned and kicked out in a screaming fury at the Trinity cat. He was spinning like a humming-top, and all she touched was the kink in his tail. He whipped round and clawed a red streak down her leg through the nylon. And then she screamed again, and began to babble through hysterical sobs that she never meant to hurt the poor old sod, that it wasn't her fault! Ever since she'd been going with young Joel she'd been seeing that little old bag going in and out, draped with her bits of gold. What in hell did an old witch like her want with jewelry? She had no *right*! At her age!

"But I never meant to hurt her! She came in too soon," lamented Connie, still and for ever the aggrieved. "What was I supposed to do? I had to get away, didn't I? *She was between me and the door!*"

She was half her size, too, and nearly four times her age! Ah, well! What the courts would do with Connie, thank God, was none of my business. I just took her in and charged her, and got her statement. Once we had her dabs it was all over, because she'd left a bunch of them sweaty and clear on that brass candlestick. But if it hadn't been for the Trinity cat and his single-minded pursuit, scaring her into that ill-judged attempt to hand us young Joel as a scapegoat, she might, she just might, have got clean away with it. At least the boy could go home now, and count his blessings.

Not that she was very bright, of course. Who but a stupid harpy, soaked in cheap perfume and gimcrack dreams, would have hung on even to the catmint mouse, mistaking it for a herbal sachet to put among her smalls?

I saw the Trinity cat only this morning, sitting grooming in the church porch. He's getting very self-important, as if he knows he's a celebrity, though throughout he was only looking after the interests of Number One, like all cats. He's lost interest in his mouse already, now most of the scent's gone.

Edgar Pangborn

MRRRAR!

Timmy ate his field mouse, washed, and climbed on a log for a cat's midsummer-night thoughts; black, ten pounds of readiness, no longer young.

Above the house beyond the hayfield a night hawk was rasping. A swaying of trees now and then released the brilliance of village lights a mile away. Down the blind thread of a nearby road swept a noise, with blazing eyes; Timmy ignored it, but tensed at something else appearing on the road—human, it was moving with unhuman quiet, slinking to Timmy's house, crouching at the back door.

Timmy had left through that door two hours ago, by request. Returning, he need only jump on the box outside it and rattle the knob. There would be delays, creaks, moanings—but The Friend would come; it was rarely necessary to wail. The Friend would open up, and say: "Well, damn it . . ."

That human shadow entered the woodshed. Nothing of importance. Timmy relaxed, yawned, and stretched . . .

The Friend used little of the house except the kitchen. His musty cot was there, and a rocking chair where Timmy could sprawl in his lap accepting the caress of crinkled hands, responding with his own baritone purr. It was a good life: Timmy could take it on his own terms.

The shadow was at the door again. A hint of smell with evil association reached Timmy, but it was too faint for complete recognition, and the memory was many days old . . .

A good life. Compatibility; a supply of milk and mixed-up meat that wasn't bad, and sometimes a sardine; mutual concessions and forbearance. Periodically one of those road-monsters stopped, with one who clattered in to spread mysteries on the table and exchange with Timmy's associate a harmless barking; after this episode something of value usually appeared in Timmy's dish. Few others ever came; when they did Timmy retired under The Friend's cot—except for The Friend he distrusted the tribe.

For one, a slab-faced roarer, he had loathing. Not long ago, The Friend had been engaged in one of his peculiar activities—prying up a floor board, lifting a black box, waving away Timmy's nose while the box rustled and jingled. The roarer had arrived during the operation, with uncharacteristic quiet. The Friend had jumped up; the atmosphere was stiff with alarm; Timmy had gone under the cot. But then the intruder had made peaceful sounds, while Timmy studied barnyard-smelling feet and a furry something dangling at the roarer's middle—a rabbit's foot, its odor not quite gone. In time, Timmy had emerged. And without warning the roarer had grabbed his tail, a wet mouth letting off a blast of noise. Timmy had gashed a thick arm and fled in swollen rage while the kitchen boiled, shrillness mingling with the roaring and a slam of the back door. Timmy had not seen the roarer again; once or twice he had caught a whiff of the same stench outdoors, and had hidden in the grass.

The shadow was of no importance. It was only making noiseless motions at the window, lifting it, climbing inside. Timmy stretched again, and wandered into the woods, the best part of the world, his feet touching leaf-mold as an owl's wing touches air.

In a moonless clearing he played make-believe with a pine cone, falling on his side to kick at it, having fun . . .

His ears warned him in time to whirl on his back—hell was loose, on an owl's down-padded wings. Timmy strove, with teeth and slashing legs—no such rabbit as the owl may have imagined. A hook stabbed; Timmy yelled, and raked a wild tufted face. The horror let go and vanished in the night.

One talon had bared a rib, going no deeper, but the gash was painful. Recovering from shock in the safety of thick brush, Timmy licked it. In due time he crept slowly home, watchful of the sky. A new thing—trouble had never before come at Timmy out of the sky. But in his careful passage he had no traffic with imaginary dangers. Timmy met danger as he should: readiness was all.

He jumped to his box. Near the house that faint Bad Smell now identified itself—slab-faced roarer and no mistake. But pain and the desire for known shelter were strongest: the door-knob had to be rattled. Here was a difficulty: normally the right paw was the knob-rattling paw, and the wound was on Timmy's right side. But he made it.

There had been dim sounds of motion in the house; instead of answering Timmy's application, they ceased. A dead moment; then a pounding of heavy steps—away. The front door banged open; feet thudded up the road. Though alarming, that was all of secondary importance.

What mattered was that The Friend had to come. Timmy rattled again; after a decent interval he wailed. The front door squealed in rising wind, but that was all . . . Timmy tried the woodshed: no good.

He considered a window-sill, but his side hurt too much when he bunched for a leap. At last his forlorn prowling brought him to the open front door; he trotted through to the kitchen, tail up, calling inquiry. He sniffed at torn-up floor boards, an empty black box, and hurried to his dish. It was overturned, but he licked some comfort from a milk puddle.

The bulk on the cot was the right size for The Friend. A dangling hand smelled almost right; Timmy saw it twitch, and arched his neck to rub against it. No answering caress, but something tumbled—a rabbit's foot on a bit of cord, fastened in some substance with marks on it that clicked as Timmy pushed it. But the atmosphere was wrong for play. Timmy batted the thing idly under the cot, and climbed up.

The bumps and hollows were wrong, unresponsive. Any position troubled the smarting side; Timmy whimpered in exasperation. The Friend was not quite there. Only a pillow at the head end—some spread of white hair above it, but the pillow had the Bad Smell. Timmy returned to his milk puddle: dried up. The front door continued its noise, squeaking and pounding . . .

A road-master hummed slowly past, stopped, and returned. Brisk footsteps, noise of a voice. Timmy went under the cot.

Below a round white glare in the kitchen doorway Timmy saw legs in a dark shining of leather. These hurried to the cot; the pillow hit the floor. A hand came into Timmy's line of vision, feeling The Friend's fingers, lifting them out of sight. The Leather Legs ran out shouting, returning with another like himself. A spitting flare bloomed into white steady light on the table—The Friend had done that every evening. The object hanging near the back door was jangled: Timmy was used to that—The Friend had often wound the crank as Leather Legs did now, and made his noises into it.

One Leather Legs peered under the cot—usual arrangements of pale skin, mouth, nose. He said; "Here, kitty, kitty!" Timmy spat.

The milk dish was righted and filled. A Leather Legs was busy at the table, but his companion stood too near the hall door—no chance to make a break for it yet. Timmy nosed the rabbit's foot, bored.

The table noises were tearing clashes and a moderate "Damn!"—as if The Friend himself were doing the miracle, a miracle now confirmed by the celestial odor and substance of sardine. Beyond the cot Timmy thrust an inquiring face like a black moon. Leather Legs retired. Watching the two with readiness, Timmy accepted . . . Then the milk. A Leather Legs reached; Timmy went under the cot. But pain was easing; thirst was appeased; he could wait it out. If The Friend had come back, Timmy might even have made overtures, to the extent of sniffing a shoe-tip. But The Friend did not come back.

Fine night odors were pouring in; the Bad Smell was almost cleaned away.

A fox barked, answered by the passion of a dog-voice in the village; the night hawk grated. Timmy worried the rabbit's foot to pass the time.

Poor stuff—no wiggle. A casual flirt of his paw sent it out into lamplight. A hand swooped down for it with a lively "Hey!"

Timmy didn't mind. What interested him was that now the doorway was clear. A Leather Legs was again booming into the jangling thing.

Timmy ran.

A shout followed him. Actually a human expression of gratitude and esteem, offering an option on a second sardine.

But to Timmy it was only a type of barking. The Friend had gone away.

He watched the sky, traveling slowly but with lessening pain. Trouble, of course, can come from any quarter of the universe: readiness is all. The forest was the best part of the world—there you sometimes even met your own kind. Timmy said: "Mrrrar. Mrrrar-aorrh?"

Ruth Rendell

LONG LIVE THE QUEEN

It was over in an instant. A flash of orange out of the green hedge, a streak across the road, a thud. The impact was felt as a surprisingly heavy jarring. There was no cry. Anna had braked, but too late and the car had been going fast. She pulled in to the side of the road, got out, walked back.

An effort was needed before she could look. The cat had been flung against the grass verge which separated road from narrow walkway. It was dead. She knew before she knelt down and felt its side that it was dead. A little blood came from its mouth. Its eyes were already glazing. It had been a fine cat of the kind called marmalade because the color is two-tone, the stripes like dark slices of peel among the clear orange. Paws, chest, and part of its face were white, the eyes gooseberry green.

It was an unfamiliar road, one she had only taken to avoid roadworks on the bridge. Anna thought, I was going too fast. There is no speed limit here but it's a country road with cottages and I shouldn't have been going so fast. The poor cat. Now she must go and admit what she had done, confront an angry or distressed owner, an owner who presumably lived in the house behind that hedge.

She opened the gate and went up the path. It was a cottage, but not a pretty one: of red brick with a low slate roof, bay windows downstairs with a green front door between them. In each bay window sat a cat, one black, one orange and white like the cat, which had run in front of her car. They stared at her, unblinking, inscrutable, as if they did not see her, as if she was not there. She could still see the black one when she was at the front door. When she put her finger to the bell and rang it, the cat did not move, nor even blink its eyes.

No one came to the door. She rang the bell again. It occurred to her that the owner might be in the back garden and she walked round the side of the house. It wasn't really a garden but a wilderness of long grass and tall weeds and wild trees. There was no one. She looked through a window into a kitchen where a tortoiseshell cat sat on top of the fridge in the sphinx position and on the floor, on a strip of matting, a brown tabby rolled sensuously, its striped paws stroking the air.

There were no cats outside as far as she could see, not living ones at least. In the left-hand corner, past a kind of lean-to coalshed and a clump of bushes, three small wooden crosses were just visible among the long grass. Anna had no doubt they were cat graves.

She looked in her bag and, finding a hairdresser's appointment card, wrote on the blank back of it her name, her parents' address and their phone number, and added, *Your cat ran out in front of my car. I'm sorry, I'm sure death was instantaneous.* Back at the front door, the black cat and the orange-and-white cat still staring out, she put the card through the letter box.

It was then that she looked in the window where the black cat was sitting. Inside was a small overfurnished living room which looked as if it smelt. Two cats lay on the hearthrug, two more were curled up together in an armchair. At either end of the mantelpiece sat a china cat, white and red with gilt whiskers. Anna thought there ought to have been another one between them, in the center of the shelf, because this was the only clear space in the room, every other corner and surface being crowded with objects, many of which had some association with the feline: cat ashtrays, cat vases, photographs of cats in silver frames, postcards of cats, mugs with cat faces on them, and ceramic, brass, silver, and glass kittens. Above the fireplace was a portrait of a marmalade-and-white cat done in oils and on the wall to the left hung a cat calendar.

Anna had an uneasy feeling that the cat in the portrait was the one that lay dead in the road. At any rate, it was very like. She could not leave the dead cat where it was. In the boot of her car were two plastic carrier bags, some sheets of newspaper, and a blanket she sometimes used for padding things she didn't want to strike against each other while she was driving. As wrapping for the cat's body, the plastic bags would look callous, the newspapers worse. She would sacrifice the blanket. It was a clean dark-blue blanket, single size, quite decent and decorous.

The cat's body wrapped in this blanket, she carried it up the path. The black cat had moved from the left-hand bay and had taken up a similar position in one of the upstairs windows. Anna took another look into the living room. A second examination of the portrait confirmed her guess that its subject was the one she was carrying. She backed away. The black cat stared down at her, turned its head, and yawned hugely. Of course it did not know she carried one of its companions, dead and now cold, wrapped in an old car blanket, having met a violent death. She had an uncomfortable feeling, a ridiculous feeling, that it would have behaved in precisely the same way if it had known.

She laid the cat's body on the roof of the coalshed. As she came back round the house, she saw a woman in the garden next door. This was a neat and tidy garden with flowers and a lawn. The woman was in her fifties, white-haired, slim, wearing a twin set.

"One of the cats ran out in front of my car," Anna said. "I'm afraid it's dead."

"Oh, dear."

"I've put the—body, the body on the coalshed. Do you know when they'll be back?"

"It's just her," the woman said. "It's just her on her own."

"Oh, well. I've written a note for her. With my name and address."

The woman was giving her an odd look. "You're very honest. Most would have just driven on. You don't have to report running over a cat, you know. It's not the same as a dog."

"I couldn't have just gone on."

"If I were you, I'd tear that note up. You can leave it to me, I'll tell her I saw you."

"I've already put it through the door," said Anna.

She said goodbye to the woman and got back into her car. She was on her way to her parents' house, where she would be staying for the next two weeks. Anna had a flat on the other side of the town, but she had promised to look after her parents' house while they were away on holiday, and—it now seemed a curious irony—her parents' cat.

If her journey had gone according to plan, if she had not been delayed for half an hour by the accident and the cat's death, she would have been in time to see her mother and father before they left for the airport. But when she got there, they had gone. On the hall table was a note for her in her mother's hand to say that they had had to leave, the cat had been fed, and there was a cold roast chicken in the fridge for Anna's supper. The cat would probably like some, too, to comfort it for missing them.

Anna did not think her mother's cat, a huge fluffy creature of a ghostly whitish-grey tabbyness named Griselda, was capable of missing anyone. She couldn't believe it had affections. It seemed to her without personality or charm, to lack endearing ways. To her knowledge, it had never uttered beyond giving an occasional thin squeak that signified hunger. It had never been known to rub its body against human legs, or even against the legs of the furniture. Anna knew that it was absurd to call an animal selfish—an animal naturally put its survival first, self-preservation being its prime instinct—yet she thought of Griselda as deeply, intensely, callously selfish. When it was not eating, it slept, and it slept in those most comfortable places where the people that owned it would have liked to sit but from which they could not bring themselves to dislodge it. At night it lay on their bed and, if they moved, dug its long sharp claws through the bedclothes into their legs.

Anna's mother didn't like hearing Griselda referred to as "it." She corrected

Anna and stroked Griselda's head. Griselda, who purred a lot when recently fed and ensconced among cushions, always stopped purring at the touch of a human hand. This would have amused Anna if she had not seen that her mother seemed hurt by it, withdrew her hand and gave an unhappy little laugh.

When she had unpacked the case she brought with her, had prepared and eaten her meal and given Griselda a chicken leg, she began to wonder if the owner of the cat she had run over would phone. The owner might feel, as people bereaved in great or small ways sometimes did feel, that nothing could bring back the dead. Discussion was useless, and so, certainly, was recrimination. It had not in fact been her fault. She had been driving fast, but not *illegally* fast, and even if she had been driving at thirty miles an hour she doubted if she could have avoided the cat which streaked so swiftly out of the hedge.

It would be better to stop thinking about it. A night's sleep, a day at work, and the memory of it would recede. She had done all she could. She was very glad she had not just driven on as the next-door neighbor had seemed to advocate. It had been some consolation to know that the woman had many cats, not just the one, so that perhaps losing one would be less of a blow.

When she had washed the dishes and phoned her friend Kate, wondered if Richard, the man who had taken her out three times and to whom she had given this number, would phone and had decided he would not, she sat down beside Griselda—not *with* Griselda but on the same sofa as she was on—and watched television. It got to ten and she thought it unlikely the cat woman—she had begun thinking of her as that—would phone now.

There was a phone extension in her parents' room but not in the spare room where she would be sleeping. It was nearly eleven-thirty and she was getting into bed when the phone rang. The chance of its being Richard, who was capable of phoning late, especially if he thought she was alone, made her go into her parents' bedroom and answer it.

A voice that sounded strange, thin, and cracked said what sounded like "Maria Yackle."

"Yes?" Anna said.

"This is Maria Yackle. It was my cat that you killed."

Anna swallowed. "Yes. I'm glad you found my note. I'm very sorry, I'm very sorry. It was an accident. The cat ran out in front of my car."

"You were going too fast."

It was a blunt statement, harshly made. Anna could not refute it. She said, "I'm very sorry about your cat."

"They don't go out much, they're happier indoors. It was a chance in a million. I should like to see you. I think you should make amends. It wouldn't be right for you just to get away with it."

415

Anna was very taken aback. Up till then the woman's remarks had seemed reasonable. She didn't know what to say.

"I think you should compensate me, don't you? I loved her, I love all my cats. I expect you thought that because I had so many cats it wouldn't hurt me so much to lose one."

That was so near what Anna had thought that she felt a kind of shock, as if this Maria Yackle or whatever she was called had read her mind. "I've told you I'm sorry. I am sorry, I was very upset, I *hated* it happening. I don't know what more I can say."

"We must meet."

"What would be the use of that?" Anna knew she sounded rude, but she was shaken by the woman's tone, her blunt, direct sentences.

There was a break in the voice, something very like a sob. "It would be of use to me."

The phone went down. Anna could hardly believe it. She had heard it go down but still she said several times over, "Hallo? Hallo?" and "Are you still there?"

She went downstairs and found the telephone directory for the area and looked up Yackle. It wasn't there. She sat down and worked her way through all the Ys. There weren't many pages of Ys, apart from Youngs, but there was no one with a name beginning with Y at that address on the rustic road among the cottages.

She couldn't get to sleep. She expected the phone to ring again, Maria Yackle to ring back. After a while, she put the bedlamp on and lay there in the light. It must have been three, and still she had not slept, when Griselda came in, got on the bed, and stretched her length along Anna's legs. She put out the light, deciding not to answer the phone if it did ring, to relax, forget the run-over cat, concentrate on nice things. As she turned face-downward and stretched her body straight, she felt Griselda's claws prickle her calves. As she shrank away from contact, curled up her legs, and left Griselda a good half of the bed, a thick rough purring began.

The first thing she thought of when she woke up was how upset that poor cat woman had been. She expected her to phone back at breakfast time but nothing happened. Anna fed Griselda, left her to her house, her cat flap, her garden and wider territory, and drove to work. Richard phoned as soon as she got in. Could they meet the following evening? She agreed, obscurely wishing he had said that night, suggesting that evening herself only to be told he had to work late, had a dinner with a client.

She had been home for ten minutes when a car drew up outside. It was an old car, at least ten years old, and not only dented and scratched but with some of the worst scars painted or sprayed over in a different shade of red. Anna, who saw it arrive from a front window, watched the woman get out of it and approach the house. She was old, or at least elderly—is elderly older than old or old older than elderly?—but dressed like a teenager. Anna got a closer look at her clothes, her hair, and her face when she opened the front door.

It was a wrinkled face, the color and texture of a chicken's wattles. Small blue eyes were buried somewhere in the strawberry redness. The bright white hair next to it was as much of a contrast as snow against scarlet cloth. She wore tight jeans with socks pulled up over the bottoms of them, dirty white trainers, and a big loose sweatshirt with a cat's face on it, a painted smiling bewhiskered mask, orange and white and green-eyed.

Anna had read somewhere the comment made by a young girl on an older woman's boast that she could wear a miniskirt because she had good legs: "It's not your legs, it's your face." She thought of this as she looked at Maria Yackle, but that was the last time for a long while she thought of anything like that.

"I've come early because we shall have a lot to talk about," Maria Yackle said and walked in. She did this in such a way as to compel Anna to open the door farther and stand aside.

"This is *your* house?"

She might have meant because Anna was so young or perhaps there was some more offensive reason for asking.

"My parents'. I'm just staying here."

"Is it this room?" She was already on the threshold of Anna's mother's living room.

Anna nodded. She had been taken aback but only for a moment. It was best to get this over. But she did not care to be dictated to. "You could have let me know. I might not have been here."

There was no reply because Maria Yackle had seen Griselda.

The cat had been sitting on the back of a wing chair between the wings, an apparently uncomfortable place though a favorite, but at sight of the newcomer had stretched, got down, and was walking toward her. Maria Yackle put out her hand. It was a horrible hand, large and red with ropelike blue veins standing out above the bones, the palm calloused, the nails black and broken and the sides of the forefinger and thumb ingrained with brownish dirt. Griselda approached and put her smoky whitish muzzle and pink nose into this hand.

"I shouldn't," Anna said rather sharply, for Maria Yackle was bending over to pick the cat up. "She isn't very nice. She doesn't like people."

"She'll like me."

And the amazing thing was that Griselda did. Maria Yackle sat down and Griselda sat on her lap. Griselda the unfriendly, the cold-hearted, the cat who

417

purred when alone and who ceased to purr when touched, the ice-eyed, the stand-offish walker-by-herself, settled down on this unknown, untried lap, having first climbed up Maria Yackle's chest and onto her shoulders and rubbed her ears and plump furry cheeks against the sweatshirt with the painted cat face.

"You seem surprised."

Anna said, "You could say that."

"There's no mystery. The explanation's simple." It was a shrill, harsh voice, cracked by the onset of old age, articulate, the usage grammatical but the accent raw cockney. "You and your mum and dad, too, no doubt, you all think you smell very nice and pretty. You have your bath every morning with bath essence and scented soap. You put talcum powder on and spray stuff in your armpits, you rub cream on your bodies and squirt on perfume. Maybe you've washed your hair, too, with shampoo and conditioner and—what-do-they-call-it?—mousse. You clean your teeth and wash your mouth, put a drop more perfume behind your ears, paint your faces—well, I daresay your dad doesn't paint his face, but he shaves, doesn't he? More mousse and then aftershave.

"You put on your clothes. All of them clean, spotless. They've either just come back from the drycleaners or else out of the washing machine with biological soap and spring-fresh fabric softener. Oh, I know, I may not do it myself but I see it on the TV.

"It all smells very fine to you, but it doesn't to her. Oh, no. To her it's just chemicals, like gas might be to you or paraffin. A nasty strong chemical smell that puts her right off and makes her shrink up in her furry skin. What's her name?"

This question was uttered on a sharp bark. "Griselda," said Anna, and, "How did you know it's a she?"

"Face," said Maria Yackle. "Look—see her little nose. See her smiley mouth and her little nose and her fat cheeks? Tomcats got a big nose, got a long muzzle. Never mind if he's been neutered, still got a big nose."

"What did you come here to say to me?" said Anna.

Griselda had curled up on the cat woman's lap, burying her head, slightly upward turned, in the crease between stomach and thigh. "I don't go in for all that stuff, you see." The big red hand stroked Griselda's head, the stripy bit between her ears. "Cat likes the smell of me because I haven't got my clothes in soapy water every day, I have a bath once a week, always have and always shall, and I don't waste my money on odorizers and deodorizers. I wash my hands when I get up in the morning and that's enough for me."

At the mention of the weekly bath, Anna had reacted instinctively and edged her chair a little farther away. Maria Yackle saw, Anna was sure she saw, but her response to this recoil was to begin on what she had in fact come about: her compensation.

"The cat you killed, she was five years old and the queen of the cats, her name was Melusina. I always have a queen. The one before was Juliana and she lived to be twelve. I wept, I mourned her, but life has to go on. 'The queen is dead,' I said, 'long live the queen!' I never promote one, I always get a new kitten. Some cats are queens, you see, and some are not. Melusina was eight weeks old when I got her from the Animal Rescue people, and I gave them a donation of twenty pounds. The vet charged me twenty-seven pounds fifty for her injections—all my cats are immunized against feline enteritis and leptospirosis—so that makes forty-seven pounds fifty. And she had her booster at age two, which was another twenty-seven fifty. I can show you the receipted bills, I always keep everything, and that makes seventy-five pounds. Then there was my petrol getting her to the vet—we'll say a straight five pounds, though it was more—and then we come to the crunch, her food. She was a good little trencherwoman."

Anna would have been inclined to laugh at this ridiculous word, but she saw to her horror that the tears were running down Maria Yackle's cheeks. They were running unchecked out of her eyes, over the rough red wrinkled skin, and one dripped unheeded onto Griselda's silvery fur.

"Take no notice. I do cry whenever I have to talk about her. I loved that cat. She was the queen of the cats. She had her own place, her throne—she used to sit in the middle of the mantelpiece with her two china ladies-in-waiting on each side of her. You'll see one day, when you come to my house.

"But we were talking about her food. She ate a large can a day—it was too much, more than she should have had, but she loved her food, she was a good little eater. Well, cat food's gone up over the years, of course, what hasn't, and I'm paying fifty pee a can now, but I reckon it'd be fair to average it out at forty pee. She was eight weeks old when I got her, so we can't say five times three hundred and sixty-five. We'll say five times three fifty-five and that's doing you a favor. I've already worked it out at home, I'm not that much of a wizard at mental arithmetic. Five three-hundred and fifty-fives are one thousand, seven hundred and seventy-five, which multiplied by forty makes seventy-one thousand pee or seven hundred and ten pounds. Add to that the seventy-five plus the vet's bill of fourteen pounds when she had a tapeworm and we get a final figure of seven hundred and ninety-nine pounds."

Anna stared at her. "You're asking me to give you nearly eight hundred pounds?"

"That's right. Of course, we'll write it down and do it properly."

"Because your cat ran under the wheels of my car?"

"You murdered her," said Maria Yackle.

"That's absurd. Of course I didn't murder her." On shaky ground, she said, "You can't murder an animal."

"You did. You said you were going too fast."

Had she? She had been, but had she said so?

Maria Yackle got up, still holding Griselda, cuddling Griselda, who nestled purring in her arms. Anna watched with distaste. You thought of cats as fastidious creatures but they were not. Only something insensitive and undiscerning would put its face against that face, nuzzle those rough grimy hands. The black fingernails brought to mind a phrase, now unpleasantly appropriate, that her grandmother had used to children with dirty hands: in mourning for the cat.

"I don't expect you to give me a check now. Is that what you thought I meant? I don't suppose you have that amount in your current account. I'll come back tomorrow or the next day."

"I'm not going to give you eight hundred pounds," said Anna.

She might as well not have spoken.

"I won't come back tomorrow, I'll come back on Wednesday." Griselda was tenderly placed on the seat of an armchair. The tears had dried on Maria's Yackle's face, leaving salt trails. She took herself out into the hall and to the front door. "You'll have thought about it by then. Anyway, I hope you'll come to the funeral. I hope there won't be any hard feelings."

That was when Anna decided Maria Yackle was mad. In one way, this was disquieting—in another, a comfort. It meant she wasn't serious about the compensation, the seven hundred and ninety-nine pounds. Sane people don't invite you to their cat's funeral. Mad people do not sue you for compensation.

"No, I shouldn't think she'd do that," said Richard when they were having dinner together. He wasn't a lawyer but had studied law. "You didn't admit you were exceeding the speed limit, did you?"

"I don't remember."

"At any rate, you didn't admit it in front of witnesses. You say she didn't threaten you?"

"Oh, no. She wasn't unpleasant. She cried, poor thing."

"Well, let's forget her, shall we, and have a nice time?"

Although no note awaited her on the doorstep, no letter came, and there were no phone calls, Anna knew the cat woman would come back on the following evening. Richard had advised her to go to the police if any threats were made. There would be no need to tell them she had been driving very fast. Anna thought the whole idea of going to the police bizarre. She rang up her friend Kate and told her all about it and Kate agreed that telling the police would be going too far.

The battered red car arrived at seven. Maria Yackle was dressed as she had been for her previous visit, but, because it was rather cold, wore a jacket made of synthetic fur as well. From its harsh, too-shiny texture there was no doubt it was synthetic, but from a distance it looked like a black cat's pelt.

She had brought an album of photographs of her cats for Anna to see. Anna looked through it—what else could she do? Some were recognizably of those she had seen through the windows. Those that were not, she supposed might be of animals now at rest under the wooden crosses in Maria Yackle's back garden. While she was looking at the pictures, Griselda came in and jumped onto the cat woman's lap.

"They're very nice, very interesting," Anna said. "I can see you're devoted to your cats."

"They're my life."

A little humoring might be in order. "When is the funeral to be?"

"I thought on Friday. Two o'clock on Friday. My sister will be there with her two. Cats don't usually take to car travel, that's why I don't often take any of mine with me, and shutting them up in cages goes against the grain—but my sister's two Burmese love the car, they'll go and sit in the car when it's parked. My friend from the Animal Rescue will come if she can get away and I've asked our vet, but I don't hold out much hope there. He has his goat clinic on Fridays. I hope you'll come along."

"I'm afraid I'll be at work."

"It's no flowers by request. Donations to the Cats' Protection League instead. Any sum, no matter how small, gratefully received. Which brings me to money. You've got a check for me."

"No, I haven't, Mrs. Yackle.'

"Miss. And it's Yakop. J-A-K-O-B. You've got a check for me for seven hundred and ninety-nine pounds."

"I'm not giving you any money, Miss Jakob. I'm very, very sorry about your cat, about Melusina, I know how fond you were of her, but giving you compensation is out of the question. I'm sorry."

The tears had come once more into Maria Jakob's eyes, had spilled over. Her face contorted with misery. It was the mention of the wretched thing's name, Anna thought. That was the trigger that started the weeping. A tear splashed onto one of the coarse red hands. Griselda opened her eyes and licked up the tear.

Maria Jakob pushed her other hand across her eyes. She blinked. "We'll have to think of something else then," she said.

"I beg your pardon?" Anna wondered if she had really heard. Things couldn't be solved so simply.

"We shall have to think of something else. A way for you to make up to me for murder."

"Look, I will give a donation to the Cats' Protection League. I'm quite prepared to give them—say, twenty pounds." Richard would be furious, but perhaps she wouldn't tell Richard. "I'll give it to you, shall I, and then you can pass it on to them?"

"I certainly hope you will. Especially if you can't come to the funeral."

That was the end of it, then. Anna felt a great sense of relief. It was only now that it was over that she realized quite how it had got to her. It had actually kept her from sleeping properly. She phoned Kate and told her about the funeral and the goat clinic, and Kate laughed and said Poor old thing. Anna slept so well that night that she didn't notice the arrival of Griselda who, when she woke, was asleep on the pillow next to her face but out of touching distance.

Richard phoned and she told him about it, omitting the part about her offer of a donation. He told her that being firm, sticking to one's guns in situations of this kind, always paid off. In the evening, she wrote a check for twenty pounds but, instead of the Cats' Protection League, made it out to Maria Jakob. If the cat woman quietly held onto it, no harm would be done. Anna went down the road to post her letter, for she had written a letter to accompany the check, in which she reiterated her sorrow about the death of the cat and added that if there was anything she could do Miss Jakob had only to let her know. Richard would have been furious.

Unlike the Jakob cats, Griselda spent a good deal of time out of doors. She was often out all evening and did not reappear until the small hours, so that it was not until the next day, not until the next evening, that Anna began to be alarmed at her absence. As far as she knew, Griselda had never been away so long before. For herself, she was unconcerned—she had never liked the cat, did not particularly like any cats, and found this one obnoxiously self-centered and cold. It was for her mother, who unaccountably loved the creature, that she was worried. She walked up and down the street calling Griselda, though the cat had never been known to come when it was called.

It did not come now. Anna walked up and down the next street, calling, and around the block and farther afield. She half expected to find Griselda's body, guessing that it might have met the same fate as Melusina. Hadn't she read somewhere that nearly forty thousand cats are killed on British roads annually?

On Saturday morning, she wrote one of those melancholy lost-cat notices and attached it to a lamp standard, wishing she had a photograph. But her mother had taken no photographs of Griselda.

Richard took her to a friend's party and afterward, when they were driving home, he said, "You know what's happened, don't you? It's been killed by that old mad woman. An eye for an eye, a cat for a cat."

"Oh, no, she wouldn't do that. She loves cats."

"Murderers love people. They just don't love the people they murder."

"I'm sure you're wrong," said Anna, but she remembered how Maria Jakob had said that if the money was not forthcoming, she must think of something else—a way to make up to her for Melusina's death. And she had not meant a donation to the Cats' Protection League.

"What shall I do?"

"I don't see that you can do anything. It's most unlikely you could prove it, she'll have seen to that. You can look at this way—she's had her pound of flesh."

"Fifteen pounds of flesh," said Anna. Griselda had been a large, heavy cat.

"Okay, fifteen pounds. She's had that, she's had her revenge. It hasn't actually caused you any grief—you'll just have to make up some story for your mother."

Anna's mother was upset, but nowhere near as upset as Maria Jakob had been over the death of Melusina. To avoid too much fuss, Anna had gone further than she intended, told her mother that she had seen Griselda's corpse and talked to the offending motorist, who had been very distressed.

A month or so later, Anna's mother got a kitten, a grey tabby tomkitten, who was very affectionate from the start, sat on her lap, purred loudly when stroked, and snuggled up in her arms, though Anna was sure her mother had not stopped having baths or using perfume. So much for the Jakob theories.

Nearly a year had gone by before she again drove down the road where Maria Jakob's house was. She had not intended to go that way. Directions had been given her to a smallholding where they sold early strawberries on a roadside stall but she must have missed her way, taken a wrong turning, and come out here.

If Maria Jakob's car had been parked in the front, she would not have stopped. There was no garage for it to be in and it was not outside, therefore the cat woman must be out. Anna thought of the funeral she had not been to—she had often thought about it, the strange people and strange cats who had attended it.

In each of the bay windows sat a cat, a tortoiseshell and a brown tabby. The black cat was eyeing her from upstairs. Anna didn't go to the front door but round the back. There, among the long grass, as she had expected, were four graves instead of three, four wooden crosses, and on the fourth was printed in black gloss paint: MELUSINA, THE QUEEN OF THE CATS. MURDERED IN HER SIXTH YEAR. RIP.

That "murdered" did not please Anna. It brought back all the resentment at the unjust accusations of eleven months before. She felt much older, she felt wiser. One thing was certain, ethics or no ethics, if she ever ran over a cat again she'd drive on—the last thing she'd do was go and confess.

She came round the side of the house and looked in at the bay window. If the tortoiseshell had still been on the windowsill, she probably would not have looked in, but the tortoiseshell had removed itself to the hearthrug.

A white cat and the marmalade-and-white lay curled up side by side in an armchair. The portrait of Melusina hung above the fireplace and this year's cat calendar was up on the left-hand wall. Light gleamed on the china cats' gilt whiskers—and between them, in the empty space that was no longer vacant, sat Griselda.

Griselda was sitting in the queen's place in the middle of the mantelpiece. She sat in the sphinx position with her eyes closed. Anna tapped on the glass and Griselda opened her eyes, stared with cold indifference, and closed them again.

The queen is dead, long live the queen!